FRECKLES

&

A GIRL *of the*

LIMBERLOST

MONCREIFFE
—— PRESS

FRECKLES &
A GIRL *of the*
LIMBERLOST

By Gene
Stratton-Porter

1904-1909

UNITED STATES

Contents

A GIRL OF
THE LIMBERLOST

CHAPTER I

"Elnora Comstock, have you lost your senses?" demanded the angry voice of Katharine Comstock while she glared at her daughter.

"Why mother!" faltered the girl.

"Don't you 'why mother' me!" cried Mrs. Comstock. "You know very well what I mean. You've given me no peace until you've had your way about this going to school business; I've fixed you good enough, and you're ready to start. But no child of mine walks the streets of Onabasha looking like a play-actress woman. You wet your hair and comb it down modest and decent and then be off, or you'll have no time to find where you belong."

Elnora gave one despairing glance at the white face, framed in a most becoming riot of reddish-brown hair, which she saw in the little kitchen mirror. Then she untied the narrow black ribbon, wet the comb and plastered the waving curls close to her head, bound them fast, pinned on the skimpy black hat and opened the back door.

"You've gone so plumb daffy you are forgetting your dinner," jeered her mother.

"I don't want anything to eat," replied Elnora.

"You'll take your dinner or you'll not go one step. Are you crazy? Walk almost three miles and no food from six in the morning until six at night. A pretty figure you'd cut if you had your way! And after I've gone and bought you this nice new pail and filled it especial to start on!"

Elnora came back with a face still whiter and picked up the lunch. "Thank you, mother! Good-bye!" she said. Mrs. Comstock did not reply. She watched the girl follow the long walk to the gate and go from sight on the road, in the bright sunshine of the first Monday of September.

"I bet a dollar she gets enough of it by night!" commented Mrs. Comstock.

Elnora walked by instinct, for her eyes were blinded with tears. She left the road where it turned south, at the corner of the Limberlost, climbed a snake fence and entered a path worn by her own feet. Dodging under willow and scrub oak branches she came at last to the faint outline of an old trail made in the days when the precious timber of the swamp was guarded by armed men. This path she followed until she reached a thick clump of bushes. From the debris in the end of a hollow log she took a key that unlocked the padlock of a large weatherbeaten old box, inside of which lay several books, a butterfly apparatus, and a small cracked mirror. The walls were lined thickly with gaudy butterflies, dragonflies, and moths. She set up the mirror and once more pulling the ribbon from her hair, she shook the bright mass over her shoulders, tossing it dry in the sunshine. Then she straightened it, bound it loosely, and replaced her hat. She tugged vainly at the low brown calico collar and gazed despairingly at the generous length of the narrow skirt. She lifted it as she would have cut it if possible. That disclosed the heavy high leather shoes, at sight of which she seemed positively ill, and hastily dropped the skirt. She opened the pail, removed the lunch, wrapped it in the napkin, and placed it in a small pasteboard box. Locking the case again she hid the key and hurried down the trail.

She followed it around the north end of the swamp and then entered a footpath crossing a farm leading in the direction of the spires of the city to the northeast. Again she climbed a fence and was on the open road. For an instant she leaned against the fence staring before her, then turned and looked back. Behind her lay the land on which she had been born to drudgery and a mother who made no pretence of loving her; before her lay the city through whose schools she hoped to find means of escape and the way to reach the things for which she cared. When she thought of how she appeared she leaned more heavily against the fence and groaned; when she thought of turning back and wearing such clothing in ignorance all the days of her life she set her teeth firmly and went hastily toward Onabasha.

On the bridge crossing a deep culvert at the suburbs she glanced around, and then kneeling she thrust the lunch box between the foundation and the flooring. This left her empty-handed as she approached the big stone high school building. She entered bravely and inquired her way to the office of the superintendent. There she learned that she should have come the previous week and arranged about her classes. There were many things incident to the opening of school, and one man unable to cope with all of them.

"Where have you been attending school?" he asked, while he advised the teacher of Domestic Science not to telephone for groceries until she knew how many she would have in her classes; wrote an order for chemicals for the students of science; and advised the leader of the orchestra to hire a professional to take the place of the bass violist, reported suddenly ill.

"I finished last spring at Brushwood school, district number nine," said Elnora. "I have been studying all summer. I am quite sure I can do the first year work, if I have a few days to get started."

"Of course, of course," assented the superintendent. "Almost invariably country pupils do good work. You may enter first year, and if it is too difficult, we will find it out speedily. Your teachers will tell you the list of books you must have, and if you will come with me I will show you the way to the auditorium. It is now time for opening exercises. Take any seat you find vacant."

Elnora stood before the entrance and stared into the largest room she ever had seen. The floor sloped to a yawning stage on which a band of musicians, grouped around a grand piano, were tuning their instruments. She had two fleeting impressions. That it was all a mistake; this was no school, but a grand display of enormous ribbon bows; and the second, that she was sinking, and had forgotten how to walk. Then a burst from the orchestra nerved her while a bevy of daintily clad, sweet-smelling things that might have been birds, or flowers, or possibly gaily dressed, happy young girls, pushed her forward. She found herself plodding across the back of the auditorium, praying for guidance, to an empty seat.

As the girls passed her, vacancies seemed to open to meet them. Their friends were moving over, beckoning and whispering invitations. Every one else was seated, but no one paid any attention to the white-faced girl stumbling half-blindly down the aisle next the farthest wall. So she went on to the very end facing the stage. No one moved, and she could not summon courage to crowd past others to several empty seats she saw. At the end of the aisle she paused in desperation, while she stared back at the whole forest of faces most of which were now turned upon her.

In a flash came the full realization of her scanty dress, her pitiful little hat and ribbon, her big, heavy shoes, her ignorance of where to go or what to do; and from a sickening wave which crept over her, she felt she was going to become very ill. Then out of the mass she saw a pair of big, brown boy eyes, three seats from her, and there was a message in them. Without moving his body he reached forward and with a pencil touched the back of the seat before him. Instantly Elnora took another step which brought her to a row of vacant front seats.

She heard laughter behind her; the knowledge that she wore the only hat in the room burned her; every matter of moment, and some of none at all, cut and stung. She had no books. Where should she go when this was over? What would she give to be on the trail going home! She was shaking with a nervous chill when the music ceased, and the superintendent arose, and coming down to the front of the flower-decked platform, opened a Bible and began to read. Elnora did not know what he was reading, and she felt that she did not care. Wildly she was racking her brain to decide whether she should sit still when the others left the room or follow, and ask some one where the Freshmen went first.

In the midst of the struggle one sentence fell on her ear. "Hide me under the shadow of Thy wings."

Elnora began to pray frantically. "Hide me, O God, hide me, under the shadow of Thy wings."

Again and again she implored that prayer, and before she realized what was coming, every one had arisen and the room was emptying rapidly. Elnora hurried after the nearest girl and in the press at the door touched her sleeve timidly.

"Will you please tell me where the Freshmen go?" she asked huskily.

The girl gave her one surprised glance, and drew away.

"Same place as the fresh women," she answered, and those nearest her laughed.

Elnora stopped praying suddenly and the colour crept into her face. "I'll wager you are the first person I meet when I find it," she said and stopped short. "Not that! Oh, I must not do that!" she thought in dismay. "Make an enemy the first thing I do. Oh, not that!"

She followed with her eyes as the young people separated in the hall, some climbing stairs, some disappearing down side halls, some entering adjoining doors. She saw the girl overtake the brown-eyed boy and speak to him. He glanced back at Elnora with a scowl on his face. Then she stood alone in the hall.

Presently a door opened and a young woman came out and entered another room. Elnora waited until she returned, and hurried to her. "Would you tell me where the Freshmen are?" she panted.

"Straight down the hall, three doors to your left," was the answer, as the girl passed.

"One minute please, oh please," begged Elnora: "Should I knock or just open the door?"

"Go in and take a seat," replied the teacher.

"What if there aren't any seats?" gasped Elnora.

"Classrooms are never half-filled, there will be plenty," was the answer.

Elnora removed her hat. There was no place to put it, so she carried it in her hand. She looked infinitely better without it. After several efforts she at last opened the door and stepping inside faced a smaller and more concentrated battery of eyes.

"The superintendent sent me. He thinks I belong here," she said to the professor in charge of the class, but she never before heard the voice with which she spoke. As she stood waiting, the girl of the hall passed on her way to the blackboard, and suppressed laughter told Elnora that her thrust had been repeated.

"Be seated," said the professor, and then because he saw Elnora was desperately embarrassed he proceeded to lend her a book and to ask her if she had studied algebra. She said she had a little, but not the same book they were using. He asked her if she felt that she could do the work they were beginning, and she said she did.

That was how it happened, that three minutes after entering the room she was told to take her place beside the girl who had gone last to the board, and whose flushed face and angry eyes avoided meeting Elnora's. Being compelled to concentrate on her proposition she forgot herself. When the professor asked that all pupils sign their work she firmly wrote "Elnora Comstock" under her demonstration. Then she took her seat and waited with white lips and trembling limbs, as one after another professor called the names on the board, while their owners arose and explained their propositions, or "flunked" if they had not found a correct solution. She was so eager to catch their forms of expression and prepare herself for her recitation, that she never looked from the work on the board, until clearly and distinctly, "Elnora Cornstock," called the professor.

The dazed girl stared at the board. One tiny curl added to the top of the first curve of the m in her name, had transformed it from a good old English patronymic that any girl might bear proudly, to Cornstock. Elnora sat speechless. When and how did it happen? She could feel the wave of smothered laughter in the air around her. A rush of anger turned her face scarlet and her soul sick. The voice of the professor addressed her directly.

"This proposition seems to be beautifully demonstrated, Miss Cornstalk," he said. "Surely, you can tell us how you did it."

That word of praise saved her. She could do good work. They might wear their pretty clothes, have their friends and make life a greater misery than it ever before had been for her, but not one of them should do better work or be more womanly. That lay with her. She was tall, straight, and handsome as she arose.

"Of course I can explain my work," she said in natural tones. "What I can't explain is how I happened to be so stupid as to make a mistake in writing my own name. I must have been a little nervous. Please excuse me."

She went to the board, swept off the signature with one stroke, then rewrote it plainly. "My name is Comstock," she said distinctly. She returned to her seat and following the formula used by the others made her first high school recitation.

As Elnora resumed her seat Professor Henley looked at her steadily. "It puzzles me," he said deliberately, "how you can write as beautiful a demonstration, and explain it as clearly as ever has been done in any of my classes and still be so disturbed as to make a mistake in your own name. Are you very sure you did that yourself, Miss Comstock?"

"It is impossible that any one else should have done it," answered Elnora.

"I am very glad you think so," said the professor. "Being Freshmen, all of you are strangers to me. I should dislike to begin the year with you feeling there was one among you small enough to do a trick like that. The next proposition, please."

When the hour had gone the class filed back to the study room and Elnora followed in desperation, because she did not know where else to go. She could not study as she had no books, and when the class again left the room to go to another professor for the next recitation, she went also. At least they could put her out if she did not belong there. Noon came at last, and she kept with the others until they dispersed on the sidewalk. She was so abnormally self-conscious she fancied all the hundreds of that laughing, throng saw and jested at her. When she passed the brown-eyed boy walking with the girl of her encounter, she knew, for she heard him say: "Did you really let that gawky piece of calico get ahead of you?" The answer was indistinct.

Elnora hurried from the city. She intended to get her lunch, eat it in the shade of the first tree, and then decide whether she would go back or go home. She knelt on the bridge and reached for her box, but it was so very light that she was prepared for the fact that it was empty, before opening it. There was one thing for which to be thankful. The boy or tramp who had seen her hide it, had left the napkin. She would not have to face her mother and account for its loss. She put it in her pocket, and threw the box into the ditch. Then she sat on the bridge and tried to think, but her brain was confused.

"Perhaps the worst is over," she said at last. "I will go back. What would mother say to me if I came home now?"

So she returned to the high school, followed some other pupils to the coat room, hung her hat, and found her way to the study where she had been in the morning. Twice that afternoon, with aching head and empty stomach, she faced strange professors, in different branches. Once she escaped notice; the second time the worst happened. She was asked a question she could not answer.

"Have you not decided on your course, and secured your books?" inquired the professor.

"I have decided on my course," replied Elnora, "I do not know where to ask for my books."

"Ask?" the professor was bewildered.

"I understood the books were furnished," faltered Elnora.

"Only to those bringing an order from the township trustee," replied the Professor.

"No! Oh no!" cried Elnora. "I will have them to-morrow," and gripped her desk for support for she knew that was not true. Four books, ranging perhaps at a dollar and a half apiece; would her mother buy them? Of course she would not—could not.

Did not Elnora know the story of old. There was enough land, but no one to do clearing and farm. Tax on all those acres, recently the new gravel road tax added, the expense of living and only the work of two women to meet all of it. She was insane to think she could come to the city to school. Her mother had been right. The girl decided that if only she lived to reach home, she would stay there and lead any sort of life to avoid more of this torture. Bad as what she wished to escape had been, it was nothing like this. She never could live down the movement that went through the class when she inadvertently revealed the fact that she had expected books to be furnished. Her mother would not secure them; that settled the question.

But the end of misery is never in a hurry to come; before the day was over the superintendent entered the room and explained that pupils from the country were charged a tuition of twenty dollars a year. That really was the end. Previously Elnora had canvassed a dozen methods for securing the money for books, ranging all the way from offering to wash the superintendent's dishes to breaking into the bank. This additional expense made her plans so wildly impossible, there was nothing to do but hold up her head until she was from sight.

Down the long corridor alone among hundreds, down the long street alone among thousands, out into the country she came at last. Across the fence and field, along the old trail once trodden by a boy's bitter agony, now stumbled a white-faced girl, sick at heart. She sat on a log and began to sob in spite of her efforts at self-control. At first it was physical breakdown, later, thought came crowding.

Oh the shame, the mortification! Why had she not known of the tuition? How did she happen to think that in the city books were furnished? Perhaps it was because she had read they were in several states. But why did she not know? Why did not her mother go with her? Other mothers—but when had her mother ever been or done anything at all like other mothers? Because she never had been it was useless to blame her now. Elnora realized she should have gone to town the week before, called on some one and learned all these things herself. She should have remembered how her clothing would look, before she wore it in public places. Now she knew, and her dreams were over. She must go home to feed chickens, calves, and pigs, wear calico and coarse shoes, and with averted head, pass a library all her life. She sobbed again.

"For pity's sake, honey, what's the matter?" asked the voice of the nearest neighbour, Wesley Sinton, as he seated himself beside Elnora. "There, there," he continued, smearing tears all over her face in an effort to dry them. "Was it as bad as that, now? Maggie has been just wild over you all day. She's got nervouser every minute. She said we were foolish to let you go. She said your clothes were not right, you ought not to carry that tin pail, and that they would laugh at you. By gum, I see they did!"

"Oh, Uncle Wesley," sobbed the girl, "why didn't she tell me?"

"Well, you see, Elnora, she didn't like to. You got such a way of holding up your head, and going through with things. She thought some way that you'd make it, till you got started, and then she begun to see a hundred things we should have done. I reckon you hadn't reached that building before she remembered that your skirt should have been pleated instead of gathered, your shoes been low, and lighter for hot September weather, and a new hat. Were your clothes right, Elnora?"

The girl broke into hysterical laughter. "Right!" she cried. "Right! Uncle Wesley, you should have seen me among them! I was a picture! They'll never forget me. No, they won't get the chance, for they'll see me again to-morrow!"

"Now that is what I call spunk, Elnora! Downright grit," said Wesley Sinton. "Don't you let them laugh you out. You've helped Margaret and me for years at harvest and busy times, what you've earned must amount to quite a sum. You can get yourself a good many clothes with it."

"Don't mention clothes, Uncle Wesley," sobbed Elnora, "I don't care now how I look. If I don't go back all of them will know it's because I am so poor I can't buy my books."

"Oh, I don't know as you are so dratted poor," said Sinton meditatively. "There are three hundred acres of good land, with fine timber as ever grew on it."

"It takes all we can earn to pay the tax, and mother wouldn't cut a tree for her life."

"Well then, maybe, I'll be compelled to cut one for her," suggested Sinton. "Anyway, stop tearing yourself to pieces and tell me. If it isn't clothes, what is it?"

"It's books and tuition. Over twenty dollars in all."

"Humph! First time I ever knew you to be stumped by twenty dollars, Elnora," said Sinton, patting her hand.

"It's the first time you ever knew me to want money," answered Elnora. "This is different from anything that ever happened to me. Oh, how can I get it, Uncle Wesley?"

"Drive to town with me in the morning and I'll draw it from the bank for you. I owe you every cent of it."

"You know you don't owe me a penny, and I wouldn't touch one from you, unless I really could earn it. For anything that's past I owe you and Aunt Margaret for all the home life and love I've ever known. I know how you work, and I'll not take your money."

"Just a loan, Elnora, just a loan for a little while until you can earn it. You can be proud with all the rest of the world, but there are no secrets between us, are there, Elnora?"

"No," said Elnora, "there are none. You and Aunt Margaret have given me all the love there has been in my life. That is the one reason above all others why you shall not give me charity. Hand me money because you find me crying for it! This isn't the first time this old trail has known tears and heartache. All of us know that story. Freckles stuck to what he undertook and won out. I stick, too. When Duncan moved away he gave me all Freckles left in the swamp, and as I have inherited his property maybe his luck will come with it. I won't touch your money, but I'll win some way. First, I'm going home and try mother. It's just possible I could find second-hand books, and perhaps all the tuition need not be paid at once. Maybe they would accept it quarterly. But oh, Uncle Wesley, you and Aunt Margaret keep on loving me! I'm so lonely, and no one else cares!"

Wesley Sinton's jaws met with a click. He swallowed hard on bitter words and changed what he would have liked to say three times before it became articulate.

"Elnora," he said at last, "if it hadn't been for one thing I'd have tried to take legal steps to make you ours when you were three years old. Maggie said then it wasn't any use, but I've always held on. You see, I was the first man there, honey, and there are things you see, that you can't ever make anybody else understand. She loved him Elnora, she just made an idol of him. There was that oozy green hole, with the thick scum broke, and two or three big bubbles slowly rising that were the breath of his body. There she was in spasms of agony, and beside her the great heavy log she'd tried to throw him. I can't ever forgive her for turning against you, and spoiling your childhood as she has, but I couldn't forgive anybody else for abusing her. Maggie has got no mercy on her, but Maggie didn't see what I did, and I've never tried to make it very clear to her. It's been a little too plain for me ever since. Whenever I look at your mother's face, I see what she saw, so I hold my tongue and say, in my heart, 'Give her a mite more time.' Some day it will come. She does love you, Elnora. Everybody does, honey. It's just that she's feeling so much, she can't express herself. You be a patient girl and wait a little longer. After all, she's your mother, and you're all she's got, but a memory, and it might do her good to let her know that she was fooled in that."

"It would kill her!" cried the girl swiftly. "Uncle Wesley, it would kill her! What do you mean?"

"Nothing," said Wesley Sinton soothingly. "Nothing, honey. That was just one of them fool things a man says, when he is trying his best to be wise. You see, she loved him mightily, and they'd been married only a year, and what she was loving was what she thought he was. She hadn't really got acquainted with the man yet. If it had been even one more year, she could have borne it, and you'd have got justice. Having been a teacher she was better educated and smarter than the rest of us, and so she was more sensitive like. She can't understand she was loving a dream. So I say it might do her good if somebody that knew, could tell her, but I swear to gracious, I never could. I've heard her out at the edge of that quagmire calling in them wild spells of hers off and on for the last sixteen years, and imploring the swamp to give him back to her, and I've got out of bed when I was pretty tired, and come down to see she didn't go in herself, or harm you. What she feels is too deep for me. I've got to respectin' her grief, and I can't get over it. Go home and tell your ma, honey, and ask her nice and kind to help you. If she won't, then you got to swallow that little lump of pride in your neck, and come to Aunt Maggie, like you been a-coming all your life."

"I'll ask mother, but I can't take your money, Uncle Wesley, indeed I can't. I'll wait a year, and earn some, and enter next year."

"There's one thing you don't consider, Elnora," said the man earnestly. "And that's what you are to Maggie. She's a little like your ma. She hasn't given up to it, and she's struggling on brave, but when we buried our second little girl the light went out of Maggie's eyes, and it's not come back. The only time I ever see a hint of it is when she thinks she's done something that makes you happy, Elnora. Now, you go easy about refusing her anything she wants to do for you. There's times in this world when it's our bounden duty to forget ourselves, and think what will help other people. Young woman, you owe me and Maggie all the comfort we can get out of you. There's the two of our own we can't ever do anything for. Don't you get the idea into your head that a fool thing you call pride is going to cut us out of all the pleasure we have in life beside ourselves."

"Uncle Wesley, you are a dear," said Elnora. "Just a dear! If I can't possibly get that money any way else on earth, I'll come and borrow it of you, and then I'll pay it back if I must dig ferns from the swamp and sell them from door to door in the city. I'll even plant them, so that they will be sure to come up in the spring. I have been sort of panic stricken all day and couldn't think. I can gather nuts and sell them. Freckles sold moths and butterflies, and I've a lot collected. Of course, I am going back to-morrow! I can find a way to get the books. Don't you worry about me. I am all right!

"Now, what do you think of that?" inquired Wesley Sinton of the swamp in general. "Here's our Elnora come back to stay. Head high and right as a trivet! You've named three ways in three minutes that you could earn ten dollars, which I figure would be enough, to start you. Let's go to supper and stop worrying!"

Elnora unlocked the case, took out the pail, put the napkin in it, pulled the ribbon from her hair, binding it down tightly again and followed to the road. From afar she could see her mother in the doorway. She blinked her eyes, and tried to smile as she answered Wesley Sinton, and indeed she did feel better. She knew now what she had to expect, where to go, and what to do. Get the books she must; when she had them, she would show those city girls and boys how to prepare and recite lessons, how to walk with a brave heart; and they could show her how to wear pretty clothes and have good times.

As she neared the door her mother reached for the pail. "I forgot to tell you to bring home your scraps for the chickens," she said.

Elnora entered. "There weren't any scraps, and I'm hungry again as I ever was in my life."

"I thought likely you would be," said Mrs. Comstock, "and so I got supper ready. We can eat first, and do the work afterward. What kept you so? I expected you an hour ago."

Elnora looked into her mother's face and smiled. It was a queer sort of a little smile, and would have reached the depths with any normal mother.

"I see you've been bawling," said Mrs. Comstock. "I thought you'd get your fill in a hurry. That's why I wouldn't go to any expense. If we keep out of the poor-house we have to cut the corners close. It's likely this Brushwood road tax will eat up all we've saved in years. Where the land tax is to come from I don't know. It gets bigger every year. If they are going to dredge the swamp ditch again they'll just have to take the land to pay for it. I can't, that's all! We'll get up early in the morning and gather and hull the beans for winter, and put in the rest of the day hoeing the turnips."

Elnora again smiled that pitiful smile.

"Do you think I didn't know that I was funny and would be laughed at?" she asked.

"Funny?" cried Mrs. Comstock hotly.

"Yes, funny! A regular caricature," answered Elnora. "No one else wore calico, not even one other. No one else wore high heavy shoes, not even one. No one else had such a funny little old hat; my hair was not right, my ribbon invisible compared with the others, I did not know where to go, or what to do, and I had no books. What a spectacle I made for them!" Elnora laughed nervously at her own picture. "But there are always two sides! The professor said in the algebra class that he never had a better solution and explanation than mine of the proposition he gave me, which scored one for me in spite of my clothes."

"Well, I wouldn't brag on myself!"

"That was poor taste," admitted Elnora. "But, you see, it is a case of whistling to keep up my courage. I honestly could see that I would have looked just as well as the rest of them if I had been dressed as they were. We can't afford that, so I have to find something else to brace me. It was rather bad, mother!"

"Well, I'm glad you got enough of it!"

"Oh, but I haven't," hurried in Elnora. "I just got a start. The hardest is over. To-morrow they won't be surprised. They will know what to expect. I am sorry to hear about the dredge. Is it really going through?"

"Yes. I got my notification today. The tax will be something enormous. I don't know as I can spare you, even if you are willing to be a laughing-stock for the town."

With every bite Elnora's courage returned, for she was a healthy young thing.

"You've heard about doing evil that good might come from it," she said. "Well, mother mine, it's something like that with me. I'm willing to bear the hard part to pay for what I'll learn. Already I have selected the ward building in which I shall teach in about four years. I am going to ask for a room with a south exposure so that the flowers and moths I take in from the swamp to show the children will do well."

"You little idiot!" said Mrs. Comstock. "How are you going to pay your expenses?"

"Now that is just what I was going to ask you!" said Elnora. "You see, I have had two startling pieces of news to-day. I did not know I would need any money. I thought the city furnished the books, and there is an out-of-town tuition, also. I need ten dollars in the morning. Will you please let me have it?"

"Ten dollars!" cried Mrs. Comstock. "Ten dollars! Why don't you say a hundred and be done with it! I could get one as easy as the other. I told you! I told you I couldn't raise a cent. Every year expenses grow bigger and bigger. I told you not to ask for money!"

"I never meant to," replied Elnora. "I thought clothes were all I needed and I could bear them. I never knew about buying books and tuition."

"Well, I did!" said Mrs. Comstock. "I knew what you would run into! But you are so bull-dog stubborn, and so set in your way, I thought I would just let you try the world a little and see how you liked it!"

Elnora pushed back her chair and looked at her mother.

"Do you mean to say," she demanded, "that you knew, when you let me go into a city classroom and reveal the fact before all of them that I expected to have my books handed out to me; do you mean to say that you knew I had to pay for them?"

Mrs. Comstock evaded the direct question.

"Anybody but an idiot mooning over a book or wasting time prowling the woods would have known you had to pay. Everybody has to pay for everything. Life is made up of pay, pay, pay! It's always and forever pay! If you don't pay one way you do another! Of course, I knew you had to pay. Of course, I knew you would come home blubbering! But you don't get a penny! I haven't one cent, and can't get one! Have your way if you are determined, but I think you will find the road somewhat rocky."

"Swampy, you mean, mother," corrected Elnora. She arose white and trembling. "Perhaps some day God will teach me how to understand you. He knows I do not now. You can't possibly realize just what you let me go through to-day, or how you let me go, but I'll tell you this: You understand enough that if you had the money, and would offer it to me, I wouldn't touch it now. And I'll tell you this much more. I'll get it myself. I'll raise it, and do it some honest way. I am going back to-morrow, the next day, and the next. You need not come out, I'll do the night work, and hoe the turnips."

It was ten o'clock when the chickens, pigs, and cattle were fed, the turnips hoed, and a heap of bean vines was stacked beside the back door.

CHAPTER II

WHEREIN WESLEY AND MARGARET GO
SHOPPING, AND ELNORA'S WARDROBE
IS REPLENISHED

Wesley Sinton walked down the road half a mile and turned at the lane leading to his home. His heart was hot and filled with indignation. He had told Elnora he did not blame her mother, but he did. His wife met him at the door.

"Did you see anything of Elnora?" she questioned.

"Most too much, Maggie," he answered. "What do you say to going to town? There's a few things has to be got right away."

"Where did you see her, Wesley?"

"Along the old Limberlost trail, my girl, torn to pieces sobbing. Her courage always has been fine, but the thing she met to-day was too much for her. We ought to have known better than to let her go that way. It wasn't only clothes; there were books, and entrance fees for out-of-town people, that she didn't know about; while there must have been jeers, whispers, and laughing. Maggie, I feel as if I'd been a traitor to those girls of ours. I ought to have gone in and seen about this school business. Don't cry, Maggie. Get me some supper, and I'll hitch up and see what we can do now."

"What can we do, Wesley?

"I don't just know. But we've got to do something. Kate Comstock will be a handful, while Elnora will be two, but between us we must see that the girl is not too hard pressed about money, and that she is dressed so she is not ridiculous. She's saved us the wages of a woman many a day, can't you make her some decent dresses?"

"Well, I'm not just what you call expert, but I could beat Kate Comstock all to pieces. I know that skirts should be pleated to the band instead of gathered, and full enough to sit in, and short enough to walk in. I could try. There are patterns for sale. Let's go right away, Wesley."

"Set me a bit of supper, while I hitch up."

Margaret built a fire, made coffee, and fried ham and eggs. She set out pie and cake and had enough for a hungry man by the time the carriage was at the door, but she had no appetite. She dressed while Wesley ate, put away the food while he dressed, and then they drove toward the city through the beautiful September evening, and as they went they planned for Elnora. The trouble was, not whether they were generous enough to buy what she needed, but whether she would accept their purchases, and what her mother would say.

They went to a drygoods store and when a clerk asked what they wanted to see neither of them knew, so they stepped aside and held a whispered consultation.

"What had we better get, Wesley?"

"Dresses," said Wesley promptly,

"But how many dresses, and what kind?"

"Blest if I know!" exclaimed Wesley. "I thought you would manage that. I know about some things I'm going to get."

At that instant several high school girls came into the store and approached them.

"There!" exclaimed Wesley breathlessly. "There, Maggie! Like them! That's what she needs! Buy like they have!"

Margaret stared. What did they wear? They were rapidly passing; they seemed to have so much, and she could not decide so quickly. Before she knew it she was among them.

"I beg your pardon, but won't you wait one minute?" she asked.

The girls stopped with wondering faces.

"It's your clothes," explained Mrs. Sinton. "You look just beautiful to me. You look exactly as I should have wanted to see my girls. They both died of diphtheria when they were little, but they had yellow hair, dark eyes and pink cheeks, and everybody thought they were lovely. If they had lived, they'd been near your age now, and I'd want them to look like you."

There was sympathy on every girl face.

"Why thank you!" said one of them. "We are very sorry for you."

"Of course you are," said Margaret. "Everybody always has been. And because I can't ever have the joy of a mother in thinking for my girls and buying pretty things for them, there is nothing left for me, but to do what I can for some one who has no mother to care for her. I know a girl, who would be just as pretty as any of you, if she had the clothes, but her mother does not think about her, so I mother her some myself."

"She must be a lucky girl," said another.

"Oh, she loves me," said Margaret, "and I love her. I want her to look just like you do. Please tell me about your clothes. Are these the dresses and hats you wear to school? What kind of goods are they, and where do you buy them?"

The girls began to laugh and cluster around Margaret. Wesley strode down the store with his head high through pride in her, but his heart was sore over the memory of two little faces under Brushwood sod. He inquired his way to the shoe department.

"Why, every one of us have on gingham or linen dresses," they said, "and they are our school clothes."

For a few moments there was a babel of laughing voices explaining to the delighted Margaret that school dresses should be bright and pretty, but simple and plain, and until cold weather they should wash.

"I'll tell you," said Ellen Brownlee, "my father owns this store, I know all the clerks. I'll take you to Miss Hartley. You tell her just how much you want to spend, and what you want to buy, and she will know how to get the most for your money. I've heard papa say she was the best clerk in the store for people who didn't know precisely what they wanted."

"That's the very thing," agreed Margaret. "But before you go, tell me about your hair. Elnora's hair is bright and wavy, but yours is silky as hackled flax. How do you do it?"

"Elnora?" asked four girls in concert.

"Yes, Elnora is the name of the girl I want these things for."

"Did she come to the high school to-day?" questioned one of them.

"Was she in your classes?" demanded Margaret without reply.

Four girls stood silent and thought fast. Had there been a strange girl among them, and had she been overlooked and passed by with indifference, because she was so very shabby? If she had appeared as much better than they, as she had looked worse, would her reception have been the same?

"There was a strange girl from the country in the Freshman class to-day," said Ellen Brownlee, "and her name was Elnora."

"That was the girl," said Margaret.

"Are her people so very poor?" questioned Ellen.

"No, not poor at all, come to think of it," answered Margaret. "It's a peculiar case. Mrs. Comstock had a great trouble and she let it change her whole life and make a different woman of her. She used to be lovely; now she is forever saving and scared to death for fear they will go to the poorhouse; but there is a big farm, covered with lots of good timber. The taxes are high for women who can't manage to clear and work the land. There ought to be enough to keep two of them in good shape all their lives, if they only knew how to do it. But no one ever told Kate Comstock anything, and never will, for she won't listen. All she does is droop all day, and walk the edge of the swamp half the night, and neglect Elnora. If you girls would make life just a little easier for her it would be the finest thing you ever did."

All of them promised they would.

"Now tell me about your hair," persisted Margaret Sinton.

So they took her to a toilet counter, and she bought the proper hair soap, also a nail file, and cold cream, for use after windy days. Then they left her with the experienced clerk, and when at last Wesley found her she was loaded with bundles and the light of other days was in her beautiful eyes. Wesley also carried some packages.

"Did you get any stockings?" he whispered.

"No, I didn't," she said. "I was so interested in dresses and hair ribbons and a—a hat——" she hesitated and glanced at Wesley. "Of course, a hat!" prompted Wesley. "That I forgot all about those horrible shoes. She's got to have decent shoes, Wesley."

"Sure!" said Wesley. "She's got decent shoes. But the man said some brown stockings ought to go with them. Take a peep, will you!"

Wesley opened a box and displayed a pair of thick-soled, beautifully shaped brown walking shoes of low cut. Margaret cried out with pleasure.

"But do you suppose they are the right size, Wesley? What did you get?"

"I just said for a girl of sixteen with a slender foot."

"Well, that's about as near as I could come. If they don't fit when she tries them, we will drive straight in and change them. Come on now, let's get home."

All the way they discussed how they should give Elnora their purchases and what Mrs. Comstock would say.

"I am afraid she will be awful mad," said Margaret.

"She'll just rip!" replied Wesley graphically. "But if she wants to leave the raising of her girl to the neighbours, she needn't get fractious if they take some pride in doing a good job. From now on I calculate Elnora shall go to school; and she shall have all the clothes and books she needs, if I go around on the back of Kate Comstock's land and cut a tree, or drive off a calf to pay for them. Why I know one tree she owns that would put Elnora in heaven for a year. Just think of it, Margaret! It's not fair. One-third of what is there belongs to Elnora by law, and if Kate Comstock raises a row I'll tell her so, and see that the girl gets it. You go to see Kate in the morning, and I'll go with you. Tell her you want Elnora's pattern, that you are going to make her a dress, for helping us. And sort of hint at a few more things. If Kate balks, I'll take a hand and settle her. I'll go to law for Elnora's share of that land and sell enough to educate her."

"Why, Wesley Sinton, you're perfectly wild."

"I'm not! Did you ever stop to think that such cases are so frequent there have been laws made to provide for them? I can bring it up in court and force Kate to educate Elnora, and board and clothe her till she's of age, and then she can take her share."

"Wesley, Kate would go crazy!"

"She's crazy now. The idea of any mother living with as sweet a girl as Elnora and letting her suffer till I find her crying like a funeral. It makes me fighting mad. All uncalled for. Not a grain of sense in it. I've offered and offered to oversee clearing her land and working her fields. Let her sell a good tree, or a few acres. Something is going to be done, right now. Elnora's been fairly happy up to this, but to spoil the school life she's planned, is to ruin all her life. I won't have it! If Elnora won't take these things, so help me, I'll tell her what she is worth, and loan her the money and she can pay me back when she comes of age. I am going to have it out with Kate Comstock in the morning. Here we are! You open up what you got while I put away the horses, and then I'll show you."

When Wesley came from the barn Margaret had four pieces of crisp gingham, a pale blue, a pink, a gray with green stripes and a rich brown and blue plaid. On each of them lay a yard and a half of wide ribbon to match. There were handkerchiefs and a brown leather belt. In her hands she held a wide-brimmed tan straw hat, having a high crown banded with velvet strips each of which fastened with a tiny gold buckle.

"It looks kind of bare now," she explained. "It had three quills on it here."

"Did you have them taken off?" asked Wesley.

"Yes, I did. The price was two and a half for the hat, and those things were a dollar and a half apiece. I couldn't pay that."

"It does seem considerable," admitted Wesley, "but will it look right without them?"

"No, it won't!" said Margaret. "It's going to have quills on it. Do you remember those beautiful peacock wing feathers that Phoebe Simms gave me? Three of them go on just where those came off, and nobody will ever know the difference. They match the hat to a moral, and they are just a little longer and richer than the ones that I had taken off. I was wondering whether I better sew them on to-night while I remember how they set, or wait till morning."

"Don't risk it!" exclaimed Wesley anxiously. "Don't you risk it! Sew them on right now!"

"Open your bundles, while I get the thread," said Margaret.

Wesley unwrapped the shoes. Margaret took them up and pinched the leather and stroked them.

"My, but they are fine!" she cried.

Wesley picked up one and slowly turned it in his big hands. He glanced at his foot and back to the shoe.

"It's a little bit of a thing, Margaret," he said softly. "Like as not I'll have to take it back. It seems as if it couldn't fit."

"It seems as if it didn't dare do anything else," said Margaret. "That's a happy little shoe to get the chance to carry as fine a girl as Elnora to high school. Now what's in the other box?"

Wesley looked at Margaret doubtfully.

"Why," he said, "you know there's going to be rainy days, and those things she has now ain't fit for anything but to drive up the cows——"

"Wesley, did you get high shoes, too?"

"Well, she ought to have them! The man said he would make them cheaper if I took both pairs at once."

Margaret laughed aloud. "Those will do her past Christmas," she exulted. "What else did you buy?"

"Well sir," said Wesley, "I saw something to-day. You told me about Kate getting that tin pail for Elnora to carry to high school and you said you told her it was a shame. I guess Elnora was ashamed all right, for to-night she stopped at the old case Duncan gave her, and took out that pail, where it had been all day, and put a napkin inside it. Coming home she confessed she was half starved because she hid her dinner under a culvert, and a tramp took it. She hadn't had a bite to eat the whole day. But she never complained at all, she was pleased that she hadn't lost the napkin. So I just inquired around till I found this, and I think it's about the ticket."

Wesley opened the package and laid a brown leather lunch box on the table. "Might be a couple of books, or drawing tools or most anything that's neat and genteel. You see, it opens this way."

It did open, and inside was a space for sandwiches, a little porcelain box for cold meat or fried chicken, another for salad, a glass with a lid which screwed on, held by a ring in a corner, for custard or jelly, a flask for tea or milk, a beautiful little knife, fork, and spoon fastened in holders, and a place for a napkin.

Margaret was almost crying over it.

"How I'd love to fill it!" she exclaimed.

"Do it the first time, just to show Kate Comstock what love is!" said Wesley. "Get up early in the morning and make one of those dresses to-morrow. Can't you make a plain gingham dress in a day? I'll pick a chicken, and you fry it and fix a little custard for the cup, and do it up brown. Go on, Maggie, you do it!"

"I never can," said Margaret. "I am slow as the itch about sewing, and these are not going to be plain dresses when it comes to making them. There are going to be edgings of plain green, pink, and brown to the bias strips, and tucks and pleats around the hips, fancy belts and collars, and all of it takes time."

"Then Kate Comstock's got to help," said Wesley. "Can the two of you make one, and get that lunch to-morrow?"

"Easy, but she'll never do it!"

"You see if she doesn't!" said Wesley. "You get up and cut it out, and soon as Elnora is gone I'll go after Kate myself. She'll take what I'll say better alone. But she'll come, and she'll help make the dress. These other things are our Christmas gifts to Elnora. She'll no doubt need them more now than she will then, and we can give them just as well. That's yours, and this is mine, or whichever way you choose."

Wesley untied a good brown umbrella and shook out the folds of a long, brown raincoat. Margaret dropped the hat, arose and took the coat. She tried it on, felt it, cooed over it and matched it with the umbrella.

"Did it look anything like rain to-night?" she inquired so anxiously that Wesley laughed.

"And this last bundle?" she said, dropping back in her chair, the coat still over her shoulders.

"I couldn't buy this much stuff for any other woman and nothing for my own," said Wesley. "It's Christmas for you, too, Margaret!" He shook out fold after fold of soft gray satiny goods that would look lovely against Margaret's pink cheeks and whitening hair.

"Oh, you old darling!" she exclaimed, and fled sobbing into his arms.

But she soon dried her eyes, raked together the coals in the cooking stove and boiled one of the dress patterns in salt water for half an hour. Wesley held the lamp while she hung the goods on the line to dry. Then she set the irons on the stove so they would be hot the first thing in the morning.

CHAPTER III

Four o'clock the following morning Elnora was shelling beans. At six she fed the chickens and pigs, swept two of the rooms of the cabin, built a fire, and put on the kettle for breakfast. Then she climbed the narrow stairs to the attic she had occupied since a very small child, and dressed in the hated shoes and brown calico, plastered down her crisp curls, ate what breakfast she could, and pinning on her hat started for town.

"There is no sense in your going for an hour yet," said her mother.

"I must try to discover some way to earn those books," replied Elnora. "I am perfectly positive I shall not find them lying beside the road wrapped in tissue paper, and tagged with my name."

She went toward the city as on yesterday. Her perplexity as to where tuition and books were to come from was worse but she did not feel quite so badly. She never again would have to face all of it for the first time. There had been times yesterday when she had prayed to be hidden, or to drop dead, and neither had happened. "I believe the best way to get an answer to prayer is to work for it," muttered Elnora grimly.

Again she followed the trail to the swamp, rearranged her hair and left the tin pail. This time she folded a couple of sandwiches in the napkin, and tied them in a neat light paper parcel which she carried in her hand. Then she hurried along the road to Onabasha and found a book-store. There she asked the prices of the list of books that she needed, and learned that six dollars would not quite supply them. She anxiously inquired for second-hand books, but was told that the only way to secure them was from the last year's Freshmen. Just then Elnora felt that she positively could not approach any of those she supposed to be Sophomores and ask to buy their old books. The only balm the girl could see for the humiliation of yesterday was to appear that day with a set of new books.

"Do you wish these?" asked the clerk hurriedly, for the store was rapidly filling with school children wanting anything from a dictionary to a pen.

"Yes," gasped Elnora, "Oh, yes! But I cannot pay for them just now. Please let me take them, and I will pay for them on Friday, or return them as perfect as they are. Please trust me for them a few days."

"I'll ask the proprietor," he said. When he came back Elnora knew the answer before he spoke.

"I'm sorry," he said, "but Mr. Hann doesn't recognize your name. You are not a customer of ours, and he feels that he can't take the risk."

Elnora clumped out of the store, the thump of her heavy shoes beating as a hammer on her brain. She tried two other dealers with the same result, and then in sick despair came into the street. What could she do? She was too frightened to think. Should she stay from school that day and canvass the homes appearing to belong to the wealthy, and try to sell beds of wild ferns, as she had suggested to Wesley Sinton? What would she dare ask for bringing in and planting a clump of ferns? How could she carry them? Would people buy them? She slowly moved past the hotel and then glanced around to see if there were a clock anywhere, for she felt sure the young people passing her constantly were on their way to school.

There it stood in a bank window in big black letters staring straight at her:

WANTED: CATERPILLARS, COCOONS, CHRYSALIDES, PUPAE CASES, BUTTERFLIES, MOTHS, INDIAN RELICS OF ALL KINDS. HIGHEST SCALE OF PRICES PAID IN CASH

Elnora caught the wicket at the cashier's desk with both hands to brace herself against disappointment.

"Who is it wants to buy cocoons, butterflies, and moths?" she panted.

"The Bird Woman," answered the cashier. "Have you some for sale?"

"I have some, I do not know if they are what she would want."

"Well, you had better see her," said the cashier. "Do you know where she lives?"

"Yes," said Elnora. "Would you tell me the time?"

"Twenty-one after eight," was the answer.

She had nine minutes to reach the auditorium or be late. Should she go to school, or to the Bird Woman? Several girls passed her walking swiftly and she remembered their faces. They were hurrying to school. Elnora caught the infection. She would see the Bird Woman at noon. Algebra came first, and that professor was kind. Perhaps she could slip to the superintendent and ask him for a book for the next lesson, and at noon—"Oh, dear Lord make it come true," prayed Elnora, at noon possibly she could sell some of those wonderful shining-winged things she had been collecting all her life around the outskirts of the Limberlost.

As she went down the long hall she noticed the professor of mathematics standing in the door of his recitation room. When she passed him he smiled and spoke to her.

"I have been watching for you," he said, and Elnora stopped bewildered.

"For me?" she questioned.

"Yes," said Professor Henley. "Step inside."

Elnora followed him into the room and closed the door behind them.

"At teachers' meeting last evening, one of the professors mentioned that a pupil had betrayed in class that she had expected her books to be furnished by the city. I thought possibly it was you. Was it?"

"Yes," breathed Elnora.

"That being the case," said Professor Henley, "it just occurred to me as you had expected that, you might require a little time to secure them, and you are too fine a mathematician to fall behind for want of supplies. So I telephoned one of our Sophomores to bring her last year's books this morning. I am sorry to say they are somewhat abused, but the text is all here. You can have them for two dollars, and pay when you are ready. Would you care to take them?"

Elnora sat suddenly, because she could not stand another instant. She reached both hands for the books, and said never a word. The professor was silent also.

At last Elnora arose, hugging those books to her heart as a mother clasps a baby.

"One thing more," said the professor. "You may pay your tuition quarterly. You need not bother about the first instalment this month. Any time in October will do."

It seemed as if Elnora's gasp of relief must have reached the soles of her brogans.

"Did any one ever tell you how beautiful you are!" she cried.

As the professor was lank, tow-haired and so near-sighted, that he peered at his pupils through spectacles, no one ever had.

"No," said Professor Henley, "I've waited some time for that; for which reason I shall appreciate it all the more. Come now, or we shall be late for opening exercises."

So Elnora entered the auditorium a second time. Her face was like the brightest dawn that ever broke over the Limberlost. No matter about the lumbering shoes and skimpy dress. No matter about anything, she had the books. She could take them home. In her garret she could commit them to memory, if need be. She could prove that clothes were not all. If the Bird Woman did not want any of the many different kinds of specimens she had collected, she was quite sure now she could sell ferns, nuts, and a great many things. Then, too, a girl made a place for her that morning, and several smiled and bowed. Elnora forgot everything save her books, and that she was where she could use them intelligently— everything except one little thing away back in her head. Her mother had known about the books and the tuition, and had not told her when she agreed to her coming.

At noon Elnora took her little parcel of lunch and started to the home of the Bird Woman. She must know about the specimens first and then she would walk to the suburbs somewhere and eat a few bites. She dropped the heavy iron knocker on the door of a big red log cabin, and her heart thumped at the resounding stroke.

"Is the Bird Woman at home?" she asked of the maid.

"She is at lunch," was the answer.

"Please ask her if she will see a girl from the Limberlost about some moths?" inquired Elnora.

"I never need ask, if it's moths," laughed the girl. "Orders are to bring any one with specimens right in. Come this way."

Elnora followed down the hall and entered a long room with high panelled wainscoting, old English fireplace with an overmantel and closets of peculiar china filling the corners. At a bare table of oak, yellow as gold, sat a woman Elnora often had watched and followed covertly around the Limberlost. The Bird Woman was holding out a hand of welcome.

"I heard!" she laughed. "A little pasteboard box, or just the mere word 'specimen,' passes you at my door. If it is moths I hope you have hundreds. I've been very busy all summer and unable to collect, and I need so many. Sit down and lunch with me, while we talk it over. From the Limberlost, did you say?"

"I live near the swamp," replied Elnora. "Since it's so cleared I dare go around the edge in daytime, though we are all afraid at night."

"What have you collected?" asked the Bird Woman, as she helped Elnora to sandwiches unlike any she ever before had tasted, salad that seemed to be made of many familiar things, and a cup of hot chocolate that would have delighted any hungry schoolgirl.

"I am afraid I am bothering you for nothing, and imposing on you," she said. "That 'collected' frightens me. I've only gathered. I always loved everything outdoors, so I made friends and playmates of them. When I learned that the moths die so soon, I saved them especially, because there seemed no wickedness in it."

"I have thought the same thing," said the Bird Woman encouragingly. Then because the girl could not eat until she learned about the moths, the Bird Woman asked Elnora if she knew what kinds she had.

"Not all of them," answered Elnora. "Before Mr. Duncan moved away he often saw me near the edge of the swamp and he showed me the box he had fixed for Freckles, and gave me the key. There were some books and things, so from that time on I studied and tried to take moths right, but I am afraid they are not what you want."

"Are they the big ones that fly mostly in June nights?" asked the Bird Woman.

"Yes," said Elnora. "Big gray ones with reddish markings, pale blue-green, yellow with lavender, and red and yellow."

"What do you mean by 'red and yellow?'" asked the Bird Woman so quickly that the girl almost jumped.

"Not exactly red," explained Elnora, with tremulous voice. "A reddish, yellowish brown, with canary-coloured spots and gray lines on their wings."

"How many of them?" It was the same quick question.

"I had over two hundred eggs," said Elnora, "but some of them didn't hatch, and some of the caterpillars died, but there must be at least a hundred perfect ones."

"Perfect! How perfect?" cried the Bird Woman.

"I mean whole wings, no down gone, and all their legs and antennae," faltered Elnora.

"Young woman, that's the rarest moth in America," said the Bird Woman solemnly. "If you have a hundred of them, they are worth a hundred dollars according to my list. I can use all that are not damaged."

"What if they are not pinned right," quavered Elnora.

"If they are perfect, that does not make the slightest difference. I know how to soften them so that I can put them into any shape I choose. Where are they? When may I see them?"

"They are in Freckles's old case in the Limberlost," said Elnora. "I couldn't carry many for fear of breaking them, but I could bring a few after school."

"You come here at four," said the Bird Woman, "and we will drive out with some specimen boxes, and a price list, and see what you have to sell. Are they your very own? Are you free to part with them?"

"They are mine," said Elnora. "No one but God knows I have them. Mr. Duncan gave me the books and the box. He told Freckles about me, and Freckles told him to give me all he left. He said for me to stick to the swamp and be brave, and my hour would come, and it has! I know most of them are all right, and oh, I do need the money!"

"Could you tell me?" asked the Bird Woman softly.

"You see the swamp and all the fields around it are so full," explained Elnora. "Every day I felt smaller and smaller, and I wanted to know more and more, and pretty soon I grew desperate, just as Freckles did. But I am better off than he was, for I have his books, and I have a mother; even if she doesn't care for me as other girls' mothers do for them, it's better than no one."

The Bird Woman's glance fell, for the girl was not conscious of how much she was revealing. Her eyes were fixed on a black pitcher filled with goldenrod in the centre of the table and she was saying what she thought.

"As long as I could go to the Brushwood school I was happy, but I couldn't go further just when things were the most interesting, so I was determined I'd come to high school and mother wouldn't consent. You see there's plenty of land, but father was drowned when I was a baby, and mother and I can't make money as men do. The taxes are higher every year, and she said it was too expensive. I wouldn't give her any rest, until at last she bought me this dress, and these shoes and I came. It was awful!"

"Do you live in that beautiful cabin at the northwest end of the swamp?" asked the Bird Woman.

"Yes," said Elnora.

"I remember the place and a story about it, now. You entered the high school yesterday?"

"Yes."

"It was rather bad?"

"Rather bad!" echoed Elnora.

The Bird Woman laughed.

"You can't tell me anything about that," she said. "I once entered a city school straight from the country. My dress was brown calico, and my shoes were heavy."

The tears began to roll down Elnora's cheeks.

"Did they——?" she faltered.

"They did!" said the Bird Woman. "All of it. I am sure they did not miss one least little thing."

Then she wiped away some tears that began coursing her cheeks, and laughed at the same time.

"Where are they now?" asked Elnora suddenly.

"They are widely scattered, but none of them have attained heights out of range. Some of the rich are poor, and some of the poor are rich. Some of the brightest died insane, and some of the dullest worked out high positions; some of the very worst to bear have gone out, and I frequently hear from others. Now I am here, able to remember it, and mingle laughter with what used to be all tears; for every day I have my beautiful work, and almost every day God sends some one like you to help me. What is your name, my girl?"

"Elnora Comstock," answered Elnora. "Yesterday on the board it changed to Cornstock, and for a minute I thought I'd die, but I can laugh over that already."

The Bird Woman arose and kissed her. "Finish your lunch," she said, "and I will bring my price lists, and make a memorandum of what you think you have, so I will know how many boxes to prepare. And remember this: What you are lies with you. If you are lazy, and accept your lot, you may live in it. If you are willing to work, you can write your name anywhere you choose, among the only ones who live beyond the grave in this world, the people who write books that help, make exquisite music, carve statues, paint pictures, and work for others. Never mind the calico dress, and the coarse shoes. Work at your books, and before long you will hear yesterday's tormentors boasting that they were once classmates of yours. 'I could a tale unfold'——!"

She laughingly left the room and Elnora sat thinking, until she remembered how hungry she was, so she ate the food, drank the hot chocolate and began to feel better.

Then the Bird Woman came back and showed Elnora a long printed slip giving a list of graduated prices for moths, butterflies, and dragonflies.

"Oh, do you want them!" exulted Elnora. "I have a few and I can get more by the thousand, with every colour in the world on their wings."

"Yes," said the Bird Woman, "I will buy them, also the big moth caterpillars that are creeping everywhere now, and the cocoons that they will spin just about this time. I have a sneaking impression that the mystery, wonder, and the urge of their pure beauty, are going to force me to picture and paint our moths and put them into a book for all the world to see and know. We Limberlost people must not be selfish with the wonders God has given to us. We must share with those poor cooped-up city people the best we can. To send them a beautiful book, that is the way, is it not, little new friend of mine?"

"Yes, oh yes!" cried Elnora. "And please God they find a way to earn the money to buy the books, as I have those I need so badly."

"I will pay good prices for all the moths you can find," said the Bird Woman, "because you see I exchange them with foreign collectors. I want a complete series of the moths of America to trade with a German scientist, another with a man in India, and another in Brazil. Others I can exchange with home collectors for those of California and Canada, so you see I can use all you can raise, or find. The banker will buy stone axes, arrow points, and Indian pipes. There was a teacher from the city grade schools here to-day for specimens. There is a fund to supply the ward buildings. I'll help you get in touch with that. They want leaves of different trees, flowers, grasses, moths, insects, birds' nests and anything about birds."

Elnora's eyes were blazing. "Had I better go back to school or open a bank account and begin being a millionaire? Uncle Wesley and I have a bushel of arrow points gathered, a stack of axes, pipes, skin-dressing tools, tubes and mortars. I don't know how I ever shall wait three hours."

"You must go, or you will be late," said the Bird Woman. "I will be ready at four."

After school closed Elnora, seated beside the Bird Woman, drove to Freckles's room in the Limberlost. One at a time the beautiful big moths were taken from the interior of the old black case. Not a fourth of them could be moved that night and it was almost dark when the last box was closed, the list figured, and into Elnora's trembling fingers were paid fifty-nine dollars and sixteen cents. Elnora clasped the money closely.

"Oh you beautiful stuff!" she cried. "You are going to buy the books, pay the tuition, and take me to high school."

Then because she was a woman, she sat on a log and looked at her shoes. Long after the Bird Woman drove away Elnora remained. She had her problem, and it was a big one. If she told her mother, would she take the money to pay the taxes? If she did not tell her, how could she account for the books, and things for which she would spend it. At last she counted out what she needed for the next day, placed the remainder in the farthest corner of the case, and locked the door. She then filled the front of her skirt from a heap of arrow points beneath the case and started home.

CHAPTER IV

WHEREIN THE SINTONS ARE DISAPPOINTED, AND MRS. COMSTOCK LEARNS THAT SHE CAN LAUGH

With the first streak of red above the Limberlost Margaret Sinton was busy with the gingham and the intricate paper pattern she had purchased. Wesley cooked the breakfast and worked until he thought Elnora would be gone, then he started to bring her mother.

"Now you be mighty careful," cautioned Margaret. "I don't know how she will take it."

"I don't either," said Wesley philosophically, "but she's got to take it some way. That dress has to be finished by school time in the morning."

Wesley had not slept well that night. He had been so busy framing diplomatic speeches to make to Mrs. Comstock that sleep had little chance with him. Every step nearer to her he approached his position seemed less enviable. By the time he reached the front gate and started down the walk between the rows of asters and lady slippers he was perspiring, and every plausible and convincing speech had fled his brain. Mrs. Comstock helped him. She met him at the door.

"Good morning," she said. "Did Margaret send you for something?"

"Yes," said Wesley. "She's got a job that's too big for her, and she wants you to help."

"Of course I will," said Mrs. Comstock. It was no one's affair how lonely the previous day had been, or how the endless hours of the present would drag. "What is she doing in such a rush?"

Now was his chance.

"She's making a dress for Elnora," answered, Wesley. He saw Mrs. Comstock's form straighten, and her face harden, so he continued hastily. "You see Elnora has been helping us at harvest time, butchering, and with unexpected visitors for years. We've made out that she's saved us a considerable sum, and as she wouldn't ever touch any pay for anything, we just went to town and got a few clothes we thought would fix her up a little for the high school. We want to get a dress done to-day mighty bad, but Margaret is slow about sewing, and she never can finish alone, so I came after you."

"And it's such a simple little matter, so dead easy; and all so between old friends like, that you can't look above your boots while you explain it," sneered Mrs. Comstock. "Wesley Sinton, what put the idea into your head that Elnora would take things bought with money, when she wouldn't take the money?"

Then Sinton's eyes came up straightly.

"Finding her on the trail last night sobbing as hard as I ever saw any one at a funeral. She wasn't complaining at all, but she's come to me all her life with her little hurts, and she couldn't hide how she'd been laughed at, twitted, and run face to face against the fact that there were books and tuition, unexpected, and nothing will ever make me believe you didn't know that, Kate Comstock."

"If any doubts are troubling you on that subject, sure I knew it! She was so anxious to try the world, I thought I'd just let her take a few knocks and see how she liked them."

"As if she'd ever taken anything but knocks all her life!" cried Wesley Sinton. "Kate Comstock, you are a heartless, selfish woman. You've never shown Elnora any real love in her life. If ever she finds out that thing you'll lose her, and it will serve you right."

"She knows it now," said Mrs. Comstock icily, "and she'll be home to-night just as usual."

"Well, you are a brave woman if you dared put a girl of Elnora's make through what she suffered yesterday, and will suffer again to-day, and let her know you did it on purpose. I admire your nerve. But I've watched this since Elnora was born, and I got enough. Things have come to a pass where they go better for her, or I interfere."

"As if you'd ever done anything but interfere all her life! Think I haven't watched you? Think I, with my heart raw in my breast, and too numb to resent it openly, haven't seen you and Mag Sinton trying to turn Elnora against me day after day? When did you ever tell her what her father meant to me? When did you ever try to make her see the wreck of my life, and what I've suffered? No indeed! Always it's been poor little abused Elnora, and cakes, kissing, extra clothes, and encouraging her to run to you with a pitiful mouth every time I tried to make a woman of her."

"Kate Comstock, that's unjust," cried Sinton. "Only last night I tried to show her the picture I saw the day she was born. I begged her to come to you and tell you pleasant what she needed, and ask you for what I happen to know you can well afford to give her."

"I can't!" cried Mrs. Comstock. "You know I can't!"

"Then get so you can!" said Wesley Sinton. "Any day you say the word you can sell six thousand worth of rare timber off this place easy. I'll see to clearing and working the fields cheap as dirt, for Elnora's sake. I'll buy you more cattle to fatten. All you've got to do is sign a lease, to pull thousands from the ground in oil, as the rest of us are doing all around you!"

"Cut down Robert's trees!" shrieked Mrs. Comstock. "Tear up his land! Cover everything with horrid, greasy oil! I'll die first."

"You mean you'll let Elnora go like a beggar, and hurt and mortify her past bearing. I've got to the place where I tell you plain what I am going to do. Maggie and I went to town last night, and we bought what things Elnora needs most urgent to make her look a little like the rest of the high school girls. Now here it is in plain English. You can help get these things ready, and let us give them to her as we want———"

"She won't touch them!" cried Mrs. Comstock.

"Then you can pay us, and she can take them as her right———"

"I won't!"

"Then I will tell Elnora just what you are worth, what you can afford, and how much of this she owns. I'll loan her the money to buy books and decent clothes, and when she is of age she can sell her share and pay me."

Mrs. Comstock gripped a chair-back and opened her lips, but no words came.

"And," Sinton continued, "if she is so much like you that she won't do that, I'll go to the county seat and lay complaint against you as her guardian before the judge. I'll swear to what you are worth, and how you are raising her, and have you discharged, or have the judge appoint some man who will see that she is comfortable, educated, and decent looking!"

"You—you wouldn't!" gasped Kate Comstock.

"I won't need to, Kate!" said Sinton, his heart softening the instant the hard words were said. "You won't show it, but you do love Elnora! You can't help it! You must see how she needs things; come help us fix them, and be friends. Maggie and I couldn't live without her, and you couldn't either. You've got to love such a fine girl as she is; let it show a little!"

"You can hardly expect me to love her," said Mrs. Comstock coldly. "But for her a man would stand back of me now, who would beat the breath out of your sneaking body for the cowardly thing with which you threaten me. After all I've suffered you'd drag me to court and compel me to tear up Robert's property. If I ever go they carry me. If they touch one tree, or put down one greasy old oil well, it will be over all I can shoot, before they begin. Now, see how quick you can clear out of here!"

"You won't come and help Maggie with the dress?"

For answer Mrs. Comstock looked around swiftly for some object on which to lay her hands. Knowing her temper, Wesley Sinton left with all the haste consistent with dignity. But he did not go home. He crossed a field, and in an hour brought another neighbour who was skilful with her needle. With sinking heart Margaret saw them coming.

"Kate is too busy to help to-day, she can't sew before to-morrow," said Wesley cheerfully as they entered.

That quieted Margaret's apprehension a little, though she had some doubts. Wesley prepared the lunch, and by four o'clock the dress was finished as far as it possibly could be until it was fitted on Elnora. If that did not entail too much work, it could be completed in two hours.

Then Margaret packed their purchases into the big market basket. Wesley took the hat, umbrella, and raincoat, and they went to Mrs. Comstock's. As they reached the step, Margaret spoke pleasantly to Mrs. Comstock, who sat reading just inside the door, but she did not answer and deliberately turned a leaf without looking up.

Wesley Sinton opened the door and went in followed by Margaret.

"Kate," he said, "you needn't take out your mad over our little racket on Maggie. I ain't told her a word I said to you, or you said to me. She's not so very strong, and she's sewed since four o'clock this morning to get this dress ready for to-morrow. It's done and we came down to try it on Elnora."

"Is that the truth, Mag Sinton?" demanded Mrs. Comstock.

"You heard Wesley say so," proudly affirmed Mrs. Sinton.

"I want to make you a proposition," said Wesley. "Wait till Elnora comes. Then we'll show her the things and see what she says."

"How would it do to see what she says without bribing her," sneered Mrs. Comstock.

"If she can stand what she did yesterday, and will to-day, she can bear 'most anything," said Wesley. "Put away the clothes if you want to, till we tell her."

"Well, you don't take this waist I'm working on," said Margaret, "for I have to baste in the sleeves and set the collar. Put the rest out of sight if you like."

Mrs. Comstock picked up the basket and bundles, placed them inside her room and closed the door.

Margaret threaded her needle and began to sew. Mrs. Comstock returned to her book, while Wesley fidgeted and raged inwardly. He could see that Margaret was nervous and almost in tears, but the lines in Mrs. Comstock's impassive face were set and cold. So they sat while the clock ticked off the time—one hour, two, dusk, and no Elnora. Just when Margaret and Wesley were discussing whether he had not better go to town to meet Elnora, they heard her coming up the walk. Wesley dropped his tilted chair and squared himself. Margaret gripped her sewing, and turned pleading eyes toward the door. Mrs. Comstock closed her book and grimly smiled.

"Mother, please open the door," called Elnora.

Mrs. Comstock arose, and swung back the screen. Elnora stepped in beside her, bent half double, the whole front of her dress gathered into a sort of bag filled with a heavy load, and one arm stacked high with books. In the dim light she did not see the Sintons.

"Please hand me the empty bucket in the kitchen, mother," she said. "I just had to bring these arrow points home, but I'm scared for fear I've spoiled my dress and will have to wash it. I'm to clean them, and take them to the banker in the morning, and oh, mother, I've sold enough stuff to pay for my books, my tuition, and maybe a dress and some lighter shoes besides. Oh, mother I'm so happy! Take the books and bring the bucket!"

Then she saw Margaret and Wesley. "Oh, glory!" she exulted. "I was just wondering how I'd ever wait to tell you, and here you are! It's too perfectly splendid to be true!"

"Tell us, Elnora," said Sinton.

"Well sir," said Elnora, doubling down on the floor and spreading out her skirt, "set the bucket here, mother. These points are brittle, and should be put in one at a time. If they are chipped I can't sell them. Well sir! I've had a time! You know I just had to have books. I tried three stores, and they wouldn't trust me, not even three days, I didn't know what in this world I could do quickly enough. Just when I was almost frantic I saw a sign in a bank window asking for caterpillars, cocoons, butterflies, arrow points, and everything. I went in, and it was this Bird Woman who wants the insects, and the banker wants the stones. I had to go to school then, but, if you'll believe it"—Elnora beamed on all of them in turn as she talked and slipped the arrow points from her dress to the pail—"if you'll believe it—but you won't, hardly, until you look at the books—there was the mathematics teacher, waiting at his door, and he had a set of books for me that he had telephoned a Sophomore to bring."

"How did he happen to do that, Elnora?" interrupted Sinton.

Elnora blushed.

"It was a fool mistake I made yesterday in thinking books were just handed out to one. There was a teachers' meeting last night and the history teacher told about that. Professor Henley thought of me. You know I told you what he said about my algebra, mother. Ain't I glad I studied out some of it myself this summer! So he telephoned and a girl brought the books. Because they are marked and abused some I get the whole outfit for two dollars. I can erase most of the marks, paste down the covers, and fix them so they look better. But I must hurry to the joy part. I didn't stop to eat, at noon, I just ran to the Bird Woman's, and I had lunch with her. It was salad, hot chocolate, and lovely things, and she wants to buy most every old scrap I ever gathered. She wants dragonflies, moths, butterflies, and he—the banker, I mean—wants everything

Indian. This very night she came to the swamp with me and took away enough stuff to pay for the books and tuition, and to-morrow she is going to buy some more."

Elnora laid the last arrow point in the pail and arose, shaking leaves and bits of baked earth from her dress. She reached into her pocket, produced her money and waved it before their wondering eyes.

"And that's the joy part!" she exulted. "Put it up in the clock till morning, mother. That pays for the books and tuition and—" Elnora hesitated, for she saw the nervous grasp with which her mother's fingers closed on the bills. Then she continued, but more slowly and thinking before she spoke.

"What I get to-morrow pays for more books and tuition, and maybe a few, just a few, things to wear. These shoes are so dreadfully heavy and hot, and they make such a noise on the floor. There isn't another calico dress in the whole building, not among hundreds of us. Why, what is that? Aunt Margaret, what are you hiding in your lap?"

She snatched the waist and shook it out, and her face was beaming. "Have you taken to waists all fancy and buttoned in the back? I bet you this is mine!"

"I bet you so too," said Margaret Sinton. "You undress right away and try it on, and if it fits, it will be done for morning. There are some low shoes, too!"

Elnora began to dance. "Oh, you dear people!" she cried. "I can pay for them to-morrow night! Isn't it too splendid! I was just thinking on the way home that I certainly would be compelled to have cooler shoes until later, and I was wondering what I'd do when the fall rains begin."

"I meant to get you some heavy dress skirts and a coat then," said Mrs. Comstock.

"I know you said so!" cried Elnora. "But you needn't, now! I can buy every single stitch I need myself. Next summer I can gather up a lot more stuff, and all winter on the way to school. I am sure I can sell ferns, I know I can nuts, and the Bird Woman says the grade rooms want leaves, grasses, birds' nests, and cocoons. Oh, isn't this world lovely! I'll be helping with the tax, next, mother!"

Elnora waved the waist and started for the bedroom. When she opened the door she gave a little cry.

"What have you people been doing?" she demanded. "I never saw so many interesting bundles in all my life. I'm 'skeered' to death for fear I can't pay for them, and will have to give up something."

"Wouldn't you take them, if you could not pay for them, Elnora?" asked her mother instantly.

"Why, not unless you did," answered Elnora. "People have no right to wear things they can't afford, have they?"

"But from such old friends as Maggie and Wesley!" Mrs. Comstock's voice was oily with triumph.

"From them least of all," cried Elnora stoutly. "From a stranger sooner than from them, to whom I owe so much more than I ever can pay now."

"Well, you don't have to," said Mrs. Comstock. "Maggie just selected these things, because she is more in touch with the world, and has got such good taste. You can pay as long as your money holds out, and if there's more necessary, maybe I can sell the butcher a calf, or if things are too costly for us, of course, they can take them back. Put on the waist now, and then you can look over the rest and see if they are suitable, and what you want."

Elnora stepped into the adjoining room and closed the door. Mrs. Comstock picked up the bucket and started for the well with it. At the bedroom she paused.

"Elnora, were you going to wash these arrow points?"

"Yes. The Bird Woman says they sell better if they are clean, so it can be seen that there are no defects in them."

"Of course," said Mrs. Comstock. "Some of them seem quite baked. Shall I put them to soak? Do you want to take them in the morning?"

"Yes, I do," answered Elnora. "If you would just fill the pail with water."

Mrs. Comstock left the room. Wesley Sinton sat with his back to the window in the west end of the cabin which overlooked the well. A suppressed sound behind him caused him to turn quickly. Then he arose and leaned over Margaret.

"She's out there laughing like a blamed monkey!" he whispered indignantly.

"Well, she can't help it!" exclaimed Margaret.

"I'm going home!" said Wesley.

"Oh no, you are not!" retorted Margaret. "You are missing the point. The point is not how you look, or feel. It is to get these things in Elnora's possession past dispute. You go now, and to-morrow Elnora will wear calico, and Kate Comstock will return these goods. Right here I stay until everything we bought is Elnora's."

"What are you going to do?" asked Wesley.

"I don't know yet, myself," said Margaret.

Then she arose and peered from the window. At the well curb stood Katharine Comstock. The strain of the day was finding reaction. Her chin was in the air, she was heaving, shaking and strangling to suppress any sound. The word that slipped between Margaret Sinton's lips shocked Wesley until he dropped on his chair, and recalled her to her senses. She was fairly composed as she turned to Elnora, and began the fitting. When she had pinched, pulled, and patted she called, "Come see if you think this fits, Kate."

Mrs. Comstock had gone around to the back door and answered from the kitchen. "You know more about it than I do. Go ahead! I'm getting supper. Don't forget to allow for what it will shrink in washing!"

"I set the colours and washed the goods last night; it can be made to fit right now," answered Margaret.

When she could find nothing more to alter she told Elnora to heat some water. After she had done that the girl began opening packages.

The hat came first.

"Mother!" cried Elnora. "Mother, of course, you have seen this, but you haven't seen it on me. I must try it on."

"Don't you dare put that on your head until your hair is washed and properly combed," said Margaret.

"Oh!" cried Elnora. "Is that water to wash my hair? I thought it was to set the colour in another dress."

"Well, you thought wrong," said Margaret simply. "Your hair is going to be washed and brushed until it shines like copper. While it dries you can eat your supper, and this dress will be finished. Then you can put on your new ribbon, and your hat. You can try your shoes now, and if they don't fit, you and Wesley can drive to town and change them. That little round bundle on the top of the basket is your stockings."

Margaret sat down and began sewing swiftly, and a little later opened the machine, and ran several long seams.

Elnora returned in a few minutes holding up her skirts and stepping daintily in the new shoes.

"Don't soil them, honey, else you're sure they fit," cautioned Wesley.

"They seem just a trifle large, maybe," said Elnora dubiously, and Wesley knelt to feel. He and Margaret thought them a fit, and then Elnora appealed to her mother. Mrs. Comstock appeared wiping her hands on her apron. She examined the shoes critically.

"They seem to fit," she said, "but they are away too fine to walk country roads."

"I think so, too," said Elnora instantly. "We had better take these back and get a cheaper pair."

"Oh, let them go for this time," said Mrs. Comstock. "They are so pretty, I hate to part with them. You can get cheaper ones after this."

Wesley and Margaret scarcely breathed for a long time.

When Wesley went to do the feeding. Elnora set the table. When the water was hot, Margaret pinned a big towel around Elnora's shoulders and washed and dried the lovely hair according to the instructions she had been given the previous night. As the hair began to dry it billowed out in a sparkling sheen that caught the light and gleamed and flashed.

"Now, the idea is to let it stand naturally, just as the curl will make it. Don't you do any of that nasty, untidy snarling, Elnora," cautioned Margaret. "Wash it this way every two weeks while you are in school, shake it out, and dry it. Then part it in the middle and turn a front quarter on each side from your face. You tie the back at your neck with a string— so, and the ribbon goes in a big, loose bow. I'll show you." One after another Margaret Sinton tied the ribbons, creasing each of them so they could not be returned, as she explained that she was trying to find the colour most becoming. Then she produced the raincoat which carried Elnora into transports.

Mrs. Comstock objected. "That won't be warm enough for cold weather, and you can't afford it and a coat, too."

"I'll tell you what I thought," said Elnora. "I was planning on the way home. These coats are fine because they keep you dry. I thought I would get one, and a warm sweater to wear under it cold days. Then I always would be dry, and warm. The sweater only costs three dollars, so I could get it and the raincoat both for half the price of a heavy cloth coat."

"You are right about that," said Mrs. Comstock. "You can change more with the weather, too. Keep the raincoat, Elnora."

"Wear it until you try the hat," said Margaret. "It will have to do until the dress is finished."

Elnora picked up the hat dubiously. "Mother, may I wear my hair as it is now?" she asked.

"Let me take a good look," said Katharine Comstock.

Heaven only knows what she saw. To Wesley and to Margaret the bright young face of Elnora, with its pink tints, its heavy dark brows, its bright blue-gray eyes, and its frame of curling reddish-brown hair was the sweetest sight on earth, and at that instant Elnora was radiant.

"So long as it's your own hair, and combed back as plain as it will go, I don't suppose it cuts much ice whether it's tied a little tighter or looser," conceded Mrs. Comstock. "If you stop right there, you may let it go at that."

Elnora set the hat on her head. It was only a wide tan straw with three exquisite peacock quills at one side. Margaret Sinton cried out, Wesley slapped his knee and sighed deeply while Mrs. Comstock stood speechless for a second.

"I wish you had asked the price before you put that on," she said impatiently. "We never can afford it."

"It's not so much as you think," said Margaret. "Don't you see what I did? I had them take off the quills, and put on some of those Phoebe Simms gave me from her peacocks. The hat will only cost you a dollar and a half."

She avoided Wesley's eyes, and looked straight at Mrs. Comstock. Elnora removed the hat to examine it.

"Why, they are those reddish-tan quills of yours!" she cried. "Mother, look how beautifully they are set on! I'd much rather have them than those from the store."

"So would I," said Mrs. Comstock. "If Margaret wants to spare them, that will make you a beautiful hat; dirt cheap, too! You must go past Mrs. Simms and show her. She would be pleased to see them."

Elnora sank into a chair and contemplated her toe. "Landy, ain't I a queen?" she murmured. "What else have I got?"

"Just a belt, some handkerchiefs, and a pair of top shoes for rainy days and colder weather," said Margaret.

"About those high shoes, that was my idea," said Wesley. "Soon as it rains, low shoes won't do, and by taking two pairs at once I could get them some cheaper. The low ones are two and the high ones two fifty, together three seventy-five. Ain't that cheap?"

"That's a real bargain," said Mrs. Comstock, "if they are good shoes, and they look it."

"This," said Wesley, producing the last package, "is your Christmas present from your Aunt Maggie. I got mine, too, but it's at the house. I'll bring it up in the morning."

He handed Margaret the umbrella, and she passed it over to Elnora who opened it and sat laughing under its shelter. Then she kissed both of them. She brought a pencil and a slip of paper to set down the prices they gave her of everything they had brought except the umbrella, added the sum, and said laughingly: "Will you please wait till to-morrow for the money? I will have it then, sure."

"Elnora," said Wesley Sinton. "Wouldn't you——"

"Elnora, hustle here a minute!" called Mrs. Comstock from the kitchen. "I need you!"

"One second, mother," answered Elnora, throwing off the coat and hat, and closing the umbrella as she ran. There were several errands to do in a hurry, and then supper. Elnora chattered incessantly, Wesley and Margaret talked all they could, while Mrs. Comstock said a word now and then, which was all she ever did. But Wesley Sinton was watching her, and time and again he saw a peculiar little twist around her mouth. He knew that for the first time in sixteen years she really was laughing over something. She had all she could do to preserve her usually sober face. Wesley knew what she was thinking.

After supper the dress was finished, the pattern for the next one discussed, and then the Sintons went home. Elnora gathered her treasures. When she started upstairs she stopped. "May I kiss you good-night, mother?" she asked lightly.

"Never mind any slobbering," said Mrs. Comstock. "I should think you'd lived with me long enough to know that I don't care for it."

"Well, I'd love to show you in some way how happy I am, and how I thank you."

"I wonder what for?" said Mrs. Comstock. "Mag Sinton chose that stuff and brought it here and you pay for it."

"Yes, but you seemed willing for me to have it, and you said you would help me if I couldn't pay all."

"Maybe I did," said Mrs. Comstock. "Maybe I did. I meant to get you some heavy dress skirts about Thanksgiving, and I still can get them. Go to bed, and for any sake don't begin mooning before a mirror, and make a dunce of yourself."

Mrs. Comstock picked up several papers and blew out the kitchen light. She stood in the middle of the sitting-room floor for a time and then went into her room and closed the door. Sitting on the edge of the bed she thought for a few minutes and then suddenly buried her face in the pillow and again heaved with laughter.

Down the road plodded Margaret and Wesley Sinton. Neither of them had words to utter their united thought.

"Done!" hissed Wesley at last. "Done brown! Did you ever feel like a bloomin', confounded donkey? How did the woman do it?"

"She didn't do it!" gulped Margaret through her tears. "She didn't do anything. She trusted to Elnora's great big soul to bring her out right, and really she was right, and so it had to bring her. She's a darling, Wesley! But she's got a time before her. Did you see Kate Comstock grab that money? Before six months she'll be out combing the Limberlost for bugs and arrow points to help pay the tax. I know her."

"Well, I don't!" exclaimed Sinton, "she's too many for me. But there is a laugh left in her yet! I didn't s'pose there was. Bet you a dollar, if we could see her this minute, she'd be chuckling over the way we got left."

Both of them stopped in the road and looked back.

"There's Elnora's light in her room," said Margaret. "The poor child will feel those clothes, and pore over her books till morning, but she'll look decent to go to school, anyway. Nothing is too big a price to pay for that."

"Yes, if Kate lets her wear them. Ten to one, she makes her finish the week with that old stuff!"

"No, she won't," said Margaret. "She'll hardly dare. Kate made some concessions, all right; big ones for her—if she did get her way in the main. She bent some, and if Elnora proves that she can walk out barehanded in the morning and come back with that much money in her pocket, an armful of books, and buy a turnout like that, she proves that she is of some consideration, and Kate's smart enough. She'll think twice before she'll do that. Elnora won't wear a calico dress to high school again. You watch and see if she does. She may have the best clothes she'll get for a time, for the least money, but she won't know it until she tries to buy goods herself at the same rates. Wesley, what about those prices? Didn't they shrink considerable?"

"You began it," said Wesley. "Those prices were all right. We didn't say what the goods cost us, we said what they would cost her. Surely, she's mistaken about being able to pay all that. Can she pick up stuff of that value around the Limberlost? Didn't the Bird Woman see her trouble, and just give her the money?"

"I don't think so," said Margaret. "Seems to me I've heard of her paying, or offering to pay those who would take the money, for bugs and butterflies, and I've known people who sold that banker Indian stuff. Once I heard that his pipe collection beat that of the Government at the Philadelphia Centennial. Those things have come to have a value."

"Well, there's about a bushel of that kind of valuables piled up in the woodshed, that belongs to Elnora. At least, I picked them up because she said she wanted them. Ain't it queer that she'd take to stones, bugs, and butterflies, and save them. Now they are going to bring her the very thing she wants the worst. Lord, but this is a funny world when you get to studying! Looks like things didn't all come by accident. Looks as if there was a plan back of it, and somebody driving that knows the road, and how to handle the lines. Anyhow, Elnora's in the wagon, and when I get out in the night and the dark closes around me, and I see the stars, I don't feel so cheap. Maggie, how the nation did Kate Comstock do that?"

"You will keep on harping, Wesley. I told you she didn't do it. Elnora did it! She walked in and took things right out of our hands. All Kate had to do was to enjoy having it go her way, and she was cute enough to put in a few questions that sort of guided Elnora. But I don't know, Wesley. This thing makes me think, too. S'pose we'd taken Elnora when she was a baby, and we'd heaped on her all the love we can't on our own, and we'd coddled, petted, and shielded her, would she have made the woman that living alone, learning to think for herself, and taking all the knocks Kate Comstock could give, have made of her?"

"You bet your life!" cried Wesley, warmly. "Loving anybody don't hurt them. We wouldn't have done anything but love her. You can't hurt a child loving it. She'd have learned to work, to study, and grown into a woman with us, without suffering like a poor homeless dog."

"But you don't see the point, Wesley. She would have grown into a fine woman with us; but as we would have raised her, would her heart ever have known the world as it does now? Where's the anguish, Wesley, that child can't comprehend? Seeing what she's seen of her mother hasn't hardened her. She can understand any mother's sorrow. Living life from the rough side has only broadened her. Where's the girl or boy burning with shame, or struggling to find a way, that will cross Elnora's path and not get a lift from her? She's had the knocks, but there'll never be any of the thing you call 'false pride' in her. I guess we better keep out. Maybe Kate Comstock knows what she's doing. Sure as you live, Elnora has grown bigger on knocks than she would on love."

"I don't s'pose there ever was a very fine point to anything but I missed it," said Wesley, "because I am blunt, rough, and have no book learning to speak of. Since you put it into words I see what you mean, but it's dinged hard on Elnora, just the same. And I don't keep out. I keep watching closer than ever. I got my slap in the face, but if I don't miss my guess, Kate Comstock learned her lesson, same as I did. She learned that I was in earnest, that I would haul her to court if she didn't loosen up a bit, and she'll loosen. You see if she doesn't. It may come hard, and the hinges creak, but she'll fix Elnora decent after this, if Elnora doesn't prove that she can fix herself. As for me, I found out that what I was doing was as much for myself as for Elnora. I wanted her to take those things from us, and love us for giving them. It didn't work, and but for you, I'd messed the whole thing and stuck like a pig in crossing a bridge. But you helped me out; Elnora's got the clothes, and by morning, maybe I won't grudge Kate the only laugh she's had in sixteen years. You been showing me the way quite a spell now, ain't you, Maggie?"

In her attic Elnora lighted two candles, set them on her little table, stacked the books, and put away the precious clothes. How lovingly she hung the hat and umbrella, folded the raincoat, and spread the new dress over a chair. She fingered the ribbons, and tried to smooth the creases from them. She put away the hose neatly folded, touched the handkerchiefs, and tried the belt. Then she slipped into her white nightdress, shook down her hair that it might become thoroughly dry, set a chair before the table, and reverently opened one of the books. A stiff draught swept the attic, for it stretched the length of the cabin, and had a window in each end. Elnora arose and going to the east window closed it. She stood for a minute looking at the stars, the sky, and the dark outline of the straggling trees of the rapidly dismantling Limberlost. In the region of her case a tiny point of light flashed and disappeared. Elnora straightened and wondered. Was it wise to leave her precious money there? The light flashed once more, wavered a few seconds, and died out. The girl waited. She did not see it again, so she turned to her books.

In the Limberlost the hulking figure of a man sneaked down the trail.

"The Bird Woman was at Freckles's room this evening," he muttered. "Wonder what for?"

He left the trail, entered the enclosure still distinctly outlined, and approached the case. The first point of light flashed from the tiny electric lamp on his vest. He took a duplicate key from his pocket, felt for the padlock and opened it. The door swung wide. The light flashed the second time. Swiftly his glance swept the interior.

"'Bout a fourth of her moths gone. Elnora must have been with the Bird Woman and given them to her." Then he stood tense. His keen eyes discovered the roll of bills hastily thrust back in the bottom of the case. He snatched them up, shut off the light, relocked the case by touch, and swiftly went down the trail. Every few seconds he paused and listened intently. Just as he reached the road, a second figure approached him.

"Is it you, Pete?" came the whispered question.

"Yes," said the first man.

"I was coming down to take a peep, when I saw your flash," he said. "I heard the Bird Woman had been at the case to-day. Anything doing?"

"Not a thing," said Pete. "She just took away about a fourth of the moths. Probably had the Comstock girl getting them for her. Heard they were together. Likely she'll get the rest to-morrow. Ain't picking gettin' bare these days?"

"Well, I should say so," said the second man, turning back in disgust. "Coming home, now?"

"No, I am going down this way," answered Pete, for his eyes caught the gleam from the window of the Comstock cabin, and he had a desire to learn why Elnora's attic was lighted at that hour.

He slouched down the road, occasionally feeling the size of the roll he had not taken time to count.

The attic was too long, the light too near the other end, and the cabin stood much too far back from the road. He could see nothing although he climbed the fence and walked back opposite the window. He knew Mrs. Comstock was probably awake, and that she sometimes went to the swamp behind her home at night. At times a cry went up from that locality that paralyzed any one near, or sent them fleeing as if for life. He did not care to cross behind the cabin. He returned to the road, passed, and again climbed the fence. Opposite the west window he could see Elnora. She sat before a small table reading from a book between two candles. Her hair fell in a bright sheen around her, and with one hand she lightly shook, and tossed it as she studied. The man stood out in the night and watched.

For a long time a leaf turned at intervals and the hair-drying went on. The man drew nearer. The picture grew more beautiful as he approached. He could not see so well as he desired, for the screen was of white mosquito netting, and it angered him. He cautiously crept closer. The elevation shut off his view. Then he remembered the large willow tree shading the well and branching across the window fit the west end of the cabin. From childhood Elnora had stepped from the sill to a limb and slid down the slanting trunk of the tree. He reached it and noiselessly swung himself up. Three steps out on the big limb the man shuddered. He was within a few feet of the girl.

He could see the throb of her breast under its thin covering and smell the fragrance of the tossing hair. He could see the narrow bed with its pieced calico cover, the whitewashed walls with gay lithographs, and every crevice stuck full of twigs with dangling cocoons. There were pegs for the few clothes, the old chest, the little table, the two chairs, the uneven floor covered with rag rugs and braided corn husk. But nothing was worth a glance except the perfect face and form within reach by one spring through the rotten mosquito bar. He gripped the limb above that on which he stood, licked his lips, and breathed through his throat to be sure he was making no sound. Elnora closed the book and laid it aside. She picked up a towel, and turning the gathered ends of her hair rubbed them across it, and dropping the towel on her lap, tossed the hair again. Then she sat in deep thought. By and by words began to come softly. Near as he was the man could not hear at first. He bent closer and listened intently.

"—ever could be so happy," murmured the soft voice. "The dress is so pretty, such shoes, the coat, and everything. I won't have to be ashamed again, not ever again, for the Limberlost is full of precious moths, and I always can collect them. The Bird Woman will buy more tomorrow, and the next day, and the next. When they are all gone, I can spend every minute gathering cocoons, and hunting other things I can sell. Oh, thank God, for my precious, precious money. Why, I didn't pray in vain after all! I thought when I asked the Lord to hide me, there in that big hall, that He wasn't doing it, because I wasn't covered from sight that instant. But I'm hidden now, I feel that." Elnora lifted her eyes to the beams above her. "I don't know much about praying properly," she muttered, "but I do thank you, Lord, for hiding me in your own time and way."

Her face was so bright that it shone with a white radiance. Two big tears welled from her eyes, and rolled down her smiling cheeks. "Oh, I do feel that you have hidden me," she breathed. Then she blew out the lights, and the little wooden bed creaked under her weight.

Pete Corson dropped from the limb and found his way to the road. He stood still a long time, then started back to the Limberlost. A tiny point of light flashed in the region of the case. He stopped with an oath.

"Another hound trying to steal from a girl," he exclaimed. "But it's likely he thinks if he gets anything it will be from a woman who can afford it, as I did."

He went on, but beside the fences, and very cautiously.

"Swamp seems to be alive to-night," he muttered. "That's three of us out."

He entered a deep place at the northwest corner, sat on the ground and taking a pencil from his pocket, he tore a leaf from a little notebook, and laboriously wrote a few lines by the light he carried. Then he went back to the region of the case and waited. Before his eyes swept the vision of the slender white creature with tossing hair. He smiled, and worshipped it, until a distant rooster faintly announced dawn.

Then he unlocked the case again, and replaced the money, laid the note upon it, and went back to concealment, where he remained until Elnora came down the trail in the morning, appearing very lovely in her new dress and hat.

CHAPTER V

It would be difficult to describe how happy Elnora was that morning as she hurried through her work, bathed and put on the neat, dainty gingham dress, and the tan shoes. She had a struggle with her hair. It crinkled, billowed, and shone, and she could not avoid seeing the becoming frame it made around her face. But in deference to her mother's feelings the girl set her teeth, and bound her hair closely to her head with a shoe-string. "Not to be changed at the case," she told herself.

That her mother was watching she was unaware. Just as she picked up the beautiful brown ribbon Mrs. Comstock spoke.

"You had better let me tie that. You can't reach behind yourself and do it right."

Elnora gave a little gasp. Her mother never before had proposed to do anything for the girl that by any possibility she could do herself. Her heart quaked at the thought of how her mother would arrange that bow, but Elnora dared not refuse. The offer was too precious. It might never be made again.

"Oh thank you!" said the girl, and sitting down she held out the ribbon. Her mother stood back and looked at her critically.

"You haven't got that like Mag Sinton had it last night," she announced. "You little idiot! You've tried to plaster it down to suit me, and you missed it. I liked it away better as Mag fixed it, after I saw it. You didn't look so peeled."

"Oh mother, mother!" laughed Elnora, with a half sob in her voice.

"Hold still, will you?" cried Mrs. Comstock. "You'll be late, and I haven't packed your dinner yet."

She untied the string and shook out the hair. It rose with electricity and clung to her fingers and hands. Mrs. Comstock jumped back as if bitten. She knew that touch. Her face grew white, and her eyes angry.

"Tie it yourself," she said shortly, "and then I'll put on the ribbon. But roll it back loose like Mag did. It looked so pretty that way."

Almost fainting Elnora stood before the glass, divided off the front parts of her hair, and rolled them as Mrs. Sinton had done; tied it at the nape of her neck, then sat while her mother arranged the ribbon.

"If I pull it down till it comes tight in these creases where she had it, it will be just right, won't it?" queried Mrs. Comstock, and the amazed Elnora stammered,

"Yes."

When she looked in the glass the bow was perfectly tied, and how the gold tone of the brown did match the lustre of the shining hair! "That's pretty," commented Mrs. Comstock's soul, but her stiff lips had said all that could be forced from them for once. Just then Wesley Sinton came to the door.

"Good morning," he cried heartily. "Elnora, you look a picture! My, but you're sweet! If any of the city boys get sassy you tell your Uncle Wesley, and he'll horsewhip them. Here's your Christmas present from me." He handed Elnora the leather lunch box, with her name carved across the strap in artistic lettering.

"Oh Uncle Wesley!" was all Elnora could say.

"Your Aunt Maggie filled it for me for a starter," he said. "Now, if you are ready, I'm going to drive past your way and you can ride almost to Onabasha with me, and save the new shoes that much."

Elnora was staring at the box. "Oh I hope it isn't impolite to open it before you," she said. "I just feel as if I must see inside."

"Don't you stand on formality with the neighbours," laughed Sinton. "Look in your box if you want to!"

Elnora slipped the strap and turned back the lid.

This disclosed the knife, fork, napkin, and spoon, the milk flask, and the interior packed with dainty sandwiches wrapped in tissue paper, and the little compartments for meat, salad, and the custard cup.

"Oh mother!" cried Elnora. "Oh mother, isn't it fine? What made you think of it, Uncle Wesley? How will I ever thank you? No one will have a finer lunch box than I. Oh I do thank you! That's the nicest gift I ever had. How I love Christmas in September!"

"It's a mighty handy thing," assented Mrs. Comstock, taking in every detail with sharp eyes. "I guess you are glad now you went and helped Mag and Wesley when you could, Elnora?"

"Deedy, yes," laughed Elnora, "and I'm going again first time they have a big day if I stay from school to do it."

"You'll do no such thing!" said the delighted Sinton. "Come now, if you're going!"

"If I ride, can you spare me time to run into the swamp to my box a minute?" asked Elnora.

The light she had seen the previous night troubled her.

"Sure," said Wesley largely. So they drove away and left a white-faced woman watching them from the door, her heart a little sorer than usual.

"I'd give a pretty to hear what he'll say to her!" she commented bitterly. "Always sticking in, always doing things I can't ever afford. Where on earth did he get that thing and what did it cost?"

Then she entered the cabin and began the day's work, but mingled with the brooding bitterness of her soul was the vision of a sweet young face, glad with a gladness never before seen on it, and over and over she repeated: "I wonder what he'll say to her!"

What he said was that she looked as fresh and sweet as a posy, and to be careful not to step in the mud or scratch her shoes when she went to the case.

Elnora found her key and opened the door. Not where she had placed it, but conspicuously in front lay her little heap of bills, and a crude scrawl of writing beside it. Elnora picked up the note in astonishment.

DERE ELNORY,

the lord amighty is hiding you all right done you ever dout it this money of yourn was took for some time las nite but it is returned with intres for god sake done ever come to the swamp at nite or late evnin or mornin or far in any time sompin worse an you know could git you

A FREND.

Elnora began to tremble. She hastily glanced around. The damp earth before the case had been trodden by large, roughly shod feet. She caught up the money and the note, thrust them into her guimpe, locked the case, and ran to the road.

She was so breathless and her face so white Sinton noticed it.

"What in the world's the matter, Elnora?" he asked.

"I am half afraid!" she panted.

"Tut, tut, child!" said Wesley Sinton. "Nothing in the world to be afraid of. What happened?"

"Uncle Wesley," said Elnora, "I had more money than I brought home last night, and I put it in my case. Some one has been there. The ground is all trampled, and they left this note."

"And took your money, I'll wager," said Sinton angrily.

"No," answered Elnora. "Read the note, and oh Uncle Wesley, tell me what it means!"

Sinton's face was a study. "I don't know what it means," he said. "Only one thing is clear. It means some beast who doesn't really want to harm you has got his eye on you, and he is telling you plain as he can, not to give him a chance. You got to keep along the roads, in the open, and not let the biggest moth that ever flew toll you out of hearing of us, or your mother. It means that, plain and distinct."

"Just when I can sell them! Just when everything is so lovely on account of them! I can't! I can't stay away from the swamp. The

Limberlost is going to buy the books, the clothes, pay the tuition, and even start a college fund. I just can't!"

"You've got to," said Sinton. "This is plain enough. You go far in the swamp at your own risk, even in daytime."

"Uncle Wesley," said the girl, "last night before I went to bed, I was so happy I tried to pray, and I thanked God for hiding me 'under the shadow of His wing.' But how in the world could any one know it?"

Wesley Sinton's heart leaped in his breast. His face was whiter than the girl's now.

"Were you praying out loud, honey?" he almost whispered.

"I might have said words," answered Elnora. "I know I do sometimes. I've never had any one to talk with, and I've played with and talked to myself all my life. You've caught me at it often, but it always makes mother angry when she does. She says it's silly. I forget and do it, when I'm alone. But Uncle Wesley, if I said anything last night, you know it was the merest whisper, because I'd have been so afraid of waking mother. Don't you see? I sat up late, and studied two lessons."

Sinton was steadying himself "I'll stop and examine the case as I come back," he said. "Maybe I can find some clue. That other—that was just accidental. It's a common expression. All the preachers use it. If I tried to pray, that would be the very first thing I'd say."

The colour returned to Elnora's face.

"Did you tell your mother about this money, Elnora?" he asked.

"No, I didn't," said Elnora. "It's dreadful not to, but I was afraid. You see they are clearing the swamp so fast. Every year it grows more difficult to find things, and Indian stuff becomes scarcer. I want to graduate, and that's four years unless I can double on the course. That means twenty dollars tuition each year, and new books, and clothes. There won't ever be so much at one time again, that I know. I just got to hang to my money. I was afraid to tell her, for fear she would want it for taxes, and she really must sell a tree or some cattle for that, mustn't she, Uncle Wesley?"

"On your life, she must!" said Wesley. "You put your little wad in the bank all safe, and never mention it to a living soul. It doesn't seem right, but your case is peculiar. Every word you say is a true word. Each year you will find less in the swamp, and things everywhere will be scarcer. If you ever get a few dollars ahead, that can start your college fund. You know you are going to college, Elnora!"

"Of course I am," said Elnora. "I settled that as soon as I knew what a college was. I will put all my money in the bank, except what I owe you. I'll pay that now."

"If your arrows are heavy," said Wesley, "I'll drive on to Onabasha with you."

"But they are not. Half of them were nicked, and this little box held all the good ones. It's so surprising how many are spoiled when you wash them."

"What does he pay?"

"Ten cents for any common perfect one, fifty for revolvers, a dollar for obsidian, and whatever is right for enormous big ones."

"Well, that sounds fair," said Sinton. "You can come down Saturday and wash the stuff at our house, and I'll take it in when we go marketing in the afternoon."

Elnora jumped from the carriage. She soon found that with her books, her lunch box, and the points she had a heavy load. She had almost reached the bridge crossing the culvert when she heard distressed screams of a child. Across an orchard of the suburbs came a small boy, after him a big dog, urged by a man in the background. Elnora's heart was with the small fleeing figure in any event whatever. She dropped her load on the bridge, and with practised hand flung a stone at the dog. The beast curled double with a howl. The boy reached the fence, and Elnora was there to help him over. As he touched the top she swung him to the ground, but he clung to her, clasping her tightly, sobbing with fear. Elnora helped him to the bridge, and sat with him in her arms. For a time his replies to her questions were indistinct, but at last he became quieter and she could understand.

He was a mite of a boy, nothing but skin-covered bones, his burned, freckled face in a mortar of tears and dust, his clothing unspeakably dirty, one great toe in a festering mass from a broken nail, and sores all over the visible portions of the small body.

"You won't let the mean old thing make his dog get me!" he wailed.

"Indeed no," said Elnora, holding him closely.

"You wouldn't set a dog on a boy for just taking a few old apples when you fed 'em to pigs with a shovel every day, would you?"

"No, I would not," said Elnora hotly.

"You'd give a boy all the apples he wanted, if he hadn't any breakfast, and was so hungry he was all twisty inside, wouldn't you?"

"Yes, I would," said Elnora.

"If you had anything to eat you would give me something right now, wouldn't you?"

"Yes," said Elnora. "There's nothing but just stones in the package. But my dinner is in that case. I'll gladly divide."

She opened the box. The famished child gave a little cry and reached both hands. Elnora caught them back.

"Did you have any supper?"

"No."

"Any dinner yesterday?"

"An apple and some grapes I stole."

"Whose boy are you?"

"Old Tom Billings's."

"Why doesn't your father get you something to eat?"

"He does most days, but he's drunk now."

"Hush, you must not!" said Elnora. "He's your father!"

"He's spent all the money to get drunk, too," said the boy, "and Jimmy and Belle are both crying for breakfast. I'd a got out all right with an apple for myself, but I tried to get some for them and the dog got too close. Say, you can throw, can't you?"

"Yes," admitted Elnora. She poured half the milk into the cup. "Drink this," she said, holding it to him.

The boy gulped the milk and swore joyously, gripping the cup with shaking fingers.

"Hush!" cried Elnora. "That's dreadful!"

"What's dreadful?"

"To say such awful words."

"Huh! pa says worser 'an that every breath he draws."

Elnora saw that the child was older than she had thought. He might have been forty judging by his hard, unchildish expression.

"Do you want to be like your father?"

"No, I want to be like you. Couldn't a angel be prettier 'an you. Can I have more milk?"

Elnora emptied the flask. The boy drained the cup. He drew a breath of satisfaction as he gazed into her face.

"You wouldn't go off and leave your little boy, would you?" he asked.

"Did some one go away and leave you?"

"Yes, my mother went off and left me, and left Jimmy and Belle, too," said the boy. "You wouldn't leave your little boy, would you?"

"No."

The boy looked eagerly at the box. Elnora lifted a sandwich and uncovered the fried chicken. The boy gasped with delight.

"Say, I could eat the stuff in the glass and the other box and carry the bread and the chicken to Jimmy and Belle," he offered.

Elnora silently uncovered the custard with preserved cherries on top and handed it and the spoon to the child. Never did food disappear faster. The salad went next, and a sandwich and half a chicken breast followed.

"I better leave the rest for Jimmy and Belle," he said, "they're 'ist fightin' hungry."

Elnora gave him the remainder of the carefully prepared lunch. The boy clutched it and ran with a sidewise hop like a wild thing. She covered the dishes and cup, polished the spoon, replaced it, and closed the case. She caught her breath in a tremulous laugh.

"If Aunt Margaret knew that, she'd never forgive me," she said. "It seems as if secrecy is literally forced upon me, and I hate it. What shall I do for lunch? I'll have to sell my arrows and keep enough money for a restaurant sandwich."

So she walked hurriedly into town, sold her points at a good price, deposited her funds, and went away with a neat little bank book and the note from the Limberlost carefully folded inside. Elnora passed down the hall that morning, and no one paid the slightest attention to her. The truth was she looked so like every one else that she was perfectly inconspicuous. But in the coat room there were members of her class. Surely no one intended it, but the whisper was too loud.

"Look at the girl from the Limberlost in the clothes that woman gave her!"

Elnora turned on them. "I beg your pardon," she said unsteadily, "I couldn't help hearing that! No one gave me these clothes. I paid for them myself."

Some one muttered, "Pardon me," but incredulous faces greeted her.

Elnora felt driven. "Aunt Margaret selected them, and she meant to give them to me," she explained, "but I wouldn't take them. I paid for them myself." There was silence.

"Don't you believe me?" panted Elnora.

"Really, it is none of our affair," said another girl. "Come on, let's go."

Elnora stepped before the girl who had spoken. "You have made this your affair," she said, "because you told a thing which was not true. No one gave me what I am wearing. I paid for my clothes myself with money I earned selling moths to the Bird Woman. I just came from the bank where I deposited what I did not use. Here is my credit." Elnora drew out and offered the little red book. "Surely you will believe that," she said.

"Why of course," said the girl who first had spoken. "We met such a lovely woman in Brownlee's store, and she said she wanted our help to buy some things for a girl, and that's how we came to know."

"Dear Aunt Margaret," said Elnora, "it was like her to ask you. Isn't she splendid?"

"She is indeed," chorused the girls. Elnora set down her lunch box and books, unpinned her hat, hanging it beside the others, and taking up the books she reached to set the box in its place and dropped it. With a little cry she snatched at it and caught the strap on top. That pulled from the fastening, the cover unrolled, the box fell away as far as it could, two porcelain lids rattled on the floor, and the one sandwich rolled like a cartwheel across the room. Elnora lifted a ghastly face. For once no one laughed. She stood an instant staring.

"It seems to be my luck to be crucified at every point of the compass," she said at last. "First two days you thought I was a pauper, now you will think I'm a fraud. All of you will believe I bought an expensive box, and then was too poor to put anything but a restaurant sandwich in it. You must stop till I prove to you that I'm not."

Elnora gathered up the lids, and kicked the sandwich into a corner.

"I had milk in that bottle, see! And custard in the cup. There was salad in the little box, fried chicken in the large one, and nut sandwiches in the tray. You can see the crumbs of all of them. A man set a dog on a child who was so starved he was stealing apples. I talked with him, and I thought I could bear hunger better, he was such a little boy, so I gave him my lunch, and got the sandwich at the restaurant."

Elnora held out the box. The girls were laughing by that time. "You goose," said one, "why didn't you give him the money, and save your lunch?"

"He was such a little fellow, and he really was hungry," said Elnora. "I often go without anything to eat at noon in the fields and woods, and never think of it."

She closed the box and set it beside the lunches of other country pupils. While her back was turned, into the room came the girl of her encounter on the first day, walked to the rack, and with an exclamation of approval took down Elnora's hat.

"Just the thing I have been wanting!" she said. "I never saw such beautiful quills in all my life. They match my new broadcloth to perfection. I've got to have that kind of quills for my hat. I never saw the like! Whose is it, and where did it come from?"

No one said a word, for Elnora's question, the reply, and her answer, had been repeated. Every one knew that the Limberlost girl had come out ahead and Sadie Reed had not been amiable, when the little flourish had been added to Elnora's name in the algebra class. Elnora's swift glance was pathetic, but no one helped her. Sadie Reed glanced from the hat to the faces around her and wondered.

"Why, this is the Freshman section, whose hat is it?" she asked again, this time impatiently.

"That's the tassel of the cornstock," said Elnora with a forced laugh.

The response was genuine. Every one shouted. Sadie Reed blushed, but she laughed also.

"Well, it's beautiful," she said, "especially the quills. They are exactly what I want. I know I don't deserve any kindness from you, but I do wish you would tell me at whose store you found those quills."

"Gladly!" said Elnora. "You can't buy quills like those at a store. They are from a living bird. Phoebe Simms gathers them in her orchard as her peacocks shed them. They are wing quills from the males."

Then there was perfect silence. How was Elnora to know that not a girl there would have told that?

"I haven't a doubt but I can get you some," she offered. "She gave Aunt Margaret a large bunch, and those are part of them. I am quite sure she has more, and would spare some."

Sadie Reed laughed shortly. "You needn't trouble," she said, "I was fooled. I thought they were expensive quills. I wanted them for a twenty-dollar velvet toque to match my new suit. If they are gathered from the ground, really, I couldn't use them."

"Only in spots!" said Elnora. "They don't just cover the earth. Phoebe Simms's peacocks are the only ones within miles of Onabasha, and they moult but once a year. If your hat cost only twenty dollars, it's scarcely good enough for those quills. You see, the Almighty made and coloured those Himself; and He puts the same kind on Phoebe Simms's peacocks that He put on the head of the family in the forests of Ceylon, away back in the beginning. Any old manufactured quill from New York or Chicago will do for your little twenty-dollar hat. You should have something infinitely better than that to be worthy of quills that are made by the Creator."

How those girls did laugh! One of them walked with Elnora to the auditorium, sat beside her during exercises, and tried to talk whenever she dared, to keep Elnora from seeing the curious and admiring looks bent upon her.

For the brown-eyed boy whistled, and there was pantomime of all sorts going on behind Elnora's back that day. Happy with her books, no one knew how much she saw, and from her absorption in her studies it was evident she cared too little to notice.

After school she went again to the home of the Bird Woman, and together they visited the swamp and carried away more specimens. This time Elnora asked the Bird Woman to keep the money until noon of the next day, when she would call for it and have it added to her bank account. She slowly walked home, for the visit to the swamp had brought back full force the experience of the morning. Again and again she examined the crude little note, for she did not know what it meant, yet it bred vague fear. The only thing of which Elnora knew herself afraid was her mother; when with wild eyes and ears deaf to childish pleading, she sometimes lost control of herself in the night and visited the pool where her husband had sunk before her, calling his name in unearthly tones and begging of the swamp to give back its dead.

CHAPTER VI

WHEREIN MRS. COMSTOCK INDULGES
IN "FRILLS," AND BILLY REAPPEARS

It was Wesley Sinton who really wrestled with Elnora's problem while he drove about his business. He was not forced to ask himself what it meant; he knew. The old Corson gang was still holding together. Elder members who had escaped the law had been joined by a younger brother of Jack's, and they met in the thickest of the few remaining fast places of the swamp to drink, gamble, and loaf. Then suddenly, there would be a robbery in some country house where a farmer that day had sold his wheat or corn and not paid a visit to the bank; or in some neighbouring village.

The home of Mrs. Comstock and Elnora adjoined the swamp. Sinton's land lay next, and not another residence or man easy to reach in case of trouble. Whoever wrote that note had some human kindness in his breast, but the fact stood revealed that he feared his strength if Elnora were delivered into his hands. Where had he been the previous night when he heard that prayer? Was that the first time he had been in such proximity? Sinton drove fast, for he wished to reach the swamp before Elnora and the Bird Woman would go there.

At almost four he came to the case, and dropping on his knees studied the ground, every sense alert. He found two or three little heel prints. Those were made by Elnora or the Bird Woman. What Sinton wanted to learn was whether all the remainder were the footprints of one man. It was easily seen, they were not. There were deep, even tracks made by fairly new shoes, and others where a well-worn heel cut deeper on the inside of the print than at the outer edge. Undoubtedly some of Corson's old gang were watching the case, and the visits of the women to it. There was no danger that any one would attack the Bird Woman. She never went to the swamp at night, and on her trips in the daytime, every one knew that she carried a revolver, understood how to use it, and pursued her work in a fearless manner.

Elnora, prowling around the swamp and lured into the interior by the flight of moths and butterflies; Elnora, without father, money, or friends save himself, to defend her—Elnora was a different proposition. For this to happen just when the Limberlost was bringing the very desire of her heart to the girl, it was too bad.

Sinton was afraid for her, yet he did not want to add the burden of fear to Katharine Comstock's trouble, or to disturb the joy of Elnora in her work. He stopped at the cabin and slowly went up the walk. Mrs. Comstock was sitting on the front steps with some sewing. The work seemed to Sinton as if she might be engaged in putting a tuck in a petticoat. He thought of how Margaret had shortened Elnora's dress to the accepted length for girls of her age, and made a mental note of Mrs. Comstock's occupation.

She dropped her work on her lap, laid her hands on it and looked into his face with a sneer.

"You didn't let any grass grow under your feet," she said.

Sinton saw her white, drawn face and comprehended.

"I went to pay a debt and see about this opening of the ditch, Kate."

"You said you were going to prosecute me."

"Good gracious, Kate!" cried Sinton. "Is that what you have been thinking all day? I told you before I left yesterday that I would not need do that. And I won't! We can't afford to quarrel over Elnora. She's all we've got. Now that she has proved that if you don't do just what I think you ought by way of clothes and schooling, she can take care of herself, I put that out of my head. What I came to see you about is a kind of scare I've had to-day. I want to ask you if you ever see anything about the swamp that makes you think the old Corson gang is still at work?"

"Can't say that I do," said Mrs. Comstock. "There's kind of dancing lights there sometimes, but I supposed it was just people passing along the road with lanterns. Folks hereabout are none too fond of the swamp. I hate it like death. I've never stayed here a night in my life without Robert's revolver, clean and loaded, under my pillow, and the shotgun, same condition, by the bed. I can't say that I'm afraid here at home. I'm not. I can take care of myself. But none of the swamp for me!"

"Well, I'm glad you are not afraid, Kate, because I must tell you something. Elnora stopped at the case this morning, and somebody had been into it in the night."

"Broke the lock?"

"No. Used a duplicate key. To-day I heard there was a man here last night. I want to nose around a little."

Sinton went to the east end of the cabin and looked up at the window. There was no way any one could have reached it without a ladder, for the logs were hewed and mortar filled the cracks even. Then he went to the west end, the willow faced him as he turned the corner. He examined the trunk carefully. There was no mistake about small particles of black swamp muck adhering to the sides of the tree. He reached the low branches and climbed the willow. There was earth on the large limb crossing Elnora's window. He stood on it, holding the branch as had been done the night before, and looked into the room. He could see very little, but he knew that if it had been dark outside and sufficiently light for Elnora to study inside he could have seen vividly. He brought his face close to the netting, and he could see the bed with its head to the east, at its foot the table with the candles and the chair before it, and then he knew where the man had been who had heard Elnora's prayer.

Mrs. Comstock had followed around the corner and stood watching him. "Do you think some slinking hulk was up there peekin' in at Elnora?" she demanded indignantly.

"There is muck on the trunk, and plenty on the limb," said Sinton. "Hadn't you better get a saw and let me take this branch off?"

"No, I hadn't," said Mrs. Comstock. "First place, Elnora's climbed from that window on that limb all her life, and it's hers. Second place, no one gets ahead of me after I've had warning. Any crow that perches on that roost again will get its feathers somewhat scattered. Look along the fence, there, and see if you can find where he came in."

The place was easy to find as was a trail leading for some distance west of the cabin.

"You just go home, and don't fret yourself," said Mrs. Comstock. "I'll take care of this. If you should hear the dinner bell at any time in the night you come down. But I wouldn't say anything to Elnora. She better keep her mind on her studies, if she's going to school."

When the work was finished that night Elnora took her books and went to her room to prepare some lessons, but every few minutes she looked toward the swamp to see if there were lights near the case. Mrs. Comstock raked together the coals in the cooking stove, got out the lunch box, and sitting down she studied it grimly. At last she arose.

"Wonder how it would do to show Mag Sinton a frill or two," she murmured.

She went to her room, knelt before a big black-walnut chest and hunted through its contents until she found an old-fashioned cook book. She tended the fire as she read and presently was in action. She first sawed an end from a fragrant, juicy, sugar-cured ham and put it to cook. Then she set a couple of eggs boiling, and after long hesitation began creaming butter and sugar in a crock. An hour later the odour of the ham, mingled with some of the richest spices of "happy Araby," in a combination that could mean nothing save spice cake, crept up to Elnora so strongly that she lifted her head and sniffed amazedly. She would have given all her precious money to have gone down and thrown her arms around her mother's neck, but she did not dare move.

Mrs. Comstock was up early, and without a word handed Elnora the case as she left the next morning.

"Thank you, mother," said Elnora, and went on her way.

She walked down the road looking straight ahead until she came to the corner, where she usually entered the swamp. She paused, glanced that way and smiled. Then she turned and looked back. There was no one coming in any direction. She followed the road until well around the corner, then she stopped and sat on a grassy spot, laid her books beside her and opened the lunch box. Last night's odours had in a measure prepared her for what she would see, but not quite. She scarcely could believe her senses. Half the bread compartment was filled with dainty sandwiches of bread and butter sprinkled with the yolk of egg and the remainder with three large slices of the most fragrant spice cake imaginable. The meat dish contained shaved cold ham, of which she knew the quality, the salad was tomatoes and celery, and the cup held preserved pear, clear as amber. There was milk in the bottle, two tissue-wrapped cucumber pickles in the folding drinking-cup, and a fresh napkin in the ring. No lunch was ever daintier or more palatable; of that Elnora was perfectly sure. And her mother had prepared it for her! "She does love me!" cried the happy girl. "Sure as you're born she loves me; only she hasn't found it out yet!"

She touched the papers daintily, and smiled at the box as if it were a living thing. As she began closing it a breath of air swept by, lifting the covering of the cake. It was like an invitation, and breakfast was several hours away. Elnora picked up a piece and ate it. That cake tasted even better than it looked. Then she tried a sandwich. How did her mother come to think of making them that way. They never had any at home. She slipped out the fork, sampled the salad, and one-quarter of pear. Then she closed the box and started down the road nibbling one of the pickles and trying to decide exactly how happy she was, but she could find no standard high enough for a measure.

She was to go to the Bird Woman's after school for the last load from the case. Saturday she would take the arrow points and specimens to the bank. That would exhaust her present supplies and give her enough money ahead to pay for books, tuition, and clothes for at least two years. She would work early and late gathering nuts. In October she would sell all the ferns she could find. She must collect specimens of all tree leaves before they fell, gather nests and cocoons later, and keep her eyes wide open for anything the grades could use. She would see the superintendent that night about selling specimens to the ward buildings. She must be ahead of any one else if she wanted to furnish these things. So she approached the bridge.

That it was occupied could be seen from a distance. As she came up she found the small boy of yesterday awaiting her with a confident smile.

"We brought you something!" he announced without greeting. "This is Jimmy and Belle—and we brought you a present."

He offered a parcel wrapped in brown paper.

"Why, how lovely of you!" said Elnora. "I supposed you had forgotten me when you ran away so fast yesterday."

"Naw, I didn't forget you," said the boy. "I wouldn't forget you, not ever! Why, I was ist a-hurrying to take them things to Jimmy and Belle. My they was glad!"

Elnora glanced at the children. They sat on the edge of the bridge, obviously clad in a garment each, very dirty and unkept, a little boy and a girl of about seven and nine. Elnora's heart began to ache.

"Say," said the boy. "Ain't you going to look what we have gave you?"

"I thought it wasn't polite to look before people," answered Elnora. "Of course, I will, if you would like to have me."

Elnora opened the package. She had been presented with a quarter of a stale loaf of baker's bread, and a big piece of ancient bologna.

"But don't you want this yourselves?" she asked in surprise.

"Gosh, no! I mean ist no," said the boy. "We always have it. We got stacks this morning. Pa's come out of it now, and he's so sorry he got more 'an ever we can eat. Have you had any before?"

"No," said Elnora, "I never did!"

The boy's eyes brightened and the girl moved restlessly.

"We thought maybe you hadn't," said the boy. "First you ever have, you like it real well; but when you don't have anything else for a long time, years an' years, you git so tired." He hitched at the string which held his trousers and watched Elnora speculatively.

"I don't s'pose you'd trade what you got in that box for ist old bread and bologna now, would you? Mebby you'd like it! And I know, I ist know, what you got would taste like heaven to Jimmy and Belle. They never had nothing like that! Not even Belle, and she's most ten! No, sir-ee, they never tasted things like you got!"

It was in Elnora's heart to be thankful for even a taste in time, as she knelt on the bridge, opened the box and divided her lunch into three equal parts, the smaller boy getting most of the milk. Then she told them it was school time and she must go.

"Why don't you put your bread and bologna in the nice box?" asked the boy.

"Of course," said Elnora. "I didn't think."

When the box was arranged to the children's satisfaction all of them accompanied Elnora to the corner where she turned toward the high school.

"Billy," said Elnora, "I would like you much better if you were cleaner. Surely, you have water! Can't you children get some soap and wash yourselves? Gentlemen are never dirty. You want to be a gentleman, don't you?"

"Is being clean all you have to do to be a gentleman?"

"No," said Elnora. "You must not say bad words, and you must be kind and polite to your sister."

"Must Belle be kind and polite to me, else she ain't a lady?"

"Yes."

"Then Belle's no lady!" said Billy succinctly.

Elnora could say nothing more just then, and she bade them good-bye and started them home.

"The poor little souls!" she mused. "I think the Almighty put them in my way to show me real trouble. I won't be likely to spend much time pitying myself while I can see them." She glanced at the lunchbox. "What on earth do I carry this for? I never had anything that was so strictly ornamental! One sure thing! I can't take this stuff to the high school. You never seem to know exactly what is going to happen to you while you are there."

As if to provide a way out of her difficulty a big dog arose from a lawn, and came toward the gate wagging his tail. "If those children ate the stuff, it can't possibly kill him!" thought Elnora, so she offered the bologna. The dog accepted it graciously, and being a beast of pedigree he trotted around to a side porch and laid the bologna before his mistress. The woman snatched it, screaming: "Come, quick! Some one is trying to poison Pedro!" Her daughter came running from the house. "Go see who is on the street. Hurry!" cried the excited mother.

Ellen Brownlee ran and looked. Elnora was half a block away, and no one nearer. Ellen called loudly, and Elnora stopped. Ellen came running toward her.

"Did you see any one give our dog something?" she cried as she approached.

Elnora saw no escape.

"I gave it a piece of bologna myself," she said. "It was fit to eat. It wouldn't hurt the dog."

Ellen stood and looked at her. "Of course, I didn't know it was your dog," explained Elnora. "I had something I wanted to throw to some dog, and that one looked big enough to manage it."

Ellen had arrived at her conclusions. "Pass over that lunch box," she demanded.

"I will not!" said Elnora.

"Then I will have you arrested for trying to poison our dog," laughed the girl as she took the box.

"One chunk of stale bread, one half mile of antique bologna contributed for dog feed; the remains of cake, salad and preserves in an otherwise empty lunch box. One ham sandwich yesterday. I think it's lovely you have the box. Who ate your lunch to-day?"

"Same," confessed Elnora, "but there were three of them this time."

"Wait, until I run back and tell mother about the dog, and get my books."

Elnora waited. That morning she walked down the hall and into the auditorium beside one of the very nicest girls in Onabasha, and it was the fourth day. But the surprise came at noon when Ellen insisted upon Elnora lunching at the Brownlee home, and convulsed her parents and family, and overwhelmed Elnora with a greatly magnified, but moderately accurate history of her lunch box.

"Gee! but it's a box, daddy!" cried the laughing girl. "It's carved leather and fastens with a strap that has her name on it. Inside are trays for things all complete, and it bears evidence of having enclosed delicious food, but Elnora never gets any. She's carried it two days now, and both times it has been empty before she reached school. Isn't that killing?"

"It is, Ellen, in more ways than one. No girl is going to eat breakfast at six o'clock, walk three miles, and do good work without her lunch. You can't tell me anything about that box. I sold it last Monday night to Wesley Sinton, one of my good country customers. He told me it was a present for a girl who was worthy of it, and I see he was right."

"He's so good to me," said Elnora. "Sometimes I look at him and wonder if a neighbour can be so kind to one, what a real father would be like. I envy a girl with a father unspeakably."

"You have cause," said Ellen Brownlee. "A father is the very dearest person in the whole round world, except a mother, who is just a dear." The girl, starting to pay tribute to her father, saw that she must include her mother, and said the thing before she remembered what Mrs. Sinton had told the girls in the store. She stopped in dismay. Elnora's face paled a trifle, but she smiled bravely.

"Then I'm fortunate in having a mother," she said.

Mr. Brownlee lingered at the table after the girls had excused themselves and returned to school.

"There's a girl Ellen can't see too much of, in my opinion," he said. "She is every inch a lady, and not a foolish notion or action about her. I can't understand just what combination of circumstances produced her in this day."

"It has been an unusual case of repression, for one thing. She waits on her elders and thinks before she speaks," said Mrs. Brownlee.

"She's mighty pretty. She looks so sound and wholesome, and she's neatly dressed."

"Ellen says she was a fright the first two days. Long brown calico dress almost touching the floor, and big, lumbering shoes. Those Sinton people bought her clothes. Ellen was in the store, and the woman stopped her crowd and asked them about their dresses. She said the girl was not poor, but her mother was selfish and didn't care for her. But Elnora showed a bank book the next day, and declared that she paid for the things herself, so the Sinton people must just have selected them. There's something peculiar about it, but nothing wrong I am sure. I'll encourage Ellen to ask her again."

"I should say so, especially if she is going to keep on giving away her lunch."

"She lunched with the Bird Woman one day this week."

"She did!"

"Yes, she lives out by the Limberlost. You know the Bird Woman works there a great deal, and probably knows her that way. I think the girl gathers specimens for her. Ellen says she knows more than the teachers about any nature question that comes up, and she is going to lead all of them in mathematics, and make them work in any branch."

When Elnora entered the coat room after having had luncheon with Ellen Brownlee there was such a difference in the atmosphere that she could feel it.

"I am almost sorry I have these clothes," she said to Ellen.

"In the name of sense, why?" cried the astonished girl.

"Every one is so nice to me in them, it sets me to wondering if in time I could have made them be equally friendly in the others."

Ellen looked at her introspectively. "I believe you could," she announced at last. "But it would have taken time and heartache, and your mind would have been less free to work on your studies. No one is happy without friends, and I just simply can't study when I am unhappy."

That night the Bird Woman made the last trip to the swamp. Every specimen she possibly could use had been purchased at a fair price, and three additions had been made to the bank book, carrying the total a little past two hundred dollars. There remained the Indian relics to sell on Saturday, and Elnora had secured the order to furnish material for nature work for the grades. Life suddenly grew very full. There was the most excitingly interesting work for every hour, and that work was to pay high school expenses and start the college fund. There was one little rift in her joy. All of it would have been so much better if she could have told her mother, and given the money into her keeping; but the struggle to get a start had been so terrible, Elnora was afraid to take the risk. When she reached home, she only told her mother that the last of the things had been sold that evening.

"I think," said Mrs. Comstock, "that we will ask Wesley to move that box over here back of the garden for you. There you are apt to get tolled farther into the swamp than you intend to go, and you might mire or something. There ought to be just the same things in our woods, and along our swampy places, as there are in the Limberlost. Can't you hunt your stuff here?"

"I can try," said Elnora. "I don't know what I can find until I do. Our woods are undisturbed, and there is a possibility they might be even better hunting than the swamp. But I wouldn't have Freckles's case moved for the world. He might come back some day, and not like it. I've tried to keep his room the best I could, and taking out the box would make a big hole in one side of it. Store boxes don't cost much. I will have Uncle Wesley buy me one, and set it up wherever hunting looks the best, early in the spring. I would feel safer at home."

"Shall we do the work or have supper first?"

"Let's do the work," said Elnora. "I can't say that I'm hungry now. Doesn't seem as if I ever could be hungry again with such a lunch. I am quite sure no one carried more delicious things to eat than I."

Mrs. Comstock was pleased. "I put in a pretty good hunk of cake. Did you divide it with any one?"

"Why, yes, I did," admitted Elnora.

"Who?"

This was becoming uncomfortable. "I ate the biggest piece myself," said Elnora, "and gave the rest to a couple of boys named Jimmy and Billy and a girl named Belle. They said it was the very best cake they ever tasted in all their lives."

Mrs. Comstock sat straight. "I used to be a master hand at spice cake," she boasted. "But I'm a little out of practice. I must get to work again. With the very weeds growing higher than our heads, we should raise plenty of good stuff to eat on this land, if we can't afford anything else but taxes."

Elnora laughed and hurried up stairs to change her dress. Margaret Sinton came that night bringing a beautiful blue one in its place, and carried away the other to launder.

"Do you mean to say those dresses are to be washed every two days?" questioned Mrs. Comstock.

"They have to be, to look fresh," replied Margaret. "We want our girl sweet as a rose."

"Well, of all things!" cried Mrs. Comstock. "Every two days! Any girl who can't keep a dress clean longer than that is a dirty girl. You'll wear the goods out and fade the colours with so much washing."

"We'll have a clean girl, anyway."

"Well, if you like the job you can have it," said Mrs. Comstock. "I don't mind the washing, but I'm so inconvenient with an iron."

Elnora sat late that night working over her lessons. The next morning she put on her blue dress and ribbon and in those she was a picture. Mrs. Comstock caught her breath with a queer stirring around her heart, and looked twice to be sure of what she saw. As Elnora gathered her books her mother silently gave her the lunch box.

"Feels heavy," said Elnora gaily. "And smelly! Like as not I'll be called upon to divide again."

"Then you divide!" said Mrs. Comstock. "Eating is the one thing we don't have to economize on, Elnora. Spite of all I can do food goes to waste in this soil every day. If you can give some of those city children a taste of the real thing, why, don't be selfish."

Elnora went down the road thinking of the city children with whom she probably would divide. Of course, the bridge would be occupied again. So she stopped and opened the box.

"I don't want to be selfish," murmured Elnora, "but it really seems as if I can't give away this lunch. If mother did not put love into it, she's substituted something that's likely to fool me."

She almost felt her steps lagging as she approached the bridge. A very hungry dog had been added to the trio of children. Elnora loved all dogs, and as usual, this one came to her in friendliness. The children said "Good morning!" with alacrity, and another paper parcel lay conspicuous.

"How are you this morning?" inquired Elnora.

"All right!" cried the three, while the dog sniffed ravenously at the lunch box, and beat a perfect tattoo with his tail.

"How did you like the bologna?" questioned Billy eagerly.

"One of the girls took me to lunch at her home yesterday," answered Elnora.

Dawn broke beautifully over Billy's streaked face. He caught the package and thrust it toward Elnora.

"Then maybe you'd like to try the bologna to-day!"

The dog leaped in glad apprehension of something, and Belle scrambled to her feet and took a step forward. The look of famished greed in her eyes was more than Elnora could endure. It was not that she cared for the food so much. Good things to eat had been in abundance all her life. She wanted with this lunch to try to absorb what she felt must be an expression of some sort from her mother, and if it were not a manifestation of love, she did not know what to think it. But it was her mother who had said "be generous." She knelt on the bridge. "Keep back the dog!" she warned the elder boy.

She opened the box and divided the milk between Billy and the girl. She gave each a piece of cake leaving one and a sandwich. Billy pressed forward eagerly, bitter disappointment on his face, and the elder boy forgot his charge.

"Aw, I thought they'd be meat!" lamented Billy.

Elnora could not endure that.

"There is!" she said gladly. "There is a little pigeon bird. I want a teeny piece of the breast, for a sort of keepsake, just one bite, and you can have the rest among you."

Elnora drew the knife from its holder and cut off the wishbone. Then she held the bird toward the girl.

"You can divide it," she said. The dog made a bound and seizing the squab sprang from the bridge and ran for life. The girl and boy hurried after him. With awful eyes Billy stared and swore tempestuously. Elnora caught him and clapped her hand over the little mouth. A delivery wagon came tearing down the street, the horse running full speed, passed the fleeing dog with the girl and boy in pursuit, and stopped at the bridge. High school girls began to roll from all sides of it.

"A rescue! A rescue!" they shouted.

It was Ellen Brownlee and her crowd, and every girl of them carried a big parcel. They took in the scene as they approached. The fleeing dog with something in its mouth, the half-naked girl and boy chasing it told the story. Those girls screamed with laughter as they watched the pursuit.

"Thank goodness, I saved the wishbone!" said Elnora. "As usual, I can prove that there was a bird." She turned toward the box. Billy had improved the time. He had the last piece of cake in one hand, and the last bite of salad disappeared in one great gulp. Then the girls shouted again.

"Let's have a sample ourselves," suggested one. She caught up the box and handed out the remaining sandwich. Another girl divided it into bites each little over an inch square, and then she lifted the cup lid and deposited a preserved strawberry on each bite. "One, two, three, altogether now!" she cried.

"You old mean things!" screamed Billy.

In an instant he was down in the road and handfuls of dust began to fly among them. The girls scattered before him.

"Billy!" cried Elnora. "Billy! I'll never give you another bite, if you throw dust on any one!"

Then Billy dropped the dust, bored both fists into his eyes, and fled sobbing into Elnora's new blue skirt. She stooped to meet him and consolation began. Those girls laughed on. They screamed and shouted until the little bridge shook.

"To-morrow might as well be a clear day," said Ellen, passing around and feeding the remaining berries to the girls as they could compose themselves enough to take them. "Billy, I admire your taste more than your temper."

Elnora looked up. "The little soul is nothing but skin and bones," she said. "I never was really hungry myself; were any of you?"

"Well, I should say so," cried a plump, rosy girl. "I'm famished right now. Let's have breakfast immediate!"

"We got to refill this box first!" said Ellen Brownlee. "Who's got the butter?" A girl advanced with a wooden tray.

"Put it in the preserve cup, a little strawberry flavour won't hurt it. Next!" called Ellen.

A loaf of bread was produced and Ellen cut off a piece which filled the sandwich box.

"Next!" A bottle of olives was unwrapped. The grocer's boy who was waiting opened that, and Ellen filled the salad dish.

"Next!"

A bag of macaroons was produced and the cake compartment filled.

"Next!"

"I don't suppose this will make quite as good dog feed as a bird," laughed a girl holding open a bag of sliced ham while Ellen filled the meat dish.

"Next!"

A box of candy was handed her and she stuffed every corner of the lunch box with chocolates and nougat. Then it was closed and formally presented to Elnora. The girls each helped themselves to candy and olives, and gave Billy the remainder of the food. Billy took one bite of ham, and approved. Belle and Jimmy had given up chasing the dog, and angry and ashamed, stood waiting half a block away.

"Come back!" cried Billy. "You great big dunces, come back! They's a new kind of meat, and cake and candy."

The boy delayed, but the girl joined Billy. Ellen wiped her fingers, stepped to the cement abutment and began reciting "Horatio at the Bridge!" substituting Elnora wherever the hero appeared in the lines.

Elnora gathered up the sacks, and gave them to Belle, telling her to take the food home, cut and spread the bread, set things on the table, and eat nicely.

Then Elnora was taken into the wagon with the girls, and driven on the run to the high school. They sang a song beginning—

"Elnora, please give me a sandwich.
I'm ashamed to ask for cake!"

as they went. Elnora did not know it, but that was her initiation. She belonged to "the crowd." She only knew that she was happy, and vaguely wondered what her mother and Aunt Margaret would have said about the proceedings.

CHAPTER VII

WHEREIN MRS. COMSTOCK
MANIPULATES MARGARET AND BILLY
ACQUIRES A RESIDENCE

Saturday morning Elnora helped her mother with the work. When she had finished Mrs. Comstock told her to go to Sintons' and wash her Indian relics, so that she would be ready to accompany Wesley to town in the afternoon. Elnora hurried down the road and was soon at the cistern with a tub busily washing arrow points, stone axes, tubes, pipes, and skin-cleaning implements.

Then she went home, dressed and was waiting when the carriage reached the gate. She stopped at the bank with the box, and Sinton went to do his marketing and some shopping for his wife.

At the dry goods store Mr. Brownlee called to him, "Hello, Sinton! How do you like the fate of your lunch box?" Then he began to laugh—

"I always hate to see a man laughing alone," said Sinton. "It looks so selfish! Tell me the fun, and let me help you."

Mr. Brownlee wiped his eyes.

"I supposed you knew, but I see she hasn't told."

Then the three days' history of the lunch box was repeated with particulars which included the dog.

"Now laugh!" concluded Mr. Brownlee.

"Blest if I see anything funny!" replied Wesley Sinton. "And if you had bought that box and furnished one of those lunches yourself, you wouldn't either. I call such a work a shame! I'll have it stopped."

"Some one must see to that, all right. They are little leeches. Their father earns enough to support them, but they have no mother, and they run wild. I suppose they are crazy for cooked food. But it is funny, and when you think it over you will see it, if you don't now."

"About where would a body find that father?" inquired Wesley Sinton grimly. Mr. Brownlee told him and he started, locating the house with little difficulty. House was the proper word, for of home there was no sign. Just a small empty house with three unkept little children racing through and around it. The girl and the elder boy hung back, but dirty little Billy greeted Sinton with: "What you want here?"

"I want to see your father," said Sinton.

"Well, he's asleep," said Billy.

"Where?" asked Sinton.

"In the house," answered Billy, "and you can't wake him."

"Well, I'll try," said Wesley.

Billy led the way. "There he is!" he said. "He is drunk again." On a dirty mattress in a corner lay a man who appeared to be strong and well. Billy was right. You could not awake him. He had gone the limit, and a little beyond.

He was now facing eternity. Sinton went out and closed the door. "Your father is sick and needs help," he said. "You stay here, and I will send a man to see him."

"If you just let him 'lone, he'll sleep it off," volunteered Billy. "He's that way all the time, but he wakes up and gets us something to eat after awhile. Only waitin' twists you up inside pretty bad."

The boy wore no air of complaint. He was merely stating facts.

Wesley Sinton looked intently at Billy. "Are you twisted up inside now?" he asked.

Billy laid a grimy hand on the region of his stomach and the filthy little waist sank close to the backbone. "Bet yer life, boss," he said cheerfully.

"How long have you been twisted?" asked Sinton.

Billy appealed to the others. "When was it we had the stuff on the bridge?"

"Yesterday morning," said the girl.

"Is that all gone?" asked Sinton.

"She went and told us to take it home," said Billy ruefully, "and 'cos she said to, we took it. Pa had come back, he was drinking some more, and he ate a lot of it—almost the whole thing, and it made him sick as a dog, and he went and wasted all of it. Then he got drunk some more, and now he's asleep again. We didn't get hardly none."

"You children sit on the steps until the man comes," said Sinton. "I'll send you some things to eat with him. What's your name, sonny?"

"Billy," said the boy.

"Well, Billy, I guess you better come with me. I'll take care of him," Sinton promised the others. He reached a hand to Billy.

"I ain't no baby, I'm a boy!" said Billy, as he shuffled along beside Sinton, taking a kick at every movable object without regard to his battered toes.

Once they passed a Great Dane dog lolling after its master, and Billy ascended Sinton as if he were a tree, and clung to him with trembling hot hands.

"I ain't afraid of that dog," scoffed Billy, as he was again placed on the walk, "but onc't he took me for a rat or somepin' and his teeth cut into my back. If I'd a done right, I'd a took the law on him."

Sinton looked down into the indignant little face. The child was bright enough, he had a good head, but oh, such a body!

"I 'bout got enough of dogs," said Billy. "I used to like 'em, but I'm getting pretty tired. You ought to seen the lickin' Jimmy and Belle and me give our dog when we caught him, for taking a little bird she gave us. We waited 'till he was asleep 'nen laid a board on him and all of us jumped on it to onc't. You could a heard him yell a mile. Belle said mebbe we could squeeze the bird out of him. But, squeeze nothing! He was holler as us, and that bird was lost long 'fore it got to his stummick. It was ist a little one, anyway. Belle said it wouldn't 'a' made a bite apiece for three of us nohow, and the dog got one good swaller. We didn't get much of the meat, either. Pa took most of that. Seems like pas and dogs gets everything."

Billy laughed dolefully. Involuntarily Wesley Sinton reached his hand. They were coming into the business part of Onabasha and the streets were crowded. Billy understood it to mean that he might lose his companion and took a grip. That little hot hand clinging tight to his, the sore feet recklessly scouring the walk, the hungry child panting for breath as he tried to keep even, the brave soul jesting in the face of hard luck, caught Sinton in a tender, empty spot.

"Say, son," he said. "How would you like to be washed clean, and have all the supper your skin could hold, and sleep in a good bed?"

"Aw, gee!" said Billy. "I ain't dead yet! Them things is in heaven! Poor folks can't have them. Pa said so."

"Well, you can have them if you want to go with me and get them," promised Sinton.

"Honest?"

"Yes, honest."

"Crost yer heart?"

"Yes," said Sinton.

"Kin I take some to Jimmy and Belle?"

"If you'll come with me and be my boy, I'll see that they have plenty."

"What will pa say?"

"Your pa is in that kind of sleep now where he won't wake up, Billy," said Sinton. "I am pretty sure the law will give you to me, if you want to come."

"When people don't ever wake up they're dead," announced Billy. "Is my pa dead?"

"Yes, he is," answered Sinton.

"And you'll take care of Jimmy and Belle, too?"

"I can't adopt all three of you," said Sinton. "I'll take you, and see that they are well provided for. Will you come?"

"Yep, I'll come," said Billy. "Let's eat, first thing we do."

"All right," agreed Sinton. "Come into this restaurant." He lifted Billy to the lunch counter and ordered the clerk to give him as many glasses of milk as he wanted, and a biscuit. "I think there's going to be fried chicken when we get home, Billy," he said, "so you just take the edge off now, and fill up later."

While Billy lunched Sinton called up the different departments and notified the proper authorities ending with the Women's Relief Association. He sent a basket of food to Belle and Jimmy, bought Billy a pair of trousers, and a shirt, and went to bring Elnora.

"Why, Uncle Wesley!" cried the girl. "Where did you find Billy?"

"I've adopted him for the time being, if not longer," replied Wesley Sinton.

"Where did you get him?"

"Well, young woman," said Wesley Sinton, "Mr. Brownlee told me the history of your lunch box. It didn't seem so funny to me as it does to the rest of them; so I went to look up the father of Billy's family, and make him take care of them, or allow the law to do it for him. It will have to be the law."

"He's deader than anything!" broke in Billy. "He can't ever take all the meat any more."

"Billy!" gasped Elnora.

"Never you mind!" said Sinton. "A child doesn't say such things about a father who loved and raised him right. When it happens, the father alone is to blame. You won't hear Billy talk like that about me when I cross over."

"You don't mean you are going to take him to keep!"

"I'll soon need help," said Wesley. "Billy will come in just about right ten years from now, and if I raise him I'll have him the way I want him."

"But Aunt Margaret doesn't like boys," objected Elnora.

"Well, she likes me, and I used to be a boy. Anyway, as I remember she has had her way about everything at our house ever since we were married. I am going to please myself about Billy. Hasn't she always done just as she chose so far as you know? Honest, Elnora!"

"Honest!" replied Elnora. "You are beautiful to all of us, Uncle Wesley; but Aunt Margaret won't like Billy. She won't want him in her home."

"In our home," corrected Wesley.

"What makes you want him?" marvelled Elnora.

"God only knows," said Sinton. "Billy ain't so beautiful, and he ain't so smart, I guess it's because he's so human. My heart goes out to him."

"So did mine," said Elnora. "I love him. I'd rather see him eat my lunch than have it myself any time."

"What makes you like him?" asked Wesley.

"Why, I don't know," pondered Elnora. "He's so little, he needs so much, he's got such splendid grit, and he's perfectly unselfish with his brother and sister. But we must wash him before Aunt Margaret sees him. I wonder if mother——"

"You needn't bother. I'm going to take him home the way he is," said Sinton. "I want Maggie to see the worst of it."

"I'm afraid——" began Elnora.

"So am I," said Wesley, "but I won't give him up. He's taken a sort of grip on my heart. I've always been crazy for a boy. Don't let him hear us."

"Don't let him be killed!" cried Elnora. During their talk Billy had wandered to the edge of the walk and barely escaped the wheels of a passing automobile in an effort to catch a stray kitten that seemed in danger.

Wesley drew Billy back to the walk, and held his hand closely. "Are you ready, Elnora?"

"Yes; you were gone a long time," she said.

Wesley glanced at a package she carried. "Have to have another book?" he asked.

"No, I bought this for mother. I've had such splendid luck selling my specimens, I didn't feel right about keeping all the money for myself, so I saved enough from the Indian relics to get a few things I wanted. I would have liked to have gotten her a dress, but I didn't dare, so I compromised on a book."

"What did you select, Elnora?" asked Wesley wonderingly.

"Well," said she, "I have noticed mother always seemed interested in anything Mark Twain wrote in the newspapers, and I thought it would cheer her up a little, so I just got his 'Innocents Abroad.' I haven't read it myself, but I've seen mention made of it all my life, and the critics say it's genuine fun."

"Good!" cried Sinton. "Good! You've made a splendid choice. It will take her mind off herself a lot. But she will scold you."

"Of course," assented Elnora. "But, possibly she will read it, and feel better. I'm going to serve her a trick. I am going to hide it until Monday, and set it on her little shelf of books the last thing before I go away. She must have all of them by heart. When she sees a new one she can't help being glad, for she loves to read, and if she has all day to become interested, maybe she'll like it so she won't scold so much."

"We are both in for it, but I guess we are prepared. I don't know what Margaret will say, but I'm going to take Billy home and see. Maybe he can win with her, as he did with us."

Elnora had doubts, but she did not say anything more. When they started home Billy sat on the front seat. He drove with the hitching strap tied to the railing of the dash-board, flourished the whip, and yelled with delight. At first Sinton laughed with him, but by the time he left Elnora with several packages at her gate, he was looking serious enough.

Margaret was at the door as they drove up the lane. Wesley left Billy in the carriage, hitched the horses and went to explain to her. He had not reached her before she cried, "Look, Wesley, that child! You'll have a runaway!"

Wesley looked and ran. Billy was standing in the carriage slashing the mettlesome horses with the whip.

"See me make 'em go!" he shouted as the whip fell a second time.

He did make them go. They took the hitching post and a few fence palings, which scraped the paint from a wheel. Sinton missed the lines at the first effort, but the dragging post impeded the horses, and he soon caught them. He led them to the barn, and ordered Billy to remain in the carriage while he unhitched. Then leading Billy and carrying his packages he entered the yard.

"You run play a few minutes, Billy," he said. "I want to talk to the nice lady."

The nice lady was looking rather stupefied as Wesley approached her.

"Where in the name of sense did you get that awful child?" she demanded.

"He is a young gentleman who has been stopping Elnora and eating her lunch every day, part of the time with the assistance of his brother and sister, while our girl went hungry. Brownlee told me about it at the store. It's happened three days running. The first time she went without anything, the second time Brownlee's girl took her to lunch, and the third a crowd of high school girls bought a lot of stuff and met them at the bridge. The youngsters seemed to think they could rob her every day, so I went to see their father about having it stopped."

"Well, I should think so!" cried Margaret.

"There were three of them, Margaret," said Wesley, "that little fellow——"

"Hyena, you mean," interpolated Margaret.

"Hyena," corrected Wesley gravely, "and another boy and a girl, all equally dirty and hungry. The man was dead. They thought he was in a drunken sleep, but he was stone dead. I brought the little boy with me, and sent the officers and other help to the house. He's half starved. I want to wash him, and put clean clothes on him, and give him some supper."

"Have you got anything to put on him?"

"Yes."

"Where did you get it?"

"Bought it. It ain't much. All I got didn't cost a dollar."

"A dollar is a good deal when you work and save for it the way we do."

"Well, I don't know a better place to put it. Have you got any hot water? I'll use this tub at the cistern. Please give me some soap and towels."

Instead Margaret pushed by him with a shriek. Billy had played by producing a cord from his pocket, and having tied the tails of Margaret's white kittens together, he had climbed on a box and hung them across the clothes line. Wild with fright the kittens were clawing each other to death, and the air was white with fur. The string had twisted and the frightened creatures could not recognize friends. Margaret stepped back with bleeding hands. Sinton cut the cord with his knife and the poor little cats raced under the house bleeding and disfigured. Margaret white with wrath faced Wesley.

"If you don't hitch up and take that animal back to town," she said, "I will."

Billy threw himself on the grass and began to scream.

"You said I could have fried chicken for supper," he wailed. "You said she was a nice lady!"

Wesley lifted him and something in his manner of handling the child infuriated Margaret. His touch was so gentle. She reached for Billy and gripped his shirt collar in the back. Wesley's hand closed over hers.

"Gently, girl!" he said. "This little body is covered with sores."

"Sores!" she ejaculated. "Sores? What kind of sores?"

"Oh, they might be from bruises made by fists or boot toes, or they might be bad blood, from wrong eating, or they might be pure filth. Will you hand me some towels?"

"No, I won't!" said Margaret.

"Well, give me some rags, then."

Margaret compromised on pieces of old tablecloth. Wesley led Billy to the cistern, pumped cold water into the tub, poured in a kettle of hot, and beginning at the head scoured him. The boy shut his little teeth, and said never a word though he twisted occasionally when the soap struck a raw spot. Margaret watched the process from the window in amazed and ever-increasing anger. Where did Wesley learn it? How could his big hands be so gentle? He came to the door.

"Have you got any peroxide?" he asked.

"A little," she answered stiffly.

"Well, I need about a pint, but I'll begin on what you have."

Margaret handed him the bottle. Wesley took a cup, weakened the drug and said to Billy: "Man, these sores on you must be healed. Then you must eat the kind of food that's fit for little men. I am going to put some medicine on you, and it is going to sting like fire. If it just runs off, I won't use any more. If it boils, there is poison in these places, and they must be tied up, dosed every day, and you must be washed, and kept mighty clean. Now, hold still, because I am going to put it on."

"I think the one on my leg is the worst," said the undaunted Billy, holding out a raw place. Sinton poured on the drug. Billy's body twisted and writhed, but he did not run.

"Gee, look at it boil!" he cried. "I guess they's poison. You'll have to do it to all of them."

Wesley's teeth were set, as he watched the boy's face. He poured the drug, strong enough to do effective work, on a dozen places over that little body and bandaged all he could. Billy's lips quivered at times, and his chin jumped, but he did not shed a tear or utter a sound other than to take a deep interest in the boiling. As Wesley put the small shirt on the boy, and fastened the trousers, he was ready to reset the hitching post and mend the fence without a word.

"Now am I clean?" asked Billy.

"Yes, you are clean outside," said Wesley. "There is some dirty blood in your body, and some bad words in your mouth, that we have to get out, but that takes time. If we put right things to eat into your stomach that will do away with the sores, and if you know that I don't like bad words you won't say them any oftener than you can help, will you Billy?"

Billy leaned against Wesley in apparent indifference.

"I want to see me!" he demanded.

Wesley led the boy into the house, and lifted him to a mirror.

"My, I'm purty good-looking, ain't I?" bragged Billy. Then as Wesley stooped to set him on the floor Billy's lips passed close to the big man's ear and hastily whispered a vehement "No!" as he ran for the door.

"How long until supper, Margaret?" asked Wesley as he followed.

"You are going to keep him for supper?" she asked

"Sure!" said Wesley. "That's what I brought him for. It's likely he never had a good square meal of decent food in his life. He's starved to the bone."

Margaret arose deliberately, removed the white cloth from the supper table and substituted an old red one she used to wrap the bread. She put away the pretty dishes they commonly used and set the table with old plates for pies and kitchen utensils. But she fried the chicken, and was generous with milk and honey, snowy bread, gravy, potatoes, and fruit.

Wesley repainted the scratched wheel. He mended the fence, with Billy holding the nails and handing the pickets. Then he filled the old hole, digged a new one and set the hitching post.

Billy hopped on one foot at his task of holding the post steady as the earth was packed around it. There was not the shadow of a trouble on his little freckled face.

Sinton threw in stones and pounded the earth solid around the post. The sound of a gulping sob attracted him to Billy. The tears were rolling down his cheeks. "If I'd a knowed you'd have to get down in a hole, and work so hard I wouldn't 'a' hit the horses," he said.

"Never you mind, Billy," said Wesley. "You will know next time, so you can think over it, and make up your mind whether you really want to before you strike."

Wesley went to the barn to put away the tools. He thought Billy was at his heels, but the boy lagged on the way. A big snowy turkey gobbler resented the small intruder in his especial preserves, and with spread tail and dragging wings came toward him threateningly. If that turkey gobbler had known the sort of things with which Billy was accustomed to holding his own, he never would have issued the challenge. Billy accepted instantly. He danced around with stiff arms at his sides and imitated the gobbler. Then came his opportunity, and he jumped on the big turkey's back. Wesley heard Margaret's scream in time to see the flying leap and admire its dexterity. The turkey tucked its tail and scampered. Billy slid from its back and as he fell he clutched wildly, caught the folded tail, and instinctively clung to it. The turkey gave one scream and relaxed its muscles. Then it fled in disfigured defeat to the haystack. Billy scrambled to his feet holding the tail, while his eyes were bulging.

"Why, the blasted old thing came off!" he said to Wesley, holding out the tail in amazed wonder.

The man, caught suddenly, forgot everything and roared. Seeing which, Billy thought a turkey tail of no account and flung that one high above him shouting in wild childish laughter, when the feathers scattered and fell.

Margaret, watching, began to cry. Wesley had gone mad. For the first time in her married life she wanted to tell her mother. When Wesley had waited until he was so hungry he could wait no longer he invaded the kitchen to find a cooked supper baking on the back of the stove, while Margaret with red eyes nursed a pair of demoralized white kittens.

"Is supper ready?" he asked.

"It has been for an hour," answered Margaret.

"Why didn't you call us?"

That "us" had too much comradeship in it. It irritated Margaret.

"I supposed it would take you even longer than this to fix things decent again. As for my turkey, and my poor little kittens, they don't matter."

"I am mighty sorry about them, Margaret, you know that. Billy is very bright, and he will soon learn——"

"Soon learn!" cried Margaret. "Wesley Sinton, you don't mean to say that you think of keeping that creature here for some time?"

"No, I think of keeping a well-behaved little boy."

Margaret set the supper on the table. Seeing the old red cloth Wesley stared in amazement. Then he understood. Billy capered around in delight.

"Ain't that pretty?" he exulted. "I wish Jimmy and Belle could see. We, why we ist eat out of our hands or off a old dry goods box, and when we fix up a lot, we have newspaper. We ain't ever had a nice red cloth like this."

Wesley looked straight at Margaret, so intently that she turned away, her face flushing. He stacked the dictionary and the geography of the world on a chair, and lifted Billy beside him. He heaped a plate generously, cut the food, put a fork into Billy's little fist, and made him eat slowly and properly. Billy did his best. Occasionally greed overcame him, and he used his left hand to pop a bite into his mouth with his fingers. These lapses Wesley patiently overlooked, and went on with his general instructions. Luckily Billy did not spill anything on his clothing or the cloth. After supper Wesley took him to the barn while he finished the night work. Then he went and sat beside Margaret on the front porch. Billy appropriated the hammock, and swung by pulling a rope tied around a tree. The very energy with which he went at the work of swinging himself appealed to Wesley.

"Mercy, but he's an active little body," he said. "There isn't a lazy bone in him. See how he works to pay for his fun."

"There goes his foot through it!" cried Margaret. "Wesley, he shall not ruin my hammock."

"Of course he shan't!" said Wesley. "Wait, Billy, let me show you."

Thereupon he explained to Billy that ladies wearing beautiful white dresses sat in hammocks, so little boys must not put their dusty feet in them. Billy immediately sat, and allowed his feet to swing.

"Margaret," said Wesley after a long silence on the porch, "isn't it true that if Billy had been a half-starved sore cat, dog, or animal of any sort, that you would have pitied, and helped care for it, and been glad to see me get any pleasure out of it I could?"

"Yes," said Margaret coldly.

"But because I brought a child with an immortal soul, there is no welcome."

"That isn't a child, it's an animal."

"You just said you would have welcomed an animal."

"Not a wild one. I meant a tame beast."

"Billy is not a beast!" said Wesley hotly. "He is a very dear little boy. Margaret, you've always done the church-going and Bible reading for this family. How do you reconcile that 'Suffer little children to come unto Me' with the way you are treating Billy?"

Margaret arose. "I haven't treated that child. I have only let him alone. I can barely hold myself. He needs the hide tanned about off him!"

"If you'd cared to look at his body, you'd know that you couldn't find a place to strike without cutting into a raw spot," said Wesley. "Besides, Billy has not done a thing for which a child should be punished. He is only full of life, no training, and with a boy's love of mischief. He did abuse your kittens, but an hour before I saw him risk his life to save one from being run over. He minds what you tell him, and doesn't do anything he is told not to. He thinks of his brother and sister right away when anything pleases him. He took that stinging medicine with the grit of a bulldog. He is just a bully little chap, and I love him."

"Oh good heavens!" cried Margaret, going into the house as she spoke.

Sinton sat still. At last Billy tired of the swing, came to him and leaned his slight body against the big knee.

"Am I going to sleep here?" he asked.

"Sure you are!" said Sinton.

Billy swung his feet as he laid across Wesley's knee. "Come on," said Wesley, "I must clean you up for bed."

"You have to be just awful clean here," announced Billy. "I like to be clean, you feel so good, after the hurt is over."

Sinton registered that remark, and worked with especial tenderness as he redressed the ailing places and washed the dust from Billy's feet and hands.

"Where can he sleep?" he asked Margaret.

"I'm sure I don't know," she answered.

"Oh, I can sleep ist any place," said Billy. "On the floor or anywhere. Home, I sleep on pa's coat on a store-box, and Jimmy and Belle they sleep on the storebox, too. I sleep between them, so's I don't roll off and crack my head. Ain't you got a storebox and a old coat?"

Wesley arose and opened a folding lounge. Then he brought an armload of clean horse blankets from a closet.

"These don't look like the nice white bed a little boy should have, Billy," he said, "but we'll make them do. This will beat a storebox all hollow."

Billy took a long leap for the lounge. When he found it bounced, he proceeded to bounce, until he was tired. By that time the blankets had to be refolded. Wesley had Billy take one end and help, while both of them seemed to enjoy the job. Then Billy lay down and curled up in his clothes like a small dog. But sleep would not come.

Finally he sat up. He stared around restlessly. Then he arose, went to Wesley, and leaned against his knee. He picked up the boy and folded his arms around him. Billy sighed in rapturous content.

"That bed feels so lost like," he said. "Jimmy always jabbed me on one side, and Belle on the other, and so I knew I was there. Do you know where they are?"

"They are with kind people who gave them a fine supper, a clean bed, and will always take good care of them."

"I wisht I was—" Billy hesitated and looked earnestly at Wesley. "I mean I wish they was here."

"You are about all I can manage, Billy," said Wesley.

Billy sat up. "Can't she manage anything?" he asked, waving toward Margaret.

"Indeed, yes," said Wesley. "She has managed me for twenty years."

"My, but she made you nice!" said Billy. "I just love you. I wisht she'd take Jimmy and Belle and make them nice as you."

"She isn't strong enough to do that, Billy. They will grow into a good boy and girl where they are."

Billy slid from Wesley's arms and walked toward Margaret until he reached the middle of the room. Then he stopped, and at last sat on the floor. Finally he lay down and closed his eyes. "This feels more like my bed; if only Jimmy and Belle was here to crowd up a little, so it wasn't so alone like."

"Won't I do, Billy?" asked Wesley in a husky voice.

Billy moved restlessly. "Seems like—seems like toward night as if a body got kind o' lonesome for a woman person—like her."

Billy indicated Margaret and then closed his eyes so tight his small face wrinkled.

Soon he was up again. "Wisht I had Snap," he said. "Oh, I ist wisht I had Snap!"

"I thought you laid a board on Snap and jumped on it," said Wesley.

"We did!" cried Billy—"oh, you ought to heard him squeal!" Billy laughed loudly, then his face clouded.

"But I want Snap to lay beside me so bad now—that if he was here I'd give him a piece of my chicken, 'fore I ate any. Do you like dogs?"

"Yes, I do," said Wesley.

Billy was up instantly. "Would you like Snap?"

"I am sure I would," said Wesley.

"Would she?" Billy indicated Margaret. And then he answered his own question. "But of course, she wouldn't, cos she likes cats, and dogs chases cats. Oh, dear, I thought for a minute maybe Snap could come here." Billy lay down and closed his eyes resolutely.

Suddenly they flew open. "Does it hurt to be dead?" he demanded.

"Nothing hurts you after you are dead, Billy," said Wesley.

"Yes, but I mean does it hurt getting to be dead?"

"Sometimes it does. It did not hurt your father, Billy. It came softly while he was asleep."

"It ist came softly?"

"Yes."

"I kind o' wisht he wasn't dead!" said Billy. "'Course I like to stay with you, and the fried chicken, and the nice soft bed, and—and everything, and I like to be clean, but he took us to the show, and he got us gum, and he never hurt us when he wasn't drunk."

Billy drew a deep breath, and tightly closed his eyes. But very soon they opened. Then he sat up. He looked at Wesley pitifully, and then he glanced at Margaret. "You don't like boys, do you?" he questioned.

"I like good boys," said Margaret.

Billy was at her knee instantly. "Well say, I'm a good boy!" he announced joyously.

"I do not think boys who hurt helpless kittens and pull out turkeys' tails are good boys."

"Yes, but I didn't hurt the kittens," explained Billy. "They got mad 'bout ist a little fun and scratched each other. I didn't s'pose they'd act like that. And I didn't pull the turkey's tail. I ist held on to the first thing I grabbed, and the turkey pulled. Honest, it was the turkey pulled." He turned to Wesley. "You tell her! Didn't the turkey pull? I didn't know its tail was loose, did I?"

"I don't think you did, Billy," said Wesley.

Billy stared into Margaret's cold face. "Sometimes at night, Belle sits on the floor, and I lay my head in her lap. I could pull up a chair and lay my head in your lap. Like this, I mean." Billy pulled up a chair, climbed on it and laid his head on Margaret's lap. Then he shut his eyes again. Margaret could have looked little more repulsed if he had been a snake. Billy was soon up.

"My, but your lap is hard," he said. "And you are a good deal fatter 'an Belle, too!" He slid from the chair and came back to the middle of the room.

"Oh but I wisht he wasn't dead!" he cried. The flood broke and Billy screamed in desperation.

Out of the night a soft, warm young figure flashed through the door and with a swoop caught him in her arms. She dropped into a chair, nestled him closely, drooped her fragrant brown head over his little bullet-eyed red one, and rocked softly while she crooned over him—

"Billy, boy, where have you been?
Oh, I have been to seek a wife,
She's the joy of my life,
But then she's a young thing and she can't leave her mammy!"

Billy clung to her frantically. Elnora wiped his eyes, kissed his face, swayed and sang.

"Why aren't you asleep?" she asked at last.

"I don't know," said Billy. "I tried. I tried awful hard cos I thought he wanted me to, but it ist wouldn't come. Please tell her I tried." He appealed to Margaret.

"He did try to go to sleep," admitted Margaret.

"Maybe he can't sleep in his clothes," suggested Elnora. "Haven't you an old dressing sacque? I could roll the sleeves."

Margaret got an old sacque, and Elnora put it on Billy. Then she brought a basin of water and bathed his face and head. She gathered him up and began to rock again.

"Have you got a pa?" asked Billy.

"No," said Elnora.

"Is he dead like mine?"

"Yes."

"Did it hurt him to die?"

"I don't know."

Billy was wide awake again. "It didn't hurt my pa," he boasted; "he ist died while he was asleep. He didn't even know it was coming."

"I am glad of that," said Elnora, pressing the small head against her breast again.

Billy escaped her hand and sat up. "I guess I won't go to sleep," he said. "It might 'come softly' and get me."

"It won't get you, Billy," said Elnora, rocking and singing between sentences. "It doesn't get little boys. It just takes big people who are sick."

"Was my pa sick?"

"Yes," said Elnora. "He had a dreadful sickness inside him that burned, and made him drink things. That was why he would forget his little boys and girl. If he had been well, he would have gotten you good things to eat, clean clothes, and had the most fun with you."

Billy leaned against her and closed his eyes, and Elnora rocked hopefully.

"If I was dead would you cry?" he was up again.

"Yes, I would," said Elnora, gripping him closer until Billy almost squealed with the embrace.

"Do you love me tight as that?" he questioned blissfully.

"Yes, bushels and bushels," said Elnora. "Better than any little boy in the whole world."

Billy looked at Margaret. "She don't!" he said. "She'd be glad if it would get me 'softly,' right now. She don't want me here 't all."

Elnora smothered his face against her breast and rocked.

"You love me, don't you?"

"I will, if you will go to sleep."

"Every single day you will give me your dinner for the bologna, won't you," said Billy.

"Yes, I will," replied Elnora. "But you will have as good lunch as I do after this. You will have milk, eggs, chicken, all kinds of good things, little pies, and cakes, maybe."

Billy shook his head. "I am going back home soon as it is light," he said, "she don't want me. She thinks I'm a bad boy. She's going to whip me—if he lets her. She said so. I heard her. Oh, I wish he hadn't died! I want to go home." Billy shrieked again.

Mrs. Comstock had started to walk slowly to meet Elnora. The girl had been so late that her mother reached the Sinton gate and followed the path until the picture inside became visible. Elnora had told her about Wesley taking Billy home. Mrs. Comstock had some curiosity to see how Margaret bore the unexpected addition to her family. Billy's voice, raised with excitement, was plainly audible. She could see Elnora holding him, and hear his excited wail. Wesley's face was drawn and haggard, and Margaret's set and defiant. A very imp of perversity entered the breast of Mrs. Comstock.

"Hoity, toity!" she said as she suddenly appeared in the door. "Blest if I ever heard a man making sounds like that before!"

Billy ceased suddenly. Mrs. Comstock was tall, angular, and her hair was prematurely white. She was only thirty-six, although she appeared fifty. But there was an expression on her usually cold face that was attractive just then, and Billy was in search of attractions.

"Have I stayed too late, mother?" asked Elnora anxiously. "I truly intended to come straight back, but I thought I could rock Billy to sleep first. Everything is strange, and he's so nervous."

"Is that your ma?" demanded Billy.

"Yes."

"Does she love you?"

"Of course!"

"My mother didn't love me," said Billy. "She went away and left me, and never came back. She don't care what happens to me. You wouldn't go away and leave your little girl, would you?" questioned Billy.

"No," said Katharine Comstock, "and I wouldn't leave a little boy, either."

Billy began sliding from Elnora's knees.

"Do you like boys?" he questioned.

"If there is anything I love it is a boy," said Mrs. Comstock assuringly. Billy was on the floor.

"Do you like dogs?"

"Yes. Almost as well as boys. I am going to buy a dog as soon as I can find a good one."

Billy swept toward her with a whoop.

"Do you want a boy?" he shouted.

Katharine Comstock stretched out her arms, and gathered him in.

"Of course, I want a boy!" she rejoiced.

"Maybe you'd like to have me?" offered Billy.

"Sure I would," triumphed Mrs. Comstock. "Any one would like to have you. You are just a real boy, Billy."

"Will you take Snap?"

"I'd like to have Snap almost as well as you."

"Mother!" breathed Elnora imploringly. "Don't! Oh, don't! He thinks you mean it!"

"And so I do mean it," said Mrs. Comstock. "I'll take him in a jiffy. I throw away enough to feed a little tyke like him every day. His chatter would be great company while you are gone. Blood soon can be purified with right food and baths, and as for Snap, I meant to buy a bulldog, but possibly Snap will serve just as well. All I ask of a dog is to bark at the right time. I'll do the rest. Would you like to come and be my boy, Billy?"

Billy leaned against Mrs. Comstock, reached his arms around her neck and gripped her with all his puny might. "You can whip me all you want to," he said. "I won't make a sound."

Mrs. Comstock held him closely and her hard face was softening; of that there could be no doubt.

"Now, why would any one whip a nice little boy like you?" she asked wonderingly.

"She"—Billy from his refuge waved toward Margaret—"she was going to whip me 'cause her cats fought, when I tied their tails together and hung them over the line to dry. How did I know her old cats would fight?"

Mrs. Comstock began to laugh suddenly, and try as she would she could not stop so soon as she desired. Billy studied her.

"Have you got turkeys?" he demanded.

"Yes, flocks of them," said Mrs. Comstock, vainly struggling to suppress her mirth, and settle her face in its accustomed lines.

"Are their tails fast?" demanded Billy.

"Why, I think so," marvelled Mrs. Comstock.

"Hers ain't!" said Billy with the wave toward Margaret that was becoming familiar. "Her turkey pulled, and its tail comed right off. She's going to whip me if he lets her. I didn't know the turkey would pull. I didn't know its tail would come off. I won't ever touch one again, will I?"

"Of course, you won't," said Mrs. Comstock. "And what's more, I don't care if you do! I'd rather have a fine little man like you than all the turkeys in the country. Let them lose their old tails if they want to, and let the cats fight. Cats and turkeys don't compare with boys, who are going to be fine big men some of these days."

Then Billy and Mrs. Comstock hugged each other rapturously, while their audience stared in silent amazement.

"You like boys!" exulted Billy, and his head dropped against Mrs. Comstock in unspeakable content.

"Yes, and if I don't have to carry you the whole way home, we must start right now," said Mrs. Comstock. "You are going to be asleep before you know it."

Billy opened his eyes and braced himself. "I can walk," he said proudly. "All right, we must start. Come, Elnora! Good-night, folks!" Mrs. Comstock set Billy on the floor, and arose gripping his hand. "You take the other side, Elnora, and we will help him as much as we can," she said.

Elnora stared piteously at Margaret, then at Wesley, and arose in white-faced bewilderment.

"Billy, are you going to leave without even saying good-bye to me?" asked Wesley, with a gulp.

Billy held tight to Mrs. Comstock and Elnora.

"Good-bye!" he said casually. "I'll come and see you some time."

Wesley Sinton gave a smothered sob, and strode from the room.

Mrs. Comstock started toward the door, dragging at Billy while Elnora pulled back, but Mrs. Sinton was before them, her eyes flashing.

"Kate Comstock, you think you are mighty smart, don't you?" she cried.

"I ain't in the lunatic asylum, where you belong, anyway," said Mrs. Comstock. "I am smart enough to tell a dandy boy when I see him, and I'm good and glad to get him. I'll love to have him!"

"Well, you won't have him!" exclaimed Margaret Sinton. "That boy is Wesley's! He found him, and brought him here. You can't come in and take him like that! Let go of him!"

"Not much, I won't!" cried Mrs. Comstock. "Leave the poor sick little soul here for you to beat, because he didn't know just how to handle things! Of course, he'll make mistakes. He must have a lot of teaching, but not the kind he'll get from you! Clear out of my way!"

"You let go of our boy," ordered Margaret.

"Why? Do you want to whip him, before he can go to sleep?" jeered Mrs. Comstock.

"No, I don't!" said Margaret. "He's Wesley's, and nobody shall touch him. Wesley!"

Wesley Sinton appeared behind Margaret in the doorway, and she turned to him. "Make Kate Comstock let go of our boy!" she demanded.

"Billy, she wants you now," said Wesley Sinton. "She won't whip you, and she won't let any one else. You can have stacks of good things to eat, ride in the carriage, and have a great time. Won't you stay with us?"

Billy drew away from Mrs. Comstock and Elnora. He faced Margaret, his eyes shrewd with unchildish wisdom. Necessity had taught him to strike the hot iron, to drive the hard bargain.

"Can I have Snap to live here always?" he demanded.

"Yes, you can have all the dogs you want," said Margaret Sinton.

"Can I sleep close enough so's I can touch you?"

"Yes, you can move your lounge up so that you can hold my hand," said Margaret.

"Do you love me now?" questioned Billy.

"I'll try to love you, if you are a good boy," said Margaret.

"Then I guess I'll stay," said Billy, walking over to her.

Out in the night Elnora and her mother went down the road in the moonlight; every few rods Mrs. Comstock laughed aloud.

"Mother, I don't understand you," sobbed Elnora.

"Well, maybe when you have gone to high school longer you will," said Mrs. Comstock. "Anyway, you saw me bring Mag Sinton to her senses, didn't you?"

"Yes, I did," answered Elnora, "but I thought you were in earnest. So did Billy, and Uncle Wesley, and Aunt Margaret."

"Well, wasn't I?" inquired Mrs. Comstock.

"But you just said you brought Aunt Margaret to!"

"Well, didn't I?"

"I don't understand you."

"That's the reason I am recommending more schooling!"

Elnora took her candle and went to bed. Mrs. Comstock was feeling too good to sleep. Twice of late she really had enjoyed herself for the first in sixteen years, and greediness for more of the same feeling crept into her blood like intoxication. As she sat brooding alone she knew the truth. She would have loved to have taken Billy. She would not have minded his mischief, his chatter, or his dog. He would have meant a distraction from herself that she greatly needed; she was even sincere about the dog. She had intended to tell Wesley to buy her one at the very first opportunity. Her last thought was of Billy. She chuckled softly, for she was not saintly, and now she knew how she could even a long score with Margaret and Wesley in a manner that would fill her soul with grim satisfaction.

CHAPTER VIII

WHEREIN THE LIMBERLOST TEMPTS
ELNORA, AND BILLY BURIES HIS FATHER

Immediately after dinner on Sunday Wesley Sinton stopped at the Comstock gate to ask if Elnora wanted to go to town with them. Billy sat beside him and he did not appear as if he were on his way to a funeral. Elnora said she had to study and could not go, but she suggested that her mother take her place. Mrs. Comstock put on her hat and went at once, which surprised Elnora. She did not know that her mother was anxious for an opportunity to speak with Sinton alone. Elnora knew why she was repeatedly cautioned not to leave their land, if she went specimen hunting.

She studied two hours and was several lessons ahead of her classes. There was no use to go further. She would take a walk and see if she could gather any caterpillars or find any freshly spun cocoons. She searched the bushes and low trees behind the garden and all around the edge of the woods on their land, and having little success, at last came to the road. Almost the first thorn bush she examined yielded a Polyphemus cocoon. Elnora lifted her head with the instinct of a hunter on the chase, and began work. She reached the swamp before she knew it, carrying five fine cocoons of different species as her reward. She pushed back her hair and gazed around longingly. A few rods inside she thought she saw cocoons on a bush, to which she went, and found several. Sense of caution was rapidly vanishing; she was in a fair way to forget everything and plunge into the swamp when she thought she heard footsteps coming down the trail. She went back, and came out almost facing Pete Corson.

That ended her difficulty. She had known him since childhood. When she sat on the front bench of the Brushwood schoolhouse, Pete had been one of the big boys at the back of the room. He had been rough and wild, but she never had been afraid of him, and often he had given her pretty things from the swamp.

"What luck!" she cried. "I promised mother I would not go inside the swamp alone, and will you look at the cocoons I've found! There are more just screaming for me to come get them, because the leaves will fall with the first frost, and then the jays and crows will begin to tear them open. I haven't much time, since I'm going to school. You will go with me, Pete! Please say yes! Just a little way!"

"What are those things?" asked the man, his keen black eyes staring at her.

"They are the cases these big caterpillars spin for winter, and in the spring they come out great night moths, and I can sell them. Oh, Pete, I can sell them for enough to take me through high school and dress me so like the others that I don't look different, and if I have very good luck I can save some for college. Pete, please go with me?"

"Why don't you go like you always have?"

"Well, the truth is, I had a little scare," said Elnora. "I never did mean to go alone; sometimes I sort of wandered inside farther than I intended, chasing things. You know Duncan gave me Freckles's books, and I have been gathering moths like he did. Lately I found I could sell them. If I can make a complete collection, I can get three hundred dollars for it. Three such collections would take me almost through college, and I've four years in the high school yet. That's a long time. I might collect them."

"Can every kind there is be found here?"

"No, not all of them, but when I get more than I need of one kind, I can trade them with collectors farther north and west, so I can complete sets. It's the only way I see to earn the money. Look what I have already. Big gray Cecropias come from this kind; brown Polyphemus from that, and green Lunas from these. You aren't working on Sunday. Go with me only an hour, Pete!"

The man looked at her narrowly. She was young, wholesome, and beautiful. She was innocent, intensely in earnest, and she needed the money, he knew that.

"You didn't tell me what scared you," he said.

"Oh, I thought I did! Why you know I had Freckles's box packed full of moths and specimens, and one evening I sold some to the Bird Woman. Next morning I found a note telling me it wasn't safe to go inside the swamp. That sort of scared me. I think I'll go alone, rather than miss the chance, but I'd be so happy if you would take care of me. Then I could go anywhere I chose, because if I mired you could pull me out. You will take care of me, Pete?"

"Yes, I'll take care of you," promised Pete Corson.

"Goody!" said Elnora. "Let's start quick! And Pete, you look at these closely, and when you are hunting or going along the road, if one dangles under your nose, you cut off the little twig and save it for me, will you?"

"Yes, I'll save you all I see," promised Pete. He pushed back his hat and followed Elnora. She plunged fearlessly among bushes, over underbrush, and across dead logs. One minute she was crying wildly, that here was a big one, the next she was reaching for a limb above her head or on her knees overturning dead leaves under a hickory or oak tree, or working aside black muck with her bare hands as she searched for buried pupae cases. For the first hour Pete bent back bushes and followed, carrying what Elnora discovered. Then he found one.

"Is this the kind of thing you are looking for?" he asked bashfully, as he presented a wild cherry twig.

"Oh Pete, that's a Promethea! I didn't even hope to find one."

"What's the bird like?" asked Pete.

"Almost black wings," said Elnora, "with clay-coloured edges, and the most wonderful wine-coloured flush over the under side if it's a male, and stronger wine above and below if it's a female. Oh, aren't I happy!"

"How would it do to make what you have into a bunch that we could leave here, and come back for them?"

"That would be all right."

Relieved of his load Pete began work. First, he narrowly examined the cocoons Elnora had found. He questioned her as to what other kinds would be like. He began to use the eyes of a trained woodman and hunter in her behalf. He saw several so easily, and moved through the forest so softly, that Elnora forgot the moths in watching him. Presently she was carrying the specimens, and he was making the trips of investigation to see which was a cocoon and which a curled leaf, or he was on his knees digging around stumps. As he worked he kept asking questions. What kind of logs were best to look beside, what trees were pupae cases most likely to be under; on what bushes did caterpillars spin most frequently? Time passed, as it always does when one's occupation is absorbing.

When the Sintons took Mrs. Comstock home, they stopped to see Elnora. She was not there. Mrs. Comstock called at the edge of her woods and received no reply. Then Wesley turned and drove back to the Limberlost. He left Margaret and Mrs. Comstock holding the team and entertaining Billy, while he entered the swamp.

Elnora and Pete had made a wide trail behind them. Before Sinton had thought of calling, he heard voices and approached with some caution. Soon he saw Elnora, her flushed face beaming as she bent with an armload of twigs and branches and talked to a kneeling man.

"Now go cautiously!" she was saying. "I am just sure we will find an Imperialis here. It's their very kind of a place. There! What did I tell you! Isn't that splendid? Oh, I am so glad you came with me!"

Wesley stood staring in speechless astonishment, for the man had arisen, brushed the dirt from his hands, and held out to Elnora a small shining dark pupa case. As his face came into view Sinton almost cried out, for he was the one man of all others Wesley knew with whom he most feared for Elnora's safety. She had him on his knees digging pupae cases for her from the swamp.

"Elnora!" called Sinton. "Elnora!"

"Oh, Uncle Wesley!" cried the girl. "See what luck we've had! I know we have a dozen and a half cocoons and we have three pupae cases. It's much harder to get the cases because you have to dig for them, and you can't see where to look. But Pete is fine at it! He's found three, and he says he will keep watch beside the roads, and through the woods while he hunts. Isn't that splendid of him? Uncle Wesley, there is a college over there on the western edge of the swamp. Look closely, and you can see the great dome up among the clouds."

"I should say you have had luck," said Wesley, striving to make his voice natural. "But I thought you were not coming to the swamp?"

"Well, I wasn't," said Elnora, "but I couldn't find many anywhere else, honest, I couldn't, and just as soon as I came to the edge I began to see them here. I kept my promise. I didn't come in alone. Pete came with me. He's so strong, he isn't afraid of anything, and he's perfectly splendid to locate cocoons! He's found half of these. Come on, Pete, it's getting dark now, and we must go."

They started toward the trail, Pete carrying the cocoons. He left them at the case, while Elnora and Wesley went on to the carriage together.

"Elnora Comstock, what does this mean?" demanded her mother.

"It's all right, one of the neighbours was with her, and she got several dollars' worth of stuff," interposed Wesley.

"You oughter seen my pa," shouted Billy. "He was ist all whited out, and he laid as still as anything. They put him away deep in the ground."

"Billy!" breathed Margaret in a prolonged groan.

"Jimmy and Belle are going to be together in a nice place. They are coming to see me, and Snap is right down here by the wheel. Here, Snap! My, but he'll be tickled to get something to eat! He's 'most twisted as me. They get new clothes, and all they want to eat, too, but they'll miss me. They couldn't have got along without me. I took care of them. I had a lot of things give to me 'cause I was the littlest, and I always divided with them. But they won't need me now."

When she left the carriage Mrs. Comstock gravely shook hands with Billy. "Remember," she said to him, "I love boys, and I love dogs. Whenever you don't have a good time up there, take your dog and come right down and be my little boy. We will just have loads of fun. You should hear the whistles I can make. If you aren't treated right you come straight to me."

Billy wagged his head sagely. "You ist bet I will!" he said.

"Mother, how could you?" asked Elnora as they walked up the path.

"How could I, missy? You better ask how couldn't I? I just couldn't! Not for enough to pay my road tax! Not for enough to pay the road tax, and the dredge tax, too!"

"Aunt Margaret always has been lovely to me, and I don't think it's fair to worry her."

"I choose to be lovely to Billy, and let her sweat out her own worries just as she has me, these sixteen years. There is nothing in all this world so good for people as taking a dose of their own medicine. The difference is that I am honest. I just say in plain English, 'if they don't treat you right, come to me.' They have only said it in actions and inferences. I want to teach Mag Sinton how her own doses taste, but she begins to sputter before I fairly get the spoon to her lips. Just you wait!"

"When I think what I owe her——" began Elnora.

"Well, thank goodness, I don't owe her anything, and so I'm perfectly free to do what I choose. Come on, and help me get supper. I'm hungry as Billy!"

Margaret Sinton rocked slowly back and forth in her chair. On her breast lay Billy's red head, one hand clutched her dress front with spasmodic grip, even after he was unconscious.

"You mustn't begin that, Margaret," said Sinton. "He's too heavy. And it's bad for him. He's better off to lie down and go to sleep alone."

"He's very light, Wesley. He jumps and quivers so. He has to be stronger than he is now, before he will sleep soundly."

CHAPTER IX

Elnora missed the little figure at the bridge the following morning. She slowly walked up the street and turned in at the wide entrance to the school grounds. She scarcely could comprehend that only a week ago she had gone there friendless, alone, and so sick at heart that she was physically ill. To-day she had decent clothing, books, friends, and her mind was at ease to work on her studies.

As she approached home that night the girl paused in amazement. Her mother had company, and she was laughing. Elnora entered the kitchen softly and peeped into the sitting-room. Mrs. Comstock sat in her chair holding a book and every few seconds a soft chuckle broke into a real laugh. Mark Twain was doing his work; while Mrs. Comstock was not lacking in a sense of humour. Elnora entered the room before her mother saw her. Mrs. Comstock looked up with flushed face.

"Where did you get this?" she demanded.

"I bought it," said Elnora.

"Bought it! With all the taxes due!"

"I paid for it out of my Indian money, mother," said Elnora. "I couldn't bear to spend so much on myself and nothing at all on you. I was afraid to buy the dress I should have liked to, and I thought the book would be company, while I was gone. I haven't read it, but I do hope it's good."

"Good! It's the biggest piece of foolishness I have read in all my life. I've laughed all day, ever since I found it. I had a notion to go out and read some of it to the cows and see if they wouldn't laugh."

"If it made you laugh, it's a wise book," said Elnora.

"Wise!" cried Mrs. Comstock. "You can stake your life it's a wise book. It takes the smartest man there is to do this kind of fooling," and she began laughing again.

Elnora, highly satisfied with her purchase, went to her room and put on her working clothes. Thereafter she made a point of bringing a book that she thought would interest her mother, from the library every week, and leaving it on the sitting-room table. Each night she carried home at least two school books and studied until she had mastered the points of her lessons. She did her share of the work faithfully, and every available minute she was in the fields searching for cocoons, for the moths promised to become her largest source of income.

She gathered baskets of nests, flowers, mosses, insects, and all sorts of natural history specimens and sold them to the grade teachers. At first she tried to tell these instructors what to teach their pupils about the specimens; but recognizing how much more she knew than they, one after another begged her to study at home, and use her spare hours in school to exhibit and explain nature subjects to their pupils. Elnora loved the work, and she needed the money, for every few days some matter of expense arose that she had not expected.

From the first week she had been received and invited with the crowd of girls in her class, and it was their custom in passing through the business part of the city to stop at the confectioners' and take turns in treating to expensive candies, ice cream sodas, hot chocolate, or whatever they fancied. When first Elnora was asked she accepted without understanding. The second time she went because she seldom had tasted these things, and they were so delicious she could not resist. After that she went because she knew all about it, and had decided to go.

She had spent half an hour on the log beside the trail in deep thought and had arrived at her conclusions. She worked harder than usual for the next week, but she seemed to thrive on work. It was October and the red leaves were falling when her first time came to treat. As the crowd flocked down the broad walk that night Elnora called, "Girls, it's my treat to-night! Come on!"

She led the way through the city to the grocery they patronized when they had a small spread, and entering came out with a basket, which she carried to the bridge on her home road. There she arranged the girls in two rows on the cement abutments and opening her basket she gravely offered each girl an exquisite little basket of bark, lined with red leaves, in one end of which nestled a juicy big red apple and in the other a spicy doughnut not an hour from Margaret Sinton's frying basket.

Another time she offered big balls of popped corn stuck together with maple sugar, and liberally sprinkled with beechnut kernels. Again it was hickory-nut kernels glazed with sugar, another time maple candy, and once a basket of warm pumpkin pies. She never made any apology, or offered any excuse. She simply gave what she could afford, and the change was as welcome to those city girls accustomed to sodas and French candy, as were these same things to Elnora surfeited on popcorn and pie. In her room was a little slip containing a record of the number of weeks in the school year, the times it would be her turn to treat and the dates on which such occasions would fall, with a number of suggestions beside each. Once the girls almost fought over a basket lined with yellow leaves, and filled with fat, very ripe red haws. In late October there was a riot over one which was lined with red leaves and contained big fragrant pawpaws frost-bitten to a perfect degree. Then hazel nuts were ripe, and once they served. One day Elnora at her wits' end, explained to her mother that the girls had given her things and she wanted to treat them. Mrs. Comstock, with characteristic stubbornness, had said she would leave a basket at the grocery for her, but firmly declined to say what would be in it. All day Elnora struggled to keep her mind on her books. For hours she wavered in tense uncertainty. What would her mother do? Should she take the girls to the confectioner's that night or risk the basket? Mrs. Comstock could make delicious things to eat, but would she?

As they left the building Elnora made a final rapid mental calculation. She could not see her way clear to a decent treat for ten people for less than two dollars and if the basket proved to be nice, then the money would be wasted. She decided to risk it. As they went to the bridge the girls were betting on what the treat would be, and crowding near Elnora like spoiled small children. Elnora set down the basket.

"Girls," she said, "I don't know what this is myself, so all of us are going to be surprised. Here goes!"

She lifted the cover and perfumes from the land of spices rolled up. In one end of the basket lay ten enormous sugar cakes the tops of which had been liberally dotted with circles cut from stick candy. The candy had melted in baking and made small transparent wells of waxy sweetness and in the centre of each cake was a fat turtle made from a raisin with cloves for head and feet. The remainder of the basket was filled with big spiced pears that could be held by their stems while they were eaten. The girls shrieked and attacked the cookies, and of all the treats Elnora offered perhaps none was quite so long remembered as that.

When Elnora took her basket, placed her books in it, and started home, all the girls went with her as far as the fence where she crossed the field to the swamp. At parting they kissed her good-bye. Elnora was a happy girl as she hurried home to thank her mother. She was happy over her books that night, and happy all the way to school the following morning.

When the music swelled from the orchestra her heart almost broke with throbbing joy. For music always had affected her strangely, and since she had been comfortable enough in her surroundings to notice things, she had listened to every note to find what it was that literally hurt her heart, and at last she knew. It was the talking of the violins. They were human voices, and they spoke a language Elnora understood. It seemed to her that she must climb up on the stage, take the instruments from the fingers of the players and make them speak what was in her heart.

That night she said to her mother, "I am perfectly crazy for a violin. I am sure I could play one, sure as I live. Did any one——" Elnora never completed that sentence.

"Hush!" thundered Mrs. Comstock. "Be quiet! Never mention those things before me again—never as long as you live! I loathe them! They are a snare of the very devil himself! They were made to lure men and women from their homes and their honour. If ever I see you with one in your fingers I will smash it in pieces."

Naturally Elnora hushed, but she thought of nothing else after she had finished her lessons. At last there came a day when for some reason the leader of the orchestra left his violin on the grand piano. That morning Elnora made her first mistake in algebra. At noon, as soon as the building was empty, she slipped into the auditorium, found the side door which led to the stage, and going through the musicians' entrance she took the violin. She carried it back into the little side room where the orchestra assembled, closed all the doors, opened the case and lifted out the instrument.

She laid it on her breast, dropped her chin on it and drew the bow softly across the strings. One after another she tested the open notes. Gradually her stroke ceased to tremble and she drew the bow firmly. Then her fingers began to fall and softly, slowly she searched up and down those strings for sounds she knew. Standing in the middle of the floor, she tried over and over. It seemed scarcely a minute before the hall was filled with the sound of hurrying feet, and she was forced to put away the violin and go to her classes. The next day she prayed that the violin would be left again, but her petition was not answered. That night when she returned from the school she made an excuse to go down to see Billy. He was engaged in hulling walnuts by driving them through holes in a board. His hands were protected by a pair of Margaret's old gloves, but he had speckled his face generously. He appeared well, and greeted Elnora hilariously.

"Me an' the squirrels are laying up our winter stores," he shouted. "Cos the cold is coming, an' the snow an' if we have any nuts we have to fix 'em now. But I'm ahead, cos Uncle Wesley made me this board, and I can hull a big pile while the old squirrel does only ist one with his teeth."

Elnora picked him up and kissed him. "Billy, are you happy?" she asked.

"Yes, and so's Snap," answered Billy. "You ought to see him make the dirt fly when he gets after a chipmunk. I bet you he could dig up pa, if anybody wanted him to."

"Billy!" gasped Margaret as she came out to them.

"Well, me and Snap don't want him up, and I bet you Jimmy and Belle don't, either. I ain't been twisty inside once since I been here, and I don't want to go away, and Snap don't, either. He told me so."

"Billy! That is not true. Dogs can't talk," cautioned Margaret.

"Then what makes you open the door when he asks you to?" demanded Billy.

"Scratching and whining isn't talking."

"Anyway, it's the best Snap can talk, and you get up and do things he wants done. Chipmunks can talk too. You ought to hear them damn things holler when Snap gets them!"

"Billy! When you want a cooky for supper and I don't give it to you it is because you said a wrong word."

"Well, for——" Billy clapped his hand over his mouth and stained his face in swipes. "Well, for—anything! Did I go an' forget again! The cookies will get all hard, won't they? I bet you ten dollars I don't say that any more."

He espied Wesley and ran to show him a walnut too big to go through the holes, and Elnora and Margaret entered the house.

They talked of many things for a time and then Elnora said suddenly: "Aunt Margaret, I like music."

"I've noticed that in you all your life," answered Margaret.

"If dogs can't talk, I can make a violin talk," announced Elnora, and then in amazement watched the face of Margaret Sinton grow pale.

"A violin!" she wavered. "Where did you get a violin?"

"They fairly seemed to speak to me in the orchestra. One day the conductor left his in the auditorium, and I took it, and Aunt Margaret, I can make it do the wind in the swamp, the birds, and the animals. I can make any sound I ever heard on it. If I had a chance to practise a little, I could make it do the orchestra music, too. I don't know how I know, but I do."

"Did—did you ever mention it to your mother?" faltered Margaret.

"Yes, and she seems prejudiced against them. But oh, Aunt Margaret, I never felt so about anything, not even going to school. I just feel as if I'd die if I didn't have one. I could keep it at school, and practise at noon a whole hour. Soon they'd ask me to play in the orchestra. I could keep it in the case and practise in the woods in summer. You'd let me play over here Sunday. Oh, Aunt Margaret, what does one cost? Would it be wicked for me to take of my money, and buy a very cheap one? I could play on the least expensive one made."

"Oh, no you couldn't! A cheap machine makes cheap music. You got to have a fine fiddle to make it sing. But there's no sense in your buying one. There isn't a decent reason on earth why you shouldn't have your fa——"

"My father's!" cried Elnora. She caught Margaret Sinton by the arm. "My father had a violin! He played it. That's why I can! Where is it! Is it in our house? Is it in mother's room?"

"Elnora!" panted Margaret. "Your mother will kill me! She always hated it."

"Mother dearly loves music," said Elnora.

"Not when it took the man she loved away from her to make it!"

"Where is my father's violin?"

"Elnora!"

"I've never seen a picture of my father. I've never heard his name mentioned. I've never had a scrap that belonged to him. Was he my father, or am I a charity child like Billy, and so she hates me?"

"She has good pictures of him. Seems she just can't bear to hear him talked about. Of course, he was your father. They lived right there when you were born. She doesn't dislike you; she merely tries to make herself think she does. There's no sense in the world in you not having his violin. I've a great notion——"

"Has mother got it?"

"No. I've never heard her mention it. It was not at home when he—when he died."

"Do you know where it is?"

"Yes. I'm the only person on earth who does, except the one who has it."

"Who is that?"

"I can't tell you, but I will see if they have it yet, and get it if I can. But if your mother finds it out she will never forgive me."

"I can't help it," said Elnora. "I want that violin."

"I'll go to-morrow, and see if it has been destroyed."

"Destroyed! Oh, Aunt Margaret! Would any one dare?"

"I hardly think so. It was a good instrument. He played it like a master."

"Tell me!" breathed Elnora.

"His hair was red and curled more than yours, and his eyes were blue. He was tall, slim, and the very imp of mischief. He joked and teased all day until he picked up that violin. Then his head bent over it, and his eyes got big and earnest. He seemed to listen as if he first heard the notes, and then copied them. Sometimes he drew the bow trembly, like he wasn't sure it was right, and he might have to try again. He could almost drive you crazy when he wanted to, and no man that ever lived could make you dance as he could. He made it all up as he went. He seemed to listen for his dancing music, too. It appeared to come to him; he'd begin to play and you had to keep time. You couldn't be still; he loved to sweep a crowd around with that bow of his. I think it was the thing you call inspiration.

I can see him now, his handsome head bent, his cheeks red, his eyes snapping, and that bow going across the strings, and driving us like sheep. He always kept his body swinging, and he loved to play. He often slighted his work shamefully, and sometimes her a little; that is why she hated it—Elnora, what are you making me do?"

The tears were rolling down Elnora's cheeks. "Oh, Aunt Margaret," she sobbed. "Why haven't you told me about him sooner? I feel as if you had given my father to me living, so that I could touch him. I can see him, too! Why didn't you ever tell me before? Go on! Go on!"

"I can't, Elnora! I'm scared silly. I never meant to say anything. If I hadn't promised her not to talk of him to you she wouldn't have let you come here. She made me swear it."

"But why? Why? Was he a shame? Was he disgraced?"

"Maybe it was that unjust feeling that took possession of her when she couldn't help him from the swamp. She had to blame some one, or go crazy, so she took it out on you. At times, those first ten years, if I had talked to you, and you had repeated anything to her, she might have struck you too hard. She was not master of herself. You must be patient with her, Elnora. God only knows what she has gone through, but I think she is a little better, lately."

"So do I," said Elnora. "She seems more interested in my clothes, and she fixes me such delicious lunches that the girls bring fine candies and cake and beg to trade. I gave half my lunch for a box of candy one day, brought it home to her, and told her. Since, she has wanted me to carry a market basket and treat the crowd every day, she was so pleased. Life has been too monotonous for her. I think she enjoys even the little change made by my going and coming. She sits up half the night to read the library books I bring, but she is so stubborn she won't even admit that she touches them. Tell me more about my father."

"Wait until I see if I can find the violin."

So Elnora went home in suspense, and that night she added to her prayers: "Dear Lord, be merciful to my father, and oh, do help Aunt Margaret to get his violin."

Wesley and Billy came in to supper tired and hungry. Billy ate heartily, but his eyes often rested on a plate of tempting cookies, and when Wesley offered them to the boy he reached for one. Margaret was compelled to explain that cookies were forbidden that night.

"What!" said Wesley. "Wrong words been coming again. Oh Billy, I do wish you could remember! I can't sit and eat cookies before a little boy who has none. I'll have to put mine back, too." Billy's face twisted in despair.

"Aw go on!" he said gruffly, but his chin was jumping, for Wesley was his idol.

"Can't do it," said Wesley. "It would choke me."

Billy turned to Margaret. "You make him," he appealed.

"He can't, Billy," said Margaret. "I know how he feels. You see, I can't myself."

Then Billy slid from his chair, ran to the couch, buried his face in the pillow and cried heart-brokenly. Wesley hurried to the barn, and Margaret to the kitchen. When the dishes were washed Billy slipped from the back door.

Wesley piling hay into the mangers heard a sound behind him and inquired, "That you, Billy?"

"Yes," answered Billy, "and it's all so dark you can't see me now, isn't it?"

"Well, mighty near," answered Wesley.

"Then you stoop down and open your mouth."

Sinton had shared bites of apple and nuts for weeks, for Billy had not learned how to eat anything without dividing with Jimmy and Belle. Since he had been separated from them, he shared with Wesley and Margaret. So he bent over the boy and received an instalment of cooky that almost choked him.

"Now you can eat it!" shouted Billy in delight. "It's all dark! I can't see what you're doing at all!"

Wesley picked up the small figure and set the boy on the back of a horse to bring his face level so that they could talk as men. He never towered from his height above Billy, but always lifted the little soul when important matters were to be discussed.

"Now what a dandy scheme," he commented. "Did you and Aunt Margaret fix it up?"

"No. She ain't had hers yet. But I got one for her. Ist as soon as you eat yours, I am going to take hers, and feed her first time I find her in the dark."

"But Billy, where did you get the cookies? You know Aunt Margaret said you were not to have any."

"I ist took them," said Billy, "I didn't take them for me. I ist took them for you and her."

Wesley thought fast. In the warm darkness of the barn the horses crunched their corn, a rat gnawed at a corner of the granary, and among the rafters the white pigeon cooed a soft sleepy note to his dusky mate.

"Did—did—I steal?" wavered Billy.

Wesley's big hands closed until he almost hurt the boy.

"No!" he said vehemently. "That is too big a word. You made a mistake. You were trying to be a fine little man, but you went at it the wrong way. You only made a mistake. All of us do that, Billy. The world grows that way. When we make mistakes we can see them; that teaches us to be more careful the next time, and so we learn."

"How wouldn't it be a mistake?"

"If you had told Aunt Margaret what you wanted to do, and asked her for the cookies she would have given them to you."

"But I was 'fraid she wouldn't, and you ist had to have it."

"Not if it was wrong for me to have it, Billy. I don't want it that much."

"Must I take it back?"

"You think hard, and decide yourself."

"Lift me down," said Billy, after a silence, "I got to put this in the jar, and tell her."

Wesley set the boy on the floor, but as he did so he paused one second and strained him close to his breast.

Margaret sat in her chair sewing; Billy slipped in and crept beside her. The little face was lined with tragedy.

"Why Billy, whatever is the matter?" she cried as she dropped her sewing and held out her arms. Billy stood back. He gripped his little fists tight and squared his shoulders. "I got to be shut up in the closet," he said.

"Oh Billy! What an unlucky day! What have you done now?"

"I stold!" gulped Billy. "He said it was ist a mistake, but it was worser 'an that. I took something you told me I wasn't to have."

"Stole!" Margaret was in despair. "What, Billy?"

"Cookies!" answered Billy in equal trouble.

"Billy!" wailed Margaret. "How could you?"

"It was for him and you," sobbed Billy. "He said he couldn't eat it 'fore me, but out in the barn it's all dark and I couldn't see. I thought maybe he could there. Then we might put out the light and you could have yours. He said I only made it worse, cos I mustn't take things, so I got to go in the closet. Will you hold me tight a little bit first? He did."

Margaret opened her arms and Billy rushed in and clung to her a few seconds, with all the force of his being, then he slipped to the floor and marched to the closet. Margaret opened the door. Billy gave one glance at the light, clinched his fists and, walking inside, climbed on a box. Margaret closed the door.

Then she sat and listened. Was the air pure enough? Possibly he might smother. She had read something once. Was it very dark? What if there should be a mouse in the closet and it should run across his foot and frighten him into spasms. Somewhere she had heard—Margaret leaned forward with tense face and listened. Something dreadful might happen. She could bear it no longer. She arose hurriedly and opened the door. Billy was drawn up on the box in a little heap, and he lifted a disapproving face to her.

"Shut that door!" he said. "I ain't been in here near long enough yet!"

CHAPTER X

WHEREIN ELNORA HAS MORE
FINANCIAL TROUBLES, AND MRS.
COMSTOCK AGAIN HEARS THE SONG OF
THE LIMBERLOST

The following night Elnora hurried to Sintons'. She threw open the back door and with anxious eyes searched Margaret's face.

"You got it!" panted Elnora. "You got it! I can see by your face that you did. Oh, give it to me!"

"Yes, I got it, honey, I got it all right, but don't be so fast. It had been kept in such a damp place it needed glueing, it had to have strings, and a key was gone. I knew how much you wanted it, so I sent Wesley right to town with it. They said they could fix it good as new, but it should be varnished, and that it would take several days for the glue to set. You can have it Saturday."

"You found it where you thought it was? You know it's his?"

"Yes, it was just where I thought, and it's the same violin I've seen him play hundreds of times. It's all right, only laying so long it needs fixing."

"Oh Aunt Margaret! Can I ever wait?"

"It does seem a long time, but how could I help it? You couldn't do anything with it as it was. You see, it had been hidden away in a garret, and it needed cleaning and drying to make it fit to play again. You can have it Saturday sure. But Elnora, you've got to promise me that you will leave it here, or in town, and not let your mother get a hint of it. I don't know what she'd do."

"Uncle Wesley can bring it here until Monday. Then I will take it to school so that I can practise at noon. Oh, I don't know how to thank you. And there's more than the violin for which to be thankful. You've given me my father. Last night I saw him plainly as life."

"Elnora you were dreaming!"

"I know I was dreaming, but I saw him. I saw him so closely that a tiny white scar at the corner of his eyebrow showed. I was just reaching out to touch him when he disappeared."

"Who told you there was a scar on his forehead?"

"No one ever did in all my life. I saw it last night as he went down. And oh, Aunt Margaret! I saw what she did, and I heard his cries! No matter what she does, I don't believe I ever can be angry with her again.

Her heart is broken, and she can't help it. Oh, it was terrible, but I am glad I saw it. Now, I will always understand."

"I don't know what to make of that," said Margaret. "I don't believe in such stuff at all, but you couldn't make it up, for you didn't know."

"I only know that I played the violin last night, as he played it, and while I played he came through the woods from the direction of Carneys'. It was summer and all the flowers were in bloom. He wore gray trousers and a blue shirt, his head was bare, and his face was beautiful. I could almost touch him when he sank."

Margaret stood perplexed. "I don't know what to think of that!" she ejaculated. "I was next to the last person who saw him before he was drowned. It was late on a June afternoon, and he was dressed as you describe. He was bareheaded because he had found a quail's nest before the bird began to brood, and he gathered the eggs in his hat and left it in a fence corner to get on his way home; they found it afterward."

"Was he coming from Carneys'?"

"He was on that side of the quagmire. Why he ever skirted it so close as to get caught is a mystery you will have to dream out. I never could understand it."

"Was he doing something he didn't want my mother to know?"

"Why?"

"Because if he had been, he might have cut close the swamp so he couldn't be seen from the garden. You know, the whole path straight to the pool where he sank can be seen from our back door. It's firm on our side. The danger is on the north and east. If he didn't want mother to know, he might have tried to pass on either of those sides and gone too close. Was he in a hurry?"

"Yes, he was," said Margaret. "He had been away longer than he expected, and he almost ran when he started home."

"And he'd left his violin somewhere that you knew, and you went and got it. I'll wager he was going to play, and didn't want mother to find it out!"

"It wouldn't make any difference to you if you knew every little thing, so quit thinking about it, and just be glad you are to have what he loved best of anything."

"That's true. Now I must hurry home. I am dreadfully late."

Elnora sprang up and ran down the road, but when she approached the cabin she climbed the fence, crossed the open woods pasture diagonally and entered at the back garden gate. As she often came that way when she had been looking for cocoons her mother asked no questions.

Elnora lived by the minute until Saturday, when, contrary to his usual custom, Wesley went to town in the forenoon, taking her along to buy some groceries. Wesley drove straight to the music store, and asked for the violin he had left to be mended.

In its new coat of varnish, with new keys and strings, it seemed much like any other violin to Sinton, but to Elnora it was the most beautiful instrument ever made, and a priceless treasure. She held it in her arms, touched the strings softly and then she drew the bow across them in whispering measure. She had no time to think what a remarkably good bow it was for sixteen years' disuse. The tan leather case might have impressed her as being in fine condition also, had she been in a state to question anything. She did remember to ask for the bill and she was gravely presented with a slip calling for four strings, one key, and a coat of varnish, total, one dollar fifty. It seemed to Elnora she never could put the precious instrument in the case and start home. Wesley left her in the music store where the proprietor showed her all he could about tuning, and gave her several beginners' sheets of notes and scales. She carried the violin in her arms as far as the crossroads at the corner of their land, then reluctantly put it under the carriage seat.

As soon as her work was done she ran down to Sintons' and began to play, and on Monday the violin went to school with her. She made arrangements with the superintendent to leave it in his office and scarcely took time for her food at noon, she was so eager to practise. Often one of the girls asked her to stay in town all night for some lecture or entertainment. She could take the violin with her, practise, and secure help. Her skill was so great that the leader of the orchestra offered to give her lessons if she would play to pay for them, so her progress was rapid in technical work. But from the first day the instrument became hers, with perfect faith that she could play as her father did, she spent half her practice time in imitating the sounds of all outdoors and improvising the songs her happy heart sang in those days.

So the first year went, and the second and third were a repetition; but the fourth was different, for that was the close of the course, ending with graduation and all its attendant ceremonies and expenses. To Elnora these appeared mountain high. She had hoarded every cent, thinking twice before she parted with a penny, but teaching natural history in the grades had taken time from her studies in school which must be made up outside. She was a conscientious student, ranking first in most of her classes, and standing high in all branches. Her interest in her violin had grown with the years. She went to school early and practised half an hour in the little room adjoining the stage, while the orchestra gathered. She put in a full hour at noon, and remained another half hour at night. She carried the violin to Sintons' on Saturday and practised all the time she could there, while Margaret watched the road to see that Mrs. Comstock was not coming. She had become so skilful that it was a delight to hear her play music of any composer, but when she played her own, that was joy inexpressible, for then the wind blew, the water rippled, the Limberlost sang her songs of sunshine, shadow, black storm, and white night.

Since her dream Elnora had regarded her mother with peculiar tenderness. The girl realized, in a measure, what had happened. She avoided anything that possibly could stir bitter memories or draw deeper a line on the hard, white face. This cost many sacrifices, much work, and sometimes delayed progress, but the horror of that awful dream remained with Elnora. She worked her way cheerfully, doing all she could to interest her mother in things that happened in school, in the city, and by carrying books that were entertaining from the public library.

Three years had changed Elnora from the girl of sixteen to the very verge of womanhood. She had grown tall, round, and her face had the loveliness of perfect complexion, beautiful eyes and hair and an added touch from within that might have been called comprehension. It was a compound of self-reliance, hard knocks, heart hunger, unceasing work, and generosity. There was no form of suffering with which the girl could not sympathize, no work she was afraid to attempt, no subject she had investigated she did not understand. These things combined to produce a breadth and depth of character altogether unusual. She was so absorbed in her classes and her music that she had not been able to gather many specimens. When she realized this and hunted assiduously, she soon found that changing natural conditions had affected such work. Men all around were clearing available land. The trees fell wherever corn would grow. The swamp was broken by several gravel roads, dotted in places around the edge with little frame houses, and the machinery of oil wells; one especially low place around the region of Freckles's room was nearly all that remained of the original. Wherever the trees fell the moisture dried, the creeks ceased to flow, the river ran low, and at times the bed was dry. With unbroken sweep the winds of the west came, gathering force with every mile and howled and raved; threatening to tear the shingles from the roof, blowing the surface from the soil in clouds of fine dust and rapidly changing everything. From coming in with two or three dozen rare moths in a day, in three years' time Elnora had grown to be delighted with finding two or three. Big pursy caterpillars could not be picked from their favourite bushes, when there were no bushes. Dragonflies would not hover over dry places, and butterflies became scarce in proportion to the flowers, while no land yields over three crops of Indian relics.

All the time the expense of books, clothing and incidentals had continued. Elnora added to her bank account whenever she could, and drew out when she was compelled, but she omitted the important feature of calling for a balance. So, one early spring morning in the last quarter of the fourth year, she almost fainted when she learned that her funds were gone. Commencement with its extra expense was coming, she had no money, and very few cocoons to open in June, which would be too late. She had one collection for the Bird Woman complete to a pair of Imperialis moths, and that was her only asset. On the day she added these big Yellow Emperors she had been promised a check for three hundred dollars, but she would not get it until these specimens were secured. She remembered that she never had found an Emperor before June.

Moreover, that sum was for her first year in college. Then she would be of age, and she meant to sell enough of her share of her father's land to finish. She knew her mother would oppose her bitterly in that, for Mrs. Comstock had clung to every acre and tree that belonged to her husband. Her land was almost complete forest where her neighbours owned cleared farms, dotted with wells that every hour sucked oil from beneath her holdings, but she was too absorbed in the grief she nursed to know or care. The Brushwood road and the redredging of the big Limberlost ditch had been more than she could pay from her income, and she had trembled before the wicket as she asked the banker if she had funds to pay it, and wondered why he laughed when he assured her she had. For Mrs. Comstock had spent no time on compounding interest, and never added the sums she had been depositing through nearly twenty years. Now she thought her funds were almost gone, and every day she worried over expenses. She could see no reason in going through the forms of graduation when pupils had all in their heads that was required to graduate. Elnora knew she had to have her diploma in order to enter the college she wanted to attend, but she did not dare utter the word, until high school was finished, for, instead of softening as she hoped her mother had begun to do, she seemed to remain very much the same.

When the girl reached the swamp she sat on a log and thought over the expense she was compelled to meet. Every member of her particular set was having a large photograph taken to exchange with the others. Elnora loved these girls and boys, and to say she could not have their pictures to keep was more than she could endure. Each one would give to all the others a handsome graduation present. She knew they would prepare gifts for her whether she could make a present in return or not. Then it was the custom for each graduating class to give a great entertainment and use the funds to present the school with a statue for the entrance hall. Elnora had been cast for and was practising a part in that performance. She was expected to furnish her dress and personal necessities. She had been told that she must have a green gauze dress, and where was it to come from?

Every girl of the class would have three beautiful new frocks for Commencement: one for the baccalaureate sermon, another, which could be plain, for graduation exercises, and a handsome one for the banquet and ball. Elnora faced the past three years and wondered how she could have spent so much money and not kept account of it. She did not realize where it had gone. She did not know what she could do now. She thought over the photographs, and at last settled that question to her satisfaction. She studied longer over the gifts, ten handsome ones there must be, and at last decided she could arrange for them. The green dress came first. The lights would be dim in the scene, and the setting deep woods. She could manage that. She simply could not have three dresses. She would have to get a very simple one for the sermon and do the best she could for graduation. Whatever she got for that must be made with a guimpe that could be taken out to make it a little more festive for the ball. But where could she get even two pretty dresses?

The only hope she could see was to break into the collection of the man from India, sell some moths, and try to replace them in June. But in her soul she knew that never would do. No June ever brought just the things she hoped it would. If she spent the college money she knew she could not replace it. If she did not, the only way was to secure a room in the grades and teach a year. Her work there had been so appreciated that Elnora felt with the recommendation she knew she could get from the superintendent and teachers she could secure a position. She was sure she could pass the examinations easily. She had once gone on Saturday, taken them and secured a license for a year before she left the Brushwood school.

She wanted to start to college when the other girls were going. If she could make the first year alone, she could manage the remainder. But make that first year herself, she must. Instead of selling any of her collection, she must hunt as she never before had hunted and find a Yellow Emperor. She had to have it, that was all. Also, she had to have those dresses. She thought of Wesley and dismissed it. She thought of the Bird Woman, and knew she could not tell her. She thought of every way in which she ever had hoped to earn money and realized that with the play, committee meetings, practising, and final examinations she scarcely had time to live, much less to do more than the work required for her pictures and gifts. Again Elnora was in trouble, and this time it seemed the worst of all.

It was dark when she arose and went home.

"Mother," she said, "I have a piece of news that is decidedly not cheerful."

"Then keep it to yourself!" said Mrs. Comstock. "I think I have enough to bear without a great girl like you piling trouble on me."

"My money is all gone!" said Elnora.

"Well, did you think it would last forever? It's been a marvel to me that it's held out as well as it has, the way you've dressed and gone."

"I don't think I've spent any that I was not compelled to," said Elnora. "I've dressed on just as little as I possibly could to keep going. I am heartsick. I thought I had over fifty dollars to put me through Commencement, but they tell me it is all gone."

"Fifty dollars! To put you through Commencement! What on earth are you proposing to do?"

"The same as the rest of them, in the very cheapest way possible."

"And what might that be?"

Elnora omitted the photographs, the gifts and the play. She told only of the sermon, graduation exercises, and the ball.

"Well, I wouldn't trouble myself over that," sniffed Mrs. Comstock. "If you want to go to a sermon, put on the dress you always use for meeting. If you need white for the exercises wear the new dress you got last spring. As for the ball, the best thing for you to do is to stay a mile away from such folly. In my opinion you'd best bring home your books, and quit right now. You can't be fixed like the rest of them, don't be so foolish as to run into it. Just stay here and let these last few days go. You can't learn enough more to be of any account."

"But, mother," gasped Elnora. "You don't understand!"

"Oh, yes, I do!" said Mrs. Comstock. "I understand perfectly. So long as the money lasted, you held up your head, and went sailing without even explaining how you got it from the stuff you gathered. Goodness knows I couldn't see. But now it's gone, you come whining to me. What have I got? Have you forgot that the ditch and the road completely strapped me? I haven't any money. There's nothing for you to do but get out of it."

"I can't!" said Elnora desperately. "I've gone on too long. It would make a break in everything. They wouldn't let me have my diploma!"

"What's the difference? You've got the stuff in your head. I wouldn't give a rap for a scrap of paper. That don't mean anything!"

"But I've worked four years for it, and I can't enter—I ought to have it to help me get a school, when I want to teach. If I don't have my grades to show, people will think I quit because I couldn't pass my examinations. I must have my diploma!"

"Then get it!" said Mrs. Comstock.

"The only way is to graduate with the others."

"Well, graduate if you are bound to!"

"But I can't, unless I have things enough like the class, that I don't look as I did that first day."

"Well, please remember I didn't get you into this, and I can't get you out. You are set on having your own way. Go on, and have it, and see how you like it!"

Elnora went upstairs and did not come down again that night, which her mother called pouting.

"I've thought all night," said the girl at breakfast, "and I can't see any way but to borrow the money of Uncle Wesley and pay it back from some that the Bird Woman will owe me, when I get one more specimen. But that means that I can't go to—that I will have to teach this winter, if I can get a city grade or a country school."

"Just you dare go dinging after Wesley Sinton for money," cried Mrs. Comstock. "You won't do any such a thing!"

"I can't see any other way. I've got to have the money!"

"Quit, I tell you!"

"I can't quit!—I've gone too far!"

"Well then, let me get your clothes, and you can pay me back."

"But you said you had no money!"

"Maybe I can borrow some at the bank. Then you can return it when the Bird Woman pays you."

"All right," said Elnora. "I don't need expensive things. Just some kind of a pretty cheap white dress for the sermon, and a white one a little better than I had last summer, for Commencement and the ball. I can use the white gloves and shoes I got myself for last year, and you can get my dress made at the same place you did that one. They have my measurements, and do perfect work. Don't get expensive things. It will be warm so I can go bareheaded."

Then she started to school, but was so tired and discouraged she scarcely could walk. Four years' plans going in one day! For she felt that if she did not start to college that fall she never would. Instead of feeling relieved at her mother's offer, she was almost too ill to go on. For the thousandth time she groaned: "Oh, why didn't I keep account of my money?"

After that the days passed so swiftly she scarcely had time to think, but several trips her mother made to town, and the assurance that everything was all right, satisfied Elnora. She worked very hard to pass good final examinations and perfect herself for the play. For two days she had remained in town with the Bird Woman in order to spend more time practising and at her work.

Often Margaret had asked about her dresses for graduation, and Elnora had replied that they were with a woman in the city who had made her a white dress for last year's Commencement when she was a junior usher, and they would be all right. So Margaret, Wesley, and Billy concerned themselves over what they would give her for a present.

Margaret suggested a beautiful dress. Wesley said that would look to every one as if she needed dresses. The thing was to get a handsome gift like all the others would have. Billy wanted to present her a five-dollar gold piece to buy music for her violin. He was positive Elnora would like that best of anything.

It was toward the close of the term when they drove to town one evening to try to settle this important question. They knew Mrs. Comstock had been alone several days, so they asked her to accompany them. She had been more lonely than she would admit, filled with unusual unrest besides, and so she was glad to go. But before they had driven a mile Billy had told that they were going to buy Elnora a graduation present, and Mrs. Comstock devoutly wished that she had remained at home. She was prepared when Billy asked: "Aunt Kate, what are you going to give Elnora when she graduates?"

"Plenty to eat, a good bed to sleep in, and do all the work while she trollops," answered Mrs. Comstock dryly.

Billy reflected. "I guess all of them have that," he said. "I mean a present you buy at the store, like Christmas?"

"It is only rich folks who buy presents at stores," replied Mrs. Comstock. "I can't afford it."

"Well, we ain't rich," he said, "but we are going to buy Elnora something as fine as the rest of them have if we sell a corner of the farm. Uncle Wesley said so."

"A fool and his land are soon parted," said Mrs. Comstock tersely. Wesley and Billy laughed, but Margaret did not enjoy the remark.

While they were searching the stores for something on which all of them could decide, and Margaret was holding Billy to keep him from saying anything before Mrs. Comstock about the music on which he was determined, Mr. Brownlee met Wesley and stopped to shake hands.

"I see your boy came out finely," he said.

"I don't allow any boy anywhere to be finer than Billy," said Wesley.

"I guess you don't allow any girl to surpass Elnora," said Mr. Brownlee. "She comes home with Ellen often, and my wife and I love her. Ellen says she is great in her part to-night. Best thing in the whole play! Of course, you are in to see it! If you haven't reserved seats, you'd better start pretty soon, for the high school auditorium only seats a thousand. It's always jammed at these home-talent plays. All of us want to see how our children perform."

"Why yes, of course," said the bewildered Wesley. Then he hurried to Margaret. "Say," he said, "there is going to be a play at the high school to-night; and Elnora is in it. Why hasn't she told us?"

"I don't know," said Margaret, "but I'm going."

"So am I," said Billy.

"Me too!" said Wesley, "unless you think for some reason she doesn't want us. Looks like she would have told us if she had. I'm going to ask her mother."

"Yes, that's what's she's been staying in town for," said Mrs. Comstock. "It's some sort of a swindle to raise money for her class to buy some silly thing to stick up in the school house hall to remember them by. I don't know whether it's now or next week, but there's something of the kind to be done."

"Well, it's to-night," said Wesley, "and we are going. It's my treat, and we've got to hurry or we won't get in. There are reserved seats, and we have none, so it's the gallery for us, but I don't care so I get to take one good peep at Elnora."

"S'pose she plays?" whispered Margaret in his ear.

"Aw, tush! She couldn't!" said Wesley.

"Well, she's been doing it three years in the orchestra, and working like a slave at it."

"Oh, well that's different. She's in the play to-night. Brownlee told me so. Come on, quick! We'll drive and hitch closest place we can find to the building."

Margaret went in the excitement of the moment, but she was troubled. When they reached the building Wesley tied the team to a railing and Billy sprang out to help Margaret. Mrs. Comstock sat still.

"Come on, Kate," said Wesley, reaching his hand.

"I'm not going anywhere," said Mrs. Comstock, settling comfortably back against the cushions.

All of them begged and pleaded, but it was no use. Not an inch would Mrs. Comstock budge. The night was warm and the carriage comfortable, the horses were securely hitched. She did not care to see what idiotic thing a pack of school children were doing, she would wait until the Sintons returned. Wesley told her it might be two hours, and she said she did not care if it were four, so they left her.

"Did you ever see such——?"

"Cookies!" cried Billy.

"Such blamed stubbornness in all your life?" demanded Wesley. "Won't come to see as fine a girl as Elnora in a stage performance. Why, I wouldn't miss it for fifty dollars!

"I think it's a blessing she didn't," said Margaret placidly. "I begged unusually hard so she wouldn't. I'm scared of my life for fear Elnora will play."

They found seats near the door where they could see fairly well. Billy stood at the back of the hall and had a good view. By and by, a great volume of sound welled from the orchestra, but Elnora was not playing.

"Told you so!" said Sinton. "Got a notion to go out and see if Kate won't come now. She can take my seat, and I'll stand with Billy."

"You sit still!" said Margaret emphatically. "This is not over yet."

So Wesley remained in his seat. The play opened and progressed very much as all high school plays have gone for the past fifty years. But Elnora did not appear in any of the scenes.

Out in the warm summer night a sour, grim woman nursed an aching heart and tried to justify herself. The effort irritated her intensely. She felt that she could not afford the things that were being done. The old fear of losing the land that she and Robert Comstock had purchased and started clearing was strong upon her. She was thinking of him, how she needed him, when the orchestra music poured from the open windows near her. Mrs. Comstock endured it as long as she could, and then slipped from the carriage and fled down the street.

She did not know how far she went or how long she stayed, but everything was still, save an occasional raised voice when she wandered back. She stood looking at the building. Slowly she entered the wide gates and followed up the walk. Elnora had been coming here for almost four years. When Mrs. Comstock reached the door she looked inside. The wide hall was lighted with electricity, and the statuary and the decorations of the walls did not seem like pieces of foolishness. The marble appeared pure, white, and the big pictures most interesting. She walked the length of the hall and slowly read the titles of the statues and the names of the pupils who had donated them. She speculated on where the piece Elnora's class would buy could be placed to advantage.

Then she wondered if they were having a large enough audience to buy marble. She liked it better than the bronze, but it looked as if it cost more. How white the broad stairway was! Elnora had been climbing those stairs for years and never told her they were marble. Of course, she thought they were wood. Probably the upper hall was even grander than this. She went over to the fountain, took a drink, climbed to the first landing and looked around her, and then without thought to the second. There she came opposite the wide-open doors and the entrance to the auditorium packed with people and a crowd standing outside. When they noticed a tall woman with white face and hair and black dress, one by one they stepped a little aside, so that Mrs. Comstock could see the stage. It was covered with curtains, and no one was doing anything. Just as she turned to go a sound so faint that every one leaned forward and listened, drifted down the auditorium. It was difficult to tell just what it was; after one instant half the audience looked toward the windows, for it seemed only a breath of wind rustling freshly opened leaves; merely a hint of stirring air.

Then the curtains were swept aside swiftly. The stage had been transformed into a lovely little corner of creation, where trees and flowers grew and moss carpeted the earth. A soft wind blew and it was the gray of dawn. Suddenly a robin began to sing, then a song sparrow joined him, and then several orioles began talking at once. The light grew stronger, the dew drops trembled, flower perfume began to creep out to the audience; the air moved the branches gently and a rooster crowed. Then all the scene was shaken with a babel of bird notes in which you could hear a cardinal whistling, and a blue finch piping. Back somewhere among the high branches a dove cooed and then a horse neighed shrilly. That set a blackbird crying, "T'check," and a whole flock answered it. The crows began to caw and a lamb bleated. Then the grosbeaks, chats, and vireos had something to say, and the sun rose higher, the light grew stronger and the breeze rustled the treetops loudly; a cow bawled and the whole barnyard answered. The guineas were clucking, the turkey gobbler strutting, the hens calling, the chickens cheeping, the light streamed down straight overhead and the bees began to hum. The air stirred strongly, and away in an unseen field a reaper clacked and rattled through ripening wheat while the driver whistled. An uneasy mare whickered to her colt, the colt answered, and the light began to decline. Miles away a rooster crowed for twilight, and dusk was coming down. Then a catbird and a brown thrush sang against a grosbeak and a hermit thrush. The air was tremulous with heavenly notes, the lights went out in the hall, dusk swept across the stage, a cricket sang and a katydid answered, and a wood pewee wrung the heart with its lonesome cry. Then a night hawk screamed, a whip-poor-will complained, a belated killdeer swept the sky, and the night wind sang a louder song. A little screech owl tuned up in the distance, a barn owl replied, and a great horned owl drowned both their voices. The moon shone and the scene was warm with mellow light. The bird voices died and soft exquisite melody began to swell and roll. In the centre of the stage, piece by piece the grasses, mosses and leaves dropped from an embankment, the foliage softly blew away, while plainer and plainer came the outlines of a lovely girl figure draped in soft clinging green. In her shower of bright hair a few green leaves and white blossoms clung, and they fell over her robe down to her feet. Her white throat and arms were bare, she leaned forward a little and swayed with the melody, her eyes fast on the clouds above her, her lips parted, a pink tinge of exercise in her cheeks as she drew her bow. She played as only a peculiar chain of circumstances puts it in the power of a very few to play. All nature had grown still, the violin sobbed, sang, danced and quavered on alone, no voice in particular; the soul of the melody of all nature combined in one great outpouring.

At the doorway, a white-faced woman endured it as long as she could and then fell senseless. The men nearest carried her down the hall to the fountain, revived her, and then placed her in the carriage to which she directed them. The girl played on and never knew. When she finished, the uproar of applause sounded a block down the street, but the half-senseless woman scarcely realized what it meant. Then the girl came to the front of the stage, bowed, and lifting the violin she played her conception of an invitation to dance. Every living soul within sound of her notes strained their nerves to sit still and let only their hearts dance with her. When that began the woman ran toward the country. She never stopped until the carriage overtook her half-way to her cabin. She said she had grown tired of sitting, and walked on ahead. That night she asked Billy to remain with her and sleep on Elnora's bed. Then she pitched headlong upon her own, and suffered agony of soul such as she never before had known. The swamp had sent back the soul of her loved dead and put it into the body of the daughter she resented, and it was almost more than she could endure and live.

CHAPTER XI

That was Friday night. Elnora came home Saturday morning and began work. Mrs. Comstock asked no questions, and the girl only told her that the audience had been large enough to more than pay for the piece of statuary the class had selected for the hall. Then she inquired about her dresses and was told they would be ready for her. She had been invited to go to the Bird Woman's to prepare for both the sermon and Commencement exercises. Since there was so much practising to do, it had been arranged that she should remain there from the night of the sermon until after she was graduated. If Mrs. Comstock decided to attend she was to drive in with the Sintons. When Elnora begged her to come she said she cared nothing about such silliness.

It was almost time for Wesley to come to take Elnora to the city, when fresh from her bath, and dressed to her outer garment, she stood with expectant face before her mother and cried: "Now my dress, mother!"

Mrs. Comstock was pale as she replied: "It's on my bed. Help yourself."

Elnora opened the door and stepped into her mother's room with never a misgiving. Since the night Margaret and Wesley had brought her clothing, when she first started to school, her mother had selected all of her dresses, with Mrs. Sinton's help made most of them, and Elnora had paid the bills. The white dress of the previous spring was the first made at a dressmaker's. She had worn that as junior usher at Commencement; but her mother had selected the material, had it made, and it had fitted perfectly and had been suitable in every way. So with her heart at rest on that point, Elnora hurried to the bed to find only her last summer's white dress, freshly washed and ironed. For an instant she stared at it, then she picked up the garment, looked at the bed beneath it, and her gaze slowly swept the room.

It was unfamiliar. Perhaps this was the third time she had been in it since she was a very small child. Her eyes ranged over the beautiful walnut dresser, the tall bureau, the big chest, inside which she never had seen, and the row of masculine attire hanging above it. Somewhere a dainty lawn or mull dress simply must be hanging: but it was not. Elnora dropped on the chest because she felt too weak to stand. In less than two hours she must be in the church, at Onabasha. She could not wear a last year's washed dress. She had nothing else. She leaned against the wall and her father's overcoat brushed her face. She caught the folds and clung to it with all her might.

"Oh father! Father!" she moaned. "I need you! I don't believe you would have done this!" At last she opened the door.

"I can't find my dress," she said.

"Well, as it's the only one there I shouldn't think it would be much trouble."

"You mean for me to wear an old washed dress to-night?"

"It's a good dress. There isn't a hole in it! There's no reason on earth why you shouldn't wear it."

"Except that I will not," said Elnora. "Didn't you provide any dress for Commencement, either?"

"If you soil that to-night, I've plenty of time to wash it again."

Wesley's voice called from the gate.

"In a minute," answered Elnora.

She ran upstairs and in an incredibly short time came down wearing one of her gingham school dresses. Her face cold and hard, she passed her mother and went into the night. Half an hour later Margaret and Billy stopped for Mrs. Comstock with the carriage. She had determined fully that she would not go before they called. With the sound of their voices a sort of horror of being left seized her, so she put on her hat, locked the door and went out to them.

"How did Elnora look?" inquired Margaret anxiously.

"Like she always does," answered Mrs. Comstock curtly.

"I do hope her dresses are as pretty as the others," said Margaret. "None of them will have prettier faces or nicer ways."

Wesley was waiting before the big church to take care of the team. As they stood watching the people enter the building, Mrs. Comstock felt herself growing ill. When they went inside among the lights, saw the flower-decked stage, and the masses of finely dressed people, she grew no better. She could hear Margaret and Billy softly commenting on what was being done.

"That first chair in the very front row is Elnora's," exulted Billy, "cos she's got the highest grades, and so she gets to lead the procession to the platform."

"The first chair!" "Lead the procession!" Mrs. Comstock was dumbfounded. The notes of the pipe organ began to fill the building in a slow rolling march. Would Elnora lead the procession in a gingham dress? Or would she be absent and her chair vacant on this great occasion? For now, Mrs. Comstock could see that it was a great occasion. Every one would remember how Elnora had played a few nights before, and they would miss her and pity her. Pity? Because she had no one to care for her. Because she was worse off than if she had no mother. For the first time in her life, Mrs. Comstock began to study herself as she would appear to others. Every time a junior girl came fluttering down the aisle, leading some one to a seat, and Mrs. Comstock saw a beautiful white dress pass, a wave of positive illness swept over her. What had she done? What would become of Elnora?

As Elnora rode to the city, she answered Wesley's questions in monosyllables so that he thought she was nervous or rehearsing her speech and did not care to talk. Several times the girl tried to tell him and realized that if she said the first word it would bring uncontrollable tears. The Bird Woman opened the screen and stared unbelievingly.

"Why, I thought you would be ready; you are so late!" she said. "If you have waited to dress here, we must hurry."

"I have nothing to put on," said Elnora.

In bewilderment the Bird Woman drew her inside.

"Did—did—" she faltered. "Did you think you would wear that?"

"No. I thought I would telephone Ellen that there had been an accident and I could not come. I don't know yet how to explain. I'm too sick to think. Oh, do you suppose I can get something made by Tuesday, so that I can graduate?"

"Yes; and you'll get something on you to-night, so that you can lead your class, as you have done for four years. Go to my room and take off that gingham, quickly. Anna, drop everything, and come help me."

The Bird Woman ran to the telephone and called Ellen Brownlee.

"Elnora has had an accident. She will be a little late," she said. "You have got to make them wait. Have them play extra music before the march."

Then she turned to the maid. "Tell Benson to have the carriage at the gate, just as soon as he can get it there. Then come to my room. Bring the thread box from the sewing-room, that roll of wide white ribbon on the cutting table, and gather all the white pins from every dresser in the house. But first come with me a minute."

"I want that trunk with the Swamp Angel's stuff in it, from the cedar closet," she panted as they reached the top of the stairs.

They hurried down the hall together and dragged the big trunk to the Bird Woman's room. She opened it and began tossing out white stuff.

"How lucky that she left these things!" she cried. "Here are white shoes, gloves, stockings, fans, everything!"

"I am all ready but a dress," said Elnora.

The Bird Woman began opening closets and pulling out drawers and boxes.

"I think I can make it this way," she said.

She snatched up a creamy lace yoke with long sleeves that recently had been made for her and held it out. Elnora slipped into it, and the Bird Woman began smoothing out wrinkles and sewing in pins. It fitted very well with a little lapping in the back. Next, from among the Angel's clothing she caught up a white silk waist with low neck and elbow sleeves, and Elnora put it on. It was large enough, but distressingly short in the waist, for the Angel had worn it at a party when she was sixteen. The Bird Woman loosened the sleeves and pushed them to a puff on the shoulders, catching them in places with pins. She began on the wide draping of the yoke, fastening it front, back and at each shoulder. She pulled down the waist and pinned it. Next came a soft white dress skirt of her own. By pinning her waist band quite four inches above Elnora's, the Bird Woman could secure a perfect Empire sweep, with the clinging silk. Then she began with the wide white ribbon that was to trim a new frock for herself, bound it three times around the high waist effect she had managed, tied the ends in a knot and let them fall to the floor in a beautiful sash.

"I want four white roses, each with two or three leaves," she cried.

Anna ran to bring them, while the Bird Woman added pins.

"Elnora," she said, "forgive me, but tell me truly. Is your mother so poor as to make this necessary?"

"No," answered Elnora. "Next year I am heir to my share of over three hundred acres of land covered with almost as valuable timber as was in the Limberlost. We adjoin it. There could be thirty oil wells drilled that would yield to us the thousands our neighbours are draining from under us, and the bare land is worth over one hundred dollars an acre for farming. She is not poor, she is—I don't know what she is. A great trouble soured and warped her. It made her peculiar. She does not in the least understand, but it is because she doesn't care to, instead of ignorance. She does not——"

Elnora stopped.

"She is—is different," finished the girl.

Anna came with the roses. The Bird Woman set one on the front of the draped yoke, one on each shoulder and the last among the bright masses of brown hair. Then she turned the girl facing the tall mirror.

"Oh!" panted Elnora. "You are a genius! Why, I will look as well as any of them."

"Thank goodness for that!" cried the Bird Woman. "If it wouldn't do, I should have been ill. You are lovely; altogether lovely! Ordinarily I shouldn't say that; but when I think of how you are carpentered, I'm admiring the result."

The organ began rolling out the march as they came in sight. Elnora took her place at the head of the procession, while every one wondered. Secretly they had hoped that she would be dressed well enough, that she would not appear poor and neglected. What this radiant young creature, gowned in the most recent style, her smooth skin flushed with excitement, and a rose-set coronet of red gold on her head, had to do with the girl they knew was difficult to decide. The signal was given and Elnora began the slow march across the vestry and down the aisle. The music welled softly, and Margaret began to sob without knowing why.

Mrs. Comstock gripped her hands together and shut her eyes. It seemed an eternity to the suffering woman before Margaret caught her arm and whispered, "Oh, Kate! For any sake look at her! Here! The aisle across!"

Mrs. Comstock opened her eyes and directing them where she was told, gazed intently, and slid down in her seat close to collapse. She was saved by Margaret's tense clasp and her command: "Here! Idiot! Stop that!"

In the blaze of light Elnora climbed the steps to the palm-embowered platform, crossed it and took her place. Sixty young men and women, each of them dressed the best possible, followed her. There were manly, fine-looking men in that class which Elnora led. There were girls of beauty and grace, but not one of them was handsomer or clothed in better taste than she.

Billy thought the time never would come when Elnora would see him, but at last she met his eye, then Margaret and Wesley had faint signs of recognition in turn, but there was no softening of the girl's face and no hint of a smile when she saw her mother.

Heartsick, Katharine Comstock tried to prove to herself that she was justified in what she had done, but she could not. She tried to blame Elnora for not saying that she was to lead a procession and sit on a platform in the sight of hundreds of people; but that was impossible, for she realized that she would have scoffed and not understood if she had been told. Her heart pained until she suffered with every breath.

When at last the exercises were over she climbed into the carriage and rode home without a word. She did not hear what Margaret and Billy were saying. She scarcely heard Wesley, who drove behind, when he told her that Elnora would not be home until Wednesday. Early the next morning Mrs. Comstock was on her way to Onabasha. She was waiting when the Brownlee store opened. She examined ready-made white dresses, but they had only one of the right size, and it was marked forty dollars. Mrs. Comstock did not hesitate over the price, but whether the dress would be suitable. She would have to ask Elnora. She inquired her way to the home of the Bird Woman and knocked.

"Is Elnora Comstock here?" she asked the maid.

"Yes, but she is still in bed. I was told to let her sleep as long as she would."

"Maybe I could sit here and wait," said Mrs. Comstock. "I want to see about getting her a dress for to-morrow. I am her mother."

"Then you don't need wait or worry," said the girl cheerfully. "There are two women up in the sewing-room at work on a dress for her right now. It will be done in time, and it will be a beauty."

Mrs. Comstock turned and trudged back to the Limberlost. The bitterness in her soul became a physical actuality, which water would not wash from her lips. She was too late! She was not needed. Another woman was mothering her girl. Another woman would prepare a beautiful dress such as Elnora had worn the previous night. The girl's love and gratitude would go to her. Mrs. Comstock tried the old process of blaming some one else, but she felt no better. She nursed her grief as closely as ever in the long days of the girl's absence. She brooded over Elnora's possession of the forbidden violin and her ability to play it until the performance could not have been told from her father's. She tried every refuge her mind could conjure, to quiet her heart and remove the fear that the girl never would come home again, but it persisted. Mrs. Comstock could neither eat nor sleep. She wandered around the cabin and garden. She kept far from the pool where Robert Comstock had sunk from sight for she felt that it would entomb her also if Elnora did not come home Wednesday morning. The mother told herself that she would wait, but the waiting was as bitter as anything she ever had known.

When Elnora awoke Monday another dress was in the hands of a seamstress and was soon fitted. It had belonged to the Angel, and was a soft white thing that with a little alteration would serve admirably for Commencement and the ball. All that day Elnora worked, helping prepare the auditorium for the exercises, rehearsing the march and the speech she was to make in behalf of the class. The following day was even busier. But her mind was at rest, for the dress was a soft delicate lace easy to change, and the marks of alteration impossible to detect.

The Bird Woman had telephoned to Grand Rapids, explained the situation and asked the Angel if she might use it. The reply had been to give the girl the contents of the chest. When the Bird Woman told Elnora, tears filled her eyes.

"I will write at once and thank her," she said. "With all her beautiful gowns she does not need them, and I do. They will serve for me often, and be much finer than anything I could afford. It is lovely of her to give me the dress and of you to have it altered for me, as I never could."

The Bird Woman laughed. "I feel religious to-day," she said. "You know the first and greatest rock of my salvation is 'Do unto others.' I'm only doing to you what there was no one to do for me when I was a girl very like you. Anna tells me your mother was here early this morning and that she came to see about getting you a dress."

"She is too late!" said Elnora coldly. "She had over a month to prepare my dresses, and I was to pay for them, so there is no excuse."

"Nevertheless, she is your mother," said the Bird Woman, softly. "I think almost any kind of a mother must be better than none at all, and you say she has had great trouble."

"She loved my father and he died," said Elnora. "The same thing, in quite as tragic a manner, has happened to thousands of other women, and they have gone on with calm faces and found happiness in life by loving others. There was something else I am afraid I never shall forget; this I know I shall not, but talking does not help. I must deliver my presents and photographs to the crowd. I have a picture and I made a present for you, too, if you would care for them."

"I shall love anything you give me," said the Bird Woman. "I know you well enough to know that whatever you do will be beautiful."

Elnora was pleased over that, and as she tried on her dress for the last fitting she was really happy. She was lovely in the dainty gown: it would serve finely for the ball and many other like occasions, and it was her very own.

The Bird Woman's driver took Elnora in the carriage and she called on all the girls with whom she was especially intimate, and left her picture and the package containing her gift to them. By the time she returned parcels for her were arriving. Friends seemed to spring from everywhere. Almost every one she knew had some gift for her, while because they so loved her the members of her crowd had made her beautiful presents. There were books, vases, silver pieces, handkerchiefs, fans, boxes of flowers and candy. One big package settled the trouble at Sinton's, for it contained a dainty dress from Margaret, a five-dollar gold piece, conspicuously labelled, "I earned this myself," from Billy, with which to buy music; and a gorgeous cut-glass perfume bottle, it would have cost five dollars to fill with even a moderate-priced scent, from Wesley.

In an expressed crate was a fine curly-maple dressing table, sent by Freckles. The drawers were filled with wonderful toilet articles from the Angel. The Bird Woman added an embroidered linen cover and a small silver vase for a few flowers, so no girl of the class had finer gifts. Elnora laid her head on the table sobbing happily, and the Bird Woman was almost crying herself. Professor Henley sent a butterfly book, the grade rooms in which Elnora had taught gave her a set of volumes covering every phase of life afield, in the woods, and water. Elnora had no time to read so she carried one of these books around with her hugging it as she went. After she had gone to dress a queer-looking package was brought by a small boy who hopped on one foot as he handed it in and said: "Tell Elnora that is from her ma."

"Who are you?" asked the Bird Woman as she took the bundle.

"I'm Billy!" announced the boy. "I gave her the five dollars. I earned it myself dropping corn, sticking onions, and pulling weeds. My, but you got to drop, and stick, and pull a lot before it's five dollars' worth."

"Would you like to come in and see Elnora's gifts?"

"Yes, ma'am!" said Billy, trying to stand quietly.

"Gee-mentley!" he gasped. "Does Elnora get all this?"

"Yes."

"I bet you a thousand dollars I be first in my class when I graduate. Say, have the others got a lot more than Elnora?"

"I think not."

"Well, Uncle Wesley said to find out if I could, and if she didn't have as much as the rest, he'd buy till she did, if it took a hundred dollars. Say, you ought to know him! He's just scrumptious! There ain't anybody any where finer 'an he is. My, he's grand!"

"I'm very sure of it!" said the Bird Woman. "I've often heard Elnora say so."

"I bet you nobody can beat this!" he boasted. Then he stopped, thinking deeply. "I don't know, though," he began reflectively. "Some of them are awful rich; they got big families to give them things and wagon loads of friends, and I haven't seen what they have. Now, maybe Elnora is getting left, after all!"

"Don't worry, Billy," she said. "I will watch, and if I find Elnora is 'getting left' I'll buy her some more things myself. But I'm sure she is not. She has more beautiful gifts now than she will know what to do with, and others will come. Tell your Uncle Wesley his girl is bountifully remembered, very happy, and she sends her dearest love to all of you. Now you must go, so I can help her dress. You will be there to-night of course?"

"Yes, sir-ee! She got me a seat, third row from the front, middle section, so I can see, and she's going to wink at me, after she gets her speech off her mind. She kissed me, too! She's a perfect lady, Elnora is. I'm going to marry her when I am big enough."

"Why isn't that splendid!" laughed the Bird Woman as she hurried upstairs.

"Dear!" she called. "Here is another gift for you."

Elnora was half disrobed as she took the package and, sitting on a couch, opened it. The Bird Woman bent over her and tested the fabric with her fingers.

"Why, bless my soul!" she cried. "Hand-woven, hand-embroidered linen, fine as silk. It's priceless! I haven't seen such things in years. My mother had garments like those when I was a child, but my sisters had them cut up for collars, belts, and fancy waists while I was small. Look at the exquisite work!"

"Where could it have come from?" cried Elnora.

She shook out a petticoat, with a hand-wrought ruffle a foot deep, then an old-fashioned chemise the neck and sleeve work of which was elaborate and perfectly wrought. On the breast was pinned a note that she hastily opened.

"I was married in these," it read, "and I had intended to be buried in them, but perhaps it would be more sensible for you to graduate and get married in them yourself, if you like. Your mother."

"From my mother!" Wide-eyed, Elnora looked at the Bird Woman. "I never in my life saw the like. Mother does things I think I never can forgive, and when I feel hardest, she turns around and does something that makes me think she just must love me a little bit, after all. Any of the girls would give almost anything to graduate in hand-embroidered linen like that. Money can't buy such things. And they came when I was thinking she didn't care what became of me. Do you suppose she can be insane?"

"Yes," said the Bird Woman. "Wildly insane, if she does not love you and care what becomes of you."

Elnora arose and held the petticoat to her. "Will you look at it?" she cried. "Only imagine her not getting my dress ready, and then sending me such a petticoat as this! Ellen would pay fifty dollars for it and never blink. I suppose mother has had it all my life, and I never saw it before."

"Go take your bath and put on those things," said the Bird Woman. "Forget everything and be happy. She is not insane. She is embittered. She did not understand how things would be. When she saw, she came at once to provide you a dress. This is her way of saying she is sorry she did not get the other. You notice she has not spent any money, so perhaps she is quite honest in saying she has none."

"Oh, she is honest!" said Elnora. "She wouldn't care enough to tell an untruth. She'd say just how things were, no matter what happened."

Soon Elnora was ready for her dress. She never had looked so well as when she again headed the processional across the flower and palm decked stage of the high school auditorium. As she sat there she could have reached over and dropped a rose she carried into the seat she had occupied that September morning when she entered the high school. She spoke the few words she had to say in behalf of the class beautifully, had the tiny wink ready for Billy, and the smile and nod of recognition for Wesley and Margaret. When at last she looked into the eyes of a white-faced woman next them, she slipped a hand to her side and raised her skirt the fraction of an inch, just enough to let the embroidered edge of a petticoat show a trifle. When she saw the look of relief which flooded her mother's face, Elnora knew that forgiveness was in her heart, and that she would go home in the morning.

It was late afternoon before she arrived, and a dray followed with a load of packages. Mrs. Comstock was overwhelmed. She sat half dazed and made Elnora show her each costly and beautiful or simple and useful gift, tell her carefully what it was and from where it came. She studied the faces of

Elnora's particular friends. The gifts from them had to be set in a group. Several times she started to speak and then stopped. At last, between her dry lips, came a harsh whisper.

"Elnora, what did you give back for these things?"

"I'll show you," said Elnora cheerfully. "I made the same gifts for the Bird Woman, Aunt Margaret and you if you care for it. But I have to run upstairs to get it."

When she returned she handed her mother an oblong frame, hand carved, enclosing Elnora's picture, taken by a schoolmate's camera. She wore her storm-coat and carried a dripping umbrella. From under it looked her bright face; her books and lunchbox were on her arm, and across the bottom of the frame was carved, "Your Country Classmate."

Then she offered another frame.

"I am strong on frames," she said. "They seemed to be the best I could do without money. I located the maple and the black walnut myself, in a little corner that had been overlooked between the river and the ditch. They didn't seem to belong to any one so I just took them. Uncle Wesley said it was all right, and he cut and hauled them for me. I gave the mill half of each tree for sawing and curing the remainder. Then I gave the wood-carver half of that for making my frames. A photographer gave me a lot of spoiled plates, and I boiled off the emulsion, and took the specimens I framed from my stuff. The man said the white frames were worth three and a half, and the black ones five. I exchanged those little framed pictures for the photographs of the others. For presents, I gave each one of my crowd one like this, only a different moth. The Bird Woman gave me the birch bark. She got it up north last summer."

Elnora handed her mother a handsome black-walnut frame a foot and a half wide by two long. It finished a small, shallow glass-covered box of birch bark, to the bottom of which clung a big night moth with delicate pale green wings and long exquisite trailers.

"So you see I did not have to be ashamed of my gifts," said Elnora. "I made them myself and raised and mounted the moths."

"Moth, you call it," said Mrs. Comstock. "I've seen a few of the things before."

"They are numerous around us every June night, or at least they used to be," said Elnora. "I've sold hundreds of them, with butterflies, dragonflies, and other specimens. Now, I must put away these and get to work, for it is almost June and there are a few more I want dreadfully. If I find them I will be paid some money for which I have been working."

She was afraid to say college at that time. She thought it would be better to wait a few days and see if an opportunity would not come when it would work in more naturally. Besides, unless she could secure the Yellow Emperor she needed to complete her collection, she could not talk college until she was of age, for she would have no money.

CHAPTER XII

"Elnora, bring me the towel, quick!" cried Mrs Comstock.

"In a minute, mother," mumbled Elnora.

She was standing before the kitchen mirror, tying the back part of her hair, while the front turned over her face.

"Hurry! There's a varmint of some kind!"

Elnora ran into the sitting-room and thrust the heavy kitchen towel into her mother's hand. Mrs. Comstock swung open the screen door and struck at some object, Elnora tossed the hair from her face so that she could see past her mother. The girl screamed wildly.

"Don't! Mother, don't!"

Mrs. Comstock struck again. Elnora caught her arm. "It's the one I want! It's worth a lot of money! Don't! Oh, you shall not!"

"Shan't, missy?" blazed Mrs. Comstock. "When did you get to bossing me?"

The hand that held the screen swept a half-circle and stopped at Elnora's cheek. She staggered with the blow, and across her face, paled with excitement, a red mark arose rapidly. The screen slammed shut, throwing the creature on the floor before them. Instantly Mrs. Comstock crushed it with her foot. Elnora stepped back. Excepting the red mark, her face was very white.

"That was the last moth I needed," she said, "to complete a collection worth three hundred dollars. You've ruined it before my eyes!"

"Moth!" cried Mrs. Comstock. "You say that because you are mad. Moths have big wings. I know a moth!"

"I've kept things from you," said Elnora, "because I didn't dare confide in you. You had no sympathy with me. But you know I never told you untruths in all my life."

"It's no moth!" reiterated Mrs. Comstock.

"It is!" cried Elnora. "It's from a case in the ground. Its wings take two or three hours to expand and harden."

"If I had known it was a moth——" Mrs. Comstock wavered.

"You did know! I told you! I begged you to stop! It meant just three hundred dollars to me."

"Bah! Three hundred fiddlesticks!"

"They are what have paid for books, tuition, and clothes for the past four years. They are what I could have started on to college. You've ruined the very one I needed. You never made any pretence of loving me. At last I'll be equally frank with you. I hate you! You are a selfish, wicked woman! I hate you!"

Elnora turned, went through the kitchen and from the back door. She followed the garden path to the gate and walked toward the swamp a short distance when reaction overtook her. She dropped on the ground and leaned against a big log. When a little child, desperate as now, she had tried to die by holding her breath. She had thought in that way to make her mother sorry, but she had learned that life was a thing thrust upon her and she could not leave it at her wish.

She was so stunned over the loss of that moth, which she had childishly named the Yellow Emperor, that she scarcely remembered the blow. She had thought no luck in all the world would be so rare as to complete her collection; now she had been forced to see a splendid Imperialis destroyed before her. There was a possibility that she could find another, but she was facing the certainty that the one she might have had and with which she undoubtedly could have attracted others, was spoiled by her mother. How long she sat there Elnora did not know or care. She simply suffered in dumb, abject misery, an occasional dry sob shaking her. Aunt Margaret was right. Elnora felt that morning that her mother never would be any different. The girl had reached the place where she realized that she could endure it no longer.

As Elnora left the room, Mrs. Comstock took one step after her.

"You little huzzy!" she gasped.

But Elnora was gone. Her mother stood staring.

"She never did lie to me," she muttered. "I guess it was a moth. And the only one she needed to get three hundred dollars, she said. I wish I hadn't been so fast! I never saw anything like it. I thought it was some deadly, stinging, biting thing. A body does have to be mighty careful here. But likely I've spilt the milk now. Pshaw! She can find another! There's no use to be foolish. Maybe moths are like snakes, where there's one, there are two."

Mrs. Comstock took the broom and swept the moth out of the door. Then she got down on her knees and carefully examined the steps, logs and the earth of the flower beds at each side. She found the place where the creature had emerged from the ground, and the hard, dark-brown case which had enclosed it, still wet inside. Then she knew Elnora had been right. It was a moth. Its wings had been damp and not expanded. Mrs. Comstock never before had seen one in that state, and she did not know how they originated. She had thought all of them came from cases spun on trees or against walls or boards. She had seen only enough to know that there were such things; as a flash of white told her that an ermine was on her premises, or a sharp "buzzzzz" warned her of a rattler. So it was from creatures like that Elnora had secured her school money. In one sickening sweep there rushed into the heart of the woman a full realization of the width of the gulf that separated her from her child. Lately many things had pointed toward it, none more plainly than when Elnora, like a reincarnation of her father, had stood fearlessly before a large city audience and played with even greater skill than he, on what Mrs. Comstock felt very certain was his violin. But that little crawling creature of earth, crushed by her before its splendid yellow and lavender wings could spread and carry it into the mystery of night, had performed a miracle.

"We are nearer strangers to each other than we are with any of the neighbours," she muttered.

So one of the Almighty's most delicate and beautiful creations was sacrificed without fulfilling the law, yet none of its species ever served so glorious a cause, for at last Mrs. Comstock's inner vision had cleared. She went through the cabin mechanically. Every few minutes she glanced toward the back walk to see if Elnora were coming. She knew arrangements had been made with Margaret to go to the city some time that day, so she grew more nervous and uneasy every moment. She was haunted by the fear that the blow might discolour Elnora's cheek; that she would tell Margaret. She went down the back walk, looking intently in all directions, left the garden and followed the swamp path. Her step was noiseless on the soft, black earth, and soon she came close enough to see Elnora. Mrs. Comstock stood looking at the girl in troubled uncertainty. Not knowing what to say, at last she turned and went back to the cabin.

Noon came and she prepared dinner, calling, as she always did, when Elnora was in the garden, but she got no response, and the girl did not come. A little after one o'clock Margaret stopped at the gate.

"Elnora has changed her mind. She is not going," called Mrs. Comstock.

She felt that she hated Margaret as she hitched her horse and came up the walk instead of driving on.

"You must be mistaken," said Margaret. "I was going on purpose for her. She asked me to take her. I had no errand. Where is she?"

"I will call her," said Mrs. Comstock.

She followed the path again, and this time found Elnora sitting on the log. Her face was swollen and discoloured, and her eyes red with crying. She paid no attention to her mother.

"Mag Sinton is here," said Mrs. Comstock harshly. "I told her you had changed your mind, but she said you asked her to go with you, and she had nothing to go for herself."

Elnora arose, recklessly waded through the deep swamp grasses and so reached the path ahead of her mother. Mrs. Comstock followed as far as the garden, but she could not enter the cabin. She busied herself among the vegetables, barely looking up when the back-door screen slammed noisily. Margaret Sinton approached colourless, her eyes so angry that Mrs. Comstock shrank back.

"What's the matter with Elnora's face?" demanded Margaret.

Mrs. Comstock made no reply.

"You struck her, did you?"

"I thought you wasn't blind!"

"I have been, for twenty long years now, Kate Comstock," said Margaret Sinton, "but my eyes are open at last. What I see is that I've done you no good and Elnora a big wrong. I had an idea that it would kill you to know, but I guess you are tough enough to stand anything. Kill or cure, you get it now!"

"What are you frothing about?" coolly asked Mrs. Comstock.

"You!" cried Margaret. "You! The woman who doesn't pretend to love her only child. Who lets her grow to a woman, as you have let Elnora, and can't be satisfied with every sort of neglect, but must add abuse yet; and all for a fool idea about a man who wasn't worth his salt!"

Mrs. Comstock picked up a hoe.

"Go right on!" she said. "Empty yourself. It's the last thing you'll ever do!"

"Then I'll make a tidy job of it," said Margaret. "You'll not touch me. You'll stand there and hear the truth at last, and because I dare face you and tell it, you will know in your soul it is truth. When Robert Comstock shaved that quagmire out there so close he went in, he wanted to keep you from knowing where he was coming from. He'd been to see Elvira Carney. They had plans to go to a dance that night——"

"Close your lips!" said Mrs. Comstock in a voice of deadly quiet.

"You know I wouldn't dare open them if I wasn't telling you the truth. I can prove what I say. I was coming from Reeds. It was hot in the woods and I stopped at Carney's as I passed for a drink. Elvira's bedridden old mother heard me, and she was so crazy for some one to talk with, I stepped in a minute. I saw Robert come down the path. Elvira saw him, too, so she ran out of the house to head him off. It looked funny, and I just deliberately moved where I could see and hear. He brought her his violin, and told her to get ready and meet him in the woods with it that night, and they would go to a dance. She took it and hid it in the loft to the well-house and promised she'd go."

"Are you done?" demanded Mrs. Comstock.

"No. I am going to tell you the whole story. You don't spare Elnora anything. I shan't spare you. I hadn't been here that day, but I can tell you just how he was dressed, which way he went and every word they said, though they thought I was busy with her mother and wouldn't notice them. Put down your hoe, Kate. I went to Elvira, told her what I knew and made her give me Comstock's violin for Elnora over three years ago. She's been playing it ever since. I won't see her slighted and abused another day on account of a man who would have broken your heart if he had lived. Six months more would have showed you what everybody else knew. He was one of those men who couldn't trust himself, and so no woman was safe with him. Now, will you drop grieving over him, and do Elnora justice?"

Mrs. Comstock grasped the hoe tighter and turning she went down the walk, and started across the woods to the home of Elvira Carney. With averted head she passed the pool, steadily pursuing her way. Elvira Carney, hanging towels across the back fence, saw her coming and went toward the gate to meet her. Twenty years she had dreaded that visit. Since Margaret Sinton had compelled her to produce the violin she had hidden so long, because she was afraid to destroy it, she had come closer expectation than dread. The wages of sin are the hardest debts on earth to pay, and they are always collected at inconvenient times and unexpected places. Mrs. Comstock's face and hair were so white, that her dark eyes seemed burned into their setting. Silently she stared at the woman before her a long time.

"I might have saved myself the trouble of coming," she said at last, "I see you are guilty as sin!"

"What has Mag Sinton been telling you?" panted the miserable woman, gripping the fence.

"The truth!" answered Mrs. Comstock succinctly. "Guilt is in every line of your face, in your eyes, all over your wretched body. If I'd taken a good look at you any time in all these past years, no doubt I could have seen it just as plain as I can now. No woman or man can do what you've done, and not get a mark set on them for every one to read."

"Mercy!" gasped weak little Elvira Carney. "Have mercy!"

"Mercy?" scoffed Mrs. Comstock. "Mercy! That's a nice word from you! How much mercy did you have on me? Where's the mercy that sent Comstock to the slime of the bottomless quagmire, and left me to see it, and then struggle on in agony all these years? How about the mercy of letting me neglect my baby all the days of her life? Mercy! Do you really dare use the word to me?"

"If you knew what I've suffered!"

"Suffered?" jeered Mrs. Comstock. "That's interesting. And pray, what have you suffered?"

"All the neighbours have suspected and been down on me. I ain't had a friend. I've always felt guilty of his death! I've seen him go down a thousand times, plain as ever you did. Many's the night I've stood on the other bank of that pool and listened to you, and I tried to throw myself in to keep from hearing you, but I didn't dare. I knew God would send me to burn forever, but I'd better done it; for now, He has set the burning on my body, and every hour it is slowly eating the life out of me. The doctor says it's a cancer——"

Mrs. Comstock exhaled a long breath. Her grip on the hoe relaxed and her stature lifted to towering height.

"I didn't know, or care, when I came here, just what I did," she said. "But my way is beginning to clear. If the guilt of your soul has come to a head, in a cancer on your body, it looks as if the Almighty didn't need any of my help in meting out His punishments. I really couldn't fix up anything to come anywhere near that. If you are going to burn until your life goes out with that sort of fire, you don't owe me anything!"

"Oh, Katharine Comstock!" groaned Elvira Carney, clinging to the fence for support.

"Looks as if the Bible is right when it says, 'The wages of sin is death,' doesn't it?" asked Mrs. Comstock. "Instead of doing a woman's work in life, you chose the smile of invitation, and the dress of unearned cloth. Now you tell me you are marked to burn to death with the unquenchable fire. And him! It was shorter with him, but let me tell you he got his share! He left me with an untruth on his lips, for he told me he was going to take his violin to Onabasha for a new key, when he carried it to you. Every vow of love and constancy he ever made me was a lie, after he touched your lips, so when he tried the wrong side of the quagmire, to hide from me the direction in which he was coming, it reached out for him, and it got him. It didn't hurry, either! It sucked him down, slow and deliberate."

"Mercy!" groaned Elvira Carney. "Mercy!"

"I don't know the word," said Mrs. Comstock. "You took all that out of me long ago. The past twenty years haven't been of the sort that taught mercy. I've never had any on myself and none on my child. Why in the name of justice, should I have mercy on you, or on him? You were both older than I, both strong, sane people, you deliberately chose your course when you lured him, and he, when he was unfaithful to me. When a Loose Man and a Light Woman face the end the Almighty ordained for them, why should they shout at me for mercy? What did I have to do with it?"

Elvira Carney sobbed in panting gasps.

"You've got tears, have you?" marvelled Mrs. Comstock. "Mine all dried long ago. I've none left to shed over my wasted life, my disfigured face and hair, my years of struggle with a man's work, my wreck of land among the tilled fields of my neighbours, or the final knowledge that the man I so gladly would have died to save, wasn't worth the sacrifice of a rattlesnake. If anything yet could wring a tear from me, it would be the thought of the awful injustice I always have done my girl. If I'd lay hand on you for anything, it would be for that."

"Kill me if you want to," sobbed Elvira Carney. "I know that I deserve it, and I don't care."

"You are getting your killing fast enough to suit me," said Mrs. Comstock. "I wouldn't touch you, any more than I would him, if I could. Once is all any man or woman deceives me about the holiest things of life. I wouldn't touch you any more than I would the black plague. I am going back to my girl."

Mrs. Comstock turned and started swiftly through the woods, but she had gone only a few rods when she stopped, and leaning on the hoe, she stood thinking deeply. Then she turned back. Elvira still clung to the fence, sobbing bitterly.

"I don't know," said Mrs. Comstock, "but I left a wrong impression with you. I don't want you to think that I believe the Almighty set a cancer to burning you as a punishment for your sins. I don't! I think a lot more of the Almighty. With a whole sky-full of worlds on His hands to manage, I'm not believing that He has time to look down on ours, and pick you out of all the millions of us sinners, and set a special kind of torture to eating you. It wouldn't be a gentlemanly thing to do, and first of all, the Almighty is bound to be a gentleman. I think likely a bruise and bad blood is what caused your trouble. Anyway, I've got to tell you that the cleanest housekeeper I ever knew, and one of the noblest Christian women, was slowly eaten up by a cancer. She got hers from the careless work of a poor doctor. The Almighty is to forgive sin and heal disease, not to invent and spread it."

She had gone only a few steps when she again turned back.

"If you will gather a lot of red clover bloom, make a tea strong as lye of it, and drink quarts, I think likely it will help you, if you are not too far gone. Anyway, it will cool your blood and make the burning easier to bear."

Then she swiftly went home. Enter the lonely cabin she could not, neither could she sit outside and think. She attacked a bed of beets and hoed until the perspiration ran from her face and body, then she began on the potatoes. When she was too tired to take another stroke she bathed and put on dry clothing. In securing her dress she noticed her husband's carefully preserved clothing lining one wall. She gathered it in an armload and carried it to the swamp. Piece by piece she pitched into the green maw of the quagmire all those articles she had dusted carefully and fought moths from for years, and stood watching as it slowly sucked them down. She went back to her room and gathered every scrap that had in any way belonged to Robert Comstock, excepting his gun and revolver, and threw it into the swamp. Then for the first time she set her door wide open.

She was too weary now to do more, but an urging unrest drove her. She wanted Elnora. It seemed to her she never could wait until the girl came and delivered her judgment. At last in an effort to get nearer to her, Mrs. Comstock climbed the stairs and stood looking around Elnora's room. It was very unfamiliar. The pictures were strange to her. Commencement had filled it with packages and bundles. The walls were covered with cocoons; moths and dragonflies were pinned everywhere. Under the bed she could see half a dozen large white boxes. She pulled out one and lifted the lid. The bottom was covered with a sheet of thin cork, and on long pins sticking in it were large, velvet-winged moths. Each one was labelled, always there were two of a kind, in many cases four, showing under and upper wings of both male and female. They were of every colour and shape.

Mrs. Comstock caught her breath sharply. When and where had Elnora found them? They were the most exquisite sight the woman ever had seen, so she opened all the boxes to feast on their beautiful contents. As she did so there came more fully a sense of the distance between her and her child. She could not understand how Elnora had gone to school, and performed so much work secretly. When it was finished, to the last moth, she, the mother who should have been the first confidant and helper, had been the one to bring disappointment. Small wonder Elnora had come to hate her.

Mrs. Comstock carefully closed and replaced the boxes; and again stood looking around the room. This time her eyes rested on some books she did not remember having seen before, so she picked up one and found that it was a moth book. She glanced over the first pages and was soon eagerly reading. When the text reached the classification of species, she laid it down, took up another and read the introductory chapters. By that time her brain was in a confused jumble of ideas about capturing moths with differing baits and bright lights.

She went down stairs thinking deeply. Being unable to sit still and having nothing else to do she glanced at the clock and began preparing supper. The work dragged. A chicken was snatched up and dressed hurriedly. A spice cake sprang into being. Strawberries that had been intended for preserves went into shortcake. Delicious odours crept from the cabin. She put many extra touches on the table and then commenced watching the road. Everything was ready, but Elnora did not come. Then began the anxious process of trying to keep cooked food warm and not spoil it. The birds went to bed and dusk came. Mrs. Comstock gave up the fire and set the supper on the table. Then she went out and sat on the front-door step watching night creep around her. She started eagerly as the gate creaked, but it was only Wesley Sinton coming.

"Katharine, Margaret and Elnora passed where I was working this afternoon, and Margaret got out of the carriage and called me to the fence. She told me what she had done. I've come to say to you that I am sorry. She has heard me threaten to do it a good many times, but I never would have got it done. I'd give a good deal if I could undo it, but I can't, so I've come to tell you how sorry I am."

"You've got something to be sorry for," said Mrs. Comstock, "but likely we ain't thinking of the same thing. It hurts me less to know the truth, than to live in ignorance. If Mag had the sense of a pewee, she'd told me long ago. That's what hurts me, to think that both of you knew Robert was not worth an hour of honest grief, yet you'd let me mourn him all these years and neglect Elnora while I did it. If I have anything to forgive you, that is what it is."

Wesley removed his hat and sat on a bench.

"Katharine," he said solemnly, "nobody ever knows how to take you."

"Would it be asking too much to take me for having a few grains of plain common sense?" she inquired. "You've known all this time that Comstock got what he deserved, when he undertook to sneak in an unused way across a swamp, with which he was none too familiar. Now I should have thought that you'd figure that knowing the same thing would be the best method to cure me of pining for him, and slighting my child."

"Heaven only knows we have thought of that, and talked of it often, but we were both too big cowards. We didn't dare tell you."

"So you have gone on year after year, watching me show indifference to Elnora, and yet a little horse-sense would have pointed out to you that she was my salvation. Why look at it! Not married quite a year. All his vows of love and fidelity made to me before the Almighty forgotten in a few months, and a dance and a Light Woman so alluring he had to lie and sneak for them. What kind of a prospect is that for a life? I know men and women. An honourable man is an honourable man, and a liar is a liar; both are born and not made. One cannot change to the other any more than that same old leopard can change its spots. After a man tells a woman the first untruth of that sort, the others come piling thick, fast, and mountain high. The desolation they bring in their wake overshadows anything I have suffered completely. If he had lived six months more I should have known him for what he was born to be. It was in the blood of him. His father and grandfather before him were fiddling, dancing people; but I was certain of him. I thought we could leave Ohio and come out here alone, and I could so love him and interest him in his work, that he would be a man. Of all the fool, fruitless jobs, making anything of a creature that begins by deceiving her, is the foolest a sane woman ever undertook. I am more than sorry you and Margaret didn't see your way clear to tell me long ago. I'd have found it out in a few more months if he had lived, and I wouldn't have borne it a day. The man who breaks his vows to me once, doesn't get the second chance. I give truth and honour. I have a right to ask it in return. I am glad I understand at last. Now, if Elnora will forgive me, we will take a new start and see what we can make out of what is left of life. If she won't, then it will be my time to learn what suffering really means."

"But she will," said Wesley. "She must! She can't help it when things are explained."

"I notice she isn't hurrying any about coming home. Do you know where she is or what she is doing?"

"I do not. But likely she will be along soon. I must go help Billy with the night work. Good-bye, Katharine. Thank the Lord you have come to yourself at last!"

They shook hands and Wesley went down the road while Mrs. Comstock entered the cabin. She could not swallow food. She stood in the back door watching the sky for moths, but they did not seem to be very numerous. Her spirits sank and she breathed unevenly. Then she heard the front screen. She reached the middle door as Elnora touched the foot of the stairs.

"Hurry, and get ready, Elnora," she said. "Your supper is almost spoiled now."

Elnora closed the stair door behind her, and for the first time in her life, threw the heavy lever which barred out anyone from down stairs. Mrs. Comstock heard the thud, and knew what it meant. She reeled slightly and caught the doorpost for support. For a few minutes she clung there, then sank to the nearest chair. After a long time she arose and stumbling half blindly, she put the food in the cupboard and covered the table. She took the lamp in one hand, the butter in the other, and started to the spring house. Something brushed close by her face, and she looked just in time to see a winged creature rise above the cabin and sail away.

"That was a night bird," she muttered. As she stopped to set the butter in the water, came another thought. "Perhaps it was a moth!" Mrs. Comstock dropped the butter and hurried out with the lamp; she held it high above her head and waited until her arms ached. Small insects of night gathered, and at last a little dusty miller, but nothing came of any size.

"I must go where they are, if I get them," muttered Mrs. Comstock.

She went to the barn after the stout pair of high boots she used in feeding stock in deep snow. Throwing these beside the back door she climbed to the loft over the spring house, and hunted an old lard oil lantern and one of first manufacture for oil. Both these she cleaned and filled. She listened until everything up stairs had been still for over half an hour. By that time it was past eleven o'clock. Then she took the lantern from the kitchen, the two old ones, a handful of matches, a ball of twine, and went from the cabin, softly closing the door.

Sitting on the back steps, she put on the boots, and then stood gazing into the perfumed June night, first in the direction of the woods on her land, then toward the Limberlost. Its outline was so dark and forbidding she shuddered and went down the garden, following the path toward the woods, but as she neared the pool her knees wavered and her courage fled. The knowledge that in her soul she was now glad Robert Comstock was at the bottom of it made a coward of her, who fearlessly had mourned him there, nights untold. She could not go on. She skirted the back of the garden, crossed a field, and came out on the road. Soon she reached the Limberlost. She hunted until she found the old trail, then followed it stumbling over logs and through clinging vines and grasses. The heavy boots clumped on her feet, overhanging branches whipped her face and pulled her hair. But her eyes were on the sky as she went straining into the night, hoping to find signs of a living creature on wing.

By and by she began to see the wavering flight of something she thought near the right size. She had no idea where she was, but she stopped, lighted a lantern and hung it as high as she could reach. A little distance away she placed the second and then the third. The objects came nearer and sick with disappointment she saw that they were bats. Crouching in the damp swamp grasses, without a thought of snakes or venomous insects, she waited, her eyes roving from lantern to lantern. Once she thought a creature of high flight dropped near the lard oil light, so she arose breathlessly waiting, but either it passed or it was an illusion. She glanced at the old lantern, then at the new, and was on her feet in an instant creeping close. Something large as a small bird was fluttering around. Mrs. Comstock began to perspire, while her hand shook wildly. Closer she crept and just as she reached for it, something similar swept past and both flew away together.

Mrs. Comstock set her teeth and stood shivering. For a long time the locusts rasped, the whip-poor-wills cried and a steady hum of night life throbbed in her ears. Away in the sky she saw something coming when it was no larger than a falling leaf. Straight toward the light it flew. Mrs. Comstock began to pray aloud.

"This way, O Lord! Make it come this way! Please! O Lord, send it lower!"

The moth hesitated at the first light, then slowly, easily it came toward the second, as if following a path of air. It touched a leaf near the lantern and settled. As Mrs. Comstock reached for it a thin yellow spray wet her hand and the surrounding leaves. When its wings raised above its back, her fingers came together. She held the moth to the light. It was nearer brown than yellow, and she remembered having seen some like it in the boxes that afternoon. It was not the one needed to complete the collection, but Elnora might want it, so Mrs. Comstock held on. Then the Almighty was kind, or nature was sufficient, as you look at it, for following the law of its being when disturbed, the moth again threw the spray by which some suppose it attracts its kind, and liberally sprinkled Mrs. Comstock's dress front and arms. From that instant, she became the best moth bait ever invented. Every Polyphemus in range hastened to her, and other fluttering creatures of night followed. The influx came her way. She snatched wildly here and there until she had one in each hand and no place to put them. She could see more coming, and her aching heart, swollen with the strain of long excitement, hurt pitifully. She prayed in broken exclamations that did not always sound reverent, but never was human soul in more intense earnest.

Moths were coming. She had one in each hand. They were not yellow, and she did not know what to do. She glanced around to try to discover some way to keep what she had, and her throbbing heart stopped and every muscle stiffened. There was the dim outline of a crouching figure not two yards away, and a pair of eyes their owner thought hidden, caught the light in a cold stream. Her first impulse was to scream and fly for life. Before her lips could open a big moth alighted on her breast while she felt another walking over her hair. All sense of caution deserted her. She did not care to live if she could not replace the yellow moth she had killed. She turned her eyes to those among the leaves.

"Here, you!" she cried hoarsely. "I need you! Get yourself out here, and help me. These critters are going to get away from me. Hustle!"

Pete Corson parted the bushes and stepped into the light.

"Oh, it's you!" said Mrs. Comstock. "I might have known! But you gave me a start. Here, hold these until I make some sort of bag for them. Go easy! If you break them I don't guarantee what will happen to you!"

"Pretty fierce, ain't you!" laughed Pete, but he advanced and held out his hands. "For Elnora, I s'pose?"

"Yes," said Mrs. Comstock. "In a mad fit, I trampled one this morning, and by the luck of the old boy himself it was the last moth she needed to complete a collection. I got to get another one or die."

"Then I guess it's your funeral," said Pete. "There ain't a chance in a dozen the right one will come. What colour was it?"

"Yellow, and big as a bird."

"The Emperor, likely," said Pete. "You dig for that kind, and they are not numerous, so's 'at you can smash 'em for fun."

"Well, I can try to get one, anyway," said Mrs. Comstock. "I forgot all about bringing anything to put them in. You take a pinch on their wings until I make a poke."

Mrs. Comstock removed her apron, tearing off the strings. She unfastened and stepped from the skirt of her calico dress. With one apron string she tied shut the band and placket. She pulled a wire pin from her hair, stuck it through the other string, and using it as a bodkin ran it around the hem of her skirt, so shortly she had a large bag. She put several branches inside to which the moths could cling, closed the mouth partially and held it toward Pete.

"Put your hand well down and let the things go!" she ordered. "But be careful, man! Don't run into the twigs! Easy! That's one. Now the other. Is the one on my head gone? There was one on my dress, but I guess it flew. Here comes a kind of a gray-looking one."

Pete slipped several more moths into the bag.

"Now, that's five, Mrs. Comstock," he said. "I'm sorry, but you'll have to make that do. You must get out of here lively. Your lights will be taken for hurry calls, and inside the next hour a couple of men will ride here like fury. They won't be nice Sunday-school men, and they won't hold bags and catch moths for you. You must go quick!"

Mrs. Comstock laid down the bag and pulled one of the lanterns lower.

"I won't budge a step," she said. "This land doesn't belong to you. You have no right to order me off it. Here I stay until I get a Yellow Emperor, and no little petering thieves of this neighbourhood can scare me away."

"You don't understand," said Pete. "I'm willing to help Elnora, and I'd take care of you, if I could, but there will be too many for me, and they will be mad at being called out for nothing."

"Well, who's calling them out?" demanded Mrs. Comstock. "I'm catching moths. If a lot of good-for-nothings get fooled into losing some sleep, why let them, they can't hurt me, or stop my work."

"They can, and they'll do both."

"Well, I'll see them do it!" said Mrs. Comstock. "I've got Robert's revolver in my dress, and I can shoot as straight as any man, if I'm mad enough. Any one who interferes with me to-night will find me mad a-plenty. There goes another!"

She stepped into the light and waited until a big brown moth settled on her and was easily taken. Then in light, airy flight came a delicate pale green thing, and Mrs. Comstock started in pursuit. But the scent was not right. The moth fluttered high, then dropped lower, still lower, and sailed away. With outstretched hands Mrs. Comstock pursued it. She hurried one way and another, then ran over an object which tripped her and she fell. She regained her feet in an instant, but she had lost sight of the moth. With livid face she turned to the crouching man.

"You nasty, sneaking son of Satan!" she cried. "Why are you hiding there? You made me lose the one I wanted most of any I've had a chance at yet. Get out of here! Go this minute, or I'll fill your worthless carcass so full of holes you'll do to sift cornmeal. Go, I say! I'm using the Limberlost to-night, and I won't be stopped by the devil himself! Cut like fury, and tell the rest of them they can just go home. Pete is going to help me, and he is all of you I need. Now go!"

The man turned and went. Pete leaned against a tree, held his mouth shut and shook inwardly. Mrs. Comstock came back panting.

"The old scoundrel made me lose that!" she said. "If any one else comes snooping around here I'll just blow them up to start with. I haven't time to talk. Suppose that had been yellow! I'd have killed that man, sure! The Limberlost isn't safe to-night, and the sooner those whelps find it out, the better it will be for them."

Pete stopped laughing to look at her. He saw that she was speaking the truth. She was quite past reason, sense, or fear. The soft night air stirred the wet hair around her temples, the flickering lanterns made her face a ghastly green. She would stop at nothing, that was evident. Pete suddenly began catching moths with exemplary industry. In putting one into the bag, another escaped.

"We must not try that again," said Mrs. Comstock. "Now, what will we do?"

"We are close to the old case," said Pete. "I think I can get into it. Maybe we could slip the rest in there."

"That's a fine idea!" said Mrs. Comstock. "They'll have so much room there they won't be likely to hurt themselves, and the books say they don't fly in daytime unless they are disturbed, so they will settle when it's light, and I can come with Elnora to get them."

They captured two more, and then Pete carried them to the case.

"Here comes a big one!" he cried as he returned.

Mrs. Comstock looked up and stepped out with a prayer on her lips. She could not tell the colour at that distance, but the moth appeared different from the others. On it came, dropping lower and darting from light to light. As it swept near her, "O Heavenly Father!" exulted Mrs. Comstock, "it's yellow! Careful Pete! Your hat, maybe!"

Pete made a long sweep. The moth wavered above the hat and sailed away. Mrs. Comstock leaned against a tree and covered her face with her shaking hands.

"That is my punishment!" she cried. "Oh, Lord, if you will give a moth like that into my possession, I'll always be a better woman!"

The Emperor again came in sight. Pete stood tense and ready. Mrs. Comstock stepped into the light and watched the mothh's course. Then a second appeared in pursuit of the first. The larger one wavered into the radius of light once more. The perspiration rolled down the man's face. He half lifted the hat.

"Pray, woman! Pray now!" he panted.

"I guess I best get over by that lard oil light and go to work," breathed Mrs. Comstock. "The Lord knows this is all in prayer, but it's no time for words just now. Ready, Pete! You are going to get a chance first!"

Pete made another long, steady sweep, but the moth darted beneath the hat. In its flight it came straight toward Mrs. Comstock. She snatched off the remnant of apron she had tucked into her petticoat band and held the calico before her. The moth struck full against it and clung to the goods. Pete crept up stealthily. The second moth followed the first, and the spray showered the apron.

"Wait!" gasped Mrs. Comstock. "I think they have settled. The books say they won't leave now."

The big pale yellow creature clung firmly, lowering and raising its wings. The other came nearer. Mrs. Comstock held the cloth with rigid hands, while Pete could hear her breathing in short gusts.

"Shall I try now?" he implored.

"Wait!" whispered the woman. "Something seems to say wait!"

The night breeze stiffened and gently waved the apron. Locusts rasped, mosquitoes hummed and frogs sang uninterruptedly. A musky odour slowly filled the air.

"Now shall I?" questioned Pete.

"No. Leave them alone. They are safe now. They are mine. They are my salvation. God and the Limberlost gave them to me! They won't move for hours. The books all say so. O Heavenly Father, I am thankful to You, and you, too, Pete Corson! You are a good man to help me. Now, I can go home and face my girl."

Instead, Mrs. Comstock dropped suddenly. She spread the apron across her knees. The moths remained undisturbed. Then her tired white head dropped, the tears she had thought forever dried gushed forth, and she sobbed for pure joy.

"Oh, I wouldn't do that now, you know!" comforted Pete. "Think of getting two! That's more than you ever could have expected. A body would think you would cry, if you hadn't got any. Come on, now. It's almost morning. Let me help you home."

Pete took the bag and the two old lanterns. Mrs. Comstock carried her moths and the best lantern and went ahead to light the way.

Elnora had sat beside her window far into the night. At last she undressed and went to bed, but sleep would not come. She had gone to the city to talk with members of the School Board about a room in the grades. There was a possibility that she might secure the moth, and so be able to start to college that fall, but if she did not, then she wanted the school. She had been given some encouragement, but she was so unhappy that nothing mattered. She could not see the way open to anything in life, save a long series of disappointments, while she remained with her mother. Yet Margaret Sinton had advised her to go home and try once more. Margaret had seemed so sure there would be a change for the better, that Elnora had consented, although she had no hope herself. So strong is the bond of blood, she could not make up her mind to seek a home elsewhere, even after the day that had passed. Unable to sleep she arose at last, and the room being warm, she sat on the floor close the window. The lights in the swamp caught her eye. She was very uneasy, for quite a hundred of her best moths were in the case. However, there was no money, and no one ever had touched a book or any of her apparatus. Watching the lights set her thinking, and before she realized it, she was in a panic of fear.

She hurried down the stairway softly calling her mother. There was no answer. She lightly stepped across the sitting-room and looked in at the open door. There was no one, and the bed had not been used. Her first thought was that her mother had gone to the pool; and the Limberlost was alive with signals. Pity and fear mingled in the heart of the girl. She opened the kitchen door, crossed the garden and ran back to the swamp. As she neared it she listened, but she could hear only the usual voices of night.

"Mother!" she called softly. Then louder, "Mother!"

There was not a sound. Chilled with fright she hurried back to the cabin. She did not know what to do. She understood what the lights in the Limberlost meant. Where was her mother? She was afraid to enter, while she was growing very cold and still more fearful about remaining outside. At last she went to her mother's room, picked up the gun, carried it into the kitchen, and crowding in a little corner behind the stove, she waited in trembling anxiety. The time was dreadfully long before she heard her mother's voice. Then she decided some one had been ill and sent for her, so she took courage, and stepping swiftly across the kitchen she unbarred the door and drew back from sight beside the table.

Mrs. Comstock entered dragging her heavy feet. Her dress skirt was gone, her petticoat wet and drabbled, and the waist of her dress was almost torn from her body. Her hair hung in damp strings; her eyes were red with crying. In one hand she held the lantern, and in the other stiffly extended before her, on a wad of calico reposed a magnificent pair of Yellow Emperors. Elnora stared, her lips parted.

"Shall I put these others in the kitchen?" inquired a man's voice.

The girl shrank back to the shadows.

"Yes, anywhere inside the door," replied Mrs. Comstock as she moved a few steps to make way for him. Pete's head appeared. He set down the moths and was gone.

"Thank you, Pete, more than ever woman thanked you before!" said Mrs. Comstock.

She placed the lantern on the table and barred the door. As she turned Elnora came into view. Mrs. Comstock leaned toward her, and held out the moths. In a voice vibrant with tones never before heard she said: "Elnora, my girl, mother's found you another moth!"

CHAPTER XIII

WHEREIN MOTHER LOVE IS BESTOWED ON ELNORA, AND SHE FINDS AN ASSISTANT IN MOTH HUNTING

Elnora awoke at dawn and lay gazing around the unfamiliar room. She noticed that every vestige of masculine attire and belongings was gone, and knew, without any explanation, what that meant. For some reason every tangible evidence of her father was banished, and she was at last to be allowed to take his place. She turned to look at her mother. Mrs. Comstock's face was white and haggard, but on it rested an expression of profound peace Elnora never before had seen. As she studied the features on the pillow beside her, the heart of the girl throbbed in tenderness. She realized as fully as any one else could what her mother had suffered. Thoughts of the night brought shuddering fear. She softly slipped from the bed, went to her room, dressed and entered the kitchen to attend the Emperors and prepare breakfast. The pair had been left clinging to the piece of calico. The calico was there and a few pieces of beautiful wing. A mouse had eaten the moths!

"Well, of all the horrible luck!" gasped Elnora.

With the first thought of her mother, she caught up the remnants of the moths, burying them in the ashes of the stove. She took the bag to her room, hurriedly releasing its contents, but there was not another yellow one. Her mother had said some had been confined in the case in the Limberlost. There was still a hope that an Emperor might be among them. She peeped at her mother, who still slept soundly.

Elnora took a large piece of mosquito netting, and ran to the swamp. Throwing it over the top of the case, she unlocked the door. She reeled, faint with distress. The living moths that had been confined there in their fluttering to escape to night and the mates they sought not only had wrecked the other specimens of the case, but torn themselves to fringes on the pins. A third of the rarest moths of the collection for the man of India were antennaless, legless, wingless, and often headless. Elnora sobbed aloud.

"This is overwhelming," she said at last. "It is making a fatalist of me. I am beginning to think things happen as they are ordained from the beginning, this plainly indicating that there is to be no college, at least, this year, for me. My life is all mountain-top or canon. I wish some one would lead me into a few days of 'green pastures.' Last night I went to sleep on mother's arm, the moths all secured, love and college, certainties. This morning I wake to find all my hopes wrecked. I simply don't dare let mother know that instead of helping me, she has ruined my collection. Everything is gone—unless the love lasts. That actually seemed true. I believe I will go see."

The love remained. Indeed, in the overflow of the long-hardened, pent-up heart, the girl was almost suffocated with tempestuous caresses and generous offerings. Before the day was over, Elnora realized that she never had known her mother. The woman who now busily went through the cabin, her eyes bright, eager, alert, constantly planning, was a stranger. Her very face was different, while it did not seem possible that during one night the acid of twenty years could disappear from a voice and leave it sweet and pleasant.

For the next few days Elnora worked at mounting the moths her mother had taken. She had to go to the Bird Woman and tell about the disaster, but Mrs. Comstock was allowed to think that Elnora delivered the moths when she made the trip. If she had told her what actually happened, the chances were that Mrs. Comstock again would have taken possession of the Limberlost, hunting there until she replaced all the moths that had been destroyed. But Elnora knew from experience what it meant to collect such a list in pairs. It would require steady work for at least two summers to replace the lost moths. When she left the Bird Woman she went to the president of the Onabasha schools and asked him to do all in his power to secure her a room in one of the ward buildings.

The next morning the last moth was mounted, and the housework finished. Elnora said to her mother, "If you don't mind, I believe I will go into the woods pasture beside Sleepy Snake Creek and see if I can catch some dragonflies or moths."

"Wait until I get a knife and a pail and I will go along," answered Mrs. Comstock. "The dandelions are plenty tender for greens among the deep grasses, and I might just happen to see something myself. My eyes are pretty sharp."

"I wish you could realize how young you are," said Elnora. "I know women in Onabasha who are ten years older than you, yet they look twenty years younger. So could you, if you would dress your hair becomingly, and wear appropriate clothes."

"I think my hair puts me in the old woman class permanently," said Mrs. Comstock.

"Well, it doesn't!" cried Elnora. "There is a woman of twenty-eight who has hair as white as yours from sick headaches, but her face is young and beautiful. If your face would grow a little fuller and those lines would go away, you'd be lovely!"

"You little pig!" laughed Mrs. Comstock. "Any one would think you would be satisfied with having a splinter new mother, without setting up a kick on her looks, first thing. Greedy!"

"That is a good word," said Elnora. "I admit the charge. I am greedy over every wasted year. I want you young, lovely, suitably dressed and enjoying life like the other girls' mothers."

Mrs. Comstock laughed softly as she pushed back her sunbonnet so that shrubs and bushes beside the way could be scanned closely. Elnora walked ahead with a case over her shoulder, a net in her hand. Her head was bare, the rolling collar of her lavender gingham dress was cut in a V at the throat, the sleeves only reached the elbows. Every few steps she paused and examined the shrubbery carefully, while Mrs. Comstock was watching until her eyes ached, but there were no dandelions in the pail she carried.

Early June was rioting in fresh grasses, bright flowers, bird songs, and gay-winged creatures of air. Down the footpath the two went through the perfect morning, the love of God and all nature in their hearts. At last they reached the creek, following it toward the bridge. Here Mrs. Comstock found a large bed of tender dandelions and stopped to fill her pail. Then she sat on the bank, picking over the greens, while she listened to the creek softly singing its June song.

Elnora remained within calling distance, and was having good success. At last she crossed the creek, following it up to a bridge. There she began a careful examination of the under sides of the sleepers and flooring for cocoons. Mrs. Comstock could see her and the creek for several rods above. The mother sat beating the long green leaves across her hand, carefully picking out the white buds, because Elnora liked them, when a splash up the creek attracted her attention.

Around the bend came a man. He was bareheaded, dressed in a white sweater, and waders which reached his waist. He walked on the bank, only entering the water when forced. He had a queer basket strapped on his hip, and with a small rod he sent a long line spinning before him down the creek, deftly manipulating with it a little floating object. He was closer Elnora than her mother, but Mrs. Comstock thought possibly by hurrying she could remain unseen and yet warn the girl that a stranger was coming. As she approached the bridge, she caught a sapling and leaned over the water to call Elnora. With her lips parted to speak she hesitated a second to watch a sort of insect that flashed past on the water, when a splash from the man attracted the girl.

She was under the bridge, one knee planted in the embankment and a foot braced to support her. Her hair was tousled by wind and bushes, her face flushed, and she lifted her arms above her head, working to loosen a cocoon she had found. The call Mrs. Comstock had intended to utter never found voice, for as Elnora looked down at the sound, "Possibly I could get that for you," suggested the man.

Mrs. Comstock drew back. He was a young man with a wonderfully attractive face, although it was too white for robust health, broad shoulders, and slender, upright frame.

"Oh, I do hope you can!" answered Elnora. "It's quite a find! It's one of those lovely pale red cocoons described in the books. I suspect it comes from having been in a dark place and screened from the weather."

"Is that so?" cried the man. "Wait a minute. I've never seen one. I suppose it's a Cecropia, from the location."

"Of course," said Elnora. "It's so cool here the moth hasn't emerged. The cocoon is a big, baggy one, and it is as red as fox tail."

"What luck!" he cried. "Are you making a collection?"

He reeled in his line, laid his rod across a bush and climbed the embankment to Elnora's side, produced a knife and began the work of whittling a deep groove around the cocoon.

"Yes. I paid my way through the high school in Onabasha with them. Now I am starting a collection which means college."

"Onabasha!" said the man. "That is where I am visiting. Possibly you know my people—Dr. Ammon's? The doctor is my uncle. My home is in Chicago. I've been having typhoid fever, something fierce. In the hospital six weeks. Didn't gain strength right, so Uncle Doc sent for me. I am to live out of doors all summer, and exercise until I get in condition again. Do you know my uncle?"

"Yes. He is Aunt Margaret's doctor, and he would be ours, only we are never ill."

"Well, you look it!" said the man, appraising Elnora at a glance.

"Strangers always mention it," sighed Elnora. "I wonder how it would seem to be a pale, languid lady and ride in a carriage."

"Ask me!" laughed the man. "It feels like the—dickens! I'm so proud of my feet. It's quite a trick to stand on them now. I have to keep out of the water all I can and stop to baby every half-mile. But with interesting outdoor work I'll be myself in a week."

"Do you call that work?" Elnora indicated the creek.

"I do, indeed! Nearly three miles, banks too soft to brag on and never a strike. Wouldn't you call that hard labour?"

"Yes," laughed Elnora. "Work at which you might kill yourself and never get a fish. Did any one tell you there were trout in Sleepy Snake Creek?"

"Uncle said I could try."

"Oh, you can," said Elnora. "You can try no end, but you'll never get a trout. This is too far south and too warm for them. If you sit on the bank and use worms you might catch some perch or catfish."

"But that isn't exercise."

"Well, if you only want exercise, go right on fishing. You will have a creel full of invisible results every night."

"I object," said the man emphatically. He stopped work again and studied Elnora. Even the watching mother could not blame him. In the shade of the bridge Elnora's bright head and her lavender dress made a picture worthy of much contemplation.

"I object!" repeated the man. "When I work I want to see results. I'd rather exercise sawing wood, making one pile grow little and the other big than to cast all day and catch nothing because there is not a fish to take. Work for work's sake doesn't appeal to me."

He digged the groove around the cocoon with skilled hand. "Now there is some fun in this!" he said. "It's going to be a fair job to cut it out, but when it comes, it is not only beautiful, but worth a price; it will help you on your way. I think I'll put up my rod and hunt moths. That would be something like! Don't you want help?"

Elnora parried the question. "Have you ever hunted moths, Mr. Ammon?"

"Enough to know the ropes in taking them and to distinguish the commonest ones. I go wild on Catocalæ. There's too many of them, all too much alike for Philip, but I know all these fellows. One flew into my room when I was about ten years old, and we thought it a miracle. None of us ever had seen one so we took it over to the museum to Dr. Dorsey. He said they were common enough, but we didn't see them because they flew at night. He showed me the museum collection, and I was so interested I took mine back home and started to hunt them. Every year after that we went to our cottage a month earlier, so I could find them, and all my family helped. I stuck to it until I went to college. Then, keeping the little moths out of the big ones was too much for the mater, so father advised that I donate mine to the museum. He bought a fine case for them with my name on it, which constitutes my sole contribution to science. I know enough to help you all right."

"Aren't you going north this year?"

"All depends on how this fever leaves me. Uncle says the nights are too cold and the days too hot there for me. He thinks I had better stay in an even temperature until I am strong again. I am going to stick pretty close to him until I know I am. I wouldn't admit it to any one at home, but I was almost gone. I don't believe anything can eat up nerve much faster than the burning of a slow fever. No, thanks, I have enough. I stay with Uncle Doc, so if I feel it coming again he can do something quickly."

"I don't blame you," said Elnora. "I never have been sick, but it must be dreadful. I am afraid you are tiring yourself over that. Let me take the knife awhile."

"Oh, it isn't so bad as that! I wouldn't be wading creeks if it were. I only need a few more days to get steady on my feet again. I'll soon have this out."

"It is kind of you to get it," said Elnora. "I should have had to peel it, which would spoil the cocoon for a specimen and ruin the moth."

"You haven't said yet whether I may help you while I am here."

Elnora hesitated.

"You better say 'yes,'" he persisted. "It would be a real kindness. It would keep me outdoors all day and give an incentive to work. I'm good at it. I'll show you if I am not in a week or so. I can 'sugar,' manipulate lights, and mirrors, and all the expert methods. I'll wager, moths are numerous in the old swamp over there."

"They are," said Elnora. "Most I have I took there. A few nights ago my mother caught a number, but we don't dare go alone."

"All the more reason why you need me. Where do you live? I can't get an answer from you, I'll go tell your mother who I am and ask her if I may help you. I warn you, young lady, I have a very effective way with mothers. They almost never turn me down."

"Then it's probable you will have a new experience when you meet mine," said Elnora. "She never was known to do what any one expected she surely would."

The cocoon came loose. Philip Ammon stepped down the embankment turning to offer his hand to Elnora. She ran down as she would have done alone, and taking the cocoon turned it end for end to learn if the imago it contained were alive. Then Ammon took back the cocoon to smooth the edges. Mrs. Comstock gave them one long look as they stood there, and returned to her dandelions. While she worked she paused occasionally, listening intently. Presently they came down the creek, the man carrying the cocoon as if it were a jewel, while Elnora made her way along the bank, taking a lesson in casting. Her face was flushed with excitement, her eyes shining, the bushes taking liberties with her hair. For a picture of perfect loveliness she scarcely could have been surpassed, and the eyes of Philip Ammon seemed to be in working order.

"Moth-er!" called Elnora.

There was an undulant, caressing sweetness in the girl's voice, as she sung out the call in perfect confidence that it would bring a loving answer, that struck deep in Mrs. Comstock's heart. She never had heard that word so pronounced before and a lump arose in her throat.

"Here!" she answered, still cleaning dandelions.

"Mother, this is Mr. Philip Ammon, of Chicago," said Elnora. "He has been ill and he is staying with Dr. Ammon in Onabasha. He came down the creek fishing and cut this cocoon from under the bridge for me. He feels that it would be better to hunt moths than to fish, until he is well. What do you think about it?"

Philip Ammon extended his hand. "I am glad to know you," he said.

"You may take the hand-shaking for granted," replied Mrs. Comstock. "Dandelions have a way of making fingers sticky, and I like to know a man before I take his hand, anyway. That introduction seems mighty comprehensive on your part, but it still leaves me unclassified. My name is Comstock."

Philip Ammon bowed.

"I am sorry to hear you have been sick," said Mrs. Comstock. "But if people will live where they have such vile water as they do in Chicago, I don't see what else they are to expect."

Philip studied her intently.

"I am sure I didn't have a fever on purpose," he said.

"You do seem a little wobbly on your legs," she observed. "Maybe you had better sit and rest while I finish these greens. It's late for the genuine article, but in the shade, among long grass they are still tender."

"May I have a leaf?" he asked, reaching for one as he sat on the bank, looking from the little creek at his feet, away through the dim cool spaces of the June forest on the opposite side. He drew a deep breath. "Glory, but this is good after almost two months inside hospital walls!"

He stretched on the grass and lay gazing up at the leaves, occasionally asking the interpretation of a bird note or the origin of an unfamiliar forest voice. Elnora began helping with the dandelions.

"Another, please," said the young man, holding out his hand.

"Do you suppose this is the kind of grass Nebuchadnezzar ate?" Elnora asked, giving the leaf.

"He knew a good thing if it is."

"Oh, you should taste dandelions boiled with bacon and served with mother's cornbread."

"Don't! My appetite is twice my size now. While it is—how far is it to Onabasha, shortest cut?"

"Three miles."

The man lay in perfect content, nibbling leaves.

"This surely is a treat," he said. "No wonder you find good hunting here. There seems to be foliage for almost every kind of caterpillar. But I suppose you have to exchange for northern species and Pacific Coast kinds?"

"Yes. And every one wants Regalis in trade. I never saw the like. They consider a Cecropia or a Polyphemus an insult, and a Luna is barely acceptable."

"What authorities have you?"

Elnora began to name text-books which started a discussion. Mrs. Comstock listened. She cleaned dandelions with greater deliberation than they ever before were examined. In reality she was taking stock of the young man's long, well-proportioned frame, his strong hands, his smooth, fine-textured skin, his thick shock of dark hair, and making mental notes of his simple manly speech and the fact that he evidently did know much about moths. It pleased her to think that if he had been a neighbour boy who had lain beside her every day of his life while she worked, he could have been no more at home. She liked the things he said, but she was proud that Elnora had a ready answer which always seemed appropriate.

At last Mrs. Comstock finished the greens.

"You are three miles from the city and less than a mile from where we live," she said. "If you will tell me what you dare eat, I suspect you had best go home with us and rest until the cool of the day before you start back. Probably some one that you can ride in with will be passing before evening."

"That is mighty kind of you," said Philip. "I think I will. It doesn't matter so much what I eat, the point is that I must be moderate. I am hungry all the time."

"Then we will go," said Mrs. Comstock, "and we will not allow you to make yourself sick with us."

Philip Ammon arose: picking up the pail of greens and his fishing rod, he stood waiting. Elnora led the way. Mrs. Comstock motioned Philip to follow and she walked in the rear. The girl carried the cocoon and the box of moths she had taken, searching every step for more. The young man frequently set down his load to join in the pursuit of a dragonfly or moth, while Mrs. Comstock watched the proceedings with sharp eyes. Every time Philip picked up the pail of greens she struggled to suppress a smile.

Elnora proceeded slowly, chattering about everything beside the trail. Philip was interested in all the objects she pointed out, noticing several things which escaped her. He carried the greens as casually when they took a short cut down the roadway as on the trail. When Elnora turned toward the gate of her home Philip Ammon stopped, took a long look at the big hewed log cabin, the vines which clambered over it, the flower garden ablaze with beds of bright bloom interspersed with strawberries and tomatoes, the trees of the forest rising north and west like a green wall and exclaimed: "How beautiful!"

Mrs. Comstock was pleased. "If you think that," she said, "perhaps you will understand how, in all this present-day rush to be modern, I have preferred to remain as I began. My husband and I took up this land, and enough trees to build the cabin, stable, and outbuildings are nearly all we ever cut. Of course, if he had lived, I suppose we should have kept up with our neighbours. I hear considerable about the value of the land, the trees which are on it, and the oil which is supposed to be under it, but as yet I haven't brought myself to change anything. So we stand for one of the few remaining homes of first settlers in this region. Come in. You are very welcome to what we have."

Mrs. Comstock stepped forward and took the lead. She had a bowl of soft water and a pair of boots to offer for the heavy waders, for outer comfort, a glass of cold buttermilk and a bench on which to rest, in the circular arbour until dinner was ready. Philip Ammon splashed in the water. He followed to the stable and exchanged boots there. He was ravenous for the buttermilk, and when he stretched on the bench in the arbour the flickering patches of sunlight so tantalized his tired eyes, while the bees made such splendid music, he was soon sound asleep. When Elnora and her mother came out with a table they stood a short time looking at him. It is probable Mrs. Comstock voiced a united thought when she said: "What a refined, decent looking young man! How proud his mother must be of him! We must be careful what we let him eat."

Then they returned to the kitchen where Mrs. Comstock proceeded to be careful. She broiled ham of her own sugar-curing, creamed potatoes, served asparagus on toast, and made a delicious strawberry shortcake. As she cooked dandelions with bacon, she feared to serve them to him, so she made an excuse that it took too long to prepare them, blanched some and made a salad. When everything was ready she touched Philip's sleeve.

"Best have something to eat, lad, before you get too hungry," she said.

"Please hurry!" he begged laughingly as he held a plate toward her to be filled. "I thought I had enough self-restraint to start out alone, but I see I was mistaken. If you would allow me, just now, I am afraid I should start a fever again. I never did smell food so good as this. It's mighty kind of you to take me in. I hope I will be man enough in a few days to do something worth while in return."

Spots of sunshine fell on the white cloth and blue china, the bees and an occasional stray butterfly came searching for food. A rose-breasted grosbeak, released from a three hours' siege of brooding, while his independent mate took her bath and recreation, mounted the top branch of a maple in the west woods from which he serenaded the dinner party with a joyful chorus in celebration of his freedom. Philip's eyes strayed to the beautiful cabin, to the mixture of flowers and vegetables stretching down to the road, and to the singing bird with his red-splotched breast of white and he said: "I can't realize now that I ever lay in ice packs in a hospital. How I wish all the sick folks could come here to grow strong!"

The grosbeak sang on, a big Turnus butterfly sailed through the arbour and poised over the table. Elnora held up a lump of sugar and the butterfly, clinging to her fingers, tasted daintily. With eager eyes and parted lips, the girl held steadily. When at last it wavered away, "That made a picture!" said Philip. "Ask me some other time how I lost my illusions concerning butterflies. I always thought of them in connection with sunshine, flower pollen, and fruit nectar, until one sad day."

"I know!" laughed Elnora. "I've seen that, too, but it didn't destroy any illusion for me. I think quite as much of the butterflies as ever."

Then they talked of flowers, moths, dragonflies, Indian relics, and all the natural wonders the swamp afforded, straying from those subjects to books and school work. When they cleared the table Philip assisted, carrying several tray loads to the kitchen. He and Elnora mounted specimens while Mrs Comstock washed the dishes. Then she came out with a ruffle she was embroidering.

"I wonder if I did not see a picture of you in Onabasha last night," Philip said to Elnora. "Aunt Anna took me to call on Miss Brownlee. She was showing me her crowd—of course, it was you! But it didn't half do you justice, although it was the nearest human of any of them. Miss Brownlee is very fond of you. She said the finest things."

Then they talked of Commencement, and at last Philip said he must go or his friends would become anxious about him.

Mrs. Comstock brought him a blue bowl of creamy milk and a plate of bread. She stopped a passing team and secured a ride to the city for him, as his exercise of the morning had been too violent, and he was forced to admit he was tired.

"May I come to-morrow afternoon and hunt moths awhile?" he asked Mrs. Comstock as he arose. "We will 'sugar' a tree and put a light beside it, if I can get stuff to make the preparation. Possibly we can take some that way. I always enjoy moth hunting, I'd like to help Miss Elnora, and it would be a charity to me. I've got to remain outdoors some place, and I'm quite sure I'd get well faster here than anywhere else. Please say I may come."

"I have no objections, if Elnora really would like help," said Mrs. Comstock.

In her heart she wished he would not come. She wanted her newly found treasure all to herself, for a time, at least. But Elnora's were eager, shining eyes. She thought it would be splendid to have help, and great fun to try book methods for taking moths, so it was arranged. As Philip rode away, Mrs. Comstock's eyes followed him. "What a nice young man!" she said.

"He seems fine," agreed Elnora.

"He comes of a good family, too. I've often heard of his father. He is a great lawyer."

"I am glad he likes it here. I need help. Possibly——"

"Possibly what?"

"We can find many moths."

"What did he mean about the butterflies?"

"That he always had connected them with sunshine, flowers, and fruits, and thought of them as the most exquisite of creations; then one day he found some clustering thickly over carrion."

"Come to think of it, I have seen butterflies——"

"So had he," laughed Elnora. "And that is what he meant."

CHAPTER XIV

WHEREIN A NEW POSITION IS
TENDERED ELNORA, AND PHILIP
AMMON IS SHOWN LIMBERLOST
VIOLETS

The next morning Mrs. Comstock called to Elnora, "The mail carrier stopped at our box."

Elnora ran down the walk and came back carrying an official letter. She tore it open and read:

MY DEAR MISS COMSTOCK:

At the weekly meeting of the Onabasha School Board last night, it was decided to add the position of Lecturer on Natural History to our corps of city teachers. It will be the duty of this person to spend two hours a week in each of the grade schools exhibiting and explaining specimens of the most prominent objects in nature: animals, birds, insects, flowers, vines, shrubs, bushes, and trees. These specimens and lectures should be appropriate to the seasons and the comprehension of the grades. This position was unanimously voted to you. I think you will find the work delightful and much easier than the routine grind of the other teachers. It is my advice that you accept and begin to prepare yourself at once. Your salary will be $750 a year, and you will be allowed $200 for expenses in procuring specimens and books. Let us know at once if you want the position, as it is going to be difficult to fill satisfactorily if you do not.

Very truly yours,

DAVID THOMPSON, President, Onabasha Schools.

"I hardly understand," marvelled Mrs. Comstock.

"It is a new position. They never have had anything like it before. I suspect it arose from the help I've been giving the grade teachers in their nature work. They are trying to teach the children something, and half the instructors don't know a blue jay from a king-fisher, a beech leaf from an elm, or a wasp from a hornet."

"Well, do you?" anxiously inquired Mrs. Comstock.

"Indeed, I do!" laughed Elnora, "and several other things beside. When Freckles bequeathed me the swamp, he gave me a bigger inheritance than he knew. While you have thought I was wandering aimlessly, I have been following a definite plan, studying hard, and storing up the stuff that will earn these seven hundred and fifty dollars. Mother dear, I am going to accept this, of course. The work will be a delight. I'd love it most of anything in teaching. You must help me. We must find nests, eggs, leaves, queer formations in plants and rare flowers. I must have flower boxes made for each of the rooms and filled with wild things. I should begin to gather specimens this very day."

Elnora's face was flushed and her eyes bright.

"Oh, what great work that will be!" she cried. "You must go with me so you can see the little faces when I tell them how the goldfinch builds its nest, and how the bees make honey."

So Elnora and her mother went into the woods behind the cabin to study nature.

"I think," said Elnora, "the idea is to begin with fall things in the fall, keeping to the seasons throughout the year."

"What are fall things?" inquired Mrs. Comstock.

"Oh, fringed gentians, asters, ironwort, every fall flower, leaves from every tree and vine, what makes them change colour, abandoned bird nests, winter quarters of caterpillars and insects, what becomes of the butterflies and grasshoppers—myriads of stuff. I shall have to be very wise to select the things it will be most beneficial for the children to learn."

"Can I really help you?" Mrs. Comstock's strong face was pathetic.

"Indeed, yes!" cried Elnora. "I never can get through it alone. There will be an immense amount of work connected with securing and preparing specimens."

Mrs. Comstock lifted her head proudly and began doing business at once. Her sharp eyes ranged from earth to heaven. She investigated everything, asking innumerable questions. At noon Mrs. Comstock took the specimens they had collected, and went to prepare dinner, while Elnora followed the woods down to the Sintons' to show her letter.

She had to explain what became of her moths, and why college would have to be abandoned for that year, but Margaret and Wesley vowed not to tell. Wesley waved the letter excitedly, explaining it to Margaret as if it were a personal possession. Margaret was deeply impressed, while Billy volunteered first aid in gathering material.

"Now anything you want in the ground, Snap can dig it out," he said. "Uncle Wesley and I found a hole three times as big as Snap, that he dug at the roots of a tree."

"We will train him to hunt pupae cases," said Elnora.

"Are you going to the woods this afternoon?" asked Billy.

"Yes," answered Elnora. "Dr. Ammon's nephew from Chicago is visiting in Onabasha. He is going to show me how men put some sort of compound on a tree, hang a light beside it, and take moths that way. It will be interesting to watch and learn."

"May I come?" asked Billy.

"Of course you may come!" answered Elnora.

"Is this nephew of Dr. Ammon a young man?" inquired Margaret.

"About twenty-six, I should think," said Elnora. "He said he had been out of college and at work in his father's law office three years."

"Does he seem nice?" asked Margaret, and Wesley smiled.

"Finest kind of a person," said Elnora. "He can teach me so much. It is very interesting to hear him talk. He knows considerable about moths that will be a help to me. He had a fever and he has to stay outdoors until he grows strong again."

"Billy, I guess you better help me this afternoon," said Margaret. "Maybe Elnora had rather not bother with you."

"There's no reason on earth why Billy should not come!" cried Elnora, and Wesley smiled again.

"I must hurry home or I won't be ready," she added.

Hastening down the road she entered the cabin, her face glowing.

"I thought you never would come," said Mrs. Comstock. "If you don't hurry Mr. Ammon will be here before you are dressed."

"I forgot about him until just now," said Elnora. "I am not going to dress. He's not coming to visit. We are only going to the woods for more specimens. I can't wear anything that requires care. The limbs take the most dreadful liberties with hair and clothing."

Mrs. Comstock opened her lips, looked at Elnora and closed them. In her heart she was pleased that the girl was so interested in her work that she had forgotten Philip Ammon's coming. But it did seem to her that such a pleasant young man should have been greeted by a girl in a fresh dress. "If she isn't disposed to primp at the coming of a man, heaven forbid that I should be the one to start her," thought Mrs. Comstock.

Philip came whistling down the walk between the cinnamon pinks, pansies, and strawberries. He carried several packages, while his face flushed with more colour than on the previous day.

"Only see what has happened to me!" cried Elnora, offering her letter.

"I'll wager I know!" answered Philip. "Isn't it great! Every one in Onabasha is talking about it. At last there is something new under the sun. All of them are pleased. They think you'll make a big success. This will give an incentive to work. In a few days more I'll be myself again, and we'll overturn the fields and woods around here."

He went on to congratulate Mrs. Comstock.

"Aren't you proud of her, though?" he asked. "You should hear what folks are saying! They say she created the necessity for the position, and every one seems to feel that it is a necessity. Now, if she succeeds, and she will, all of the other city schools will have such departments, and first thing you know she will have made the whole world a little better. Let me rest a few seconds; my feet are acting up again. Then we will cook the moth compound and put it to cool."

He laughed as he sat breathing shortly.

"It doesn't seem possible that a fellow could lose his strength like this. My knees are actually trembling, but I'll be all right in a minute. Uncle Doc said I could come. I told him how you took care of me, and he said I would be safe here."

Then he began unwrapping packages and explaining to Mrs. Comstock how to cook the compound to attract the moths. He followed her into the kitchen, kindled the fire, and stirred the preparation as he talked. While the mixture cooled, he and Elnora walked through the vegetable garden behind the cabin and strayed from there into the woods.

"What about college?" he asked. "Miss Brownlee said you were going."

"I had hoped to," replied Elnora, "but I had a streak of dreadful luck, so I'll have to wait until next year. If you won't speak of it, I'll tell you."

Philip promised, so Elnora recited the history of the Yellow Emperor. She was so interested in doing the Emperor justice she did not notice how many personalities went into the story. A few pertinent questions told him the remainder. He looked at the girl in wonder. In face and form she was as lovely as any one of her age and type he ever had seen. Her school work far surpassed that of most girls of her age he knew. She differed in other ways. This vast store of learning she had gathered from field and forest was a wealth of attraction no other girl possessed. Her frank, matter-of-fact manner was an inheritance from her mother, but there was something more. Once, as they talked he thought "sympathy" was the word to describe it and again "comprehension." She seemed to possess a large sense of brotherhood for all human and animate creatures. She spoke to him as if she had known him all her life. She talked to the grosbeak in exactly the same manner, as she laid strawberries and potato bugs on the fence for his family. She did not swerve an inch from her way when a snake slid past her, while the squirrels came down from the trees and took corn from her fingers. She might as well have been a boy, so lacking was she in any touch of feminine coquetry toward him. He studied her wonderingly. As they went along the path they reached a large slime-covered pool surrounded by decaying stumps and logs thickly covered with water hyacinths and blue flags. Philip stopped.

"Is that the place?" he asked.

Elnora assented. "The doctor told you?"

"Yes. It was tragic. Is that pool really bottomless?"

"So far as we ever have been able to discover."

Philip stood looking at the water, while the long, sweet grasses, thickly sprinkled with blue flag bloom, over which wild bees clambered, swayed around his feet. Then he turned to the girl. She had worked hard. The same lavender dress she had worn the previous day clung to her in limp condition. But she was as evenly coloured and of as fine grain as a wild rose petal, her hair was really brown, but never was such hair touched with a redder glory, while her heavy arching brows added a look of strength to her big gray-blue eyes.

"And you were born here?"

He had not intended to voice that thought.

"Yes," she said, looking into his eyes. "Just in time to prevent my mother from saving the life of my father. She came near never forgiving me."

"Ah, cruel!" cried Philip.

"I find much in life that is cruel, from our standpoints," said Elnora. "It takes the large wisdom of the Unfathomable, the philosophy of the Almighty, to endure some of it. But there is always right somewhere, and at last it seems to come."

"Will it come to you?" asked Philip, who found himself deeply affected.

"It has come," said the girl serenely. "It came a week ago. It came in fullest measure when my mother ceased to regret that I had been born. Now, work that I love has come—that should constitute happiness. A little farther along is my violet bed. I want you to see it."

As Philip Ammon followed he definitely settled upon the name of the unusual feature of Elnora's face. It should be called "experience." She had known bitter experiences early in life. Suffering had been her familiar more than joy. He watched her earnestly, his heart deeply moved. She led him into a swampy half-open space in the woods, stopped and stepped aside. He uttered a cry of surprised delight.

A few decaying logs were scattered around, the grass grew in tufts long and fine. Blue flags waved, clusters of cowslips nodded gold heads, but the whole earth was purple with a thick blanket of violets nodding from stems a foot in length. Elnora knelt and slipping her fingers between the leaves and grasses to the roots, gathered a few violets and gave them to Philip.

"Can your city greenhouses surpass them?" she asked.

He sat on a log to examine the blooms.

"They are superb!" he said. "I never saw such length of stem or such rank leaves, while the flowers are the deepest blue, the truest violet I ever saw growing wild. They are coloured exactly like the eyes of the girl I am going to marry."

Elnora handed him several others to add to those he held. "She must have wonderful eyes," she commented.

"No other blue eyes are quite so beautiful," he said. "In fact, she is altogether lovely."

"Is it customary for a man to think the girl he is going to marry lovely? I wonder if I should find her so."

"You would," said Philip. "No one ever fails to. She is tall as you, very slender, but perfectly rounded; you know about her eyes; her hair is black and wavy—while her complexion is clear and flushed with red."

"Why, she must be the most beautiful girl in the whole world!" she cried.

"No, indeed!" he said. "She is not a particle better looking in her way than you are in yours. She is a type of dark beauty, but you are equally as perfect. She is unusual in her combination of black hair and violet eyes, although every one thinks them black at a little distance. You are quite as unusual with your fair face, black brows, and brown hair; indeed, I know many people who would prefer your bright head to her dark one. It's all a question of taste—and being engaged to the girl," he added.

"That would be likely to prejudice one," laughed Elnora.

"Edith has a birthday soon; if these last will you let me have a box of them to send her?"

"I will help gather and pack them for you, so they will carry nicely. Does she hunt moths with you?"

Back went Philip Ammon's head in a gale of laughter.

"No!" he cried. "She says they are 'creepy.' She would go into a spasm if she were compelled to touch those caterpillars I saw you handling yesterday."

"Why would she?" marvelled Elnora. "Haven't you told her that they are perfectly clean, helpless, and harmless as so much animate velvet?"

"No, I have not told her. She wouldn't care enough about caterpillars to listen."

"In what is she interested?"

"What interests Edith Carr? Let me think! First, I believe she takes pride in being a little handsomer and better dressed than any girl of her set. She is interested in having a beautiful home, fine appointments, in being petted, praised, and the acknowledged leader of society.

"She likes to find new things which amuse her, and to always and in all circumstances have her own way about everything."

"Good gracious!" cried Elnora, staring at him. "But what does she do? How does she spend her time?"

"Spend her time!" repeated Philip. "Well, she would call that a joke. Her days are never long enough. There is endless shopping, to find the pretty things; regular visits to the dressmakers, calls, parties, theatres, entertainments. She is always rushed. I never am able to be with her half as much as I would like."

"But I mean work," persisted Elnora. "In what is she interested that is useful to the world?"

"Me!" cried Philip promptly.

"I can understand that," laughed Elnora. "What I can't understand is how you can be in——" She stopped in confusion, but she saw that he had finished the sentence as she had intended. "I beg your pardon!" she cried. "I didn't intend to say that. But I cannot understand these people I hear about who live only for their own amusement. Perhaps it is very great; I'll never have a chance to know. To me, it seems the only pleasure in this world worth having is the joy we derive from living for those we love, and those we can help. I hope you are not angry with me."

Philip sat silently looking far away, with deep thought in his eyes.

"You are angry," faltered Elnora.

His look came back to her as she knelt before him among the flowers and he gazed at her steadily.

"No doubt I should be," he said, "but the fact is I am not. I cannot understand a life purely for personal pleasure myself. But she is only a girl, and this is her playtime. When she is a woman in her own home, then she will be different, will she not?"

Elnora never resembled her mother so closely as when she answered that question.

"I would have to be well acquainted with her to know, but I should hope so. To make a real home for a tired business man is a very different kind of work from that required to be a leader of society. It demands different talent and education. Of course, she means to change, or she would not have promised to make a home for you. I suspect our dope is cool now, let's go try for some butterflies."

As they went along the path together Elnora talked of many things but Philip answered absently. Evidently he was thinking of something else. But the moth bait recalled him and he was ready for work as they made their way back to the woods. He wanted to try the Limberlost, but Elnora was firm about remaining on home ground. She did not tell him that lights hung in the swamp would be a signal to call up a band of men whose presence she dreaded. So they started, Ammon carrying the dope, Elnora the net, Billy and Mrs. Comstock following with cyanide boxes and lanterns.

First they tried for butterflies and captured several fine ones without trouble. They also called swarms of ants, bees, beetles, and flies. When it grew dusk, Mrs. Comstock and Philip went to prepare supper. Elnora and Billy remained until the butterflies disappeared. Then they lighted the lanterns, repainted the trees and followed the home trail.

"Do you 'spec you'll get just a lot of moths?" asked Billy, as he walked beside Elnora.

"I am sure I hardly know," said the girl. "This is a new way for me. Perhaps they will come to the lights, but few moths eat; and I have some doubt about those which the lights attract settling on the right trees. Maybe the smell of that dope will draw them. Between us, Billy, I think I like my old way best. If I can find a hidden moth, slip up and catch it unawares, or take it in full flight, it's my captive, and I can keep it until it dies naturally. But this way you seem to get it under false pretences, it has no chance, and it will probably ruin its wings struggling for freedom before morning."

"Well, any moth ought to be proud to be taken anyway, by you," said Billy. "Just look what you do! You can make everybody love them. People even quit hating caterpillars when they see you handle them and hear you tell all about them. You must have some to show people how they are. It's not like killing things to see if you can, or because you want to eat them, the way most men kill birds. I think it is right for you to take enough for collections, to show city people, and to illustrate the Bird Woman's books. You go on and take them! The moths don't care. They're glad to have you. They like it!"

"Billy, I see your future," said Elnora. "We will educate you and send you up to Mr. Ammon to make a great lawyer. You'd beat the world as a special pleader. You actually make me feel that I am doing the moths a kindness to take them."

"And so you are!" cried Billy. "Why, just from what you have taught them Uncle Wesley and Aunt Margaret never think of killing a caterpillar until they look whether it's the beautiful June moth kind, or the horrid tent ones. That's what you can do. You go straight ahead!"

"Billy, you are a jewel!" cried Elnora, throwing her arm across his shoulders as they came down the path.

"My, I was scared!" said Billy with a deep breath.

"Scared?" questioned Elnora.

"Yes sir-ee! Aunt Margaret scared me. May I ask you a question?"

"Of course, you may!"

"Is that man going to be your beau?"

"Billy! No! What made you think such a thing?"

"Aunt Margaret said likely he would fall in love with you, and you wouldn't want me around any more. Oh, but I was scared! It isn't so, is it?"

"Indeed, no!"

"I am your beau, ain't I?"

"Surely you are!" said Elnora, tightening her arm.

"I do hope Aunt Kate has ginger cookies," said Billy with a little skip of delight.

CHAPTER XV

WHEREIN MRS. COMSTOCK FACES THE
ALMIGHTY, AND PHILIP AMMON WRITES
A LETTER

Mrs. Comstock and Elnora were finishing breakfast the following morning when they heard a cheery whistle down the road. Elnora with surprised eyes looked at her mother.

"Could that be Mr. Ammon?" she questioned.

"I did not expect him so soon," commented Mrs. Comstock.

It was sunrise, but the musician was Philip Ammon. He appeared stronger than on yesterday.

"I hope I am not too early," he said. "I am consumed with anxiety to learn if we have made a catch. If we have, we should beat the birds to it. I promised Uncle Doc to put on my waders and keep dry for a few days yet, when I go to the woods. Let's hurry! I am afraid of crows. There might be a rare moth."

The sun was topping the Limberlost when they started. As they neared the place Philip stopped.

"Now we must use great caution," he said. "The lights and the odours always attract numbers that don't settle on the baited trees. Every bush, shrub, and limb may hide a specimen we want."

So they approached with much care.

"There is something, anyway!" cried Philip.

"There are moths! I can see them!" exulted Elnora.

"Those you see are fast enough. It's the ones for which you must search that will escape. The grasses are dripping, and I have boots, so you look beside the path while I take the outside," suggested Ammon.

Mrs. Comstock wanted to hunt moths, but she was timid about making a wrong movement, so she wisely sat on a log and watched Philip and Elnora to learn how they proceeded. Back in the deep woods a hermit thrush was singing his chant to the rising sun. Orioles were sowing the pure, sweet air with notes of gold, poured out while on wing. The robins were only chirping now, for their morning songs had awakened all the other birds an hour ago. Scolding red-wings tilted on half the bushes. Excepting late species of haws, tree bloom was almost gone, but wild flowers made the path border and all the wood floor a riot of colour. Elnora, born among such scenes, worked eagerly, but to the city man, recently from a hospital, they seemed too good to miss. He frequently stooped to examine a flower face, paused to listen intently to the thrush or lifted his head to see the gold flash which accompanied the oriole's trailing notes. So Elnora uttered the first cry, as she softly lifted branches and peered among the grasses.

"My find!" she called. "Bring the box, mother!"

Philip came hurrying also. When they reached her she stood on the path holding a pair of moths. Her eyes were wide with excitement, her cheeks pink, her red lips parted, and on the hand she held out to them clung a pair of delicate blue-green moths, with white bodies, and touches of lavender and straw colour. All around her lay flower-brocaded grasses, behind the deep green background of the forest, while the sun slowly sifted gold from heaven to burnish her hair. Mrs. Comstock heard a sharp breath behind her.

"Oh, what a picture!" exulted Philip at her shoulder. "She is absolutely and altogether lovely! I'd give a small fortune for that faithfully set on canvas!"

He picked the box from Mrs. Comstock's fingers and slowly advanced with it. Elnora held down her hand and transferred the moths. Philip closed the box carefully, but the watching mother saw that his eyes were following the girl's face. He was not making the slightest attempt to conceal his admiration.

"I wonder if a woman ever did anything lovelier than to find a pair of Luna moths on a forest path, early on a perfect June morning," he said to Mrs. Comstock, when he returned the box.

She glanced at Elnora who was intently searching the bushes.

"Look here, young man," said Mrs. Comstock. "You seem to find that girl of mine about right."

"I could suggest no improvement," said Philip. "I never saw a more attractive girl anywhere. She seems absolutely perfect to me."

"Then suppose you don't start any scheme calculated to spoil her!" proposed Mrs. Comstock dryly. "I don't think you can, or that any man could, but I'm not taking any risks. You asked to come here to help in this work. We are both glad to have you, if you confine yourself to work; but it's the least you can do to leave us as you find us."

"I beg your pardon!" said Philip. "I intended no offence. I admire her as I admire any perfect creation."

"And nothing in all this world spoils the average girl so quickly and so surely," said Mrs. Comstock. She raised her voice. "Elnora, fasten up that tag of hair over your left ear. These bushes muss you so you remind me of a sheep poking its nose through a hedge fence."

Mrs. Comstock started down the path toward the log again, when she reached it she called sharply: "Elnora, come here! I believe I have found something myself."

The "something" was a Citheronia Regalis which had emerged from its case on the soft earth under the log. It climbed up the wood, its stout legs dragging a big pursy body, while it wildly flapped tiny wings the size of a man's thumb-nail. Elnora gave one look and a cry which brought Philip.

"That's the rarest moth in America!" he announced. "Mrs. Comstock, you've gone up head. You can put that in a box with a screen cover to-night, and attract half a dozen, possibly."

"Is it rare, Elnora?" inquired Mrs. Comstock, as if no one else knew.

"It surely is," answered Elnora. "If we can find it a mate to-night, it will lay from two hundred and fifty to three hundred eggs to-morrow. With any luck at all I can raise two hundred caterpillars from them. I did once before. And they are worth a dollar apiece."

"Was the one I killed like that?"

"No. That was a different moth, but its life processes were the same as this. The Bird Woman calls this the King of the Poets."

"Why does she?"

"Because it is named for Citheron who was a poet, and regalis refers to a king. You mustn't touch it or you may stunt wing development. You watch and don't let that moth out of sight, or anything touch it. When the wings are expanded and hardened we will put it in a box."

"I am afraid it will race itself to death," objected Mrs. Comstock.

"That's a part of the game," said Philip. "It is starting circulation now. When the right moment comes, it will stop and expand its wings. If you watch closely you can see them expand."

Presently the moth found a rough projection of bark and clung with its feet, back down, its wings hanging. The body was an unusual orange red, the tiny wings were gray, striped with the red and splotched here and there with markings of canary yellow. Mrs. Comstock watched breathlessly. Presently she slipped from the log and knelt to secure a better view.

"Are its wings developing?" called Elnora.

"They are growing larger and the markings coming stronger every minute."

"Let's watch, too," said Elnora to Philip.

They came and looked over Mrs. Comstock's shoulder. Lower drooped the gay wings, wider they spread, brighter grew the markings as if laid off in geometrical patterns. They could hear Mrs. Comstock's tense breath and see her absorbed expression.

"Young people," she said solemnly, "if your studying science and the elements has ever led you to feel that things just happen, kind of evolve by chance, as it were, this sight will be good for you. Maybe earth and air accumulate, but it takes the wisdom of the Almighty God to devise the wing of a moth. If there ever was a miracle, this whole process is one. Now, as I understand it, this creature is going to keep on spreading those wings, until they grow to size and harden to strength sufficient to bear its body. Then it flies away, mates with its kind, lays its eggs on the leaves of a certain tree, and the eggs hatch tiny caterpillars which eat just that kind of leaves, and the worms grow and grow, and take on different forms and colours until at last they are big caterpillars six inches long, with large horns. Then they burrow into the earth, build a water-proof house around themselves from material which is inside them, and lie through rain and freezing cold for months. A year from egg laying they come out like this, and begin the process all over again. They don't eat, they don't see distinctly, they live but a few days, and fly only at night; then they drop off easy, but the process goes on."

A shivering movement went over the moth. The wings drooped and spread wider. Mrs. Comstock sank into soft awed tones.

"There never was a moment in my life," she said, "when I felt so in the Presence, as I do now. I feel as if the Almighty were so real, and so near, that I could reach out and touch Him, as I could this wonderful work of His, if I dared. I feel like saying to Him: 'To the extent of my brain power I realize Your presence, and all it is in me to comprehend of Your power. Help me to learn, even this late, the lessons of Your wonderful creations. Help me to unshackle and expand my soul to the fullest realization of Your wonders. Almighty God, make me bigger, make me broader!'"

The moth climbed to the end of the projection, up it a little way, then suddenly reversed its wings, turned the hidden sides out and dropped them beside its abdomen, like a large fly. The upper side of the wings, thus exposed, was far richer colour, more exquisite texture than the under, and they slowly half lifted and drooped again. Mrs. Comstock turned her face to Philip.

"Am I an old fool, or do you feel it, too?" she half whispered.

"You are wiser than you ever have been before," answered he. "I feel it, also."

"And I," breathed Elnora.

The moth spread its wings, shivered them tremulously, opening and closing them rapidly. Philip handed the box to Elnora.

She shook her head.

"I can't take that one," she said. "Give her freedom."

"But, Elnora," protested Mrs. Comstock, "I don't want to let her go. She's mine. She's the first one I ever found this way. Can't you put her in a big box, and let her live, without hurting her? I can't bear to let her go. I want to learn all about her."

"Then watch while we gather these on the trees," said Elnora. "We will take her home until night and then decide what to do. She won't fly for a long time yet."

Mrs. Comstock settled on the ground, gazing at the moth. Elnora and Philip went to the baited trees, placing several large moths and a number of smaller ones in the cyanide jar, and searching the bushes beyond where they found several paired specimens of differing families. When they returned Elnora showed her mother how to hold her hand before the moth so that it would climb upon her fingers. Then they started back to the cabin, Elnora and Philip leading the way; Mrs. Comstock followed slowly, stepping with great care lest she stumble and injure the moth. Her face wore a look of comprehension, in her eyes was an exalted light. On she came to the blue-bordered pool lying beside her path.

A turtle scrambled from a log and splashed into the water, while a red-wing shouted, "O-ka-lee!" to her. Mrs. Comstock paused and looked intently at the slime-covered quagmire, framed in a flower riot and homed over by sweet-voiced birds. Then she gazed at the thing of incomparable beauty clinging to her fingers and said softly: "If you had known about wonders like these in the days of your youth, Robert Comstock, could you ever have done what you did?"

Elnora missed her mother, and turning to look for her, saw her standing beside the pool. Would the old fascination return? A panic of fear seized the girl. She went back swiftly.

"Are you afraid she is going?" Elnora asked. "If you are, cup your other hand over her for shelter. Carrying her through this air and in the hot sunshine will dry her wings and make them ready for flight very quickly. You can't trust her in such air and light as you can in the cool dark woods."

While she talked she took hold of her mother's sleeve, anxiously smiling a pitiful little smile that Mrs. Comstock understood. Philip set his load at the back door, returning to hold open the garden gate for Elnora and Mrs. Comstock. He reached it in time to see them standing together beside the pool. The mother bent swiftly and kissed the girl on the lips. Philip turned and was busily hunting moths on the raspberry bushes when they reached the gate. And so excellent are the rewards of attending your own business, that he found a Promethea on a lilac in a corner; a moth of such rare wine-coloured, velvety shades that it almost sent Mrs. Comstock to her knees again. But this one was fully developed, able to fly, and had to be taken into the cabin hurriedly. Mrs. Comstock stood in the middle of the room holding up her Regalis.

"Now what must I do?" she asked.

Elnora glanced at Philip Ammon. Their eyes met and both of them smiled; he with amusement at the tall, spare figure, with dark eyes and white crown, asking the childish question so confidingly; and Elnora with pride. She was beginning to appreciate the character of her mother.

"How would you like to sit and see her finish development? I'll get dinner," proposed the girl.

After they had dined, Philip and Elnora carried the dishes to the kitchen, brought out boxes, sheets of cork, pins, ink, paper slips and everything necessary for mounting and classifying the moths they had taken. When the housework was finished Mrs. Comstock with her ruffle sat near, watching and listening. She remembered all they said that she understood, and when uncertain she asked questions. Occasionally she laid down her work to straighten some flower which needed attention or to search the garden for a bug for the grosbeak. In one of these absences Elnora said to Philip: "These replace quite a number of the moths I lost for the man of India. With a week of such luck, I could almost begin to talk college again."

"There is no reason why you should not have the week and the luck," said he. "I have taken moths until the middle of August, though I suspect one is more likely to find late ones in the north where it is colder than here. The next week is hay-time, but we can count on a few double-brooders and strays, and by working the exchange method for all it is worth, I think we can complete the collection again."

"You almost make me hope," said Elnora, "but I must not allow myself. I don't truly think I can replace all I lost, not even with your help. If I could, I scarcely see my way clear to leave mother this winter. I have found her so recently, and she is so precious, I can't risk losing her again. I am going to take the nature position in the Onabasha schools, and I shall be most happy doing the work. Only, these are a temptation."

"I wish you might go to college this fall with the other girls," said Philip. "I feel that if you don't you never will. Isn't there some way?"

"I can't see it if there is, and I really don't want to leave mother."

"Well, mother is mighty glad to hear it," said Mrs. Comstock, entering the arbour.

Philip noticed that her face was pale, her lips quivering, her voice cold.

"I was telling your daughter that she should go to college this winter," he explained, "but she says she doesn't want to leave you."

"If she wants to go, I wish she could," said Mrs. Comstock, a look of relief spreading over her face.

"Oh, all girls want to go to college," said Philip. "It's the only proper place to learn bridge and embroidery; not to mention midnight lunches of mixed pickles and fruit cake, and all the delights of the sororities."

"I have thought for years of going to college," said Elnora, "but I never thought of any of those things."

"That is because your education in fudge and bridge has been sadly neglected," said Philip. "You should hear my sister Polly! This was her final year! Lunches and sororities were all I heard her mention, until Tom Levering came on deck; now he is the leading subject. I can't see from her daily conversation that she knows half as much really worth knowing as you do, but she's ahead of you miles on fun."

"Oh, we had some good times in the high school," said Elnora. "Life hasn't been all work and study. Is Edith Carr a college girl?"

"No. She is the very selectest kind of a private boarding-school girl."

"Who is she?" asked Mrs. Comstock.

Philip opened his lips.

"She is a girl in Chicago, that Mr. Ammon knows very well," said Elnora. "She is beautiful and rich, and a friend of his sister's. Or, didn't you say that?"

"I don't remember, but she is," said Philip. "This moth needs an alcohol bath to remove the dope."

"Won't the down come, too?" asked Elnora anxiously.

"No. You watch and you will see it come out, as Polly would say, 'a perfectly good' moth."

"Is your sister younger than you?" inquired Elnora.

"Yes," said Philip, "but she is three years older than you. She is the dearest sister in all the world. I'd love to see her now."

"Why don't you send for her," suggested Elnora. "Perhaps she'd like to help us catch moths."

"Yes, I think Polly in a Virot hat, Picot embroidered frock and three-inch heels would take more moths than any one who ever tried the Limberlost," laughed Philip.

"Well, you find many of them, and you are her brother."

"Yes, but that is different. Father was reared in Onabasha, and he loved the country. He trained me his way and mother took charge of Polly. I don't quite understand it. Mother is a great home body herself, but she did succeed in making Polly strictly ornamental."

"Does Tom Levering need a 'strictly ornamental' girl?"

"You are too matter of fact! Too 'strictly' material. He needs a darling girl who will love him plenty, and Polly is that."

"Well, then, does the Limberlost need a 'strictly ornamental' girl?"

"No!" cried Philip. "You are ornament enough for the Limberlost. I have changed my mind. I don't want Polly here. She would not enjoy catching moths, or anything we do."

"She might," persisted Elnora. "You are her brother, and surely you care for these things."

"The argument does not hold," said Philip. "Polly and I do not like the same things when we are at home, but we are very fond of each other. The member of my family who would go crazy about this is my father. I wish he could come, if only for a week. I'd send for him, but he is tied up in preparing some papers for a great corporation case this summer. He likes the country. It was his vote that brought me here."

Philip leaned back against the arbour, watching the grosbeak as it hunted food between a tomato vine and a day lily. Elnora set him to making labels, and when he finished them he asked permission to write a letter. He took no pains to conceal his page, and from where she sat opposite him, Elnora could not look his way without reading: "My dearest Edith." He wrote busily for a time and then sat staring across the garden.

"Have you run out of material so quickly?" asked Elnora.

"That's about it," said Philip. "I have said that I am getting well as rapidly as possible, that the air is fine, the folks at Uncle Doc's all well, and entirely too good to me; that I am spending most of my time in the country helping catch moths for a collection, which is splendid exercise; now I can't think of another thing that will be interesting."

There was a burst of exquisite notes in the maple.

"Put in the grosbeak," suggested Elnora. "Tell her you are so friendly with him you feed him potato bugs."

Philip lowered the pen to the sheet, bent forward, then hesitated.

"Blest if I do!" he cried. "She'd think a grosbeak was a depraved person with a large nose. She'd never dream that it was a black-robed lover, with a breast of snow and a crimson heart. She doesn't care for hungry babies and potato bugs. I shall write that to father. He will find it delightful."

Elnora deftly picked up a moth, pinned it and placed its wings. She straightened the antennae, drew each leg into position and set it in perfectly lifelike manner. As she lifted her work to see if she had it right, she glanced at Philip. He was still frowning and hesitating over the paper.

"I dare you to let me dictate a couple of paragraphs."

"Done!" cried Philip. "Go slowly enough that I can write it."

Elnora laughed gleefully.

"I am writing this," she began, "in an old grape arbour in the country, near a log cabin where I had my dinner. From where I sit I can see directly into the home of the next-door neighbour on the west. His name is R. B. Grosbeak. From all I have seen of him, he is a gentleman of the old school; the oldest school there is, no doubt. He always wears a black suit and cap and a white vest, decorated with one large red heart, which I think must be the emblem of some ancient order. I have been here a number of times, and I never have seen him wear anything else, or his wife appear in other than a brown dress with touches of white.

"It has appealed to me at times that she was a shade neglectful of her home duties, but he does not seem to feel that way. He cheerfully stays in the sitting-room, while she is away having a good time, and sings while he cares for the four small children. I must tell you about his music. I am sure he never saw inside a conservatory. I think he merely picked up what he knows by ear and without vocal training, but there is a tenderness in his tones, a depth of pure melody, that I never have heard surpassed. It may be that I think more of his music than that of some other good vocalists hereabout, because I see more of him and appreciate his devotion to his home life.

"I just had an encounter with him at the west fence, and induced him to carry a small gift to his children. When I see the perfect harmony in which he lives, and the depth of content he and the brown lady find in life, I am almost persuaded to— Now this is going to be poetry," said Elnora. "Move your pen over here and begin with a quote and a cap."

Philip's face had been an interesting study while he wrote her sentences. Now he gravely set the pen where she indicated, and Elnora dictated—

"Buy a nice little home in the country,
And settle down there for life."

"That's the truth!" cried Philip. "It's as big a temptation as I ever had. Go on!"

"That's all," said Elnora. "You can finish. The moths are done. I am going hunting for whatever I can find for the grades."

"Wait a minute," begged Philip. "I am going, too."

"No. You stay with mother and finish your letter."

"It is done. I couldn't add anything to that."

"Very well! Sign your name and come on. But I forgot to tell you all the bargain. Maybe you won't send the letter when you hear that. The remainder is that you show me the reply to my part of it."

"Oh, that's easy! I wouldn't have the slightest objection to showing you the whole letter."

He signed his name, folded the sheets and slipped them into his pocket.

"Where are we going and what do we take?"

"Will you go, mother?" asked Elnora.

"I have a little work that should be done," said Mrs. Comstock. "Could you spare me? Where do you want to go?"

"We will go down to Aunt Margaret's and see her a few minutes and get Billy. We will be back in time for supper."

Mrs. Comstock smiled as she watched them down the road. What a splendid-looking pair of young creatures they were! How finely proportioned, how full of vitality! Then her face grew troubled as she saw them in earnest conversation. Just as she was wishing she had not trusted her precious girl with so much of a stranger, she saw Elnora stoop to lift a branch and peer under. The mother grew content. Elnora was thinking only of her work. She was to be trusted utterly.

CHAPTER XVI

WHEREIN THE LIMBERLOST SINGS FOR PHILIP, AND THE TALKING TREES TELL GREAT SECRETS

A few days later Philip handed Elnora a sheet of paper and she read: "In your condition I should think the moth hunting and life at that cabin would be very good for you, but for any sake keep away from that Grosbeak person, and don't come home with your head full of granger ideas. No doubt he has a remarkable voice, but I can't bear untrained singers, and don't you get the idea that a June song is perennial. You are not hearing the music he will make when the four babies have the scarlet fever and the measles, and the gadding wife leaves him at home to care for them then. Poor soul, I pity her! How she exists where rampant cows bellow at you, frogs croak, mosquitoes consume you, the butter goes to oil in summer and bricks in winter, while the pump freezes every day, and there is no earthly amusement, and no society! Poor things! Can't you influence him to move? No wonder she gads when she has a chance! I should die. If you are thinking of settling in the country, think also of a woman who is satisfied with white and brown to accompany you! Brown! Of all deadly colours! I should go mad in brown."

Elnora laughed while she read. Her face was dimpling, as she returned the sheet. "Who's ahead?" she asked.

"Who do you think?" he parried.

"She is," said Elnora. "Are you going to tell her in your next that R. B. Grosbeak is a bird, and that he probably will spend the winter in a wild plum thicket in Tennessee?"

"No," said Philip. "I shall tell her that I understand her ideas of life perfectly, and, of course, I never shall ask her to deal with oily butter and frozen pumps—"

"—and measley babies," interpolated Elnora.

"Exactly!" said Philip. "At the same time I find so much to counterbalance those things, that I should not object to bearing them myself, in view of the recompense. Where do we go and what do we do to-day?"

"We will have to hunt beside the roads and around the edge of the Limberlost to-day," said Elnora. "Mother is making strawberry preserves, and she can't come until she finishes. Suppose we go down to the swamp and I'll show you what is left of the flower-room that Terence O'More, the big lumber man of Great Rapids, made when he was a homeless boy here. Of course, you have heard the story?"

"Yes, and I've met the O'Mores who are frequently in Chicago society. They have friends there. I think them one ideal couple."

"That sounds as if they might be the only one," said Elnora, "and, indeed, they are not. I know dozens. Aunt Margaret and Uncle Wesley are another, the Brownlees another, and my mathematics professor and his wife. The world is full of happy people, but no one ever hears of them. You must fight and make a scandal to get into the papers. No one knows about all the happy people. I am happy myself, and look how perfectly inconspicuous I am."

"You only need go where you will be seen," began Philip, when he remembered and finished. "What do we take to-day?"

"Ourselves," said Elnora. "I have a vagabond streak in my blood and it's in evidence. I am going to show you where real flowers grow, real birds sing, and if I feel quite right about it, perhaps I shall raise a note or two myself."

"Oh, do you sing?" asked Philip politely.

"At times," answered Elnora. "'As do the birds; because I must,' but don't be scared. The mood does not possess me often. Perhaps I shan't raise a note."

They went down the road to the swamp, climbed the snake fence, followed the path to the old trail and then turned south upon it. Elnora indicated to Philip the trail with remnants of sagging barbed wire.

"It was ten years ago," she said. "I was a little school girl, but I wandered widely even then, and no one cared. I saw him often. He had been in a city institution all his life, when he took the job of keeping timber thieves out of this swamp, before many trees had been cut. It was a strong man's work, and he was a frail boy, but he grew hardier as he lived out of doors. This trail we are on is the path his feet first wore, in those days when he was insane with fear and eaten up with loneliness, but he stuck to his work and won out. I used to come down to the road and creep among the bushes as far as I dared, to watch him pass. He walked mostly, at times he rode a wheel.

"Some days his face was dreadfully sad, others it was so determined a little child could see the force in it, and once he was radiant. That day the Swamp Angel was with him. I can't tell you what she was like. I never saw any one who resembled her. He stopped close here to show her a bird's nest. Then they went on to a sort of flower-room he had made, and he sang for her. By the time he left, I had gotten bold enough to come out on the trail, and I met the big Scotchman Freckles lived with. He saw me catching moths and butterflies, so he took me to the flower-room and gave me everything there. I don't dare come alone often, so I can't keep it up as he did, but you can see something of how it was."

Elnora led the way and Philip followed. The outlines of the room were not distinct, because many of the trees were gone, but Elnora showed how it had been as nearly as she could.

"The swamp is almost ruined now," she said. "The maples, walnuts, and cherries are all gone. The talking trees are the only things left worth while."

"The 'talking trees!' I don't understand," commented Philip.

"No wonder!" laughed Elnora. "They are my discovery. You know all trees whisper and talk during the summer, but there are two that have so much to say they keep on the whole winter, when the others are silent. The beeches and oaks so love to talk, they cling to their dead, dry leaves. In the winter the winds are stiffest and blow most, so these trees whisper, chatter, sob, laugh, and at times roar until the sound is deafening. They never cease until new leaves come out in the spring to push off the old ones. I love to stand beneath them with my ear to the trunks, interpreting what they say to fit my moods. The beeches branch low, and their leaves are small so they only know common earthly things; but the oaks run straight above almost all other trees before they branch, their arms are mighty, their leaves large. They meet the winds that travel around the globe, and from them learn the big things."

Philip studied the girls face. "What do the beeches tell you, Elnora?" he asked gently.

"To be patient, to be unselfish, to do unto others as I would have them do to me."

"And the oaks?"

"They say 'be true,' 'live a clean life,' 'send your soul up here and the winds of the world will teach it what honour achieves.'"

"Wonderful secrets, those!" marvelled Philip. "Are they telling them now? Could I hear?"

"No. They are only gossiping now. This is play-time. They tell the big secrets to a white world, when the music inspires them."

"The music?"

"All other trees are harps in the winter. Their trunks are the frames, their branches the strings, the winds the musicians. When the air is cold and clear, the world very white, and the harp music swelling, then the talking trees tell the strengthening, uplifting things."

"You wonderful girl!" cried Philip. "What a woman you will be!"

"If I am a woman at all worth while, it will be because I have had such wonderful opportunities," said Elnora. "Not every girl is driven to the forest to learn what God has to say there. Here are the remains of Freckles's room. The time the Angel came here he sang to her, and I listened. I never heard music like that. No wonder she loved him. Every one who knew him did, and they do yet. Try that log, it makes a fairly good seat. This old store box was his treasure house, just as it's now mine. I will show you my dearest possession. I do not dare take it home because mother can't overcome her dislike for it. It was my father's, and in some ways I am like him. This is the strongest."

Elnora lifted the violin and began to play. She wore a school dress of green gingham, with the sleeves rolled to the elbows. She seemed a part of the setting all around her. Her head shone like a small dark sun, and her face never had seemed so rose-flushed and fair. From the instant she drew the bow, her lips parted and her eyes turned toward something far away in the swamp, and never did she give more of that impression of feeling for her notes and repeating something audible only to her. Philip was too close to get the best effect. He arose and stepped back several yards, leaning against a large tree, looking and listening intently.

As he changed positions he saw that Mrs. Comstock had followed them, and was standing on the trail, where she could not have helped hearing everything Elnora had said.

So to Philip before her and the mother watching on the trail, Elnora played the Song of the Limberlost. It seemed as if the swamp hushed all its other voices and spoke only through her dancing bow. The mother out on the trail had heard it all, once before from the girl, many times from her father. To the man it was a revelation. He stood so stunned he forgot Mrs. Comstock. He tried to realize what a city audience would say to that music, from such a player, with a similar background, and he could not imagine.

He was wondering what he dared say, how much he might express, when the last note fell and the girl laid the violin in the case, closed the door, locked it and hid the key in the rotting wood at the end of a log. Then she came to him. Philip stood looking at her curiously.

"I wonder," he said, "what people would say to that?"

"I played that in public once," said Elnora. "I think they liked it, fairly well. I had a note yesterday offering me the leadership of the high school orchestra in Onabasha. I can take it as well as not. None of my talks to the grades come the first thing in the morning. I can play a few minutes in the orchestra and reach the rooms in plenty of time. It will be more work that I love, and like finding the money. I would gladly play for nothing, merely to be able to express myself."

"With some people it makes a regular battlefield of the human heart—this struggle for self-expression," said Philip. "You are going to do beautiful work in the world, and do it well. When I realize that your violin belonged to your father, that he played it before you were born, and it no doubt affected your mother strongly, and then couple with that the years you have roamed these fields and swamps finding in nature all you had to lavish your heart upon, I can see how you evolved. I understand what you mean by self-expression. I know something of what you have to express. The world never so wanted your message as it does now. It is hungry for the things you know. I can see easily how your position came to you. What you have to give is taught in no college, and I am not sure but you would spoil yourself if you tried to run your mind through a set groove with hundreds of others. I never thought I should say such a thing to any one, but I do say to you, and I honestly believe it; give up the college idea. Your mind does not need that sort of development. Stick close to your work in the woods. You are becoming so infinitely greater on it, than the best college girl I ever knew, that there is no comparison. When you have money to spend, take that violin and go to one of the world's great masters and let the Limberlost sing to him; if he thinks he can improve it, very well. I have my doubts."

"Do you really mean that you would give up all idea of going to college, in my place?"

"I really mean it," said Philip. "If I now held the money in my hands to send you, and could give it to you in some way you would accept I would not. I do not know why it is the fate of the world always to want something different from what life gives them. If you only could realize it, my girl, you are in college, and have been always. You are in the school of experience, and it has taught you to think, and given you a heart. God knows I envy the man who wins it! You have been in the college of the Limberlost all your life, and I never met a graduate from any other institution who could begin to compare with you in sanity, clarity, and interesting knowledge. I wouldn't even advise you to read too many books on your lines. You acquire your material first hand, and you know that you are right. What you should do is to begin early to practise self-expression. Don't wait too long to tell us about the woods as you know them."

"Follow the course of the Bird Woman, you mean?" asked Elnora.

"In your own way; with your own light. She won't live forever. You are younger, and you will be ready to begin where she ends. The swamp has given you all you need so far; now you give it to the world in payment. College be confounded! Go to work and show people what there is in you!"

Not until then did he remember Mrs. Comstock.

"Should we go out to the trail and see if your mother is coming?" he asked.

"Here she is now," said Elnora. "Gracious, it's a mercy I got that violin put away in time! I didn't expect her so soon," whispered the girl as she turned and went toward her mother. Mrs. Comstock's expression was peculiar as she looked at Elnora.

"I forgot that you were making sun-preserves and they didn't require much cooking," she said. "We should have waited for you."

"Not at all!" answered Mrs. Comstock. "Have you found anything yet?"

"Nothing that I can show you," said Elnora. "I am almost sure I have found an idea that will revolutionize the whole course of my work, thought, and ambitions."

"'Ambitions!' My, what a hefty word!" laughed Mrs. Comstock. "Now who would suspect a little red-haired country girl of harbouring such a deadly germ in her body? Can you tell mother about it?"

"Not if you talk to me that way, I can't," said Elnora.

"Well, I guess we better let ambition lie. I've always heard it was safest asleep. If you ever get a bona fide attack, it will be time to attend it. Let's hunt specimens. It is June. Philip and I are in the grades. You have an hour to put an idea into our heads that will stick for a lifetime, and grow for good. That's the way I look at your job. Now, what are you going to give us? We don't want any old silly stuff that has been hashed over and over, we want a big new idea to plant in our hearts. Come on, Miss Teacher, what is the boiled-down, double-distilled essence of June? Give it to us strong. We are large enough to furnish it developing ground. Hurry up! Time is short and we are waiting. What is the miracle of June? What one thing epitomizes the whole month, and makes it just a little different from any other?"

"The birth of these big night moths," said Elnora promptly.

Philip clapped his hands. The tears started to Mrs. Comstock's eyes. She took Elnora in her arms, and kissed her forehead.

"You'll do!" she said. "June is June, not because it has bloom, bird, fruit, or flower, exclusive to it alone.

"It's half May and half July in all of them. But to me, it's just June, when it comes to these great, velvet-winged night moths which sweep its moonlit skies, consummating their scheme of creation, and dropping like a bloomed-out flower. Give them moths for June. Then make that the basis of your year's work. Find the distinctive feature of each month, the one thing which marks it a time apart, and hit them squarely between the eyes with it. Even the babies of the lowest grades can comprehend moths when they see a few emerge, and learn their history, as it can be lived before them. You should show your specimens in pairs, then their eggs, the growing caterpillars, and then the cocoons. You want to dig out the red heart of every month in the year, and hold it pulsing before them.

"I can't name all of them off-hand, but I think of one more right now. February belongs to our winter birds. It is then the great horned owl of the swamp courts his mate, the big hawks pair, and even the crows begin to take notice. These are truly our birds. Like the poor we have them always with us. You should hear the musicians of this swamp in February, Philip, on a mellow night. Oh, but they are in earnest! For twenty-one years I've listened by night to the great owls, all the smaller sizes, the foxes, coons, and every resident left in these woods, and by day to the hawks, yellow-hammers, sap-suckers, titmice, crows, and other winter birds. Only just now it's come to me that the distinctive feature of February is not linen bleaching, nor sugar making; it's the love month of our very own birds. Give them hawks and owls for February, Elnora."

With flashing eyes the girl looked at Philip. "How's that?" she said. "Don't you think I will succeed, with such help? You should hear the concert she is talking about! It is simply indescribable when the ground is covered with snow, and the moonlight white."

"It's about the best music we have," said Mrs. Comstock. "I wonder if you couldn't copy that and make a strong, original piece out of it for your violin, Elnora?"

There was one tense breath, then—— "I could try," said Elnora simply.

Philip rushed to the rescue. "We must go to work," he said, and began examining a walnut branch for Luna moth eggs. Elnora joined him while Mrs. Comstock drew her embroidery from her pocket and sat on a log. She said she was tired, they could come for her when they were ready to go. She could hear their voices around her until she called them at supper time. When they came to her she stood waiting on the trail, the sewing in one hand, the violin in the other. Elnora became very white, but followed the trail without a word. Philip, unable to see a woman carry a heavier load than he, reached for the instrument. Mrs. Comstock shook her head. She carried the violin home, took it into her room and closed the door. Elnora turned to Philip.

"If she destroys that, I shall die!" cried the girl.

"She won't!" said Philip. "You misunderstand her. She wouldn't have said what she did about the owls, if she had meant to. She is your mother. No one loves you as she does. Trust her! Myself—I think she's simply great!"

Mrs. Comstock returned with serene face, and all of them helped with the supper. When it was over Philip and Elnora sorted and classified the afternoon's specimens, and made a trip to the woods to paint and light several trees for moths. When they came back Mrs. Comstock sat in the arbour, and they joined her. The moonlight was so intense, print could have been read by it. The damp night air held odours near to earth, making flower and tree perfume strong. A thousand insects were serenading, and in the maple the grosbeak occasionally said a reassuring word to his wife, while she answered that all was well. A whip-poor-will wailed in the swamp and beside the blue-bordered pool a chat complained disconsolately. Mrs. Comstock went into the cabin, but she returned immediately, laying the violin and bow across Elnora's lap. "I wish you would give us a little music," she said.

CHAPTER XVII

WHEREIN MRS. COMSTOCK DANCES IN THE MOONLIGHT, AND ELNORA MAKES A CONFESSION

Billy was swinging in the hammock, at peace with himself and all the world, when he thought he heard something. He sat bolt upright, his eyes staring. Once he opened his lips, then thought again and closed them. The sound persisted. Billy vaulted the fence, and ran down the road with his queer sidewise hop. When he neared the Comstock cabin, he left the warm dust of the highway and stepped softly at slower pace over the rank grasses of the roadside. He had heard aright. The violin was in the grape arbour, singing a perfect jumble of everything, poured out in an exultant tumult. The strings were voicing the joy of a happy girl heart.

Billy climbed the fence enclosing the west woods and crept toward the arbour. He was not a spy and not a sneak. He merely wanted to satisfy his child-heart as to whether Mrs. Comstock was at home, and Elnora at last playing her loved violin with her mother's consent. One peep sufficed. Mrs. Comstock sat in the moonlight, her head leaning against the arbour; on her face was a look of perfect peace and contentment. As he stared at her the bow hesitated a second and Mrs. Comstock spoke:

"That's all very melodious and sweet," she said, "but I do wish you could play Money Musk and some of the tunes I danced as a girl."

Elnora had been carefully avoiding every note that might be reminiscent of her father. At the words she laughed softly and began "Turkey in the Straw." An instant later Mrs. Comstock was dancing in the moon light. Ammon sprang to her side, caught her in his arms, while to Elnora's laughter and the violin's impetus they danced until they dropped panting on the arbour bench.

Billy scarcely knew when he reached the road. His light feet barely touched the soft way, so swiftly he flew. He vaulted the fence and burst into the house.

"Aunt Margaret! Uncle Wesley!" he screamed. "Listen! Listen! She's playing it! Elnora's playing her violin at home! And Aunt Kate is dancing like anything before the arbour! I saw her in the moonlight! I ran down! Oh, Aunt Margaret!"

Billy fled sobbing to Margaret's breast.

"Why Billy!" she chided. "Don't cry, you little dunce! That's what we've all prayed for these many years; but you must be mistaken about Kate. I can't believe it."

Billy lifted his head. "Well, you just have to!" he said. "When I say I saw anything, Uncle Wesley knows I did. The city man was dancing with her. They danced together and Elnora laughed. But it didn't look funny to me; I was scared."

"Who was it said 'wonders never cease,'" asked Wesley. "You mark my word, once you get Kate Comstock started, you can't stop her. There's a wagon load of penned-up force in her. Dancing in the moonlight! Well, I'll be hanged!"

Billy was at his side instantly. "Whoever does it will have to hang me, too," he cried.

Sinton threw his arm around Billy and drew him closely. "Tell us all about it, son," he said. Billy told. "And when Elnora just stopped a breath, 'Can't you play some of the old things I knew when I was a girl?' said her ma. Then Elnora began to do a thing that made you want to whirl round and round, and quicker 'an scat there was her ma a-whirling. The city man, he ups and grabs her and whirls, too, and back in the woods I was going just like they did. Elnora begins to laugh, and I ran to tell you, cos I knew you'd like to know. Now, all the world is right, ain't it?" ended Billy in supreme satisfaction.

"You just bet it is!" said Wesley.

Billy looked steadily at Margaret. "Is it, Aunt Margaret?"

Margaret Sinton smiled at him bravely.

An hour later when Billy was ready to climb the stairs to his room, he went to Margaret to say good night. He leaned against her an instant, then brought his lips to her ear. "Wish I could get your little girls back for you!" he whispered and dashed toward the stairs.

Down at the Comstock cabin the violin played on until Elnora was so tired she scarcely could lift the bow. Then Philip went home. The women walked to the gate with him, and stood watching him from sight.

"That's what I call one decent young man!" said Mrs. Comstock. "To see him fit in with us, you'd think he'd been brought up in a cabin; but it's likely he's always had the very cream o' the pot."

"Yes, I think so," laughed Elnora, "but it hasn't hurt him. I've never seen anything I could criticise. He's teaching me so much, unconsciously. You know he graduated from Harvard, and has several degrees in law. He's coming in the morning, and we are going to put in a big day on Catocalæ."

"Which is——?"

"Those gray moths with wings that fold back like big flies, and they appear as if they had been carved from old wood. Then, when they fly, the lower wings flash out and they are red and black, or gold and black, or pink and black, or dozens of bright, beautiful colours combined with black. No one ever has classified all of them and written their complete history, unless the Bird Woman is doing it now. She wants everything she can get about them."

"I remember," said Mrs. Comstock. "They are mighty pretty things. I've started up slews of them from the vines covering the logs, all my life. I must be cautious and catch them after this, but they seem powerful spry. I might get hold of something rare." She thought intently and added, "And wouldn't know it if I did. It would just be my luck. I've had the rarest thing on earth in reach this many a day and only had the wit to cinch it just as it was going. I'll bet I don't let anything else escape me."

Next morning Philip came early, and he and Elnora went at once to the fields and woods. Mrs. Comstock had come to believe so implicitly in him that she now stayed at home to complete the work before she joined them, and when she did she often sat sewing, leaving them wandering hours at a time. It was noon before she finished, and then she packed a basket of lunch. She found Elnora and Philip near the violet patch, which was still in its prime. They all lunched together in the shade of a wild crab thicket, with flowers spread at their feet, and the gold orioles streaking the air with flashes of light and trailing ecstasy behind them, while the red-wings, as always, asked the most impertinent questions. Then Mrs. Comstock carried the basket back to the cabin, and Philip and Elnora sat on a log, resting a few minutes. They had unexpected luck, and both were eager to continue the search.

"Do you remember your promise about these violets?" asked he. "To-morrow is Edith's birthday, and if I'd put them special delivery on the morning train, she'd get them in the late afternoon. They ought to keep that long. She leaves for the North next day."

"Of course, you may have them," said Elnora. "We will quit long enough before supper to gather a large bunch. They can be packed so they will carry all right. They should be perfectly fresh, especially if we gather them this evening and let them drink all night."

Then they went back to hunt Catocalæ. It was a long and a happy search. It led them into new, unexplored nooks of the woods, past a red-poll nest, and where goldfinches prospected for thistledown for the cradles they would line a little later. It led them into real forest, where deep, dark pools lay, where the hermit thrush and the wood robin extracted the essence from all other bird melody, and poured it out in their pure bell-tone notes. It seemed as if every old gray tree-trunk, slab of loose bark, and prostrate log yielded the flashing gray treasures; while of all others they seemed to take alarm most easily, and be most difficult to capture.

Philip came to Elnora at dusk, daintily holding one by the body, its dark wings showing and its long slender legs trying to clasp his fingers and creep from his hold.

"Oh for mercy's sake!" cried Elnora, staring at him.

"I half believe it!" exulted Ammon.

"Did you ever see one?"

"Only in collections, and very seldom there."

Elnora studied the black wings intently. "I surely believe that's Sappho," she marvelled. "The Bird Woman will be overjoyed."

"We must get the cyanide jar quickly," said Philip.

"I wouldn't lose her for anything. Such a chase as she led me!"

Elnora brought the jar and began gathering up paraphernalia.

"When you make a find like that," she said, "it's the right time to quit and feel glorious all the rest of that day. I tell you I'm proud! We will go now. We have barely time to carry out our plans before supper. Won't mother be pleased to see that we have a rare one?"

"I'd like to see any one more pleased than I am!" said Philip Ammon. "I feel as if I'd earned my supper to-night. Let's go."

He took the greater part of the load and stepped aside for Elnora to precede him. She followed the path, broken by the grazing cattle, toward the cabin and nearest the violet patch she stopped, laid down her net, and the things she carried. Philip passed her and hurried straight toward the back gate.

"Aren't you going to——?" began Elnora.

"I'm going to get this moth home in a hurry," he said. "This cyanide has lost its strength, and it's not working well. We need some fresh in the jar."

He had forgotten the violets! Elnora stood looking after him, a curious expression on her face. One second so—then she picked up the net and followed. At the blue-bordered pool she paused and half turned back, then she closed her lips firmly and went on. It was nine o'clock when Philip said good-bye, and started to town. His gay whistle floated to them from the farthest corner of the Limberlost. Elnora complained of being tired, so she went to her room and to bed. But sleep would not come. Thought was racing in her brain and the longer she lay the wider awake she grew. At last she softly slipped from bed, lighted her lamp and began opening boxes. Then she went to work. Two hours later a beautiful birch bark basket, strongly and artistically made, stood on her table. She set a tiny alarm clock at three, returned to bed and fell asleep instantly with a smile on her lips.

She was on the floor with the first tinkle of the alarm, and hastily dressing, she picked up the basket and a box to fit it, crept down the stairs, and out to the violet patch. She was unafraid as it was growing light, and lining the basket with damp mosses she swiftly began picking, with practised hands, the best of the flowers. She scarcely could tell which were freshest at times, but day soon came creeping over the Limberlost and peeped at her. The robins awoke all their neighbours, and a babel of bird notes filled the air. The dew was dripping, while the first strong rays of light fell on a world in which Elnora worshipped. When the basket was filled to overflowing, she set it in the stout pasteboard box, packed it solid with mosses, tied it firmly and slipped under the cord a note she had written the previous night.

Then she took a short cut across the woods and walked swiftly to Onabasha. It was after six o'clock, but all of the city she wished to avoid were asleep. She had no trouble in finding a small boy out, and she stood at a distance waiting while he rang Dr. Ammon's bell and delivered the package for Philip to a maid, with the note which was to be given him at once.

On the way home through the woods passing some baited trees she collected the captive moths. She entered the kitchen with them so naturally that Mrs. Comstock made no comment. After breakfast Elnora went to her room, cleared away all trace of the night's work and was out in the arbour mounting moths when Philip came down the road. "I am tired sitting," she said to her mother. "I think I will walk a few rods and meet him."

"Who's a trump?" he called from afar.

"Not you!" retorted Elnora. "Confess that you forgot!"

"Completely!" said Philip. "But luckily it would not have been fatal. I wrote Polly last week to send Edith something appropriate to-day, with my card. But that touch from the woods will be very effective. Thank you more than I can say. Aunt Anna and I unpacked it to see the basket, and it was a beauty. She says you are always doing such things."

"Well, I hope not!" laughed Elnora. "If you'd seen me sneaking out before dawn, not to awaken mother and coming in with moths to make her think I'd been to the trees, you'd know it was a most especial occasion."

Then Philip understood two things: Elnora's mother did not know of the early morning trip to the city, and the girl had come to meet him to tell him so.

"You were a brick to do it!" he whispered as he closed the gate behind them. "I'll never forget you for it. Thank you ever so much."

"I did not do that for you," said Elnora tersely. "I did it mostly to preserve my own self-respect. I saw you were forgetting. If I did it for anything besides that, I did it for her."

"Just look what I've brought!" said Philip, entering the arbour and greeting Mrs. Comstock. "Borrowed it of the Bird Woman. And it isn't hers. A rare edition of Catocalæ with coloured plates. I told her the best I could, and she said to try for Sappho here. I suspect the Bird Woman will be out presently. She was all excitement."

Then they bent over the book together and with the mounted moth before them determined her family. The Bird Woman did come later, and carried the moth away, to put into a book and Elnora and Philip were freshly filled with enthusiasm.

So these days were the beginning of the weeks that followed. Six of them flying on Time's wings, each filled to the brim with interest. After June, the moth hunts grew less frequent; the fields and woods were searched for material for Elnora's grade work. The most absorbing occupation they found was in carrying out Mrs. Comstock's suggestion to learn the vital thing for which each month was distinctive, and make that the key to the nature work. They wrote out a list of the months, opposite each the things all of them could suggest which seemed to pertain to that month alone, and then tried to sift until they found something typical. Mrs. Comstock was a great help. Her mother had been Dutch and had brought from Holland numerous quaint sayings and superstitions easily traceable to Pliny's Natural History; and in Mrs. Comstock's early years in Ohio she had heard much Indian talk among her elders, so she knew the signs of each season, and sometimes they helped. Always her practical thought and sterling common sense were useful. When they were afield until exhausted they came back to the cabin for food, to prepare specimens and classify them, and to talk over the day. Sometimes Philip brought books and read while Elnora and her mother worked, and every night Mrs. Comstock asked for the violin. Her perfect hunger for music was sufficient evidence of how she had suffered without it. So the days crept by, golden, filled with useful work and pure pleasure.

The grosbeak had led the family in the maple abroad and a second brood, in a wild grape vine clambering over the well, was almost ready for flight. The dust lay thick on the country roads, the days grew warmer; summer was just poising to slip into fall, and Philip remained, coming each day as if he had belonged there always.

One warm August afternoon Mrs. Comstock looked up from the ruffle on which she was engaged to see a blue-coated messenger enter the gate.

"Is Philip Ammon here?" asked the boy.

"He is," said Mrs. Comstock.

"I have a message for him."

"He is in the woods back of the cabin. I will ring the bell. Do you know if it is important?"

"Urgent," said the boy; "I rode hard."

Mrs. Comstock stepped to the back door and clanged the dinner bell sharply, paused a second, and rang again. In a short time Philip and Elnora ran down the path.

"Are you ill, mother?" cried Elnora.

Mrs. Comstock indicated the boy. "There is an important message for Philip," she said.

He muttered an excuse and tore open the telegram. His colour faded slightly. "I have to take the first train," he said. "My father is ill and I am needed."

He handed the sheet to Elnora. "I have about two hours, as I remember the trains north, but my things are all over Uncle Doc's house, so I must go at once."

"Certainly," said Elnora, giving back the message. "Is there anything I can do to help? Mother, bring Philip a glass of buttermilk to start on. I will gather what you have here."

"Never mind. There is nothing of importance. I don't want to be hampered. I'll send for it if I miss anything I need."

Philip drank the milk, said good-bye to Mrs. Comstock; thanked her for all her kindness, and turned to Elnora.

"Will you walk to the edge of the Limberlost with me?" he asked. Elnora assented. Mrs. Comstock followed to the gate, urged him to come again soon, and repeated her good-bye. Then she went back to the arbour to await Elnora's return. As she watched down the road she smiled softly.

"I had an idea he would speak to me first," she thought, "but this may change things some. He hasn't time. Elnora will come back a happy girl, and she has good reason. He is a model young man. Her lot will be very different from mine."

She picked up her embroidery and began setting dainty precise little stitches, possible only to certain women.

On the road Elnora spoke first. "I do hope it is nothing serious," she said. "Is he usually strong?"

"Quite strong," said Philip. "I am not at all alarmed but I am very much ashamed. I have been well enough for the past month to have gone home and helped him with some critical cases that were keeping him at work in this heat. I was enjoying myself so I wouldn't offer to go, and he would not ask me to come, so long as he could help it. I have allowed him to overtax himself until he is down, and mother and Polly are north at our cottage. He's never been sick before, and it's probable I am to blame that he is now."

"He intended you to stay this long when you came," urged Elnora.

"Yes, but it's hot in Chicago. I should have remembered him. He is always thinking of me. Possibly he has needed me for days. I am ashamed to go to him in splendid condition and admit that I was having such a fine time I forgot to come home."

"You have had a fine time, then?" asked Elnora.

They had reached the fence. Philip vaulted over to take a short cut across the fields. He turned and looked at her.

"The best, the sweetest, and most wholesome time any man ever had in this world," he said. "Elnora, if I talked hours I couldn't make you understand what a girl I think you are. I never in all my life hated anything as I hate leaving you. It seems to me that I have not strength to do it."

"If you have learned anything worth while from me," said Elnora, "that should be it. Just to have strength to go to your duty, and to go quickly."

He caught the hand she held out to him in both his. "Elnora, these days we have had together, have they been sweet to you?"

"Beautiful days!" said Elnora. "Each like a perfect dream to be thought over and over all my life. Oh, they have been the only really happy days I've ever known; these days rich with mother's love, and doing useful work with your help. Good-bye! You must hurry!"

Philip gazed at her. He tried to drop her hand, only clutched it closer. Suddenly he drew her toward him. "Elnora," he whispered, "will you kiss me good-bye?"

Elnora drew back and stared at him with wide eyes. "I'd strike you sooner!" she said. "Have I ever said or done anything in your presence that made you feel free to ask that, Philip Ammon?"

"No!" panted Philip. "No! I think so much of you I wanted to touch your lips once before I left you. You know, Elnora——"

"Don't distress yourself," said Elnora calmly. "I am broad enough to judge you sanely. I know what you mean. It would be no harm to you. It would not matter to me, but here we will think of some one else. Edith Carr would not want your lips to-morrow if she knew they had touched mine to-day. I was wise to say: 'Go quickly!'"

Philip still clung to her. "Will you write me?" he begged.

"No," said Elnora. "There is nothing to say, save good-bye. We can do that now."

He held on. "Promise that you will write me only one letter," he urged. "I want just one message from you to lock in my desk, and keep always. Promise you will write once, Elnora."

She looked into his eyes, and smiled serenely. "If the talking trees tell me this winter, the secret of how a man may grow perfect, I will write you what it is, Philip. In all the time I have known you, I never have liked you so little. Good-bye."

She drew away her hand and swiftly turned back to the road. Philip Ammon, wordless, started toward Onabasha on a run.

Elnora crossed the road, climbed the fence and sought the shelter of their own woods. She chose a diagonal course and followed it until she came to the path leading past the violet patch. She went down this hurriedly. Her hands were clenched at her side, her eyes dry and bright, her cheeks red-flushed, and her breath coming fast. When she reached the patch she turned into it and stood looking around her.

The mosses were dry, the flowers gone, weeds a foot high covered it. She turned away and went on down the path until she was almost in sight of the cabin.

Mrs. Comstock smiled and waited in the arbour until it occurred to her that Elnora was a long time coming, so she went to the gate. The road stretched away toward the Limberlost empty and lonely. Then she knew that Elnora had gone into their own woods and would come in the back way. She could not understand why the girl did not hurry to her with what she would have to tell. She went out and wandered around the garden. Then she stepped into the path and started along the way leading to the woods, past the pool now framed in a thick setting of yellow lilies. Then she saw, and stopped, gasping for breath. Her hands flew up and her lined face grew ghastly. She stared at the sky and then at the prostrate girl figure. Over and over she tried to speak, but only a dry breath came. She turned and fled back to the garden.

In the familiar enclosure she gazed around her like a caged animal seeking escape. The sun beat down on her bare head mercilessly, and mechanically she moved to the shade of a half-grown hickory tree that voluntarily had sprouted beside the milk house. At her feet lay an axe with which she made kindlings for fires. She stooped and picked it up. The memory of that prone figure sobbing in the grass caught her with a renewed spasm. She shut her eyes as if to close it out. That made hearing so acute she felt certain she heard Elnora moaning beside the path. The eyes flew open. They looked straight at a few spindling tomato plants set too near the tree and stunted by its shade. Mrs. Comstock whirled on the hickory and swung the axe. Her hair shook down, her clothing became disarranged, in the heat the perspiration streamed, but stroke fell on stroke until the tree crashed over, grazing a corner of the milk house and smashing the garden fence on the east.

At the sound Elnora sprang to her feet and came running down the garden walk. "Mother!" she cried. "Mother! What in the world are you doing?"

Mrs. Comstock wiped her ghastly face on her apron. "I've laid out to cut that tree for years," she said. "It shades the beets in the morning, and the tomatoes in the afternoon!"

Elnora uttered one wild little cry and fled into her mother's arms. "Oh mother!" she sobbed. "Will you ever forgive me?"

Mrs. Comstock's arms swept together in a tight grip around Elnora.

"There isn't a thing on God's footstool from a to izzard I won't forgive you, my precious girl!" she said. "Tell mother what it is!"

Elnora lifted her wet face. "He told me," she panted, "just as soon as he decently could—that second day he told me. Almost all his life he's been engaged to a girl at home. He never cared anything about me. He was only interested in the moths and growing strong."

Mrs. Comstock's arms tightened. With a shaking hand she stroked the bright hair.

"Tell me, honey," she said. "Is he to blame for a single one of these tears?"

"Not one!" sobbed Elnora. "Oh mother, I won't forgive you if you don't believe that. Not one! He never said, or looked, or did anything all the world might not have known. He likes me very much as a friend. He hated to go dreadfully!"

"Elnora!" the mother's head bent until the white hair mingled with the brown. "Elnora, why didn't you tell me at first?"

Elnora caught her breath in a sharp snatch. "I know I should!" she sobbed. "I will bear any punishment for not, but I didn't feel as if I possibly could. I was afraid."

"Afraid of what?" the shaking hand was on the hair again.

"Afraid you wouldn't let him come!" panted Elnora. "And oh, mother, I wanted him so!"

CHAPTER XVIII

WHEREIN MRS. COMSTOCK
EXPERIMENTS WITH REJUVENATION,
AND ELNORA TEACHES NATURAL
HISTORY

For the following week Mrs. Comstock and Elnora worked so hard there was no time to talk, and they were compelled to sleep from physical exhaustion. Neither of them made any pretence of eating, for they could not swallow without an effort, so they drank milk and worked. Elnora kept on setting bait for Catacolae and Sphinginae, which, unlike the big moths of June, live several months. She took all the dragonflies and butterflies she could, and when she went over the list for the man of India, she found, to her amazement, that with Philip's help she once more had it complete save a pair of Yellow Emperors.

This circumstance was so surprising she had a fleeting thought of writing Philip and asking him to see if he could not secure her a pair. She did tell the Bird Woman, who from every source at her command tried to complete the series with these moths, but could not find any for sale.

"I think the mills of the Gods are grinding this grist," said Elnora, "and we might as well wait patiently until they choose to send a Yellow Emperor."

Mrs. Comstock invented work. When she had nothing more to do, she hoed in the garden although the earth was hard and dry and there were no plants that really needed attention. Then came a notification that Elnora would be compelled to attend a week's session of the Teachers' Institute held at the county seat twenty miles north of Onabasha the following week. That gave them something of which to think and real work to do. Elnora was requested to bring her violin. As she was on the programme of one of the most important sessions for a talk on nature work in grade schools, she was driven to prepare her speech, also to select and practise some music. Her mother turned her attention to clothing.

They went to Onabasha together and purchased a simple and appropriate fall suit and hat, goods for a dainty little coloured frock, and a dress skirt and several fancy waists. Margaret Sinton came down and the sewing began. When everything was finished and packed, Elnora kissed her mother good-bye at the depot, and entered the train. Mrs. Comstock went into the waiting-room and dropped into a seat to rest.

Her heart was so sore her whole left side felt tender. She was half starved for the food she had no appetite to take. She had worked in dogged determination until she was exhausted. For a time she simply sat and rested. Then she began to think. She was glad Elnora had gone where she would be compelled to fix her mind on other matters for a few days. She remembered the girl had said she wanted to go.

School would begin the following week. She thought over what Elnora would have to do to accomplish her work successfully. She would be compelled to arise at six o'clock, walk three miles through varying weather, lead the high school orchestra, and then put in the remainder of the day travelling from building to building over the city, teaching a specified length of time every week in each room. She must have her object lessons ready, and she must do a certain amount of practising with the orchestra. Then a cold lunch at noon, and a three-mile walk at night.

"Humph!" said Mrs. Comstock, "to get through that the girl would have to be made of cast-iron. I wonder how I can help her best?"

She thought deeply.

"The less she sees of what she's been having all summer, the sooner she'll feel better about it," she muttered.

She arose, went to the bank and inquired for the cashier.

"I want to know just how I am fixed here," she said.

The cashier laughed. "You haven't been in a hurry," he replied. "We have been ready for you any time these twenty years, but you didn't seem to pay much attention. Your account is rather flourishing. Interest, when it gets to compounding, is quite a money breeder. Come back here to a table and I will show you your balances."

Mrs. Comstock sank into a chair and waited while the cashier read a jumble of figures to her. It meant that her deposits had exceeded her expenses from one to three hundred dollars a year, according to the cattle, sheep, hogs, poultry, butter, and eggs she had sold. The aggregate of these sums had been compounding interest throughout the years. Mrs. Comstock stared at the total with dazed and unbelieving eyes. Through her sick heart rushed the realization, that if she merely had stood before that wicket and asked one question, she would have known that all those bitter years of skimping for Elnora and herself had been unnecessary. She arose and went back to the depot.

"I want to send a message," she said. She picked up the pencil, and with rash extravagance, wrote, "Found money at bank didn't know about. If you want to go to college, come on first train and get ready." She hesitated a second and then she said to herself grimly, "Yes, I'll pay for that, too," and recklessly added, "With love, Mother." Then she sat waiting for the answer. It came in less than an hour. "Will teach this winter. With dearest love, Elnora."

Mrs. Comstock held the message a long time. When she arose she was ravenously hungry, but the pain in her heart was a little easier. She went to a restaurant and ate some food, then to a dressmaker where she ordered four dresses: two very plain every-day ones, a serviceable dark gray cloth suit, and a soft light gray silk with touches of lavender and lace. She made a heavy list of purchases at Brownlee's, and the remainder of the day she did business in her direct and spirited way. At night she was so tired she scarcely could walk home, but she built a fire and cooked and ate a hearty meal.

Later she went out beside the west fence and gathered an armful of tansy which she boiled to a thick green tea. Then she stirred in oatmeal until it was a stiff paste. She spread a sheet over her bed and began tearing strips of old muslin. She bandaged each hand and arm with the mixture and plastered the soggy, evil-smelling stuff in a thick poultice over her face and neck. She was so tired she went to sleep, and when she awoke she was half skinned. She bathed her face and hands, did the work and went back to town, coming home at night to go through the same process.

By the third morning she was a raw even red, the fourth she had faded to a brilliant pink under the soothing influence of a cream recommended. That day came a letter from Elnora saying that she would remain where she was until Saturday morning, and then come to Ellen Brownlee's at Onabasha and stay for the Saturday's session of teachers to arrange their year's work. Sunday was Ellen's last day at home, and she wanted Elnora very much. She had to call together the orchestra and practise them Sunday; and could not come home until after school Monday night. Mrs. Comstock at once answered the letter saying those arrangements suited her.

The following day she was a pale pink, later a delicate porcelain white. Then she went to a hairdresser and had the rope of snowy hair which covered her scalp washed, dressed, and fastened with such pins and combs as were decided to be most becoming. She took samples of her dresses, went to a milliner, and bought a street hat to match her suit, and a gray satin with lavender orchids to wear with the silk dress. Her last investment was a loose coat of soft gray broadcloth with white lining, and touches of lavender on the embroidered collar, and gray gloves to match.

Then she went home, rested and worked by turns until Monday. When school closed on that evening, Elnora, so tired she almost trembled, came down the long walk after a late session of teachers' meeting, to be stopped by a messenger boy.

"There's a lady wants to see you most important. I am to take you to the place," he said.

Elnora groaned. She could not imagine who wanted her, but there was nothing to do but find out; tired and anxious to see her mother as she was.

"This is the place," said the boy, and went his way whistling. Elnora was three blocks from the high school building on the same street. She was before a quaint old house, fresh with paint and covered with vines. There was a long wide lot, grass-covered, closely set with trees, and a barn and chicken park at the back that seemed to be occupied. Elnora stepped on the veranda which was furnished with straw rugs, bent-hickory chairs, hanging baskets, and a table with a work-box and magazines, and knocked at the screen door.

Inside she could see polished floors, walls freshly papered in low-toned harmonious colours, straw rugs and madras curtains. It seemed to be a restful, homelike place to which she had come. A second later down an open stairway came a tall, dark-eyed woman with cheeks faintly pink and a crown of fluffy snow-white hair. She wore a lavender gingham dress with white collar and cuffs, and she called as she advanced: "That screen isn't latched! Open it and come see your brand-new mother, my girl."

Elnora stepped inside the door. "Mother!" she cried. "You my mother! I don't believe it!"

"Well, you better!" said Mrs. Comstock, "because it's true! You said you wished I were like the other girls' mothers, and I've shot as close the mark as I could without any practice. I thought that walk would be too much for you this winter, so I just rented this house and moved in, to be near you, and help more in case I'm needed. I've only lived here a day, but I like it so well I've a mortal big notion to buy the place."

"But mother!" protested Elnora, clinging to her wonderingly. "You are perfectly beautiful, and this house is a little paradise, but how will we ever pay for it? We can't afford it!"

"Humph! Have you forgotten I telegraphed you I'd found some money I didn't know about? All I've done is paid for, and plenty more to settle for all I propose to do."

Mrs. Comstock glanced around with satisfaction.

"I may get homesick as a pup before spring," she said, "but if I do I can go back. If I don't, I'll sell some timber and put a few oil wells where they don't show much. I can have land enough cleared for a few fields and put a tenant on our farm, and we will buy this and settle here. It's for sale."

"You don't look it, but you've surely gone mad!"

"Just the reverse, my girl," said Mrs. Comstock, "I've gone sane. If you are going to undertake this work, you must be convenient to it. And your mother should be where she can see that you are properly dressed, fed, and cared for. This is our—let me think—reception-room. How do you like it? This door leads to your workroom and study. I didn't do much there because I wasn't sure of my way. But I knew you would want a rug, curtains, table, shelves for books, and a case for your specimens, so I had a carpenter shelve and enclose that end of it. Looks pretty neat to me. The dining-room and kitchen are back, one of the cows in the barn, and some chickens in the coop. I understand that none of the other girls' mothers milk a cow, so a neighbour boy will tend to ours for a third of the milk. There are three bedrooms, and a bath upstairs. Go take one, put on some fresh clothes, and come to supper. You can find your room because your things are in it."

Elnora kissed her mother over and over, and hurried upstairs. She identified her room by the dressing-case. There were a pretty rug, and curtains, white iron bed, plain and rocking chairs to match her case, a shirtwaist chest, and the big closet was filled with her old clothing and several new dresses. She found the bathroom, bathed, dressed in fresh linen and went down to a supper that was an evidence of Mrs. Comstock's highest art in cooking. Elnora was so hungry she ate her first real meal in two weeks. But the bites went down slowly because she forgot about them in watching her mother.

"How on earth did you do it?" she asked at last. "I always thought you were naturally brown as a nut."

"Oh, that was tan and sunburn!" explained Mrs. Comstock. "I always knew I was white underneath it. I hated to shade my face because I hadn't anything but a sunbonnet, and I couldn't stand for it to touch my ears, so I went bareheaded and took all the colour I accumulated. But when I began to think of moving you in to your work, I saw I must put up an appearance that wouldn't disgrace you, so I thought I'd best remove the crust. It took some time, and I hope I may die before I ever endure the feel and the smell of the stuff I used again, but it skinned me nicely. What you now see is my own with a little dust of rice powder, for protection. I'm sort of tender yet."

"And your lovely, lovely hair?" breathed Elnora.

"Hairdresser did that!" said Mrs. Comstock. "It cost like smoke. But I watched her, and with a little help from you I can wash it alone next time, though it will be hard work. I let her monkey with it until she said she had found 'my style.' Then I tore it down and had her show me how to build it up again three times. I thought my arms would drop. When I paid the bill for her work, the time I'd taken, the pins, and combs she'd used, I nearly had heart failure, but I didn't turn a hair before her. I just smiled at her sweetly and said, 'How reasonable you are!' Come to think of it, she was! She might have charged me ten dollars for what she did quite as well as nine seventy-five. I couldn't have helped myself. I had made no bargain to begin on."

Then Elnora leaned back in her chair and shouted, in a gust of hearty laughter, so a little of the ache ceased in her breast. There was no time to think, the remainder of that evening, she was so tired she had to sleep, while her mother did not awaken her until she barely had time to dress, breakfast and reach school. There was nothing in the new life to remind her of the old. It seemed as if there never came a minute for retrospection, but her mother appeared on the scene with more work, or some entertaining thing to do.

Mrs. Comstock invited Elnora's friends to visit her, and proved herself a bright and interesting hostess. She digested a subject before she spoke; and when she advanced a view, her point was sure to be original and tersely expressed. Before three months people waited to hear what she had to say. She kept her appearance so in mind that she made a handsome and a distinguished figure.

Elnora never mentioned Philip Ammon, neither did Mrs. Comstock. Early in December came a note and a big box from him. It contained several books on nature subjects which would be of much help in school work, a number of conveniences Elnora could not afford, and a pair of glass-covered plaster casts, for each large moth she had. In these the upper and underwings of male and female showed. He explained that she would break her specimens easily, carrying them around in boxes. He had seen these and thought they would be of use. Elnora was delighted with them, and at once began the tedious process of softening the mounted moths and fitting them to the casts moulded to receive them. Her time was so taken in school, she progressed slowly, so her mother undertook this work. After trying one or two very common ones she learned to handle the most delicate with ease. She took keen pride in relaxing the tense moths, fitting them to the cases, polishing the glass covers to the last degree and sealing them. The results were beautiful to behold.

Soon after Elnora wrote to Philip:

DEAR FRIEND:

I am writing to thank you for the books, and the box of conveniences sent me for my work. I can use everything with fine results. Hope I am giving good satisfaction in my position. You will be interested to learn that when the summer's work was classified and pinned, I again had my complete collection for the man of India, save a Yellow Emperor. I have tried everywhere I know, so has the Bird Woman. We cannot find a pair for sale. Fate is against me, at least this season. I shall have to wait until next year and try again.

Thank you very much for helping me with my collection and for the books and cases.

Sincerely yours,

ELNORA COMSTOCK.

Philip was disappointed over that note and instead of keeping it he tore it into bits and dropped them into the waste basket.

That was precisely what Elnora had intended he should do. Christmas brought beautiful cards of greeting to Mrs. Comstock and Elnora, Easter others, and the year ran rapidly toward spring. Elnora's position had been intensely absorbing, while she had worked with all her power. She had made a wonderful success and won new friends. Mrs. Comstock had helped in every way she could, so she was very popular also.

Throughout the winter they had enjoyed the city thoroughly, and the change of life it afforded, but signs of spring did wonderful things to the hearts of the country-bred women. A restlessness began on bright February days, calmed during March storms and attacked full force in April. When neither could bear it any longer they were forced to discuss the matter and admit they were growing ill with pure homesickness. They decided to keep the city house during the summer, but to return to the farm to live as soon as school closed.

So Mrs. Comstock would prepare breakfast and lunch and then slip away to the farm to make up beds in her ploughed garden, plant seeds, trim and tend her flowers, and prepare the cabin for occupancy. Then she would go home and make the evening as cheerful as possible for Elnora; in these days she lived only for the girl.

Both of them were glad when the last of May came and the schools closed. They packed the books and clothing they wished to take into a wagon and walked across the fields to the old cabin. As they approached it, Mrs. Comstock said to Elnora: "You are sure you won't be lonely here?"

Elnora knew what she really meant.

"Quite sure," she said. "For a time last fall I was glad to be away, but that all wore out with the winter. Spring made me homesick as I could be. I can scarcely wait until we get back again."

So they began that summer as they had begun all others—with work. But both of them took a new joy in everything, and the violin sang by the hour in the twilight.

CHAPTER XIX

WHEREIN PHILIP AMMON GIVES A BALL
IN HONOUR OF EDITH CARR, AND HART
HENDERSON APPEARS ON THE SCENE

Edith Carr stood in a vine-enclosed side veranda of the Lake Shore
Club House waiting while Philip Ammon gave some important orders.
In a few days she would sail for Paris to select a wonderful trousseau she
had planned for her marriage in October. To-night Philip was giving a
club dance in her honour. He had spent days in devising new and
exquisite effects in decorations, entertainment, and supper. Weeks before
the favoured guests had been notified. Days before they had received the
invitations asking them to participate in this entertainment by Philip
Ammon in honour of Miss Carr. They spoke of it as "Phil's dance for
Edith!"

She could hear the rumble of carriages and the panting of automobiles
as in a steady stream they rolled to the front entrance. She could catch
glimpses of floating draperies of gauze and lace, the flash of jewels, and
the passing of exquisite colour. Every one was newly arrayed in her
honour in the loveliest clothing, and the most expensive jewels they could
command. As she thought of it she lifted her head a trifle higher and her
eyes flashed proudly.

She was robed in a French creation suggested and designed by Philip.
He had said to her: "I know a competent judge who says the distinctive
feature of June is her exquisite big night moths. I want you to be the very
essence of June that night, as you will be the embodiment of love. Be a
moth. The most beautiful of them is either the pale-green Luna or the
Yellow Imperialis. Be my moon lady, or my gold Empress."

He took her to the museum and showed her the moths. She instantly
decided on the yellow. Because she knew the shades would make her
more startlingly beautiful than any other colour. To him she said: "A
moon lady seems so far away and cold. I would be of earth and very near
on that night. I choose the Empress."

So she matched the colours exactly, wrote out the idea and forwarded
the order to Paquin. To-night when Philip Ammon came for her, he
stood speechless a minute and then silently kissed her hands.

For she stood tall, lithe, of grace inborn, her dark waving hair high
piled and crossed by gold bands studded with amethyst and at one side

an enamelled lavender orchid rimmed with diamonds, which flashed and sparkled. The soft yellow robe of lightest weight velvet fitted her form perfectly, while from each shoulder fell a great velvet wing lined with lavender, and flecked with embroidery of that colour in imitation of the moth. Around her throat was a wonderful necklace and on her arms were bracelets of gold set with amethyst and rimmed with diamonds. Philip had said that her gloves, fan, and slippers must be lavender, because the feet of the moth were that colour. These accessories had been made to order and embroidered with gold. It had been arranged that her mother, Philip's, and a few best friends should receive his guests. She was to appear when she led the grand march with Philip Ammon. Miss Carr was positive that she would be the most beautiful, and most exquisitely gowned woman present. In her heart she thought of herself as "Imperialis Regalis," as the Yellow Empress. In a few moments she would stun her world into feeling it as Philip Ammon had done, for she had taken pains that the history of her costume should be whispered to a few who would give it circulation. She lifted her head proudly and waited, for was not Philip planning something unusual and unsurpassed in her honour? Then she smiled.

But of all the fragmentary thoughts crossing her brain the one that never came was that of Philip Ammon as the Emperor. Philip the king of her heart; at least her equal in all things. She was the Empress—yes, Philip was but a mere man, to devise entertainments, to provide luxuries, to humour whims, to kiss hands!

"Ah, my luck!" cried a voice behind her.

Edith Carr turned and smiled.

"I thought you were on the ocean," she said.

"I only reached the dock," replied the man, "when I had a letter that recalled me by the first limited."

"Oh! Important business?"

"The only business of any importance in all the world to me. I'm triumphant that I came. Edith, you are the most superb woman in every respect that I have ever seen. One glimpse is worth the whole journey."

"You like my dress?" She moved toward him and turned, lifting her arms. "Do you know what it is intended to represent?"

"Yes, Polly Ammon told me. I knew when I heard about it how you would look, so I started a sleuth hunt, to get the first peep. Edith, I can become intoxicated merely with looking at you to-night."

He half-closed his eyes and smilingly stared straight at her. He was taller than she, a lean man, with close-cropped light hair, steel-gray eyes, a square chin and "man of the world" written all over him.

Edith Carr flushed. "I thought you realized when you went away that you were to stop that, Hart Henderson," she cried.

"I did, but this letter of which I tell you called me back to start it all over again."

She came a step closer. "Who wrote that letter, and what did it contain concerning me?" she demanded.

"One of your most intimate chums wrote it. It contained the hazard that possibly I had given up too soon. It said that in a fit of petulance you had broken your engagement with Ammon twice this winter, and he had come back because he knew you did not really mean it. I thought deeply there on the dock when I read that, and my boat sailed without me. I argued that anything so weak as an engagement twice broken and patched up again was a mighty frail affair indeed, and likely to smash completely at any time, so I came on the run. I said once I would not see you marry any other man. Because I could not bear it, I planned to go into exile of any sort to escape that. I have changed my mind. I have come back to haunt you until the ceremony is over. Then I go, not before. I was insane!"

The girl laughed merrily. "Not half so insane as you are now, Hart!" she cried gaily. "You know that Philip Ammon has been devoted to me all my life. Now I'll tell you something else, because this looks serious for you. I love him with all my heart. Not while he lives shall he know it, and I will laugh at him if you tell him, but the fact remains: I intend to marry him, but no doubt I shall tease him constantly. It's good for a man to be uncertain. If you could see Philip's face at the quarterly return of his ring, you would understand the fun of it. You had better have taken your boat."

"Possibly," said Henderson calmly. "But you are the only woman in the world for me, and while you are free, as I now see my light, I remain near you. You know the old adage."

"But I'm not 'free!'" cried Edith Carr. "I'm telling you I am not. This night is my public acknowledgment that Phil and I are promised, as our world has surmised since we were children. That promise is an actual fact, because of what I just have told you. My little fits of temper don't count with Phil. He's been reared on them. In fact, I often invent one in a perfect calm to see him perform. He is the most amusing spectacle. But, please, please, do understand that I love him, and always shall, and that we shall be married."

"Just the same, I'll wait and see it an accomplished fact," said Henderson. "And Edith, because I love you, with the sort of love it is worth a woman's while to inspire, I want your happiness before my own. So I am going to say this to you, for I never dreamed you were capable of the feeling you have displayed for Phil. If you do love him, and have loved him always, a disappointment would cut you deeper than you know. Go careful from now on! Don't strain that patched engagement of yours any further. I've known Philip all my life. I've known him through boyhood, in college, and since. All men respect him. Where the rest of us confess our sins, he stands clean. You can go to his arms with nothing to forgive. Mark this thing! I have heard him say, 'Edith is my slogan,' and I have seen him march home strong in the strength of his love for you, in the face of temptations before which every other man of us fell. Before the gods! that ought to be worth something to a girl, if she really is the delicate, sensitive, refined thing she would have man believe. It would take a woman with the organism of an ostrich to endure some of the men here to-night, if she knew them as I do; but Phil is sound to the core. So this is what I would say to you: first, your instincts are right in loving him, why not let him feel it in the ways a woman knows? Second, don't break your engagement again. As men know the man, any of us would be afraid to the soul. He loves you, yes! He is long-suffering for you, yes! But men know he has a limit. When the limit is reached, he will stand fast, and all the powers can't move him. You don't seem to think it, but you can go too far!"

"Is that all?" laughed Edith Carr sarcastically.

"No, there is one thing more," said Henderson. "Here or here-after, now and so long as I breathe, I am your slave. You can do anything you choose and know that I will kneel before you again. So carry this in the depths of your heart; now or at any time, in any place or condition, merely lift your hand, and I will come. Anything you want of me, that thing will I do. I am going to wait; if you need me, it is not necessary to speak; only give me the faintest sign. All your life I will be somewhere near you waiting for it."

"Idjit! You rave!" laughed Edith Carr. "How you would frighten me! What a bugbear you would raise! Be sensible and go find what keeps Phil. I was waiting patiently, but my patience is going. I won't look nearly so well as I do now when it is gone."

At that instant Philip Ammon entered. He was in full evening dress and exceptionally handsome. "Everything is ready," he said; "they are waiting for us to lead the march. It is formed."

Edith Carr smiled entrancingly. "Do you think I am ready?"

Philip looked what he thought, and offered his arm. Edith Carr nodded carelessly to Hart Henderson, and moved away. Attendants parted the curtains and the Yellow Empress bowing right and left, swept the length of the ballroom and took her place at the head of the formed procession. The large open dancing pavilion was draped with yellow silk caught up with lilac flowers. Every corner was filled with bloom of those colours. The music was played by harpers dressed in yellow and violet, so the ball opened.

The midnight supper was served with the same colours and the last half of the programme was being danced. Never had girl been more complimented and petted in the same length of time than Edith Carr. Every minute she seemed to grow more worthy of praise. A partners' dance was called and the floor was filled with couples waiting for the music. Philip stood whispering delightful things to Edith facing him. From out of the night, in at the wide front entrance to the pavilion, there swept in slow wavering flight a large yellow moth and fluttered toward the centre cluster of glaring electric lights. Philip Ammon and Edith Carr saw it at the same instant.

"Why, isn't that——?" she began excitedly.

"It's a Yellow Emperor! This is fate!" cried Philip. "The last one Elnora needs for her collection. I must have it! Excuse me!"

He ran toward the light. "Hats! Handkerchiefs! Fans! Anything!" he panted. "Every one hold up something and stop that! It's a moth; I've got to catch it!"

"It's yellow! He wants it for Edith!" ran in a murmur around the hall. The girl's face flushed, while she bit her lips in vexation.

Instantly every one began holding up something to keep the moth from flying back into the night. One fan held straight before it served, and the moth gently settled on it.

"Hold steady!" cried Philip. "Don't move for your life!" He rushed toward the moth, made a quick sweep and held it up between his fingers. "All right!" he called. "Thanks, every one! Excuse me a minute."

He ran to the office.

"An ounce of gasolene, quick!" he ordered. "A cigar box, a cork, and the glue bottle."

He poured some glue into the bottom of the box, set the cork in it firmly, dashed the gasolene over the moth repeatedly, pinned it to the cork, poured the remainder of the liquid over it, closed the box, and fastened it. Then he laid a bill on the counter.

"Pack that box with cork around it, in one twice its size, tie securely and express to this address at once."

He scribbled on a sheet of paper and shoved it over.

"On your honour, will you do that faithfully as I say?" he asked the clerk.

"Certainly," was the reply.

"Then keep the change," called Philip as he ran back to the pavilion.

Edith Carr stood where he left her, thinking rapidly. She heard the murmur that arose when Philip started to capture the exquisite golden creature she was impersonating. She saw the flash of surprise that went over unrestrained faces when he ran from the room, without even showing it to her. "The last one Elnora needs," rang in her ears. He had told her that he helped collect moths the previous summer, but she had understood that the Bird Woman, with whose work Miss Carr was familiar, wanted them to put in a book.

He had spoken of a country girl he had met who played the violin wonderfully, and at times, he had shown a disposition to exalt her as a standard of womanhood. Miss Carr had ignored what he said, and talked of something else. But that girl's name had been Elnora. It was she who was collecting moths! No doubt she was the competent judge who was responsible for the yellow costume Philip had devised. Had Edith Carr been in her room, she would have torn off the dress at the thought.

Being in a circle of her best friends, which to her meant her keenest rivals and harshest critics, she grew rigid with anger. Her breath hurt her paining chest. No one thought to speak to the musicians, and seeing the floor filled, they began the waltz. Only part of the guests could see what had happened, and at once the others formed and commenced to dance. Gay couples came whirling past her.

Edith Carr grew very white as she stood alone. Her lips turned pale, while her dark eyes flamed with anger. She stood perfectly still where Philip had left her, and the approaching men guided their partners around her, while the girls, looking back, could be seen making exclamations of surprise.

The idolized only daughter of the Carr family hoped that she would drop dead from mortification, but nothing happened. She was too perverse to step aside and say that she was waiting for Philip. Then came Tom Levering dancing with Polly Ammon. Being in the scales with the Ammon family, Tom scented trouble from afar, so he whispered to Polly: "Edith is standing in the middle of the floor, and she's awful mad about something."

"That won't hurt her," laughed Polly. "It's an old pose of hers. She knows she looks superb when she is angry, so she keeps herself furious half the time on purpose."

"She looks like the mischief!" answered Tom. "Hadn't we better steer over and wait with her? She's the ugliest sight I ever saw!"

"Why, Tom!" cried Polly. "Stop, quickly!"

They hurried to Edith.

"Come dear," said Polly. "We are going to wait with you until Phil returns. Let's go after a drink. I am so thirsty!"

"Yes, do!" begged Tom, offering his arm. "Let's get out of here until Phil comes."

There was the opportunity to laugh and walk away, but Edith Carr would not accept it.

"My betrothed left me here," she said. "Here I shall remain until he returns for me, and then—he will be my betrothed no longer!"

Polly grasped Edith's arm.

"Oh, Edith!" she implored. "Don't make a scene here, and to-night. Edith, this has been the loveliest dance ever given at the club house. Every one is saying so. Edith! Darling, do come! Phil will be back in a second. He can explain! It's only a breath since I saw him go out. I thought he had returned."

As Polly panted these disjointed ejaculations, Tom Levering began to grow angry on her account.

"He has been gone just long enough to show every one of his guests that he will leave me standing alone, like a neglected fool, for any passing whim of his. Explain! His explanation would sound well! Do you know for whom he caught that moth? It is being sent to a girl he flirted with all last summer. It has just occurred to me that the dress I am wearing is her suggestion. Let him try to explain!"

Speech unloosed the fountain. She stripped off her gloves to free her hands. At that instant the dancers parted to admit Philip. Instinctively they stopped as they approached and with wondering faces walled in Edith and Philip, Polly and Tom.

"Mighty good of you to wait!" cried Philip, his face showing his delight over his success in capturing the Yellow Emperor. "I thought when I heard the music you were going on."

"How did you think I was going on?" demanded Edith Carr in frigid tones.

"I thought you would step aside and wait a few seconds for me, or dance with Henderson. It was most important to have that moth. It completes a valuable collection for a person who needs the money. Come!"

He held out his arms.

"I 'step aside' for no one!" stormed Edith Carr. "I await no other girl's pleasure! You may 'complete the collection' with that!"

She drew her engagement ring from her finger and reached to place it on one of Philip's outstretched hands. He saw and drew back. Instantly Edith dropped the ring. As it fell, almost instinctively Philip caught it in air. With amazed face he looked closely at Edith Carr. Her distorted features were scarcely recognizable. He held the ring toward her.

"Edith, for the love of mercy, wait until I can explain," he begged. "Put on your ring and let me tell you how it is."

"I know perfectly 'how it is,'" she answered. "I never shall wear that ring again."

"You won't even hear what I have to say? You won't take back your ring?" he cried.

"Never! Your conduct is infamous!"

"Come to think of it," said Philip deliberately, "it is 'infamous' to cut a girl, who has danced all her life, out of a few measures of a waltz. As for asking forgiveness for so black a sin as picking up a moth, and starting it to a friend who lives by collecting them, I don't see how I could! I have not been gone three minutes by the clock, Edith. Put on your ring and finish the dance like a dear girl."

He thrust the glittering ruby into her fingers and again held out his arms. She dropped the ring, and it rolled some distance from them. Hart Henderson followed its shining course, and caught it before it was lost.

"You really mean it?" demanded Philip in a voice as cold as hers ever had been.

"You know I mean it!" cried Edith Carr.

"I accept your decision in the presence of these witnesses," said Philip Ammon. "Where is my father?" The elder Ammon with a distressed face hurried to him. "Father, take my place," said Philip. "Excuse me to my guests. Ask all my friends to forgive me. I am going away for awhile."

He turned and walked from the pavilion. As he went Hart Henderson rushed to Edith Carr and forced the ring into her fingers. "Edith, quick. Come, quick!" he implored. "There's just time to catch him. If you let him go that way, he never will return in this world. Remember what I told you."

"Great prophet! aren't you, Hart?" she sneered. "Who wants him to return? If that ring is thrust upon me again I shall fling it into the lake. Signal the musicians to begin, and dance with me."

Henderson put the ring into his pocket, and began the dance. He could feel the muscular spasms of the girl in his arms, her face was cold and hard, but her breath burned with the scorch of fever. She finished the dance and all others, taking Phil's numbers with Henderson, who had arrived too late to arrange a programme. She left with the others, merely inclining her head as she passed Ammon's father taking his place, and entered the big touring car for which Henderson had telephoned. She sank limply into a seat and moaned softly.

"Shall I drive awhile in the night air?" asked Henderson.

She nodded. He instructed the chauffeur.

She raised her head in a few seconds. "Hart, I'm going to pieces," she said. "Won't you put your arm around me a little while?"

Henderson gathered her into his arms and her head fell on his shoulder. "Closer!" she cried.

Henderson held her until his arms were numb, but he did not know it. The tricks of fate are cruel enough, but there scarcely could have been a worse one than that: To care for a woman as he loved Edith Carr and have her given into his arms because she was so numb with misery over her trouble with another man that she did not know or care what she did. Dawn was streaking the east when he spoke to her.

"Edith, it is growing light."

"Take me home," she said.

Henderson helped her up the steps and rang the bell.

"Miss Carr is ill," he said to the footman. "Arouse her maid instantly, and have her prepare something hot as quickly as possible."

"Edith," he cried, "just a word. I have been thinking. It isn't too late yet. Take your ring and put it on. I will go find Phil at once and tell him you have, that you are expecting him, and he will come."

"Think what he said!" she cried. "He accepted my decision as final, 'in the presence of witnesses,' as if it were court. He can return it to me, if I ever wear it again."

"You think that now, but in a few days you will find that you feel very differently. Living a life of heartache is no joke, and no job for a woman. Put on your ring and send me to tell him to come."

"No."

"Edith, there was not a soul who saw that, but sympathized with Phil. It was ridiculous for you to get so angry over a thing which was never intended for the slightest offence, and by no logical reasoning could have been so considered."

"Do you think that?" she demanded.

"I do!" said Henderson. "If you had laughed and stepped aside an instant, or laughed and stayed where you were, Phil would have been back; or, if he needed punishment in your eyes, to have found me having one of his dances would have been enough. I was waiting. You could have called me with one look. But to publicly do and say what you did, my lady—I know Phil, and I know you went too far. Put on that ring, and send him word you are sorry, before it is too late."

"I will not! He shall come to me."

"Then God help you!" said Henderson, "for you are plunging into misery whose depth you do not dream. Edith, I beg of you——"

She swayed where she stood. Her maid opened the door and caught her. Henderson went down the hall and out to his car.

CHAPTER XX

WHEREIN THE ELDER AMMON OFFERS ADVICE, AND EDITH CARR EXPERIENCES REGRETS

Philip Ammon walked from among his friends a humiliated and a wounded man. Never before had Edith Carr appeared quite so beautiful. All evening she had treated him with unusual consideration. Never had he loved her so deeply. Then in a few seconds everything was different. Seeing the change in her face, and hearing her meaningless accusations, killed something in his heart. Warmth went out and a cold weight took its place. But even after that, he had offered the ring to her again, and asked her before others to reconsider. The answer had been further insult.

He walked, paying no heed to where he went. He had traversed many miles when he became aware that his feet had chosen familiar streets. He was passing his home. Dawn was near, but the first floor was lighted. He staggered up the steps and was instantly admitted. The library door stood open, while his father sat with a book pretending to read. At Philip's entrance the father scarcely glanced up.

"Come on!" he called. "I have just told Banks to bring me a cup of coffee before I turn in. Have one with me!"

Philip sat beside the table and leaned his head on his hands, but he drank a cup of steaming coffee and felt better.

"Father," he said, "father, may I talk with you a little while?"

"Of course," answered Mr. Ammon. "I am not at all tired. I think I must have been waiting in the hope that you would come. I want no one's version of this but yours. Tell me the straight of the thing, Phil."

Philip told all he knew, while his father sat in deep thought.

"On my life I can't see any occasion for such a display of temper, Phil. It passed all bounds of reason and breeding. Can't you think of anything more?"

"I cannot!"

"Polly says every one expected you to carry the moth you caught to Edith. Why didn't you?"

"She screams if a thing of that kind comes near her. She never has taken the slightest interest in them. I was in a big hurry. I didn't want to miss one minute of my dance with her. The moth was not so uncommon, but by a combination of bad luck it had become the rarest in America for a friend of mine, who is making a collection to pay college expenses. For an instant last June the series was completed; when a woman's uncontrolled temper ruined this specimen and the search for it began over. A few days later a pair was secured, and again the money was in sight for several hours. Then an accident wrecked one-fourth of the collection. I helped replace those last June, all but this Yellow Emperor which we could not secure, and we haven't been able to find, buy or trade for one since. So my friend was compelled to teach this past winter instead of going to college. When that moth came flying in there to-night, it seemed to me like fate. All I thought of was, that to secure it would complete the collection and secure the money. So I caught the Emperor and started it to Elnora. I declare to you that I was not out of the pavilion over three minutes at a liberal estimate. If I only had thought to speak to the orchestra! I was sure I would be back before enough couples gathered and formed for the dance."

The eyes of the father were very bright.

"The friend for whom you wanted the moth is a girl?" he asked indifferently, as he ran the book leaves through his fingers.

"The girl of whom I wrote you last summer, and told you about in the fall. I helped her all the time I was away."

"Did Edith know of her?"

"I tried many times to tell her, to interest her, but she was so indifferent that it was insulting. She would not hear me."

"We are neither one in any condition to sleep. Why don't you begin at the first and tell me about this girl? To think of other matters for a time may clear our vision for a sane solution of this. Who is she, just what is she doing, and what is she like? You know I was reared among those Limberlost people, I can understand readily. What is her name and where does she live?"

Philip gave a man's version of the previous summer, while his father played with the book industriously.

"You are very sure as to her refinement and education?"

"In almost two months' daily association, could a man be mistaken? She can far and away surpass Polly, Edith, or any girl of our set on any common, high school, or supplementary branch, and you know high schools have French, German, and physics now. Besides, she is a graduate of two other institutions. All her life she has been in the school of Hard Knocks. She has the biggest, tenderest, most human heart I ever knew in a girl. She has known life in its most cruel phases, and instead of hardening her, it has set her trying to save other people suffering. Then this nature position of which I told you; she graduated in the School of the Woods, before she secured that. The Bird Woman, whose work you know, helped her there. Elnora knows more interesting things in a minute than any other girl I ever met knew in an hour, provided you are a person who cares to understand plant and animal life."

The book leaves slid rapidly through his fingers as the father drawled: "What sort of looking girl is she?"

"Tall as Edith, a little heavier, pink, even complexion, wide open blue-gray eyes with heavy black brows, and lashes so long they touch her cheeks. She has a rope of waving, shining hair that makes a real crown on her head, and it appears almost red in the light. She is as handsome as any fair woman I ever saw, but she doesn't know it. Every time any one pays her a compliment, her mother, who is a caution, discovers that, for some reason, the girl is a fright, so she has no appreciation of her looks."

"And you were in daily association two months with a girl like that! How about it, Phil?"

"If you mean, did I trifle with her, no!" cried Philip hotly. "I told her the second time I met her all about Edith. Almost every day I wrote to Edith in her presence. Elnora gathered violets and made a fancy basket to put them in for Edith's birthday. I started to err in too open admiration for Elnora, but her mother brought me up with a whirl I never forgot. Fifty times a day in the swamps and forests Elnora made a perfect picture, but I neither looked nor said anything. I never met any girl so downright noble in bearing and actions. I never hated anything as I hated leaving her, for we were dear friends, like two wholly congenial men. Her mother was almost always with us. She knew how much I admired Elnora, but so long as I concealed it from the girl, the mother did not care."

"Yet you left such a girl and came back whole-hearted to Edith Carr!"

"Surely! You know how it has been with me about Edith all my life."

"Yet the girl you picture is far her superior to an unprejudiced person, when thinking what a man would require in a wife to be happy."

"I never have thought what I would 'require' to be happy! I only thought whether I could make Edith happy. I have been an idiot! What I've borne you'll never know! To-night is only one of many outbursts like that, in varying and lesser degrees."

"Phil, I love you, when you say you have thought only of Edith! I happen to know that it is true. You are my only son, and I have had a right to watch you closely. I believe you utterly. Any one who cares for you as I do, and has had my years of experience in this world over yours, knows that in some ways, to-night would be a blessed release, if you could take it; but you cannot! Go to bed now, and rest. To-morrow, go back to her and fix it up."

"You heard what I said when I left her! I said it because something in my heart died a minute before that, and I realized that it was my love for Edith Carr. Never again will I voluntarily face such a scene. If she can act like that at a ball, before hundreds, over a thing of which I thought nothing at all, she would go into actual physical fits and spasms, over some of the household crises I've seen the mater meet with a smile. Sir, it is truth that I have thought only of her up to the present. Now, I will admit I am thinking about myself. Father, did you see her? Life is too short, and it can be too sweet, to throw it away in a battle with an unrestrained woman. I am no fighter—where a girl is concerned, anyway. I respect and love her or I do nothing. Never again is either respect or love possible between me and Edith Carr. Whenever I think of her in the future, I will see her as she was to-night. But I can't face the crowd just yet. Could you spare me a few days?"

"It is only ten days until you were to go north for the summer, go now."

"I don't want to go north. I don't want to meet people I know. There, the story would precede me. I do not need pitying glances or rough condolences. I wonder if I could not hide at Uncle Ed's in Wisconsin for awhile?"

The book closed suddenly. The father leaned across the table and looked into the son's eyes.

"Phil, are you sure of what you just have said?"

"Perfectly sure!"

"Do you think you are in any condition to decide to-night?"

"Death cannot return to life, father. My love for Edith Carr is dead. I hope never to see her again."

"If I thought you could be certain so soon! But, come to think of it, you are very like me in many ways. I am with you in this. Public scenes and disgraces I would not endure. It would be over with me, were I in your position, that I know."

"It is done for all time," said Philip Ammon. "Let us not speak of it further."

"Then, Phil," the father leaned closer and looked at the son tenderly, "Phil, why don't you go to the Limberlost?"

"Father!"

"Why not? No one can comfort a hurt heart like a tender woman; and, Phil, have you ever stopped to think that you may have a duty in the Limberlost, if you are free? I don't know! I only suggest it. But, for a country schoolgirl, unaccustomed to men, two months with a man like you might well awaken feelings of which you do not think. Because you were safe-guarded is no sign the girl was. She might care to see you. You can soon tell. With you, she comes next to Edith, and you have made it clear to me that you appreciate her in many ways above. So I repeat it, why not go to the Limberlost?"

A long time Philip Ammon sat in deep thought. At last he raised his head.

"Well, why not!" he said. "Years could make me no surer than I am now, and life is short. Please ask Banks to get me some coffee and toast, and I will bathe and dress so I can take the early train."

"Go to your bath. I will attend to your packing and everything. And Phil, if I were you, I would leave no addresses."

"Not an address!" said Philip. "Not even Polly."

When the train pulled out, the elder Ammon went home to find Hart Henderson waiting.

"Where is Phil?" he demanded.

"He did not feel like facing his friends at present, and I am just back from driving him to the station. He said he might go to Siam, or Patagonia. He would leave no address."

Henderson almost staggered. "He's not gone? And left no address? You don't mean it! He'll never forgive her!"

"Never is a long time, Hart," said Mr. Ammon. "And it seems even longer to those of us who are well acquainted with Phil. Last night was not the last straw. It was the whole straw-stack. It crushed Phil so far as she is concerned. He will not see her again voluntarily, and he will not forget if he does. You can take it from him, and from me, we have accepted the lady's decision. Will you have a cup of coffee?"

Twice Henderson opened his lips to speak of Edith Carr's despair. Twice he looked into the stern, inflexible face of Mr. Ammon and could not betray her. He held out the ring.

"I have no instructions as to that," said the elder Ammon, drawing back. "Possibly Miss Carr would have it as a keepsake."

"I am sure not," said Henderson curtly.

"Then suppose you return it to Peacock. I will phone him. He will give you the price of it, and you might add it to the children's Fresh Air Fund. We would be obliged if you would do that. No one here cares to handle the object."

"As you choose," said Henderson. "Good morning!"

Then he went to his home, but he could not think of sleep. He ordered breakfast, but he could not eat. He paced the library for a time, but it was too small. Going on the streets he walked until exhausted, then he called a hansom and was driven to his club. He had thought himself familiar with every depth of suffering; that night had taught him that what he felt for himself was not to be compared with the anguish which wrung his heart over the agony of Edith Carr. He tried to blame Philip Ammon, but being an honest man, Henderson knew that was unjust. The fault lay wholly with her, but that only made it harder for him, as he realized it would in time for her.

As he sauntered into the room an attendant hurried to him.

"You are wanted most urgently at the 'phone, Mr. Henderson," he said. "You have had three calls from Main 5770."

Henderson shivered as he picked down the receiver and gave the call.

"Is that you, Hart?" came Edith's voice.

"Yes."

"Did you find Phil?"

"No."

"Did you try?"

"Yes. As soon as I left you I went straight there."

"Wasn't he home yet?"

"He has been home and gone again."

"Gone!"

The cry tore Henderson's heart.

"Shall I come and tell you, Edith?"

"No! Tell me now."

"When I reached the house Banks said Mr. Ammon and Phil were out in the motor, so I waited. Mr. Ammon came back soon. Edith, are you alone?"

"Yes. Go on!"

"Call your maid. I can't tell you until some one is with you."

"Tell me instantly!"

"Edith, he said he had been to the station. He said Phil had started to Siam or Patagonia, he didn't know which, and left no address. He said——"

Distinctly Henderson heard her fall. He set the buzzer ringing, and in a few seconds heard voices, so he knew she had been found. Then he crept into a private den and shook with a hard, nervous chill.

The next day Edith Carr started on her trip to Europe. Henderson felt certain she hoped to meet Philip there. He was sure she would be disappointed, though he had no idea where Ammon could have gone. But after much thought he decided he would see Edith soonest by remaining at home, so he spent the summer in Chicago.

CHAPTER XXI

WHEREIN PHILIP AMMON RETURNS TO
THE LIMBERLOST, AND ELNORA
STUDIES THE SITUATION

"We must be thinking about supper, mother," said Elnora, while she set the wings of a Cecropia with much care. "It seems as if I can't get enough to eat, or enough of being at home. I enjoyed that city house. I don't believe I could have done my work if I had been compelled to walk back and forth. I thought at first I never wanted to come here again. Now, I feel as if I could not live anywhere else."

"Elnora," said Mrs. Comstock, "there's some one coming down the road."

"Coming here, do you think?"

"Yes, coming here, I suspect."

Elnora glanced quickly at her mother and then turned to the road as Philip Ammon reached the gate.

"Careful, mother!" the girl instantly warned. "If you change your treatment of him a hair's breadth, he will suspect. Come with me to meet him."

She dropped her work and sprang up.

"Well, of all the delightful surprises!" she cried.

She was a trifle thinner than during the previous summer. On her face there was a more mature, patient look, but the sun struck her bare head with the same ray of red gold. She wore one of the old blue gingham dresses, open at the throat and rolled to the elbows. Mrs. Comstock did not appear at all the same woman, but Philip saw only Elnora; heard only her greeting. He caught both hands where she offered but one.

"Elnora," he cried, "if you were engaged to me, and we were at a ball, among hundreds, where I offended you very much, and didn't even know I had done anything, and if I asked you before all of them to allow me to explain, to forgive me, to wait, would your face grow distorted and unfamiliar with anger? Would you drop my ring on the floor and insult me repeatedly? Oh Elnora, would you?"

Elnora's big eyes seemed to leap, while her face grew very white. She drew away her hands.

"Hush, Phil! Hush!" she protested. "That fever has you again! You are dreadfully ill. You don't know what you are saying."

"I am sleepless and exhausted; I'm heartsick; but I am well as I ever was. Answer me, Elnora, would you?"

"Answer nothing!" cried Mrs. Comstock. "Answer nothing! Hang your coat there on your nail, Phil, and come split some kindling. Elnora, clean away that stuff, and set the table. Can't you see the boy is starved and tired? He's come home to rest and eat a decent meal. Come on, Phil!"

Mrs. Comstock marched away, and Philip hung his coat in its old place and followed. Out of sight and hearing she turned on him.

"Do you call yourself a man or a hound?" she flared.

"I beg your pardon——" stammered Philip Ammon.

"I should think you would!" she ejaculated. "I'll admit you did the square thing and was a man last summer, though I'd liked it better if you'd faced up and told me you were promised; but to come back here babying, and take hold of Elnora like that, and talk that way because you have had a fuss with your girl, I don't tolerate. Split that kindling and I'll get your supper, and then you better go. I won't have you working on Elnora's big heart, because you have quarrelled with some one else. You'll have it patched up in a week and be gone again, so you can go right away."

"Mrs. Comstock, I came to ask Elnora to marry me."

"The more fool you, then!" cried Mrs. Comstock. "This time yesterday you were engaged to another woman, no doubt. Now, for some little flare-up you come racing here to use Elnora as a tool to spite the other girl. A week of sane living, and you will be sorry and ready to go back to Chicago, or, if you really are man enough to be sure of yourself, she will come to claim you. She has her rights. An engagement of years is a serious matter, and not broken for a whim. If you don't go, she'll come. Then, when you patch up your affairs and go sailing away together, where does my girl come in?"

"I am a lawyer, Mrs. Comstock," said Philip. "It appeals to me as beneath your ordinary sense of justice to decide a case without hearing the evidence. It is due me that you hear me first."

"Hear your side!" flashed Mrs. Comstock. "I'd a heap sight rather hear the girl!"

"I wish to my soul that you had heard and seen her last night, Mrs. Comstock," said Ammon. "Then, my way would be clear. I never even thought of coming here to-day. I'll admit I would have come in time, but not for many months. My father sent me."

"Your father sent you! Why?"

"Father, mother, and Polly were present last night. They, and all my friends, saw me insulted and disgraced in the worst exhibition of uncontrolled temper any of us ever witnessed. All of them knew it was the end. Father liked what I had told him of Elnora, and he advised me to come here, so I came. If she does not want me, I can leave instantly, but, oh I hoped she would understand!"

"You people are not splitting wood," called Elnora.

"Oh yes we are!" answered Mrs. Comstock. "You set out the things for biscuit, and lay the table." She turned again to Philip. "I know considerable about your father," she said. "I have met your Uncle's family frequently this winter. I've heard your Aunt Anna say that she didn't at all like Miss Carr, and that she and all your family secretly hoped that something would happen to prevent your marrying her. That chimes right in with your saying that your father sent you here. I guess you better speak your piece."

Philip gave his version of the previous night.

"Do you believe me?" he finished.

"Yes," said Mrs. Comstock.

"May I stay?"

"Oh, it looks all right for you, but what about her?"

"Nothing, so far as I am concerned. Her plans were all made to start to Europe to-day. I suspect she is on the way by this time. Elnora is very sensible, Mrs. Comstock. Hadn't you better let her decide this?"

"The final decision rests with her, of course," admitted Mrs. Comstock. "But look you one thing! She's all I have. As Solomon says, 'she is the one child, the only child of her mother.' I've suffered enough in this world that I fight against any suffering which threatens her. So far as I know you've always been a man, and you may stay. But if you bring tears and heartache to her, don't have the assurance to think I'll bear it tamely. I'll get right up and fight like a catamount, if things go wrong for Elnora!"

"I have no doubt but you will," replied Philip, "and I don't blame you in the least if you do. I have the utmost devotion to offer Elnora, a good home, fair social position, and my family will love her dearly. Think it over. I know it is sudden, but my father advised it."

"Yes, I reckon he did!" said Mrs. Comstock dryly. "I guess instead of me being the catamount, you had the genuine article up in Chicago, masquerading in peacock feathers, and posing as a fine lady, until her time came to scratch. Human nature seems to be the same the world over. But I'd give a pretty to know that secret thing you say you don't, that set her raving over your just catching a moth for Elnora. You might get that crock of strawberries in the spring house."

They prepared and ate supper. Afterward they sat in the arbour and talked, or Elnora played until time for Philip to go.

"Will you walk to the gate with me?" he asked Elnora as he arose.

"Not to-night," she answered lightly. "Come early in the morning if you like, and we will go over to Sleepy Snake Creek and hunt moths and gather dandelions for dinner."

Philip leaned toward her. "May I tell you to-morrow why I came?" he asked.

"I think not," replied Elnora. "The fact is, I don't care why you came. It is enough for me that we are your very good friends, and that in trouble, you have found us a refuge. I fancy we had better live a week or two before you say anything. There is a possibility that what you have to say may change in that length of time.

"It will not change one iota!" cried Philip.

"Then it will have the grace of that much age to give it some small touch of flavour," said the girl. "Come early in the morning."

She lifted the violin and began to play.

"Well bless my soul!" ejaculated the astounded Mrs. Comstock. "To think I was worrying for fear you couldn't take care of yourself!"

Elnora laughed while she played.

"Shall I tell you what he said?"

"Nope! I don't want to hear it!" said Elnora. "He is only six hours from Chicago. I'll give her a week to find him and fix it up, if he stays that long. If she doesn't put in an appearance then, he can tell me what he wants to say, and I'll take my time to think it over. Time in plenty, too! There are three of us in this, and one must be left with a sore heart for life. If the decision rests with me I propose to be very sure that it is the one who deserves such hard luck."

The next morning Philip came early, dressed in the outing clothing he had worn the previous summer, and aside from a slight paleness seemed very much the same as when he left. Elnora met him on the old footing, and for a week life went on exactly as it had the previous summer. Mrs. Comstock made mental notes and watched in silence. She could see that Elnora was on a strain, though she hoped Philip would not. The girl grew restless as the week drew to a close. Once when the gate clicked she suddenly lost colour and moved nervously. Billy came down the walk.

Philip leaned toward Mrs. Comstock and said: "I am expressly forbidden to speak to Elnora as I would like. Would you mind telling her for me that I had a letter from my father this morning saying that Miss Carr is on her way to Europe for the summer?"

"Elnora," said Mrs. Comstock promptly, "I have just heard that Carr woman is on her way to Europe, and I wish to my gracious stars she'd stay there!"

Philip Ammon shouted, but Elnora arose hastily and went to meet Billy. They came into the arbour together and after speaking to Mrs.

Comstock and Philip, Billy said: "Uncle Wesley and I found something funny, and we thought you'd like to see."

"I don't know what I should do without you and Uncle Wesley to help me," said Elnora. "What have you found now?"

"Something I couldn't bring. You have to come to it. I tried to get one and I killed it. They are a kind of insecty things, and they got a long tail that is three fine hairs. They stick those hairs right into the hard bark of trees, and if you pull, the hairs stay fast and it kills the bug."

"We will come at once," laughed Elnora. "I know what they are, and I can use some in my work."

"Billy, have you been crying?" inquired Mrs. Comstock.

Billy lifted a chastened face. "Yes, ma'am," he replied. "This has been the worst day."

"What's the matter with the day?"

"The day is all right," admitted Billy. "I mean every single thing has gone wrong with me."

"Now that is too bad!" sympathized Mrs. Comstock.

"Began early this morning," said Billy. "All Snap's fault, too."

"What has poor Snap been doing?" demanded Mrs. Comstock, her eyes beginning to twinkle.

"Digging for woodchucks, like he always does. He gets up at two o'clock to dig for them. He was coming in from the woods all tired and covered thick with dirt. I was going to the barn with the pail of water for Uncle Wesley to use in milking. I had to set down the pail to shut the gate so the chickens wouldn't get into the flower beds, and old Snap stuck his dirty nose into the water and began to lap it down. I knew Uncle Wesley wouldn't use that, so I had to go 'way back to the cistern for more, and it pumps awful hard. Made me mad, so I threw the water on Snap."

"Well, what of it?"

"Nothing, if he'd stood still. But it scared him awful, and when he's afraid he goes a-humping for Aunt Margaret. When he got right up against her he stiffened out and gave a big shake. You oughter seen the nice blue dress she had put on to go to Onabasha!"

Mrs. Comstock and Philip laughed, but Elnora put her arms around the boy. "Oh Billy!" she cried. "That was too bad!"

"She got up early and ironed that dress to wear because it was cool. Then, when it was all dirty, she wouldn't go, and she wanted to real bad." Billy wiped his eyes. "That ain't all, either," he added.

"We'd like to know about it, Billy," suggested Mrs. Comstock, struggling with her face.

"Cos she couldn't go to the city, she's most worked herself to death. She's done all the dirty, hard jobs she could find. She's fixing her grape juice now."

"Sure!" cried Mrs. Comstock. "When a woman is disappointed she always works like a dog to gain sympathy!"

"Well, Uncle Wesley and I are sympathizing all we know how, without her working so. I've squeezed until I almost busted to get the juice out from the seeds and skins. That's the hard part. Now, she has to strain it through white flannel and seal it in bottles, and it's good for sick folks. Most wish I'd get sick myself, so I could have a glass. It's so good!"

Elnora glanced swiftly at her mother.

"I worked so hard," continued Billy, "that she said if I would throw the leavings in the woods, then I could come after you to see about the bugs. Do you want to go?"

"We will all go," said Mrs. Comstock. "I am mightily interested in those bugs myself."

From afar commotion could be seen at the Sinton home. Wesley and Margaret were running around wildly and peculiar sounds filled the air.

"What's the trouble?" asked Philip, hurrying to Wesley.

"Cholera!" groaned Sinton. "My hogs are dying like flies."

Margaret was softly crying. "Wesley, can't I fix something hot? Can't we do anything? It means several hundred dollars and our winter meat."

"I never saw stock taken so suddenly and so hard," said Wesley. "I have 'phoned for the veterinary to come as soon as he can get here."

All of them hurried to the feeding pen into which the pigs seemed to be gathering from the woods. Among the common stock were big white beasts of pedigree which were Wesley's pride at county fairs. Several of these rolled on their backs, pawing the air feebly and emitting little squeaks. A huge Berkshire sat on his haunches, slowly shaking his head, the water dropping from his eyes, until he, too, rolled over with faint grunts. A pair crossing the yard on wavering legs collided, and attacked each other in anger, only to fall, so weak they scarcely could squeal. A fine snowy Plymouth Rock rooster, after several attempts, flew to the fence, balanced with great effort, wildly flapped his wings and started a guttural crow, but fell sprawling among the pigs, too helpless to stand.

"Did you ever see such a dreadful sight?" sobbed Margaret.

Billy climbed on the fence, took one long look and turned an astounded face to Wesley.

"Why them pigs is drunk!" he cried. "They act just like my pa!"

Wesley turned to Margaret.

"Where did you put the leavings from that grape juice?" he demanded.

"I sent Billy to throw it in the woods."

"Billy——" began Wesley.

"Threw it just where she told me to," cried Billy. "But some of the pigs came by there coming into the pen, and some were close in the fence corners."

"Did they eat it?" demanded Wesley.

"They just chanked into it," replied Billy graphically. "They pushed, and squealed, and fought over it. You couldn't blame 'em! It was the best stuff I ever tasted!"

"Margaret," said Wesley, "run 'phone that doctor he won't be needed. Billy, take Elnora and Mr. Ammon to see the bugs. Katharine, suppose you help me a minute."

Wesley took the clothes basket from the back porch and started in the direction of the cellar. Margaret returned from the telephone.

"I just caught him," she said. "There's that much saved. Why Wesley, what are you going to do?"

"You go sit on the front porch a little while," said Wesley. "You will feel better if you don't see this."

"Wesley," cried Margaret aghast. "Some of that wine is ten years old. There are days and days of hard work in it, and I couldn't say how much sugar. Dr. Ammon keeps people alive with it when nothing else will stay on their stomachs."

"Let 'em die, then!" said Wesley. "You heard the boy, didn't you?"

"It's a cold process. There's not a particle of fermentation about it."

"Not a particle of fermentation! Great day, Margaret! Look at those pigs!"

Margaret took a long look. "Leave me a few bottles for mince-meat," she wavered.

"Not a smell for any use on this earth! You heard the boy! He shan't say, when he grows to manhood, that he learned to like it here!"

Wesley threw away the wine, Mrs. Comstock cheerfully assisting. Then they walked to the woods to see and learn about the wonderful insects. The day ended with a big supper at Sintons', and then they went to the Comstock cabin for a concert. Elnora played beautifully that night. When the Sintons left she kissed Billy with particular tenderness. She was so moved that she was kinder to Philip than she had intended to be, and Elnora as an antidote to a disappointed lover was a decided success in any mood.

However strong the attractions of Edith Carr had been, once the bond was finally broken, Philip Ammon could not help realizing that Elnora was the superior woman, and that he was fortunate to have escaped, when he regarded his ties strongest. Every day, while working with Elnora, he saw more to admire. He grew very thankful that he was free to try to win her, and impatient to justify himself to her.

Elnora did not evince the slightest haste to hear what he had to say, but waited the week she had set, in spite of Philip's hourly manifest impatience. When she did consent to listen, Philip felt before he had talked five minutes, that she was putting herself in Edith Carr's place, and judging him from what the other girl's standpoint would be. That was so disconcerting, he did not plead his cause nearly so well as he had hoped, for when he ceased Elnora sat in silence.

"You are my judge," he said at last. "What is your verdict?"

"If I could hear her speak from her heart as I just have heard you, then I could decide," answered Elnora.

"She is on the ocean," said Philip. "She went because she knew she was wholly in the wrong. She had nothing to say, or she would have remained."

"That sounds plausible," reasoned Elnora, "but it is pretty difficult to find a woman in an affair that involves her heart with nothing at all to say. I fancy if I could meet her, she would say several things. I should love to hear them. If I could talk with her three minutes, I could tell what answer to make you."

"Don't you believe me, Elnora?"

"Unquestioningly," answered Elnora. "But I would believe her also. If only I could meet her I soon would know."

"I don't see how that is to be accomplished," said Philip, "but I am perfectly willing. There is no reason why you should not meet her, except that she probably would lose her temper and insult you."

"Not to any extent," said Elnora calmly. "I have a tongue of my own, while I am not without some small sense of personal values."

Philip glanced at her and began to laugh. Very different of facial formation and colouring, Elnora at times closely resembled her mother. She joined in his laugh ruefully.

"The point is this," she said. "Some one is going to be hurt, most dreadfully. If the decision as to whom it shall be rests with me, I must know it is the right one. Of course, no one ever hinted it to you, but you are a very attractive man, Philip. You are mighty good to look at, and you have a trained, refined mind, that makes you most interesting. For years Edith Carr has felt that you were hers. Now, how is she going to change? I have been thinking—thinking deep and long, Phil. If I were in her place, I simply could not give you up, unless you had made yourself unworthy of love. Undoubtedly, you never seemed so desirable to her as just now, when she is told she can't have you. What I think is that she will come to claim you yet."

"You overlook the fact that it is not in a woman's power to throw away a man and pick him up at pleasure," said Philip with some warmth. "She publicly and repeatedly cast me off. I accepted her decision as publicly as it was made. You have done all your thinking from a wrong viewpoint. You seem to have an idea that it lies with you to decide what I shall do, that if you say the word, I shall return to Edith. Put that thought out of your head! Now, and for all time to come, she is a matter of indifference to me. She killed all feeling in my heart for her so completely that I do not even dread meeting her.

"If I hated her, or was angry with her, I could not be sure the feeling would not die. As it is, she has deadened me into a creature of indifference. So you just revise your viewpoint a little, Elnora. Cease thinking it is for you to decide what I shall do, and that I will obey you. I make my own decisions in reference to any woman, save you. The question you are to decide is whether I may remain here, associating with you as I did last summer; but with the difference that it is understood that I am free; that it is my intention to care for you all I please, to make you return my feeling for you if I can. There is just one question for you to decide, and it is not triangular. It is between us. May I remain? May I love you? Will you give me the chance to prove what I think of you?"

"You speak very plainly," said Elnora.

"This is the time to speak plainly," said Philip Ammon. "There is no use in allowing you to go on threshing out a problem which does not exist. If you do not want me here, say so and I will go. Of course, I warn you before I start, that I will come back. I won't yield without the stiffest fight it is in me to make. But drop thinking it lies in your power to send me back to Edith Carr. If she were the last woman in the world, and I the last man, I'd jump off the planet before I would give her further opportunity to exercise her temper on me. Narrow this to us, Elnora. Will you take the place she vacated? Will you take the heart she threw away? I'd give my right hand and not flinch, if I could offer you my life, free from any contact with hers, but that is not possible. I can't undo things which are done. I can only profit by experience and build better in the future."

"I don't see how you can be sure of yourself," said Elnora. "I don't see how I could be sure of you. You loved her first, you never can care for me anything like that. Always I'd have to be afraid you were thinking of her and regretting."

"Folly!" cried Philip. "Regretting what? That I was not married to a woman who was liable to rave at me any time or place, without my being conscious of having given offence? A man does relish that! I am likely to pine for more!"

"You'd be thinking she'd learned a lesson. You would think it wouldn't happen again."

"No, I wouldn't be 'thinking,'" said, Philip. "I'd be everlastingly sure! I wouldn't risk what I went through that night again, not to save my life! Just you and me, Elnora. Decide for us."

"I can't!" cried Elnora. "I am afraid!"

"Very well," said Philip. "We will wait until you feel that you can. Wait until fear vanishes. Just decide now whether you would rather have me go for a few months, or remain with you. Which shall it be, Elnora?"

"You can never love me as you did her," wailed Elnora.

"I am happy to say I cannot," replied he. "I've cut my matrimonial teeth. I'm cured of wanting to swell in society. I'm over being proud of a woman for her looks alone. I have no further use for lavishing myself on a beautiful, elegantly dressed creature, who thinks only of self. I have learned that I am a common man. I admire beauty and beautiful clothing quite as much as I ever did; but, first, I want an understanding, deep as the lowest recess of my soul, with the woman I marry. I want to work for you, to plan for you, to build you a home with every comfort, to give you all good things I can, to shield you from every evil. I want to interpose my body between yours and fire, flood, or famine. I want to give you everything; but I hate the idea of getting nothing at all on which I can depend in return. Edith Carr had only good looks to offer, and when anger overtook her, beauty went out like a snuffed candle.

"I want you to love me. I want some consideration. I even crave respect. I've kept myself clean. So far as I know how to be, I am honest and scrupulous. It wouldn't hurt me to feel that you took some interest in these things. Rather fierce temptations strike a man, every few days, in this world. I can keep decent, for a woman who cares for decency, but when I do, I'd like to have the fact recognized, by just enough of a show of appreciation that I could see it. I am tired of this one-sided business. After this, I want to get a little in return for what I give. Elnora, you have love, tenderness, and honest appreciation of the finest in life. Take what I offer, and give what I ask."

"You do not ask much," said Elnora.

"As for not loving you as I did Edith," continued Philip, "as I said before, I hope not! I have a newer and a better idea of loving. The feeling I offer you was inspired by you. It is a Limberlost product. It is as much bigger, cleaner, and more wholesome than any feeling I ever had for Edith Carr, as you are bigger than she, when you stand before your classes and in calm dignity explain the marvels of the Almighty, while she stands on a ballroom floor, and gives way to uncontrolled temper. Ye gods, Elnora, if you could look into my soul, you would see it leap and rejoice over my escape! Perhaps it isn't decent, but it's human; and I'm only a common human being. I'm the gladdest man alive that I'm free! I would turn somersaults and yell if I dared. What an escape! Stop straining after Edith Carr's viewpoint and take a look from mine. Put yourself in my place and try to study out how I feel.

"I am so happy I grow religious over it. Fifty times a day I catch myself whispering, 'My soul is escaped!' As for you, take all the time you want. If you prefer to be alone, I'll take the next train and stay away as long as I can bear it, but I'll come back. You can be most sure of that. Straight as your pigeons to their loft, I'll come back to you, Elnora. Shall I go?"

"Oh, what's the use to be extravagant?" murmured Elnora.

CHAPTER XXII

WHEREIN PHILIP AMMON KNEELS TO ELNORA, AND STRANGERS COME TO THE LIMBERLOST

The month which followed was a reproduction of the previous June. There were long moth hunts, days of specimen gathering, wonderful hours with great books, big dinners all of them helped to prepare, and perfect nights filled with music. Everything was as it had been, with the difference that Philip was now an avowed suitor. He missed no opportunity to advance himself in Elnora's graces. At the end of the month he was no nearer any sort of understanding with her than he had been at the beginning. He revelled in the privilege of loving her, but he got no response. Elnora believed in his love, yet she hesitated to accept him, because she could not forget Edith Carr.

One afternoon early in July, Philip came across the fields, through the Comstock woods, and entered the garden. He inquired for Elnora at the back door and was told that she was reading under the willow. He went around the west end of the cabin to her. She sat on a rustic bench they had made and placed beneath a drooping branch. He had not seen her before in the dress she was wearing. It was clinging mull of pale green, trimmed with narrow ruffles and touched with knots of black velvet; a simple dress, but vastly becoming. Every tint of her bright hair, her luminous eyes, her red lips, and her rose-flushed face, neck, and arms grew a little more vivid with the delicate green setting.

He stopped short. She was so near, so temptingly sweet, he lost control. He went to her with a half-smothered cry after that first long look, dropped on one knee beside her and reached an arm behind her to the bench back, so that he was very near. He caught her hands.

"Elnora!" he cried tensely, "end it now! Say this strain is over. I pledge you that you will be happy. You don't know! If you only would say the word, you would awake to new life and great joy! Won't you promise me now, Elnora?"

The girl sat staring into the west woods, while strong in her eyes was her father's look of seeing something invisible to others. Philip's arm slipped from the bench around her. His fingers closed firmly over hers. "Elnora," he pleaded, "you know me well enough. You have had time in plenty. End it now. Say you will be mine!" He gathered her closer, pressing his face against hers, his breath on her cheek. "Can't you quite promise yet, my girl of the Limberlost?"

Elnora shook her head. Instantly he released her.

"Forgive me," he begged. "I had no intention of thrusting myself upon you, but, Elnora, you are the veriest Queen of Love this afternoon. From the tips of your toes to your shining crown, I worship you. I want no woman save you. You are so wonderful this afternoon, I couldn't help urging. Forgive me. Perhaps it was something that came this morning for you. I wrote Polly to send it. May we try if it fits? Will you tell me if you like it?"

He drew a little white velvet box from his pocket and showed her a splendid emerald ring.

"It may not be right," he said. "The inside of a glove finger is not very accurate for a measure, but it was the best I could do. I wrote Polly to get it, because she and mother are home from the East this week, but next they will go on to our cottage in the north, and no one knows what is right quite so well as Polly." He laid the ring in Elnora's hand. "Dearest," he said, "don't slip that on your finger; put your arms around my neck and promise me, all at once and abruptly, or I'll keel over and die of sheer joy."

Elnora smiled.

"I won't! Not all those venturesome things at once; but, Phil, I'm ashamed to confess that ring simply fascinates me. It is the most beautiful one I ever saw, and do you know that I never owned a ring of any kind in my life? Would you think me unwomanly if I slip it on for a second, before I can say for sure? Phil, you know I care! I care very much! You know I will tell you the instant I feel right about it."

"Certainly you will," agreed Philip promptly. "It is your right to take all the time you choose. I can't put that ring on you until it means a bond between us. I'll shut my eyes and you try it on, so we can see if it fits." Philip turned his face toward the west woods and tightly closed his eyes. It was a boyish thing to do, and it caught the hesitating girl in the depths of her heart as the boy element in a man ever appeals to a motherly woman. Before she quite realized what she was doing, the ring slid on her finger. With both arms she caught Philip and drew him to her breast, holding him closely. Her head drooped over his, her lips were on his hair. So an instant, then her arms dropped. He lifted a convulsed, white face.

"Dear Lord!" he whispered. "You—you didn't mean that, Elnora! You—— What made you do it?"

"You—you looked so boyish!" panted Elnora. "I didn't mean it! I—I forgot that you were older than Billy. Look—look at the ring!"

"'The Queen can do no wrong,'" quoted Philip between his set teeth. "But don't you do that again, Elnora, unless you do mean it. Kings are not so good as queens, and there is a limit with all men. As you say, we will look at your ring. It seems very lovely to me. Suppose you leave it on until time for me to go. Please do! I have heard of mute appeals; perhaps it will plead for me. I am wild for your lips this afternoon. I am going to take your hands."

He caught both of them and covered them with kisses.

"Elnora," he said, "Will you be my wife?"

"I must have a little more time," she whispered. "I must be absolutely certain, for when I say yes, and give myself to you, only death shall part us. I would not give you up. So I want a little more time—but, I think I will."

"Thank you," said Philip. "If at any time you feel that you have reached a decision, will you tell me? Will you promise me to tell me instantly, or shall I keep asking you until the time comes?"

"You make it difficult," said Elnora. "But I will promise you that. Whenever the last doubt vanishes, I will let you know instantly—if I can."

"Would it be difficult for you?" whispered Ammon.

"I—I don't know," faltered Elnora.

"It seems as if I can't be man enough to put this thought aside and give up this afternoon," said Philip. "I am ashamed of myself, but I can't help it. I am going to ask God to make that last doubt vanish before I go this night. I am going to believe that ring will plead for me. I am going to hope that doubt will disappear suddenly. I will be watching. Every second I will be watching. If it happens and you can't speak, give me your hand. Just the least movement toward me, I will understand. Would it help you to talk this over with your mother? Shall I call her? Shall I——?"

Honk! Honk! Honk! Hart Henderson set the horn of the big automobile going as it shot from behind the trees lining the Brushwood road. The picture of a vine-covered cabin, a large drooping tree, a green-clad girl and a man bending over her very closely flashed into view. Edith Carr caught her breath with a snap. Polly Ammon gave Tom Levering a quick touch and wickedly winked at him.

Several days before, Edith had returned from Europe suddenly. She and Henderson had called at the Ammon residence saying that they were going to motor down to the Limberlost to see Philip a few hours, and urged that Polly and Tom accompany them. Mrs. Ammon knew that her husband would disapprove of the trip, but it was easy to see that Edith Carr had determined on going. So the mother thought it better to have Polly along to support Philip than to allow him to confront Edith unexpectedly and alone. Polly was full of spirit. She did not relish the thought of Edith as a sister. Always they had been in the same set, always Edith, because of greater beauty and wealth, had patronized Polly. Although it had rankled, she had borne it sweetly. But two days before, her father had extracted a promise of secrecy, given her Philip's address and told her to send him the finest emerald ring she could select. Polly knew how that ring would be used. What she did not know was that the girl who accompanied her went back to the store afterward, made an excuse to the clerk that she had been sent to be absolutely sure that the address was right, and so secured it for Edith Carr.

Two days later Edith had induced Hart Henderson to take her to Onabasha. By the aid of maps they located the Comstock land and passed it, merely to see the place. Henderson hated that trip, and implored Edith not to take it, but she made no effort to conceal from him what she suffered, and it was more than he could endure. He pointed out that Philip had gone away without leaving an address, because he did not wish to see her, or any of them. But Edith was so sure of her power, she felt certain Philip needed only to see her to succumb to her beauty as he always had done, while now she was ready to plead for forgiveness. So they came down the Brushwood road, and Henderson had just said to Edith beside him: "This should be the Comstock land on our left."

A minute later the wood ended, while the sunlight, as always pitiless, etched with distinctness the scene at the west end of the cabin. Instinctively, to save Edith, Henderson set the horn blowing. He had thought to drive to the city, but Polly Ammon arose crying: "Phil! Phil!" Tom Levering was on his feet shouting and waving, while Edith in her most imperial manner ordered him to turn into the lane leading through the woods beside the cabin.

"Find some way for me to have a minute alone with her," she commanded as he stopped the car.

"That is my sister Polly, her fiance Tom Levering, a friend of mine named Henderson, and——" began Philip,

"—and Edith Carr," volunteered Elnora.

"And Edith Carr," repeated Philip Ammon. "Elnora, be brave, for my sake. Their coming can make no difference in any way. I won't let them stay but a few minutes. Come with me!"

"Do I seem scared?" inquired Elnora serenely. "This is why you haven't had your answer. I have been waiting just six weeks for that motor. You may bring them to me at the arbour."

Philip glanced at her and broke into a laugh. She had not lost colour. Her self-possession was perfect. She deliberately turned and walked toward the grape arbour, while he sprang over the west fence and ran to the car.

Elnora standing in the arbour entrance made a perfect picture, framed in green leaves and tendrils. No matter how her heart ached, it was good to her, for it pumped steadily, and kept her cheeks and lips suffused with colour. She saw Philip reach the car and gather his sister into his arms.

Past her he reached a hand to Levering, then to Edith Carr and Henderson. He lifted his sister to the ground, and assisted Edith to alight. Instantly, she stepped beside him, and Elnora's heart played its first trick.

She could see that Miss Carr was splendidly beautiful, while she moved with the hauteur and grace supposed to be the prerogatives of royalty. And she had instantly taken possession of Philip. But he also had a brain which was working with rapidity. He knew Elnora was watching, so he turned to the others.

"Give her up, Tom!" he cried. "I didn't know I wanted to see the little nuisance so badly, but I do. How are father and mother? Polly, didn't the mater send me something?"

"She did!" said Polly Ammon, stopping on the path and lifting her chin as a little child, while she drew away her veil.

Philip caught her in his arms and stooped for his mother's kiss.

"Be good to Elnora!" he whispered.

"Umhu!" assented Polly. And aloud—"Look at that ripping green and gold symphony! I never saw such a beauty! Thomas Asquith Levering, you come straight here and take my hand!"

Edith's move to compel Philip to approach Elnora beside her had been easy to see; also its failure. Henderson stepped into Philip's place as he turned to his sister. Instead of taking Polly's hand Levering ran to open the gate. Edith passed through first, but Polly darted in front of her on the run, with Phil holding her arm, and swept up to Elnora. Polly looked for the ring and saw it. That settled matters with her.

"You lovely, lovely, darling girl!" she cried, throwing her arms around Elnora and kissing her. With her lips close Elnora's ear, Polly whispered, "Sister! Dear, dear sister!"

Elnora drew back, staring at Polly in confused amazement. She was a beautiful girl, her eyes were sparkling and dancing, and as she turned to make way for the others, she kept one of Elnora's hands in hers. Polly would have dropped dead in that instant if Edith Carr could have killed with a look, for not until then did she realize that Polly would even many a slight, and that it had been a great mistake to bring her.

Edith bowed low, muttered something and touched Elnora's fingers. Tom took his cue from Polly.

"I always follow a good example," he said, and before any one could divine his intention he kissed Elnora as he gripped her hand and cried: "Mighty glad to meet you! Like to meet you a dozen times a day, you know!"

Elnora laughed and her heart pumped smoothly. They had accomplished their purpose. They had let her know they were there through compulsion, but on her side. In that instant only pity was in Elnora's breast for the flashing dark beauty, standing with smiling face while her heart must have been filled with exceeding bitterness. Elnora stepped back from the entrance.

"Come into the shade," she urged. "You must have found it warm on these country roads. Won't you lay aside your dust-coats and have a cool drink? Philip, would you ask mother to come, and bring that pitcher from the spring house?"

They entered the arbour exclaiming at the dim, green coolness. There was plenty of room and wide seats around the sides, a table in the centre, on which lay a piece of embroidery, magazines, books, the moth apparatus, and the cyanide jar containing several specimens. Polly rejoiced in the cooling shade, slipped off her duster, removed her hat, rumpled her pretty hair and seated herself to indulge in the delightful occupation of paying off old scores. Tom Levering followed her example. Edith took a seat but refused to remove her hat and coat, while Henderson stood in the entrance.

"There goes something with wings! Should you have that?" cried Levering.

He seized a net from the table and raced across the garden after a butterfly. He caught it and came back mightily pleased with himself. As the creature struggled in the net, Elnora noted a repulsed look on Edith Carr's face. Levering helped the situation beautifully.

"Now what have I got?" he demanded. "Is it just a common one that every one knows and you don't keep, or is it the rarest bird off the perch?"

"You must have had practice, you took that so perfectly," said Elnora. "I am sorry, but it is quite common and not of a kind I keep. Suppose all of you see how beautiful it is and then it may go nectar hunting again."

She held the butterfly where all of them could see, showed its upper and under wing colours, answered Polly's questions as to what it ate, how long it lived, and how it died. Then she put it into Polly's hand saying: "Stand there in the light and loosen your hold slowly and easily."

Elnora caught a brush from the table and began softly stroking the creature's sides and wings. Delighted with the sensation the butterfly opened and closed its wings, clinging to Polly's soft little fingers, while every one cried out in surprise. Elnora laid aside the brush, and the butterfly sailed away.

"Why, you are a wizard! You charm them!" marvelled Levering.

"I learned that from the Bird Woman," said Elnora. "She takes soft brushes and coaxes butterflies and moths into the positions she wants for the illustrations of a book she is writing. I have helped her often. Most of the rare ones I find go to her."

"Then you don't keep all you take?" questioned Levering.

"Oh, dear, no!" cried Elnora. "Not a tenth! For myself, a pair of each kind to use in illustrating the lectures I give in the city schools in the winter, and one pair for each collection I make. One might as well keep the big night moths of June, for they only live four or five days anyway. For the Bird Woman, I only save rare ones she has not yet secured. Sometimes I think it is cruel to take such creatures from freedom, even for an hour, but it is the only way to teach the masses of people how to distinguish the pests they should destroy, from the harmless ones of great beauty. Here comes mother with something cool to drink."

Mrs. Comstock came deliberately, talking to Philip as she approached. Elnora gave her one searching look, but could discover only an extreme brightness of eye to denote any unusual feeling. She wore one of her lavender dresses, while her snowy hair was high piled. She had taken care of her complexion, and her face had grown fuller during the winter. She might have been any one's mother with pride, and she was perfectly at ease.

Polly instantly went to her and held up her face to be kissed. Mrs. Comstock's eyes twinkled and she made the greeting hearty.

The drink was compounded of the juices of oranges and berries from the garden. It was cool enough to frost glasses and pitcher and delicious to dusty tired travellers. Soon the pitcher was empty, and Elnora picked it up and went to refill it. While she was gone Henderson asked Philip about some trouble he was having with his car. They went to the woods and began a minute examination to find a defect which did not exist. Polly and Levering were having an animated conversation with Mrs. Comstock. Henderson saw Edith arise, follow the garden path next the woods and stand waiting under the willow which Elnora would pass on her return. It was for that meeting he had made the trip. He got down on the ground, tore up the car, worked, asked for help, and kept Philip busy screwing bolts and applying the oil can. All the time Henderson kept an eye on Edith and Elnora under the willow. But he took pains to lay the work he asked Philip to do where that scene would be out of his sight. When Elnora came around the corner with the pitcher, she found herself facing Edith Carr.

"I want a minute with you," said Miss Carr.

"Very well," replied Elnora, walking on.

"Set the pitcher on the bench there," commanded Edith Carr, as if speaking to a servant.

"I prefer not to offer my visitors a warm drink," said Elnora. "I'll come back if you really wish to speak with me."

"I came solely for that," said Edith Carr.

"It would be a pity to travel so far in this dust and heat for nothing. I'll only be gone a second."

Elnora placed the pitcher before her mother. "Please serve this," she said. "Miss Carr wishes to speak with me."

"Don't you pay the least attention to anything she says," cried Polly. "Tom and I didn't come here because we wanted to. We only came to checkmate her. I hoped I'd get the opportunity to say a word to you, and now she has given it to me. I just want to tell you that she threw Phil over in perfectly horrid way. She hasn't any right to lay the ghost of a claim to him, has she, Tom?"

"Nary a claim," said Tom Levering earnestly. "Why, even you, Polly, couldn't serve me as she did Phil, and ever get me back again. If I were you, Miss Comstock, I'd send my mother to talk with her and I'd stay here."

Tom had gauged Mrs. Comstock rightly. Polly put her arms around Elnora. "Let me go with you, dear," she begged.

"I promised I would speak with her alone," said Elnora, "and she must be considered. But thank you, very much."

"How I shall love you!" exulted Polly, giving Elnora a parting hug.

The girl slowly and gravely walked back to the willow. She could not imagine what was coming, but she was promising herself that she would be very patient and control her temper.

"Will you be seated?" she asked politely.

Edith Carr glanced at the bench, while a shudder shook her.

"No. I prefer to stand," she said. "Did Mr. Ammon give you the ring you are wearing, and do you consider yourself engaged to him?"

"By what right do you ask such personal questions as those?" inquired Elnora.

"By the right of a betrothed wife. I have been promised to Philip Ammon ever since I wore short skirts. All our lives we have expected to marry. An agreement of years cannot be broken in one insane moment. Always he has loved me devotedly. Give me ten minutes with him and he will be mine for all time."

"I seriously doubt that," said Elnora. "But I am willing that you should make the test. I will call him."

"Stop!" commanded Edith Carr. "I told you that it was you I came to see."

"I remember," said Elnora.

"Mr. Ammon is my betrothed," continued Edith Carr. "I expect to take him back to Chicago with me."

"You expect considerable," murmured Elnora. "I will raise no objection to your taking him, if you can—but, I tell you frankly, I don't think it possible."

"You are so sure of yourself as that," scoffed Edith Carr. "One hour in my presence will bring back the old spell, full force. We belong to each other. I will not give him up."

"Then it is untrue that you twice rejected his ring, repeatedly insulted him, and publicly renounced him?"

"That was through you!" cried Edith Carr. "Phil and I never had been so near and so happy as we were on that night. It was your clinging to him for things that caused him to desert me among his guests, while he tried to make me await your pleasure. I realize the spell of this place, for a summer season. I understand what you and your mother have done to inveigle him. I know that your hold on him is quite real. I can see just how you have worked to ensnare him!"

"Men would call that lying," said Elnora calmly. "The second time I met Philip Ammon he told me of his engagement to you, and I respected it. I did by you as I would want you to do by me. He was here parts of each day, almost daily last summer. The Almighty is my witness that never once, by word or look, did I ever make the slightest attempt to interest him in my person or personality. He wrote you frequently in my presence. He forgot the violets for which he asked to send you. I gathered them and carried them to him. I sent him back to you in unswerving devotion, and the Almighty is also my witness that I could have changed his heart last summer, if I had tried. I wisely left that work for you. All my life I shall be glad that I lived and worked on the square. That he ever would come back to me free, by your act, I never dreamed. When he left me I did not hope or expect to see him again," Elnora's voice fell soft and low, "and, behold! You sent him—and free!"

"You exult in that!" cried Edith Carr. "Let me tell you he is not free! We have belonged for years. We always shall. If you cling to him, and hold him to rash things he has said and done, because he thought me still angry and unforgiving with him, you will ruin all our lives. If he married you, before a month you would read heart-hunger for me in his eyes. He could not love me as he has done, and give me up for a little scene like that!"

"There is a great poem," said Elnora, "one line of which reads, 'For each man kills the thing he loves.' Let me tell you that a woman can do that also. He did love you—that I concede. But you killed his love everlastingly, when you disgraced him in public. Killed it so completely he does not even feel resentment toward you. To-day, he would do you a favour, if he could; but love you, no! That is over!"

Edith Carr stood truly regal and filled with scorn. "You are mistaken! Nothing on earth could kill that!" she cried, and Elnora saw that the girl really believed what she said.

"You are very sure of yourself!" said Elnora.

"I have reason to be sure," answered Edith Carr.

"We have lived and loved too long. I have had years with him to match against your days. He is mine! His work, his ambitions, his friends, his place in society are with me. You may have a summer charm for a sick man in the country; if he tried placing you in society, he soon would see you as others will. It takes birth to position, schooling, and endless practice to meet social demands gracefully. You would put him to shame in a week."

"I scarcely think I should follow your example so far," said Elnora dryly. "I have a feeling for Philip that would prevent my hurting him purposely, either in public or private. As for managing a social career for him he never mentioned that he desired such a thing. What he asked of me was that I should be his wife. I understood that to mean that he desired me to keep him a clean house, serve him digestible food, mother his children, and give him loving sympathy and tenderness."

"Shameless!" cried Edith Carr.

"To which of us do you intend that adjective to apply?" inquired Elnora. "I never was less ashamed in all my life. Please remember I am in my own home, and your presence here is not on my invitation."

Miss Carr lifted her head and struggled with her veil. She was very pale and trembling violently, while Elnora stood serene, a faint smile on her lips.

"Such vulgarity!" panted Edith Carr. "How can a man like Philip endure it?"

"Why don't you ask him?" inquired Elnora. "I can call him with one breath; but, if he judged us as we stand, I should not be the one to tremble at his decision. Miss Carr, you have been quite plain. You have told me in carefully selected words what you think of me. You insult my birth, education, appearance, and home. I assure you I am legitimate. I will pass a test examination with you on any high school or supplementary branch, or French or German. I will take a physical examination beside you. I will face any social emergency you can mention with you. I am acquainted with a whole world in which Philip Ammon is keenly interested, that you scarcely know exists. I am not afraid to face any audience you can get together anywhere with my violin. I am not repulsive to look at, and I have a wholesome regard for the proprieties and civilities of life. Philip Ammon never asked anything more of me, why should you?"

"It is plain to see," cried Edith Carr, "that you took him when he was hurt and angry and kept his wound wide open. Oh, what have you not done against me?"

"I did not promise to marry him when an hour ago he asked me, and offered me this ring, because there was so much feeling in my heart for you, that I knew I never could be happy, if I felt that in any way I had failed in doing justice to your interests. I did slip on this ring, which he had just brought, because I never owned one, and it is very beautiful, but I made him no promise, nor shall I make any, until I am quite, quite sure, that you fully realize he never would marry you if I sent him away this hour."

"You know perfectly that if your puny hold on him were broken, if he were back in his home, among his friends, and where he was meeting me, in one short week he would be mine again, as he always has been. In your heart you don't believe what you say. You don't dare trust him in my presence. You are afraid to allow him out of your sight, because you know what the results would be. Right or wrong, you have made up your mind to ruin him and me, and you are going to be selfish enough to do it. But——"

"That will do!" said Elnora. "Spare me the enumeration of how I will regret it. I shall regret nothing. I shall not act until I know there will be nothing to regret. I have decided on my course. You may return to your friends."

"What do you mean?" demanded Edith Carr.

"That is my affair," replied Elnora. "Only this! When your opportunity comes, seize it! Any time you are in Philip Ammon's presence, exert the charms of which you boast, and take him. I grant you are justified in doing it if you can. I want nothing more than I want to see you marry Philip if he wants you. He is just across the fence under that automobile. Go spread your meshes and exert your wiles. I won't stir to stop you. Take him to Onabasha, and to Chicago with you. Use every art you possess. If the old charm can be revived I will be the first to wish both of you well. Now, I must return to my visitors. Kindly excuse me."

Elnora turned and went back to the arbour. Edith Carr followed the fence and passed through the gate into the west woods where she asked Henderson about the car. As she stood near him she whispered: "Take Phil back to Onabasha with us."

"I say, Ammon, can't you go to the city with us and help me find a shop where I can get this pinion fixed?" asked Henderson. "We want to lunch and start back by five. That will get us home about midnight. Why don't you bring your automobile here?"

"I am a working man," said Philip. "I have no time to be out motoring. I can't see anything the matter with your car, myself; but, of course you don't want to break down in the night, on strange roads, with women on your hands. I'll see."

Philip went into the arbour, where Polly took possession of his lap, fingered his hair, and kissed his forehead and lips.

"When are you coming to the cottage, Phil?" she asked. "Come soon, and bring Miss Comstock for a visit. All of us will be so glad to have her."

Philip beamed on Polly. "I'll see about that," he said. "Sounds pretty good. Elnora, Henderson is in trouble with his automobile. He wants me to go to Onabasha with him to show him where the doctor lives, and make repairs so he can start back this evening. It will take about two hours. May I go?"

"Of course, you must go," she said, laughing lightly. "You can't leave your sister. Why don't you return to Chicago with them? There is plenty of room, and you could have a fine visit."

"I'll be back in just two hours," said Philip. "While I am gone, you be thinking over what we were talking of when the folks came."

"Miss Comstock can go with us as well as not," said Polly. "That back seat was made for three, and I can sit on your lap."

"Come on! Do come!" urged Philip instantly, and Tom Levering joined him, but Henderson and Edith silently waited at the gate.

"No, thank you," laughed Elnora. "That would crowd you, and it's warm and dusty. We will say good-bye here."

She offered her hand to all of them, and when she came to Philip she gave him one long steady look in the eyes, then shook hands with him also.

CHAPTER XXIII

WHEREIN ELNORA REACHES A
DECISION, AND FRECKLES AND THE
ANGEL APPEAR

"Well, she came, didn't she?" remarked Mrs. Comstock to Elnora as they watched the automobile speed down the road. As it turned the Limberlost corner, Philip arose and waved to them.

"She hasn't got him yet, anyway," said Mrs. Comstock, taking heart. "What's that on your finger, and what did she say to you?"

Elnora explained about the ring as she drew it off.

"I have several letters to write, then I am going to change my dress and walk down toward Aunt Margaret's for a little exercise. I may meet some of them, and I don't want them to see this ring. You keep it until Philip comes," said Elnora. "As for what Miss Carr said to me, many things, two of importance: one, that I lacked every social requirement necessary for the happiness of Philip Ammon, and that if I married him I would see inside a month that he was ashamed of me——"

"Aw, shockins!" scorned Mrs. Comstock. "Go on!"

"The other was that she has been engaged to him for years, that he belongs to her, and she refuses to give him up. She said that if he were in her presence one hour, she would have him under a mysterious thing she calls 'her spell' again; if he were where she could see him for one week, everything would be made up. It is her opinion that he is suffering from wounded pride, and that the slightest concession on her part will bring him to his knees before her."

Mrs. Comstock giggled. "I do hope the boy isn't weak-kneed," she said. "I just happened to be passing the west window this afternoon——"

Elnora laughed. "Nothing save actual knowledge ever would have made me believe there was a girl in all this world so infatuated with herself. She speaks casually of her power over men, and boasts of 'bringing a man to his knees' as complacently as I would pick up a net and say: 'I am going to take a butterfly.' She honestly believes that if Philip were with her a short time she could rekindle his love for her and awaken in him every particle of the old devotion. Mother, the girl is honest! She is absolutely sincere! She so believes in herself and the strength of Phil's love for her, that all her life she will believe in and brood over that thought, unless she is taught differently. So long as she thinks that, she will nurse wrong ideas and pine over her blighted life. She must be taught that Phil is absolutely free, and yet he will not go to her."

"But how on earth are you proposing to teach her that?"

"The way will open."

"Lookey here, Elnora!" cried Mrs. Comstock. "That Carr girl is the handsomest dark woman I ever saw. She's got to the place where she won't stop at anything. Her coming here proves that. I don't believe there was a thing the matter with that automobile. I think that was a scheme she fixed up to get Phil where she could see him alone, as she worked to see you. If you are going deliberately to put Philip under her influence again, you've got to brace yourself for the possibility that she may win. A man is a weak mortal, where a lovely woman is concerned, and he never denied that he loved her once. You may make yourself downright miserable."

"But mother, if she won, it wouldn't make me half so miserable as to marry Phil myself, and then read hunger for her in his eyes! Some one has got to suffer over this. If it proves to be me, I'll bear it, and you'll never hear a whisper of complaint from me. I know the real Philip Ammon better in our months of work in the fields than she knows him in all her years of society engagements. So she shall have the hour she asked, many, many of them, enough to make her acknowledge that she is wrong. Now I am going to write my letters and take my walk."

Elnora threw her arms around her mother and kissed her repeatedly. "Don't you worry about me," she said. "I will get along all right, and whatever happens, I always will be your girl and you my darling mother."

She left two sealed notes on her desk. Then she changed her dress, packed a small bundle which she dropped with her hat from the window beside the willow, and softly went down stairs. Mrs. Comstock was in the garden. Elnora picked up the hat and bundle, hurried down the road a few rods, then climbed the fence and entered the woods. She took a diagonal course, and after a long walk reached a road two miles west and one south. There she straightened her clothing, put on her hat and a thin dark veil and waited the passing of the next trolley. She left it at the first town and took a train for Fort Wayne. She made that point just in time to climb on the evening train north, as it pulled from the station. It was after midnight when she left the car at Grand Rapids, and went into the depot to await the coming of day.

Tired out, she laid her head on her bundle and fell asleep on a seat in the women's waiting-room. Long after light she was awakened by the roar and rattle of trains. She washed, re-arranged her hair and clothing, and went into the general waiting-room to find her way to the street. She saw him as he entered the door. There was no mistaking the tall, lithe figure, the bright hair, the lean, brown-splotched face, the steady gray eyes. He was dressed for travelling, and carried a light overcoat and a bag. Straight to him Elnora went speeding.

"Oh, I was just starting to find you!" she cried.

"Thank you!" he said.

"You are going away?" she panted.

"Not if I am needed. I have a few minutes. Can you be telling me briefly?"

"I am the Limberlost girl to whom your wife gave the dress for Commencement last spring, and both of you sent lovely gifts. There is a reason, a very good reason, why I must be hidden for a time, and I came straight to you—as if I had a right."

"You have!" answered Freckles. "Any boy or girl who ever suffered one pang in the Limberlost has a claim to the best drop of blood in my heart. You needn't be telling me anything more. The Angel is at our cottage on Mackinac. You shall tell her and play with the babies while you want shelter. This way!"

They breakfasted in a luxurious car, talked over the swamp, the work of the Bird Woman; Elnora told of her nature lectures in the schools, and soon they were good friends. In the evening they left the train at Mackinaw City and crossed the Straits by boat. Sheets of white moonlight flooded the water and paved a molten path across the breast of it straight to the face of the moon.

The island lay a dark spot on the silver surface, its tall trees sharply outlined on the summit, and a million lights blinked around the shore. The night guns boomed from the white fort and a dark sentinel paced the ramparts above the little city tucked down close to the water. A great tenor summering in the north came out on the upper deck of the big boat, and baring his head, faced the moon and sang: "Oh, the moon shines bright on my old Kentucky home!" Elnora thought of the Limberlost, of Philip, and her mother, and almost choked with the sobs that would arise in her throat. On the dock a woman of exquisite beauty swept into the arms of Terence O'More.

"Oh, Freckles!" she cried. "You've been gone a month!"

"Four days, Angel, only four days by the clock," remonstrated Freckles. "Where are the children?"

"Asleep! Thank goodness! I'm worn to a thread. I never saw such inventive, active children. I can't keep track of them!"

"I have brought you help," said Freckles. "Here is the Limberlost girl in whom the Bird Woman is interested. Miss Comstock needs a rest before beginning her school work for next year, so she came to us."

"You dear thing! How good of you!" cried the Angel. "We shall be so happy to have you!"

In her room that night, in a beautiful cottage furnished with every luxury, Elnora lifted a tired face to the Angel.

"Of course, you understand there is something back of this?" she said. "I must tell you."

"Yes," agreed the Angel. "Tell me! If you get it out of your system, you will stand a better chance of sleeping."

Elnora stood brushing the copper-bright masses of her hair as she talked. When she finished the Angel was almost hysterical.

"You insane creature!" she cried. "How crazy of you to leave him to her! I know both of them. I have met them often. She may be able to make good her boast. But it is perfectly splendid of you! And, after all, really it is the only way. I can see that. I think it is what I should have done myself, or tried to do. I don't know that I could have done it! When I think of walking away and leaving Freckles with a woman he once loved, to let her see if she can make him love her again, oh, it gives me a graveyard heart. No, I never could have done it! You are bigger than I ever was. I should have turned coward, sure."

"I am a coward," admitted Elnora. "I am soul-sick! I am afraid I shall lose my senses before this is over. I didn't want to come! I wanted to stay, to go straight into his arms, to bind myself with his ring, to love him with all my heart. It wasn't my fault that I came. There was something inside that just pushed me. She is beautiful——"

"I quite agree with you!"

"You can imagine how fascinating she can be. She used no arts on me. Her purpose was to cower me. She found she could not do that, but she did a thing which helped her more: she proved that she was honest, perfectly sincere in what she thought. She believes that if she merely beckons to Philip, he will go to her. So I am giving her the opportunity to learn from him what he will do. She never will believe it from any one else. When she is satisfied, I shall be also."

"But, child! Suppose she wins him back!"

"That is the supposition with which I shall eat and sleep for the coming few weeks. Would one dare ask for a peep at the babies before going to bed?"

"Now, you are perfect!" announced the Angel. "I never should have liked you all I can, if you had been content to go to sleep in this house without asking to see the babies. Come this way. We named the first boy for his father, of course, and the girl for Aunt Alice. The next boy is named for my father, and the baby for the Bird Woman. After this we are going to branch out."

Elnora began to laugh.

"Oh, I suspect there will be quite a number of them," said the Angel serenely. "I am told the more there are the less trouble they make. The big ones take care of the little ones. We want a large family. This is our start."

She entered a dark room and held aloft a candle. She went to the side of a small white iron bed in which lay a boy of eight and another of three. They were perfectly formed, rosy children, the elder a replica of his mother, the other very like. Then they came to a cradle where a baby girl of almost two slept soundly, and made a picture.

"But just see here!" said the Angel. She threw the light on a sleeping girl of six. A mass of red curls swept the pillow. Line and feature the face was that of Freckles. Without asking, Elnora knew the colour and expression of the closed eyes. The Angel handed Elnora the candle, and stooping, straightened the child's body. She ran her fingers through the bright curls, and lightly touched the aristocratic little nose.

"The supply of freckles holds out in my family, you see!" she said. "Both of the girls will have them, and the second boy a few."

She stood an instant longer, then bending, ran her hand caressingly down a rosy bare leg, while she kissed the babyish red mouth. There had been some reason for touching all of them, the kiss fell on the lips which were like Freckles's.

To Elnora she said a tender good-night, whispering brave words of encouragement and making plans to fill the days to come. Then she went away. An hour later there was a light tap on the girl's door.

"Come!" she called as she lay staring into the dark.

The Angel felt her way to the bedside, sat down and took Elnora's hands.

"I just had to come back to you," she said. "I have been telling Freckles, and he is almost hurting himself with laughing. I didn't think it was funny, but he does. He thinks it's the funniest thing that ever happened. He says that to run away from Mr. Ammon, when you had made him no promise at all, when he wasn't sure of you, won't send him home to her; it will set him hunting you! He says if you had combined the wisdom of Solomon, Socrates, and all the remainder of the wise men, you couldn't have chosen any course that would have sealed him to you so surely. He feels that now Mr. Ammon will perfectly hate her for coming down there and driving you away. And you went to give her the chance she wanted. Oh, Elnora! It is becoming funny! I see it, too!"

The Angel rocked on the bedside. Elnora faced the dark in silence.

"Forgive me," gulped the Angel. "I didn't mean to laugh. I didn't think it was funny, until all at once it came to me. Oh, dear! Elnora, it *is* funny! I've got to laugh!"

"Maybe it is," admitted Elnora "to others; but it isn't very funny to me. And it won't be to Philip, or to mother."

That was very true. Mrs. Comstock had been slightly prepared for stringent action of some kind, by what Elnora had said. The mother instantly had guessed where the girl would go, but nothing was said to Philip. That would have been to invalidate Elnora's test in the beginning, and Mrs. Comstock knew her child well enough to know that she never would marry Philip unless she felt it right that she should. The only way was to find out, and Elnora had gone to seek the information. There was nothing to do but wait until she came back, and her mother was not in the least uneasy but that the girl would return brave and self-reliant, as always.

Philip Ammon hurried back to the Limberlost, strong in the hope that now he might take Elnora into his arms and receive her promise to become his wife. His first shock of disappointment came when he found her gone. In talking with Mrs. Comstock he learned that Edith Carr had made an opportunity to speak with Elnora alone. He hastened down the road to meet her, coming back alone, an agitated man. Then search revealed the notes. His read:

DEAR PHILIP:

I find that I am never going to be able to answer your question of this afternoon fairly to all of us, when you are with me. So I am going away a few weeks to think over matters alone. I shall not tell you, or even mother, where I am going, but I shall be safe, well cared for, and happy. Please go back home and live among your friends, just as you always have done, and on or before the first of September, I will write you where I am, and what I have decided. Please do not blame Edith Carr for this, and do not avoid her. I hope you will call on her and be friends. I think she is very sorry, and covets your friendship at least. Until September, then, as ever,

ELNORA.

Mrs. Comstock's note was much the same. Philip was ill with disappointment. In the arbour he laid his head on the table, among the implements of Elnora's loved work, and gulped down dry sobs he could not restrain. Mrs. Comstock never had liked him so well. Her hand involuntarily crept toward his dark head, then she drew back. Elnora would not want her to do anything whatever to influence him.

"What am I going to do to convince Edith Carr that I do not love her, and Elnora that I am hers?" he demanded.

"I guess you have to figure that out yourself," said Mrs. Comstock. "I'd be glad to help you if I could, but it seems to be up to you."

Philip sat a long time in silence. "Well, I have decided!" he said abruptly. "Are you perfectly sure Elnora had plenty of money and a safe place to go?"

"Absolutely!" answered Mrs. Comstock. "She has been taking care of herself ever since she was born, and she always has come out all right, so far; I'll stake all I'm worth on it, that she always will. I don't know where she is, but I'm not going to worry about her safety."

"I can't help worrying!" cried Philip. "I can think of fifty things that may happen to her when she thinks she is safe. This is distracting! First, I am going to run up to see my father. Then, I'll let you know what we have decided. Is there anything I can do for you?"

"Nothing!" said Mrs. Comstock.

But the desire to do something for him was so strong with her she scarcely could keep her lips closed or her hands quiet. She longed to tell him what Edith Carr had said, how it had affected Elnora, and to comfort him as she felt she could. But loyalty to the girl held her. If Elnora truly felt that she could not decide until Edith Carr was convinced, then Edith Carr would have to yield or triumph. It rested with Philip. So Mrs. Comstock kept silent, while Philip took the night limited, a bitterly disappointed man.

By noon the next day he was in his father's offices. They had a long conference, but did not arrive at much until the elder Ammon suggested sending for Polly. Anything that might have happened could be explained after Polly had told of the private conference between Edith and Elnora.

"Talk about lovely woman!" cried Philip Ammon. "One would think that after such a dose as Edith gave me, she would be satisfied to let me go my way, but no! Not caring for me enough herself to save me from public disgrace, she must now pursue me to keep any other woman from loving me. I call that too much! I am going to see her, and I want you to go with me, father."

"Very well," said Mr. Ammon, "I will go."

When Edith Carr came into her reception-room that afternoon, gowned for conquest, she expected only Philip, and him penitent. She came hurrying toward him, smiling, radiant, ready to use every allurement she possessed, and paused in dismay when she saw his cold face and his father. "Why, Phil!" she cried. "When did you come home?"

"I am not at home," answered Philip. "I merely ran up to see my father on business, and to inquire of you what it was you said to Miss Comstock yesterday that caused her to disappear before I could return to the Limberlost."

"Miss Comstock disappear! Impossible!" cried Edith Carr. "Where could she go?"

"I thought perhaps you could answer that, since it was through you that she went."

"Phil, I haven't the faintest idea where she is," said the girl gently.

"But you know perfectly why she went! Kindly tell me that."

"Let me see you alone, and I will."

"Here and now, or not at all."

"Phil!"

"What did you say to the girl I love?"

Then Edith Carr stretched out her arms.

"Phil, I am the girl you love!" she cried. "All your life you have loved me. Surely it cannot be all gone in a few weeks of misunderstanding. I was jealous of her! I did not want you to leave me an instant that night for any other girl living. That was the moth I was representing. Every one knew it! I wanted you to bring it to me. When you did not, I knew instantly it had been for her that you worked last summer, she who suggested my dress, she who had power to take you from me, when I wanted you most. The thought drove me mad, and I said and did those insane things. Phil, I beg your pardon! I ask your forgiveness. Yesterday she said that you had told her of me at once. She vowed both of you had been true to me and Phil, I couldn't look into her eyes and not see that it was the truth. Oh, Phil, if you understood how I have suffered you would forgive me. Phil, I never knew how much I cared for you! I will do anything—anything!"

"Then tell me what you said to Elnora yesterday that drove her, alone and friendless, into the night, heaven knows where!"

"You have no thought for any one save her?"

"Yes," said Philip. "I have. Because I once loved you, and believed in you, my heart aches for you. I will gladly forgive anything you ask. I will do anything you want, except to resume our former relations. That is impossible. It is hopeless and useless to ask it."

"You truly mean that!"

"Yes."

"Then find out from her what I said!"

"Come, father," said Philip, rising.

"You were going to show Miss Comstock's letter to Edith!" suggested Mr. Ammon.

"I have not the slightest interest in Miss Comstock's letter," said Edith Carr.

"You are not even interested in the fact that she says you are not responsible for her going, and that I am to call on you and be friends with you?"

"That is interesting, indeed!" sneered Miss Carr.

She took the letter, read and returned it.

"She has done what she could for my cause, it seems," she said coldly. "How very generous of her! Do you propose calling out Pinkertons and instituting a general search?"

"No," replied Philip. "I simply propose to go back to the Limberlost and live with her mother, until Elnora becomes convinced that I am not courting you, and never shall be. Then, perhaps, she will come home to us. Good-bye. Good luck to you always!"

CHAPTER XXIV

WHEREIN EDITH CARR WAGES A
BATTLE, AND HART HENDERSON
STANDS GUARD

Many people looked, a few followed, when Edith Carr slowly came down the main street of Mackinac, pausing here and there to note the glow of colour in one small booth after another, overflowing with gay curios. That street of packed white sand, winding with the curves of the shore, outlined with brilliant shops, and thronged with laughing, bare-headed people in outing costumes was a picturesque and fascinating sight. Thousands annually made long journeys and paid exorbitant prices to take part in that pageant.

As Edith Carr passed, she was the most distinguished figure of the old street. Her clinging black gown was sufficiently elaborate for a dinner dress. On her head was a large, wide, drooping-brimmed black hat, with immense floating black plumes, while on the brim, and among the laces on her breast glowed velvety, deep red roses. Some way these made up for the lack of colour in her cheeks and lips, and while her eyes seemed unnaturally bright, to a close observer they appeared weary. Despite the effort she made to move lightly she was very tired, and dragged her heavy feet with an effort.

She turned at the little street leading to the dock, and went to meet the big lake steamer ploughing up the Straits from Chicago. Past the landing place, on to the very end of the pier she went, then sat down, leaned against a dock support and closed her tired eyes. When the steamer came very close she languidly watched the people lining the railing. Instantly she marked one lean anxious face turned toward hers, and with a throb of pity she lifted a hand and waved to Hart Henderson. He was the first man to leave the boat, coming to her instantly. She spread her trailing skirts and motioned him to sit beside her. Silently they looked across the softly lapping water. At last she forced herself to speak to him.

"Did you have a successful trip?"

"I accomplished my purpose."

"You didn't lose any time getting back."

"I never do when I am coming to you."

"Do you want to go to the cottage for anything?"

"No."

"Then let us sit here and wait until the Petoskey steamer comes in. I like to watch the boats. Sometimes I study the faces, if I am not too tired."

"Have you seen any new types to-day?"

She shook her head. "This has not been an easy day, Hart."

"And it's going to be worse," said Henderson bitterly. "There's no use putting it off. Edith, I saw some one to-day."

"You should have seen thousands," she said lightly.

"I did. But of them all, only one will be of interest to you."

"Man or woman?"

"Man."

"Where?"

"Lake Shore private hospital."

"An accident?"

"No. Nervous and physical breakdown."

"Phil said he was going back to the Limberlost."

"He went. He was there three weeks, but the strain broke him. He has an old letter in his hands that he has handled until it is ragged. He held it up to me and said: 'You can see for yourself that she says she will be well and happy, but we can't know until we see her again, and that may never be. She may have gone too near that place her father went down, some of that Limberlost gang may have found her in the forest, she may lie dead in some city morgue this instant, waiting for me to find her body.'"

"Hart! For pity sake stop!"

"I can't," cried Henderson desperately. "I am forced to tell you. They are fighting brain fever. He did go back to the swamp and he prowled it night and day. The days down there are hot now, and the nights wet with dew and cold. He paid no attention and forgot his food. A fever started and his uncle brought him home. They've never had a word from her, or found a trace of her. Mrs. Comstock thought she had gone to O'Mores' at Great Rapids, so when Phil broke down she telegraphed there. They had been gone all summer, so her mother is as anxious as Phil."

"The O'Mores are here," said Edith. "I haven't seen any of them, because I haven't gone out much in the few days since we came, but this is their summer home."

"Edith, they say at the hospital that it will take careful nursing to save Phil. He is surrounded by stacks of maps and railroad guides. He is trying to frame up a plan to set the entire detective agency of the country to work. He says he will stay there just two days longer. The doctors say he will kill himself when he goes. He is a sick man, Edith. His hands are burning and shaky and his breath was hot against my face."

"Why are you telling me?" It was a cry of acute anguish.

"He thinks you know where she is."

"I do not! I haven't an idea! I never dreamed she would go away when she had him in her hand! I should not have done it!"

"He said it was something you said to her that made her go."

"That may be, but it doesn't prove that I know where she went."

Henderson looked across the water and suffered keenly. At last he turned to Edith and laid a firm, strong hand over hers.

"Edith," he said, "do you realize how serious this is?"

"I suppose I do."

"Do you want as fine a fellow as Philip driven any further? If he leaves that hospital now, and goes out to the exposure and anxiety of a search for her, there will be a tragedy that no after regrets can avert. Edith, what did you say to Miss Comstock that made her run away from Phil?"

The girl turned her face from him and sat still, but the man gripping her hands and waiting in agony could see that she was shaken by the jolting of the heart in her breast.

"Edith, what did you say?"

"What difference can it make?"

"It might furnish some clue to her action."

"It could not possibly."

"Phil thinks so. He has thought so until his brain is worn enough to give way. Tell me, Edith!"

"I told her Phil was mine! That if he were away from her an hour and back in my presence, he would be to me as he always has been."

"Edith, did you believe that?"

"I would have staked my life, my soul on it!"

"Do you believe it now?"

There was no answer. Henderson took her other hand and holding both of them firmly he said softly: "Don't mind me, dear. I don't count! I'm just old Hart! You can tell me anything. Do you still believe that?"

The beautiful head barely moved in negation. Henderson gathered both her hands in one of his and stretched an arm across her shoulders to the post to support her. She dragged her hands from him and twisted them together.

"Oh, Hart!" she cried. "It isn't fair! There is a limit! I have suffered my share. Can't you see? Can't you understand?"

"Yes," he panted. "Yes, my girl! Tell me just this one thing yet, and I'll cheerfully kill any one who annoys you further. Tell me, Edith!"

Then she lifted her big, dull, pain-filled eyes to his and cried: "No! I do not believe it now! I know it is not true! I killed his love for me. It is dead and gone forever. Nothing will revive it! Nothing in all this world. And that is not all. I did not know how to touch the depths of his nature. I never developed in him those things he was made to enjoy. He admired me. He was proud to be with me. He thought, and I thought, that he worshipped me; but I know now that he never did care for me as he cares for her. Never! I can see it! I planned to lead society, to make his home a place sought for my beauty and popularity. She plans to advance his political ambitions, to make him comfortable physically, to stimulate his intellect, to bear him a brood of red-faced children. He likes her and her plans as he never did me and mine. Oh, my soul! Now, are you satisfied?"

She dropped back against his arm exhausted. Henderson held her and learned what suffering truly means. He fanned her with his hat, rubbed her cold hands and murmured broken, incoherent things. By and by slow tears slipped from under her closed lids, but when she opened them her eyes were dull and hard.

"What a rag one is when the last secret of the soul is torn out and laid bare!" she cried.

Henderson thrust his handkerchief into her fingers and whispered, "Edith, the boat has been creeping up. It's very close. Maybe some of our crowd are on it. Hadn't we better slip away from here before it lands?"

"If I can walk," she said. "Oh, I am so dead tired, Hart!

"Yes, dear," said Henderson soothingly. "Just try to pass the landing before the boat anchors. If I only dared carry you!"

They struggled through the waiting masses, but directly opposite the landing there was a backward movement in the happy, laughing crowd, the gang-plank came down with a slam, and people began hurrying from the boat. Crowded against the fish house on the dock, Henderson could only advance a few steps at a time. He was straining every nerve to protect and assist Edith. He saw no one he recognized near them, so he slipped his arm across her back to help support her. He felt her stiffen against him and catch her breath. At the same instant, the clearest, sweetest male voice he ever had heard called: "Be careful there, little men!"

Henderson sent a swift glance toward the boat. Terence O'More had stepped from the gang-plank, leading a little daughter, so like him, it was comical. There followed a picture not easy to describe. The Angel in the full flower of her beauty, richly dressed, a laugh on her cameo face, the setting sun glinting on her gold hair, escorted by her eldest son, who held her hand tightly and carefully watched her steps. Next came Elnora, dressed with equal richness, a trifle taller and slenderer, almost the same type of colouring, but with different eyes and hair, facial lines and expression. She was led by the second O'More boy who convulsed the crowd by saying: "Tareful, Elnora! Don't 'oo be 'teppin' in de water!"

People surged around them, purposely closing them in.

"What lovely women! Who are they? It's the O'Mores. The lightest one is his wife. Is that her sister? No, it is his! They say he has a title in England."

Whispers ran fast and audible. As the crowd pressed around the party an opening was left beside the fish sheds. Edith ran down the dock. Henderson sprang after her, catching her arm and assisting her to the street.

"Up the shore! This way!" she panted. "Every one will go to dinner the first thing they do."

They left the street and started around the beach, but Edith was breathless from running, while the yielding sand made difficult walking.

"Help me!" she cried, clinging to Henderson. He put his arm around her, almost carrying her from sight into a little cove walled by high rocks at the back, while there was a clean floor of white sand, and logs washed from the lake for seats. He found one of these with a back rest, and hurrying down to the water he soaked his handkerchief and carried it to her. She passed it across her lips, over her eyes, and then pressed the palms of her hands upon it. Henderson removed the heavy hat, fanned her with his, and wet the handkerchief again.

"Hart, what makes you?" she said wearily. "My mother doesn't care. She says this is good for me. Do you think this is good for me, Hart?"

"Edith, you know I would give my life if I could save you this," he said, and could not speak further.

She leaned against him, closed her eyes and lay silent so long the man fell into panic.

"Edith, you are not unconscious?" he whispered, touching her.

"No, just resting. Please don't leave me."

He held her carefully, gently fanning her. She was suffering almost more than either of them could endure.

"I wish you had your boat," she said at last. "I want to sail with the wind in my face."

"There is no wind. I can bring my motor around in a few minutes."

"Then get it."

"Lie on the sand. I can 'phone from the first booth. It won't take but a little while."

Edith lay on the white sand, and Henderson covered her face with her hat. Then he ran to the nearest booth and talked imperatively. Presently he was back bringing a hot drink that was stimulating. Shortly the motor ran close to the beach and stopped. Henderson's servant brought a row-boat ashore and took them to the launch. It was filled with cushions and wraps. Henderson made a couch and soon, warmly covered, Edith sped out over the water in search of peace.

Hour after hour the boat ran up and down the shore. The moon arose and the night air grew very chilly. Henderson put on an overcoat and piled more covers on Edith.

"You must take me home," she said at last. "The folks will be uneasy."

He was compelled to take her to the cottage with the battle still raging. He went back early the next morning, but already she had wandered out over the island. Instinctively Henderson felt that the shore would attract her. There was something in the tumult of rough little Huron's waves that called to him. It was there he found her, crouching so close the water the foam was dampening her skirts.

"May I stay?" he asked.

"I have been hoping you would come," she answered. "It's bad enough when you are here, but it is a little easier than bearing it alone."

"Thank God for that!" said Henderson sitting beside her. "Shall I talk to you?"

She shook her head. So they sat by the hour. At last she spoke: "Of course, you know there is something I have got to do, Hart!"

"You have not!" cried Henderson, violently. "That's all nonsense! Give me just one word of permission. That is all that is required of you."

"'Required?' You grant, then, that there is something 'required?'"

"One word. Nothing more."

"Did you ever know one word could be so big, so black, so desperately bitter? Oh, Hart!"

"No."

"But you know it now, Hart!"

"Yes."

"And still you say that it is 'required?'"

Henderson suffered unspeakably. At last he said: "If you had seen and heard him, Edith, you, too, would feel that it is 'required.' Remember——"

"No! No! No!" she cried. "Don't ask me to remember even the least of my pride and folly. Let me forget!"

She sat silent for a long time.

"Will you go with me?" she whispered.

"Of course."

At last she arose.

"I might as well give up and have it over," she faltered.

That was the first time in her life that Edith Carr ever had proposed to give up anything she wanted.

"Help me, Hart!"

Henderson started around the beach assisting her all he could. Finally he stopped.

"Edith, there is no sense in this! You are too tired to go. You know you can trust me. You wait in any of these lovely places and send me. You will be safe, and I'll run. One word is all that is necessary."

"But I've got to say that word myself, Hart!"

"Then write it, and let me carry it. The message is not going to prove who went to the office and sent it."

"That is quite true," she said, dropping wearily, but she made no movement to take the pen and paper he offered.

"Hart, you write it," she said at last.

Henderson turned away his face. He gripped the pen, while his breath sucked between his dry teeth.

"Certainly!" he said when he could speak. "Mackinac, August 27, 1908. Philip Ammon, Lake Shore Hospital, Chicago." He paused with suspended pen and glanced at Edith. Her white lips were working, but no sound came. "Miss Comstock is with the Terence O'Mores, on Mackinac Island," prompted Henderson.

Edith nodded.

"Signed, Henderson," continued the big man.

Edith shook her head.

"Say, 'She is well and happy,' and sign, Edith Carr!" she panted.

"Not on your life!" flashed Henderson.

"For the love of mercy, Hart, don't make this any harder! It is the least I can do, and it takes every ounce of strength in me to do it."

"Will you wait for me here?" he asked.

She nodded, and, pulling his hat lower over his eyes, Henderson ran around the shore. In less than an hour he was back. He helped her a little farther to where the Devil's Kitchen lay cut into the rocks; it furnished places to rest, and cool water. Before long his man came with the boat. From it they spread blankets on the sand for her, and made chafing-dish tea. She tried to refuse it, but the fragrance overcame her for she drank ravenously. Then Henderson cooked several dishes and spread an appetizing lunch. She was young, strong, and almost famished for food. She was forced to eat. That made her feel much better. Then Henderson helped her into the boat and ran it through shady coves of the shore, where there were refreshing breezes. When she fell asleep the girl did not know, but the man did. Sadly in need of rest himself, he ran that boat for five hours through quiet bays, away from noisy parties, and where the shade was cool and deep. When she awoke he took her home, and as they went she knew that she had been mistaken. She would not die. Her heart was not even broken. She had suffered horribly; she would suffer more; but eventually the pain must wear out. Into her head crept a few lines of an old opera:

> "Hearts do not break, they sting and ache,
> For old love's sake, but do not die,
> As witnesseth the living I."

That evening they were sailing down the Straits before a stiff breeze and Henderson was busy with the tiller when she said to him: "Hart, I want you to do something more for me."

"You have only to tell me," he said.

"Have I only to tell you, Hart?" she asked softly.

"Haven't you learned that yet, Edith?"

"I want you to go away."

"Very well," he said quietly, but his face whitened visibly.

"You say that as if you had been expecting it."

"I have. I knew from the beginning that when this was over you would dislike me for having seen you suffer. I have grown my Gethsemane in a full realization of what was coming, but I could not leave you, Edith, so long as it seemed to me that I was serving you. Does it make any difference to you where I go?"

"I want you where you will be loved, and good care taken of you."

"Thank you!" said Henderson, smiling grimly. "Have you any idea where such a spot might be found?"

"It should be with your sister at Los Angeles. She always has seemed very fond of you."

"That is quite true," said Henderson, his eyes brightening a little. "I will go to her. When shall I start?"

"At once."

Henderson began to tack for the landing, but his hands shook until he scarcely could manage the boat. Edith Carr sat watching him indifferently, but her heart was throbbing painfully. "Why is there so much suffering in the world?" she kept whispering to herself. Inside her door Henderson took her by the shoulders almost roughly.

"For how long is this, Edith, and how are you going to say good-bye to me?"

She raised tired, pain-filled eyes to his.

"I don't know for how long it is," she said. "It seems now as if it had been a slow eternity. I wish to my soul that God would be merciful to me and make something 'snap' in my heart, as there did in Phil's, that would give me rest. I don't know for how long, but I'm perfectly shameless with you, Hart. If peace ever comes and I want you, I won't wait for you to find it out yourself, I'll cable, Marconigraph, anything. As for how I say good-bye; any way you please, I don't care in the least what happens to me."

Henderson studied her intently.

"In that case, we will shake hands," he said. "Good-bye, Edith. Don't forget that every hour I am thinking of you and hoping all good things will come to you soon."

CHAPTER XXV

WHEREIN PHILIP FINDS ELNORA, AND EDITH CARR OFFERS A YELLOW EMPEROR

"Oh, I need my own violin," cried Elnora. "This one may be a thousand times more expensive, and much older than mine; but it wasn't inspired and taught to sing by a man who knew how. It doesn't know 'beans,' as mother would say, about the Limberlost."

The guests in the O'More music-room laughed appreciatively.

"Why don't you write your mother to come for a visit and bring yours?" suggested Freckles.

"I did that three days ago," acknowledged Elnora. "I am half expecting her on the noon boat. That is one reason why this violin grows worse every minute. There is nothing at all the matter with me."

"Splendid!" cried the Angel. "I've begged and begged her to do it. I know how anxious these mothers become. When did you send? What made you? Why didn't you tell me?"

"'When?' Three days ago. 'What made me?' You. 'Why didn't I tell you?' Because I can't be sure in the least that she will come. Mother is the most individual person. She never does what every one expects she will. She may not come, and I didn't want you to be disappointed."

"How did I make you?" asked the Angel.

"Loving Alice. It made me realize that if you cared for your girl like that, with Mr. O'More and three other children, possibly my mother, with no one, might like to see me. I know I want to see her, and you had told me to so often, I just sent for her. Oh, I do hope she comes! I want her to see this lovely place."

"I have been wondering what you thought of Mackinac," said Freckles.

"Oh, it is a perfect picture, all of it! I should like to hang it on the wall, so I could see it whenever I wanted to; but it isn't real, of course; it's nothing but a picture."

"These people won't agree with you," smiled Freckles.

"That isn't necessary," retorted Elnora. "They know this, and they love it; but you and I are acquainted with something different. The Limberlost is life. Here it is a carefully kept park. You motor, sail, and golf, all so secure and fine. But what I like is the excitement of choosing a path carefully, in the fear that the quagmire may reach out and suck me down;

to go into the swamp naked-handed and wrest from it treasures that bring me books and clothing, and I like enough of a fight for things that I always remember how I got them. I even enjoy seeing a canny old vulture eyeing me as if it were saying: 'Ware the sting of the rattler, lest I pick your bones as I did old Limber's.' I like sufficient danger to put an edge on life. This is so tame. I should have loved it when all the homes were cabins, and watchers for the stealthy Indian canoes patrolled the shores. You wait until mother comes, and if my violin isn't angry with me for leaving it, to-night we shall sing you the Song of the Limberlost. You shall hear the big gold bees over the red, yellow, and purple flowers, bird song, wind talk, and the whispers of Sleepy Snake Creek, as it goes past you. You will know!" Elnora turned to Freckles.

He nodded. "Who better?" he asked. "This is secure while the children are so small, but when they grow larger, we are going farther north, into real forest, where they can learn self-reliance and develop backbone."

Elnora laid away the violin. "Come along, children," she said. "We must get at that backbone business at once. Let's race to the playhouse."

With the brood at her heels Elnora ran, and for an hour lively sounds stole from the remaining spot of forest on the Island, which lay beside the O'More cottage. Then Terry went to the playroom to bring Alice her doll. He came racing back, dragging it by one leg, and crying: "There's company! Someone has come that mamma and papa are just tearing down the house over. I saw through the window."

"It could not be my mother, yet," mused Elnora. "Her boat is not due until twelve. Terry, give Alice that doll——"

"It's a man-person, and I don't know him, but my father is shaking his hand right straight along, and my mother is running for a hot drink and a cushion. It's a kind of a sick person, but they are going to make him well right away, any one can see that. This is the best place.

"I'll go tell him to come lie on the pine needles in the sun and watch the sails go by. That will fix him!"

"Watch sails go by," chanted Little Brother. "'A fix him! Elnora fix him, won't you?"

"I don't know about that," answered Elnora. "What sort of person is he, Terry?"

"A beautiful white person; but my father is going to 'colour him up,' I heard him say so. He's just out of the hospital, and he is a bad person, 'cause he ran away from the doctors and made them awful angry. But father and mother are going to doctor him better. I didn't know they could make sick people well."

"'Ey do anyfing!" boasted Little Brother.

Before Elnora missed her, Alice, who had gone to investigate, came flying across the shadows and through the sunshine waving a paper. She thurst it into Elnora's hand.

"There is a man-person—a stranger-person!" she shouted. "But he knows you! He sent you that! You are to be the doctor! He said so! Oh, do hurry! I like him heaps!"

Elnora read Edith Carr's telegram to Philip Ammon and understood that he had been ill, that she had been located by Edith who had notified him. In so doing she had acknowledged defeat. At last Philip was free. Elnora looked up with a radiant face.

"I like him 'heaps' myself!" she cried. "Come on children, we will go tell him so."

Terry and Alice ran, but Elnora had to suit her steps to Little Brother, who was her loyal esquire, and would have been heartbroken over desertion and insulted at being carried. He was rather dragged, but he was arriving, and the emergency was great, he could see that.

"She's coming!" shouted Alice.

"She's going to be the doctor!" cried Terry.

"She looked just like she'd seen angels when she read the letter," explained Alice.

"She likes you 'heaps!' She said so!" danced Terry. "Be waiting! Here she is!"

Elnora helped Little Brother up the steps, then deserted him and came at a rush. The stranger-person stood holding out trembling arms.

"Are you sure, at last, runaway?" asked Philip Ammon.

"Perfectly sure!" cried Elnora.

"Will you marry me now?"

"This instant! That is, any time after the noon boat comes in."

"Why such unnecessary delay?" demanded Ammon.

"It is almost September," explained Elnora. "I sent for mother three days ago. We must wait until she comes, and we either have to send for Uncle Wesley and Aunt Margaret, or go to them. I couldn't possibly be married properly without those dear people."

"We will send," decided Ammon. "The trip will be a treat for them. O'More, would you get off a message at once?"

Every one met the noon boat. They went in the motor because Philip was too weak to walk so far. As soon as people could be distinguished at all Elnora and Philip sighted an erect figure, with a head like a snowdrift. When the gang-plank fell the first person across it was a lean, red-haired boy of eleven, carrying a violin in one hand and an enormous bouquet of yellow marigolds and purple asters in the other. He was beaming with broad smiles until he saw Philip. Then his expression changed.

"Aw, say!" he exclaimed reproachfully. "I bet you Aunt Margaret is right. He is going to be your beau!"

Elnora stooped to kiss Billy as she caught her mother.

"There, there!" cried Mrs. Comstock. "Don't knock my headgear into my eye. I'm not sure I've got either hat or hair. The wind blew like bizzem coming up the river."

She shook out her skirts, straightened her hat, and came forward to meet Philip, who took her into his arms and kissed her repeatedly. Then he passed her along to Freckles and the Angel to whom her greetings were mingled with scolding and laughter over her wind-blown hair.

"No doubt I'm a precious spectacle!" she said to the Angel. "I saw your pa a little before I started, and he sent you a note. It's in my satchel. He said he was coming up next week. What a lot of people there are in this world! And what on earth are all of them laughing about? Did none of them ever hear of sickness, or sorrow, or death? Billy, don't you go to playing Indian or chasing woodchucks until you get out of those clothes. I promised Margaret I'd bring back that suit good as new."

Then the O'More children came crowding to meet Elnora's mother.

"Merry Christmas!" cried Mrs. Comstock, gathering them in. "Got everything right here but the tree, and there seems to be plenty of them a little higher up. If this wind would stiffen just enough more to blow away the people, so one could see this place, I believe it would be right decent looking."

"See here," whispered Elnora to Philip. "You must fix this with Billy. I can't have his trip spoiled."

"Now, here is where I dust the rest of 'em!" complacently remarked Mrs. Comstock, as she climbed into the motor car for her first ride, in company with Philip and Little Brother. "I have been the one to trudge the roads and hop out of the way of these things for quite a spell."

She sat very erect as the car rolled into the broad main avenue, where only stray couples were walking. Her eyes began to twinkle and gleam. Suddenly she leaned forward and touched the driver on the shoulder.

"Young man," she said, "just you toot that horn suddenly and shave close enough a few of those people, so that I can see how I look when I leap for ragweed and snake fences."

The amazed chauffeur glanced questioningly at Philip who slightly nodded. A second later there was a quick "honk!" and a swerve at a corner. A man engrossed in conversation grabbed the woman to whom he was talking and dashed for the safety of a lawn. The woman tripped in her skirts, and as she fell the man caught and dragged her. Both of them turned red faces to the car and berated the driver. Mrs. Comstock laughed in unrestrained enjoyment. Then she touched the chauffeur again.

"That's enough," she said. "It seems a mite risky." A minute later she added to Philip, "If only they had been carrying six pounds of butter and ten dozen eggs apiece, wouldn't that have been just perfect?"

Billy had wavered between Elnora and the motor, but his loyal little soul had been true to her, so the walk to the cottage began with him at her side. Long before they arrived the little O'Mores had crowded around and captured Billy, and he was giving them an expurgated version of Mrs. Comstock's tales of Big Foot and Adam Poe, boasting that Uncle Wesley had been in the camps of Me-shin-go-me-sia and knew Wa-ca-co-nah before he got religion and dressed like white men; while the mighty prowess of Snap as a woodchuck hunter was done full justice. When they reached the cottage Philip took Billy aside, showed him the emerald ring and gravely asked his permission to marry Elnora. Billy struggled to be just, but it was going hard with him, when Alice, who kept close enough to hear, intervened.

"Why don't you let them get married?" she asked. "You are much too small for her. You wait for me!"

Billy studied her intently. At last he turned to Ammon. "Aw, well! Go on, then!" he said gruffly. "I'll marry Alice!"

Alice reached her hand. "If you got that settled let's put on our Indian clothes, call the boys, and go to the playhouse."

"I haven't got any Indian clothes," said Billy ruefully.

"Yes, you have," explained Alice. "Father bought you some coming from the dock. You can put them on in the playhouse. The boys do."

Billy examined the playhouse with gleaming eyes.

Never had he encountered such possibilities. He could see a hundred amusing things to try, and he could not decide which to do first. The most immediate attraction seemed to be a dead pine, held perpendicularly by its fellows, while its bark had decayed and fallen, leaving a bare, smooth trunk.

"If we just had some grease that would make the dandiest pole to play Fourth of July with!" he shouted.

The children remembered the Fourth. It had been great fun.

"Butter is grease. There is plenty in the 'frigerator," suggested Alice, speeding away.

Billy caught the cold roll and began to rub it against the tree excitedly.

"How are you going to get it greased to the top?" inquired Terry.

Billy's face lengthened. "That's so!" he said. "The thing is to begin at the top and grease down. I'll show you!"

Billy put the butter in his handkerchief and took the corners between his teeth. He climbed the pole, greasing it as he slid down.

"Now, I got to try first," he said, "because I'm the biggest and so I have the best chance; only the one that goes first hasn't hardly any chance at all, because he has to wipe off the grease on himself, so the others can get up at last. See?"

"All right!" said Terry. "You go first and then I will and then Alice. Phew! It's slick. He'll never get up."

Billy wrestled manfully, and when he was exhausted he boosted Terry, and then both of them helped Alice, to whom they awarded a prize of her own doll. As they rested Billy remembered.

"Do your folks keep cows?" he asked.

"No, we buy milk," said Terry.

"Gee! Then what about the butter? Maybe your ma needs it for dinner!"

"No, she doesn't!" cried Alice. "There's stacks of it! I can have all the butter I want."

"Well, I'm mighty glad of it!" said Billy. "I didn't just think. I'm afraid we've greased our clothes, too."

"That's no difference," said Terry. "We can play what we please in these things."

"Well, we ought to be all dirty, and bloody, and have feathers on us to be real Indians," said Billy.

Alice tried a handful of dirt on her sleeve and it streaked beautifully. Instantly all of them began smearing themselves.

"If we only had feathers," lamented Billy.

Terry disappeared and shortly returned from the garage with a feather duster. Billy fell on it with a shriek. Around each one's head he firmly tied a twisted handkerchief, and stuck inside it a row of stiffly upstanding feathers.

"Now, if we just only had some pokeberries to paint us red, we'd be real, for sure enough Indians, and we could go on the warpath and fight all the other tribes and burn a lot of them at the stake."

Alice sidled up to him. "Would huckleberries do?" she asked softly.

"Yes!" shouted Terry, wild with excitement. "Anything that's a colour."

Alice made another trip to the refrigerator. Billy crushed the berries in his hands and smeared and streaked all their faces liberally.

"Now are we ready?" asked Alice.

Billy collapsed. "I forgot the ponies! You got to ride ponies to go on the warpath!"

"You ain't neither!" contradicted Terry. "It's the very latest style to go on the warpath in a motor. Everybody does! They go everywhere in them. They are much faster and better than any old ponies."

Billy gave one genuine whoop. "Can we take your motor?"

Terry hesitated.

"I suppose you are too little to run it?" said Billy.

"I am not!" flashed Terry. "I know how to start and stop it, and I drive lots for Stephens. It is hard to turn over the engine when you start."

"I'll turn it," volunteered Billy. "I'm strong as anything."

"Maybe it will start without. If Stephens has just been running it, sometimes it will. Come on, let's try."

Billy straightened up, lifted his chin and cried: "Houpe! Houpe! Houpe!"

The little O'Mores stared in amazement.

"Why don't you come on and whoop?" demanded Billy. "Don't you know how? You are great Indians! You got to whoop before you go on the warpath. You ought to kill a bat, too, and see if the wind is right. But maybe the engine won't run if we wait to do that. You can whoop, anyway. All together now!"

They did whoop, and after several efforts the cry satisfied Billy, so he led the way to the big motor, and took the front seat with Terry. Alice and Little Brother climbed into the back.

"Will it go?" asked Billy, "or do we have to turn it?"

"It will go," said Terry as the machine gently slid out into the avenue and started under his guidance.

"This is no warpath!" scoffed Billy. "We got to go a lot faster than this, and we got to whoop. Alice, why don't you whoop?"

Alice arose, took hold of the seat in front and whooped.

"If I open the throttle, I can't squeeze the bulb to scare people out of our way," said Terry. "I can't steer and squeeze, too."

"We'll whoop enough to get them out of the way. Go faster!" urged Billy.

Billy also stood, lifted his chin and whooped like the wildest little savage that ever came out of the West. Alice and Little Brother added their voices, and when he was not absorbed with the steering gear, Terry joined in.

"Faster!" shouted Billy.

Intoxicated with the speed and excitement, Terry threw the throttle wider and the big car leaped forward and sped down the avenue. In it four black, feather-bedecked children whooped in wild glee until suddenly Terry's war cry changed to a scream of panic.

"The lake is coming!"

"Stop!" cried Billy. "Stop! Why don't you stop?"

Paralyzed with fear Terry clung to the steering gear and the car sped onward.

"You little fool! Why don't you stop?" screamed Billy, catching Terry's arm. "Tell me how to stop!"

A bicycle shot beside them and Freckles standing on the pedals shouted: "Pull out the pin in that little circle at your feet!"

Billy fell on his knees and tugged and the pin yielded at last. Just as the wheels struck the white sand the bicycle sheered close, Freckles caught the lever and with one strong shove set the brake. The water flew as the car struck Huron, but luckily it was shallow and the beach smooth. Hub deep the big motor stood quivering as Freckles climbed in and backed it to dry sand.

Then he drew a deep breath and stared at his brood.

"Terence, would you kindly be explaining?" he said at last.

Billy looked at the panting little figure of Terry.

"I guess I better," he said. "We were playing Indians on the warpath, and we hadn't any ponies, and Terry said it was all the style to go in automobiles now, so we——"

Freckles's head went back, and he did some whooping himself.

"I wonder if you realize how nearly you came to being four drowned children?" he said gravely, after a time.

"Oh, I think I could swim enough to get most of us out," said Billy. "Anyway, we need washing."

"You do indeed," said Freckles. "I will head this procession to the garage, and there we will remove the first coat." For the remainder of Billy's visit the nurse, chauffeur, and every servant of the O'More household had something of importance on their minds, and Billy's every step was shadowed.

"I have Billy's consent," said Philip to Elnora, "and all the other consent you have stipulated. Before you think of something more, give me your left hand, please."

Elnora gave it gladly, and the emerald slipped on her finger. Then they went together into the forest to tell each other all about it, and talk it over.

"Have you seen Edith?" asked Philip.

"No," answered Elnora. "But she must be here, or she may have seen me when we went to Petoskey a few days ago. Her people have a cottage over on the bluff, but the Angel never told me until to-day. I didn't want to make that trip, but the folks were so anxious to entertain me, and it was only a few days until I intended to let you know myself where I was."

"And I was going to wait just that long, and if I didn't hear then I was getting ready to turn over the country. I can scarcely realize yet that Edith sent me that telegram."

"No wonder! It's a difficult thing to believe. I can't express how I feel for her."

"Let us never speak of it again," said Philip. "I came nearer feeling sorry for her last night than I have yet. I couldn't sleep on that boat coming over, and I couldn't put away the thought of what sending that message cost her. I never would have believed it possible that she would do it. But it is done. We will forget it."

"I scarcely think I shall," said Elnora. "It is something I like to remember. How suffering must have changed her! I would give anything to bring her peace."

"Henderson came to see me at the hospital a few days ago. He's gone a rather wild pace, but if he had been held from youth by the love of a good woman he might have lived differently. There are things about him one cannot help admiring."

"I think he loves her," said Elnora softly.

"He does! He always has! He never made any secret of it. He will cut in now and do his level best, but he told me that he thought she would send him away. He understands her thoroughly."

Edith Carr did not understand herself. She went to her room after her good-bye to Henderson, lay on her bed and tried to think why she was suffering as she was.

"It is all my selfishness, my unrestrained temper, my pride in my looks, my ambition to be first," she said. "That is what has caused this trouble."

Then she went deeper.

"How does it happen that I am so selfish, that I never controlled my temper, that I thought beauty and social position the vital things of life?" she muttered. "I think that goes a little past me. I think a mother who allows a child to grow up as I did, who educates it only for the frivolities of life, has a share in that child's ending. I think my mother has some responsibility in this," Edith Carr whispered to the night. "But she will recognize none. She would laugh at me if I tried to tell her what I have suffered and the bitter, bitter lesson I have learned. No one really cares, but Hart. I've sent him away, so there is no one! No one!"

Edith pressed her fingers across her burning eyes and lay still.

"He is gone!" she whispered at last. "He would go at once. He would not see me again. I should think he never would want to see me any more. But I will want to see him! My soul! I want him now! I want him every minute! He is all I have. And I've sent him away. Oh, these dreadful days to come, alone! I can't bear it. Hart! Hart!" she cried aloud. "I want you! No one cares but you. No one understands but you. Oh, I want you!"

She sprang from her bed and felt her way to her desk.

"Get me some one at the Henderson cottage," she said to Central, and waited shivering.

"They don't answer."

"They are there! You must get them. Turn on the buzzer."

After a time the sleepy voice of Mrs. Henderson answered.

"Has Hart gone?" panted Edith Carr.

"No! He came in late and began to talk about starting to California. He hasn't slept in weeks to amount to anything. I put him to bed. There is time enough to start to California when he awakens. Edith, what are you planning to do next with that boy of mine?"

"Will you tell him I want to see him before he goes?"

"Yes, but I won't wake him."

"I don't want you to. Just tell him in the morning."

"Very well."

"You will be sure?"

"Sure!"

Hart was not gone. Edith fell asleep. She arose at noon the next day, took a cold bath, ate her breakfast, dressed carefully, and leaving word that she had gone to the forest, she walked slowly across the leaves. It was cool and quiet there, so she sat where she could see him coming, and waited. She was thinking deep and fast.

Henderson came swiftly down the path. A long sleep, food, and Edith's message had done him good. He had dressed in new light flannels that were becoming. Edith arose and went to meet him.

"Let us walk in the forest," she said.

They passed the old Catholic graveyard, and entered the deepest wood of the Island, where all shadows were green, all voices of humanity ceased, and there was no sound save the whispering of the trees, a few bird notes and squirrel rustle. There Edith seated herself on a mossy old log, and Henderson studied her. He could detect a change. She was still pale and her eyes tired, but the dull, strained look was gone. He wanted to hope, but he did not dare. Any other man would have forced her to speak. The mighty tenderness in Henderson's heart shielded her in every way.

"What have you thought of that you wanted yet, Edith?" he asked lightly as he stretched himself at her feet.

"You!"

Henderson lay tense and very still.

"Well, I am here!"

"Thank Heaven for that!"

Henderson sat up suddenly, leaning toward her with questioning eyes. Not knowing what he dared say, afraid of the hope which found birth in his heart, he tried to shield her and at the same time to feel his way.

"I am more thankful than I can express that you feel so," he said. "I would be of use, of comfort, to you if I knew how, Edith."

"You are my only comfort," she said. "I tried to send you away. I thought I didn't want you. I thought I couldn't bear the sight of you, because of what you have seen me suffer. But I went to the root of this thing last night, Hart, and with self in mind, as usual, I found that I could not live without you."

Henderson began breathing lightly. He was afraid to speak or move.

"I faced the fact that all this is my own fault," continued Edith, "and came through my own selfishness. Then I went farther back and realized that I am as I was reared. I don't want to blame my parents, but I was carefully trained into what I am. If Elnora Comstock had been like me, Phil would have come back to me. I can see how selfish I seem to him, and how I appear to you, if you would admit it."

"Edith," said Henderson desperately, "there is no use to try to deceive you. You have known from the first that I found you wrong in this. But it's the first time in your life I ever thought you wrong about anything—and it's the only time I ever shall. Understand, I think you the bravest, most beautiful woman on earth, the one most worth loving."

"I'm not to be considered in the same class with her."

"I don't grant that, but if I did, you, must remember how I compare with Phil. He's my superior at every point. There's no use in discussing that. You wanted to see me, Edith. What did you want?"

"I wanted you to not go away."

"Not at all?"

"Not at all! Not ever! Not unless you take me with you, Hart."

She slightly extended one hand to him. Henderson took that hand, kissing it again and again.

"Anything you want, Edith," he said brokenly. "Just as you wish it. Do you want me to stay here, and go on as we have been?"

"Yes, only with a difference."

"Can you tell me, Edith?"

"First, I want you to know that you are the dearest thing on earth to me, right now. I would give up everything else, before I would you. I can't honestly say that I love you with the love you deserve. My heart is too sore. It's too soon to know. But I love you some way. You are necessary to me. You are my comfort, my shield. If you want me, as you know me to be, Hart, you may consider me yours. I give you my word of honour I will try to be as you would have me, just as soon as I can."

Henderson kissed her hand passionately. "Don't, Edith," he begged. "Don't say those things. I can't bear it. I understand. Everything will come right in time. Love like mine must bring a reward. You will love me some day. I can wait. I am the most patient fellow."

"But I must say it," cried Edith. "I—I think, Hart, that I have been on the wrong road to find happiness. I planned to finish life as I started it with Phil; and you see how glad he was to change. He wanted the other sort of girl far more than he ever wanted me. And you, Hart, honest, now—I'll know if you don't tell me the truth! Would you rather have a wife as I planned to live life with Phil, or would you rather have her as Elnora Comstock intends to live with him?"

"Edith!" cried the man, "Edith!"

"Of course, you can't say it in plain English," said the girl. "You are far too chivalrous for that. You needn't say anything. I am answered. If you could have your choice you wouldn't have a society wife, either. In your heart you'd like the smaller home of comfort, the furtherance of your ambitions, the palatable meals regularly served, and little children around you. I am sick of all we have grown up to, Hart. When your hour of trouble comes, there is no comfort for you. I am tired to death. You find out what you want to do, and be, that is a man's work in the world, and I will plan our home, with no thought save your comfort. I'll be the other kind of a girl, as fast as I can learn. I can't correct all my faults in one day, but I'll change as rapidly as I can."

"God knows, I will be different, too, Edith. You shall not be the only generous one. I will make all the rest of life worthy of you. I will change, too!"

"Don't you dare!" said Edith Carr, taking his head between her hands and holding it against her knees, while the tears slid down her cheeks. "Don't you dare change, you big-hearted, splendid lover! I am little and selfish. You are the very finest, just as you are!"

Henderson was not talking then, so they sat through a long silence. At last he heard Edith draw a quick breath, and lifting his head he looked where she pointed. Up a fern stalk climbed a curious looking object. They watched breathlessly. By lavender feet clung a big, pursy, lavender-splotched, yellow body. Yellow and lavender wings began to expand and take on colour. Every instant great beauty became more apparent. It was one of those double-brooded freaks, which do occur on rare occasions, or merely an Eacles Imperialis moth that in the cool damp northern forest had failed to emerge in June. Edith Carr drew back with a long, shivering breath. Henderson caught her hands and gripped them firmly. Steadily she looked the thought of her heart into his eyes.

"By all the powers, you shall not!" swore the man. "You have done enough. I will smash that thing!"

"Oh no you won't!" cried the girl, clinging to his hands. "I am not big enough yet, Hart, but before I leave this forest I shall have grown to breadth and strength to carry that to her. She needs two of each kind. Phil only sent her one!"

"Edith I can't bear it! That's not demanded! Let me take it!"

"You may go with me. I know where the O'More cottage is. I have been there often."

"I'll say you sent it!"

"You may watch me deliver it!"

"Phil may be there by now."

"I hope he is! I should like him to see me do one decent thing by which to remember me."

"I tell you that is not necessary!"

"'Not necessary!'" cried the girl, her big eyes shining. "Not necessary? Then what on earth is the thing doing here? I just have boasted that I would change, that I would be like her, that I would grow bigger and broader. As the words are spoken God gives me the opportunity to prove whether I am sincere. This is my test, Hart! Don't you see it? If I am big enough to carry that to her, you will believe that there is some good in me. You will not be loving me in vain. This is an especial Providence, man! Be my strength! Help me, as you always have done!"

Henderson arose and shook the leaves from his clothing. He drew Edith Carr to her feet and carefully picked the mosses from her skirts. He went to the water and moistened his handkerchief to bathe her face.

"Now a dust of powder," he said when the tears were washed away.

From a tiny book Edith tore leaves that she passed over her face.

"All gone!" cried Henderson, critically studying her. "You look almost half as lovely as you really are!"

Edith Carr drew a wavering breath. She stretched one hand to him.

"Hold tight, Hart!" she said. "I know they handle these things, but I would quite as soon touch a snake."

Henderson clenched his teeth and held steadily. The moth had emerged too recently to be troublesome. It climbed on her fingers quietly and obligingly clung there without moving. So hand in hand they went down the dark forest path. When they came to the avenue, the first person they met paused with an ejaculation of wonder. The next stopped also, and every one following. They could make little progress on account of marvelling, interested people. A strange excitement took possession of Edith. She began to feel proud of the moth.

"Do you know," she said to Henderson, "this is growing easier every step. Its clinging is not disagreeable as I thought it would be. I feel as if I were saving it, protecting it. I am proud that we are taking it to be put into a collection or a book. It seems like doing a thing worth while. Oh, Hart, I wish we could work together at something for which people would care as they seem to for this. Hear what they say! See them lift their little children to look at it!"

"Edith, if you don't stop," said Henderson, "I will take you in my arms here on the avenue. You are adorable!"

"Don't you dare!" laughed Edith Carr. The colour rushed to her cheeks and a new light leaped in her eyes.

"Oh, Hart!" she cried. "Let's work! Let's do something! That's the way she makes people love her so. There's the place, and thank goodness, there is a crowd."

"You darling!" whispered Henderson as they passed up the walk. Her face was rose-flushed with excitement and her eyes shone.

"Hello, everyone!" she cried as she came on the wide veranda. "Only see what we found up in the forest! We thought you might like to have it for some of your collections."

She held out the moth as she walked straight to Elnora, who arose to meet her, crying: "How perfectly splendid! I don't even know how to begin to thank you."

Elnora took the moth. Edith shook hands with all of them and asked Philip if he were improving. She said a few polite words to Freckles and the Angel, declined to remain on account of an engagement, and went away, gracefully.

"Well bully for her!" said Mrs. Comstock. "She's a little thoroughbred after all!"

"That was a mighty big thing for her to be doing," said Freckles in a hushed voice.

"If you knew her as well as I do," said Philip Ammon, "you would have a better conception of what that cost."

"It was a terror!" cried the Angel. "I never could have done it."

"'Never could have done it!'" echoed Freckles. "Why, Angel, dear, that is the one thing of all the world you would have done!"

"I have to take care of this," faltered Elnora, hurrying toward the door to hide the tears which were rolling down her cheeks.

"I must help," said Philip, disappearing also. "Elnora," he called, catching up with her, "take me where I may cry, too. Wasn't she great?"

"Superb!" exclaimed Elnora. "I have no words. I feel so humbled!"

"So do I," said Philip. "I think a brave deed like that always makes one feel so. Now are you happy?"

"Unspeakably happy!" answered Elnora.

THE END

FRECKLES

CHARACTERS

FRECKLES, a plucky waif who guards the Limberlost timber leases and dreams of Angels.

THE SWAMP ANGEL, in whom Freckles' sweetest dream materializes.

MCLEAN, a member of a Grand Rapids lumber company, who befriends Freckles.

MRS. DUNCAN, who gives mother-love and a home to Freckles.

DUNCAN, head teamster of McLean's timber gang.

THE BIRD WOMAN, who is collecting camera studies of birds for a book.

LORD AND LADY O'MORE, who come from Ireland in quest of a lost relative.

THE MAN OF AFFAIRS, brusque of manner, but big of heart.

WESSNER, a Dutch timber-thief who wants rascality made easy.

BLACK JACK, a villain to whom thought of repentance comes too late.

SEARS, camp cook.

CHAPTER I

WHEREIN GREAT RISKS ARE TAKEN
AND THE LIMBERLOST GUARD IS HIRED

Freckles came down the corduroy that crosses the lower end of the Limberlost. At a glance he might have been mistaken for a tramp, but he was truly seeking work. He was intensely eager to belong somewhere and to be attached to almost any enterprise that would furnish him food and clothing.

Long before he came in sight of the camp of the Grand Rapids Lumber Company, he could hear the cheery voices of the men, the neighing of the horses, and could scent the tempting odors of cooking food. A feeling of homeless friendlessness swept over him in a sickening wave. Without stopping to think, he turned into the newly made road and followed it to the camp, where the gang was making ready for supper and bed.

The scene was intensely attractive. The thickness of the swamp made a dark, massive background below, while above towered gigantic trees. The men were calling jovially back and forth as they unharnessed tired horses that fell into attitudes of rest and crunched, in deep content, the grain given them. Duncan, the brawny Scotch head-teamster, lovingly wiped the flanks of his big bays with handfuls of pawpaw leaves, as he softly whistled, "O wha will be my dearie, O!" and a cricket beneath the leaves at his feet accompanied him. The green wood fire hissed and crackled merrily. Wreathing tongues of flame wrapped around the big black kettles, and when the cook lifted the lids to plunge in his testing-fork, gusts of savory odors escaped.

Freckles approached him.

"I want to speak with the Boss," he said.

The cook glanced at him and answered carelessly: "He can't use you."

The color flooded Freckles' face, but he said simply: "If you will be having the goodness to point him out, we will give him a chance to do his own talking."

With a shrug of astonishment, the cook led the way to a rough board table where a broad, square-shouldered man was bending over some account-books.

"Mr. McLean, here's another man wanting to be taken on the gang, I suppose," he said.

"All right," came the cheery answer. "I never needed a good man more than I do just now."

The manager turned a page and carefully began a new line.

"No use of your bothering with this fellow," volunteered the cook. "He hasn't but one hand."

The flush on Freckles' face burned deeper. His lips thinned to a mere line. He lifted his shoulders, took a step forward, and thrust out his right arm, from which the sleeve dangled empty at the wrist.

"That will do, Sears," came the voice of the Boss sharply. "I will interview my man when I finish this report."

He turned to his work, while the cook hurried to the fires. Freckles stood one instant as he had braced himself to meet the eyes of the manager; then his arm dropped and a wave of whiteness swept him. The Boss had not even turned his head. He had used the possessive. When he said "my man," the hungry heart of Freckles went reaching toward him.

The boy drew a quivering breath. Then he whipped off his old hat and beat the dust from it carefully. With his left hand he caught the right sleeve, wiped his sweaty face, and tried to straighten his hair with his fingers. He broke a spray of ironwort beside him and used the purple bloom to beat the dust from his shoulders and limbs. The Boss, busy over his report, was, nevertheless, vaguely alive to the toilet being made behind him, and scored one for the man.

McLean was a Scotchman. It was his habit to work slowly and methodically. The men of his camps never had known him to be in a hurry or to lose his temper. Discipline was inflexible, but the Boss was always kind. His habits were simple. He shared camp life with his gangs. The only visible signs of wealth consisted of a big, shimmering diamond stone of ice and fire that glittered and burned on one of his fingers, and the dainty, beautiful thoroughbred mare he rode between camps and across the country on business.

No man of McLean's gangs could honestly say that he ever had been overdriven or underpaid. The Boss never had exacted any deference from his men, yet so intense was his personality that no man of them ever had attempted a familiarity. They all knew him to be a thorough gentleman, and that in the great timber city several millions stood to his credit.

He was the only son of that McLean who had sent out the finest ships ever built in Scotland. That his son should carry on this business after the father's death had been his ambition. He had sent the boy through the universities of Oxford and Edinburgh, and allowed him several years' travel before he should attempt his first commission for the firm.

Then he was ordered to southern Canada and Michigan to purchase a consignment of tall, straight timber for masts, and south to Indiana for oak beams. The young man entered these mighty forests, parts of which lay untouched since the dawn of the morning of time. The clear, cool, pungent atmosphere was intoxicating. The intense silence, like that of a great empty cathedral, fascinated him. He gradually learned that, to the shy wood creatures that darted across his path or peeped inquiringly from leafy ambush, he was brother. He found himself approaching, with a feeling of reverence, those majestic trees that had stood through ages of sun, wind, and snow. Soon it became difficult to fell them. When he had filled his order and returned home, he was amazed to learn that in the swamps and forests he had lost his heart and it was calling—forever calling him.

When he inherited his father's property, he promptly disposed of it, and, with his mother, founded a home in a splendid residence in the outskirts of Grand Rapids. With three partners, he organized a lumber company. His work was to purchase, fell, and ship the timber to the mills. Marshall managed the milling process and passed the lumber to the factory. From the lumber, Barthol made beautiful and useful furniture, which Uptegrove scattered all over the world from a big wholesale house. Of the thousands who saw their faces reflected on the polished surfaces of that furniture and found comfort in its use, few there were to whom it suggested mighty forests and trackless swamps, and the man, big of soul and body, who cut his way through them, and with the eye of experience doomed the proud trees that were now entering the homes of civilization for service.

When McLean turned from his finished report, he faced a young man, yet under twenty, tall, spare, heavily framed, closely freckled, and red-haired, with a homely Irish face, but in the steady gray eyes, straightly meeting his searching ones of blue, there was unswerving candor and the appearance of longing not to be ignored. He was dressed in the roughest of farm clothing, and seemed tired to the point of falling.

"You are looking for work?" questioned McLean.

"Yis," answered Freckles.

"I am very sorry," said the Boss with genuine sympathy in his every tone, "but there is only one man I want at present—a hardy, big fellow with a stout heart and a strong body. I hoped that you would do, but I am afraid you are too young and scarcely strong enough."

Freckles stood, hat in hand, watching McLean.

"And what was it you thought I might be doing?" he asked.

The Boss could scarcely repress a start. Somewhere before accident and poverty there had been an ancestor who used cultivated English, even with an accent. The boy spoke in a mellow Irish voice, sweet and pure. It was scarcely definite enough to be called brogue, yet there was a trick in the turning of the sentence, the wrong sound of a letter here and there, that was almost irresistible to McLean, and presaged a misuse of infinitives and possessives with which he was very familiar and which touched him nearly. He was of foreign birth, and despite years of alienation, in times of strong feeling he committed inherited sins of accent and construction.

"It's no child's job," answered McLean. "I am the field manager of a big lumber company. We have just leased two thousand acres of the Limberlost. Many of these trees are of great value. We can't leave our camp, six miles south, for almost a year yet; so we have blazed a trail and strung barbed wires securely around this lease. Before we return to our work, I must put this property in the hands of a reliable, brave, strong man who will guard it every hour of the day, and sleep with one eye open at night. I shall require the entire length of the trail to be walked at least twice each day, to make sure that our lines are up and that no one has been trespassing."

Freckles was leaning forward, absorbing every word with such intense eagerness that he was beguiling the Boss into explanations he had never intended making.

"But why wouldn't that be the finest job in the world for me?" he pleaded. "I am never sick. I could walk the trail twice, three times every day, and I'd be watching sharp all the while."

"It's because you are scarcely more than a boy, and this will be a trying job for a work-hardened man," answered McLean. "You see, in the first place, you would be afraid. In stretching our lines, we killed six rattlesnakes almost as long as your body and as thick as your arm. It's the price of your life to start through the marshgrass surrounding the swamp unless you are covered with heavy leather above your knees.

"You should be able to swim in case high water undermines the temporary bridge we have built where Sleepy Snake Creek enters the swamp. The fall and winter changes of weather are abrupt and severe, while I would want strict watch kept every day. You would always be alone, and I don't guarantee what is in the Limberlost. It is lying here as it has lain since the beginning of time, and it is alive with forms and voices. I don't pretend to say what all of them come from; but from a few slinking shapes I've seen, and hair-raising yells I've heard, I'd rather not confront their owners myself; and I am neither weak nor fearful.

"Worst of all, any man who will enter the swamp to mark and steal timber is desperate. One of my employees at the south camp, John Carter, compelled me to discharge him for a number of serious reasons. He came here, entered the swamp alone, and succeeded in locating and marking a number of valuable trees that he was endeavoring to sell to a rival company when we secured the lease. He has sworn to have these trees if he has to die or to kill others to get them; and he is a man that the strongest would not care to meet."

"But if he came to steal trees, wouldn't he bring teams and men enough: that all anyone could do would be to watch and be after you?" queried the boy.

"Yes," replied McLean.

"Then why couldn't I be watching just as closely, and coming as fast, as an older, stronger man?" asked Freckles.

"Why, by George, you could!" exclaimed McLean. "I don't know as the size of a man would be half so important as his grit and faithfulness, come to think of it. Sit on that log there and we will talk it over. What is your name?"

Freckles shook his head at the proffer of a seat, and folding his arms, stood straight as the trees around him. He grew a shade whiter, but his eyes never faltered.

"Freckles!" he said.

"Good enough for everyday," laughed McLean, "but I scarcely can put 'Freckles' on the company's books. Tell me your name."

"I haven't any name," replied the boy.

"I don't understand," said McLean.

"I was thinking from the voice and the face of you that you wouldn't," said Freckles slowly. "I've spent more time on it than I ever did on anything else in all me life, and I don't understand. Does it seem to you that anyone would take a newborn baby and row over it, until it was bruised black, cut off its hand, and leave it out in a bitter night on the steps of a charity home, to the care of strangers? That's what somebody did to me."

McLean stared aghast. He had no reply ready, and presently in a low voice he suggested: "And after?"

"The Home people took me in, and I was there the full legal age and several years over. For the most part we were a lot of little Irishmen together. They could always find homes for the other children, but nobody would ever be wanting me on account of me arm."

"Were they kind to you?" McLean regretted the question the minute it was asked.

"I don't know," answered Freckles. The reply sounded so hopeless, even to his own ears, that he hastened to qualify it by adding: "You see, it's like this, sir. Kindnesses that people are paid to lay off in job lots and that belong equally to several hundred others, ain't going to be soaking into any one fellow so much."

"Go on," said McLean, nodding comprehendingly.

"There's nothing worth the taking of your time to tell," replied Freckles. "The Home was in Chicago, and I was there all me life until three months ago. When I was too old for the training they gave to the little children, they sent me to the closest ward school as long as the law would let them; but I was never like any of the other children, and they all knew it. I'd to go and come like a prisoner, and be working around the Home early and late for me board and clothes. I always wanted to learn mighty bad, but I was glad when that was over.

"Every few days, all me life, I'd to be called up, looked over, and refused a home and love, on account of me hand and ugly face; but it was all the home I'd ever known, and I didn't seem to belong to any place else.

"Then a new superintendent was put in. He wasn't for being like any of the others, and he swore he'd weed me out the first thing he did. He made a plan to send me down the State to a man he said he knew who needed a boy. He wasn't for remembering to tell that man that I was a hand short, and he knocked me down the minute he found I was the boy who had been sent him. Between noon and that evening, he and his son close my age had me in pretty much the same shape in which I was found in the beginning, so I lay awake that night and ran away. I'd like to have squared me account with that boy before I left, but I didn't dare for fear of waking the old man, and I knew I couldn't handle the two of them; but I'm hoping to meet him alone some day before I die."

McLean tugged at his mustache to hide the smile on his lips, but he liked the boy all the better for this confession.

"I didn't even have to steal clothes to get rid of starting in me Home ones," Freckles continued, "for they had already taken all me clean, neat things for the boy and put me into his rags, and that went almost as sore as the beatings, for where I was we were always kept tidy and sweet-smelling, anyway. I hustled clear into this State before I learned that man couldn't have kept me if he'd wanted to. When I thought I was good and away from him, I commenced hunting work, but it is with everybody else just as it is with you, sir. Big, strong, whole men are the only ones for being wanted."

"I have been studying over this matter," answered McLean. "I am not so sure but that a man no older than you and similar in every way could do this work very well, if he were not a coward, and had it in him to be trustworthy and industrious."

Freckles came forward a step.

"If you will give me a job where I can earn me food, clothes, and a place to sleep," he said, "if I can have a Boss to work for like other men, and a place I feel I've a right to, I will do precisely what you tell me or die trying."

He spoke so convincingly that McLean believed, although in his heart he knew that to employ a stranger would be wretched business for a man with the interests he had involved.

"Very well," the Boss found himself answering, "I will enter you on my pay rolls. We'll have supper, and then I will provide you with clean clothing, wading-boots, the wire-mending apparatus, and a revolver. The first thing in the morning, I will take you the length of the trail myself and explain fully what I want done. All I ask of you is to come to me at once at the south camp and tell me as a man if you find this job too hard for you. It will not surprise me. It is work that few men would perform faithfully. What name shall I put down?"

Freckles' gaze never left McLean's face, and the Boss saw the swift spasm of pain that swept his lonely, sensitive features.

"I haven't any name," he said stubbornly, "no more than one somebody clapped on to me when they put me on the Home books, with not the thought or care they'd name a house cat. I've seen how they enter those poor little abandoned devils often enough to know. What they called me is no more my name than it is yours. I don't know what mine is, and I never will; but I am going to be your man and do your work, and I'll be glad to answer to any name you choose to call me. Won't you please be giving me a name, Mr. McLean?"

The Boss wheeled abruptly and began stacking his books. What he was thinking was probably what any other gentleman would have thought in the circumstances. With his eyes still downcast, and in a voice harsh with huskiness, he spoke.

"I will tell you what we will do, my lad," he said. "My father was my ideal man, and I loved him better than any other I have ever known. He went out five years ago, but that he would have been proud to leave you his name I firmly believe. If I give to you the name of my nearest kin and the man I loved best—will that do?"

Freckles' rigid attitude relaxed suddenly. His head dropped, and big tears splashed on the soiled calico shirt. McLean was not surprised at the silence, for he found that talking came none too easily just then.

"All right," he said. "I will write it on the roll—James Ross McLean."

"Thank you mightily," said Freckles. "That makes me feel almost as if I belonged, already."

"You do," said McLean. "Until someone armed with every right comes to claim you, you are mine. Now, come and take a bath, have some supper, and go to bed."

As Freckles followed into the lights and sounds of the camp, his heart and soul were singing for joy.

CHAPTER II

WHEREIN FRECKLES PROVES HIS
METTLE AND FINDS FRIENDS

Next morning found Freckles in clean, whole clothing, fed, and rested. Then McLean outfitted him and gave him careful instruction in the use of his weapon. The Boss showed him around the timber-line, and engaged him a place to board with the family of his head teamster, Duncan, whom he had brought from Scotland with him, and who lived in a small clearing he was working out between the swamp and the corduroy. When the gang was started for the south camp, Freckles was left to guard a fortune in the Limberlost. That he was under guard himself those first weeks he never knew.

Each hour was torture to the boy. The restricted life of a great city orphanage was the other extreme of the world compared with the Limberlost. He was afraid for his life every minute. The heat was intense. The heavy wading-boots rubbed his feet until they bled. He was sore and stiff from his long tramp and outdoor exposure. The seven miles of trail was agony at every step. He practiced at night, under the direction of Duncan, until he grew sure in the use of his revolver. He cut a stout hickory cudgel, with a knot on the end as big as his fist; this never left his hand. What he thought in those first days he himself could not recall clearly afterward.

His heart stood still every time he saw the beautiful marsh-grass begin a sinuous waving AGAINST the play of the wind, as McLean had told him it would. He bolted half a mile with the first boom of the bittern, and his hat lifted with every yelp of the sheitpoke. Once he saw a lean, shadowy form following him, and fired his revolver. Then he was frightened worse than ever for fear it might have been Duncan's collie.

The first afternoon that he found his wires down, and he was compelled to plunge knee deep into the black swamp-muck to restring them, he became so ill from fear and nervousness that he scarcely could control his shaking hand to do the work. With every step, he felt that he would miss secure footing and be swallowed in that clinging sea of blackness. In dumb agony he plunged forward, clinging to the posts and trees until he had finished restringing and testing the wire. He had consumed much time. Night closed in. The Limberlost stirred gently, then shook herself, growled, and awoke around him.

There seemed to be a great owl hooting from every hollow tree, and a little one screeching from every knothole. The bellowing of big bullfrogs was not sufficiently deafening to shut out the wailing of whip-poor-wills that seemed to come from every bush. Nighthawks swept past him with their shivering cry, and bats struck his face. A prowling wildcat missed its catch and screamed with rage. A straying fox bayed incessantly for its mate.

The hair on the back of Freckles' neck arose as bristles, and his knees wavered beneath him. He could not see whether the dreaded snakes were on the trail, or, in the pandemonium, hear the rattle for which McLean had cautioned him to listen. He stood motionless in an agony of fear. His breath whistled between his teeth. The perspiration ran down his face and body in little streams.

Something big, black, and heavy came crashing through the swamp close to him, and with a yell of utter panic Freckles ran—how far he did not know; but at last he gained control over himself and retraced his steps. His jaws set stiffly and the sweat dried on his body. When he reached the place from which he had started to run, he turned and with measured steps made his way down the line. After a time he realized that he was only walking, so he faced that sea of horrors again. When he came toward the corduroy, the cudgel fell to test the wire at each step.

Sounds that curdled his blood seemed to encompass him, and shapes of terror to draw closer and closer. Fear had so gained the mastery that he did not dare look behind him; and just when he felt that he would fall dead before he ever reached the clearing, came Duncan's rolling call: "Freckles! Freckles!" A shuddering sob burst in the boy's dry throat; but he only told Duncan that finding the wire down had caused the delay.

The next morning he started on time. Day after day, with his heart pounding, he ducked, dodged, ran when he could, and fought when he was brought to bay. If he ever had an idea of giving up, no one knew it; for he clung to his job without the shadow of wavering. All these things, in so far as he guessed them, Duncan, who had been set to watch the first weeks of Freckles' work, carried to the Boss at the south camp; but the innermost, exquisite torture of the thing the big Scotchman never guessed, and McLean, with his finer perceptions, came only a little closer.

After a few weeks, when Freckles learned that he was still living, that he had a home, and the very first money he ever had possessed was safe in his pockets, he began to grow proud. He yet side-stepped, dodged, and hurried to avoid being late again, but he was gradually developing the fearlessness that men ever acquire of dangers to which they are hourly accustomed.

His heart seemed to be leaping when his first rattler disputed the trail with him, but he mustered courage to attack it with his club. After its head had been crushed, he mastered an Irishman's inborn repugnance for snakes sufficiently to cut off its rattles to show Duncan. With this victory, his greatest fear of them was gone.

Then he began to realize that with the abundance of food in the swamp, flesh-hunters would not come on the trail and attack him, and he had his revolver for defence if they did. He soon learned to laugh at the big, floppy birds that made horrible noises. One day, watching behind a tree, he saw a crane solemnly performing a few measures of a belated nuptial song-and-dance with his mate. Realizing that it was intended in tenderness, no matter how it appeared, the lonely, starved heart of the boy sympathized with them.

Before the first month passed, he was fairly easy about his job; by the next he rather liked it. Nature can be trusted to work her own miracle in the heart of any man whose daily task keeps him alone among her sights, sounds, and silences.

When day after day the only thing that relieved his utter loneliness was the companionship of the birds and beasts of the swamp, it was the most natural thing in the world that Freckles should turn to them for friendship. He began by instinctively protecting the weak and helpless. He was astonished at the quickness with which they became accustomed to him and the disregard they showed for his movements, when they learned that he was not a hunter, while the club he carried was used more frequently for their benefit than his own. He scarcely could believe what he saw.

From the effort to protect the birds and animals, it was only a short step to the possessive feeling, and with that sprang the impulse to caress and provide. Through fall, when brooding was finished and the upland birds sought the swamp in swarms to feast on its seeds and berries, Freckles was content with watching them and speculating about them. Outside of half a dozen of the very commonest they were strangers to him. The likeness of their actions to humanity was an hourly surprise.

When black frost began stripping the Limberlost, cutting the ferns, shearing the vines from the trees, mowing the succulent green things of the swale, and setting the leaves swirling down, he watched the departing troops of his friends with dismay. He began to realize that he would be left alone. He made especial efforts toward friendliness with the hope that he could induce some of them to stay. It was then that he conceived the idea of carrying food to the birds; for he saw that they were leaving for lack of it; but he could not stop them. Day after day, flocks gathered and departed: by the time the first snow whitened his trail around the Limberlost, there were left only the little black-and-white juncos, the sapsuckers, yellow-hammers, a few patriarchs among the flaming cardinals, the blue jays, the crows, and the quail.

Then Freckles began his wizard work. He cleared a space of swale, and twice a day he spread a birds' banquet. By the middle of December the strong winds of winter had beaten most of the seed from the grass and bushes. The snow fell, covering the swamp, and food was very scarce and difficult to find. The birds scarcely waited until Freckles' back was turned to attack his provisions. In a few weeks they flew toward the clearing to meet him. During the bitter weather of January they came halfway to the cabin every morning, and fluttered around him as doves all the way to the feeding-ground. Before February they were so accustomed to him, and so hunger-driven, that they would perch on his head and shoulders, and the saucy jays would try to pry into his pockets.

Then Freckles added to wheat and crumbs, every scrap of refuse food he could find at the cabin. He carried to his pets the parings of apples, turnips, potatoes, stray cabbage-leaves, and carrots, and tied to the bushes meat-bones having scraps of fat and gristle. One morning, coming to his feeding-ground unusually early, he found a gorgeous cardinal and a rabbit side by side sociably nibbling a cabbage-leaf, and that instantly gave to him the idea of cracking nuts, from the store he had gathered for Duncan's children, for the squirrels, in the effort to add them to his family. Soon he had them coming—red, gray, and black; then he became filled with a vast impatience that he did not know their names or habits.

So the winter passed. Every week McLean rode to the Limberlost; never on the same day or at the same hour. Always he found Freckles at his work, faithful and brave, no matter how severe the weather.

The boy's earnings constituted his first money; and when the Boss explained to him that he could leave them safe at a bank and carry away a scrap of paper that represented the amount, he went straight on every payday and made his deposit, keeping out barely what was necessary for his board and clothing. What he wanted to do with his money he did not know, but it gave to him a sense of freedom and power to feel that it was there—it was his and he could have it when he chose. In imitation of McLean, he bought a small pocket account-book, in which he carefully set down every dollar he earned and every penny he spent. As his expenses were small and the Boss paid him generously, it was astonishing how his little hoard grew.

That winter held the first hours of real happiness in Freckles' life. He was free. He was doing a man's work faithfully, through every rigor of rain, snow, and blizzard. He was gathering a wonderful strength of body, paying his way, and saving money. Every man of the gang and of that locality knew that he was under the protection of McLean, who was a power, this had the effect of smoothing Freckles' path in many directions.

Mrs. Duncan showed him that individual kindness for which his hungry heart was longing. She had a hot drink ready for him when he came from a freezing day on the trail. She knit him a heavy mitten for his left hand, and devised a way to sew and pad the right sleeve that protected the maimed arm in bitter weather. She patched his clothing—frequently torn by the wire—and saved kitchen scraps for his birds, not because she either knew or cared anything about them, but because she herself was close enough to the swamp to be touched by its utter loneliness. When Duncan laughed at her for this, she retorted: "My God, mannie, if Freckles hadna the birds and the beasts he would be always alone. It was never meant for a human being to be so solitary. He'd get touched in the head if he hadna them to think for and to talk to."

"How much answer do ye think he gets to his talkin', lass?" laughed Duncan.

"He gets the answer that keeps the eye bright, the heart happy, and the feet walking faithful the rough path he's set them in," answered Mrs. Duncan earnestly.

Duncan walked away appearing very thoughtful. The next morning he gave an ear from the corn he was shelling for his chickens to Freckles, and told him to carry it to his wild chickens in the Limberlost. Freckles laughed delightedly.

"Me chickens!" he said. "Why didn't I ever think of that before? Of course they are! They are just little, brightly colored cocks and hens! But 'wild' is no good. What would you say to me 'wild chickens' being a good deal tamer than yours here in your yard?"

"Hoot, lad!" cried Duncan.

"Make yours light on your head and eat out of your hands and pockets," challenged Freckles.

"Go and tell your fairy tales to the wee people! They're juist brash on believin' things," said Duncan. "Ye canna invent any story too big to stop them from callin' for a bigger."

"I dare you to come see!" retorted Freckles.

"Take ye!" said Duncan. "If ye make juist ane bird licht on your heid or eat frae your hand, ye are free to help yoursel' to my corn-crib and wheat bin the rest of the winter."

Freckles sprang in air and howled in glee.

"Oh, Duncan! You're too, aisy" he cried. "When will you come?"

"I'll come next Sabbath," said Duncan. "And I'll believe the birds of the Limberlost are tame as barnyard fowl when I see it, and no sooner!"

After that Freckles always spoke of the birds as his chickens, and the Duncans followed his example. The very next Sabbath, Duncan, with his wife and children, followed Freckles to the swamp. They saw a sight so wonderful it will keep them talking all the remainder of their lives, and make them unfailing friends of all the birds.

Freckles' chickens were awaiting him at the edge of the clearing. They cut the frosty air around his head into curves and circles of crimson, blue, and black. They chased each other from Freckles, and swept so closely themselves that they brushed him with their outspread wings.

At their feeding-ground Freckles set down his old pail of scraps and swept the snow from a small level space with a broom improvised of twigs. As soon as his back was turned, the birds clustered over the food, snatching scraps to carry to the nearest bushes. Several of the boldest, a big crow and a couple of jays, settled on the rim and feasted at leisure, while a cardinal, that hesitated to venture, fumed and scolded from a twig overhead.

Then Freckles scattered his store. At once the ground resembled the spread mantle of Montezuma, except that this mass of gaily colored feathers was on the backs of living birds. While they feasted, Duncan gripped his wife's arm and stared in astonishment; for from the bushes and dry grass, with gentle cheeping and queer, throaty chatter, as if to encourage each other, came flocks of quail. Before anyone saw it arrive, a big gray rabbit sat in the midst of the feast, contentedly gnawing a cabbage-leaf.

"Weel, I be drawed on!" came Mrs. Duncan's tense whisper.

"Shu-shu," cautioned Duncan.

Lastly Freckles removed his cap. He began filling it with handfuls of wheat from his pockets. In a swarm the grain-eaters arose around him as a flock of tame pigeons. They perched on his arms and the cap, and in the stress of hunger, forgetting all caution, a brilliant cock cardinal and an equally gaudy jay fought for a perching-place on his head.

"Weel, I'm beat," muttered Duncan, forgetting the silence imposed on his wife. "I'll hae to give in. 'Seein' is believin'. A man wad hae to see that to believe it. We mauna let the Boss miss that sight, for it's a chance will no likely come twice in a life. Everything is snowed under and thae craturs near starved, but trustin' Freckles that complete they are tamer than our chickens. Look hard, bairns!" he whispered. "Ye winna see the like o' yon again, while God lets ye live. Notice their color against the ice and snow, and the pretty skippin' ways of them! And spunky! Weel, I'm heat fair!"

Freckles emptied his cap, turned his pockets and scattered his last grain. Then he waved his watching friends good-bye and started down the timber-line.

A week later, Duncan and Freckles arose from breakfast to face the bitterest morning of the winter. When Freckles, warmly capped and gloved, stepped to the corner of the kitchen for his scrap-pail, he found a big pan of steaming boiled wheat on the top of it. He wheeled to Mrs. Duncan with a shining face.

"Were you fixing this warm food for me chickens or yours?" he asked.

"It's for yours, Freckles," she said. "I was afeared this cold weather they wadna lay good without a warm bite now and then."

Duncan laughed as he stepped to the other room for his pipe; but Freckles faced Mrs. Duncan with a trace of every pang of starved mother-hunger he ever had suffered written large on his homely, splotched, narrow features.

"Oh, how I wish you were my mother!" he cried.

Mrs. Duncan attempted an echo of her husband's laugh.

"Lord love the lad!" she exclaimed. "Why, Freckles, are ye no bright enough to learn without being taught by a woman that I am your mither? If a great man like yoursel' dinna ken that, learn it now and ne'er forget it. Ance a woman is the wife of any man, she becomes wife to all men for having had the wifely experience she kens! Ance a man-child has beaten his way to life under the heart of a woman, she is mither to all men, for the hearts of mithers are everywhere the same. Bless ye, laddie, I am your mither!"

She tucked the coarse scarf she had knit for him closer over his chest and pulled his cap lower over his ears, but Freckles, whipping it off and holding it under his arm, caught her rough, reddened hand and pressed it to his lips in a long kiss. Then he hurried away to hide the happy, embarrassing tears that were coming straight from his swelling heart.

Mrs. Duncan, sobbing unrestrainedly, swept into the adjoining room and threw herself into Duncan's arms.

"Oh, the puir lad!" she wailed. "Oh, the puir mither-hungry lad! He breaks my heart!"

Duncan's arms closed convulsively around his wife. With a big, brown hand he lovingly stroked her rough, sorrel hair.

"Sarah, you're a guid woman!" he said. "You're a michty guid woman! Ye hae a way o' speakin' out at times that's like the inspired prophets of the Lord. If that had been put to me, now, I'd 'a' felt all I kent how to and been keen enough to say the richt thing; but dang it, I'd 'a' stuttered and stammered and got naething out that would ha' done onybody a mite o' good. But ye, Sarah! Did ye see his face, woman? Ye sent him off lookin' leke a white light of holiness had passed ower and settled on him. Ye sent the lad away too happy for mortal words, Sarah. And ye made me that proud o' ye! I wouldna trade ye an' my share o' the Limberlost with ony king ye could mention."

He relaxed his clasp, and setting a heavy hand on each shoulder, he looked straight into her eyes.

"Ye're prime, Sarah! Juist prime!" he said.

Sarah Duncan stood alone in the middle of her two-roomed log cabin and lifted a bony, clawlike pair of hands, reddened by frequent immersion in hot water, cracked and chafed by exposure to cold, black-lined by constant battle with swamp-loam, calloused with burns, and stared at them wonderingly.

"Pretty-lookin' things ye are!" she whispered. "But ye hae juist been kissed. And by such a man! Fine as God ever made at His verra best. Duncan wouldna trade wi' a king! Na! Nor I wadna trade with a queen wi' a palace, an' velvet gowns, an' diamonds big as hazelnuts, an' a hundred visitors a day into the bargain. Ye've been that honored I'm blest if I can bear to souse ye in dish-water. Still, that kiss winna come off! Naething can take it from me, for it's mine till I dee. Lord, if I amna proud! Kisses on these old claws! Weel, I be drawed on!"

CHAPTER III

WHEREIN A FEATHER FALLS AND A
SOUL IS BORN

So Freckles fared through the bitter winter. He was very happy. He had hungered for freedom, love, and appreciation so long! He had been unspeakably lonely at the Home; and the utter loneliness of a great desert or forest is not so difficult to endure as the loneliness of being constantly surrounded by crowds of people who do not care in the least whether one is living or dead.

All through the winter Freckles' entire energy was given to keeping up his lines and his "chickens" from freezing or starving. When the first breath of spring touched the Limberlost, and the snow receded before it; when the catkins began to bloom; when there came a hint of green to the trees, bushes, and swale; when the rushes lifted their heads, and the pulse of the newly resurrected season beat strongly in the heart of nature, something new stirred in the breast of the boy.

Nature always levies her tribute. Now she laid a powerful hand on the soul of Freckles, to which the boy's whole being responded, though he had not the least idea what was troubling him. Duncan accepted his wife's theory that it was a touch of spring fever, but Freckles knew better. He never had been so well. Clean, hot, and steady the blood pulsed in his veins. He was always hungry, and his most difficult work tired him not at all. For long months, without a single intermission, he had tramped those seven miles of trail twice each day, through every conceivable state of weather. With the heavy club he gave his wires a sure test, and between sections, first in play, afterward to keep his circulation going, he had acquired the skill of an expert drum major. In his work there was exercise for every muscle of his body each hour of the day, at night a bath, wholesome food, and sound sleep in a room that never knew fire. He had gained flesh and color, and developed a greater strength and endurance than anyone ever could have guessed.

Nor did the Limberlost contain last year's terrors. He had been with her in her hour of desolation, when stripped bare and deserted, she had stood shivering, as if herself afraid. He had made excursions into the interior until he was familiar with every path and road that ever had been cut. He had sounded the depths of her deepest pools, and had learned why the trees grew so magnificently. He had found that places of swamp and swale were few compared with miles of solid timber-land, concealed by summer's luxuriant undergrowth.

The sounds that at first had struck cold fear into his soul he now knew had left on wing and silent foot at the approach of winter. As flock after flock of the birds returned and he recognized the old echoes reawakening, he found to his surprise that he had been lonely for them and was hailing their return with great joy. All his fears were forgotten. Instead, he was possessed of an overpowering desire to know what they were, to learn where they had been, and whether they would make friends with him as the winter birds had done; and if they did, would they be as fickle? For, with the running sap, creeping worm, and winging bug, most of Freckles' "chickens" had deserted him, entered the swamp, and feasted to such a state of plethora on its store that they cared little for his supply, so that in the strenuous days of mating and nest-building the boy was deserted.

He chafed at the birds' ingratitude, but he found speedy consolation in watching and befriending the newcomers. He surely would have been proud and highly pleased if he had known that many of the former inhabitants of the interior swamp now grouped their nests beside the timber-line solely for the sake of his protection and company.

The yearly resurrection of the Limberlost is a mighty revival. Freckles stood back and watched with awe and envy the gradual reclothing and repopulation of the swamp. Keen-eyed and alert through danger and loneliness, he noted every stage of development, from the first piping frog and unsheathing bud, to full leafage and the return of the last migrant.

The knowledge of his complete loneliness and utter insignificance was hourly thrust upon him. He brooded and fretted until he was in a fever; yet he never guessed the cause. He was filled with a vast impatience, a longing that he scarcely could endure.

It was June by the zodiac, June by the Limberlost, and by every delight of a newly resurrected season it should have been June in the hearts of all men. Yet Freckles scowled darkly as he came down the trail, and the running TAP, TAP that tested the sagging wire and telegraphed word of his coming to his furred and feathered friends of the swamp, this morning carried the story of his discontent a mile ahead of him.

Freckles' special pet, a dainty, yellow-coated, black-sleeved, cock goldfinch, had remained on the wire for several days past the bravest of all; and Freckles, absorbed with the cunning and beauty of the tiny fellow, never guessed that he was being duped. For the goldfinch was skipping, flirting, and swinging for the express purpose of so holding his attention that he would not look up and see a small cradle of thistledown and wool perilously near his head. In the beginning of brooding, the spunky little homesteader had clung heroically to the wire when he was almost paralyzed with fright. When day after day passed and brought only softly whistled repetitions of his call, a handful of crumbs on the top of a locust line-post, and gently worded coaxings, he grew in confidence. Of late he had sung and swung during the passing of Freckles, who, not dreaming of the nest and the solemn-eyed little hen so close above, thought himself unusually gifted in his power to attract the birds. This morning the goldfinch scarcely could believe his ears, and clung to the wire until an unusually vicious rap sent him spinning a foot in air, and his "PTSEET" came with a squall of utter panic.

The wires were ringing with a story the birds could not translate, and Freckles was quite as ignorant of the trouble as they.

A peculiar movement beneath a small walnut tree caught his attention. He stopped to investigate. There was an unusually large Luna cocoon, and the moth was bursting the upper end in its struggles to reach light and air. Freckles stood and stared.

"There's something in there trying to get out," he muttered. "Wonder if I could help it? Guess I best not be trying. If I hadn't happened along, there wouldn't have been anyone to do anything, and maybe I'd only be hurting it. It's—it's———Oh, skaggany! It's just being born!"

Freckles gasped with surprise. The moth cleared the opening, and with many wabblings and contortions climbed up the tree. He stared speechless with amazement as the moth crept around a limb and clung to the under side. There was a big pursy body, almost as large as his thumb, and of the very snowiest white that Freckles ever had seen. There was a band of delicate lavender across its forehead, and its feet were of the same colour; there were antlers, like tiny, straw-colored ferns, on its head, and from its shoulders hung the crumpled wet wings. As Freckles gazed, tense with astonishment, he saw that these were expanding, drooping, taking on color, and small, oval markings were beginning to show.

The minutes passed. Freckles' steady gaze never wavered. Without realizing it, he was trembling with eagerness and anxiety. As he saw what was taking place, "It's going to fly," he breathed in hushed wonder. The morning sun fell on the moth and dried its velvet down, while the warm air made it fluffy. The rapidly growing wings began to show the most delicate green, with lavender fore-ribs, transparent, eye-shaped markings, edged with lines of red, tan, and black, and long, crisp trailers.

Freckles was whispering to himself for fear of disturbing the moth. It began a systematic exercise of raising and lowering its exquisite wings to dry them and to establish circulation. The boy realized that soon it would be able to spread them and sail away. His long-coming soul sent up its first shivering cry.

"I don't know what it is! Oh, I wish I knew! How I wish I knew! It must be something grand! It can't be a butterfly! It's away too big. Oh, I wish there was someone to tell me what it is!"

He climbed on the locust post, and balancing himself with the wire, held a finger in the line of the moth's advance up the twig. It unhesitatingly climbed on, so he stepped to the path, holding it to the light and examining it closely. Then he held it in the shade and turned it, gloating over its markings and beautiful coloring. When he held the moth to the limb, it climbed on, still waving those magnificent wings.

"My, but I'd like to be staying with you!" he said. "But if I was to stand here all day you couldn't grow any prettier than you are right now, and I wouldn't grow smart enough to tell what you are. I suppose there's someone who knows. Of course there is! Mr. McLean said there were people who knew every leaf, bird, and flower in the Limberlost. Oh Lord! How I wish You'd be telling me just this one thing!"

The goldfinch had ventured back to the wire, for there was his mate, only a few inches above the man-creature's head; and indeed, he simply must not be allowed to look up, so the brave little fellow rocked on the wire and piped, as he had done every day for a week: "SEE ME? SEE ME?"

"See you! Of course I see you," growled Freckles. "I see you day after day, and what good is it doing me? I might see you every morning for a year, and then not be able to be telling anyone about it. 'Seen a bird with black silk wings—little, and yellow as any canary.' That's as far as I'd get. What you doing here, anyway? Have you a mate? What's your name? 'See you?' I reckon I see you; but I might as well be blind, for any good it's doing me!"

Freckles impatiently struck the wire. With a screech of fear, the goldfinch fled precipitately. His mate arose from the nest with a whirr— Freckles looked up and saw it.

"O—ho!" he cried. "So THAT'S what you are doing here! You have a wife. And so close my head I have been mighty near wearing a bird on my bonnet, and never knew it!"

Freckles laughed at his own jest, while in better humor he climbed to examine the neat, tiny cradle and its contents. The hen darted at him in a frenzy. "Now, where do you come in?" he demanded, when he saw that she was not similar to the goldfinch.

"You be clearing out of here! This is none of your fry. This is the nest of me little, yellow friend of the wire, and you shan't be touching it. Don't blame you for wanting to see, though. My, but it's a fine nest and beauties of eggs. Will you be keeping away, or will I fire this stick at you?"

Freckles dropped to the trail. The hen darted to the nest and settled on it with a tender, coddling movement. He of the yellow coat flew to the edge to make sure that everything was right. It would have been plain to the veriest novice that they were partners in that cradle.

"Well, I'll be switched!" muttered Freckles. "If that ain't both their nest! And he's yellow and she's green, or she's yellow and he's green. Of course, I don't know, and I haven't any way to find out, but it's plain as the nose on your face that they are both ready to be fighting for that nest, so, of course, they belong. Doesn't that beat you? Say, that's what's been sticking me all of this week on that grass nest in the thorn tree down the line. One day a blue bird is setting, so I think it is hers. The next day a brown bird is on, and I chase it off because the nest is blue's. Next day the brown bird is on again, and I let her be, because I think it must be hers. Next day, be golly, blue's on, and off I send her because it's brown's; and now, I bet my hat, it's both their nest and I've only been bothering them and making a big fool of mesilf. Pretty specimen I am, pretending to be a friend to the birds, and so blamed ignorant I don't know which ones go in pairs, and blue and brown are a pair, of course, if yellow and green are—and there's the red birds! I never thought of them! He's red and she's gray—and now I want to be knowing, are they all different? Why no! Of course, they ain't! There's the jays all blue, and the crows all black."

The tide of Freckles' discontent welled until he almost choked with anger and chagrin. He plodded down the trail, scowling blackly and viciously spanging the wire. At the finches' nest he left the line and peered into the thorn tree. There was no bird brooding. He pressed closer to take a peep at the snowy, spotless little eggs he had found so beautiful, when at the slight noise up raised four tiny baby heads with wide-open mouths, uttering hunger cries. Freckles stepped back. The brown bird alighted on the edge and closed one cavity with a wiggling green worm, while not two minutes later the blue filled another with a white. That settled it. The blue and brown were mates. Once again Freckles repeated his "How I wish I knew!"

Around the bridge spanning Sleepy Snake Creek the swale spread widely, the timber was scattering, and willows, rushes, marsh-grass, and splendid wild flowers grew abundantly. Here lazy, big, black water snakes, for which the creek was named, sunned on the bushes, wild ducks and grebe chattered, cranes and herons fished, and muskrats plowed the bank in queer, rolling furrows. It was always a place full of interest, so Freckles loved to linger on the bridge, watching the marsh and water people. He also transacted affairs of importance with the wild flowers and sweet marsh-grass. He enjoyed splashing through the shallow pools on either side of the bridge.

Then, too, where the creek entered the swamp was a place of unusual beauty. The water spread in darksome, mossy, green pools. Water-plants and lilies grew luxuriantly, throwing up large, rank, green leaves. Nowhere else in the Limberlost could be found frog-music to equal that of the mouth of the creek. The drumming and piping rolled in never-ending orchestral effect, while the full chorus rang to its accompaniment throughout the season.

Freckles slowly followed the path leading from the bridge to the line. It was the one spot at which he might relax his vigilance. The boldest timber thief the swamp ever had known would not have attempted to enter it by the mouth of the creek, on account of the water and because there was no protection from surrounding trees. He was bending the rank grass with his cudgel, and thinking of the shade the denser swamp afforded, when he suddenly dodged sidewise; the cudgel whistled sharply through the air and Freckles sprang back.

From the clear sky above him, first level with his face, then skimming, dipping, tilting, whirling until it struck, quill down, in the path in front of him, came a glossy, iridescent, big black feather. As it touched the ground, Freckles snatched it up with almost a continuous movement facing the sky. There was not a tree of any size in a large open space. There was no wind to carry it. From the clear sky it had fallen, and Freckles, gazing eagerly into the arch of June blue with a few lazy clouds floating high in the sea of ether, had neither mind nor knowledge to dream of a bird hanging as if frozen there. He turned the big quill questioningly, and again his awed eyes swept the sky.

"A feather dropped from Heaven!" he breathed reverently. "Are the holy angels moulting? But no; if they were, it would be white. Maybe all the angels are not for being white. What if the angels of God are white and those of the devil are black? But a black one has no business up there. Maybe some poor black angel is so tired of being punished it's for slipping to the gates, beating its wings trying to make the Master hear!"

Again and again Freckles searched the sky, but there was no answering gleam of golden gates, no form of sailing bird; then he went slowly on his way, turning the feather and wondering about it. It was a wing quill, eighteen inches in length, with a heavy spine, gray at the base, shading to jet black at the tip, and it caught the play of the sun's rays in slanting gleams of green and bronze. Again Freckles' "old man of the sea" sat sullen and heavy on his shoulders and weighted him down until his step lagged and his heart ached.

"Where did it come from? What is it? Oh, how I wish I knew!" he kept repeating as he turned and studied the feather, with almost unseeing eyes, so intently was he thinking.

Before him spread a large, green pool, filled with rotting logs and leaves, bordered with delicate ferns and grasses among which lifted the creamy spikes of the arrow-head, the blue of water-hyacinth, and the delicate yellow of the jewel-flower. As Freckles leaned, handling the feather and staring at it, then into the depths of the pool, he once more gave voice to his old query: "I wonder what it is!"

Straight across from him, couched in the mosses of a soggy old log, a big green bullfrog, with palpitant throat and batting eyes, lifted his head and bellowed in answer. "FIN' DOUT! FIN' DOUT!"

"Wha—what's that?" stammered Freckles, almost too much bewildered to speak. "I—I know you are only a bullfrog, but, be jabbers, that sounded mightily like speech. Wouldn't you please to be saying it over?"

The bullfrog cuddled contentedly in the ooze. Then suddenly he lifted his voice, and, as an imperative drumbeat, rolled it again: "FIN' DOUT! FIN' DOUT! FIN DOUT!"

Freckles had the answer. Something seemed to snap in his brain. There was a wavering flame before his eyes. Then his mind cleared. His head lifted in a new poise, his shoulders squared, while his spine straightened. The agony was over. His soul floated free. Freckles came into his birthright.

"Before God, I will!" He uttered the oath so impressively that the recording angel never winced as he posted it in the prayer column.

Freckles set his hat over the top of one of the locust posts used between trees to hold up the wire while he fastened the feather securely in the band. Then he started down the line, talking to himself as men who have worked long alone always fall into the habit of doing.

"What a fool I have been!" he muttered. "Of course that's what I have to do! There wouldn't likely anybody be doing it for me. Of course I can! What am I a man for? If I was a four-footed thing of the swamp, maybe I couldn't; but a man can do anything if he's the grit to work hard enough and stick at it, Mr. McLean is always saying, and here's the way I am to do it. He said, too, that there were people that knew everything in the swamp. Of course they have written books! The thing for me to be doing is to quit moping and be buying some. Never bought a book in me life, or anything else of much account, for that matter. Oh, ain't I glad I didn't waste me money! I'll surely be having enough to get a few. Let me see."

Freckles sat on a log, took his pencil and account-book, and figured on a back page. He had walked the timber-line ten months. His pay was thirty dollars a month, and his board cost him eight. That left twenty-two dollars a month, and his clothing had cost him very little. At the least he had two hundred dollars in the bank. He drew a deep breath and smiled at the sky with satisfaction.

"I'll be having a book about all the birds, trees, flowers, butterflies, and——Yes, by gummy! I'll be having one about the frogs—if it takes every cent I have," he promised himself.

He put away the account-book, that was his most cherished possession, caught up his stick, and started down the line. The even tap, tap, and the cheery, gladsome whistle carried far ahead of him the message that Freckles was himself again.

He fell into a rapid pace, for he had lost time that morning; when he rounded the last curve he was almost running. There was a chance that the Boss might be there for his weekly report.

Then, wavering, flickering, darting here and there over the sweet marsh-grass, came a large black shadow, sweeping so closely before him that for the second time that morning Freckles dodged and sprang back. He had seen some owls and hawks of the swamp that he thought might be classed as large birds, but never anything like this, for six feet it spread its big, shining wings. Its strong feet could be seen drawn among its feathers. The sun glinted on its sharp, hooked beak. Its eyes glowed, caught the light, and seemed able to pierce the ground at his feet. It cared no more for Freckles than if he had not been there; for it perched on a low tree, while a second later it awkwardly hopped to the trunk of a lightning-riven elm, turned its back, and began searching the blue.

Freckles looked just in time to see a second shadow sweep the grass; and another bird, a trifle smaller and not quite so brilliant in the light, slowly sailed down to perch beside the first. Evidently they were mates, for with a queer, rolling hop the first-comer shivered his bronze wings, sidled to the new arrival, and gave her a silly little peck on her wing. Then he coquettishly drew away and ogled her. He lifted his head, waddled from her a few steps, awkwardly ambled back, and gave her such a simple sort of kiss on her beak that Freckles burst into a laugh, but clapped his hand over his mouth to stifle the sound.

The lover ducked and side-stepped a few feet. He spread his wings and slowly and softly waved them precisely as if he were fanning his charmer, which was indeed the result he accomplished. Then a wave of uncontrollable tenderness moved him so he hobbled to his bombardment once more. He faced her squarely this time, and turned his head from side to side with queer little jerks and indiscriminate peckings at her wings and head, and smirkings that really should have been irresistible. She yawned and shuffled away indifferently. Freckles reached up, pulled the quill from his hat, and looking from it to the birds, nodded in settled conviction.

"So you're me black angels, ye spalpeens! No wonder you didn't get in! But I'll back you to come closer it than any other birds ever did. You fly higher than I can see. Have you picked the Limberlost for a good thing and come to try it? Well, you can be me chickens if you want to, but I'm blest if you ain't cool for new ones. Why don't you take this stick for a gun and go skinning a mile?"

Freckles broke into an unrestrained laugh, for the bird-lover was keen about his courting, while evidently his mate was diffident. When he approached too boisterously, she relieved him of a goodly tuft of feathers and sent him backward in a series of squirmy little jumps that gave the boy an idea of what had happened up-sky to send the falling feather across his pathway.

"Score one for the lady! I'll be umpiring this," volunteered Freckles.

With a ravishing swagger, half-lifted wings, and deep, guttural hissing, the lover approached again. He suddenly lifted his body, but she coolly rocked forward on the limb, glided gracefully beneath him, and slowly sailed into the Limberlost. He recovered himself and gazed after her in astonishment.

Freckles hurried down the trail, shaking with laughter. When he neared the path to the clearing and saw the Boss sitting motionless on the mare that was the pride of his heart, the boy broke into a run.

"Oh, Mr. McLean!" he cried. "I hope I haven't kept you waiting very long! And the sun is getting hot! I have been so slow this morning! I could have gone faster, only there were that many things to keep me, and I didn't know you would be here. I'll hurry after this. I've never had to be giving excuses before. The line wasn't down, and there wasn't a sign of trouble; it was other things that were making me late."

McLean, smiling on the boy, immediately noticed the difference in him. This flushed, panting, talkative lad was not the same creature who had sought him in despair and bitterness. He watched in wonder as Freckles mopped the perspiration from his forehead and began to laugh. Then, forgetting all his customary reserve with the Boss, the pent-up boyishness in the lad broke forth. With an eloquence of which he never dreamed he told his story. He talked with such enthusiasm that McLean never took his eyes from his face or shifted in the saddle until he described the strange bird-lover, and then the Boss suddenly bent over the pommel and laughed with the boy.

Freckles decorated his story with keen appreciation and rare touches of Irish wit and drollery that made it most interesting as well as very funny. It was a first attempt at descriptive narration. With an inborn gift for striking the vital point, a naturalist's dawning enthusiasm for the wonders of the Limberlost, and the welling joy of his newly found happiness, he made McLean see the struggles of the moth and its freshly painted wings, the dainty, brilliant bird-mates of different colors, the feather sliding through the clear air, the palpitant throat and batting eyes of the frog; while his version of the big bird's courtship won for the Boss the best laugh he had enjoyed for years.

"They're in the middle of a swamp now" said Freckles. "Do you suppose there is any chance of them staying with me chickens? If they do, they'll be about the queerest I have; but I tell you, sir, I am finding some plum good ones. There's a new kind over at the mouth of the creek that uses its wings like feet and walks on all fours. It travels like a thrashing machine. There's another, tall as me waist, with a bill a foot long, a neck near two, not the thickness of me wrist and an elegant color. He's some blue and gray, touched up with black, white, and brown. The voice of him is such that if he'd be going up and standing beside a tree and crying at it a few times he could be sawing it square off. I don't know but it would be a good idea to try him on the gang, sir."

McLean laughed. "Those must be blue herons, Freckles," he said. "And it doesn't seem possible, but your description of the big black birds sounds like genuine black vultures. They are common enough in the South. I've seen them numerous around the lumber camps of Georgia, but I never before heard of any this far north. They must be strays. You have described perfectly our nearest equivalent to a branch of these birds called in Europe Pharaoh's Chickens, but if they are coming to the Limberlost they will have to drop Pharaoh and become Freckles' Chickens, like the remainder of the birds; won't they? Or are they too odd and ugly to interest you?"

"Oh, not at all, at all!" cried Freckles, bursting into pure brogue in his haste. "I don't know as I'd be calling them exactly pretty, and they do move like a rocking-horse loping, but they are so big and fearless. They have a fine color for black birds, and their feet and beaks seem so strong. You never saw anything so keen as their eyes! And fly? Why, just think, sir, they must be flying miles straight up, for they were out of sight completely when the feather fell. I don't suppose I've a chicken in the swamp that can go as close heaven as those big, black fellows, and then——"

Freckles' voice dragged and he hesitated.

"Then what?" interestedly urged McLean.

"He was loving her so," answered Freckles in a hushed voice. "I know it looked awful funny, and I laughed and told on him, but if I'd taken time to think I don't believe I'd have done it. You see, I've seen such a little bit of loving in me life. You easily can be understanding that at the Home it was every day the old story of neglect and desertion. Always people that didn't even care enough for their children to keep them, so you see, sir, I had to like him for trying so hard to make her know how he loved her. Of course, they're only birds, but if they are caring for each other like that, why, it's just the same as people, ain't it?"

Freckles lifted his brave, steady eyes to the Boss.

"If anybody loved me like that, Mr. McLean, I wouldn't be spending any time on how they looked or moved. All I'd be thinking of would be how they felt toward me. If they will stay, I'll be caring as much for them as any chickens I have. If I did laugh at them I thought he was just fine!"

The face of McLean was a study; but the honest eyes of the boy were so compelling that he found himself answering: "You are right, Freckles. He's a gentleman, isn't he? And the only real chicken you have. Of course he'll remain! The Limberlost will be paradise for his family. And now, Freckles, what has been the trouble all spring? You have done your work as faithfully as anyone could ask, but I can't help seeing that there is something wrong. Are you tired of your job?"

"I love it," answered Freckles. "It will almost break me heart when the gang comes and begins tearing up the swamp and scaring away me chickens."

"Then what is the trouble?" insisted McLean.

"I think, sir, it's been books," answered Freckles. "You see, I didn't realize it meself until the bullfrog told me this morning. I hadn't ever even heard about a place like this. Anyway, I wasn't understanding how it would be, if I had. Being among these beautiful things every day, I got so anxious like to be knowing and naming them, that it got to eating into me and went and made me near sick, when I was well as I could be. Of course, I learned to read, write, and figure some at school, but there was nothing there, or in any of the city that I ever got to see, that would make a fellow even be dreaming of such interesting things as there are here. I've seen the parks—but good Lord, they ain't even beginning to be in it with the Limberlost! It's all new and strange to me. I don't know a thing about any of it. The bullfrog told me to 'find out,' plain as day, and books are the only way; ain't they?"

"Of course," said McLean, astonished at himself for his heartfelt relief. He had not guessed until that minute what it would have meant to him to have Freckles give up. "You know enough to study out what you want yourself, if you have the books; don't you?"

"I am pretty sure I do," said Freckles. "I learned all I'd the chance at in the Home, and me schooling was good as far as it went. Wouldn't let you go past fourteen, you know. I always did me sums perfect, and loved me history books. I had them almost by heart. I never could get me grammar to suit them. They said it was just born in me to go wrong talking, and if it hadn't been I suppose I would have picked it up from the other children; but I'd the best voice of any of them in the Home or at school. I could knock them all out singing. I was always leader in the Home, and once one of the superintendents gave me carfare and let me go into the city and sing in a boys' choir. The master said I'd the swatest voice of them all until it got rough like, and then he made me quit for awhile, but he said it would be coming back by now, and I'm railly thinking it is, sir, for I've tried on the line a bit of late and it seems to go smooth again and lots stronger. That and me chickens have been all the company I've been having, and it will be all I'll want if I can have some books and learn the real names of things, where they come from, and why they do such interesting things. It's been fretting me more than I knew to be shut up here among all these wonders and not knowing a thing. I wanted to ask you what some books would cost me, and if you'd be having the goodness to get me the right ones. I think I have enough money."

Freckles offered his account-book and the Boss studied it gravely.

"You needn't touch your account, Freckles," he said. "Ten dollars from this month's pay will provide you everything you need to start on. I will write a friend in Grand Rapids today to select you the very best and send them at once."

Freckles' eyes were shining.

"Never owned a book in me life!" he said. "Even me schoolbooks were never mine. Lord! How I used to wish I could have just one of them for me very own! Won't it be fun to see me sawbird and me little yellow fellow looking at me from the pages of a book, and their real names and all about them printed alongside? How long will it be taking, sir?"

"Ten days should do it nicely," said McLean. Then, seeing Freckles' lengthening face, he added: "I'll have Duncan bring you a ten-bushel store-box the next time he goes to town. He can haul it to the west entrance and set it up wherever you want it. You can put in your spare time filling it with the specimens you find until the books come, and then you can study out what you have. I suspect you could collect specimens that I could send to naturalists in the city and sell for you; things like that winged creature, this morning. I don't know much in that line, but it must have been a moth, and it might have been rare. I've seen them by the thousand in museums, and in all nature I don't remember rarer coloring than their wings. I'll order you a butterfly-net and box and show you how scientists pin specimens. Possibly you can make a fine collection of these swamp beauties. It will be all right for you to take a pair of different moths and butterflies, but I don't want to hear of your killing any birds. They are protected by heavy fines."

McLean rode away leaving Freckles staring aghast. Then he saw the point and smiled. Standing on the trail, he twirled the feather and thought over the morning.

"Well, if life ain't getting to be worth living!" he said wonderingly. "Biggest streak of luck I ever had! 'Bout time something was coming my way, but I wouldn't ever thought anybody could strike such magnificent prospects through only a falling feather."

CHAPTER IV

WHEREIN FRECKLES FACES TROUBLE
BRAVELY AND OPENS THE WAY FOR
NEW EXPERIENCES

On Duncan's return from his next trip to town there was a big store-box loaded on the back of his wagon. He drove to the west entrance of the swamp, set the box on a stump that Freckles had selected in a beautiful, sheltered place, and made it secure on its foundations with a tree at its back.

"It seems most a pity to nail into that tree," said Duncan. "I haena the time to examine into the grain of it, but it looks as if it might be a rare ane. Anyhow, the nailin' winna hurt it deep, and havin' the case by it will make it safer if it is a guid ane."

"Isn't it an oak?" asked Freckles.

"Ay," said Duncan. "It looks like it might be ane of thae fine-grained white anes that mak' such grand furniture."

When the body of the case was secure, Duncan made a door from the lid and fastened it with hinges. He drove a staple, screwed on a latch, and gave Freckles a small padlock—so that he might fasten in his treasures safely. He made a shelf at the top for his books, and last of all covered the case with oil-cloth.

It was the first time in Freckles' life that anyone ever had done that much for his pleasure, and it warmed his heart with pure joy. If the interior of the box already had been covered with the rarest treasures of the Limberlost he could have been no happier.

When the big teamster stood back to look at his work he laughingly quoted, "'Neat, but no' gaudy,' as McLean says. All we're, needing now is a coat of paint to make a cupboard that would turn Sarah green with envy. Ye'll find that safe an' dry, lad, an' that's all that's needed."

"Mr. Duncan," said Freckles, "I don't know why you are being so mighty good to me; but if you have any jobs at the cabin that I could do for you or Mrs. Duncan, hours off the line, it would make me mighty happy."

Duncan laughed. "Ye needna feel ye are obliged to me, lad. Ye mauna think I could take a half-day off in the best hauling season and go to town for boxes to rig up, and spend of my little for fixtures."

"I knew Mr. McLean sent you," said Freckles, his eyes wide and bright with happiness. "It's so good of him. How I wish I could do something that would please him as much!"

"Why, Freckles," said Duncan, as he knelt and began collecting his tools, "I canna see that it will hurt ye to be told that ye are doing every day a thing that pleases the Boss as much as anything ye could do. Ye're being uncommon faithful, lad, and honest as old Father Time. McLean is trusting ye as he would his own flesh and blood."

"Oh, Duncan!" cried the happy boy. "Are you sure?"

"Why I know," answered Duncan. "I wadna venture to say so else. In those first days he cautioned me na to tell ye, but now he wadna care. D'ye ken, Freckles, that some of the single trees ye are guarding are worth a thousand dollars?"

Freckles caught his breath and stood speechless.

"Ye see," said Duncan, "that's why they maun be watched so closely. They tak', say, for instance, a burl maple—bird's eye they call it in the factory, because it's full o' wee knots and twists that look like the eye of a bird. They saw it out in sheets no muckle thicker than writin' paper. Then they make up the funiture out of cheaper wood and cover it with the maple—veneer, they call it. When it's all done and polished ye never saw onythin' grander. Gang into a retail shop the next time ye are in town and see some. By sawin' it thin that way they get finish for thousands of dollars' worth of furniture from a single tree. If ye dinna watch faithful, and Black Jack gets out a few he has marked, it means the loss of more money than ye ever dreamed of, lad. The other night, down at camp, some son of Balaam was suggestin' that ye might be sellin' the Boss out to Jack and lettin' him tak' the trees secretly, and nobody wad ever ken till the gang gets here."

A wave of scarlet flooded Freckles' face and he blazed hotly at the insult.

"And the Boss," continued Duncan, coolly ignoring Freckles' anger, "he lays back just as cool as cowcumbers an' says: 'I'll give a thousand dollars to ony man that will show me a fresh stump when we reach the Limberlost,' says he. Some of the men just snapped him op that they'd find some. So you see bow the Boss is trustin' ye, lad."

"I am gladder than I can ever expriss," said Freckles. "And now will I be walking double time to keep some of them from cutting a tree to get all that money!"

"Mither o' Moses!" howled Duncan. "Ye can trust the Scotch to bungle things a'thegither. McLean was only meanin' to show ye all confidence and honor. He's gone and set a high price for some dirty whelp to ruin ye. I was just tryin' to show ye how he felt toward ye, and

I've gone an' give ye that worry to bear. Damn the Scotch! They're so slow an' so dumb!"

"Exciptin' prisint company?" sweetly inquired Freckles.

"No!" growled Duncan. "Headin' the list! He'd nae business to set a price on ye, lad, for that's about the amount of it, an' I'd nae right to tell ye. We've both done ye ill, an' both meanin' the verra best. Juist what I'm always sayin' to Sarah."

"I am mighty proud of what you have been telling me, Duncan," said Freckles. "I need the warning, sure. For with the books coming I might be timpted to neglect me work when double watching is needed. Thank you more than I can say for putting me on to it. What you've told me may be the saving of me. I won't stop for dinner now. I'll be getting along the east line, and when I come around about three, maybe Mother Duncan will let me have a glass of milk and a bite of something."

"Ye see now!" cried Duncan in disgust. "Ye'll start on that seven-mile tramp with na bite to stay your stomach. What was it I told ye?"

"You told me that the Scotch had the hardest heads and the softest hearts of any people that's living," answered Freckles.

Duncan grunted in gratified disapproval.

Freckles picked up his club and started down the line, whistling cheerily, for he had an unusually long repertoire upon which to draw.

Duncan went straight to the lower camp, and calling McLean aside, repeated the conversation verbatim, ending: "And nae matter what happens now or ever, dinna ye dare let onythin' make ye believe that Freckles hasna guarded faithful as ony man could."

"I don't think anything could shake my faith in the lad," answered McLean.

Freckles was whistling merrily. He kept one eye religiously on the line. The other he divided between the path, his friends of the wire, and a search of the sky for his latest arrivals. Every day since their coming he had seen them, either hanging as small, black clouds above the swamp or bobbing over logs and trees with their queer, tilting walk. Whenever he could spare time, he entered the swamp and tried to make friends with them, for they were the tamest of all his unnumbered subjects. They ducked, dodged, and ambled around him, over logs and bushes, and not even a near approach would drive them to flight.

For two weeks he had found them circling over the Limberlost regularly, but one morning the female was missing and only the big black chicken hung sentinel above the swamp. His mate did not reappear in the following days, and Freckles grew very anxious. He spoke of it to Mrs. Duncan, and she quieted his fears by raising a delightful hope in their stead.

"Why, Freckles, if it's the hen-bird ye are missing, it's ten to one she's safe," she said. "She's laid, and is setting, ye silly! Watch him and mark whaur he lichts. Then follow and find the nest. Some Sabbath we'll all gang see it."

Accepting this theory, Freckles began searching for the nest. Because these "chickens" were large, as the hawks, he looked among the treetops until he almost sprained the back of his neck. He had half the crow and hawk nests in the swamp located. He searched for this nest instead of collecting subjects for his case. He found the pair the middle of one forenoon on the elm where he had watched their love-making. The big black chicken was feeding his mate; so it was proved that they were a pair, they were both alive, and undoubtedly she was brooding. After that Freckles' nest-hunting continued with renewed zeal, but as he had no idea where to look and Duncan could offer no helpful suggestion, the nest was no nearer to being found.

Coming from a long day on the trail, Freckles saw Duncan's children awaiting him much closer the swale than they usually ventured, and from their wild gestures he knew that something had happened. He began to run, but the cry that reached him was: "The books have come!"

How they hurried! Freckles lifted the youngest to his shoulder, the second took his club and dinner pail, and when they reached Mrs. Duncan they found her at work on a big box. She had loosened the lid, and then she laughingly sat on it.

"Ye canna have a peep in here until ye have washed and eaten supper," she said. "It's all ready on the table. Ance ye begin on this, ye'll no be willin' to tak' your nose o' it till bedtime, and I willna get my work done the nicht. We've eaten long ago."

It was difficult work, but Freckles smiled bravely. He made himself neat, swallowed a few bites, then came so eagerly that Mrs. Duncan yielded, although she said she very well knew all the time that his supper would be spoiled.

Lifting the lid, they removed the packing and found in that box books on birds, trees, flowers, moths, and butterflies. There was also one containing Freckles' bullfrog, true to life. Besides these were a butterfly-net, a naturalist's tin specimen-box, a bottle of cyanide, a box of cotton, a paper of long, steel specimen-pins, and a letter telling what all these things were and how to use them.

At the discovery of each new treasure, Freckles shouted: "Will you be looking at this, now?"

Mrs. Duncan cried: "Weel, I be drawed on!"

The eldest boy turned a somersault for every extra, while the baby, trying to follow his example, bunched over in a sidewise sprawl and cut his foot on the axe with which his mother had prized up the box-lid. That sobered them, they carried the books indoors. Mrs. Duncan had a top shelf in her closet cleared for them, far above the reach of meddling little fingers.

When Freckles started for the trail next morning, the shining new specimen-box flashed on his back. The black "chicken," a mere speck in the blue, caught the gleam of it. The folded net hung beside the boy's hatchet, and the bird book was in the box. He walked the line and tested each section scrupulously, watching every foot of the trail, for he was determined not to slight his work; but if ever a boy "made haste slowly" in a hurry, it was Freckles that morning. When at last he reached the space he had cleared and planted around his case, his heart swelled with the pride of possessing even so much that he could call his own, while his quick eyes feasted on the beauty of it.

He had made a large room with the door of the case set even with one side of it. On three sides, fine big bushes of wild rose climbed to the lower branches of the trees. Part of his walls were mallow, part alder, thorn, willow, and dogwood. Below there filled in a solid mass of pale pink sheep-laurel, and yellow St. John's wort, while the amber threads of the dodder interlaced everywhere. At one side the swamp came close, here cattails grew in profusion. In front of them he had planted a row of water-hyacinths without disturbing in the least the state of their azure bloom, and where the ground arose higher for his floor, a row of foxfire, that soon would be open.

To the left he had discovered a queer natural arrangement of the trees, that grew to giant size and were set in a gradually narrowing space so that a long, open vista stretched away until lost in the dim recesses of the swamp. A little trimming of underbush, rolling of dead logs, levelling of floor and carpeting with moss, made it easy to understand why Freckles had named this the "cathedral"; yet he never had been taught that "the groves were God's first temples."

On either side of the trees that constituted the first arch of this dim vista of the swamp he planted ferns that grew waist-high thus early in the season, and so skilfully the work had been done that not a frond drooped because of the change. Opposite, he cleared a space and made a flower bed. He filled one end with every delicate, lacy vine and fern he could transplant successfully. The body of the bed was a riot of color. Here he set growing dainty blue-eyed-Marys and blue-eyed grass side by side. He planted harebells; violets, blue, white, and yellow; wild geranium, cardinal-flower, columbine, pink snake's mouth, buttercups, painted trilliums, and orchis. Here were blood-root, moccasin-flower, hepatica, pitcher-plant, Jack-in-the-pulpit, and every other flower of the Limberlost that was in bloom or bore a bud presaging a flower. Every day saw the addition of new specimens. The place would have driven a botanist wild with envy.

On the line side he left the bushes thick for concealment, entering by a narrow path he and Duncan had cleared in setting up the case. He called this the front door, though he used every precaution to hide it. He built rustic seats between several of the trees, leveled the floor, and thickly carpeted it with rank, heavy, woolly-dog moss. Around the case he planted wild clematis, bittersweet, and wild-grapevines, and trained them over it until it was almost covered. Every day he planted new flowers, cut back rough bushes, and coaxed out graceful ones. His pride in his room was very great, but he had no idea how surprisingly beautiful it would appear to anyone who had not witnessed its growth and construction.

This morning Freckles walked straight to his case, unlocked it, and set his apparatus and dinner inside. He planted a new specimen he had found close the trail, and, bringing his old scrap-bucket from the corner in which it was hidden, from a near-by pool he dipped water to pour over his carpet and flowers.

Then he took out the bird book, settled comfortably on a bench, and with a deep sigh of satisfaction turned to the section headed. "V." Past "veery" and "vireo" he went, down the line until his finger, trembling with eagerness, stopped at "vulture."

"'Great black California vulture,'" he read.

"Humph! This side the Rockies will do for us."

"'Common turkey-buzzard.'"

"Well, we ain't hunting common turkeys. McLean said chickens, and what he says goes."

"'Black vulture of the South.'"

"Here we are arrived at once."

Freckles' finger followed the line, and he read scraps aloud.

"'Common in the South. Sometimes called Jim Crow. Nearest equivalent to C-a-t-h-a-r-t-e-s A-t-r-a-t-a.'"

"How the divil am I ever to learn them corkin' big words by mesel'?"

"'—the Pharaoh's Chickens of European species. Sometimes stray north as far as Virginia and Kentucky——'"

"And sometimes farther," interpolated Freckles, "'cos I got them right here in Indiana so like these pictures I can just see me big chicken bobbing up to get his ears boxed. Hey?"

"'Light-blue eggs'——'"

"Golly! I got to be seeing them!"

"'—big as a common turkey's, but shaped like a hen's, heavily splotched with chocolate——'"

"Caramels, I suppose. And——'"

"'—in hollow logs or stumps.'"

"Oh, hagginy! Wasn't I barking up the wrong tree, though? Ought to been looking close the ground all this time. Now it's all to do over, and I suspect the sooner I start the sooner I'll be likely to find them."

Freckles put away his book, dampened the smudge-fire, without which the mosquitoes made the swamp almost unbearable, took his cudgel and lunch, and went to the line. He sat on a log, ate at dinner-time and drank his last drop of water. The heat of June was growing intense. Even on the west of the swamp, where one had full benefit of the breeze from the upland, it was beginning to be unpleasant in the middle of the day.

He brushed the crumbs from his knees and sat resting awhile and watching the sky to see if his big chicken were hanging up there. But he came to the earth abruptly, for there were steps coming down the trail that were neither McLean's nor Duncan's—and there never had been others. Freckles' heart leaped hotly. He ran a quick hand over his belt to feel if his revolver and hatchet were there, caught up his cudgel and laid it across his knees—then sat quietly, waiting. Was it Black Jack, or someone even worse? Forced to do something to brace his nerves, he puckered his stiffening lips and began whistling a tune he had led in his clear tenor every year of his life at the Home Christmas exercises.

"Who comes this way, so blithe and gay,
Upon a merry Christmas day?"

His quick Irish wit roused to the ridiculousness of it until he broke into a laugh that steadied him amazingly.

Through the bushes he caught a glimpse of the oncoming figure. His heart flooded with joy, for it was a man from the gang. Wessner had been his bunk-mate the night he came down the corduroy. He knew him as well as any of McLean's men. This was no timber-thief. No doubt the Boss had sent him with a message. Freckles sprang up and called cheerily, a warm welcome on his face.

"Well, it's good telling if you're glad to see me," said Wessner, with something very like a breath of relief. "We been hearing down at the camp you were so mighty touchy you didn't allow a man within a rod of the line."

"No more do I," answered Freckles, "if he's a stranger, but you're from McLean, ain't you?"

"Oh, damn McLean!" said Wessner.

Freckles gripped the cudgel until his knuckles slowly turned purple.

"And are you railly saying so?" he inquired with elaborate politeness.

"Yes, I am," said Wessner. "So would every man of the gang if they wasn't too big cowards to say anything, unless maybe that other slobbering old Scotchman, Duncan. Grinding the lives out of us! Working us like dogs, and paying us starvation wages, while he rolls up his millions and lives like a prince!"

Green lights began to play through the gray of Freckles' eyes.

"Wessner," he said impressively, "you'd make a fine pattern for the father of liars! Every man on that gang is strong and hilthy, paid all he earns, and treated with the courtesy of a gentleman! As for the Boss living like a prince, he shares fare with you every day of your lives!"

Wessner was not a born diplomat, but he saw he was on the wrong tack, so he tried another.

"How would you like to make a good big pile of money, without even lifting your hand?" he asked.

"Humph!" said Freckles. "Have you been up to Chicago and cornered wheat, and are you offering me a friendly tip on the invistment of me fortune?"

Wessner came close.

"Freckles, old fellow," he said, "if you let me give you a pointer, I can put you on to making a cool five hundred without stepping out of your tracks."

Freckles drew back.

"You needn't be afraid of speaking up," he said. "There isn't a soul in the Limberlost save the birds and the beasts, unless some of your sort's come along and's crowding the privileges of the legal tinints."

"None of my friends along," said Wessner. "Nobody knew I came but Black, I—I mean a friend of mine. If you want to hear sense and act with reason, he can see you later, but it ain't necessary. We can make all the plans needed. The trick's so dead small and easy."

"Must be if you have the engineering of it," said Freckles. But he heard, with a sigh of relief, that they were alone.

Wessner was impervious. "You just bet it is! Why, only think, Freckles, slavin' away at a measly little thirty dollars a month, and here is a chance to clear five hundred in a day! You surely won't be the fool to miss it!"

"And how was you proposing for me to stale it?" inquired Freckles. "Or am I just to find it laying in me path beside the line?"

"That's it, Freckles," blustered the Dutchman, "you're just to find it. You needn't do a thing. You needn't know a thing. You name a morning when you will walk up the west side of the swamp and then turn round and walk back down the same side again and the money is yours. Couldn't anything be easier than that, could it?"

"Depinds entirely on the man," said Freckles. The lilt of a lark hanging above the swale beside them was not sweeter than the sweetness of his voice. "To some it would seem to come aisy as breathing; and to some, wringin' the last drop of their heart's blood couldn't force thim! I'm not the man that goes into a scheme like that with the blindfold over me eyes, for, you see, it manes to break trust with the Boss; and I've served him faithful as I knew. You'll have to be making the thing very clear to me understanding."

"It's so dead easy," repeated Wessner, "it makes me tired of the simpleness of it. You see there's a few trees in the swamp that's real gold mines. There's three especial. Two are back in, but one's square on the line. Why, your pottering old Scotch fool of a Boss nailed the wire to it with his own hands! He never noticed where the bark had been peeled, or saw what it was. If you will stay on this side of the trail just one day we can have it cut, loaded, and ready to drive out at night. Next morning you can find it, report, and be the busiest man in the search for us. We know where to fix it all safe and easy. Then McLean has a bet up with a couple of the gang that there can't be a raw stump found in the Limberlost. There's plenty of witnesses to swear to it, and I know three that will. There's a cool thousand, and this tree is worth all of that, raw. Say, it's a gold mine, I tell you, and just five hundred of it is yours. There's no danger on earth to you, for you've got McLean that bamboozled you could sell out the whole swamp and he'd never mistrust you. What do you say?"

Freckles' soul was satisfied. "Is that all?" he asked.

"No, it ain't," said Wessner. "If you really want to brace up and be a man and go into the thing for keeps, you can make five times that in a week. My friend knows a dozen others we could get out in a few days, and all you'd have to do would be to keep out of sight. Then you could take your money and skip some night, and begin life like a gentleman somewhere else. What do you think about it?"

Freckles purred like a kitten.

"'Twould be a rare joke on the Boss," he said, "to be stalin' from him the very thing he's trusted me to guard, and be getting me wages all winter throwed in free. And you're making the pay awful high. Me to be getting five hundred for such a simple little thing as that. You're trating me most royal indade! It's away beyond all I'd be expecting. Sivinteen cints would be a big price for that job. It must be looked into thorough. Just you wait here until I do a minute's turn in the swamp, and then I'll be eschorting you out of the clearing and giving you the answer."

Freckles lifted the overhanging bushes and hurried to the case. He unslung the specimen-box and laid it inside with his hatchet and revolver. He slipped the key in his pocket and went back to Wessner.

"Now for the answer," he said. "Stand up!"

There was iron in his voice, and he was commanding as an outraged general. "Anything, you want to be taking off?" he questioned.

Wessner looked the astonishment he felt. "Why, no, Freckles," he said.

"Have the goodness to be calling me Mister McLean," snapped Freckles. "I'm after resarvin' me pet name for the use of me friends! You may stand with your back to the light or be taking any advantage you want."

"Why, what do you mean?" spluttered Wessner.

"I'm manin'," said Freckles tersely, "to lick a quarter-section of hell out of you, and may the Holy Vargin stay me before I leave you here carrion, for your carcass would turn the stummicks of me chickens!"

At the camp that morning, Wessner's conduct had been so palpable an excuse to force a discharge that Duncan moved near McLean and whispered, "Think of the boy, sir?"

McLean was so troubled that, an hour later, he mounted Nellie and followed Wessner to his home in Wildcat Hollow, only to find that he had left there shortly before, heading for the Limberlost. McLean rode at top speed. When Mrs. Duncan told him that a man answering Wessner's description had gone down the west side of the swamp close noon, he left the mare in her charge and followed on foot. When he heard voices he entered the swamp and silently crept close just in time to hear Wessner whine: "But I can't fight you, Freckles. I hain't done nothing to you. I'm away bigger than you, and you've only one hand."

The Boss slid off his coat and crouched among the bushes, ready to spring; but as Freckles' voice reached him he held himself, with a strong effort, to learn what mettle was in the boy.

"Don't you be wasting of me good time in the numbering of me hands," cried Freckles. "The stringth of me cause will make up for the weakness of me mimbers, and the size of a cowardly thief doesn't count. You'll think all the wildcats of the Limberlost are turned loose on you whin I come against you, and as for me cause——I slept with you, Wessner, the night I came down the corduroy like a dirty, friendless tramp, and the Boss was for taking me up, washing, clothing, and feeding me, and giving me a home full of love and tinderness, and a master to look to, and good, well-earned money in the bank. He's trusting me his heartful, and here comes you, you spotted toad of the big road, and insults me, as is an honest Irish gintleman, by hinting that you concaive I'd be willing to shut me eyes and hold fast while you rob him of the thing I was set and paid to guard, and then act the sneak and liar to him, and ruin and eternally blacken the soul of me. You damned rascal," raved Freckles, "be fighting before I forget the laws of a gintlemin's game and split your dirty head with me stick!"

Wessner backed away, mumbling, "But I don't want to hurt you, Freckles!"

"Oh, don't you!" raged the boy, now fairly frothing. "Well, you ain't resembling me none, for I'm itching like death to git me fingers in the face of you."

He danced up, and as Wessner lunged in self-defense, ducked under his arm as a bantam and punched him in the pit of the stomach so that he doubled with a groan. Before Wessner could straighten himself, Freckles was on him, fighting like the wildest fury that ever left the beautiful island. The Dutchman dealt thundering blows that sometimes landed and sent Freckles reeling, and sometimes missed, while he went plunging into the swale with the impetus of them. Freckles could not strike with half Wessner's force, but he could land three blows to the Dutchman's one. It was here that the boy's days of alert watching on the line, the perpetual swinging of the heavy cudgel, and the endurance of all weather stood him in good stead; for he was tough, and agile. He skipped, ducked, and dodged. For the first five minutes he endured fearful punishment. Then Wessner's breath commenced to whistle between his teeth, when Freckles only had begun fighting. He sprang back with shrill laughter.

"Begolly! and will your honor be whistling the hornpipe for me to be dancing of?" he cried.

SPANG! went his fist into Wessner's face, and he was past him into the swale.

"And would you be pleased to tune up a little livelier?" he gasped, and clipped his ear as he sprang back. Wessner lunged at him in blind fury. Freckles, seeing an opening, forgot the laws of a gentleman's game and drove the toe of his heavy wading-boot in Wessner's middle until he doubled and fell heavily. In a flash Freckles was on him. For a time McLean could not see what was happening. "Go! Go to him now!" he commanded himself, but so intense was his desire to see the boy win alone that he did not stir.

At last Freckles sprang up and backed away. "Time!" he yelled as a fury. "Be getting up, Mr. Wessner, and don't be afraid of hurting me. I'll let you throw in an extra hand and lick you to me complate satisfaction all the same. Did you hear me call the limit? Will you get up and be facing me?"

As Wessner struggled to his feet, he resembled a battlefield, for his clothing was in ribbons and his face and hands streaming blood.

"I—I guess I got enough," he mumbled.

"Oh, you do?" roared Freckles. "Well this ain't your say. You come on to me ground, lying about me Boss and intimatin' I'd stale from his very pockets. Now will you be standing up and taking your medicine like a man, or getting it poured down the throat of you like a baby? I ain't got enough! This is only just the beginning with me. Be looking out there!"

He sprang against Wessner and sent him rolling. He attacked the unresisting figure and fought him until he lay limp and quiet and Freckles had no strength left to lift an arm. Then he arose and stepped back, gasping for breath. With his first lungful of air he shouted: "Time!" But the figure of Wessner lay motionless.

Freckles watched him with regardful eye and saw at last that he was completely exhausted. He bent over him, and catching him by the back of the neck, jerked him to his knees. Wessner lifted the face of a whipped cur, and fearing further punishment, burst into shivering sobs, while the tears washed tiny rivulets through the blood and muck. Freckles stepped back, glaring at Wessner, but suddenly the scowl of anger and the ugly disfiguring red faded from the boy's face. He dabbed at a cut on his temple from which issued a tiny crimson stream, and jauntily shook back his hair. His face took on the innocent look of a cherub, and his voice rivaled that of a brooding dove, but into his eyes crept a look of diabolical mischief.

He glanced vaguely around him until he saw his club, seized and twirled it as a drum major, stuck it upright in the muck, and marched on tiptoe to Wessner, mechanically, as a puppet worked by a string. Bending over, Freckles reached an arm around Wessner's waist and helped him to his feet.

"Careful, now" he cautioned, "be careful, Freddy; there's danger of you hurting me."

Drawing a handkerchief from a back pocket, Freckles tenderly wiped Wessner's eyes and nose.

"Come, Freddy, me child," he admonished Wessner, "it's time little boys were going home. I've me work to do, and can't be entertaining you any more today. Come back tomorrow, if you ain't through yet, and we'll repate the perfarmance. Don't be staring at me so wild like! I would eat you, but I can't afford it. Me earnings, being honest, come slow, and I've no money to be squanderin' on the pailful of Dyspeptic's Delight it would be to taking to work you out of my innards!"

Again an awful wrenching seized McLean. Freckles stepped back as Wessner, tottering and reeling, as a thoroughly drunken man, came toward the path, appearing indeed as if wildcats had attacked him.

The cudgel spun high in air, and catching it with an expertness acquired by long practice on the line, the boy twirled it a second, shook back his thick hair bonnily, and stepping into the trail, followed Wessner. Because Freckles was Irish, it was impossible to do it silently, so presently his clear tenor rang out, though there were bad catches where he was hard pressed for breath:

> *"It was the Dutch. It was the Dutch.*
> *Do you think it was the Irish hollered help?*
> *Not much!*
> *It was the Dutch. It was the Dutch————"*

Wessner turned and mumbled: "What you following me for? What are you going to do with me?"

Freckles called the Limberlost to witness: "How's that for the ingratitude of a beast? And me troubling mesilf to show him off me territory with the honors of war!"

Then he changed his tone completely and added: "Belike it's this, Freddy. You see, the Boss might come riding down this trail any minute, and the little mare's so wheedlesome that if she'd come on to you in your prisint state all of a sudden, she'd stop that short she'd send Mr. McLean out over the ears of her. No disparagement intinded to the sinse of the mare!" he added hastily.

Wessner belched a fearful oath, while Freckles laughed merrily.

"That's a sample of the thanks a generous act's always for getting," he continued. "Here's me neglictin' me work to eschort you out proper, and you saying such awful words Freddy," he demanded sternly, "do you want me to soap out your mouth? You don't seem to be realizing it, but if you was to buck into Mr. McLean in your prisint state, without me there to explain matters the chance is he'd cut the liver out of you; and I shouldn't think you'd be wanting such a fine gintleman as him to see that it's white!"

Wessner grew ghastly under his grime and broke into a staggering run.

"And now will you be looking at the manners of him?" questioned Freckles plaintively. "Going without even a 'thank you,' right in the face of all the pains I've taken to make it interesting for him!"

Freckles twirled the club and stood as a soldier at attention until Wessner left the clearing, but it was the last scene of that performance. When the boy turned, there was deathly illness on his face, while his legs wavered beneath his weight. He staggered to the case, and opening it he took out a piece of cloth. He dipped it into the water, and sitting on a bench, he wiped the blood and grime from his face, while his breath sucked between his clenched teeth. He was shivering with pain and excitement in spite of himself. He unbuttoned the band of his right sleeve, and turning it back, exposed the blue-lined, calloused whiteness of his maimed arm, now vividly streaked with contusions, while in a series of circular dots the blood oozed slowly. Here Wessner had succeeded in setting his teeth. When Freckles saw what it was he forgave himself the kick in the pit of Wessner's stomach, and cursed fervently and deep.

"Freckles, Freckles," said McLean's voice.

Freckles snatched down his sleeve and arose to his feet.

"Excuse me, sir," he said. "You'll surely be belavin' I thought meself alone."

McLean pushed him carefully to the seat, and bending over him, opened a pocket-case that he carried as regularly as his revolver and watch, for cuts and bruises were of daily occurrence among the gang.

Taking the hurt arm, he turned back the sleeve and bathed and bound the wounds. He examined Freckles' head and body and convinced himself that there was no permanent injury, although the cruelty of the punishment the boy had borne set the Boss shuddering. Then he closed the case, shoved it into his pocket, and sat beside Freckles. All the indescribable beauty of the place was strong around him, but he saw only the bruised face of the suffering boy, who had hedged for the information he wanted as a diplomat, argued as a judge, fought as a sheik, and triumphed as a devil.

When the pain lessened and breath relieved Freckles' pounding heart, he watched the Boss covertly. How had McLean gotten there and how long had he been there? Freckles did not dare ask. At last he arose, and going to the case, took out his revolver and the wire-mending apparatus and locked the door. Then he turned to McLean.

"Have you any orders, sir?" he asked.

"Yes," said McLean, "I have, and you are to follow them to the letter. Turn over that apparatus to me and go straight home. Soak yourself in the hottest bath your skin will bear and go to bed at once. Now hurry."

"Mr. McLean," said Freckles, "it's sorry I am to be telling you, but the afternoon's walking of the line ain't done. You see, I was just for getting to me feet to start, and I was on time, when up came a gintleman, and we got into a little heated argument. It's either settled, or it's just begun, but between us, I'm that late I haven't started for the afternoon yet. I must be going at once, for there's a tree I must find before the day's over."

"You plucky little idiot," growled McLean. "You can't walk the line! I doubt if you can reach Duncan's. Don't you know when you are done up? You go to bed; I'll finish your work."

"Niver!" protested Freckles. "I was just a little done up for the prisint, a minute ago. I'm all right now. Riding-boots are far too low. The day's hot and the walk a good seven miles, sir. Niver!"

As he reached for the outfit he pitched forward and his eyes closed. McLean stretched him on the moss and applied restoratives. When Freckles returned to consciousness, McLean ran to the cabin to tell Mrs. Duncan to have a hot bath ready, and to bring Nellie. That worthy woman promptly filled the wash-boiler, starting a roaring fire under it. She pushed the horse-trough from its base and rolled it to the kitchen.

By the time McLean came again, leading Nelie and holding Freckles on her back, Mrs. Duncan was ready for business. She and the Boss laid Freckles in the trough and poured on hot water until he squirmed. They soaked and massaged him. Then they drew off the hot water and closed his pores with cold. Lastly they stretched him on the floor and chafed, rubbed, and kneaded him until he cried out for mercy. As they rolled him into bed, his eyes dropped shut, but a little later they flared open.

"Mr. McLean," he cried, "the tree! Oh, do be looking after the tree!"

McLean bent over him. "Which tree, Freckles?"

"I don't know exact sir; but it's on the east line, and the wire is fastened to it. He bragged that you nailed it yourself, sir. You'll know it by the bark having been laid open to the grain somewhere low down. Five hundred dollars he offered me—to be—selling you out—sir!"

Freckles' head rolled over and his eyes dropped shut. McLean towered above the lad. His bright hair waved on the pillow. His face was swollen, and purple with bruises. His left arm, with the hand battered almost out of shape, stretched beside him, and the right, with no hand at all, lay across a chest that was a mass of purple welts. McLean's mind traveled to the night, almost a year before, when he had engaged Freckles, a stranger.

The Boss bent, covering the hurt arm with one hand and laying the other with a caress on the boy's forehead. Freckles stirred at his touch, and whispered as softly as the swallows under the eaves: "If you're coming this way—tomorrow—be pleased to step over—and we'll repate—the chorus softly!"

"Bless the gritty devil," muttered McLean.

Then he went out and told Mrs. Duncan to keep close watch on Freckles, also to send Duncan to him at the swamp the minute he came home. Following the trail to the line and back to the scent of the fight, the Boss entered Freckles' study quietly, as if his spirit, keeping there, might be roused, and gazed around with astonished eyes.

How had the boy conceived it? What a picture he had wrought in living colors! He had the heart of a painter. He had the soul of a poet. The Boss stepped carefully over the velvet carpet to touch the walls of crisp verdure with gentle fingers. He stood long beside the flower bed, and gazed at the banked wall of bright bloom as if he doubted its reality.

Where had Freckles ever found, and how had he transplanted such ferns? As McLean turned from them he stopped suddenly.

He had reached the door of the cathedral. That which Freckles had attempted would have been patent to anyone. What had been in the heart of the shy, silent boy when he had found that long, dim stretch of forest, decorated its entrance, cleared and smoothed its aisle, and carpeted its altar? What veriest work of God was in these mighty living pillars and the arched dome of green! How similar to stained cathedral windows were the long openings between the trees, filled with rifts of blue, rays of gold, and the shifting emerald of leaves! Where could be found mosaics to match this aisle paved with living color and glowing light? Was Freckles a devout Christian, and did he worship here? Or was he an untaught heathen, and down this vista of entrancing loveliness did Pan come piping, and dryads, nymphs, and fairies dance for him?

Who can fathom the heart of a boy? McLean had been thinking of Freckles as a creature of unswerving honesty, courage, and faithfulness. Here was evidence of a heart aching for beauty, art, companionship, worship. It was writ large all over the floor, walls, and furnishing of that little Limberlost clearing.

When Duncan came, McLean told him the story of the fight, and they laughed until they cried. Then they started around the line in search of the tree.

Said Duncan: "Now the boy is in for sore trouble!"

"I hope not," answered McLean. "You never in all your life saw a cur whipped so completely. He won't come back for the repetition of the chorus. We surely can find the tree. If we can't, Freckles can. I will bring enough of the gang to take it out at once. That will insure peace for a time, at least, and I am hoping that in a month more the whole gang may be moved here. It soon will be fall, and then, if he will go, I intend to send Freckles to my mother to be educated. With his quickness of mind and body and a few years' good help he can do anything. Why, Duncan, I'd give a hundred-dollar bill if you could have been here and seen for yourself."

"Yes, and I'd 'a' done murder," muttered the big teamster. "I hope, sir, ye will make good your plans for Freckles, though I'd as soon see ony born child o' my ain taken from our home. We love the lad, me and Sarah."

Locating the tree was easy, because it was so well identified. When the rumble of the big lumber wagons passing the cabin on the way to the swamp wakened Freckles next morning, he sprang up and was soon following them. He was so sore and stiff that every movement was torture at first, but he grew easier, and shortly did not suffer so much. McLean scolded him for coming, yet in his heart triumphed over every new evidence of fineness in the boy.

The tree was a giant maple, and so precious that they almost dug it out by the roots. When it was down, cut in lengths, and loaded, there was yet an empty wagon. As they were gathering up their tools to go, Duncan said: "There's a big hollow tree somewhere mighty close here that I've been wanting for a watering-trough for my stock; the one I have is so small. The Portland company cut this for elm butts last year, and it's six feet diameter and hollow for forty feet. It was a buster! While the men are here and there is an empty wagon, why mightn't I load it on and tak' it up to the barn as we pass?"

McLean said he was very willing, ordered the driver to break line and load the log, detailing men to assist. He told Freckles to ride on a section of the maple with him, but now the boy asked to enter the swamp with Duncan.

"I don't see why you want to go," said McLean. "I have no business to let you out today at all."

"It's me chickens," whispered Freckles in distress. "You see, I was just after finding yesterday, from me new book, how they do be nesting in hollow trees, and there ain't any too many in the swamp. There's just a chance that they might be in that one."

"Go ahead," said McLean. "That's a different story. If they happen to be there, why tell Duncan he must give up the tree until they have finished with it."

Then he climbed on a wagon and was driven away. Freckles hurried into the swamp. He was a little behind, yet he could see the men. Before he overtook them, they had turned from the west road and had entered the swamp toward the east.

They stopped at the trunk of a monstrous prostrate log. It had been cut three feet from the ground, over three-fourths of the way through, and had fallen toward the east, the body of the log still resting on the stump. The underbrush was almost impenetrable, but Duncan plunged in and with a crowbar began tapping along the trunk to decide how far it was hollow, so that they would know where to cut. As they waited his decision, there came from the mouth of it—on wings—a large black bird that swept over their heads.

Freckles danced wildly. "It's me chickens! Oh, it's me chickens!" he shouted. "Oh, Duncan, come quick! You've found the nest of me precious chickens!"

Duncan hurried to the mouth of the log, but Freckles was before him. He crashed through poison-vines and underbrush regardless of any danger, and climbed on the stump. When Duncan came he was shouting like a wild man.

"It's hatched!" he yelled. "Oh, me big chicken has hatched out me little chicken, and there's another egg. I can see it plain, and oh, the funny little white baby! Oh, Duncan, can you see me little white chicken?"

Duncan could easily see it; so could everyone else. Freckles crept into the log and tenderly carried the hissing, blinking little bird to the light in a leaf-lined hat. The men found it sufficiently wonderful to satisfy even Freckles, who had forgotten he was ever sore or stiff, and coddled over it with every blarneying term of endearment he knew.

Duncan gathered his tools. "Deal's off, boys!" he said cheerfully. "This log mauna be touched until Freckles' chaukies have finished with it. We might as weel gang. Better put it back, Freckles. It's just out, and it may chill. Ye will probably hae twa the morn."

Freckles crept into the log and carefully deposited the baby beside the egg. When he came back, he said: "I made a big mistake not to be bringing the egg out with the baby, but I was fearing to touch it. It's shaped like a hen's egg, and it's big as a turkey's, and the beautifulest blue—just splattered with big brown splotches, like me book said, precise. Bet you never saw such a sight as it made on the yellow of the rotten wood beside that funny leathery-faced little white baby."

"Tell you what, Freckles," said one of the teamsters. "Have you ever heard of this Bird Woman who goes all over the country with a camera and makes pictures? She made some on my brother Jim's place last summer, and Jim's so wild about them he quits plowing and goes after her about every nest he finds. He helps her all he can to take them, and then she gives him a picture. Jim's so proud of what he has he keeps them in the Bible. He shows them to everybody that comes, and brags about how he helped. If you're smart, you'll send for her and she'll come and make a picture just like life. If you help her, she will give you one. It would be uncommon pretty to keep, after your birds are gone. I dunno what they are. I never see their like before. They must be something rare. Any you fellows ever see a bird like that hereabouts?"

No one ever had.

"Well," said the teamster, "failing to get this log lets me off till noon, and I'm going to town. I go right past her place. I've a big notion to stop and tell her. If she drives straight back in the swamp on the west road, and turns east at this big sycamore, she can't miss finding the tree, even if Freckles ain't here to show her. Jim says her work is a credit to the State she lives in, and any man is a measly creature who isn't willing to help her all he can. My old daddy used to say that all there was to religion was doing to the other fellow what you'd want him to do to you, and if I was making a living taking bird pictures, seems to me I'd be mighty glad for a chance to take one like that. So I'll just stop and tell her, and by gummy! maybe she will give me a picture of the little white sucker for my trouble."

Freckles touched his arm.

"Will she be rough with it?" he asked.

"Government land! No!" said the teamster. "She's dead down on anybody that shoots a bird or tears up a nest. Why, she's half killing herself in all kinds of places and weather to teach people to love and protect the birds. She's that plum careful of them that Jim's wife says she has Jim a standin' like a big fool holding an ombrelly over them when they are young and tender until she gets a focus, whatever that is. Jim says there ain't a bird on his place that don't actually seem to like having her around after she has wheedled them a few days, and the pictures she takes nobody would ever believe who didn't stand by and see."

"Will you he sure to tell her to come?" asked Freckles.

Duncan slept at home that night. He heard Freckles slipping out early the next morning, but he was too sleepy to wonder why, until he came to do his morning chores. When he found that none of his stock was at all thirsty, and saw the water-trough brimming, he knew that the boy was trying to make up to him for the loss of the big trough that he had been so anxious to have.

"Bless his fool little hot heart!" said Duncan. "And him so sore it is tearing him to move for anything. Nae wonder he has us all loving him!"

Freckles was moving briskly, and his heart was so happy that he forgot all about the bruises. He hurried around the trail, and on his way down the east side he went to see the chickens. The mother bird was on the nest. He was afraid the other egg might be hatching, so he did not venture to disturb her. He made the round and reached his study early. He ate his lunch, but did not need to start on the second trip until the middle of the afternoon. He would have long hours to work on his flower bed, improve his study, and learn about his chickens. Lovingly he set his room in order and watered the flowers and carpet. He had chosen for his resting-place the coolest spot on the west side, where there was almost always a breeze; but today the heat was so intense that it penetrated even there.

"I'm mighty glad there's nothing calling me inside!" he said. "There's no bit of air stirring, and it will just be steaming. Oh, but it's luck Duncan found the nest before it got so unbearing hot! I might have missed it altogether. Wouldn't it have been a shame to lose that sight? The cunning little divil! When he gets to toddling down that log to meet me, won't he be a circus? Wonder if he'll be as graceful a performer afoot as his father and mother?"

The heat became more insistent. Noon came; Freckles ate his dinner and settled for an hour or two on a bench with a book.

CHAPTER V

WHEREIN AN ANGEL MATERIALIZES
AND A MAN WORSHIPS

Perhaps there was a breath of sound—Freckles never afterward could remember—but for some reason he lifted his head as the bushes parted and the face of an angel looked between. Saints, nymphs, and fairies had floated down his cathedral aisle for him many times, with forms and voices of exquisite beauty.

Parting the wild roses at the entrance was beauty of which Freckles never had dreamed. Was it real or would it vanish as the other dreams? He dropped his book, and rising to his feet, went a step closer, gazing intently. This was real flesh and blood. It was in every way kin to the Limberlost, for no bird of its branches swung with easier grace than this dainty young thing rocked on the bit of morass on which she stood. A sapling beside her was not straighter or rounder than her slender form. Her soft, waving hair clung around her face from the heat, and curled over her shoulders. It was all of one piece with the gold of the sun that filtered between the branches. Her eyes were the deepest blue of the iris, her lips the reddest red of the foxfire, while her cheeks were exactly of the same satin as the wild rose petals caressing them. She was smiling at Freckles in perfect confidence, and she cried:

"Oh, I'm so delighted that I've found you!"

The wildly leaping heart of Freckles burst from his body and fell in the black swamp-muck at her feet with such a thud that he did not understand how she could avoid hearing. He really felt that if she looked down she would see.

Incredulous, he quavered: "An'—an' was you looking for me?"

"I hoped I might find you," said the Angel. "You see, I didn't do as I was told, and I'm lost. The Bird Woman said I should wait in the carriage until she came back. She's been gone hours. It's a perfect Turkish bath in there, and I'm all lumpy with mosquito bites. Just when I thought that I couldn't bear it another minute, along came the biggest Papilio Ajax you ever saw. I knew how pleased she'd be, so I ran after it. It flew so slow and so low that I thought a dozen times I had it. Then all at once it went from sight above the trees, and I couldn't find my way back to save me. I think I've walked more than an hour. I have been mired to my knees. A thorn raked my arm until it is bleeding, and I'm so tired and warm."

She parted the bushes farther. Freckles saw that her blue cotton frock clung to her, limp with perspiration. It was torn across the breast. One sleeve hung open from shoulder to elbow. A thorn had torn her arm until it was covered with blood, and the gnats and mosquitoes were clustering around it. Her feet were in lace hose and low shoes. Freckles gasped. In the Limberlost in low shoes! He caught an armful of moss from his carpet and buried it in the ooze in front of her for a footing.

"Come out here so I can see where you are stepping. Quick, for the life of you!" he ordered.

She smiled on him indulgently.

"Why?" she inquired.

"Did anybody let you come here and not be telling you of the snakes?" urged Freckles.

"We met Mr. McLean on the corduroy, and he did say something about snakes, I believe. The Bird Woman put on leather leggings, and a nice, parboiled time she must be having! Worst dose I ever endured, and I'd nothing to do but swelter."

"Will you be coming out of there?" groaned Freckles.

She laughed as if it were a fine joke.

"Maybe if I'd be telling you I killed a rattler curled upon that same place you're standing, as long as me body and the thickness of me arm, you'd be moving where I can see your footing," he urged insistently.

"What a perfectly delightful little brogue you speak," she said. "My father is Irish, and half should be enough to entitle me to that much. 'Maybe—if I'd—be telling you,'" she imitated, rounding and accenting each word carefully.

Freckles was beginning to feel a wildness in his head. He had derided Wessner at that same hour yesterday. Now his own eyes were filling with tears.

"If you were understanding the danger!" he continued desperately.

"Oh, I don't think there is much!"

She tilted on the morass.

"If you killed one snake here, it's probably all there is near; and anyway, the Bird Woman says a rattlesnake is a gentleman and always gives warning before he strikes. I don't hear any rattling. Do you?"

"Would you be knowing it if you did?" asked Freckles, almost impatiently.

How the laugh of the young thing rippled!

"'Would I be knowing it?'" she mocked. "You should see the swamps of Michigan where they dump rattlers from the marl-dredgers three and four at a time!"

Freckles stood astounded. She did know. She was not in the least afraid. She was depending on a rattlesnake to live up to his share of the contract and rattle in time for her to move. The one characteristic an Irishman admires in a woman, above all others, is courage. Freckles worshiped anew. He changed his tactics.

"I'd be pleased to be receiving you at me front door," he said, "but as you have arrived at the back, will you come in and be seated?"

He waved toward a bench. The Angel came instantly.

"Oh, how lovely and cool!" she cried.

As she moved across his room, Freckles had difficult work to keep from falling on his knees; for they were very weak, while he was hard driven by an impulse to worship.

"Did you arrange this?" she asked.

"Yis," said Freckles simply.

"Someone must come with a big canvas and copy each side of it," she said. "I never saw anything so beautiful! How I wish I might remain here with you! I will, some day, if you will let me; but now, if you can spare the time, will you help me find the carriage? If the Bird Woman comes back and I am gone, she will be almost distracted."

"Did you come on the west road?" asked Freckles.

"I think so," she said. "The man who told the Bird Woman said that was the only place the wires were down. We drove away in, and it was dreadful—over stumps and logs, and we mired to the hubs. I suppose you know, though. I should have stayed in the carriage, but I was so tired. I never dreamed of getting lost. I suspect I will be scolded finely. I go with the Bird Woman half the time during the summer vacations. My father says I learn a lot more than I do at school, and get it straight. I never came within a smell of being lost before. I thought, at first, it was going to be horrid; but since I've found you, maybe it will be good fun after all."

Freckles was amazed to hear himself excusing: "It was so hot in there. You couldn't be expected to bear it for hours and not be moving. I can take you around the trail almost to where you were. Then you can sit in the carriage, and I will go find the Bird Woman."

"You'll be killed if you do! When she stays this long, it means that she has a focus on something. You see, when she has a focus, and lies in the weeds and water for hours, and the sun bakes her, and things crawl over her, and then someone comes along and scares her bird away just as she has it coaxed up—why, she kills them. If I melt, you won't go after her. She's probably blistered and half eaten up; but she never will quit until she is satisfied."

"Then it will be safer to be taking care of you," suggested Freckles.

"Now you're talking sense!" said the Angel.

"May I try to help your arm?" he asked.

"Have you any idea how it hurts?" she parried.

"A little," said Freckles.

"Well, Mr. McLean said We'd probably find his son here"

"His son!" cried Freckles.

"That's what he said. And that you would do anything you could for us; and that we could trust you with our lives. But I would have trusted you anyway, if I hadn't known a thing about you. Say, your father is rampaging proud of you, isn't he?"

"I don't know," answered the dazed Freckles.

"Well, call on me if you want reliable information. He's so proud of you he is all swelled up like the toad in AEsop's Fables. If you have ever had an arm hurt like this, and can do anything, why, for pity sake, do it!"

She turned back her sleeve, holding toward Freckles an arm of palest cameo, shaped so exquisitely that no sculptor could have chiseled it.

Freckles unlocked his case, and taking out some cotton cloth, he tore it in strips. Then he brought a bucket of the cleanest water he could find. She yielded herself to his touch as a baby, and he bathed away the blood and bandaged the ugly, ragged wound. He finished his surgery by lapping the torn sleeve over the cloth and binding it down with a piece of twine, with the Angel's help about the knots.

Freckles worked with trembling fingers and a face tense with earnestness.

"Is it feeling any better?" he asked.

"Oh, it's well now!" cried the Angel. "It doesn't hurt at all, any more."

"I'm mighty glad," said Freckles. "But you had best go and be having your doctor fix it right; the minute you get home."

"Oh, bother! A little scratch like that!" jeered the Angel. "My blood is perfectly pure. It will heal in three days."

"It's cut cruel deep. It might be making a scar," faltered Freckles, his eyes on the ground. "'Twould—'twould be an awful pity. A doctor might know something to prevent it."

"Why, I never thought of that!" exclaimed the Angel.

"I noticed you didn't," said Freckles softly. "I don't know much about it, but it seems as if most girls would."

The Angel thought intently, while Freckles still knelt beside her. Suddenly she gave herself an impatient little shake, lifted her glorious eyes full to his, and the smile that swept her sweet, young face was the loveliest thing that Freckles ever had seen.

"Don't let's bother about it," she proposed, with the faintest hint of a confiding gesture toward him. "It won't make a scar. Why, it couldn't, when you have dressed it so nicely."

The velvety touch of her warm arm was tingling in Freckles' fingertips. Dainty lace and fine white ribbon peeped through her torn dress. There were beautiful rings on her fingers. Every article she wore was of the finest material and in excellent taste. There was the trembling Limberlost guard in his coarse clothing, with his cotton rags and his old pail of swamp water. Freckles was sufficiently accustomed to contrasts to notice them, and sufficiently fine to be hurt by them always.

He lifted his eyes with a shadowy pain in them to hers, and found them of serene, unconscious purity. What she had said was straight from a kind, untainted, young heart. She meant every word of it. Freckles' soul sickened. He scarcely knew whether he could muster strength to stand.

"We must go and hunt for the carriage," said the Angel, rising.

In instant alarm for her, Freckles sprang up, grasped the cudgel, and led the way, sharply watching every step. He went as close the log as he felt that he dared, and with a little searching found the carriage. He cleared a path for the Angel, and with a sigh of relief saw her enter it safely. The heat was intense. She pushed the damp hair from her temples.

"This is a shame!" said Freckles. "You'll never be coming here again."

"Oh yes I shall!" said the Angel. "The Bird Woman says that these birds remain over a month in the nest and she would like to make a picture every few days for seven or eight weeks, perhaps."

Freckles barely escaped crying aloud for joy.

"Then don't you ever be torturing yourself and your horse to be coming in here again," he said. "I'll show you a way to drive almost to the nest on the east trail, and then you can come around to my room and stay while the Bird Woman works. It's nearly always cool there, and there's comfortable seats, and water."

"Oh! did you have drinking-water there?" she cried. "I was never so thirsty or so hungry in my life, but I thought I wouldn't mention it."

"And I had not the wit to be seeing!" wailed Freckles. "I can be getting you a good drink in no time."

He turned to the trail.

"Please wait a minute," called the Angel. "What's your name? I want to think about you while you are gone." Freckles lifted his face with the brown rift across it and smiled quizzically.

"Freckles?" she guessed, with a peal of laughter. "And mine is——"

"I'm knowing yours," interrupted Freckles.

"I don't believe you do. What is it?" asked the girl.

"You won't be getting angry?"

"Not until I've had the water, at least."

It was Freckles' turn to laugh. He whipped off his big, floppy straw hat, stood uncovered before her, and said, in the sweetest of all the sweet tones of his voice: "There's nothing you could be but the Swamp Angel."

The girl laughed happily.

Once out of her sight, Freckles ran every step of the way to the cabin. Mrs. Duncan gave him a small bucket of water, cool from the well. He carried it in the crook of his right arm, and a basket filled with bread and butter, cold meat, apple pie, and pickles, in his left hand.

"Pickles are kind o' cooling," said Mrs. Duncan.

Then Freckles ran again.

The Angel was on her knees, reaching for the bucket, as he came up.

"Be drinking slow," he cautioned her.

"Oh!" she cried, with a long breath of satisfaction. "It's so good! You are more than kind to bring it!"

Freckles stood blinking in the dazzling glory of her smile until he scarcely could see to lift the basket.

"Mercy!" she exclaimed. "I think I had better be naming you the 'Angel.' My Guardian Angel."

"Yis," said Freckles. "I look the character every day—but today most emphatic!"

"Angels don't go by looks," laughed the girl. "Your father told us you had been scrapping. But he told us why. I'd gladly wear all your cuts and bruises if I could do anything that would make my father look as peacocky as yours did. He strutted about proper. I never saw anyone look prouder."

"Did he say he was proud of me?" marveled Freckles.

"He didn't need to," answered the Angel. "He was radiating pride from every pore. Now, have you brought me your dinner?"

"I had my dinner two hours ago," answered Freckles.

"Honest Injun?" bantered the Angel.

"Honest! I brought that on purpose for you."

"Well, if you knew how hungry I am, you would know how thankful I am, to the dot," said the Angel.

"Then you be eating," cried the happy Freckles.

The Angel sat on a big camera, spread the lunch on the carriage seat, and divided it in halves. The daintiest parts she could select she carefully put back into the basket. The remainder she ate. Again Freckles found her of the swamp, for though she was almost ravenous, she managed her food as gracefully as his little yellow fellow, and her every movement was easy and charming. As he watched her with famished eyes, Freckles told her of his birds, flowers, and books, and never realized what he was doing.

He led the horse to a deep pool that he knew of, and the tortured creature drank greedily, and lovingly rubbed him with its nose as he wiped down its welted body with grass. Suddenly the Angel cried: "There comes the Bird Woman!"

Freckles had intended leaving before she came, but now he was glad indeed to be there, for a warmer, more worn, and worse bitten creature he never had seen. She was staggering under a load of cameras and paraphernalia. Freckles ran to her aid. He took all he could carry of her load, stowed it in the back of the carriage, and helped her in. The Angel gave her water, knelt and unfastened the leggings, bathed her face, and offered the lunch.

Freckles brought the horse. He was not sure about the harness, but the Angel knew, and soon they left the swamp. Then he showed them how to reach the chicken tree from the outside, indicated a cooler place for the horse, and told them how, the next time they came, the Angel could find his room while she waited.

The Bird Woman finished her lunch, and lay back, almost too tired to speak.

"Were you for getting Little Chicken's picture?" Freckles asked.

"Finely!" she answered. "He posed splendidly. But I couldn't do anything with his mother. She will require coaxing."

"The Lord be praised!" muttered Freckles under his breath.

The Bird Woman began to feel better.

"Why do you call the baby vulture 'Little Chicken'?" she asked, leaning toward Freckles in an interested manner.

"'Twas Duncan began it," said Freckles. "You see, through the fierce cold of winter the birds of the swamp were almost starving. It is mighty lonely here, and they were all the company I was having. I got to carrying scraps and grain down to them. Duncan was that ginerous he was giving me of his wheat and corn from his chickens' feed, and he called the birds me swamp chickens. Then when these big black fellows came, Mr. McLean said they were our nearest kind to some in the old world that they called 'Pharaoh's Chickens,' and he called mine 'Freckles' Chickens.'"

"Good enough!" cried the Bird Woman, her splotched purple face lighting with interest. "You must shoot something for them occasionally, and I'll bring more food when I come. If you will help me keep them until I get my series, I'll give you a copy of each study I make, mounted in a book."

Freckles drew a deep breath.

"I'll be doing me very best," he promised, and from the deeps he meant it.

"I wonder if that other egg is going to hatch?" mused the Bird Woman. "I am afraid not. It should have pipped today. Isn't it a beauty! I never before saw either an egg or the young. They are rare this far north."

"So Mr. McLean said," answered Freckles.

Before they drove away, the Bird Woman thanked him for his kindness to the Angel and to her. She gave him her hand at parting, and Freckles joyfully realized that this was going to be another person for him to love. He could not remember, after they had driven away, that they even had noticed his missing hand, and for the first time in his life he had forgotten it.

When the Bird Woman and the Angel were on the home road, she told of the little corner of paradise into which she had strayed and of her new name. The Bird Woman looked at the girl and guessed its appropriateness.

"Did you know Mr. McLean had a son?" asked the Angel. "Isn't the little accent he has, and the way he twists a sentence, too dear? And isn't it too old-fashioned and funny to hear him call his father 'mister'?"

"It sounds too good to be true," said the Bird Woman, answering the last question first. "I am so tired of these present-day young men who patronizingly call their fathers 'Dad,' 'Governor,' 'Old Man' and 'Old Chap,' that the boy's attitude of respect and deference appealed to me as being fine as silk. There must be something rare about that young man."

She did not find it necessary to tell the Angel that for several years she had known the man who so proudly proclaimed himself Freckles' father to be a bachelor and a Scotchman. The Bird Woman had a fine way of attending strictly to her own business.

Freckles turned to the trail, but he stopped at every wild brier to study the pink satin of the petals. She was not of his world, and better than any other he knew it; but she might be his Angel, and he was dreaming of naught but blind, silent worship. He finished the happiest day of his life, and that night he returned to the swamp as if drawn by invisible force. That Wessner would try for his revenge, he knew. That he would be abetted by Black Jack was almost certain, but fear had fled the happy heart of Freckles. He had kept his trust. He had won the respect of the Boss. No one ever could wipe from his heart the flood of holy adoration that had welled with the coming of his Angel. He would do his best, and trust for strength to meet the dark day of reckoning that he knew would come sooner or later. He swung round the trail, briskly tapping the wire, and singing in a voice that scarcely could have been surpassed for sweetness.

At the edge of the clearing he came into the bright moonlight and there sat McLean on his mare. Freckles hurried to him.

"Is there trouble?" he inquired anxiously.

"That's what I wanted to ask you," said the Boss. "I stopped at the cabin to see you a minute, before I turned in, and they said you had come down here. You must not do it, Freckles. The swamp is none too healthful at any time, and at night it is rank poison."

Freckles stood combing his fingers through Nellie's mane, while the dainty creature was twisting her head for his caresses. He pushed back his hat and looked into McLean's face. "It's come to the 'sleep with one eye open,' sir. I'm not looking for anything to be happening for a week or two, but it's bound to come, and soon. If I'm to keep me trust as I've promised you and meself, I've to live here mostly until the gang comes. You must be knowing that, sir."

"I'm afraid it's true, Freckles," said McLean. "And I've decided to double the guard until we come. It will be only a few weeks, now; and I'm so anxious for you that you must not be left alone further. If anything should happen to you, Freckles, it would spoil one of the very dearest plans of my life."

Freckles heard with dismay the proposition to place a second guard.

"Oh! no, no, Mr. McLean," he cried. "Not for the world! I wouldn't be having a stranger around, scaring me birds and tramping up me study, and disturbing all me ways, for any money! I am all the guard you need! I will be faithful! I will turn over the lease with no tree missing—on me life, I will! Oh, don't be sending another man to set them saying I turned coward and asked for help. It will just kill the honor of me heart if you do it. The only thing I want is another gun. If it railly comes to trouble, six cartridges ain't many, and you know I am slow-like about reloading." McLean reached into his hip pocket and handed a shining big revolver to Freckles, who slipped it beside the one already in his belt.

Then the Boss sat brooding.

"Freckles," he said at last, "we never know the timber of a man's soul until something cuts into him deeply and brings the grain out strong. You've the making of a mighty fine piece of furniture, my boy, and you shall have your own way these few weeks yet. Then, if you will go, I intend to take you to the city and educate you, and you are to be my son, my lad—my own son!"

Freckles twisted his finger in Nellie's mane to steady himself.

"But why should you be doing that, sir?" he faltered.

McLean slid his arm around the boy's shoulder and gathered him close.

"Because I love you, Freckles," he said simply.

Freckles lifted a white face. "My God, sir!" he whispered. "Oh, my God!"

McLean tightened his clasp a second longer, then he rode down the trail.

Freckles lifted his hat and faced the sky. The harvest moon looked down, sheeting the swamp in silver glory. The Limberlost sang her night song. The swale softly rustled in the wind. Winged things of night brushed his face; and still Freckles gazed upward, trying to fathom these things that had come to him. There was no help from the sky. It seemed far away, cold, and blue. The earth, where flowers blossomed, angels walked, and love could be found, was better. But to One, above, he must make acknowledgment for these miracles. His lips moved and he began talking softly.

"Thank You for each separate good thing that has come to me," he said, "and above all for the falling of the feather. For if it didn't really fall from an angel, its falling brought an Angel, and if it's in the great heart of you to exercise yourself any further about me, oh, do please to be taking good care of her!"

CHAPTER VI

WHEREIN A FIGHT OCCURS AND
WOMEN SHOOT STRAIGHT

The following morning Freckles, inexpressibly happy, circled the Limberlost. He kept snatches of song ringing, as well as the wires. His heart was so full that tears of joy glistened in his eyes. He rigorously strove to divide his thought evenly between McLean and the Angel. He realized to the fullest the debt he already owed the Boss and the magnitude of last night's declaration and promises. He was hourly planning to deliver his trust and then enter with equal zeal on whatever task his beloved Boss saw fit to set him next. He wanted to be ready to meet every device that Wessner and Black Jack could think of to outwit him. He recognized their double leverage, for if they succeeded in felling even one tree McLean became liable for his wager.

Freckles' brow wrinkled in his effort to think deeply and strongly, but from every swaying wild rose the Angel beckoned to him. When he crossed Sleepy Snake Creek and the goldfinch, waiting as ever, challenged: "SEE ME?" Freckles saw the dainty swaying grace of the Angel instead. What is a man to do with an Angel who dismembers herself and scatters over a whole swamp, thrusting a vivid reminder upon him at every turn?

Freckles counted the days. This first one he could do little but test his wires, sing broken snatches, and dream; but before the week would bring her again he could do many things. He would carry all his books to the swamp to show to her. He would complete his flower bed, arrange every detail he had planned for his room, and make of it a bower fairies might envy. He must devise a way to keep water cool. He would ask Mrs. Duncan for a double lunch and an especially nice one the day of her next coming, so that if the Bird Woman happened to be late, the Angel might not suffer from thirst and hunger. He would tell her to bring heavy leather leggings, so that he might take her on a trip around the trail. She should make friends with all of his chickens and see their nests.

On the line he talked of her incessantly.

"You needn't be thinking," he said to the goldfinch, "that because I'm coming down this line alone day after day, it's always to be so. Some of these times you'll be swinging on this wire, and you'll see me coming, and you'll swing, skip, and flirt yourself around, and chip up right spunky: 'SEE ME?' I'll be saying 'See you? Oh, Lord! See her!' You'll look, and there she'll stand. The sunshine won't look gold any more, or the roses pink, or the sky blue, because she'll be the pinkest, bluest, goldest thing of all. You'll be yelling yourself hoarse with the jealousy of her. The sawbird will stretch his neck out of joint, and she'll turn the heads of all the flowers. Wherever she goes, I can go back afterward and see the things she's seen, walk the path she's walked, hear the grasses whispering over all she's said; and if there's a place too swampy for her bits of feet; Holy Mother! Maybe—maybe she'd be putting the beautiful arms of her around me neck and letting me carry her over!"

Freckles shivered as with a chill. He sent the cudgel whirling skyward, dexterously caught it, and set it spinning.

"You damned presumptuous fool!" he cried. "The thing for you to be thinking of would be to stretch in the muck for the feet of her to be walking over, and then you could hold yourself holy to be even of that service to her.

"Maybe she'll be wanting the cup me blue-and-brown chickens raised their babies in. Perhaps she'd like to stop at the pool and see me bullfrog that had the goodness to take on human speech to show me the way out of me trouble. If there's any feathers falling that day, why, it's from the wings of me chickens—it's sure to be, for the only Angel outside the gates will be walking this timberline, and every step of the way I'll be holding me breath and praying that she don't unfold wings and sail away before the hungry eyes of me."

So Freckles dreamed his dreams, made his plans, and watched his line. He counted not only the days, but the hours of each day. As he told them off, every one bringing her closer, he grew happier in the prospect of her coming. He managed daily to leave some offering at the big elm log for his black chickens. He slipped under the line at every passing, and went to make sure that nothing was molesting them. Though it was a long trip, he paid them several extra visits a day for fear a snake, hawk, or fox might have found the baby. For now his chickens not only represented all his former interest in them, but they furnished the inducement that was bringing his Angel.

Possibly he could find other subjects that the Bird Woman wanted. The teamster had said that his brother went after her every time he found a nest. He never had counted the nests that he knew of, and it might be that among all the birds of the swamp some would be rare to her.

The feathered folk of the Limberlost were practically undisturbed save by their natural enemies. It was very probable that among his chickens others as odd as the big black ones could be found. If she wanted pictures of half-grown birds, he could pick up fifty in one morning's trip around the line, for he had fed, handled, and made friends with them ever since their eyes opened.

He had gathered bugs and worms all spring as he noticed them on the grass and bushes, and dropped them into the first little open mouth he had found. The babies gladly had accepted this queer tri-parent addition to their natural providers.

When the week had passed, Freckles had his room crisp and glowing with fresh living things that represented every color of the swamp. He carried bark and filled all the muckiest places of the trail.

It was middle July. The heat of the past few days had dried the water around and through the Limberlost, so that it was possible to cross it on foot in almost any direction—if one had an idea of direction and did not become completely lost in its rank tangle of vegetation and bushes. The brighter-hued flowers were opening. The trumpet-creepers were flaunting their gorgeous horns of red and gold sweetness from the tops of lordly oak and elm, and below entire pools were pink-sheeted in mallow bloom.

The heat was doing one other thing that was bound to make Freckles, as a good Irishman, shiver. As the swale dried, its inhabitants were seeking the cooler depths of the swamp. They liked neither the heat nor leaving the field mice, moles, and young rabbits of their chosen location. He saw them crossing the trail every day as the heat grew intense. The rattlers were sadly forgetting their manners, for they struck on no provocation whatever, and did not even remember to rattle afterward. Daily Freckles was compelled to drive big black snakes and blue racers from the nests of his chickens. Often the terrified squalls of the parent birds would reach him far down the line and he would run to rescue the babies.

He saw the Angel when the carriage turned from the corduroy into the clearing. They stopped at the west entrance to the swamp, waiting for him to precede them down the trail, as he had told them it was safest for the horse that he should do. They followed the east line to a point opposite the big chickens' tree, and Freckles carried in the cameras and showed the Bird Woman a path he had cleared to the log. He explained to her the effect the heat was having on the snakes, and creeping back to Little Chicken, brought him to the light. As she worked at setting up her camera, he told her of the birds of the line, while she stared at him, wide-eyed and incredulous.

They arranged that Freckles should drive the carriage into the east entrance in the shade and then take the horse toward the north to a better place he knew. Then he was to entertain the Angel at his study or on the line until the Bird Woman finished her work and came to them.

"This will take only a little time," she said. "I know where to set the camera now, and Little Chicken is big enough to be good and too small to run away or to act very ugly, so I will be coming soon to see about those nests. I have ten plates along, and I surely won't use more than two on him; so perhaps I can get some nests or young birds this morning."

Freckles almost flew, for his dream had come true so soon. He was walking the timber-line and the Angel was following him. He asked to be excused for going first, because he wanted to be sure the trail was safe for her. She laughed at his fears, telling him that it was the polite thing for him to do, anyway.

"Oh!" said Freckles, "so you was after knowing that? Well, I didn't s'pose you did, and I was afraid you'd think me wanting in respect to be preceding you!"

The astonished Angel looked at him, caught the irrepressible gleam of Irish fun in his eyes, so they stood and laughed together.

Freckles did not realize how he was talking that morning. He showed her many of the beautiful nests and eggs of the line. She could identify a number of them, but of some she was ignorant, so they made notes of the number and color of the eggs, material, and construction of nest, color, size, and shape of the birds, and went to find them in the book.

At his room, when Freckles had lifted the overhanging bushes and stepped back for her to enter, his heart was all out of time and place. The study was vastly more beautiful than a week previous. The Angel drew a deep breath and stood gazing first at one side, then at another, then far down the cathedral aisle. "It's just fairyland!" she cried ecstatically. Then she turned and stared at Freckles as she had at his handiwork.

"What are you planning to be?" she asked wonderingly.

"Whatever Mr. McLean wants me to," he replied.

"What do you do most?" she asked.

"Watch me lines."

"I don't mean work!"

"Oh, in me spare time I keep me room and study in me books."

"Do you work on the room or the books most?"

"On the room only what it takes to keep it up, and the rest of the time on me books."

The Angel studied him closely. "Well, maybe you are going to be a great scholar," she said, "but you don't look it. Your face isn't right for that, but it's got something big in it—something really great. I must find out what it is and then you must work on it. Your father is expecting you to do something. One can tell by the way he talks. You should begin right away. You've wasted too much time already."

Poor Freckles hung his head. He never had wasted an hour in his life. There never had been one that was his to waste.

The Angel, studying him intently, read the thought in his face. "Oh, I don't mean that!" she cried, with the frank dismay of sixteen. "Of course, you're not lazy! No one ever would think that from your appearance. It's this I mean: there is something fine, strong, and full of power in your face. There is something you are to do in this world, and no matter how you work at all these other things, or how successfully you do them, it is all wasted until you find the ONE THING that you can do best. If you hadn't a thing in the world to keep you, and could go anywhere you please and do anything you want, what would you do?" persisted the Angel.

"I'd go to Chicago and sing in the First Episcopal choir," answered Freckles promptly.

The Angel dropped on a seat—the hat she had removed and held in her fingers rolled to her feet. "There!" she exclaimed vehemently. "You can see what I'm going to be. Nothing! Absolutely nothing! You can sing? Of course you can sing! It is written all over you."

"Anyone with half wit could have seen he could sing, without having to be told," she thought. "It's in the slenderness of his fingers and his quick nervous touch. It is in the brightness of his hair, the fire of his eyes, the breadth of his chest, the muscles of his throat and neck; and above all, it's in every tone of his voice, for even as he speak it's the sweetest sound I ever heard from the throat of a mortal."

"Will you do something for me?" she asked.

"I'll do anything in the world you want me to," said Freckles largely, "and if I can't do what you want, I'll go to work at once and I'll try 'til I can."

"Good! That's business!" said the Angel. "You go over there and stand before that hedge and sing something. Just anything you think of first."

Freckles faced the Angel from his banked wall of brown, blue, and crimson, with its background of solid green, and lifting his face to the sky, he sang the first thing that came into his mind. It was a children's song that he had led for the little folks at the Home many times, recalled to his mind by the Angel's exclamation:

> "To fairyland we go,
> With a song of joy, heigh-o.
> In dreams we'll stand upon that shore
> And all the realm behold;
> We'll see the sights so grand
> That belong to fairyland,
> Its mysteries we will explore,
> Its beauties will unfold.
>
> "Oh, tra, la, la, oh, ha, ha, ha!
> We're happy now as we can be,
> Our welcome song we will prolong,
> And greet you with our melody.

> *O fairyland, sweet fairyland,*
> *We love to sing———*"

No song could have given the intense sweetness and rollicking quality of Freckles' voice better scope. He forgot everything but pride in his work. He was singing the chorus, and the Angel was shivering in ecstasy, when clip! clip! came the sharply beating feet of a swiftly ridden horse down the trail from the north. They both sprang toward the entrance.

"Freckles! Freckles!" called the voice of the Bird Woman.

They were at the trail on the instant.

"Both those revolvers loaded?" she asked.

"Yes," said Freckles.

"Is there a way you can cut across the swamp and reach the chicken tree in a few minutes, and with little noise?"

"Yes."

"Then go flying," said the Bird Woman. "Give the Angel a lift behind me, and we will ride the horse back where you left him and wait for you. I finished Little Chicken in no time and put him back. His mother came so close, I felt sure she would enter the log. The light was fine, so I set and focused the camera and covered it with branches, attached the long hose, and went away over a hundred feet and hid in some bushes to wait. A short, stout man and a tall, dark one passed me so closely I almost could have reached out and touched them. They carried a big saw on their shoulders. They said they could work until near noon, and then they must lay off until you passed and then try to load and get out at night. They went on—not entirely from sight—and began cutting a tree. Mr. McLean told me the other day what would probably happen here, and if they fell that tree he loses his wager on you. Keep to the east and north and hustle. We'll meet you at the carriage. I always am armed. Give Angel one of your revolvers, and you keep the other. We will separate and creep toward them from different sides and give them a fusillade that will send them flying. You hurry, now!"

She lifted the reins and started briskly down the trail. The Angel, hatless and with sparkling eyes, was clinging around her waist.

Freckles wheeled and ran. He worked his way with much care, dodging limbs and bushes with noiseless tread, and cutting as closely where he thought the men were as he felt that he dared if he were to remain unseen. As he ran he tried to think. It was Wessner, burning for his revenge, aided by the bully of the locality, that he was going to meet. He was accustomed to that thought but not to the complication of having two women on his hands who undoubtedly would have to be taken care of in spite of the Bird Woman's offer to help him. His heart was jarring as it never had before with running. He must follow the Bird Woman's plan and meet them at the carriage, but if they really did intend to try to help him, he must not allow it. Allow the Angel to try to handle a revolver in his defence? Never! Not for all the trees in the Limberlost! She might shoot herself. She might forget to watch sharply and run across a snake that was not particularly well behaved that morning. Freckles permitted himself a grim smile as he went speeding on.

When he reached the carriage, the Bird Woman and the Angel had the horse hitched, the outfit packed, and were calmly waiting. The Bird Woman held a revolver in her hand. She wore dark clothing. They had pinned a big focusing cloth over the front of the Angel's light dress.

"Give Angel one of your revolvers, quick!" said the Bird Woman. "We will creep up until we are in fair range. The underbrush is so thick and they are so busy that they will never notice us, if we don't make a noise. You fire first, then I will pop in from my direction, and then you, Angel, and shoot quite high, or else very low. We mustn't really hit them. We'll go close enough to the cowards to make it interesting, and keep it up until we have them going."

Freckles protested.

The Bird Woman reached over, and, taking the smaller revolver from his belt, handed it to the Angel. "Keep your nerve steady, dear; watch where you step, and shoot high," she said. "Go straight at them from where you are. Wait until you hear Freckles' first shot, then follow me as closely as you can, to let them know that we outnumber them. If you want to save McLean's wager on you, now you go!" she commanded Freckles, who, with an agonized glance at the Angel, ran toward the east.

The Bird Woman chose the middle distance, and for a last time cautioned the Angel as she moved away to lie down and shoot high.

Through the underbrush the Bird Woman crept even more closely than she had intended, found a clear range, and waited for Freckles' shot. There was one long minute of sickening suspense. The men straightened for breath. Work was difficult with a handsaw in the heat of the swamp. As they rested, the big dark fellow took a bottle from his pocket and began oiling the saw.

"We got to keep mighty quiet," he said, "and wait to fell it until that damned guard has gone to his dinner."

Again they bent to their work. Freckles' revolver spat fire. Lead spanged on steel. The saw-handle flew from Wessner's hand and he reeled from the jar of the shock. Black Jack straightened, uttering a fearful oath. The hat sailed from his head from the far northeast. The Angel had not waited for the Bird Woman, and her shot scarcely could have been called high. At almost the same instant the third shot whistled from the east. Black Jack sprang into the air with a yell of complete panic, for it ripped a heel from his boot. Freckles emptied his second chamber, and the earth spattered over Wessner. Shots poured in rapidly. Without even reaching for a weapon, both men ran toward the east road in great leaping bounds, while leaden slugs sung and hissed around them in deadly earnest.

Freckles was trimming his corners as closely as he dared, but if the Angel did not really intend to hit, she was taking risks in a scandalous manner.

When the men reached the trail, Freckles yelled at the top of his voice: "Head them off on the south, boys! Fire from the south!"

As he had hoped, Jack and Wessner instantly plunged into the swale. A spattering of lead followed them. They crossed the swale, running low, with not even one backward glance, and entered the woods beyond the corduroy.

Then the little party gathered at the tree.

"I'd better fix this saw so they can't be using it if they come back," said Freckles, taking out his hatchet and making saw-teeth fly.

"Now we must leave here without being seen," said the Bird Woman to the Angel. "It won't do for me to make enemies of these men, for I am likely to meet them while at work any day."

"You can do it by driving straight north on this road," said Freckles. "I will go ahead and cut the wires for you. The swale is almost dry. You will only be sinking a little. In a few rods you will strike a cornfield. I will take down the fence and let you into that. Follow the furrows and drive straight across it until you come to the other side. Be following the fence south until you come to a road through the woods east of it. Then take that road and follow east until you reach the pike. You will come out on your way back to town, and two miles north of anywhere they are likely to be. Don't for your lives ever let it out that you did this," he earnestly cautioned, "for it's black enemies you would be making."

Freckles clipped the wires and they drove through. The Angel leaned from the carriage and held out his revolver. Freckles looked at her in surprise. Her eyes were black, while her face was a deeper rose than usual. He felt that his own was white.

"Did I shoot high enough?" she asked sweetly. "I really forgot about lying down."

Freckles winced. Did the child know how close she had gone? Surely she could not! Or was it possible that she had the nerve and skill to fire like that purposely?

"I will send the first reliable man I meet for McLean," said the Bird Woman, gathering up the lines. "If I don't meet one when we reach town, we will send a messenger. If it wasn't for having the gang see me, I would go myself; but I will promise you that you will have help in a little over two hours. You keep well hidden. They must think some of the gang is with you now. There isn't a chance that they will be back, but don't run any risks. Remain under cover. If they should come, it probably would be for their saw." She laughed as at a fine joke.

CHAPTER VII

WHEREIN FRECKLES WINS HONOR AND
FINDS A FOOTPRINT ON THE TRAIL

Round-eyed, Freckles watched the Bird Woman and the Angel drive away. After they were from sight and he was safely hidden among the branches of a small tree, he remembered that he neither had thanked them nor said good-bye. Considering what they had been through, they never would come again. His heart sank until he had palpitation in his wading-boots.

Stretching the length of the limb, he thought deeply, though he was not thinking of Black Jack or Wessner. Would the Bird Woman and the Angel come again? No other woman whom he ever had known would. But did they resemble any other women he ever had known? He thought of the Bird Woman's unruffled face and the Angel's revolver practice, and presently he was not so sure that they would not return.

What were the people in the big world like? His knowledge was so very limited. There had been people at the Home, who exchanged a stilted, perfunctory kindness for their salaries. The visitors who called on receiving days he had divided into three classes: the psalm-singing kind, who came with a tear in the eye and hypocrisy in every feature of their faces; the kind who dressed in silks and jewels, and handed to those poor little mother-hungry souls worn toys that their children no longer cared for, in exactly the same spirit in which they pitched biscuits to the monkeys at the zoo, and for the same reason—to see how they would take them and be amused by what they would do; and the third class, whom he considered real people. They made him feel they cared that he was there, and that they would have been glad to see him elsewhere.

Now here was another class, that had all they needed of the world's best and were engaged in doing work that counted. They had things worth while to be proud of; and they had met him as a son and brother. With them he could, for the only time in his life, forget the lost hand that every day tortured him with a new pang. What kind of people were they and where did they belong among the classes he knew? He failed to decide, because he never had known others similar to them; but how he loved them!

In the world where he was going soon, were the majority like them, or were they of the hypocrite and bun-throwing classes?

He had forgotten the excitement of the morning and the passing of time when distant voices aroused him, and he gently lifted his head. Nearer and nearer they came, and as the heavy wagons rumbled down the east trail he could hear them plainly. The gang were shouting themselves hoarse for the Limberlost guard. Freckles did not feel that he deserved it. He would have given much to be able to go to the men and explain, but to McLean only could he tell his story.

At the sight of Freckles the men threw up their hats and cheered. McLean shook hands with him warmly, but big Duncan gathered him into his arms and hugged him as a bear and choked over a few words of praise. The gang drove in and finished felling the tree. McLean was angry beyond measure at this attempt on his property, for in their haste to fell the tree the thieves had cut too high and wasted a foot and a half of valuable timber.

When the last wagon rolled away, McLean sat on the stump and Freckles told the story he was aching to tell. The Boss scarcely could believe his senses. Also, he was much disappointed.

"I have been almost praying all the way over, Freckles," he said, "that you would have some evidence by which we could arrest those fellows and get them out of our way, but this will never do. We can't mix up those women in it. They have helped you save me the tree and my wager as well. Going across the country as she does, the Bird Woman never could be expected to testify against them."

"No, indeed; nor the Angel, either, sir," said Freckles.

"The Angel?" queried the astonished McLean.

The Boss listened in silence while Freckles told of the coming and christening of the Angel.

"I know her father well," said McLean at last, "and I have often seen her. You are right; she is a beautiful young girl, and she appears to be utterly free from the least particle of false pride or foolishness. I do not understand why her father risks such a jewel in this place."

"He's daring it because she is a jewel, sir," said Freckles, eagerly. "Why, she's trusting a rattlesnake to rattle before it strikes her, and of course, she thinks she can trust mankind as well. The man isn't made who wouldn't lay down the life of him for her. She doesn't need any care. Her face and the pretty ways of her are all the protection she would need in a band of howling savages."

"Did you say she handled one of the revolvers?" asked McLean.

"She scared all the breath out of me body," admitted Freckles. "Seems that her father has taught her to shoot. The Bird Woman told her distinctly to lie low and blaze away high, just to help scare them. The spunky little thing followed them right out into the west road, spitting lead like hail, and clipping all around the heads and heels of them; and

I'm damned, sir, if I believe she'd cared a rap if she'd hit. I never saw much shooting, but if that wasn't the nearest to miss I ever want to see! Scared the life near out of me body with the fear that she'd drop one of them. As long as I'd no one to help me but a couple of women that didn't dare be mixed up in it, all I could do was to let them get away."

"Now, will they come back?" asked McLean.

"Of course!" said Freckles. "They're not going to be taking that. You could stake your life on it, they'll be coming back. At least, Black Jack will. Wessner may not have the pluck, unless he is half drunk. Then he'd be a terror. And the next time—" Freckles hesitated.

"What?"

"It will be a question of who shoots first and straightest."

"Then the only thing for me to do is to double the guard and bring the gang here the first minute possible. As soon as I feel that we have the rarest of the stuff out below, we will come. The fact is, in many cases, until it is felled it's difficult to tell what a tree will prove to be. It won't do to leave you here longer alone. Jack has been shooting twenty years to your one, and it stands to reason that you are no match for him. Who of the gang would you like best to have with you?"

"No one, sir," said Freckles emphatically. "Next time is where I run. I won't try to fight them alone. I'll just be getting wind of them, and then make tracks for you. I'll need to come like lightning, and Duncan has no extra horse, so I'm thinking you'd best get me one—or perhaps a wheel would be better. I used to do extra work for the Home doctor, and he would let me take his bicycle to ride around the place. And at times the head nurse would loan me his for an hour. A wheel would cost less and be faster than a horse, and would take less care. I believe, if you are going to town soon, you had best pick up any kind of an old one at some second-hand store, for if I'm ever called to use it in a hurry there won't be the handlebars left after crossing the corduroy."

"Yes," said McLean; "and if you didn't have a first-class wheel, you never could cross the corduroy on it at all."

As they walked to the cabin, McLean insisted on another guard, but Freckles was stubbornly set on fighting his battle alone. He made one mental condition. If the Bird Woman was going to give up the Little Chicken series, he would yield to the second guard, solely for the sake of her work and the presence of the Angel in the Limberlost. He did not propose to have a second man unless it were absolutely necessary, for he had been alone so long that he loved the solitude, his chickens, and flowers. The thought of having a stranger to all his ways come and meddle with his arrangements, frighten his pets, pull his flowers, and interrupt him when he wanted to study, so annoyed him that he was blinded to his real need for help.

With McLean it was a case of letting his sober, better judgment be overridden by the boy he was growing so to love that he could not endure to oppose him, and to have Freckles keep his trust and win alone meant more than any money the Boss might lose.

The following morning McLean brought the wheel, and Freckles took it to the trail to test it. It was new, chainless, with as little as possible to catch in hurried riding, and in every way the best of its kind. Freckles went skimming around the trail on it on a preliminary trip before he locked it in his case and started his minute examination of his line on foot. He glanced around his room as he left it, and then stood staring.

On the moss before his prettiest seat lay the Angel's hat. In the excitement of yesterday all of them had forgotten it. He went and picked it up, oh! so carefully, gazing at it with hungry eyes, but touching it only to carry it to his case, where he hung it on the shining handlebar of the new wheel and locked it among his treasures. Then he went to the trail, with a new expression on his face and a strange throbbing in his heart. He was not in the least afraid of anything that morning. He felt he was the veriest Daniel, but all his lions seemed weak and harmless.

What Black Jack's next move would be he could not imagine, but that there would be a move of some kind was certain. The big bully was not a man to give up his purpose, or to have the hat swept from his head with a bullet and bear it meekly. Moreover, Wessner would cling to his revenge with a Dutchman's singleness of mind.

Freckles tried to think connectedly, but there were too many places on the trail where the Angel's footprints were yet visible. She had stepped in one mucky spot and left a sharp impression. The afternoon sun had baked it hard, and the horses' hoofs had not obliterated any part of it, as they had in so many places. Freckles stood fascinated, gazing at it. He measured it lovingly with his eye. He would not have ventured a caress on her hat any more than on her person, but this was different. Surely a footprint on a trail might belong to anyone who found and wanted it. He stooped under the wires and entered the swamp. With a little searching, he found a big piece of thick bark loose on a log and carefully peeling it, carried it out and covered the print so that the first rain would not obliterate it.

When he reached his room, he tenderly laid the hat upon his bookshelf, and to wear off his awkwardness, mounted his wheel and went spinning on trail again. It was like flying, for the path was worn smooth with his feet and baked hard with the sun almost all the way. When he came to the bark, he veered far to one side and smiled at it in passing. Suddenly he was off the wheel, kneeling beside it. He removed his hat, carefully lifted the bark, and gazed lovingly at the imprint.

"I wonder what she was going to say of me voice," he whispered. "She never got it said, but from the face of her, I believe she was liking it fairly well. Perhaps she was going to say that singing was the big thing I was to be doing. That's what they all thought at the Home. Well, if it is, I'll just shut me eyes, think of me little room, the face of her watching, and the heart of her beating, and I'll raise them. Damn them, if singing will do it, I'll raise them from the benches!"

With this dire threat, Freckles knelt, as at a wayside spring, and deliberately laid his lips on the footprint. Then he arose, appearing as if he had been drinking at the fountain of gladness.

CHAPTER VIII

WHEREIN FRECKLES MEETS A MAN OF AFFAIRS AND LOSES NOTHING BY THE ENCOUNTER

"Weel, I be drawed on!" exclaimed Mrs. Duncan.

Freckles stood before her, holding the Angel's hat.

"I've been thinking this long time that ye or Duncan would see that sunbonnets werena braw enough for a woman of my standing, and ye're a guid laddie to bring me this beautiful hat."

She turned it around, examining the weave of the straw and the foliage trimmings, passing her rough fingers over the satin ties delightedly. As she held it up, admiring it, Freckles' astonished eyes saw a new side of Sarah Duncan. She was jesting, but under the jest the fact loomed strong that, though poor, overworked, and with none but God-given refinement, there was something in her soul crying after that bit of feminine finery, and it made his heart ache for her. He resolved that when he reached the city he would send her a hat, if it took fifty dollars to do it.

She lingeringly handed it back to him.

"It's unco guid of ye to think of me," she said lightly, "but I maun question your taste a wee. D'ye no think ye had best return this and get a woman with half her hair gray a little plainer headdress? Seems like that's far ower gay for me. I'm no' saying that it's no' exactly what I'd like to hae, but I mauna mak mysel' ridiculous. Ye'd best give this to somebody young and pretty, say about sixteen. Where did ye come by it, Freckles? If there's anything been dropping lately, ye hae forgotten to mention it."

"Do you see anything heavenly about that hat?" queried Freckles, holding it up.

The morning breeze waved the ribbons gracefully, binding one around Freckles' sleeve and the other across his chest, where they caught and clung as if magnetized.

"Yes," said Sarah Duncan. "It's verra plain and simple, but it juist makes ye feel that it's all of the finest stuff. It's exactly what I'd call a heavenly hat."

"Sure," said Freckles, "for it's belonging to an Angel!"

Then he told her about the hat and asked her what he should do with it.

"Take it to her, of course!" said Sarah Duncan. "Like it's the only ane she has and she may need it badly."

Freckles smiled. He had a clear idea about the hat being the only one the Angel had. However, there was a thing he felt he should do and wanted to do, but he was not sure.

"You think I might be taking it home?" he said.

"Of course ye must," said Mrs. Duncan. "And without another hour's delay. It's been here two days noo, and she may want it, and be too busy or afraid to come."

"But how can I take it?" asked Freckles.

"Gang spinning on your wheel. Ye can do it easy in an hour."

"But in that hour, what if——?"

"Nonsense!" interrupted Sarah Duncan. "Ye've watched that timber-line until ye're grown fast to it, lad. Give me your boots and club and I'll gae walk the south end and watch doon the east and west sides until ye come back."

"Mrs. Duncan! You never would be doing it," cried Freckles.

"Why not?" inquired she.

"But you know you're mortal afraid of snakes and a lot of other things in the swamp."

"I am afraid of snakes," said Mrs. Duncan, "but likely they've gone into the swamp this hot weather. I'll juist stay on the trail and watch, and ye might hurry the least bit. The day's so bright it feels like storm. I can put the bairns on the woodpile to play until I get back. Ye gang awa and take the blessed little angel her beautiful hat."

"Are you sure it will be all right?" urged Freckles. "Do you think if Mr. McLean came he would care?"

"Na," said Mrs. Duncan; "I dinna. If ye and me agree that a thing ought to be done, and I watch in your place, why, it's bound to be all right with McLean. Let me pin the hat in a paper, and ye jump on your wheel and gang flying. Ought ye put on your Sabbath-day clothes?"

Freckles shook his head. He knew what he should do, but there was no use in taking time to try to explain it to Mrs. Duncan while he was so hurried. He exchanged his wading-boots for shoes, gave her his club, and went spinning toward town. He knew very well where the Angel lived. He had seen her home many times, and he passed it again without even raising his eyes from the street, steering straight for her father's place of business.

Carrying the hat, Freckles passed a long line of clerks, and at the door of the private office asked to see the proprietor. When he had waited a moment, a tall, spare, keen-eyed man faced him, and in brisk, nervous tones asked: "How can I serve you, sir?"

Freckles handed him the package and answered, "By delivering to your daughter this hat, which she was after leaving at me place the other day, when she went away in a hurry. And by saying to her and the Bird Woman that I'm more thankful than I'll be having words to express for the brave things they was doing for me. I'm McLean's Limberlost guard, sir."

"Why don't you take it yourself?" questioned the Man of Affairs.

Freckles' clear gray eyes met those of the Angel's father squarely, and he asked: "If you were in my place, would you take it to her yourself?"

"No, I would not," said that gentleman quickly.

"Then why ask why I did not?" came Freckles' lamb-like query.

"Bless me!" said the Angel's father. He stared at the package, then at the lifted chin of the boy, and then at the package again, and muttered, "Excuse me!"

Freckles bowed.

"It would be favoring me greatly if you would deliver the hat and the message. Good morning, sir," and he turned away.

"One minute," said the Angel's father. "Suppose I give you permission to return this hat in person and make your own acknowledgments."

Freckles stood one moment thinking intently, and then he lifted those eyes of unswerving truth and asked: "Why should you, sir? You are kind, indade, to mention it, and it's thanking you I am for your good intintions, but my wanting to go or your being willing to have me ain't proving that your daughter would be wanting me or care to bother with me."

The Angel's father looked keenly into the face of this extraordinary young man, for he found it to his liking.

"There's one other thing I meant to say," said Freckles. "Every day I see something, and at times a lot of things, that I think the Bird Woman would be wanting pictures of badly, if she knew. You might be speaking of it to her, and if she'd want me to, I can send her word when I find things she wouldn't likely get elsewhere."

"If that's the case," said the Angel's father, "and you feel under obligations for her assistance the other day, you can discharge them in that way. She is spending all her time in the fields and woods searching for subjects. If you run across things, perhaps rarer than she may find, about your work, it would save her the time she spends searching for subjects, and she could work in security under your protection. By all means let her know if you find subjects you think she could use, and we will do anything we can for you, if you will give her what help you can and see that she is as safe as possible."

"It's hungry for human beings I am," said Freckles, "and it's like Heaven to me to have them come. Of course, I'll be telling or sending her word every time me work can spare me. Anything I can do it would make me uncommon happy, but"—again truth had to be told, because it was Freckles who was speaking—"when it comes to protecting them, I'd risk me life, to be sure, but even that mightn't do any good in some cases. There are many dangers to be reckoned with in the swamp, sir, that call for every person to look sharp. If there wasn't really thieving to guard against, why, McLean wouldn't need be paying out good money for a guard. I'd love them to be coming, and I'll do all I can, but you must be told that there's danger of them running into timber thieves again any day, sir."

"Yes," said the Angel's father, "and I suppose there's danger of the earth opening up and swallowing the town any day, but I'm damned if I quit business for fear it will, and the Bird Woman won't, either. Everyone knows her and her work, and there is no danger in the world of anyone in any way molesting her, even if he were stealing a few of McLean's gold-plated trees. She's as safe in the Limberlost as she is at home, so far as timber thieves are concerned. All I am ever uneasy about are the snakes, poison-vines, and insects; and those are risks she must run anywhere. You need not hesitate a minute about that. I shall be glad to tell them what you wish. Thank you very much, and good day, sir."

There was no way in which Freckles could know it, but by following his best instincts and being what he conceived a gentleman should be, he surprised the Man of Affairs into thinking of him and seeing his face over his books many times that morning; whereas, if he had gone to the Angel as he had longed to do, her father never would have given him a second thought.

On the street he drew a deep breath. How had he acquitted himself? He only knew that he had lived up to his best impulse, and that is all anyone can do. He glanced over his wheel to see that it was all right, and just as he stepped to the curb to mount he heard a voice that thrilled him through and through: "Freckles! Oh Freckles!"

The Angel separated from a group of laughing, sweet-faced girls and came hurrying to him. She was in snowy white—a quaint little frock, with a marvel of soft lace around her throat and wrists. Through the sheer sleeves of it her beautiful, rounded arms showed distinctly, and it was cut just to the base of her perfect neck. On her head was a pure white creation of fancy braid, with folds on folds of tulle, soft and silken as cobwebs, lining the brim; while a mass of white roses clustered against the gold of her hair, crept around the crown, and fell in a riot to her shoulders at the back. There were gleams of gold with settings of blue on her fingers, and altogether she was the daintiest, sweetest sight he ever had seen. Freckles, standing on the curb, forgot himself in his cotton shirt, corduroys, and his belt to which his wire-cutter and pliers were hanging, and gazed as a man gazes when first he sees the woman he adores with all her charms enhanced by appropriate and beautiful clothing.

"Oh Freckles," she cried as she came to him. "I was wondering about you the other day. Do you know I never saw you in town before. You watch that old line so closely! Why did you come? Is there any trouble? Are you just starting to the Limberlost?"

"I came to bring your hat," said Freckles. "You forgot it in the rush the other day. I have left it with your father, and a message trying to ixpriss the gratitude of me for how you and the Bird Woman were for helping me out."

The Angel nodded gravely, then Freckles saw that he had done the proper thing in going to her father. His heart bounded until it jarred his body, for she was saying that she scarcely could wait for the time to come for the next picture of the Little Chicken series. "I want to hear the remainder of that song, and I hadn't even begun seeing your room yet," she complained. "As for singing, if you can sing like that every day, I never can get enough of it. I wonder if I couldn't bring my banjo and some of the songs I like best. I'll play and you sing, and we'll put the birds out of commission."

Freckles stood on the curb with drooped eyes, for he felt that if he lifted them the tumult of tender adoration in them would show and frighten her.

"I was afraid your ixperience the other day would scare you so that you'd never be coming again," he found himself saying.

The Angel laughed gaily.

"Did I seem scared?" she questioned.

"No," said Freckles, "you did not."

"Oh, I just enjoyed that," she cried. "Those hateful, stealing old things! I had a big notion to pink one of them, but I thought maybe someway it would be best for you that I shouldn't. They needed it. That didn't scare me; and as for the Bird Woman, she's accustomed to finding snakes, tramps, cross dogs, sheep, cattle, and goodness knows what! You can't frighten her when she's after a picture. Did they come back?"

"No," said Freckles. "The gang got there a little after noon and took out the tree, but I must tell you, and you must tell the Bird Woman, that there's no doubt but they will be coming back, and they will have to make it before long now, for it's soon the gang will be there to work on the swamp."

"Oh, what a shame!" cried the Angel. "They'll clear out roads, cut down the beautiful trees, and tear up everything. They'll drive away the birds and spoil the cathedral. When they have done their worst, then all these mills close here will follow in and take out the cheap timber. Then the landowners will dig a few ditches, build some fires, and in two summers more the Limberlost will be in corn and potatoes."

They looked at each other, and groaned despairingly in unison.

"You like it, too," said Freckles.

"Yes," said the Angel, "I love it. Your room is a little piece right out of the heart of fairyland, and the cathedral is God's work, not yours. You only found it and opened the door after He had it completed. The birds, flowers, and vines are all so lovely. The Bird Woman says it is really a fact that the mallows, foxfire, iris, and lilies are larger and of richer coloring there than in the remainder of the country. She says it's because of the rich loam and muck. I hate seeing the swamp torn up, and to you it will be like losing your best friend; won't it?"

"Something like," said Freckles. "Still, I've the Limberlost in me heart so that all of it will be real to me while I live, no matter what they do to it. I'm glad past telling if you will be coming a few more times, at least until the gang arrives. Past that time I don't allow mesilf to be thinking."

"Come, have a cool drink before you start back," said the Angel.

"I couldn't possibly," said Freckles. "I left Mrs. Duncan on the trail, and she's terribly afraid of a lot of things. If she even sees a big snake, I don't know what she'll do."

"It won't take but a minute, and you can ride fast enough to make up for it. Please. I want to think of something fine for you, to make up a little for what you did for me that first day."

Freckles looked in sheer wonderment into the beautiful face of the Angel. Did she truly mean it? Would she walk down that street with him, crippled, homely, in mean clothing, with the tools of his occupation on him, and share with him the treat she was offering? He could not believe it, even of the Angel. Still, in justice to the candor of her pure, sweet face, he would not think that she would make the offer and not mean it. She really did mean just what she said, but when it came to carrying out her offer and he saw the stares of her friends, the sneers of her enemies—if such as she could have enemies—and heard the whispered jeers of the curious, then she would see her mistake and be sorry. It would be only a manly thing for him to think this out, and save her from the results of her own blessed bigness of heart.

"I railly must be off," said Freckles earnestly, "but I'm thanking you more than you'll ever know for your kindness. I'll just be drinking bowls of icy things all me way home in the thoughts of it."

Down came the Angel's foot. Her eyes flashed indignantly. "There's no sense in that," she said. "How do you think you would have felt when you knew I was warm and thirsty and you went and brought me a drink and I wouldn't take it because—because goodness knows why! You can ride faster to make up for the time. I've just thought out what I want to fix for you."

She stepped to his side and deliberately slipped her hand under his arm—that right arm that ended in an empty sleeve.

"You are coming," she said firmly. "I won't have it."

Freckles could not have told how he felt, neither could anyone else. His blood rioted and his head swam, but he kept his wits. He bent over her.

"Please don't, Angel," he said softly. "You don't understand."

How Freckles came to understand was a problem.

"It's this," he persisted. "If your father met me on the street, in my station and dress, with you on me arm, he'd have every right to be caning me before the people, and not a finger would I lift to stay him."

The Angel's eyes snapped. "If you think my father cares about my doing anything that is right and kind, and that makes me happy to do— why, then you completely failed in reading my father, and I'll ask him and just show you."

She dropped Freckles' arm and turned toward the entrance to the building. "Why, look there!" she exclaimed.

Her father stood in a big window fronting the street, a bundle of papers in his hand, interestedly watching the little scene, with eyes that comprehended quite as thoroughly as if he had heard every word. The Angel caught his glance and made a despairing little gesture toward Freckles. The Man of Affairs answered her with a look of infinite tenderness. He nodded his head and waved the papers in the direction she had indicated, and the veriest dolt could have read the words his lips formed: "Take him along!"

A sudden trembling seized Freckles. At sight of the Angel's father he had stepped back as far from her as he could, leaned the wheel against him, and snatched off his hat.

The Angel turned on him with triumphing eyes.

She was highly strung and not accustomed to being thwarted. "Did You see that?" she demanded. "Now are you satisfied? Will you come, or must I call a policeman to bring you?"

Freckles went. There was nothing else to do. Guiding his wheel, he walked down the street beside her. On every hand she was kept busy giving and receiving the cheeriest greetings. She walked into the parlors exactly as if she owned them. A clerk came hurrying to meet her.

"There's a table vacant beside a window where it is cool. I'll save it for you," and he started back.

"Please not," said the Angel. "I've taken this man unawares, when he's in a rush. I'm afraid if we sit down we'll take too much time and afterward he will blame me."

She walked to the fountain, and a long row of people stared with all the varying degrees of insolence and curiosity that Freckles had felt they would. He glanced at the Angel. NOW would she see?

"On my soul!" he muttered under his breath. "They don't aven touch her!"

She laid down her sunshade and gloves. She walked to the end of the counter and turned the full battery of her eyes on the attendant.

"Please," she said.

The white-aproned individual stepped back and gave delighted assent. The Angel stepped beside him, and selecting a tall, flaring glass, of almost paper thinness, she stooped and rolled it in a tray of cracked ice.

"I want to mix a drink for my friend," she said. "He has a long, hot ride before him, and I don't want him started off with one of those old palate-teasing sweetnesses that you mix just on purpose to drive a man back in ten minutes." There was an appreciative laugh from the line at the counter.

"I want a clear, cool, sparkling drink that has a tang of acid in it. Where's the cherry phosphate? That, not at all sweet, would be good; don't you think?"

The attendant did think. He pointed out the different taps, and the Angel compounded the drink, while Freckles, standing so erect he almost leaned backward, gazed at her and paid no attention to anyone else. When she had the glass brimming, she tilted a little of its contents into a second glass and tasted it.

"That's entirely too sweet for a thirsty man," she said.

She poured out half the mixture, and refilling the glass, tasted it a second time. She submitted that result to the attendant. "Isn't that about the thing?" she asked.

He replied enthusiastically. "I'd get my wages raised ten a month if I could learn that trick."

The Angel carried the brimming, frosty glass to Freckles. He removed his hat, and lifting the icy liquid even with her eyes and looking straight into them, he said in the mellowest of all the mellow tones of his voice: "I'll be drinking it to the Swamp Angel."

As he had said to her that first day, she now cautioned him: "Be drinking slowly."

When the screen-door swung behind them, one of the men at the counter asked of the attendant: "Now, what did that mean?"

"Exactly what you saw," replied he, rather curtly. "We're accustomed to it here. Hardly a day passes, this hot weather, but she's picking up some poor, god-forsaken mortal and bringing him in. Then she comes behind the counter herself and fixes up a drink to suit the occasion. She's all sorts of fancies about what's what for all kinds of times and conditions, and you bet she can just hit the spot! Ain't a clerk here can put up a drink to touch her. She's a sort of knack at it. Every once in a while, when the Boss sees her, he calls out to her to mix him a drink."

"And does she?" asked the man with an interested grin.

"Well, I guess! But first she goes back and sees how long it is since he's had a drink. What he drank last. How warm he is. When he ate last. Then she comes here and mixes a glass of fizz with a little touch of acid, and a bit of cherry, lemon, grape, pineapple, or something sour and cooling, and it hits the spot just as no spot was ever hit before. I honestly believe that the INTEREST she takes in it is half the trick, for I watch her closely and I can't come within gunshot of her concoctions. She has a running bill here. Her father settles once a month. She gives nine-tenths of it away. Hardly ever touches it herself, but when she does she makes me mix it. She's just old persimmons. Even the scrub-boy of this establishment would fight for her. It lasts the year round, for in winter it's some poor, frozen cuss that she's warming up on hot coffee or chocolate."

"Mighty queer specimen she had this time," volunteered another. "Irish, hand off, straight as a ramrod, and something worth while in his face. Notice that hat peel off, and the eyes of him? There's a case of 'fight for her!' Wonder who he is?"

"I think," said a third, "that he's McLean's Limberlost guard, and I suspect she's gone to the swamp with the Bird Woman for pictures and knows him that way. I've heard that he is a master hand with the birds, and that would just suit the Bird Woman to a T."

On the street the Angel walked beside Freckles to the first crossing and there she stopped. "Now, will you promise to ride fast enough to make up for the five minutes that took?" she asked. "I am a little uneasy about Mrs. Duncan."

Freckles turned his wheel into the street. It seemed to him he had poured that delicious icy liquid into every vein in his body instead of his stomach. It even went to his brain.

"Did you insist on fixing that drink because you knew how intoxicating 'twould be?" he asked.

There was subtlety in the compliment and it delighted the Angel. She laughed gleefully.

"Next time, maybe you won't take so much coaxing," she teased.

"I wouldn't this, if I had known your father and been understanding you better. Do you really think the Bird Woman will be coming again?"

The Angel jeered. "Wild horses couldn't drag her away," she cried. "She will have hard work to wait the week out. I shouldn't be in the least surprised to see her start any hour."

Freckles could not endure the suspense; it had to come.

"And you?" he questioned, but he dared not lift his eyes.

"Wild horses me, too," she laughed, "couldn't keep me away either! I dearly love to come, and the next time I am going to bring my banjo, and I'll play, and you sing for me some of the songs I like best; won't you?"

"Yis," said Freckles, because it was all he was capable of saying just then.

"It's beginning to act stormy," she said. "If you hurry you will just about make it. Now, good-bye."

CHAPTER IX

Freckles was halfway to the Limberlost when he dismounted. He could ride no farther, because he could not see the road. He sat under a tree, and, leaning against it, sobs shook, twisted, and rent him. If they would remind him of his position, speak condescendingly, or notice his hand, he could endure it, but this—it surely would kill him! His hot, pulsing Irish blood was stirred deeply. What did they mean? Why did they do it? Were they like that to everyone? Was it pity?

It could not be, for he knew that the Bird Woman and the Angel's father must know that he was not really McLean's son, and it did not matter to them in the least. In spite of accident and poverty, they evidently expected him to do something worth while in the world. That must be his remedy. He must work on his education. He must get away. He must find and do the great thing of which the Angel talked. For the first time, his thoughts turned anxiously toward the city and the beginning of his studies. McLean and the Duncans spoke of him as "the boy," but he was a man. He must face life bravely and act a man's part. The Angel was a mere child. He must not allow her to torture him past endurance with her frank comradeship that meant to him high heaven, earth's richness, and all that lay between, and NOTHING to her.

There was an ominous growl of thunder, and amazed at himself, Freckles snatched up his wheel and raced toward the swamp. He was worried to find his boots lying at the cabin door; the children playing on the woodpile told him that "mither" said they were so heavy she couldn't walk in them, and she had come back and taken them off. Thoroughly frightened, he stopped only long enough to slip them on, and then sped with all his strength for the Limberlost. To the west, the long, black, hard-beaten trail lay clear; but far up the east side, straight across the path, he could see what was certainly a limp, brown figure. Freckles spun with all his might.

Face down, Sarah Duncan lay across the trail. When Freckles turned her over, his blood chilled at the look of horror settled on her face. There was a low humming and something spatted against him. Glancing around, Freckles shivered in terror, for there was a swarm of wild bees settled on a scrub-thorn only a few yards away. The air was filled with excited, unsettled bees making ready to lead farther in search of a suitable location. Then he thought he understood, and with a prayer of thankfulness in his heart that she had escaped, even so narrowly, he caught her up and hurried down the trail until they were well out of danger. He laid her in the shade, and carrying water from the swamp in the crown of his hat, he bathed her face and hands; but she lay in unbroken stillness, without a sign of life.

She had found Freckles' boots so large and heavy that she had gone back and taken them off, although she was mortally afraid to approach the swamp without them. The thought of it made her nervous, and the fact that she never had been there alone added to her fears. She had not followed the trail many rods when her trouble began. She was not Freckles, so not a bird of the line was going to be fooled into thinking she was.

They began jumping from their nests and darting from unexpected places around her head and feet, with quick whirs, that kept her starting and dodging. Before Freckles was halfway to the town, poor Mrs. Duncan was hysterical, and the Limberlost had neither sung nor performed for her.

But there was trouble brewing. It was quiet and intensely hot, with that stifling stillness that precedes a summer storm, and feathers and fur were tense and nervous. The birds were singing only a few broken snatches, and flying around, seeking places of shelter. One moment everything seemed devoid of life, the next there was an unexpected whir, buzz, and sharp cry. Inside, a pandemonium of growling, spatting, snarling, and grunting broke loose.

The swale bent flat before heavy gusts of wind, and the big black chicken swept lower and lower above the swamp. Patches of clouds gathered, shutting out the sun and making it very dark, and the next moment were swept away. The sun poured with fierce, burning brightness, and everything was quiet. It was at the first growl of thunder that Freckles really had noticed the weather, and putting his own troubles aside resolutely, raced for the swamp.

Sarah Duncan paused on the line. "Weel, I wouldna stay in this place for a million a month," she said aloud, and the sound of her voice brought no comfort, for it was so little like she had thought it that she glanced hastily around to see if it had really been she that spoke. She tremblingly wiped the perspiration from her face with the skirt of her sunbonnet.

"Awfu' hot," she panted huskily. "B'lieve there's going to be a big storm. I do hope Freckles will hurry."

Her chin was quivering as a terrified child's. She lifted her bonnet to replace it and brushed against a bush beside her. WHIRR, almost into her face, went a nighthawk stretched along a limb for its daytime nap. Mrs. Duncan cried out and sprang down the trail, alighting on a frog that was hopping across. The horrible croak it gave as she crushed it sickened her. She screamed wildly and jumped to one side. That carried her into the swale, where the grasses reached almost to her waist, and her horror of snakes returning, she made a flying leap for an old log lying beside the line. She alighted squarely, but it was so damp and rotten that she sank straight through it to her knees. She caught at the wire as she went down, and missing, raked her wrist across a barb until she tore a bleeding gash. Her fingers closed convulsively around the second strand. She was too frightened to scream now. Her tongue stiffened. She clung frantically to the sagging wire, and finally managed to grasp it with the other hand. Then she could reach the top wire, and so she drew herself up and found solid footing. She picked up the club that she had dropped in order to extricate herself. Leaning heavily on it, she managed to return to the trail, but she was trembling so that she scarcely could walk. Going a few steps farther, she came to the stump of the first tree that had been taken out.

She sat bolt upright and very still, trying to collect her thoughts and reason away her terror. A squirrel above her dropped a nut, and as it came rattling down, bouncing from branch to branch, every nerve in her tugged wildly. When the disgusted squirrel barked loudly, she sprang to the trail.

The wind arose higher, the changes from light to darkness were more abrupt, while the thunder came closer and louder at every peal. In swarms the blackbirds arose from the swale and came flocking to the interior, with a clamoring cry: "T'CHECK, T'CHECK." Grackles marshaled to the tribal call: "TRALL-A-HEE, TRALL-A-HEE." Red-winged blackbirds swept low, calling to belated mates: "FOL-LOW-ME, FOL-LOW-ME." Big, jetty crows gathered close to her, crying, as if warning her to flee before it was everlastingly too late. A heron, fishing the near-by pool for Freckles' "find-out" frog, fell into trouble with a muskrat and uttered a rasping note that sent Mrs. Duncan a rod down the line without realizing that she had moved. She was too shaken to run far. She stopped and looked around her fearfully.

Several bees struck her and were angrily buzzing before she noticed them. Then the humming swelled on all sides. A convulsive sob shook her, and she ran into the bushes, now into the swale, anywhere to avoid the swarming bees, ducking, dodging, fighting for her very life. Presently the humming seemed to become a little fainter. She found the trail again, and ran with all her might from a few of her angry pursuers.

As she ran, straining every muscle, she suddenly became aware that, crossing the trail before her, was a big, round, black body, with brown markings on its back, like painted geometrical patterns. She tried to stop, but the louder buzzing behind warned her she dared not. Gathering her skirts higher, with hair flying around her face and her eyes almost bursting from their sockets, she ran straight toward it. The sound of her feet and the humming of the bees alarmed the rattler, so it stopped across the trail, lifting its head above the grasses of the swale and rattling inquiringly— rattled until the bees were outdone.

Straight toward it went the panic-stricken woman, running wildly and uncontrollably. She took one leap, clearing its body on the path, then flew ahead with winged feet. The snake, coiled to strike, missed Mrs. Duncan and landed among the bees instead. They settled over and around it, and realizing that it had found trouble, it sank among the grasses and went threshing toward its den in the deep willow-fringed low ground. The swale appeared as if a reaper were cutting a wide swath. The mass of enraged bees darted angrily around, searching for it, and striking the scrub-thorn, began a temporary settling there to discover whether it were a suitable place. Completely exhausted, Mrs. Duncan staggered on a few steps farther, fell facing the path, where Freckles found her, and lay quietly.

Freckles worked over her until she drew a long, quivering breath and opened her eyes.

When she saw him bending above her, she closed them tightly, and gripping him, struggled to her feet. He helped her, and with his arm around and half carrying her, they made their way to the clearing. She clung to him with all her remaining strength, but open her eyes she would not until her children came clustering around her. Then, brawny, big Scotswoman though she was, she quietly keeled over again. The children added their wailing to Freckles' panic.

This time he was so close the cabin that he could carry her into the house and lay her on the bed. He sent the oldest boy scudding down the corduroy for the nearest neighbor, and between them they undressed Mrs. Duncan and discovered that she was not bitten. They bathed and bound the bleeding wrist and coaxed her back to consciousness. She lay sobbing and shuddering. The first intelligent word she said was: "Freckles, look at that jar on the kitchen table and see if my yeast is no running ower."

Several days passed before she could give Duncan and Freckles any detailed account of what had happened to her, even then she could not do it without crying as the least of her babies. Freckles was almost heartbroken, and nursed her as well as any woman could have done; while big Duncan, with a heart full for them both, worked early and late to chink every crack of the cabin and examine every spot that possibly could harbor a snake. The effects of her morning on the trail kept her shivering half the time. She could not rest until she sent for McLean and begged him to save Freckles from further risk, in that place of horrors. The Boss went to the swamp with his mind fully determined to do so.

Freckles stood and laughed at him. "Why, Mr. McLean, don't you let a woman's nervous system set you worrying about me," he said. "I'm not denying how she felt, because I've been through it meself, but that's all over and gone. It's the height of me glory to fight it out with the old swamp, and all that's in it, or will be coming to it, and then to turn it over to you as I promised you and meself I'd do, sir. You couldn't break the heart of me entire quicker than to be taking it from me now, when I'm just on the home-stretch. It won't be over three or four weeks yet, and when I've gone it almost a year, why, what's that to me, sir? You mustn't let a woman get mixed up with business, for I've always heard about how it's bringing trouble."

McLean smiled. "What about that last tree?" he said.

Freckles blushed and grinned appreciatively.

"Angels and Bird Women don't count in the common run, sir," he affirmed shamelessly.

McLean sat in the saddle and laughed.

CHAPTER X

WHEREIN FRECKLES STRIVES MIGHTILY
AND THE SWAMP ANGEL REWARDS HIM

The Bird Woman and the Angel did not seem to count in the common run, for they arrived on time for the third of the series and found McLean on the line talking to Freckles. The Boss was filled with enthusiasm over a marsh article of the Bird Woman's that he just had read. He begged to be allowed to accompany her into the swamp and watch the method by which she secured an illustration in such a location.

The Bird Woman explained to him that it was an easy matter with the subject she then had in hand; and as Little Chicken was too small to be frightened by him, and big enough to be growing troublesome, she was glad for his company. They went to the chicken log together, leaving to the happy Freckles the care of the Angel, who had brought her banjo and a roll of songs that she wanted to hear him sing. The Bird Woman told them that they might practice in Freckles' room until she finished with Little Chicken, and then she and McLean would come to the concert.

It was almost three hours before they finished and came down the west trail for their rest and lunch. McLean walked ahead, keeping sharp watch on the trail and clearing it of fallen limbs from overhanging trees. He sent a big piece of bark flying into the swale, and then stopped short and stared at the trail.

The Bird Woman bent forward. Together they studied that imprint of the Angel's foot. At last their eyes met, the Bird Woman's filled with astonishment, and McLean's humid with pity. Neither said a word, but they knew. McLean entered the swale and hunted up the bark. He replaced it, and the Bird Woman carefully stepped over. As they reached the bushes at the entrance, the voice of the Angel stopped them, for it was commanding and filled with much impatience.

"Freckles James Ross McLean!" she was saying. "You fill me with dark-blue despair! You're singing as if your voice were glass and might break at any minute. Why don't you sing as you did a week ago? Answer me that, please."

Freckles smiled confusedly at the Angel, who sat on one of his fancy seats, playing his accompaniment on her banjo.

"You are a fraud," she said. "Here you went last week and led me to think that there was the making of a great singer in you, and now you are singing—do you know how badly you are singing?"

"Yis," said Freckles meekly. "I'm thinking I'm too happy to be singing well today. The music don't come right only when I'm lonesome and sad. The world's for being all sunshine at prisint, for among you and Mr. McLean and the Bird Woman I'm after being THAT happy that I can't keep me thoughts on me notes. It's more than sorry I am to be disappointing you. Play it over, and I'll be beginning again, and this time I'll hold hard."

"Well," said the Angel disgustedly, "it seems to me that if I had all the things to be proud of that you have, I'd lift up my head and sing!"

"And what is it I've to be proud of, ma'am?" politely inquired Freckles.

"Why, a whole worldful of things," cried the Angel explosively. "For one thing, you can be good and proud over the way you've kept the timber thieves out of this lease, and the trust your father has in you. You can be proud that you've never even once disappointed him or failed in what he believed you could do. You can be proud over the way everyone speaks of you with trust and honor, and about how brave of heart and strong of body you are I heard a big man say a few days ago that the Limberlost was full of disagreeable things—positive dangers, unhealthful as it could be, and that since the memory of the first settlers it has been a rendezvous for runaways, thieves, and murderers. This swamp is named for a man that was lost here and wandered around 'til he starved. That man I was talking with said he wouldn't take your job for a thousand dollars a month—in fact, he said he wouldn't have it for any money, and you've never missed a day or lost a tree. Proud! Why, I should think you would just parade around about proper over that!

"And you can always be proud that you are born an Irishman. My father is Irish, and if you want to see him get up and strut give him a teeny opening to enlarge on his race. He says that if the Irish had decent territory they'd lead the world. He says they've always been handicapped by lack of space and of fertile soil. He says if Ireland had been as big and fertile as Indiana, why, England wouldn't ever have had the upper hand. She'd only be an appendage. Fancy England an appendage! He says Ireland has the finest orators and the keenest statesmen in Europe today, and when England wants to fight, with whom does she fill her trenches? Irishmen, of course! Ireland has the greenest grass and trees, the finest stones and lakes, and they've jaunting-cars. I don't know just exactly what they are, but Ireland has all there are, anyway. They've a lot of great actors, and a few singers, and there never was a sweeter poet than one of theirs. You should hear my father recite 'Dear Harp of My Country.' He does it this way."

The Angel arose, made an elaborate old-time bow, and holding up the banjo, recited in clipping feet and meter, with rhythmic swing and a touch of brogue that was simply irresistible:

"Dear harp of my country" [The Angel ardently clasped the banjo],

"In darkness I found thee" [She held it to the light],

"The cold chain of silence had hung o'er thee long" [She muted the strings with her rosy palm];

"Then proudly, my own Irish harp, I unbound thee" [She threw up her head and swept a ringing harmony];

"And gave all thy chords to light, freedom, and song" [She crashed into the notes of the accompaniment she had been playing for Freckles].

"That's what you want to be thinking of!" she cried. "Not darkness, and lonesomeness, and sadness, but 'light, freedom, and song.' I can't begin to think offhand of all the big, splendid things an Irishman has to be proud of; but whatever they are, they are all yours, and you are a part of them. I just despise that 'saddest-when-I-sing' business. You can sing! Now you go over there and do it! Ireland has had her statesmen, warriors, actors, and poets; now you be her voice! You stand right out there before the cathedral door, and I'm going to come down the aisle playing that accompaniment, and when I stop in front of you—you sing!"

The Angel's face wore an unusual flush. Her eyes were flashing and she was palpitating with earnestness.

She parted the bushes and disappeared. Freckles, straight and tense, stood waiting. Presently, before he saw she was there, she was coming down the aisle toward him, playing compellingly, and rifts of light were touching her with golden glory. Freckles stood as if transfixed.

The cathedral was majestically beautiful, from arched dome of frescoed gold, green, and blue in never-ending shades and harmonies, to the mosaic aisle she trod, richly inlaid in choicest colors, and gigantic pillars that were God's handiwork fashioned and perfected through ages of sunshine and rain. But the fair young face and divinely molded form of the Angel were His most perfect work of all. Never had she appeared so surpassingly beautiful. She was smiling encouragingly now, and as she came toward him, she struck the chords full and strong.

The heart of poor Freckles almost burst with dull pain and his great love for her. In his desire to fulfill her expectations he forgot everything else, and when she reached his initial chord he was ready. He literally burst forth:

> *"Three little leaves of Irish green,*
> *United on one stem,*
> *Love, truth, and valor do they mean,*
> *They form a magic gem."*

The Angel's eyes widened curiously and her lips parted. A deep color swept into her cheeks. She had intended to arouse him. She had more than succeeded. She was too young to know that in the effort to rouse a man, women frequently kindle fires that they neither can quench nor control. Freckles was looking over her head now and singing that song, as it never had been sung before, for her alone; and instead of her helping him, as she had intended, he was carrying her with him on the waves of his voice, away, away into another world. When he struck into the chorus, wide-eyed and panting, she was swaying toward him and playing with all her might.

> *"Oh, do you love? Oh, say you love*
> *You love the shamrock green!"*

At the last note, Freckles' voice ceased and he looked at the Angel. He had given his best and his all. He fell on his knees and folded his arms across his breast. The Angel, as if magnetized, walked straight down the aisle to him, and running her fingers into the crisp masses of his red hair, tilted his head back and laid her lips on his forehead.

Then she stepped back and faced him. "Good boy!" she said, in a voice that wavered from the throbbing of her shaken heart. "Dear boy! I knew you could do it! I knew it was in you! Freckles, when you go into the world, if you can face a big audience and sing like that, just once, you will be immortal, and anything you want will be yours."

"Anything!" gasped Freckles.

"Anything," said the Angel.

Freckles arose, muttered something, and catching up his old bucket, plunged into the swamp blindly on a pretence of bringing water. The Angel walked slowly across the study, sat on the rustic bench, and, through narrowed lids, intently studied the tip of her shoe.

On the trail the Bird Woman wheeled to McLean with a dumbfounded look.

"God!" muttered he.

At last the Bird Woman spoke.

"Do you think the Angel knew she did that?" she asked softly.

"No," said McLean; "I do not. But the poor boy knew it. Heaven help him!"

The Bird Woman stared across the gently waving swale. "I don't see how I am going to blame her," she said at last. "It's so exactly what I would have done myself."

"Say the remainder," demanded McLean hoarsely. "Do him justice."

"He was born a gentleman," conceded the Bird Woman. "He took no advantage. He never even offered to touch her. Whatever that kiss meant to him, he recognized that it was the loving impulse of a child under stress of strong emotion. He was fine and manly as any man ever could have been."

McLean lifted his hat. "Thank you," he said simply, and parted the bushes for her to enter Freckles' room.

It was her first visit. Before she left she sent for her cameras and made studies of each side of it and of the cathedral. She was entranced with the delicate beauty of the place, while her eyes kept following Freckles as if she could not believe that it could be his conception and work.

That was a happy day. The Bird Woman had brought a lunch, and they spread it, with Freckles' dinner, on the study floor and sat, resting and enjoying themselves. But the Angel put her banjo into its case, silently gathered her music, and no one mentioned the concert.

The Bird Woman left McLean and the Angel to clear away the lunch, and with Freckles examined the walls of his room and told him all she knew about his shrubs and flowers. She analyzed a cardinal-flower and showed him what he had wanted to know all summer—why the bees buzzed ineffectually around it while the humming-birds found in it an ever-ready feast. Some of his specimens were so rare that she was unfamiliar with them, and with the flower book between them they knelt, studying the different varieties. She wandered the length of the cathedral aisle with him, and it was at her suggestion that he lighted his altar with a row of flaming foxfire.

As Freckles came to the cabin from his long day at the swamp he saw Mrs. Chicken sweeping to the south and wondered where she was going. He stepped into the bright, cosy little kitchen, and as he reached down the wash-basin he asked Mrs. Duncan a question.

"Mother Duncan, do kisses wash off?"

So warm a wave swept her heart that a half-flush mantled her face. She straightened her shoulders and glanced at her hands tenderly.

"Lord, na! Freckles," she cried. "At least, the anes ye get from people ye love dinna. They dinna stay on the outside. They strike in until they find the center of your heart and make their stopping-place there, and naething can take them from ye—I doubt if even death——Na, lad, ye can be reet sure kisses dinna wash off!"

Freckles set the basin down and muttered as he plunged his hot, tired face into the water, "I needn't be afraid to be washing, then, for that one struck in."

CHAPTER XI

WHEREIN THE BUTTERFLIES GO ON A
SPREE AND FRECKLES INFORMS THE
BIRD WOMAN

"I wish," said Freckles at breakfast one morning, "that I had some way to be sending a message to the Bird Woman. I've something at the swamp that I'm believing never happened before, and surely she'll be wanting it."

"What now, Freckles?" asked Mrs. Duncan.

"Why, the oddest thing you ever heard of," said Freckles; "the whole insect tribe gone on a spree. I'm supposing it's my doings, but it all happened by accident, like. You see, on the swale side of the line, right against me trail, there's one of these scrub wild crabtrees. Where the grass grows thick around it, is the finest place you ever conceived of for snakes. Having women about has set me trying to clean out those fellows a bit, and yesterday I noticed that tree in passing. It struck me that it would be a good idea to be taking it out. First I thought I'd take me hatchet and cut it down, for it ain't thicker than me upper arm. Then I remembered how it was blooming in the spring and filling all the air with sweetness. The coloring of the blossoms is beautiful, and I hated to be killing it. I just cut the grass short all around it. Then I started at the ground, trimmed up the trunk near the height of me shoulder, and left the top spreading. That made it look so truly ornamental that, idle like, I chips off the rough places neat, and this morning, on me soul, it's a sight! You see, cutting off the limbs and trimming up the trunk sets the sap running. In this hot sun it ferments in a few hours. There isn't much room for more things to crowd on that tree than there are, and to get drunker isn't noways possible."

"Weel, I be drawed on!" exclaimed Mrs. Duncan. "What kind of things do ye mean, Freckles?"

"Why, just an army of black ants. Some of them are sucking away like old topers. Some of them are setting up on their tails and hind legs, fiddling with their fore-feet and wiping their eyes. Some are rolling around on the ground, contented. There are quantities of big blue-bottle flies over the bark and hanging on the grasses around, too drunk to steer a course flying; so they just buzz away like flying, and all the time sitting still. The snake-feeders are too full to feed anything—even more sap to themselves. There's a lot of hard-backed bugs—beetles, I guess—colored like the brown, blue, and black of a peacock's tail. They hang on until the legs of them are so wake they can't stick a minute longer, and then they break away and fall to the ground. They just lay there on their backs, fably clawing air. When it wears off a bit, up they get, and go crawling back for more, and they so full they bump into each other and roll over. Sometimes they can't climb the tree until they wait to sober up a little. There's a lot of big black-and-gold bumblebees, done for entire, stumbling over the bark and rolling on the ground. They just lay there on their backs, rocking from side to side, singing to themselves like fat, happy babies. The wild bees keep up a steady buzzing with the beating of their wings.

"The butterflies are the worst old topers of them all. They're just a circus! You never saw the like of the beauties! They come every color you could be naming, and every shape you could be thinking up. They drink and drink until, if I'm driving them away, they stagger as they fly and turn somersaults in the air. If I lave them alone, they cling to the grasses, shivering happy like; and I'm blest, Mother Duncan, if the best of them could be unlocking the front door with a lead pencil, even."

"I never heard of anything sae surprising," said Mrs. Duncan.

"It's a rare sight to watch them, and no one ever made a picture of a thing like that before, I'm for thinking," said Freckles earnestly.

"Na," said Mrs. Duncan. "Ye can be pretty sure there didna. The Bird Woman must have word in some way, if ye walk the line and I walk to town and tell her. If ye think ye can wait until after supper, I am most sure ye can gang yoursel', for Duncan is coming home and he'd be glad to watch for ye. If he does na come, and na ane passes that I can send word with today, I really will gang early in the morning and tell her mysel'."

Freckles took his lunch and went to the swamp. He walked and watched eagerly. He could find no trace of anything, yet he felt a tense nervousness, as if trouble might be brooding. He examined every section of the wire, and kept watchful eyes on the grasses of the swale, in an effort to discover if anyone had passed through them; but he could discover no trace of anything to justify his fears.

He tilted his hat brim to shade his face and looked for his chickens. They were hanging almost beyond sight in the sky.

"Gee!" he said. "If I only had your sharp eyes and convenient location now, I wouldn't need be troubling so."

He reached his room and cautiously scanned the entrance before he stepped in. Then he pushed the bushes apart with his right arm and entered, his left hand on the butt of his favorite revolver. Instantly he knew that someone had been there. He stepped to the center of the room, closely scanning each wall and the floor. He could find no trace of a clue to confirm his belief, yet so intimate was he with the spirit of the place that he knew.

How he knew he could not have told, yet he did know that someone had entered his room, sat on his benches, and walked over his floor. He was surest around the case. Nothing was disturbed, yet it seemed to Freckles that he could see where prying fingers had tried the lock. He stepped behind the case, carefully examining the ground all around it, and close beside the tree to which it was nailed he found a deep, fresh footprint in the spongy soil—a long, narrow print, that was never made by the foot of Wessner. His heart tugged in his breast as he mentally measured the print, but he did not linger, for now the feeling arose that he was being watched. It seemed to him that he could feel the eyes of some intruder at his back. He knew he was examining things too closely: if anyone were watching, he did not want him to know that he felt it.

He took the most open way, and carried water for his flowers and moss as usual; but he put himself into no position in which he was fully exposed, and his hand was close his revolver constantly. Growing restive at last under the strain, he plunged boldly into the swamp and searched minutely all around his room, but he could not discover the least thing to give him further cause for alarm. He unlocked his case, took out his wheel, and for the remainder of the day he rode and watched as he never had before. Several times he locked the wheel and crossed the swamp on foot, zigzagging to cover all the space possible. Every rod he traveled he used the caution that sprang from knowledge of danger and the direction from which it probably would come. Several times he thought of sending for McLean, but for his life he could not make up his mind to do it with nothing more tangible than one footprint to justify him.

He waited until he was sure Duncan would be at home, if he were coming for the night, before he went to supper. The first thing he saw as he crossed the swale was the big bays in the yard.

There had been no one passing that day, and Duncan readily agreed to watch until Freckles rode to town. He told Duncan of the footprint, and urged him to guard closely. Duncan said he might rest easy, and filling his pipe and taking a good revolver, the big man went to the Limberlost.

Freckles made himself clean and neat, and raced to town, but it was night and the stars were shining before he reached the home of the Bird Woman. From afar he could see that the house was ablaze with lights. The lawn and veranda were strung with fancy lanterns and alive with people. He thought his errand important, so to turn back never occurred to Freckles. This was all the time or opportunity he would have. He must see the Bird Woman, and see her at once. He leaned his wheel inside the fence and walked up the broad front entrance. As he neared the steps, he saw that the place was swarming with young people, and the Angel, with an excuse to a group that surrounded her, came hurrying to him.

"Oh Freckles!" she cried delightedly. "So you could come? We were so afraid you could not! I'm as glad as I can be!"

"I don't understand," said Freckles. "Were you expecting me?"

"Why of course!" exclaimed the Angel. "Haven't you come to my party? Didn't you get my invitation? I sent you one."

"By mail?" asked Freckles.

"Yes," said the Angel. "I had to help with the preparations, and I couldn't find time to drive out; but I wrote you a letter, and told you that the Bird Woman was giving a party for me, and we wanted you to come, surely. I told them at the office to put it with Mr. Duncan's mail."

"Then that's likely where it is at present," said Freckles. "Duncan comes to town only once a week, and at times not that. He's home tonight for the first in a week. He's watching an hour for me until I come to the Bird Woman with a bit of work I thought she'd be caring to hear about bad. Is she where I can see her?"

The Angel's face clouded.

"What a disappointment!" she cried. "I did so want all my friends to know you. Can't you stay anyway?"

Freckles glanced from his wading-boots to the patent leathers of some of the Angel's friends, and smiled whimsically, but there was no danger of his ever misjudging her again.

"You know I cannot, Angel," he said.

"I am afraid I do," she said ruefully. "It's too bad! But there is a thing I want for you more than to come to my party, and that is to hang on and win with your work. I think of you every day, and I just pray that those thieves are not getting ahead of you. Oh, Freckles, do watch closely!"

She was so lovely a picture as she stood before him, ardent in his cause, that Freckles could not take his eyes from her to notice what her friends were thinking. If she did not mind, why should he? Anyway, if they really were the Angel's friends, probably they were better accustomed to her ways than he.

Her face and bared neck and arms were like the wild rose bloom. Her soft frock of white tulle lifted and stirred around her with the gentle evening air. The beautiful golden hair, that crept around her temples and ears as if it loved to cling there, was caught back and bound with broad blue satin ribbon. There was a sash of blue at her waist, and knots of it catching up her draperies.

"Must I go after the Bird Woman?" she pleaded.

"Indade, you must," answered Freckles firmly.

The Angel went away, but returned to say that the Bird Woman was telling a story to those inside and she could not come for a short time.

"You won't come in?" she pleaded.

"I must not," said Freckles. "I am not dressed to be among your friends, and I might be forgetting meself and stay too long."

"Then," said the Angel, "we mustn't go through the house, because it would disturb the story; but I want you to come the outside way to the conservatory and have some of my birthday lunch and some cake to take to Mrs. Duncan and the babies. Won't that be fun?"

Freckles thought that it would be more than fun, and followed delightedly.

The Angel gave him a big glass, brimming with some icy, sparkling liquid that struck his palate as it never had been touched before, because a combination of frosty fruit juices had not been a frequent beverage with him. The night was warm, and the Angel most beautiful and kind. A triple delirium of spirit, mind, and body seized upon him and developed a boldness all unnatural. He slightly parted the heavy curtains that separated the conservatory from the company and looked between. He almost stopped breathing. He had read of things like that, but he never had seen them.

The open space seemed to stretch through half a dozen rooms, all ablaze with lights, perfumed with flowers, and filled with elegantly dressed people. There were glimpses of polished floors, sparkling glass, and fine furnishings. From somewhere, the voice of his beloved Bird Woman arose and fell.

The Angel crowded beside him and was watching also.

"Doesn't it look pretty?" she whispered.

"Do you suppose Heaven is any finer than that?" asked Freckles.

The Angel began to laugh.

"Do you want to be laughing harder than that?" queried Freckles.

"A laugh is always good," said the Angel. "A little more avoirdupois won't hurt me. Go ahead."

"Well then," said Freckles, "it's only that I feel all over as if I belonged there. I could wear fine clothes, and move over those floors, and hold me own against the best of them."

"But where does my laugh come in?" demanded the Angel, as if she had been defrauded.

"And you ask me where the laugh comes in, looking me in the face after that," marveled Freckles.

"I wouldn't be so foolish as to laugh at such a manifest truth as that," said the Angel. "Anyone who knows you even half as well as I do, knows that you are never guilty of a discourtesy, and you move with twice the grace of any man here. Why shouldn't you feel as if you belonged where people are graceful and courteous?"

"On me soul!" said Freckles, "you are kind to be thinking it. You are doubly kind to be saying it."

The curtains parted and a woman came toward them. Her silks and laces trailed across the polished floors. The lights gleamed on her neck and arms, and flashed from rare jewels. She was smiling brightly; and until she spoke, Freckles had not realized fully that it was his loved Bird Woman.

Noticing his bewilderment, she cried: "Why, Freckles! Don't you know me in my war clothes?"

"I do in the uniform in which you fight the Limberlost," said Freckles.

The Bird Woman laughed. Then he told her why he had come, but she scarcely could believe him. She could not say exactly when she would go, but she would make it as soon as possible, for she was most anxious for the study.

While they talked, the Angel was busy packing a box of sandwiches, cake, fruit, and flowers. She gave him a last frosty glass, thanked him repeatedly for bringing news of new material; then Freckles went into the night. He rode toward the Limberlost with his eyes on the stars. Presently he removed his hat, hung it to his belt, and ruffled his hair to the sweep of the night wind. He filled the air all the way with snatches of oratorios, gospel hymns, and dialect and coon songs, in a startlingly varied programme. The one thing Freckles knew that he could do was to sing. The Duncans heard him coming a mile up the corduroy and could not believe their senses. Freckles unfastened the box from his belt, and gave Mrs. Duncan and the children all the eatables it contained, except one big piece of cake that he carried to the sweet-loving Duncan. He put the flowers back in the box and set it among his books. He did not say anything, but they understood it was not to be touched.

"Thae's Freckles' flow'rs," said a tiny Scotsman, "but," he added cheerfully, "it's oor sweeties!"

Freckles' face slowly flushed as he took Duncan's cake and started toward the swamp. While Duncan ate, Freckles told him something about the evening, as well as he could find words to express himself, and the big man was so amazed he kept forgetting the treat in his hands.

Then Freckles mounted his wheel and began a spin that terminated only when the biggest Plymouth Rock in Duncan's coop saluted a new day, and long lines of light reddened the east. As he rode he sang, while he sang he worshiped, but the god he tried to glorify was a dim and faraway mystery. The Angel was warm flesh and blood.

Every time he passed the little bark-covered imprint on the trail he dismounted, removed his hat, solemnly knelt and laid his lips on the impression. Because he kept no account himself, only the laughing-faced old man of the moon knew how often it happened; and as from the beginning, to the follies of earth that gentleman has ever been kind.

With the near approach of dawn Freckles tuned his last note. Wearied almost to falling, he turned from the trail into the path leading to the cabin for a few hours' rest.

CHAPTER XII

WHEREIN BLACK JACK CAPTURES FRECKLES AND THE ANGEL CAPTURES JACK

As Freckles left the trail, from the swale close the south entrance, four large muscular men arose and swiftly and carefully entered the swamp by the wagon road. Two of them carried a big saw, the third, coils of rope and wire, and all of them were heavily armed. They left one man on guard at the entrance. The other three made their way through the darkness as best they could, and were soon at Freckles' room. He had left the swamp on his wheel from the west trail. They counted on his returning on the wheel and circling the east line before he came there.

A little below the west entrance to Freckles' room, Black Jack stepped into the swale, and binding a wire tightly around a scrub oak, carried it below the waving grasses, stretched it taut across the trail, and fastened it to a tree in the swamp. Then he obliterated all signs of his work, and arranged the grass over the wire until it was so completely covered that only minute examination would reveal it. They entered Freckles' room with coarse oaths and jests. In a few moments, his specimen case with its precious contents was rolled into the swamp, while the saw was eating into one of the finest trees of the Limberlost.

The first report from the man on watch was that Duncan had driven to the South camp; the second, that Freckles was coming. The man watching was sent to see on which side the boy turned into the path; as they had expected, he took the east. He was a little tired and his head was rather stupid, for he had not been able to sleep as he had hoped, but he was very happy. Although he watched until his eyes ached, he could see no sign of anyone having entered the swamp.

He called a cheery greeting to all his chickens. At Sleepy Snake Creek he almost fell from his wheel with surprise: the saw-bird was surrounded by four lanky youngsters clamoring for breakfast. The father was strutting with all the importance of a drum major.

"No use to expect the Bird Woman today," said Freckles; "but now wouldn't she be jumping for a chance at that?"

As soon as Freckles was far down the east line, the watch was posted below the room on the west to report his coming. It was only a few moments before the signal came. Then the saw stopped, and the rope was brought out and uncoiled close to a sapling. Wessner and Black Jack crowded to the very edge of the swamp a little above the wire, and crouched, waiting.

They heard Freckles before they saw him. He came gliding down the line swiftly, and as he rode he was singing softly:

> *"Oh, do you love,*
> *Oh, say you love———"*

He got no farther. The sharply driven wheel struck the tense wire and bounded back. Freckles shot over the handlebar and coasted down the trail on his chest. As he struck, Black Jack and Wessner were upon him. Wessner caught off an old felt hat and clapped it over Freckles' mouth, while Black Jack twisted the boy's arms behind him and they rushed him into his room. Almost before he realized that anything had happened, he was trussed to a tree and securely gagged.

Then three of the men resumed work on the tree. The other followed the path Freckles had worn to Little Chicken's tree, and presently he reported that the wires were down and two teams with the loading apparatus coming to take out the timber. All the time the saw was slowly eating, eating into the big tree.

Wessner went to the trail and removed the wire. He picked up Freckles' wheel, that did not seem to be injured, and leaned it against the bushes so that if anyone did pass on the trail he would not see it doubled in the swamp-grass.

Then he came and stood in front of Freckles and laughed in devilish hate. To his own amazement, Freckles found himself looking fear in the face, and marveled that he was not afraid. Four to one! The tree halfway eaten through, the wagons coming up the inside road—he, bound and gagged! The men with Black Jack and Wessner had belonged to McLean's gang when last he had heard of them, but who those coming with the wagons might be he could not guess.

If they secured that tree, McLean lost its value, lost his wager, and lost his faith in him. The words of the Angel hammered in his ears. "Oh, Freckles, do watch closely!"

The saw worked steadily.

When the tree was down and loaded, what would they do? Pull out, and leave him there to report them? It was not to be hoped for. The place always had been lawless. It could mean but one thing.

A mist swept before his eyes, while his head swam. Was it only last night that he had worshiped the Angel in a delirium of happiness? And now, what? Wessner, released from a turn at the saw, walked to the flower bed, and tearing up a handful of rare ferns by the roots, started toward

Freckles. His intention was obvious. Black Jack stopped him, with an oath.

"You see here, Dutchy," he bawled, "mebby you think you'll wash his face with that, but you won't. A contract's a contract. We agreed to take out these trees and leave him for you to dispose of whatever way you please, provided you shut him up eternally on this deal. But I'll not see a tied man tormented by a fellow that he can lick up the ground with, loose, and that's flat. It raises my gorge to think what he'll get when we're gone, but you needn't think you're free to begin before. Don't you lay a hand on him while I'm here! What do you say, boys?"

"I say yes," growled one of McLean's latest deserters. "What's more, we're a pack of fools to risk the dirty work of silencing him. You had him face down and you on his back; why the hell didn't you cover his head and roll him into the bushes until we were gone? When I went into this, I didn't understand that he was to see all of us and that there was murder on the ticket. I'm not up to it. I don't mind lifting trees we came for, but I'm cursed if I want blood on my hands."

"Well, you ain't going to get it," bellowed Jack. "You fellows only contracted to help me get out my marked trees. He belong to Wessner, and it ain't in our deal what happens to him."

"Yes, and if Wessner finishes him safely, we are practically in for murder as well as stealing the trees; and if he don't, all hell's to pay. I think you've made a damnable bungle of this thing; that's what I think!"

"Then keep your thoughts to yourself," cried Jack. "We're doing this, and it's all planned safe and sure. As for killing that buck—come to think of it, killing is what he needs. He's away too good for this world of woe, anyhow. I tell you, it's all safe enough. His dropping out won't be the only secret the old Limberlost has never told. It's too dead easy to make it look like he helped take the timber and then cut. Why, he's played right into our hands. He was here at the swamp all last night, and back again in an hour or so. When we get our plan worked out, even old fool Duncan won't lift a finger to look for his carcass. We couldn't have him going in better shape."

"You just bet," said Wessner. "I owe him all he'll get, and be damned to you, but I'll pay!" he snarled at Freckles.

So it was killing, then. They were not only after this one tree, but many, and with his body it was their plan to kill his honor. To brand him a thief, with them, before the Angel, the Bird Woman, the dear Boss, and the Duncans—Freckles, in sick despair, sagged against the ropes.

Then he gathered his forces and thought swiftly. There was no hope of McLean's coming. They had chosen a day when they knew he had a big contract at the South camp. The Boss could not come before tomorrow by any possibility, and there would be no tomorrow for the boy. Duncan was on his way to the South camp, and the Bird Woman had said she would come as soon as she could. After the fatigue of the party, it was useless to expect her and the Angel today, and God save them from coming! The Angel's father had said they would be as safe in the Limberlost as at home. What would he think of this?

The sweat broke on Freckles' forehead. He tugged at the ropes whenever he felt that he dared, but they were passed around the tree and his body several times, and knotted on his chest. He was helpless. There was no hope, no help. And after they had conspired to make him appear a runaway thief to his loved ones, what was it that Wessner would do to him?

Whatever it was, Freckles lifted his head and resolved that he would bear in mind what he had once heard the Bird Woman say. He would go out bonnily. Never would he let them see, if he grew afraid. After all, what did it matter what they did to his body if by some scheme of the devil they could encompass his disgrace?

Then hope suddenly rose high in Freckles' breast. They could not do that! The Angel would not believe. Neither would McLean. He would keep up his courage. Kill him they could; dishonor him they could not.

Yet, summon all the fortitude he might, that saw eating into the tree rasped his nerves worse and worse. With whirling brain he gazed into the Limberlost, searching for something, he knew not what, and in blank horror found his eyes focusing on the Angel. She was quite a distance away, but he could see her white lips and angry expression.

Last week he had taken her and the Bird Woman across the swamp over the path he followed in going from his room to the chicken tree. He had told them the night before, that the butterfly tree was on the line close to this path. In figuring on their not coming that day, he failed to reckon with the enthusiasm of the Bird Woman. They must be there for the study, and the Angel had risked crossing the swamp in search of him. Or was there something in his room they needed? The blood surged in his ears as the roar of the Limberlost in the wrath of a storm.

He looked again, and it had been a dream. She was not there. Had she been? For his life, Freckles could not tell whether he really had seen the Angel, or whether his strained senses had played him the most cruel trick of all. Or was it not the kindest? Now he could go with the vision of her lovely face fresh with him.

"Thank You for that, oh God!" whispered Freckles. "'Twas more than kind of You and I don't s'pose I ought to be wanting anything else; but if You can, oh, I wish I could know before this ends, if 'twas me mother"— Freckles could not even whisper the words, for he hesitated a second and ended—"IF 'TWAS ME MOTHER DID IT!"

"Freckles! Freckles! Oh, Freckles!" the voice of the Angel came calling. Freckles swayed forward and wrenched at the rope until it cut deeply into his body.

"Hell!" cried Black Jack. "Who is that? Do you know?"

Freckles nodded.

Jack whipped out a revolver and snatched the gag from Freckles' mouth.

"Say quick, or it's up with you right now, and whoever that is with you!"

"It's the girl the Bird Woman takes with her," whispered Freckles through dry, swollen lips.

"They ain't due here for five days yet," said Wessner. "We got on to that last week."

"Yes," said Freckles, "but I found a tree covered with butterflies and things along the east line yesterday that I thought the Bird Woman would want extra, and I went to town to tell her last night. She said she'd come soon, but she didn't say when. They must be here. I take care of the girl while the Bird Woman works. Untie me quick until she is gone. I'll try to send her back, and then you can go on with your dirty work."

"He ain't lying," volunteered Wessner. "I saw that tree covered with butterflies and him watching around it when we were spying on him yesterday."

"No, he leaves lying to your sort," snapped Black Jack, as he undid the rope and pitched it across the room. "Remember that you're covered every move you make, my buck," he cautioned.

"Freckles! Freckles!" came the Angel's impatient voice, closer and closer.

"I must be answering," said Freckles, and Jack nodded. "Right here!" he called, and to the men: "You go on with your work, and remember one thing yourselves. The work of the Bird Woman is known all over the world. This girl's father is a rich man, and she is all he has. If you offer hurt of any kind to either of them, this world has no place far enough away or dark enough for you to be hiding in. Hell will be easy to what any man will get if he touches either of them!"

"Freckles, where are you?" demanded the Angel.

Soulsick with fear for her, Freckles went toward her and parted the bushes that she might enter. She came through without apparently giving him a glance, and the first words she said were: "Why have the gang come so soon? I didn't know you expected them for three weeks yet. Or is this some especial tree that Mr. McLean needs to fill an order right now?"

Freckles hesitated. Would a man dare lie to save himself? No. But to save the Angel—surely that was different. He opened his lips, but the

Angel was capable of saving herself. She walked among them, exactly as if she had been reared in a lumber camp, and never waited for an answer.

"Why, your specimen case!" she cried. "Look! Haven't you noticed that it's tipped over? Set it straight, quickly!"

A couple of the men stepped out and carefully righted the case.

"There! That's better," she said. "Freckles, I'm surprised at your being so careless. It would be a shame to break those lovely butterflies for one old tree! Is that a valuable tree? Why didn't you tell us last night you were going to take out a tree this morning? Oh, say, did you put your case there to protect that tree from that stealing old Black Jack and his gang? I bet you did! Well, if that wasn't bright! What kind of a tree is it?"

"It's a white oak," said Freckles.

"Like those they make dining-tables and sideboards from?"

"Yes."

"My! How interesting!" she cried. "I don't know a thing about timber, but my father wants me to learn just everything I can. I am going to ask him to let me come here and watch you until I know enough to boss a gang myself. Do you like to cut trees, gentlemen?" she asked with angelic sweetness of the men.

Some of them appeared foolish and some grim, but one managed to say they did.

Then the Angel's eyes turned full on Black Jack, and she gave the most natural little start of astonishment.

"Oh! I almost thought that you were a ghost!" she cried. "But I see now that you are really and truly. Were you ever in Colorado?"

"No," said Jack.

"I see you aren't the same man," said the Angel. "You know, we were in Colorado last year, and there was a cowboy who was the handsomest man anywhere around. He'd come riding into town every night, and all we girls just adored him! Oh, but he was a beauty! I thought at first glance you were really he, but I see now he wasn't nearly so tall nor so broad as you, and only half as handsome."

The men began to laugh while Jack flushed crimson. The Angel joined in the laugh.

"Well, I'll leave it to you! Isn't he handsome?" she challenged. "As for that cowboy's face, it couldn't be compared with yours. The only trouble with you is that your clothes are spoiling you. It's the dress those cowboys wear that makes half their attraction. If you were properly clothed, you could break the heart of the prettiest girl in the country."

With one accord the other men looked at Black Jack, and for the first time realized that he was a superb specimen of manhood, for he stood six feet tall, was broad, well-rounded, and had dark, even skin, big black eyes, and full red lips.

"I'll tell you what!" exclaimed the Angel. "I'd just love to see you on horseback. Nothing sets a handsome man off so splendidly. Do you ride?"

"Yes," said Jack, and his eyes were burning on the Angel as if he would fathom the depths of her soul.

"Well," said the Angel winsomely, "I know what I just wish you'd do. I wish you would let your hair grow a little longer. Then wear a blue flannel shirt a little open at the throat, a red tie, and a broad-brimmed felt hat, and ride past my house of evenings. I'm always at home then, and almost always on the veranda, and, oh! but I would like to see you! Will you do that for me?" It is impossible to describe the art with which the Angel asked the question. She was looking straight into Jack's face, coarse and hardened with sin and careless living, which was now taking on a wholly different expression. The evil lines of it were softening and fading under her clear gaze. A dull red flamed into his bronze cheeks, while his eyes were growing brightly tender.

"Yes," he said, and the glance he gave the men was of such a nature that no one saw fit even to change countenance.

"Oh, goody!" she cried, tilting on her toes. "I'll ask all the girls to come see, but they needn't stick in! We can get along without them, can't we?"

Jack leaned toward her. He was the charmed fluttering bird, while the Angel was the snake.

"Well, I rather guess!" he cried.

The Angel drew a deep breath and surveyed him rapturously.

"My, but you're tall!" she commented. "Do you suppose I ever will grow to reach your shoulders?"

She stood on tiptoe and measured the distance with her eyes. Then she developed timid confusion, while her glance sought the ground.

"I wish I could do something," she half whispered.

Jack seemed to increase an inch in height.

"What?" he asked hoarsely.

"Lariat Bill used always to have a bunch of red flowers in his shirt pocket. The red lit up his dark eyes and olive cheeks and made him splendid. May I put some red flowers on you?"

Freckles stared as he wheezed for breath. He wished the earth would open and swallow him. Was he dead or alive? Since his Angel had seen Black Jack she never had glanced his way. Was she completely bewitched? Would she throw herself at the man's feet before them all? Couldn't she give him even one thought? Hadn't she seen that he was gagged and bound? Did she truly think that these were McLean's men? Why, she could not! It was only a few days ago that she had been close enough to this man and angry enough with him to peel the hat from his head with a shot! Suddenly a thing she had said jestingly to him one day came back with startling force: "You must take Angels on trust." Of course you must! She was his Angel. She must have seen! His life, and what was far more, her own, was in her hands. There was nothing he could do but trust her. Surely she was working out some plan.

The Angel knelt beside his flower bed and recklessly tore up by the roots a big bunch of foxfire.

"These stems are so tough and sticky," she said. "I can't break them. Loan me your knife," she ordered Freckles.

As she reached for the knife, her back was for one second toward the men. She looked into his eyes and deliberately winked.

She severed the stems, tossed the knife to Freckles, and walking to Jack, laid the flowers over his heart.

Freckles broke into a sweat of agony. He had said she would be safe in a herd of howling savages. Would she? If Black Jack even made a motion toward touching her, Freckles knew that from somewhere he would muster the strength to kill him. He mentally measured the distance to where his club lay and set his muscles for a spring. But no—by the splendor of God! The big fellow was baring his head with a hand that was unsteady. The Angel pulled one of the long silver pins from her hat and fastened her flowers securely.

Freckles was quaking. What was to come next? What was she planning, and oh! did she understand the danger of her presence among those men; the real necessity for action?

As the Angel stepped from Jack, she turned her head to one side and peered at him, quite as Freckles had seen the little yellow fellow do on the line a hundred times, and said: "Well, that does the trick! Isn't that fine? See how it sets him off, boys? Don't you forget the tie is to be red, and the first ride soon. I can't wait very long. Now I must go. The Bird Woman will be ready to start, and she will come here hunting me next, for she is busy today. What did I come here for anyway?"

She glanced inquiringly around, and several of the men laughed. Oh, the delight of it! She had forgotten her errand for him! Jack had a second increase in height. The Angel glanced helplessly as if seeking a clue. Then her eyes fell, as if by accident, on Freckles, and she cried, "Oh, I know now! It was those magazines the Bird Woman promised you. I came to tell you that we put them under the box where we hide things, at the entrance to the swamp as we came in. I knew I would need my hands crossing the swamp, so I hid them there. You'll find them at the same old place."

Then Freckles spoke.

"It's mighty risky for you to be crossing the swamp alone," he said. "I'm surprised that the Bird Woman would be letting you try it. I know it's a little farther, but it's begging you I am to be going back by the trail. That's bad enough, but it's far safer than the swamp."

The Angel laughed merrily.

"Oh stop your nonsense!" she cried. "I'm not afraid! Not in the least! The Bird Woman didn't want me to try following a path that I'd been over only once, but I was sure I could do it, and I'm rather proud of the performance. Now, don't go babying! You know I'm not afraid!"

"No," said Freckles gently, "I know you're not; but that has nothing to do with the fact that your friends are afraid for you. On the trail you can see your way a bit ahead, and you've all the world a better chance if you meet a snake."

Then Freckles had an inspiration. He turned to Jack imploringly.

"You tell her!" he pleaded. "Tell her to go by the trail. She will for you."

The implication of this statement was so gratifying to Black Jack that he seemed again to expand and take on increase before their very eyes.

"You bet!" exclaimed Jack. And to the Angel: "You better take Freckles' word for it, miss. He knows the old swamp better than any of us, except me, and if he says 'go by the trail,' you'd best do it."

The Angel hesitated. She wanted to recross the swamp and try to reach the horse. She knew Freckles would brave any danger to save her crossing the swamp alone, but she really was not afraid, while the trail added over a mile to the walk. She knew the path. She intended to run for dear life the instant she felt herself from their sight, and tucked in the folds of her blouse was a fine little 32-caliber revolver that her father had presented her for her share in what he was pleased to call her military exploit. One last glance at Freckles showed her the agony in his eyes, and immediately she imagined he had some other reason. She would follow the trail.

"All right," she said, giving Jack a thrilling glance. "If you say so, I'll return by the trail to please you. Good-bye, everybody."

She lifted the bushes and started toward the entrance.

"You damned fool! Stop her!" growled Wessner. "Keep her till we're loaded, anyhow. You're playing hell! Can't you see that when this thing is found out, there she'll be to ruin all of us. If you let her go, every man of us has got to cut, and some of us will be caught sure."

Jack sprang forward. Freckles' heart muffled in his throat. The Angel seemed to divine Jack's coming. She was humming a little song. She deliberately stopped and began pulling the heads of the curious grasses that grew all around her. When she straightened, she took a step backward and called: "Ho! Freckles, the Bird Woman wants that natural history pamphlet returned. It belongs to a set she is going to have bound. That's one of the reasons we put it under the box. You be sure to get them as you go home tonight, for fear it rains or becomes damp with the heavy dews."

"All right," said Freckles, but it was in a voice that he never had heard before.

Then the Angel turned and sent a parting glance at Jack. She was overpoweringly human and bewitchingly lovely.

"You won't forget that ride and the red tie," she half asserted, half questioned.

Jack succumbed. Freckles was his captive, but he was the Angel's, soul and body. His face wore the holiest look it ever had known as he softly re-echoed Freckles' "All right." With her head held well up, the Angel walked slowly away, and Jack turned to the men.

"Drop your damned staring and saw wood," he shouted. "Don't you know anything at all about how to treat a lady?" It might have been a question which of the cronies that crouched over green wood fires in the cabins of Wildcat Hollow, eternally sucking a corncob pipe and stirring the endless kettles of stewing coon and opossum, had taught him to do even as well as he had by the Angel.

The men muttered and threatened among themselves, but they began working desperately. Someone suggested that a man be sent to follow the Angel and to watch her and the Bird Woman leave the swamp. Freckles' heart sank within him, but Jack was in a delirium and past all caution.

"Yes," he sneered. "Mebby all of you had better give over on the saw and run after the girl. I guess not! Seems to me I got the favors. I didn't see no bouquets on the rest of you! If anybody follows her, I do, and I'm needed here among such a pack of idiots. There's no danger in that baby face. She wouldn't give me away! You double and work like forty, while me and Wessner will take the axes and begin to cut in on the other side."

"What about the noise?" asked Wessner.

"No difference about the noise," answered Jack. "She took us to be from McLean's gang, slick as grease. Make the chips fly!"

So all of them attacked the big tree.

Freckles sat on one of his benches and waited. In their haste to fell the tree and load it, so that the teamsters could start, and leave them free to attack another, they had forgotten to rebind him.

The Angel was on the trail and safely started. The cold perspiration made Freckles' temples clammy and ran in little streams down his chest. It would take her more time to follow the trail, but her safety was Freckles' sole thought in urging her to go that way. He tried to figure on how long it would require to walk to the carriage. He wondered if the Bird Woman had unhitched. He followed the Angel every step of the way. He figured on when she would cross the path of the clearing, pass the deep pool where his "find-out" frog lived, cross Sleepy Snake Creek, and reach the carriage.

He wondered what she would say to the Bird Woman, and how long it would take them to pack and start. He knew now that they would understand, and the Angel would try to get the Boss there in time to save his wager. She could never do it, for the saw was over half through, and Jack and Wessner cutting into the opposite side of the tree. It appeared as if they could fell at least that tree, before McLean could come, and if they did he lost his wager.

When it was down, would they rebind him and leave him for Wessner to wreak his insane vengeance on, or would they take him along to the next tree and dispose of him when they had stolen all the timber they could? Jack had said that he should not be touched until he left. Surely he would not run all that risk for one tree, when he had many others of far greater value marked. Freckles felt that he had some hope to cling to now, but he found himself praying that the Angel would hurry.

Once Jack came to Freckles and asked if he had any water. Freckles arose and showed him where he kept his drinking-water. Jack drank in great gulps, and as he passed back the bucket, he said: "When a man's got a chance of catching a fine girl like that, he ought not be mixed up in any dirty business. I wish to God I was out of this!"

Freckles answered heartily: "I wish I was, too!"

Jack stared at him a minute and then broke into a roar of rough laughter.

"Blest if I blame you," he said. "But you had your chance! We offered you a fair thing and you gave Wessner his answer. I ain't envying you when he gives you his."

"You're six to one," answered Freckles. "It will be easy enough for you to be killing the body of me, but, curse you all, you can't blacken me soul!"

"Well, I'd give anything you could name if I had your honesty," said Jack.

When the mighty tree fell, the Limberlost shivered and screamed with the echo. Freckles groaned in despair, but the gang took heart. That was so much accomplished. They knew where to dispose of it safely, with no questions asked. Before the day was over, they could remove three others, all suitable for veneer and worth far more than this. Then they would leave Freckles to Wessner and scatter for safety, with more money than they had ever hoped for in their possession.

CHAPTER XIII

WHEREIN THE ANGEL RELEASES
FRECKLES, AND THE CURSE OF BLACK
JACK FALLS UPON HER

On the line, the Angel gave one backward glance at Black Jack, to see that he had returned to his work. Then she gathered her skirts above her knees and leaped forward on the run. In the first three yards she passed Freckles' wheel. Instantly she imagined that was why he had insisted on her coming by the trail. She seized it and sprang on. The saddle was too high, but she was an expert rider and could catch the pedals as they came up. She stopped at Duncan's cabin long enough to remedy this, telling Mrs. Duncan while working what was happening, and for her to follow the east trail until she found the Bird Woman, and told her that she had gone after McLean and for her to leave the swamp as quickly as possible.

Even with her fear for Freckles to spur her, Sarah Duncan blanched and began shivering at the idea of facing the Limberlost. The Angel looked her in the eyes.

"No matter how afraid you are, you have to go," she said. "If you don't the Bird Woman will go to Freckles' room, hunting me, and they will have trouble with her. If she isn't told to leave at once, they may follow me, and, finding I'm gone, do some terrible thing to Freckles. I can't go—that's flat—for if they caught me, then there'd be no one to go for help. You don't suppose they are going to take out the trees they're after and then leave Freckles to run and tell? They are going to murder the boy; that's what they are going to do. You run, and run for life! For Freckles' life! You can ride back with the Bird Woman."

The Angel saw Mrs. Duncan started; then began her race.

Those awful miles of corduroy! Would they never end? She did not dare use the wheel too roughly, for if it broke she never could arrive on time afoot. Where her way was impassable for the wheel, she jumped off, and pushing it beside her or carrying it, she ran as fast as she could. The day was fearfully warm. The sun poured with the fierce baking heat of August. The bushes claimed her hat, and she did not stop for it.

Where it was at all possible, the Angel mounted and pounded over the corduroy again. She was panting for breath and almost worn out when she reached the level pike. She had no idea how long she had been—and only two miles covered. She leaned over the bars, almost standing on the pedals, racing with all the strength in her body. The blood surged in her ears while her head swam, but she kept a straight course, and rode and rode. It seemed to her that she was standing still, while the trees and houses were racing past her.

Once a farmer's big dog rushed angrily into the road and she swerved until she almost fell, but she regained her balance, and setting her muscles, pedaled as fast as she could. At last she lifted her head. Surely it could not be over a mile more. She had covered two of corduroy and at least three of gravel, and it was only six in all.

She was reeling in the saddle, but she gripped the bars with new energy, and raced desperately. The sun beat on her bare head and hands. Just when she was choking with dust, and almost prostrate with heat and exhaustion—crash, she ran into a broken bottle. Snap! went the tire; the wheel swerved and pitched over. The Angel rolled into the thick yellow dust of the road and lay quietly.

From afar, Duncan began to notice a strange, dust-covered object in the road, as he headed toward town with the first load of the day's felling.

He chirruped to the bays and hurried them all he could. As he neared the Angel, he saw it was a woman and a broken wheel. He was beside her in an instant. He carried her to a shaded fence-corner, stretched her on the grass, and wiped the dust from the lovely face all dirt-streaked, crimson, and bearing a startling whiteness around the mouth and nose.

Wheels were common enough. Many of the farmers' daughters owned and rode them, but he knew these same farmers' daughters; this face was a stranger's. He glanced at the Angel's tumbled clothing, the silkiness of her hair, with its pale satin ribbon, and noticed that she had lost her hat. Her lips tightened in an ominous quiver. He left her and picked up the wheel: as he had surmised, he knew it. This, then, was Freckles' Swamp Angel. There was trouble in the Limberlost, and she had broken down racing to McLean. Duncan turned the bays into a fence-corner, tied one of them, unharnessed the other, fastened up the trace chains, and hurried to the nearest farmhouse to send help to the Angel. He found a woman, who took a bottle of camphor, a jug of water, and some towels, and started on the run.

Then Duncan put the bay to speed and raced to camp.

The Angel, left alone, lay still for a second, then she shivered and opened her eyes. She saw that she was on the grass and the broken wheel beside her. Instantly she realized that someone had carried her there and gone after help. She sat up and looked around. She noticed the load of logs and the one horse. Someone was riding after help for her!

"Oh, poor Freckles!" she wailed. "They may be killing him by now. Oh, how much time have I wasted?"

She hurried to the other bay, her fingers flying as she set him free. Snatching up a big blacksnake whip that lay on the ground, she caught the hames, stretched along the horse's neck, and, for the first time, the fine, big fellow felt on his back the quality of the lash that Duncan was accustomed to crack over him. He was frightened, and ran at top speed.

The Angel passed a wildly waving, screaming woman on the road, and a little later a man riding as if he, too, were in great haste. The man called to her, but she only lay lower and used the whip. Soon the feet of the man's horse sounded farther and farther away.

At the South camp they were loading a second wagon, when the Angel appeared riding one of Duncan's bays, lathered and dripping, and cried: "Everybody go to Freckles! There are thieves stealing trees, and they had him bound. They're going to kill him!"

She wheeled the horse toward the Limberlost. The alarm sounded through camp. The gang were not unprepared. McLean sprang to Nellie's back and raced after the Angel. As they passed Duncan, he wheeled and followed. Soon the pike was an irregular procession of barebacked riders, wildly driving flying horses toward the swamp.

The Boss rode neck-and-neck with the Angel. He repeatedly commanded her to stop and fall out of line, until he remembered that he would need her to lead him to Freckles. Then he gave up and rode beside her, for she was sending the bay at as sharp a pace as the other horses could keep and hold out. He could see that she was not hearing him. He glanced back and saw that Duncan was close. There was something terrifying in the appearance of the big man, and the manner in which he sat his beast and rode. It would be a sad day for the man on whom Duncan's wrath broke. There were four others close behind him, and the pike filling with the remainder of the gang; so McLean took heart and raced beside the Angel. Over and over he asked her where the trouble was, but she only gripped the hames, leaned along the bay's neck, and slashed away with the blacksnake. The steaming horse, with crimson nostrils and heaving sides, stretched out and ran for home with all the speed there was in him.

When they passed the cabin, the Bird Woman's carriage was there and Mrs. Duncan in the door wringing her hands, but the Bird Woman was nowhere to be seen. The Angel sent the bay along the path and turned into the west trail, while the men bunched and followed her. When she reached the entrance to Freckles' room, there were four men with her, and two more very close behind. She slid from the horse, and snatching the little revolver from her pocket, darted toward the bushes. McLean caught them back, and with drawn weapon, pressed beside her. There they stopped in astonishment.

The Bird Woman blocked the entrance. Over a small limb lay her revolver. It was trained at short range on Black Jack and Wessner, who stood with their hands above their heads.

Freckles, with the blood trickling down his face, from an ugly cut in his temple, was gagged and bound to the tree again; the remainder of the men were gone. Black Jack was raving as a maniac, and when they looked closer it was only the left arm that he raised. His right, with the hand shattered, hung helpless at his side, while his revolver lay at Freckles' feet. Wessner's weapon was in his belt, and beside him Freckles' club.

Freckles' face was white, with colorless lips, but in his eyes was the strength of undying courage. McLean pushed past the Bird Woman crying. "Hold steady on them only one minute more!"

He snatched the revolver from Wessner's belt, and stooped for Jack's.

At that instant the Angel rushed past. She tore the gag from Freckles, and seizing the rope knotted on his chest, she tugged at it desperately. Under her fingers it gave way, and she hurled it to McLean. The men were crowding in, and Duncan seized Wessner. As the Angel saw Freckles stand out, free, she reached her arms to him and pitched forward. A fearful oath burst from the lips of Black Jack. To have saved his life, Freckles could not have avoided the glance of triumph he gave Jack, when folding the Angel in his arms and stretching her on the mosses.

The Bird Woman cried out sharply for water as she ran to them. Someone sprang to bring that, and another to break open the case for brandy. As McLean arose from binding Wessner, there was a cry that Jack was escaping.

He was already far in the swamp, running for its densest part in leaping bounds. Every man who could be spared plunged after him.

Other members of the gang arriving, were sent to follow the tracks of the wagons. The teamsters had driven from the west entrance, and crossing the swale, had taken the same route the Bird Woman and the Angel had before them. There had been ample time for the drivers to reach the road; after that they could take any one of four directions. Traffic was heavy, and lumber wagons were passing almost constantly, so the men turned back and joined the more exciting hunt for a man. The remainder of the gang joined them, also farmers of the region and travelers attracted by the disturbance.

Watchers were set along the trail at short intervals. They patrolled the line and roads through the swamp that night, with lighted torches, and the next day McLean headed as thorough a search as he felt could be made of one side, while Duncan covered the other; but Black Jack could not be found. Spies were set around his home, in Wildcat Hollow, to ascertain if he reached there or aid was being sent in any direction to him;

but it was soon clear that his relatives were ignorant of his hiding-place, and were searching for him.

Great is the elasticity of youth. A hot bath and a sound night's sleep renewed Freckles' strength, and it needed but little more to work the same result with the Angel. Freckles was on the trail early the next morning. Besides a crowd of people anxious to witness Jack's capture, he found four stalwart guards, one at each turn. In his heart he was compelled to admit that he was glad to have them there. Close noon, McLean placed his men in charge of Duncan, and taking Freckles, drove to town to see how the Angel fared. McLean visited a greenhouse and bought an armload of its finest products; but Freckles would have none of them. He would carry his message in a glowing mass of the Limberlost's first goldenrod.

The Bird Woman received them, and in answer to their eager inquiries, said that the Angel was in no way seriously injured, only so bruised and shaken that their doctor had ordered her to lie quietly for the day. Though she was sore and stiff, they were having work to keep her in bed. Her callers sent up their flowers with their grateful regards, and the Angel promptly returned word that she wanted to see them.

She reached both hands to McLean. "What if one old tree is gone? You don't care, sir? You feel that Freckles has kept his trust as nobody ever did before, don't you? You won't forget all those long first days of fright that you told us of, the fearful cold of winter, the rain, heat, and lonesomeness, and the brave days, and lately, nights, too, and let him feel that his trust is broken? Oh, Mr. McLean," she begged, "say something to him! Do something to make him feel that it isn't for nothing he has watched and suffered it out with that old Limberlost. Make him see how great and fine it is, and how far, far better he has done than you or any of us expected! What's one old tree, anyway?" she cried passionately.

"I was thinking before you came. Those other men were rank big cowards. They were scared for their lives. If they were the drivers, I wager you gloves against gloves they never took those logs out to the pike. My coming upset them. Before you feel bad any more, you go look and see if they didn't lose courage the minute they left Wessner and Black Jack, dump that timber and run. I don't believe they ever had the grit to drive out with it in daylight. Go see if they didn't figure on leaving the way we did the other morning, and you'll find the logs before you reach the road. They never risked taking them into the open, when they got away and had time to think. Of course they didn't!

"And, then, another thing. You haven't lost your wager! It never will be claimed, because you made it with a stout, dark, red-faced man who drives a bay and a gray. He was right back of you, Mr. McLean, when I came yesterday. He went deathly white and shook on his feet when he saw those men probably would be caught. Some one of them was something to him, and you can just spot him for one of the men at the bottom of your troubles, and urging those younger fellows to steal from you. I suppose he'd promised to divide. You settle with him, and that business will stop."

She turned to Freckles. "And you be the happiest man alive, because you have kept your trust. Go look where I tell you and you'll find the logs. I can see just about where they are. When they go up that steep little hill, into the next woods after the cornfield, why, they could unloose the chains and the logs would roll from the wagons themselves. Now, you go look; and Mr. McLean, you do feel that Freckles has been brave and faithful? You won't love him any the less even if you don't find the logs."

The Angel's nerve gave way and she began to cry. Freckles could not endure it. He almost ran from the room, with the tears in his eyes; but McLean took the Angel from the Bird Woman's arms, and kissed her brave little face, stroked her hair, and petted her into quietness before he left.

As they drove to the swamp, McLean so earnestly seconded all that the Angel had said that he soon had the boy feeling much better.

"Freckles, your Angel has a spice of the devil in her, but she's superb! You needn't spend any time questioning or bewailing anything she does. Just worship blindly, my boy. By heaven! she's sense, courage, and beauty for half a dozen girls," said McLean.

"It's altogether right you are, sir," affirmed Freckles heartily. Presently he added, "There's no question but the series is over now."

"Don't think it!" answered McLean. "The Bird Woman is working for success, and success along any line is not won by being scared out. She will be back on the usual day, and ten to one, the Angel will be with her. They are made of pretty stern stuff, and they don't scare worth a cent. Before I left, I told the Bird Woman it would be safe; and it will. You may do your usual walking, but those four guards are there to remain. They are under your orders absolutely. They are prohibited from firing on any bird or molesting anything that you want to protect, but there they remain, and this time it is useless for you to say one word. I have listened to your pride too long. You are too precious to me, and that voice of yours is too precious to the world to run any more risks."

"I am sorry to have anything spoil the series," said Freckles, "and I'd love them to be coming, the Angel especial, but it can't be. You'll have to tell them so. You see, Jack would have been ready to stake his life she meant what she said and did to him. When the teams pulled out, Wessner seized me; then he and Jack went to quarreling over whether they should finish me then or take me to the next tree they were for felling. Between them they were pulling me around and hurting me bad. Wessner wanted to get at me right then, and Jack said he shouldn't be touching me till the last tree was out and all the rest of them gone. I'm belaying Jack really hated to see me done for in the beginning; and I think, too, he was afraid if Wessner finished me then he'd lose his nerve and cut, and they couldn't be managing the felling without him; anyway, they were hauling me round like I was already past all feeling, and they tied me up again. To keep me courage up, I twits Wessner about having to tie me and needing another man to help handle me. I told him what I'd do to him if I was free, and he grabs up me own club and lays open me head with it. When the blood came streaming, it set Jack raving, and he cursed and damned Wessner for a coward and a softy. Then Wessner turned on Jack and gives it to him for letting the Angel make a fool of him. Tells him she was just playing with him, and beyond all manner of doubt she'd gone after you, and there was nothing to do on account of his foolishness but finish me, get out, and let the rest of the timber go, for likely you was on the way right then. That drove Jack plum crazy.

"I don't think he was for having a doubt of the Angel before, but then he just raved. He grabbed out his gun and turned on Wessner. Spang! It went out of his fist, and the order comes: 'Hands up!' Wessner reached for kingdom come like he was expecting to grab hold and pull himself up. Jack puts up what he has left. Then he leans over to me and tells me what he'll do to me if he ever gets out of there alive. Then, just like a snake hissing, he spits out what he'll do to her for playing him. He did get away, and with his strength, that wound in his hand won't be bothering him long. He'll do to me just what he said, and when he hears it really was she that went after you, why, he'll keep his oath about her.

"He's lived in the swamp all his life, sir, and everybody says it's always been the home of cutthroats, outlaws, and runaways. He knows its most secret places as none of the others. He's alive. He's in there now, sir. Some way he'll keep alive. If you'd seen his face, all scarlet with passion, twisted with pain, and black with hate, and heard him swearing that oath, you'd know it was a sure thing. I ain't done with him yet, and I've brought this awful thing on her."

"And I haven't begun with him yet," said McLean, setting his teeth. "I've been away too slow and too easy, believing there'd be no greater harm than the loss of a tree. I've sent for a couple of first-class detectives. We will put them on his track, and rout him out and rid the country of him. I don't propose for him to stop either our work or our pleasure. As for his being in the swamp now, I don't believe it. He'd find a way out last night, in spite of us. Don't you worry! I am at the helm now, and I'll see to that gentleman in my own way."

"I wish to my soul you had seen and heard him!" said Freckles, unconvinced.

They entered the swamp, taking the route followed by the Bird Woman and the Angel. They really did find the logs, almost where the Angel had predicted they would be. McLean went to the South camp and had an interview with Crowen that completely convinced him that the Angel was correct there also. But he had no proof, so all he could do was to discharge the man, although his guilt was so apparent that he offered to withdraw the wager.

Then McLean sent for a pack of bloodhounds and put them on the trail of Black Jack. They clung to it, on and on, into the depths of the swamp, leading their followers through what had been considered impassable and impenetrable ways, and finally, around near the west entrance and into the swale. Here the dogs bellowed, raved, and fell over each other in their excitement. They raced back and forth from swamp to swale, but follow the scent farther they would not, even though cruelly driven. At last their owner attributed their actions to snakes, and as they were very valuable dogs, abandoned the effort to urge them on. So that all they really established was the fact that Black Jack had eluded their vigilance and crossed the trail some time in the night. He had escaped to the swale; from there he probably crossed the corduroy, and reaching the lower end of the swamp, had found friends. It was a great relief to feel that he was not in the swamp, and it raised the spirits of every man on the line, though many of them expressed regrets that he who was undoubtedly most to blame should escape, while Wessner, who in the beginning was only his tool, should be left to punishment.

But for Freckles, with Jack's fearful oath ringing in his ears, there was neither rest nor peace. He was almost ill when the day for the next study of the series arrived and he saw the Bird Woman and the Angel coming down the corduroy. The guards of the east line he left at their customary places, but those of the west he brought over and placed, one near Little Chicken's tree, and the other at the carriage. He was firm about the Angel's remaining in the carriage, that he did not offer to have unhitched. He went with the Bird Woman to secure the picture, which was the easiest matter it had been at any time yet, for the simple reason that the placing of the guards and the unusual movement around the swamp had made Mr. and Mrs. Chicken timid, and they had not carried Little Chicken the customary amount of food. Freckles, in the anxiety of the past few days, had neglected him, and he had been so hungry, much of the time, that when the Bird Woman held up a sweet-bread, although he had started toward the recesses of the log at her coming, he stopped; with slightly opened beak, he waited anxiously for the treat, and gave a study of great value, showing every point of his head, also his wing and tail development.

When the Bird Woman proposed to look for other subjects close about the line, Freckles went so far as to tell her that Jack had made fearful threats against the Angel. He implored her to take the Angel home and keep her under unceasing guard until Jack was located. He wanted to tell her all about it, but he knew how dear the Angel was to her, and he dreaded to burden her with his fears when they might prove groundless. He allowed her to go, but afterward blamed himself severely for having done so.

CHAPTER XIV

WHEREIN FRECKLES NURSES A
HEARTACHE AND BLACK JACK DROPS
OUT

"McLean," said Mrs. Duncan, as the Boss paused to greet her in passing the cabin, "do you know that Freckles hasna been in bed the past five nights and all he's eaten in that many days ye could pack into a pint cup?"

"Why, what does the boy mean?" demanded McLean. "There's no necessity for him being on guard, with the watch I've set on the line. I had no idea he was staying down there."

"He's no there," said Mrs. Duncan. "He goes somewhere else. He leaves on his wheel juist after we're abed and rides in close cock-crow or a little earlier, and he's looking like death and nothing short of it."

"But where does he go?" asked McLean in astonishment.

"I'm no given to bearing tales out of school," said Sarah Duncan, "but in this case I'd tell ye if I could. What the trouble is I dinna ken. If it is no' stopped, he's in for dreadful sickness, and I thought ye could find out and help him. He's in sair trouble; that's all I know."

McLean sat brooding as he stroked Nellie's neck.

At last he said: "I suspect I understand. At any rate, I think I can find out. Thank you for telling me."

"Ye'll no need telling, once ye clap your eyes on him," prophesied Mrs. Duncan. "His face is all a glist'ny yellow, and he's peaked as a starving caged bird."

McLean rode to the Limberlost, and stopping in the shade, sat waiting for Freckles, whose hour for passing the foot of the lease had come.

Along the north line came Freckles, fairly staggering. When he turned east and reached Sleepy Snake Creek, sliding through the swale as the long black snake for which it was named, he sat on the bridge and closed his burning eyes, but they would not remain shut. As if pulled by wires, the heavy lids flew open, while the outraged nerves and muscles of his body danced, twitched, and tingled.

He bent forward and idly watched the limpid little stream flowing beneath his feet. Stretching into the swale, it came creeping between an impenetrable wall of magnificent wild flowers, vines, and ferns. Milkweed, goldenrod, ironwort, fringed gentians, cardinal-flowers, and turtle-head stood on the very edge of the creek, and every flower of them had a double in the water. Wild clematis crowned with snow the heads of trees scattered here and there on the bank.

From afar the creek appeared to be murky, dirty water. Really it was clear and sparkling. The tinge of blackness was gained from its bed of muck showing through the transparent current. He could see small and wonderfully marked fish. What became of them when the creek spread into the swamp? For one thing, they would make mighty fine eating for the family of that self-satisfied old blue heron.

Freckles sat so quietly that soon the brim of his hat was covered with snake-feeders, rasping their crisp wings and singing while they rested. Some of them settled on the club, and one on his shoulder. He was so motionless; feathers, fur, and gauze were so accustomed to him, that all through the swale they continued their daily life and forgot he was there.

The heron family were wading the mouth of the creek. Freckles idly wondered whether the nerve-racking rasps they occasionally emitted indicated domestic felicity or a raging quarrel. He could not decide. A sheitpoke, with flaring crest, went stalking across a bare space close to the creek's mouth. A stately brown bittern waded into the clear-flowing water, lifting his feet high at every step, and setting them down carefully, as if he dreaded wetting them, and with slightly parted beak, stood eagerly watching around him for worms. Behind him were some mighty trees of the swamp above, and below the bank glowed a solid wall of goldenrod.

No wonder the ancients had chosen yellow as the color to represent victory, for the fierce, conquering hue of the sun was in it. They had done well, too, in selecting purple as the emblem of royalty. It was a dignified, compelling color, while in its warm tone there was a hint of blood.

It was the Limberlost's hour to proclaim her sovereignty and triumph. Everywhere she flaunted her yellow banner and trailed the purple of her mantle, that was paler in the thistle-heads, took on strength in the first opening asters, and glowed and burned in the ironwort.

He gazed into her damp, mossy recesses where high-piled riven trees decayed under coats of living green, where dainty vines swayed and clambered, and here and there a yellow leaf, fluttering down, presaged the coming of winter. His love of the swamp laid hold of him and shook him with its force.

Compellingly beautiful was the Limberlost, but cruel withal; for inside bleached the uncoffined bones of her victims, while she had missed cradling him, oh! so narrowly.

He shifted restlessly; the movement sent the snake-feeders skimming. The hum of life swelled and roared in his strained ears. Small turtles, that had climbed on a log to sun, splashed clumsily into the water. Somewhere in the timber of the bridge a bloodthirsty little frog cried sharply. "KEEL'IM! KEEL'IM!"

Freckles muttered: "It's worse than that Black Jack swore to do to me, little fellow."

A muskrat waddled down the bank and swam for the swamp, its pointed nose riffling the water into a shining trail in its wake.

Then, below the turtle-log, a dripping silver-gray head, with shining eyes, was cautiously lifted, and Freckles' hand slid to his revolver. Higher and higher came the head, a long, heavy, furcoated body arose, now half, now three-fourths from the water. Freckles looked at his shaking hand and doubted, but he gathered his forces, the shot rang, and the otter lay quiet. He hurried down and tried to lift it. He scarcely could muster strength to carry it to the bridge. The consciousness that he really could go no farther with it made Freckles realize the fact that he was close the limit of human endurance. He could bear it little, if any, longer. Every hour the dear face of the Angel wavered before him, and behind it the awful distorted image of Black Jack, as he had sworn to the punishment he would mete out to her. He must either see McLean, or else make a trip to town and find her father. Which should he do? He was almost a stranger, so the Angel's father might not be impressed with what he said as he would if McLean went to him. Then he remembered that McLean had said he would come that morning. Freckles never had forgotten before. He hurried on the east trail as fast as his tottering legs would carry him.

He stopped when he came to the first guard, and telling him of his luck, asked him to get the otter and carry it to the cabin, as he was anxious to meet McLean.

Freckles passed the second guard without seeing him, and hurried to the Boss. He took off his hat, wiped his forehead, and stood silent under the eyes of McLean.

The Boss was dumbfounded. Mrs. Duncan had led him to expect that he would find a change in Freckles, but this was almost deathly. The fact was apparent that the boy scarcely knew what he was doing. His eyes had a glazed, far-sighted appearance, that wrung the heart of the man who loved him. Without a thought of preliminaries, McLean leaned in the saddle and drew Freckles to him.

"My poor lad!" he said. "My poor, dear lad! tell me, and we will try to right it!"

Freckles had twisted his fingers in Nellie's mane. At the kind words his face dropped on McLean's thigh and he shook with a nervous chill. McLean gathered him closer and waited.

When the guard came with the otter, McLean without a word motioned him to lay it down and leave them.

"Freckles," said McLean at last, "will you tell me, or must I set to work in the dark and try to find the trouble?"

"Oh, I want to tell you! I must tell you, sir," shuddered Freckles. "I cannot be bearing it the day out alone. I was coming to you when I remembered you would be here."

He lifted his face and gazed across the swale, with his jaws set firmly a minute, as if gathering his forces. Then he spoke.

"It's the Angel, sir," he said.

Instinctively McLean's grip on him tightened, and Freckles looked into the Boss's face in wonder.

"I tried, the other day," said Freckles, "and I couldn't seem to make you see. It's only that there hasn't been an hour, waking or sleeping, since the day she parted the bushes and looked into me room, that the face of her hasn't been before me in all the tinderness, beauty, and mischief of it. She talked to me friendly like. She trusted me entirely to take right care of her. She helped me with things about me books. She traited me like I was born a gintleman, and shared with me as if I were of her own blood. She walked the streets of the town with me before her friends with all the pride of a queen. She forgot herself and didn't mind the Bird Woman, and run big risks to help me out that first day, sir. This last time she walked into that gang of murderers, took their leader, and twisted him to the will of her. She outdone him and raced the life almost out of her trying to save me.

"Since I can remimber, whatever the thing was that happened to me in the beginning has been me curse. I've been bitter, hard, and smarting under it hopelessly. She came by, and found me voice, and put hope of life and success like other men into me in spite of it."

Freckles held up his maimed arm.

"Look at it, sir!" he said. "A thousand times I've cursed it, hanging there helpless. She took it on the street, before all the people, just as if she didn't see that it was a thing to hide and shrink from. Again and again I've had the feeling with her, if I didn't entirely forget it, that she didn't see it was gone and I must be pointing it out to her. Her touch on it was so sacred-like, at times since I've caught meself looking at the awful thing near like I was proud of it, sir. If I had been born your son she couldn't be traiting me more as her equal, and she can't help knowing you ain't truly me father. Nobody can know the homeliness or the ignorance of me better than I do, and all me lack of birth, relatives, and money, and what's it all to her?"

Freckles stepped back, squared his shoulders, and with a royal lift of his head looked straight into the Boss's eyes.

"You saw her in the beautiful little room of her, and you can't be forgetting how she begged and plead with you for me. She touched me body, and 'twas sanctified. She laid her lips on my brow, and 'twas sacrament. Nobody knows the height of her better than me. Nobody's studied my depths closer. There's no bridge for the great distance between us, sir, and clearest of all, I'm for realizing it: but she risked terrible things when she came to me among that gang of thieves. She wore herself past bearing to save me from such an easy thing as death! Now, here's me, a man, a big, strong man, and letting her live under that fearful oath, so worse than any death 'twould be for her, and lifting not a finger to save her. I cannot hear it, sir. It's killing me by inches! Black Jack's hand may not have been hurt so bad. Any hour he may be creeping up behind her! Any minute the awful revenge he swore to be taking may in some way fall on her, and I haven't even warned her father. I can't stay here doing nothing another hour. The five nights gone I've watched under her windows, but there's the whole of the day. She's her own horse and little cart, and's free to be driving through the town and country as she pleases. If any evil comes to her through Black Jack, it comes from her angel-like goodness to me. Somewhere he's hiding! Somewhere he is waiting his chance! Somewhere he is reaching out for her! I tell you I cannot, I dare not be bearing it longer!"

"Freckles, be quiet!" said McLean, his eyes humid and his voice quivering with the pity of it all. "Believe me, I did not understand. I know the Angel's father well. I will go to him at once. I have transacted business with him for the past three years. I will make him see! I am only beginning to realize your agony, and the real danger there is for the Angel. Believe me, I will see that she is fully protected every hour of the day and night until Jack is located and disposed of. And I promise you further, that if I fail to move her father or make him understand the danger, I will maintain a guard over her until Jack is caught. Now will you go bathe, drink some milk, go to bed, and sleep for hours, and then be my brave, bright old boy again?"

"Yis," said Freckles simply.

But McLean could see the flesh was twitching on the lad's bones.

"What was it the guard brought there?" McLean asked in an effort to distract Freckles' thoughts.

"Oh!" Freckles said, glancing where the Boss pointed, "I forgot it! 'Tis an otter, and fine past believing, for this warm weather. I shot it at the creek this morning. 'Twas a good shot, considering. I expected to miss."

Freckles picked up the animal and started toward McLean with it, but Nellie pricked up her dainty little ears, danced into the swale, and snorted with fright. Freckles dropped the otter and ran to her head.

"For pity's sake, get her on the trail, sir," he begged. "She's just about where the old king rattler crosses to go into the swamp—the old buster Duncan and I have been telling you of. I haven't a doubt but it was the one Mother Duncan met. 'Twas down the trail there, just a little farther on, that I found her, and it's sure to be close yet."

McLean slid from Nellie's back, led her into the trail farther down the line, and tied her to a bush. Then he went to examine the otter. It was a rare, big specimen, with exquisitely fine, long, silky hair.

"What do you want to do with it, Freckles?" asked McLean, as he stroked the soft fur lingeringly. "Do you know that it is very valuable?"

"I was for almost praying so, sir," said Freckles. "As I saw it coming up the bank I thought this: Once somewhere in a book there was a picture of a young girl, and she was just a breath like the beautifulness of the Angel. Her hands were in a muff as big as her body, and I thought it was so pretty. I think she was some queen, or the like. Do you suppose I could have this skin tanned and made into such a muff as that?—an enormous big one, sir?"

"Of course you can," said McLean. "That's a fine idea and it's easy enough. We must box and express the otter, cold storage, by the first train. You stand guard a minute and I'll tell Hall to carry it to the cabin. I'll put Nellie to Duncan's rig, and we'll drive to town and call on the Angel's father. Then we'll start the otter while it is fresh, and I'll write your instructions later. It would be a mighty fine thing for you to give to the Angel as a little reminder of the Limberlost before it is despoiled, and as a souvenir of her trip for you."

Freckles lifted a face with a glow of happy color creeping into it and eyes lighting with a former brightness. Throwing his arms around McLean, he cried: "Oh, how I love you! Oh, I wish I could make you know how I love you!"

McLean strained him to his breast.

"God bless you, Freckles," he said. "I do know! We're going to have some good old times out of this world together, and we can't begin too soon. Would you rather sleep first, or have a bite of lunch, take the drive with me, and then rest? I don't know but sleep will come sooner and deeper to take the ride and have your mind set at ease before you lie down. Suppose you go."

"Suppose I do," said Freckles, with a glimmer of the old light in his eyes and newly found strength to shoulder the otter. Together they turned into the trail.

McLean noticed and spoke of the big black chickens.

"They've been hanging round out there for several days past," said Freckles. "I'll tell you what I think it means. I think the old rattler has killed something too big for him to swallow, and he's keeping guard and won't let me chickens have it. I'm just sure, from the way the birds have acted out there all summer, that it is the rattler's den. You watch them now. See the way they dip and then rise, frightened like!"

Suddenly McLean turned toward him with blanching face
"Freckles!" he cried.

"My God, sir!" shuddered Freckles.

He dropped the otter, caught up his club, and plunged into the swale. Reaching for his revolver, McLean followed. The chickens circled higher at their coming, and the big snake lifted his head and rattled angrily. It sank in sinuous coils at the report of McLean's revolver, and together he and Freckles stood beside Black Jack. His fate was evident and most horrible.

"Come," said the Boss at last. "We don't dare touch him. We will get a sheet from Mrs. Duncan and tuck over him, to keep these swarms of insects away, and set Hall on guard, while we find the officers."

Freckles' lips closed resolutely. He deliberately thrust his club under Black Jack's body, and, raising him, rested it on his knee. He pulled a long silver pin from the front of the dead man's shirt and sent it spinning into the swale. Then he gathered up a few crumpled bright flowers and dropped them into the pool far away.

"My soul is sick with the horror of this thing," said McLean, as he and Freckles drove toward town. "I can't understand how Jack dared risk creeping through the swale, even in desperation. No one knew its dangers better than he. And why did he choose the rankest, muckiest place to cross the swamp?"

"Don't you think, sir, it was because it was on a line with the Limberlost south of the corduroy? The grass was tallest there, and he counted on those willows to screen him. Once he got among them, he would have been safe to walk by stooping. If he'd made it past that place, he'd been sure to get out."

"Well, I'm as sorry for Jack as I know how to be," said McLean, "but I can't help feeling relieved that our troubles are over, for now they are. With so dreadful a punishment for Jack, Wessner under arrest, and warrants for the others, we can count on their going away and remaining. As for anyone else, I don't think they will care to attempt stealing my timber after the experience of these men. There is no other man here with Jack's fine ability in woodcraft. He was an expert."

"Did you ever hear of anyone who ever tried to locate any trees excepting him?" asked Freckles.

"No, I never did," said McLean. "I am sure there was no one besides him. You see, it was only with the arrival of our company that the other fellows scented good stuff in the Limberlost, and tried to work in. Jack knew the swamp better than anyone here. When he found there were two companies trying to lease, he wanted to stand in with the one from which he could realize the most. Even then he had trees marked that he was trying to dispose of. I think his sole intention in forcing me to discharge him from my gang was to come here and try to steal timber. We had no idea, when we took the lease, what a gold mine it was."

"That's exactly what Wessner said that first day," said Freckles eagerly. "That 'twas a 'gold mine'! He said he didn't know where the marked trees were, but he knew a man who did, and if I would hold off and let them get the marked ones, there were a dozen they could get out in a few days."

"Freckles!" cried McLean. "You don't mean a dozen!"

"That's what he said, sir—a dozen. He said they couldn't tell how the grain of all of them would work up, of course, but they were all worth taking out, and five or six were real gold mines. This makes three they've tried, so there must be nine more marked, and several of them for being just fine."

"Well, I wish I knew which they are," said McLean, "so I could get them out first."

"I have been thinking," said Freckles. "I believe if you will leave one of the guards on the line—say Hall—that I will begin on the swamp, at the north end, and lay it off in sections, and try to hunt out the marked trees. I suppose they are all marked something like that first maple on the line was. Wessner mentioned another good one not so far from that. He said it was best of all. I'd be having the swelled head if I could find that. Of course, I don't know a thing about the trees, but I could hunt for the marks. Jack was so good at it he could tell some of them by the bark, but all he wanted to take that we've found so far have just had a deep chip cut out, rather low down, and where the bushes were thick over it. I believe I could be finding some of them."

"Good head!" said McLean. "We will do that. You may begin as soon as you are rested. And about things you come across in the swamp, Freckles—the most trifling little thing that you think the Bird Woman would want, take your wheel and go after her at any time. I'll leave two men on the line, so that you will have one on either side, and you can come and go as you please. Have you stopped to think of all we owe her, my boy?"

"Yis; and the Angel—we owe her a lot, too," said Freckles. "I owe her me life and honor. It's lying awake nights I'll have to be trying to think how I'm ever to pay her up."

"Well, begin with the muff," suggested McLean. "That should be fine."

He bent down and ruffled the rich fur of the otter lying at his feet.

"I don't exactly see how it comes to be in such splendid fur in summer. Their coats are always thick in cold weather, but this scarcely could be improved. I'll wire Cooper to be watching for it. They must have it fresh. When it's tanned we won't spare any expense in making it up. It should be a royal thing, and some way I think it will exactly suit the Angel. I can't think of anything that would be more appropriate for her."

"Neither can I," agreed Freckles heartily. "When I reach the city there's one other thing, if I've the money after the muff is finished."

He told McLean of Mrs. Duncan's desire for a hat similar to the Angel's. He hesitated a little in the telling, keeping sharp watch on McLean's face. When he saw the Boss's eyes were full of comprehension and sympathy, he loved him anew, for, as ever, McLean was quick to understand. Instead of laughing, he said: "I think you'll have to let me in on that, too. You mustn't be selfish, you know. I'll tell you what we'll do. Send it for Christmas. I'll be home then, and we can fill a box. You get the hat. I'll add a dress and wrap. You buy Duncan a hat and gloves. I'll send him a big overcoat, and we'll put in a lot of little stuff for the babies. Won't that be fun?"

Freckles fairly shivered with delight.

"That would be away too serious for fun," he said. "That would be heavenly. How long will it be?"

He began counting the time, and McLean deliberately set himself to encourage Freckles and keep his thoughts from the trouble of the past few days, for he had been overwrought and needed quiet and rest.

CHAPTER XV

WHEREIN FRECKLES AND THE ANGEL
TRY TAKING A PICTURE, AND LITTLE
CHICKEN FURNISHES THE SUBJECT

A week later everything at the Limberlost was precisely as it had been before the tragedy, except the case in Freckles' room now rested on the stump of the newly felled tree. Enough of the vines were left to cover it prettily, and every vestige of the havoc of a few days before was gone. New guards were patrolling the trail. Freckles was roughly laying off the swamp in sections and searching for marked trees. In that time he had found one deeply chipped and the chip cunningly replaced and tacked in. It promised to be quite rare, so he was jubilant. He also found so many subjects for the Bird Woman that her coming was of almost daily occurrence, and the hours he spent with her and the Angel were nothing less than golden.

The Limberlost was now arrayed as the Queen of Sheba in all her glory. The first frosts of autumn had bejewelled her crown in flashing topaz, ruby, and emerald. Around her feet trailed the purple of her garments, while in her hand was her golden scepter. Everything was at full tide. It seemed as if nothing could grow lovelier, and it was all standing still a few weeks, waiting coming destruction.

The swamp was palpitant with life. Every pair of birds that had flocked to it in the spring was now multiplied by from two to ten. The young were tame from Freckles' tri-parenthood, and so plump and sleek that they were quite as beautiful as their elders, even if in many cases they lacked their brilliant plumage. It was the same story of increase everywhere. There were chubby little ground-hogs scudding on the trail. There were cunning baby coons and opossums peeping from hollow logs and trees. Young muskrats followed their parents across the lagoons.

If you could come upon a family of foxes that had not yet disbanded, and see the young playing with a wild duck's carcass that their mother had brought, and note the pride and satisfaction in her eyes as she lay at one side guarding them, it would be a picture not to be forgotten. Freckles never tired of studying the devotion of a fox mother to her babies. To him, whose early life had been so embittered by continual proof of neglect and cruelty in human parents toward their children, the love of these furred and feathered folk of the Limberlost was even more of a miracle than to the Bird Woman and the Angel.

The Angel liked the baby rabbits and squirrels. Earlier in the season, when the young were yet very small, it so happened that at times Freckles could give into her hands one of these little ones. Then it was pure joy to stand back and watch her heaving breast, flushed cheek, and shining eyes. Hers were such lovely eyes. Freckles had discovered lately that they were not so dark as he had thought them at first, but that the length and thickness of lash, by which they were shaded, made them appear darker than they really were. They were forever changing. Now sparkling and darkling with wit, now humid with sympathy, now burning with the fire of courage, now taking on strength of color with ambition, now flashing indignantly at the abuse of any creature.

She had carried several of the squirrel and bunny babies home, and had littered the conservatory with them. Her care of them was perfect. She was learning her natural history from nature, and having much healthful exercise. To her, they were the most interesting of all, but the Bird Woman preferred the birds, with a close second in the moths and butterflies.

Brown butterfly time had come. The edge of the swale was filled with milkweed, and other plants beloved of them, and the air was golden with the flashing satin wings of the monarch, viceroy, and argynnis. They outnumbered those of any other color three to one.

Among the birds it really seemed as if the little yellow fellows were in the preponderance. At least, they were until the redwinged blackbirds and bobolinks, that had nested on the upland, suddenly saw in the swamp the garden of the Lord and came swarming by hundreds to feast and adventure upon it these last few weeks before migration. Never was there a finer feast spread for the birds. The grasses were filled with seeds: so, too, were weeds of every variety. Fall berries were ripe. Wild grapes and black haws were ready. Bugs were creeping everywhere. The muck was yeasty with worms. Insects filled the air. Nature made glorious pause for holiday before her next change, and by none of the frequenters of the swamp was this more appreciated than by the big black chickens.

They seemed to feel the new reign of peace and fullness most of all. As for food, they did not even have to hunt for themselves these days, for the feasts now being spread before Little Chicken were more than he could use, and he was glad to have his parents come down and help him.

He was a fine, big, overgrown fellow, and his wings, with quills of jetty black, gleaming with bronze, were so strong they almost lifted his body. He had three inches of tail, and his beak and claws were sharp. His muscles began to clamor for exercise. He raced the forty feet of his home back and forth many times every hour of the day. After a few days of that, he began lifting and spreading his wings, and flopping them until the down on his back was filled with elm fiber. Then he commenced jumping. The funny little hops, springs, and sidewise bounds he gave set Freckles and the Angel, hidden in the swamp, watching him, into smothered chuckles of delight.

Sometimes he fell to coquetting with himself; and that was the funniest thing of all, for he turned his head up, down, from side to side, and drew in his chin with prinky little jerks and tilts. He would stretch his neck, throw up his head, turn it to one side and smirk—actually smirk, the most complacent and self-satisfied smirk that anyone ever saw on the face of a bird. It was so comical that Freckles and the Angel told the Bird Woman of it one day.

When she finished her work on Little Chicken, she left them the camera ready for use, telling them they might hide in the bushes and watch. If Little Chicken came out and truly smirked, and they could squeeze the bulb at the proper moment to snap him, she would be more than delighted.

Freckles and the Angel quietly curled beside a big log, and with eager eyes and softest breathing they patiently waited; but Little Chicken had feasted before they told of his latest accomplishment. He was tired and sleepy, so he went into the log to bed, and for an hour he never stirred.

They were becoming anxious, for the light soon would be gone, and they had so wanted to try for the picture. At last Little Chicken lifted his head, opened his beak, and gaped widely. He dozed a minute or two more. The Angel said that was his beauty sleep. Then he lazily gaped again and stood up, stretching and yawning. He ambled leisurely toward the gateway, and the Angel said: "Now, we may have a chance, at last."

"I do hope so," shivered Freckles.

With one accord they arose to their knees and trained their eyes on the mouth of the log. The light was full and strong. Little Chicken prospected again with no results. He dressed his plumage, polished his beak, and when he felt fine and in full toilet he began to flirt with himself. Freckles' eyes snapped and his breath sucked between his clenched teeth.

"He's going to do it!" whispered the Angel. "That will come next. You'll best give me that bulb!"

"Yis," assented Freckles, but he was looking at the log and he made no move to relinquish the bulb.

Little Chicken nodded daintily and ruffled his feathers. He gave his head sundry little sidewise jerks and rapidly shifted his point of vision. Once there was the fleeting little ghost of a smirk.

"Now!—No!" snapped the Angel.

Freckles leaned toward the bird. Tensely he waited. Unconsciously the hand of the Angel clasped his. He scarcely knew it was there. Suddenly

Little Chicken sprang straight in the air and landed with a thud. The Angel started slightly, but Freckles was immovable. Then, as if in approval of his last performance, the big, overgrown baby wheeled until he was more than three-quarters, almost full side, toward the camera, straightened on his legs, squared his shoulders, stretched his neck full height, drew in his chin and smirked his most pronounced smirk, directly in the face of the lens.

Freckles' fingers closed on the bulb convulsively, and the Angel's closed on his at the instant. Then she heaved a great sigh of relief and lifted her hands to push back the damp, clustering hair from her face.

"How soon do you s'pose it will be finished?" came Freckles' strident whisper.

For the first time the Angel looked at him. He was on his knees, leaning forward, his eyes directed toward the bird, the perspiration running in little streams down his red, mosquito-bitten face. His hat was awry, his bright hair rampant, his breast heaving with excitement, while he yet gripped the bulb with every ounce of strength in his body.

"Do you think we were for getting it?" he asked.

The Angel could only nod. Freckles heaved a deep sigh of relief.

"Well, if that ain't the hardest work I ever did in me life!" he exclaimed. "It's no wonder the Bird Woman's for coming out of the swamp looking as if she's been through a fire, a flood, and a famine, if that's what she goes through day after day. But if you think we got it, why, it's worth all it took, and I'm glad as ever you are, sure!"

They put the holders in the case, carefully closed the camera, set it in also, and carried it to the road.

Then Freckles exulted.

"Now, let's be telling the Bird Woman about it!" he shouted, wildly dancing and swinging his hat.

"We got it! We got it! I bet a farm we got it!"

Hand in hand they ran to the north end of the swamp, yelling "We got it!" like young Comanches, and never gave a thought to what they might do until a big blue-gray bird, with long neck and trailing legs, arose on flapping wings and sailed over the Limberlost.

The Angel became white to the lips and gripped Freckles with both hands. He gulped with mortification and turned his back.

To frighten her subject away carelessly! It was the head crime in the Bird Woman's category. She extended her hands as she arose, baked, blistered, and dripping, and exclaimed: "Bless you, my children! Bless you!" And it truly sounded as if she meant it.

"Why, why——" stammered the bewildered Angel.

Freckles hurried into the breach.

"You must be for blaming it every bit on me. I was thinking we got Little Chicken's picture real good. I was so drunk with the joy of it I lost all me senses and, 'Let's run tell the Bird Woman,' says I. Like a fool I was for running, and I sort of dragged the Angel along."

"Oh Freckles!" expostulated the Angel. "Are you loony? Of course, it was all my fault! I've been with her hundreds of times. I knew perfectly well that I wasn't to let anything—NOT ANYTHING—scare her bird away! I was so crazy I forgot. The blame is all mine, and she'll never forgive me."

"She will, too!" cried Freckles. "Wasn't you for telling me that very first day that when people scared her birds away she just killed them! It's all me foolishness, and I'll never forgive meself!"

The Bird Woman plunged into the swale at the mouth of Sleepy Snake Creek, and came wading toward them, with a couple of cameras and dripping tripods.

"If you will permit me a word, my infants," she said, "I will explain to you that I have had three shots at that fellow."

The Angel heaved a deep sigh of relief, and Freckles' face cleared a little.

"Two of them," continued the Bird Woman, "in the rushes—one facing, crest lowered; one light on back, crest flared; and the last on wing, when you came up. I simply had been praying for something to make him arise from that side, so that he would fly toward the camera, for he had waded around until in my position I couldn't do it myself. See? Behold in yourselves the answer to the prayers of the long-suffering!"

Freckles took a step toward her.

"Are you really meaning that?" he asked wonderingly. "Only think, Angel, we did the right thing! She won't lose her picture through the carelessness of us, when she's waited and soaked nearly two hours. She's not angry with us!"

"Never was in a sweeter temper in my life," said the Bird Woman, busily cleaning and packing the cameras.

Freckles removed his hat and solemnly held out his hand. With equal solemnity the Angel grasped it. The Bird Woman laughed alone, for to them the situation had been too serious to develop any of the elements of fun.

Then they loaded the carriage, and the Bird Woman and the Angel started for their homes. It had been a difficult time for all of them, so they were very tired, but they were joyful. Freckles was so happy it seemed to him that life could hold little more. As the Bird Woman was ready to drive away he laid his hand on the lines and looked into her face.

"Do you suppose we got it?" he asked, so eagerly that she would have given much to be able to say yes with conviction.

"Why, my dear, I don't know," she said. "I've no way to judge. If you made the exposure just before you came to me, there was yet a fine light. If you waited until Little Chicken was close the entrance, you should have something good, even if you didn't catch just the fleeting expression for which you hoped. Of course, I can't say surely, but I think there is every reason to believe that you have it all right. I will develop the plate tonight, make you a proof from it early in the morning, and bring it when we come. It's only a question of a day or two now until the gang arrives. I want to work in all the studies I can before that time, for they are bound to disturb the birds. Mr. McLean will need you then, and I scarcely see how we are to do without you."

Moved by an impulse she never afterward regretted, she bent and laid her lips on Freckles' forehead, kissing him gently and thanking him for his many kindnesses to her in her loved work. Freckles started away so happy that he felt inclined to keep watching behind to see if the trail were not curling up and rolling down the line after him.

CHAPTER XVI

WHEREIN THE ANGEL LOCATES A RARE
TREE AND DINES WITH THE GANG

From afar Freckles saw them coming. The Angel was standing, waving her hat. He sprang on his wheel and raced, jolting and pounding, down the corduroy to meet them. The Bird Woman stopped the horse and the Angel gave him the bit of print paper. Freckles leaned the wheel against a tree and took the proof with eager fingers. He never before had seen a study from any of his chickens. He stood staring. When he turned his face toward them it was transfigured with delight.

"You see!" he exclaimed, and began gazing again. "Oh, me Little Chicken!" he cried. "Oh me ilegant Little Chicken! I'd be giving all me money in the bank for you!"

Then he thought of the Angel's muff and Mrs. Duncan's hat, and added, "or at least, all but what I'm needing bad for something else. Would you mind stopping at the cabin a minute and showing this to Mother Duncan?" he asked.

"Give me that little book in your pocket," said the Bird Woman.

She folded the outer edges of the proof so that it would fit into the book, explaining as she did so its perishable nature in that state. Freckles went hurrying ahead, and they arrived in time to see Mrs. Duncan gazing as if awestruck, and to hear her bewildered "Weel I be drawed on!"

Freckles and the Angel helped the Bird Woman to establish herself for a long day at the mouth of Sleepy Snake Creek. Then she sent them away and waited what luck would bring to her.

"Now, what shall we do?" inquired the Angel, who was a bundle of nerves and energy.

"Would you like to go to me room awhile?" asked Freckles.

"If you don't care to very much, I'd rather not," said the Angel. "I'll tell you. Let's go help Mrs. Duncan with dinner and play with the baby. I love a nice, clean baby."

They started toward the cabin. Every few minutes they stopped to investigate something or to chatter over some natural history wonder. The Angel had quick eyes; she seemed to see everything, but Freckles' were even quicker; for life itself had depended on their sharpness ever since the beginning of his work at the swamp. They saw it at the same time.

"Someone has been making a flagpole," said the Angel, running the toe of her shoe around the stump, evidently made that season. "Freckles, what would anyone cut a tree as small as that for?"

"I don't know," said Freckles.

"Well, but I want to know!" said the Angel. "No one came away here and cut it for fun. They've taken it away. Let's go back and see if we can see it anywhere around there."

She turned, retraced her footsteps, and began eagerly searching. Freckles did the same.

"There it is!" he exclaimed at last, "leaning against the trunk of that big maple."

"Yes, and leaning there has killed a patch of dried bark," said the Angel. "See how dried it appears?"

Freckles stared at her.

"Angel!" he shouted, "I bet you it's a marked tree!"

"Course it is!" cried the Angel. "No one would cut that sapling and carry it away there and lean it up for nothing. I'll tell you! This is one of Jack's marked trees. He's climbed up there above anyone's head, peeled the bark, and cut into the grain enough to be sure. Then he's laid the bark back and fastened it with that pole to mark it. You see, there're a lot of other big maples close around it. Can you climb to that place?"

"Yes," said Freckles; "if I take off my wading-boots I can."

"Then take them off," said the Angel, "and do hurry! Can't you see that I am almost crazy to know if this tree is a marked one?"

When they pushed the sapling over, a piece of bark as big as the crown of Freckles' hat fell away.

"I believe it looks kind of nubby," encouraged the Angel, backing away, with her face all screwed into a twist in an effort to intensify her vision.

Freckles reached the opening, then slid rapidly to the ground. He was almost breathless while his eyes were flashing.

"The bark's been cut clean with a knife, the sap scraped away, and a big chip taken out deep. The trunk is the twistiest thing you ever saw. It's full of eyes as a bird is of feathers!"

The Angel was dancing and shaking his hand.

"Oh, Freckles," she cried, "I'm so delighted that you found it!"

"But I didn't," said the astonished Freckles. "That tree isn't my find; it's yours. I forgot it and was going on; you wouldn't give up, and kept talking about it, and turned back. You found it!"

"You'd best be looking after your reputation for truth and veracity," said the Angel. "You know you saw that sapling first!"

"Yes, after you took me back and set me looking for it," scoffed Freckles.

The clear, ringing echo of strongly swung axes came crashing through the Limberlost.

"'Tis the gang!" shouted Freckles. "They're clearing a place to make the camp. Let's go help!"

"Hadn't we better mark that tree again?" cautioned the Angel. "It's away in here. There's such a lot of them, and all so much alike. We'd feel good and green to find it and then lose it."

Freckles lifted the sapling to replace it, but the Angel motioned him away.

"Use your hatchet," she said. "I predict this is the most valuable tree in the swamp. You found it. I'm going to play that you're my knight. Now, you nail my colors on it."

She reached up, and pulling a blue bow from her hair, untied and doubled it against the tree. Freckles turned his eyes from her and managed the fastening with shaking fingers. The Angel had called him her knight! Dear Lord, how he loved her! She must not see his face, or surely her quick eyes would read what he was fighting to hide. He did not dare lay his lips on that ribbon then, but that night he would return to it. When they had gone a little distance, they both looked back, and the morning breeze set the bit of blue waving them a farewell.

They walked at a rapid pace.

"I am sorry about scaring the birds," said the Angel, "but it's almost time for them to go anyway. I feel dreadfully over having the swamp ruined, but isn't it a delight to hear the good, honest ring of those axes, instead of straining your ears for stealthy sounds? Isn't it fine to go openly and freely, with nothing worse than a snake or a poison-vine to fear?"

"Ah!" said Freckles, with a long breath, "it's better than you can dream, Angel. Nobody will ever be guessing some of the things I've been through trying to keep me promise to the Boss, and to hold out until this day. That it's come with only one fresh stump, and the log from that saved, and this new tree to report, isn't it grand? Maybe Mr. McLean will be forgetting that stump when he sees this tree, Angel!"

"He can't forget it," said the Angel; and in answer to Freckles' startled eyes she added, "because he never had any reason to remember it. He couldn't have done a whit better himself. My father says so. You're all right, Freckles!"

She reached him her hand, and as two children, they broke into a run when they came closer the gang. They left the swamp by the west road and followed the trail until they found the men. To the Angel it seemed complete charm. In the shadiest spot on the west side of the line, at the edge of the swamp and very close Freckles' room, they were cutting bushes and clearing space for a big tent for the men's sleeping-quarters, another for a dining-hall, and a board shack for the cook. The teamsters were unloading, the horses were cropping leaves from the bushes, while each man was doing his part toward the construction of the new Limberlost quarters.

Freckles helped the Angel climb on a wagonload of canvas in the shade. She removed her leggings, wiped her heated face, and glowed with happiness and interest.

The gang had been sifted carefully. McLean now felt that there was not a man in it who was not trustworthy.

They all had heard of the Angel's plucky ride for Freckles' relief; several of them had been in the rescue party. Others, new since that time, had heard the tale rehearsed in its every aspect around the smudge-fires at night. Almost all of them knew the Angel by sight from her trips with the Bird Woman to their leases. They all knew her father, her position, and the luxuries of her home. Whatever course she had chosen with them they scarcely would have resented it, but the Angel never had been known to choose a course. Her spirit of friendliness was inborn and inbred. She loved everyone, so she sympathized with everyone. Her generosity was only limited by what was in her power to give.

She came down the trail, hand in hand with the red-haired, freckled timber guard whom she had worn herself past the limit of endurance to save only a few weeks before, racing in her eagerness to reach them, and laughing her "Good morning, gentlemen," right and left. When she was ensconced on the wagonload of tenting, she sat on a roll of canvas as a queen on her throne. There was not a man of the gang who did not respect her. She was a living exponent of universal brotherhood. There was no man among them who needed her exquisite face or dainty clothing to teach him that the deference due a gentlewoman should be paid her. That the spirit of good fellowship she radiated levied an especial tribute of its own, and it became their delight to honor and please her.

As they raced toward the wagon—"Let me tell about the tree, please?" she begged Freckles.

"Why, sure!" said Freckles.

He probably would have said the same to anything she suggested. When McLean came, he found the Angel flushed and glowing, sitting on the wagon, her hands already filled. One of the men, who was cutting a scrub-oak, had carried to her a handful of crimson leaves. Another had gathered a bunch of delicate marsh-grass heads for her. Someone else, in taking out a bush, had found a daintily built and lined little nest, fresh as when made.

She held up her treasures and greeted McLean, "Good morning, Mr. Boss of the Limberlost!"

The gang shouted, while he bowed profoundly before her.

"Everyone listen!" cried the Angel, climbing a roll of canvas. "I have something to say! Freckles has been guarding here over a year now, and he presents the Limberlost to you, with every tree in it saved; for good measure he has this morning located the rarest one of them all: the one in from the east line, that Wessner spoke of the first day—nearest the one you took out. All together! Everyone! Hurrah for Freckles!"

With flushing cheeks and gleaming eyes, gaily waving the grass above her head, she led in three cheers and a tiger. Freckles slipped into the swamp and hid himself, for fear he could not conceal his pride and his great surging, throbbing love for her.

The Angel subsided on the canvas and explained to McLean about the maple. The Boss was mightily pleased. He took Freckles and set out to re-locate and examine the tree. The Angel was interested in the making of the camp, so she preferred to remain with the men. With her sharp eyes she was watching every detail of construction; but when it came to the stretching of the dining-hall canvas she proceeded to take command. The men were driving the rope-pins, when the Angel arose on the wagon and, leaning forward, spoke to Duncan, who was directing the work.

"I believe if you will swing that around a few feet farther, you will find it better, Mr. Duncan," she said. "That way will let the hot sun in at noon, while the sides will cut off the best breeze."

"That's a fact," said Duncan, studying the conditions.

So, by shifting the pins a little, they obtained comfort for which they blessed the Angel every day. When they came to the sleeping-tent, they consulted her about that. She explained the general direction of the night breeze and indicated the best position for the tent. Before anyone knew how it happened, the Angel was standing on the wagon, directing the location and construction of the cooking-shack, the erection of the crane for the big boiling-pots, and the building of the store-room. She superintended the laying of the floor of the sleeping-tent lengthwise, so that it would be easier to sweep, and suggested a new arrangement of the cots that would afford all the men an equal share of night breeze. She left the wagon, and climbing on the newly erected dining-table, advised with the cook in placing his stove, table, and kitchen utensils.

When Freckles returned from the tree to join in the work around the camp, he caught glimpses of her enthroned on a soapbox, cleaning beans. She called to him that they were invited for dinner, and that they had accepted the invitation.

When the beans were steaming in the pot, the Angel advised the cook to soak them overnight the next time, so that they would cook more quickly and not burst. She was sure their cook at home did that way, and the CHEF of the gang thought it would be a good idea. The next Freckles saw of her she was paring potatoes. A little later she arranged the table.

She swept it with a broom, instead of laying a cloth; took the hatchet and hammered the deepest dents from the tin plates, and nearly skinned her fingers scouring the tinware with rushes. She set the plates an even distance apart, and laid the forks and spoons beside them. When the cook threw away half a dozen fruit-cans, she gathered them up and melted off the tops, although she almost blistered her face and quite blistered her fingers doing it. Then she neatly covered these improvised vases with the Manila paper from the groceries, tying it with wisps of marshgrass. These she filled with fringed gentians, blazing-star, asters, goldenrod, and ferns, placing them the length of the dining-table. In one of the end cans she arranged her red leaves, and in the other the fancy grass. Two men, watching her, went away proud of themselves and said that she was "a born lady." She laughingly caught up a paper bag and fitted it jauntily to her head in imitation of a cook's cap. Then she ground the coffee, and beat a couple of eggs to put in, "because there is company," she gravely explained to the cook. She asked that delighted individual if he did not like it best that way, and he said he did not know, because he never had a chance to taste it. The Angel said that was her case exactly—she never had, either; she was not allowed anything stronger than milk. Then they laughed together.

She told the cook about camping with her father, and explained that he made his coffee that way. When the steam began to rise from the big boiler, she stuffed the spout tightly with clean marshgrass, to keep the aroma in, placed the boiler where it would only simmer, and explained why. The influence of the Angel's visit lingered with the cook through the remainder of his life, while the men prayed for her frequent return.

She was having a happy time, when McLean came back jubilant, from his trip to the tree. How jubilant he told only the Angel, for he had been obliged to lose faith in some trusted men of late, and had learned discretion by what he suffered. He planned to begin clearing out a road to the tree that same afternoon, and to set two guards every night, for it promised to be a rare treasure, so he was eager to see it on the way to the mills.

"I am coming to see it felled," cried the Angel. "I feel a sort of motherly interest in that tree."

McLean was highly amused. He would have staked his life on the honesty of either the Angel or Freckles; yet their versions of the finding of the tree differed widely.

"Tell me, Angel," the Boss said jestingly. "I think I have a right to know. Who really did locate that tree?"

"Freckles," she answered promptly and emphatically.

"But he says quite as positively that it was you. I don't understand."

The Angel's legal look flashed into her face. Her eyes grew tense with earnestness. She glanced around, and seeing no towel or basin, held out her hand for Sears to pour water over them. Then, using the skirt of her dress to dry them, she climbed on the wagon.

"I'll tell you, word for word, how it happened," she said, "and then you shall decide, and Freckles and I will agree with you."

When she had finished her version, "Tell us, 'oh, most learned judge!'" she laughingly quoted, "which of us located that tree?"

"Blest if I know who located it!" exclaimed McLean. "But I have a fairly accurate idea as to who put the blue ribbon on it."

The Boss smiled significantly at Freckles, who just had come, for they had planned that they would instruct the company to reserve enough of the veneer from that very tree to make the most beautiful dressing table they could design for the Angel's share of the discovery.

"What will you have for yours?" McLean had asked of Freckles.

"If it's all the same to you, I'll be taking mine out in music lessons— begging your pardon—voice culture," said Freckles with a grimace.

McLean laughed, for Freckles needed to see or hear only once to absorb learning as the thirsty earth sucks up water.

The Angel placed McLean at the head of the table. She took the foot, with Freckles on her right, while the lumber gang, washed, brushed, and straightened until they felt unfamiliar with themselves and each other, filled the sides. That imposed a slight constraint. Then, too, the men were afraid of the flowers, the polished tableware, and above all, of the dainty grace of the Angel. Nowhere do men so display lack of good breeding and culture as in dining. To sprawl on the table, scoop with their knives, chew loudly, gulp coffee, and duck their heads as snapping-turtles for every bite, had not been noticed by them until the Angel, sitting straightly, suddenly made them remember that they, too, were possessed of spines. Instinctively every man at the table straightened.

CHAPTER XVII

WHEREIN FRECKLES OFFERS HIS LIFE
FOR HIS LOVE AND GETS A BROKEN
BODY

To reach the tree was a more difficult task than McLean had supposed. The gang could approach nearest on the outside toward the east, but after they reached the end of the east entrance there was yet a mile of most impenetrable thicket, trees big and little, and bushes of every variety and stage of growth. In many places the muck had to be filled to give the horses and wagons a solid foundation over which to haul heavy loads. It was several days before they completed a road to the noble, big tree and were ready to fell it.

When the sawing began, Freckles was watching down the road where it met the trail leading from Little Chicken's tree. He had gone to the tree ahead of the gang to remove the blue ribbon. Carefully folded, it now lay over his heart. He was promising himself much comfort with that ribbon, when he would leave for the city next month to begin his studies and dream the summer over again. It would help to make things tangible. When he was dressed as other men, and at his work, he knew where he meant to home that precious bit of blue. It should be his good-luck token, and he would wear it always to keep bright in memory the day on which the Angel had called him her knight.

How he would study, and oh, how he would sing! If only he could fulfill McLean's expectations, and make the Angel proud of him! If only he could be a real knight!

He could not understand why the Angel had failed to come. She had wanted to see their tree felled. She would be too late if she did not arrive soon. He had told her it would be ready that morning, and she had said she surely would be there. Why, of all mornings, was she late on this?

McLean had ridden to town. If he had been there, Freckles would have asked that they delay the felling, but he scarcely liked to ask the gang. He really had no authority, although he thought the men would wait; but some way he found such embarrassment in framing the request that he waited until the work was practically ended. The saw was out, and the men were cutting into the felling side of the tree when the Boss rode in.

His first word was to inquire for the Angel. When Freckles said she had not yet come, the Boss at once gave orders to stop work on the tree until she arrived; for he felt that she virtually had located it, and if she desired to see it felled, she should. As the men stepped back, a stiff morning breeze caught the top, that towered high above its fellows. There was an ominous grinding at the base, a shiver of the mighty trunk, then directly in line of its fall the bushes swung apart and the laughing face of the Angel looked on them.

A groan of horror burst from the dry throats of the men, and reading the agony in their faces, she stopped short, glanced up, and understood.

"South!" shouted McLean. "Run south!"

The Angel was helpless. It was apparent that she did not know which way south was. There was another slow shiver of the big tree. The remainder of the gang stood motionless, but Freckles sprang past the trunk and went leaping in big bounds. He caught up the Angel and dashed through the thicket for safety. The swaying trunk was half over when, for an instant, a near-by tree stayed its fall. They saw Freckles' foot catch, and with the Angel he plunged headlong.

A terrible cry broke from the men, while McLean covered his face. Instantly Freckles was up, with the Angel in his arms, struggling on. The outer limbs were on them when they saw Freckles hurl the Angel, face down, in the muck, as far from him as he could send her. Springing after, in an attempt to cover her body with his own, he whirled to see if they were yet in danger, and with outstretched arms braced himself for the shock. The branches shut them from sight, and the awful crash rocked the earth.

McLean and Duncan ran with axes and saws. The remainder of the gang followed, and they worked desperately. It seemed a long time before they caught a glimpse of the Angel's blue dress, but it renewed their vigor. Duncan fell on his knees beside her and tore the muck from underneath her with his hands. In a few seconds he dragged her out, choking and stunned, but surely not fatally hurt.

Freckles lay a little farther under the tree, a big limb pinning him down. His eyes were wide open. He was perfectly conscious. Duncan began mining beneath him, but Freckles stopped him.

"You can't be moving me," he said. "You must cut off the limb and lift it. I know."

Two men ran for the big saw. A number of them laid hold of the limb and bore up. In a short time it was removed, and Freckles lay free.

The men bent over to lift him, but he motioned them away.

"Don't be touching me until I rest a bit," he pleaded.

Then he twisted his head until he saw the Angel, who was wiping muck from her eyes and face on the skirt of her dress.

"Try to get up," he begged.

McLean laid hold of the Angel and helped her to her feet.

"Do you think any bones are broken?" gasped Freckles.

The Angel shook her head and wiped muck.

"You see if you can find any, sir," Freckles commanded.

The Angel yielded herself to McLean's touch, and he assured Freckles that she was not seriously injured.

Freckles settled back, a smile of ineffable tenderness on his face.

"Thank the Lord!" he hoarsely whispered.

The Angel leaned toward him.

"Now, Freckles, you!" she cried. "It's your turn. Please get up!"

A pitiful spasm swept Freckles' face. The sight of it washed every vestige of color from the Angel's. She took hold of his hands.

"Freckles, get up!" It was half command, half entreaty.

"Easy, Angel, easy! Let me rest a bit first!" implored Freckles.

She knelt beside him. He reached his arm around her and drew her closely. He looked at McLean in an agony of entreaty that brought the Boss to his knees on the other side.

"Oh, Freckles!" McLean cried. "Not that! Surely we can do something! We must! Let me see!"

He tried to unfasten Freckles' neckband, but his fingers shook so clumsily that the Angel pushed them away and herself laid Freckles' chest bare. With one hasty glance she gathered the clothing together and slipped her arm under his head. Freckles lifted his eyes of agony to hers.

"You see?" he said.

The Angel nodded dumbly.

Freckles turned to McLean.

"Thank you for everything," he panted. "Where are the boys?"

"They are all here," said the Boss, "except a couple who have gone for doctors, Mrs. Duncan and the Bird Woman."

"It's no use trying to do anything," said Freckles. "You won't forget the muff and the Christmas box. The muff especial?"

There was a movement above them so pronounced that it attracted Freckles' attention, even in that extreme hour. He looked up, and a pleased smile flickered on his drawn face.

"Why, if it ain't me Little Chicken!" he cried hoarsely. "He must be making his very first trip from the log. Now Duncan can have his big watering-trough."

"It was Little Chicken that made me late," faltered the Angel. "I was so anxious to get here early I forgot to bring his breakfast from the carriage. He must have been hungry, for when I passed the log he started after me. He was so wabbly, and so slow flying from tree to tree and through the bushes, I just had to wait on him, for I couldn't drive him back."

"Of course you couldn't! Me bird has too amazing good sinse to go back when he could be following you," exulted Freckles, exactly as if he did not realize what the delay had cost him. Then he lay silently thinking, but presently he asked slowly: "And so 'twas me Little Chicken that was making you late, Angel?"

"Yes," said the Angel.

A spasm of fierce pain shook Freckles, and a look of uncertainty crossed his face.

"All summer I've been thanking God for the falling of the feather and all the delights it's brought me," he muttered, "but this looks as if——"

He stopped short and raised questioning eyes to McLean.

"I can't help being Irish, but I can help being superstitious," he said. "I mustn't be laying it to the Almighty, or to me bird, must I?"

"No, dear lad," said McLean, stroking the brilliant hair. "The choice lay with you. You could have stood a rooted dolt like all the remainder of us. It was through your great love and your high courage that you made the sacrifice."

"Don't you be so naming it, sir!" cried Freckles. "It's just the reverse. If I could be giving me body the hundred times over to save hers from this, I'd be doing it and take joy with every pain."

He turned with a smile of adoring tenderness to the Angel. She was ghastly white, and her eyes were dull and glazed. She scarcely seemed to hear or understand what was coming, but she bravely tried to answer that smile.

"Is my forehead covered with dirt?" he asked.

She shook her head.

"You did once," he gasped.

Instantly she laid her lips on his forehead, then on each cheek, and then in a long kiss on his lips.

McLean bent over him.

"Freckles," he said brokenly, "you will never know how I love you. You won't go without saying good-bye to me?"

That word stung the Angel to quick comprehension. She started as if arousing from sleep.

"Good-bye?" she cried sharply, her eyes widening and the color rushing into her white face. "Good-bye! Why, what do you mean? Who's saying good-bye? Where could Freckles go, when he is hurt like this, save to the hospital? You needn't say good-bye for that. Of course, we will all go with him! You call up the men. We must start right away."

"It's no use, Angel," said Freckles. "I'm thinking ivry bone in me breast is smashed. You'll have to be letting me go!"

"I will not," said the Angel flatly. "It's no use wasting precious time talking about it. You are alive. You are breathing; and no matter how badly your bones are broken, what are great surgeons for but to fix you up and make you well again? You promise me that you'll just grit your teeth and hang on when we hurt you, for we must start with you as quickly as it can be done. I don't know what has been the matter with me. Here's good time wasted already."

"Oh, Angel!" moaned Freckles, "I can't! You don't know how bad it is. I'll die the minute you are for trying to lift me!"

"Of course you will, if you make up your mind to do it," said the Angel. "But if you are determined you won't, and set yourself to breathing deep and strong, and hang on to me tight, I can get you out. Really you must, Freckles, no matter how it hurts, for you did this for me, and now I must save you, so you might as well promise."

She bent over him, trying to smile encouragement with her fear-stiffened lips.

"You will promise, Freckles?"

Big drops of cold sweat ran together on Freckles' temples.

"Angel, darlin' Angel," he pleaded, taking her hand in his. "You ain't understanding, and I can't for the life of me be telling you, but indade, it's best to be letting me go. This is my chance. Please say good-bye, and let me slip off quick!"

He appealed to McLean.

"Dear Boss, you know! You be telling her that, for me, living is far worse pain than dying. Tell her you know death is the best thing that could ever be happening to me!"

"Merciful Heaven!" burst in the Angel. "I can't endure this delay!"

She caught Freckles' hand to her breast, and bending over him, looked deeply into his stricken eyes.

"'Angel, I give you my word of honor that I will keep right on breathing.' That's what you are going to promise me," she said. "Do you say it?"

Freckles hesitated.

"Freckles!" imploringly commanded the Angel, "YOU DO SAY IT!"

"Yis," gasped Freckles.

The Angel sprang to her feet.

"Then that's all right," she said, with a tinge of her old-time briskness. "You just keep breathing away like a steam engine, and I will do all the remainder."

The eager men gathered around her.

"It's going to be a tough pull to get Freckles out," she said, "but it's our only chance, so listen closely and don't for the lives of you fail me in doing quickly what I tell you. There's no time to spend falling down over each other; we must have some system. You four there get on those wagon horses and ride to the sleeping-tent. Get the stoutest cot, a couple of comforts, and a pillow. Ride back with them some way to save time. If you meet any other men of the gang, send them here to help carry the cot. We won't risk the jolt of driving with him. The others clear a path out to the road; and Mr. McLean, you take Nellie and ride to town. Tell my father how Freckles is hurt and that he risked it to save me. Tell him I'm going to take Freckles to Chicago on the noon train, and I want him to hold it if we are a little late. If he can't, then have a special ready at the station and another on the Pittsburgh at Fort Wayne, so we can go straight through. You needn't mind leaving us. The Bird Woman will be here soon. We will rest awhile."

She dropped into the muck beside Freckles and began stroking his hair and hand. He lay with his face of agony turned to hers, and fought to smother the groans that would tell her what he was suffering.

When they stood ready to lift him, the Angel bent over him in a passion of tenderness.

"Dear old Limberlost guard, we're going to lift you now," she said. "I suspect you will faint from the pain of it, but we will be as easy as ever we can, and don't you dare forget your promise!"

A whimsical half-smile touched Freckles' quivering lips.

"Angel, can a man be remembering a promise when he ain't knowing?" he asked.

"You can," said the Angel stoutly, "because a promise means so much more to you than it does to most men."

A look of strength flashed into Freckles' face at her words.

"I am ready," he said.

With the first touch his eyes closed, a mighty groan was wrenched from him, and he lay senseless. The Angel gave Duncan one panic-stricken look. Then she set her lips and gathered her forces again.

"I guess that's a good thing," she said. "Maybe he won't feel how we are hurting him. Oh boys, are you being quick and gentle?"

She stepped to the side of the cot and bathed Freckles' face. Taking his hand in hers, she gave the word to start. She told the men to ask every able-bodied man they met to join them so that they could change carriers often and make good time.

The Bird Woman insisted upon taking the Angel into the carriage and following the cot, but she refused to leave Freckles, and suggested that the Bird Woman drive ahead, pack them some clothing, and be at the station ready to accompany them to Chicago. All the way the Angel walked beside the cot, shading Freckles' face with a branch, and holding his hand. At every pause to change carriers she moistened his face and lips and watched each breath with heart-breaking anxiety.

She scarcely knew when her father joined them, and taking the branch from her, slipped an arm around her waist and almost carried her. To the city streets and the swarm of curious, staring faces she paid no more attention than she had to the trees of the Limberlost. When the train came and the gang placed Freckles aboard, big Duncan made a place for the Angel beside the cot.

With the best physician to be found, and with the Bird Woman and McLean in attendance, the four-hours' run to Chicago began. The Angel constantly watched over Freckles; bathed his face, stroked his hand, and gently fanned him. Not for an instant would she yield her place, or allow anyone else to do anything for him. The Bird Woman and McLean regarded her in amazement. There seemed to be no end to her resources and courage. The only time she spoke was to ask McLean if he were sure the special would be ready on the Pittsburgh road. He replied that it was made up and waiting.

At five o'clock Freckles lay stretched on the operating-table of Lake View Hospital, while three of the greatest surgeons in Chicago bent over him. At their command, McLean picked up the unwilling Angel and carried her to the nurses to be bathed, have her bruises attended, and to be put to bed.

In a place where it is difficult to surprise people, they were astonished women as they removed the Angel's dainty stained and torn clothing, drew off hose muck-baked to her limbs, soaked the dried loam from her silken hair, and washed the beautiful scratched, bruised, dirt-covered body. The Angel fell fast asleep long before they had finished, and lay deeply unconscious, while the fight for Freckles' life was being waged.

Three days later she was the same Angel as of old, except that Freckles was constantly in her thoughts. The anxiety and responsibility that she felt for his condition had bred in her a touch of womanliness and authority that was new. That morning she arose early and hovered near Freckles' door. She had been allowed to remain with him constantly, for the nurses and surgeons had learned, with his returning consciousness, that for her alone would the active, highly strung, pain-racked sufferer be quiet and obey orders. When she was dropping from loss of sleep, the threat that she would fall ill had to be used to send her to bed. Then by telling Freckles that the Angel was asleep and they would waken her the moment he moved, they were able to control him for a short time.

The surgeon was with Freckles. The Angel had been told that the word he brought that morning would be final, so she curled in a window seat, dropped the curtains behind her, and in dire anxiety, waited the opening of the door.

Just as it unclosed, McLean came hurrying down the hall and to the surgeon, but with one glance at his face he stepped back in dismay; while the Angel, who had arisen, sank to the seat again, too dazed to come forward. The men faced each other. The Angel, with parted lips and frightened eyes, bent forward in tense anxiety.

"I—I thought he was doing nicely?" faltered McLean.

"He bore the operation well," replied the surgeon, "and his wounds are not necessarily fatal. I told you that yesterday, but I did not tell you that something else probably would kill him; and it will. He need not die from the accident, but he will not live the day out."

"But why? What is it?" asked McLean hurriedly. "We all dearly love the boy. We have millions among us to do anything that money can accomplish. Why must he die, if those broken bones are not the cause?"

"That is what I am going to give you the opportunity to tell me," replied the surgeon. "He need not die from the accident, yet he is dying as fast as his splendid physical condition will permit, and it is because he so evidently prefers death to life. If he were full of hope and ambition to live, my work would be easy. If all of you love him as you prove you do, and there is unlimited means to give him anything he wants, why should he desire death?"

"Is he dying?" demanded McLean.

"He is," said the surgeon. "He will not live this day out, unless some strong reaction sets in at once. He is so low, that preferring death to life, nature cannot overcome his inertia. If he is to live, he must be made to desire life. Now he undoubtedly wishes for death, and that it come quickly."

"Then he must die," said McLean.

His broad shoulders shook convulsively. His strong hands opened and closed mechanically.

"Does that mean that you know what he desires and cannot, or will not, supply it?"

McLean groaned in misery.

"It means," he said desperately, "that I know what he wants, but it is as far removed from my power to help him as it would be to give him a star. The thing for which he will die, he can never have."

"Then you must prepare for the end very shortly" said the surgeon, turning abruptly away.

McLean caught his arm roughly.

"You look here!" he cried in desperation. "You say that as if I could do something if I would. I tell you the boy is dear to me past expression. I would do anything—spend any sum. You have noticed and repeatedly commented on the young girl with me. It is that child that he wants! He worships her to adoration, and knowing he can never be anything to her, he prefers death to life. In God's name, what can I do about it?"

"Barring that missing hand, I never examined a finer man," said the surgeon, "and she seemed perfectly devoted to him; why cannot he have her?"

"Why?" echoed McLean. "Why? Well, for many reasons! I told you he was my son. You probably knew that he was not. A little over a year ago I never had seen him. He joined one of my lumber gangs from the road. He is a stray, left at one of your homes for the friendless here in Chicago. When he grew up the superintendent bound him to a brutal man. He ran away and landed in one of my lumber camps. He has no name or knowledge of legal birth. The Angel—we have talked of her. You see what she is, physically and mentally. She has ancestors reaching back to Plymouth Rock, and across the sea for generations before that. She is an idolized, petted only child, and there is great wealth. Life holds everything for her, nothing for him. He sees it more plainly than anyone else could. There is nothing for the boy but death, if it is the Angel that is required to save him."

The Angel stood between them.

"Well, I just guess not!" she cried. "If Freckles wants me, all he has to do is to say so, and he can have me!"

The amazed men stepped back, staring at her.

"That he will never say," said McLean at last, "and you don't understand, Angel. I don't know how you came here. I wouldn't have had you hear that for the world, but since you have, dear girl, you must be told that it isn't your friendship or your kindness Freckles wants; it is your love."

The Angel looked straight into the great surgeon's eyes with her clear, steady orbs of blue, and then into McLean's with unwavering frankness.

"Well, I do love him," she said simply.

McLean's arms dropped helplessly.

"You don't understand," he reiterated patiently. "It isn't the love of a friend, or a comrade, or a sister, that Freckles wants from you; it is the love of a sweetheart. And if to save the life he has offered for you, you are thinking of being generous and impulsive enough to sacrifice your future—in the absence of your father, it will become my plain duty, as the protector in whose hands he has placed you, to prevent such rashness. The very words you speak, and the manner in which you say them, prove that you are a mere child, and have not dreamed what love is."

Then the Angel grew splendid. A rosy flush swept the pallor of fear from her face. Her big eyes widened and dilated with intense lights. She seemed to leap to the height and the dignity of superb womanhood before their wondering gaze.

"I never have had to dream of love," she said proudly. "I never have known anything else, in all my life, but to love everyone and to have everyone love me. And there never has been anyone so dear as Freckles. If you will remember, we have been through a good deal together. I do love Freckles, just as I say I do. I don't know anything about the love of sweethearts, but I love him with all the love in my heart, and I think that will satisfy him."

"Surely it should!" muttered the man of knives and lancets.

McLean reached to take hold of the Angel, but she saw the movement and swiftly stepped back.

"As for my father," she continued, "he at once told me what he learned from you about Freckles. I've known all you know for several weeks. That knowledge didn't change your love for him a particle. I think the Bird Woman loved him more. Why should you two have all the fine perceptions there are? Can't I see how brave, trustworthy, and splendid he is? Can't I see how his soul vibrates with his music, his love of beautiful things and the pangs of loneliness and heart hunger? Must you two love him with all the love there is, and I give him none? My father is never unreasonable. He won't expect me not to love Freckles, or not to tell him so, if the telling will save him."

She darted past McLean into Freckles' room, closed the door, and turned the key.

CHAPTER XVIII

WHEREIN FRECKLES REFUSES LOVE
WITHOUT KNOWLEDGE OF
HONORABLE BIRTH, AND THE ANGEL
GOES IN QUEST OF IT

Freckles lay on a flat pillow, his body immovable in a plaster cast, his maimed arm, as always, hidden. His greedy gaze fastened at once on the Angel's face. She crossed to him with light step and bent over him with infinite tenderness. Her heart ached at the change in his appearance. He seemed so weak, heart hungry, so utterly hopeless, so alone. She could see that the night had been one long terror.

For the first time she tried putting herself in Freckles' place. What would it mean to have no parents, no home, no name? No name! That was the worst of all. That was to be lost—indeed—utterly and hopelessly lost. The Angel lifted her hands to her dazed head and reeled, as she tried to face that proposition. She dropped on her knees beside the bed, slipped her arm under the pillow, and leaning over Freckles, set her lips on his forehead. He smiled faintly, but his wistful face appeared worse for it. It hurt the Angel to the heart.

"Dear Freckles," she said, "there is a story in your eyes this morning, tell me?"

Freckles drew a long, wavering breath.

"Angel," he begged, "be generous! Be thinking of me a little. I'm so homesick and worn out, dear Angel, be giving me back me promise. Let me go?"

"Why Freckles!" faltered the Angel. "You don't know what you are asking. 'Let you go!' I cannot! I love you better than anyone, Freckles. I think you are the very finest person I ever knew. I have our lives all planned. I want you to be educated and learn all there is to know about singing, just as soon as you are well enough. By the time you have completed your education I will have finished college, and then I want," she choked a second, "I want you to be my real knight, Freckles, and come to me and tell me that you—like me—a little. I have been counting on you for my sweetheart from the very first, Freckles. I can't give you up, unless you don't like me. But you do like me—just a little—don't you, Freckles?"

Freckles lay whiter than the coverlet, his staring eyes on the ceiling and his breath wheezing between dry lips. The Angel awaited his answer a second, and when none came, she dropped her crimsoning face beside him on the pillow and whispered in his ear:

"Freckles, I—I'm trying to make love to you. Oh, can't you help me only a little bit? It's awful hard all alone! I don't know how, when I really mean it, but Freckles, I love you. I must have you, and now I guess—I guess maybe I'd better kiss you next."

She lifted her shamed face and bravely laid her feverish, quivering lips on his. Her breath, like clover-bloom, was in his nostrils, and her hair touched his face. Then she looked into his eyes with reproach.

"Freckles," she panted, "Freckles! I didn't think it was in you to be mean!"

"Mean, Angel! Mean to you?" gasped Freckles.

"Yes," said the Angel. "Downright mean. When I kiss you, if you had any mercy at all you'd kiss back, just a little bit."

Freckles' sinewy fist knotted into the coverlet. His chin pointed ceilingward while his head rocked on the pillow.

"Oh, Jesus!" burst from him in agony. "You ain't the only one that was crucified!"

The Angel caught Freckles' hand and carried it to her breast.

"Freckles!" she wailed in terror, "Freckles! It is a mistake? Is it that you don't want me?"

Freckles' head rolled on in wordless suffering.

"Wait a bit, Angel?" he panted at last. "Be giving me a little time!"

The Angel arose with controlled features. She bathed his face, straightened his hair, and held water to his lips. It seemed a long time before he reached toward her. Instantly she knelt again, carried his hand to her breast, and leaned her cheek upon it.

"Tell me, Freckles," she whispered softly.

"If I can," said Freckles in agony. "It's just this. Angels are from above. Outcasts are from below. You've a sound body and you're beautifulest of all. You have everything that loving, careful raising and money can give you. I have so much less than nothing that I don't suppose I had any right to be born. It's a sure thing—nobody wanted me afterward, so of course, they didn't before. Some of them should have been telling you long ago."

"If that's all you have to say, Freckles, I've known that quite a while," said the Angel stoutly. "Mr. McLean told my father, and he told me. That only makes me love you more, to pay for all you've missed."

"Then I'm wondering at you," said Freckles in a voice of awe. "Can't you see that if you were willing and your father would come and offer you to me, I couldn't be touching the soles of your feet, in love—me, whose people brawled over me, cut off me hand, and throwed me away to freeze and to die! Me, who has no name just as much because I've no RIGHT to any, as because I don't know it. When I was little, I planned to find me father and mother when I grew up. Now I know me mother deserted me, and me father was maybe a thief and surely a liar. The pity for me suffering and the watching over me have gone to your head, dear Angel, and it's me must be thinking for you. If you could be forgetting me lost hand, where I was raised, and that I had no name to give you, and if you would be taking me as I am, some day people such as mine must be, might come upon you. I used to pray ivery night and morning and many times the day to see me mother. Now I only pray to die quickly and never risk the sight of her. 'Tain't no ways possible, Angel! It's a wildness of your dear head. Oh, do for mercy sake, kiss me once more and be letting me go!"

"Not for a minute!" cried the Angel. "Not for a minute, if those are all the reasons you have. It's you who are wild in your head, but I can understand just how it happened. Being shut in that Home most of your life, and seeing children every day whose parents did neglect and desert them, makes you sure yours did the same; and yet there are so many other things that could have happened so much more easily than that. There are thousands of young couples who come to this country and start a family with none of their relatives here. Chicago is a big, wicked city, and grown people could disappear in many ways, and who would there ever be to find to whom their little children belonged? The minute my father told me how you felt, I began to study this thing over, and I've made up my mind you are dead wrong. I meant to ask my father or the Bird Woman to talk to you before you went away to school, but as matters are right now I guess I'll just do it myself. It's all so plain to me. Oh, if I could only make you see!"

She buried her face in the pillow and presently lifted it, transfigured.

"Now I have it!" she cried. "Oh, dear heart! I can make it so plain! Freckles, can you imagine you see the old Limberlost trail? Well when we followed it, you know there were places where ugly, prickly thistles overgrew the path, and you went ahead with your club and bent them back to keep them from stinging through my clothing. Other places there were big shining pools where lovely, snow-white lilies grew, and you waded in and gathered them for me. Oh dear heart, don't you see? It's this! Everywhere the wind carried that thistledown, other thistles sprang up and grew prickles; and wherever those lily seeds sank to the mire, the pure white of other lilies bloomed. But, Freckles, there was never a place anywhere in the Limberlost, or in the whole world, where the thistledown floated and sprang up and blossomed into white lilies! Thistles grow from thistles, and lilies from other lilies. Dear Freckles, think hard! You must see it! You are a lily, straight through. You never, never could have drifted from the thistle-patch.

"Where did you find the courage to go into the Limberlost and face its terrors? You inherited it from the blood of a brave father, dear heart. Where did you get the pluck to hold for over a year a job that few men would have taken at all? You got it from a plucky mother, you bravest of boys. You attacked single-handed a man almost twice your size, and fought as a demon, merely at the suggestion that you be deceptive and dishonest. Could your mother or your father have been untruthful? Here you are, so hungry and starved that you are dying for love. Where did you get all that capacity for loving? You didn't inherit it from hardened, heartless people, who would disfigure you and purposely leave you to die, that's one sure thing. You once told me of saving your big bullfrog from a rattlesnake. You knew you risked a horrible death when you did it. Yet you will spend miserable years torturing yourself with the idea that your own mother might have cut off that hand. Shame on you, Freckles! Your mother would have done this——"

The Angel deliberately turned back the cover, slipped up the sleeve, and laid her lips on the scars.

"Freckles! Wake up!" she cried, almost shaking him. "Come to your senses! Be a thinking, reasoning man! You have brooded too much, and been all your life too much alone. It's all as plain as plain can be to me. You must see it! Like breeds like in this world! You must be some sort of a reproduction of your parents, and I am not afraid to vouch for them, not for a minute!

"And then, too, if more proof is needed, here it is: Mr. McLean says that you never once have failed in tact and courtesy. He says that you are the most perfect gentleman he ever knew, and he has traveled the world over. How does it happen, Freckles? No one at that Home taught you. Hundreds of men couldn't be taught, even in a school of etiquette; so it must be instinctive with you. If it is, why, that means that it is born in you, and a direct inheritance from a race of men that have been gentlemen for ages, and couldn't be anything else.

"Then there's your singing. I don't believe there ever was a mortal with a sweeter voice than yours, and while that doesn't prove anything, there is a point that does. The little training you had from that choirmaster won't account for the wonderful accent and ease with which you sing. Somewhere in your close blood is a marvelously trained vocalist; we every one of us believe that, Freckles.

"Why does my father refer to you constantly as being of fine perceptions and honor? Because you are, Freckles. Why does the Bird Woman leave her precious work and come here to help look after you? I never heard of her losing any time over anyone else. It's because she loves you. And why does Mr. McLean turn all of his valuable business over to hired men and watch you personally? And why is he hunting excuses every day to spend money on you? My father says McLean is full Scotch-close with a dollar. He is a hard-headed business man, Freckles, and he is doing it because he finds you worthy of it. Worthy of all we all can do and more than we know how to do, dear heart! Freckles, are you listening to me? Oh! won't you see it? Won't you believe it?"

"Oh, Angel!" chattered the bewildered Freckles, "are you truly maning it? Could it be?"

"Of course it could," flashed the Angel, "because it just is!"

"But you can't prove it," wailed Freckles. "It ain't giving me a name, or me honor!"

"Freckles," said the Angel sternly, "you are unreasonable! Why, I did prove every word I said! Everything proves it! You look here! If you knew for sure that I could give you a name and your honor, and prove to you that your mother did love you, why, then, would you just go to breathing like perpetual motion and hang on for dear life and get well?"

A bright light shone in Freckles' eyes.

"If I knew that, Angel," he said solemnly, "you couldn't be killing me if you felled the biggest tree in the Limberlost smash on me!"

"Then you go right to work," said the Angel, "and before night I'll prove one thing to you: I can show you easily enough how much your mother loved you. That will be the first step, and then the remainder will all come. If my father and Mr. McLean are so anxious to spend some money, I'll give them a chance. I don't see why we haven't comprehended how you felt and so have been at work weeks ago. We've been awfully selfish. We've all been so comfortable, we never stopped to think what other people were suffering before our eyes. None of us has understood. I'll hire the finest detective in Chicago, and we'll go to work together. This is nothing compared with things people do find out. We'll go at it, beak and claw, and we'll show you a thing or two."

Freckles caught her sleeve.

"Me mother, Angel! Me mother!" he marveled hoarsely. "Did you say you could be finding out today if me mother loved me? How? Oh, Angel! Nothing matters, IF ONLY ME MOTHER DIDN'T DO IT!"

"Then you rest easy," said the Angel, with large confidence. "Your mother didn't do it! Mothers of sons such as you don't do things like that. I'll go to work at once and prove it to you. The first thing to do is to go to that Home where you were and get the clothes you wore the night you were left there. I know that they are required to save those things carefully. We can find out almost all there is to know about your mother from them. Did you ever see them?"

"Yis," he replied.

"Freckles! Were they white?" she cried.

"Maybe they were once. They're all yellow with laying, and brown with blood-stains now" said Freckles, the old note of bitterness creeping in. "You can't be telling anything at all by them, Angel!"

"Well, but I just can!" said the Angel positively. "I can see from the quality what kind of goods your mother could afford to buy. I can see from the cut whether she had good taste. I can see from the care she took in making them how much she loved and wanted you."

"But how? Angel, tell me how!" implored Freckles with trembling eagerness.

"Why, easily enough," said the Angel. "I thought you'd understand. People that can afford anything at all, always buy white for little new babies—linen and lace, and the very finest things to be had. There's a young woman living near us who cut up her wedding clothes to have fine things for her baby. Mothers who love and want their babies don't buy little rough, ready-made things, and they don't run up what they make on an old sewing machine. They make fine seams, and tucks, and put on lace and trimming by hand. They sit and stitch, and stitch—little, even stitches, every one just as careful. Their eyes shine and their faces glow. When they have to quit to do something else, they look sorry, and fold up their work so particularly. There isn't much worth knowing about your mother that those little clothes won't tell. I can see her putting the little stitches into them and smiling with shining eyes over your coming. Freckles, I'll wager you a dollar those little clothes of yours are just alive with the dearest, tiny handmade stitches."

A new light dawned in Freckles' eyes. A tinge of warm color swept into his face. Renewed strength was noticeable in his grip of her hands.

"Oh Angel! Will you go now? Will you be hurrying?" he cried.

"Right away," said the Angel. "I won't stop for a thing, and I'll hurry with all my might."

She smoothed his pillow, straightened the cover, gave him one steady look in the eyes, and went quietly from the room.

Outside the door, McLean and the surgeon anxiously awaited her. McLean caught her shoulders.

"Angel, what have you done?" he demanded.

The Angel smiled defiance into his eyes.

"What have I done?" she repeated. "I've tried to save Freckles."

"What will your father say?" groaned McLean.

"It strikes me," said the Angel, "that what Freckles said would be to the point."

"Freckles!" exclaimed McLean. "What could he say?"

"He seemed to be able to say several things," answered the Angel sweetly. "I fancy the one that concerns you most at present was, that if my father should offer me to him he would not have me."

"And no one knows why better than I do," cried McLean. "Every day he must astonish me with some new fineness."

He turned to the surgeon. "Save him!" he commanded. "Save him!" he implored. "He is too fine to be sacrificed."

"His salvation lies here," said the surgeon, stroking the Angel's sunshiny hair, "and I can read in the face of her that she knows how she is going to work it out. Don't trouble for the boy. She will save him!"

The Angel laughingly sped down the hall, and into the street, just as she was.

"I have come," she said to the matron of the Home, "to ask if you will allow me to examine, or, better yet, to take with me, the little clothes that a boy you called Freckles, discharged last fall, wore the night he was left here."

The woman looked at her in greater astonishment than the occasion demanded.

"Well, I'd be glad to let you see them," she said at last, "but the fact is we haven't them. I do hope we haven't made some mistake. I was thoroughly convinced, and so was the superintendent. We let his people take those things away yesterday. Who are you, and what do you want with them?"

The Angel stood dazed and speechless, staring at the matron.

"There couldn't have been a mistake," continued the matron, seeing the Angel's distress. "Freckles was here when I took charge, ten years ago. These people had it all proved that he belonged to them. They had him traced to where he ran away in Illinois last fall, and there they completely lost track of him. I'm sorry you seem so disappointed, but it is all right. The man is his uncle, and as like the boy as he possibly could be. He is almost killed to go back without him. If you know where Freckles is, they'd give big money to find out."

The Angel laid a hand along each cheek to steady her chattering teeth.

"Who are they?" she stammered. "Where are they going?"

"They are Irish folks, miss," said the matron. "They have been in Chicago and over the country for the past three months, hunting him everywhere. They have given up, and are starting home today. They——
"

"Did they leave an address? Where could I find them?" interrupted the Angel.

"They left a card, and I notice the morning paper has the man's picture and is full of them. They've advertised a great deal in the city papers. It's a wonder you haven't seen something."

"Trains don't run right. We never get Chicago papers," said the Angel. "Please give me that card quickly. They may escape me. I simply must catch them!"

The matron hurried to the secretary and came back with a card.

"Their addresses are there," she said. "Both in Chicago and at their home. They made them full and plain, and I was to cable at once if I got the least clue of him at any time. If they've left the city, you can stop them in New York. You're sure to catch them before they sail—if you hurry."

The matron caught up a paper and thrust it into the Angel's hand as she ran to the street.

The Angel glanced at the card. The Chicago address was Suite Eleven, Auditorium. She laid her hand on her driver's sleeve and looked into his eyes.

"There is a fast-driving limit?" she asked.

"Yes, miss."

"Will you crowd it all you can without danger of arrest? I will pay well. I must catch some people!"

Then she smiled at him. The hospital, an Orphans' Home, and the Auditorium seemed a queer combination to that driver, but the Angel was always and everywhere the Angel, and her methods were strictly her own.

"I will take you there as quickly as any man could with a team," he said promptly.

The Angel clung to the card and paper, and as best she could in the lurching, swaying cab, read the addresses over.

"O'More, Suite Eleven, Auditorium."

"'O'More,'" she repeated. "Seems to fit Freckles to a dot. Wonder if that could be his name? 'Suite Eleven' means that you are pretty well fixed. Suites in the Auditorium come high."

Then she turned the card and read on its reverse, Lord Maxwell O'More, M. P., Killvany Place, County Clare, Ireland.

The Angel sat on the edge of the seat, bracing her feet against the one opposite, as the cab pitched and swung around corners and past vehicles. She mechanically fingered the pasteboard and stared straight ahead. Then she drew a deep breath and read the card again.

"A Lord-man!" she groaned despairingly. "A Lord-man! Bet my hoecake's scorched! Here I've gone and pledged my word to Freckles I'd find him some decent relatives, that he could be proud of, and now there isn't a chance out of a dozen that he'll have to be ashamed of them after all. It's too mean!"

The tears of vexation rolled down the tired, nerve-racked Angel's cheeks.

"This isn't going to do," she said, resolutely wiping her eyes with the palm of her hand and gulping down the nervous spasm in her throat. "I must read this paper before I meet Lord O'More."

She blinked back the tears and spreading the paper on her knee, read: "After three months' fruitless search, Lord O'More gives up the quest of his lost nephew, and leaves Chicago today for his home in Ireland."

She read on, and realized every word. The likeness settled any doubt. It was Freckles over again, only older and well dressed.

"Well, I must catch you if I can," muttered the Angel. "But when I do, if you are a gentleman in name only, you shan't have Freckles; that's flat. You're not his father and he is twenty. Anyway, if the law will give him to you for one year, you can't spoil him, because nobody could, and," she added, brightening, "he'll probably do you a lot of good. Freckles and I both must study years yet, and you should be something that will save him. I guess it will come out all right. At least, I don't believe you can take him away if I say no."

"Thank you; and wait, no matter how long," she said to her driver.

Catching up the paper, she hurried to the desk and laid down Lord O'More's card.

"Has my uncle started yet?" she asked sweetly.

The surprised clerk stepped back on a bellboy, and covertly kicked him for being in the way.

"His lordship is in his room," he said, with a low bow.

"All right," said the Angel, picking up the card. "I thought he might have started. I'll see him."

The clerk shoved the bellboy toward the Angel.

"Show her ladyship to the elevator and Lord O'More's suite," he said, bowing double.

"Aw, thanks," said the Angel with a slight nod, as she turned away.

"I'm not sure," she muttered to herself as the elevator sped upward, "whether it's the Irish or the English who say: 'Aw, thanks,' but it's probable he isn't either; and anyway, I just had to do something to counteract that 'All right.' How stupid of me!"

At the bellboy's tap, the door swung open and the liveried servant thrust a cardtray before the Angel. The opening of the door created a current that swayed a curtain aside, and in an adjoining room, lounging in a big chair, with a paper in his hand, sat a man who was, beyond question, of Freckles' blood and race.

With perfect control the Angel dropped Lord O'More's card in the tray, stepped past his servant, and stood before his lordship.

"Good morning," she said with tense politeness.

Lord O'More said nothing. He carelessly glanced her over with amused curiosity, until her color began to deepen and her blood to run hotly.

"Well, my dear," he said at last, "how can I serve you?"

Instantly the Angel became indignant. She had been so shielded in the midst of almost entire freedom, owing to the circumstances of her life, that the words and the look appeared to her as almost insulting. She lifted her head with a proud gesture.

"I am not your 'dear,'" she said with slow distinctness. "There isn't a thing in the world you can do for me. I came here to see if I could do something—a very great something—for you; but if I don't like you, I won't do it!"

Then Lord O'More did stare. Suddenly he broke into a ringing laugh. Without a change of attitude or expression, the Angel stood looking steadily at him.

There was a silken rustle, then a beautiful woman with cheeks of satiny pink, dark hair, and eyes of pure Irish blue, moved to Lord O'More's side, and catching his arm, shook him impatiently.

"Terence! Have you lost your senses?" she cried. "Didn't you understand what the child said? Look at her face! See what she has!"

Lord O'More opened his eyes widely and sat up. He did look at the Angel's face intently, and suddenly found it so good that it was difficult to follow the next injunction. He arose instantly.

"I beg your pardon," he said. "The fact is, I am leaving Chicago sorely disappointed. It makes me bitter and reckless. I thought you one more of those queer, useless people who have thrust themselves on me constantly, and I was careless. Forgive me, and tell me why you came."

"I will if I like you," said the Angel stoutly, "and if I don't, I won't!"

"But I began all wrong, and now I don't know how to make you like me," said his lordship, with sincere penitence in his tone.

The Angel found herself yielding to his voice. He spoke in a soft, mellow, smoothly flowing Irish tone, and although his speech was perfectly correct, it was so rounded, and accented, and the sentences so turned, that it was Freckles over again. Still, it was a matter of the very greatest importance, and she must be sure; so she looked into the beautiful woman's face.

"Are you his wife?" she asked.

"Yes," said the woman, "I am his wife."

"Well," said the Angel judicially, "the Bird Woman says no one in the whole world knows all a man's bignesses and all his littlenesses as his wife does. What you think of him should do for me. Do you like him?"

The question was so earnestly asked that it met with equal earnestness. The dark head moved caressingly against Lord O'More's sleeve.

"Better than anyone in the whole world," said Lady O'More promptly.

The Angel mused a second, and then her legal tinge came to the fore again.

"Yes, but have you anyone you could like better, if he wasn't all right?" she persisted.

"I have three of his sons, two little daughters, a father, mother, and several brothers and sisters," came the quick reply.

"And you like him best?" persisted the Angel with finality.

"I love him so much that I would give up every one of them with dry eyes if by so doing I could save him," cried Lord O'More's wife.

"Oh!" cried the Angel. "Oh, my!"

She lifted her clear eyes to Lord O'More's and shook her head.

"She never, never could do that!" she said. "But it's a mighty big thing to your credit that she THINKS she could. I guess I'll tell you why I came."

She laid down the paper, and touched the portrait.

"When you were only a boy, did people call you Freckles?" she asked.

"Dozens of good fellows all over Ireland and the Continent are doing it today," answered Lord O'More.

The Angel's face wore her most beautiful smile.

"I was sure of it," she said winningly. "That's what we call him, and he is so like you, I doubt if any one of those three boys of yours are more so. But it's been twenty years. Seems to me you've been a long time coming!"

Lord O'More caught the Angel's wrists and his wife slipped her arms around her.

"Steady, my girl!" said the man's voice hoarsely. "Don't make me think you've brought word of the boy at this last hour, unless you know surely."

"It's all right," said the Angel. "We have him, and there's no chance of a mistake. If I hadn't gone to that Home for his little clothes, and heard of you and been hunting you, and had met you on the street, or anywhere, I would have stopped you and asked you who you were, just because you are so like him. It's all right. I can tell you where Freckles is; but whether you deserve to know—that's another matter!"

Lord O'More did not hear her. He dropped in his chair, and covering his face, burst into those terrible sobs that shake and rend a strong man. Lady O'More hovered over him, weeping.

"Umph! Looks pretty fair for Freckles," muttered the Angel. "Lots of things can be explained; now perhaps they can explain this."

They did explain so satisfactorily that in a few minutes the Angel was on her feet, hurrying Lord and Lady O'More to reach the hospital. "You said Freckles' old nurse knew his mother's picture instantly," said the Angel. "I want that picture and the bundle of little clothes."

Lady O'More gave them into her hands.

The likeness was a large miniature, painted on ivory, with a frame of beaten gold. Surrounded by masses of dark hair was a delicately cut face.

In the upper part of it there was no trace of Freckles, but the lips curving in a smile were his very own. The Angel gazed at it steadily. Then with a quivering breath she laid the portrait aside and reached both hands to Lord O'More.

"That will save Freckles' life and insure his happiness," she said positively. "Thank you, oh thank you for coming!"

She opened the bundle of yellow and brown linen and gave only a glance at the texture and work. Then she gathered the little clothes and the picture to her heart and led the way to the cab.

Ushering Lord and Lady O'More into the reception room, she said to McLean, "Please go call up my father and ask him to come on the first train."

She closed the door after him.

"These are Freckles' people," she said to the Bird Woman. "You can find out about each other; I'm going to him."

CHAPTER XIX

WHEREIN FRECKLES FINDS HIS
BIRTHRIGHT AND THE ANGEL LOSES
HER HEART

The nurse left the room quietly, as the Angel entered, carrying the bundle and picture. When they were alone, she turned to Freckles and saw that the crisis was indeed at hand.

That she had good word to give him was his salvation, for despite the heavy plaster jacket that held his body immovable, his head was lifted from the pillow. Both arms reached for her. His lips and cheeks flamed, while his eyes flashed with excitement.

"Angel," he panted. "Oh Angel! Did you find them? Are they white? Are the little stitches there? OH ANGEL! DID ME MOTHER LOVE ME?"

The words seemed to leap from his burning lips. The Angel dropped the bundle on the bed and laid the picture face down across his knees. She gently pushed his head to the pillow and caught his arms in a firm grasp.

"Yes, dear heart," she said with fullest assurance. "No little clothes were ever whiter. I never in all my life saw such dainty, fine, little stitches; and as for loving you, no boy's mother ever loved him more!"

A nervous trembling seized Freckles.

"Sure? Are you sure?" he urged with clicking teeth.

"I know," said the Angel firmly. "And Freckles, while you rest and be glad, I want to tell you a story. When you feel stronger we will look at the clothes together. They are here. They are all right. But while I was at the Home getting them, I heard of some people that were hunting a lost boy. I went to see them, and what they told me was all so exactly like what might have happened to you that I must tell you. Then you'll understand that things could be very different from what you always have tortured yourself with thinking. Are you strong enough to listen? May I tell you?"

"Maybe 'twasn't me mother! Maybe someone else made those little stitches!"

"Now, goosie, don't you begin that," said the Angel, "because I know that it was!"

"Know!" cried Freckles, his head springing from the pillow. "Know! How can you know?"

The Angel gently soothed him back.

"Why, because nobody else would ever sit and do it the way it is done. That's how I know," she said emphatically. "Now you listen while I tell you about this lost boy and his people, who have hunted for months and can't find him."

Freckles lay quietly under her touch, but he did not hear a word that she was saying until his roving eyes rested on her face; he immediately noticed a remarkable thing. For the first time she was talking to him and avoiding his eyes. That was not like the Angel at all. It was the delight of hearing her speak that she looked one squarely in the face and with perfect frankness. There were no side glances and down-drooping eyes when the Angel talked; she was business straight through. Instantly Freckles' wandering thoughts fastened on her words.

"—and he was a sour, grumpy, old man," she was saying. "He always had been spoiled, because he was an only son, so he had a title, and a big estate. He would have just his way, no matter about his sweet little wife, or his boys, or anyone. So when his elder son fell in love with a beautiful girl having a title, the very girl of all the world his father wanted him to, and added a big adjoining estate to his, why, that pleased him mightily.

"Then he went and ordered his younger son to marry a poky kind of a girl, that no one liked, to add another big estate on the other side, and that was different. That was all the world different, because the elder son had been in love all his life with the girl he married, and, oh, Freckles, it's no wonder, for I saw her! She's a beauty and she has the sweetest way.

"But that poor younger son, he had been in love with the village vicar's daughter all his life. That's no wonder either, for she was more beautiful yet. She could sing as the angels, but she hadn't a cent. She loved him to death, too, if he was bony and freckled and red-haired—I don't mean that! They didn't say what color his hair was, but his father's must have been the reddest ever, for when he found out about them, and it wasn't anything so terrible, HE JUST CAVED!

"The old man went to see the girl—the pretty one with no money, of course—and he hurt her feelings until she ran away. She went to London and began studying music. Soon she grew to be a fine singer, so she joined a company and came to this country.

"When the younger son found that she had left London, he followed her. When she got here all alone, and afraid, and saw him coming to her, why, she was so glad she up and married him, just like anybody else would have done. He didn't want her to travel with the troupe, so when they reached Chicago they thought that would be a good place, and they stopped, while he hunted work. It was slow business, because he never had been taught to do a useful thing, and he didn't even know how to hunt work, least of all to do it when he found it; so pretty soon things were going wrong. But if he couldn't find work, she could always sing, so she sang at night, and made little things in the daytime. He didn't like her to sing in public, and he wouldn't allow her when he could HELP himself; but winter came, it was very cold, and fire was expensive. Rents went up, and they had to move farther out to cheaper and cheaper places; and you were coming—I mean, the boy that is lost was coming—and they were almost distracted. Then the man wrote and told his father all about it; and his father sent the letter back unopened with a line telling him never to write again. When the baby came, there was very little left to pawn for food and a doctor, and nothing at all for a nurse; so an old neighbor woman went in and took care of the young mother and the little baby, because she was so sorry for them. By that time they were away in the suburbs on the top floor of a little wooden house, among a lot of big factories, and it kept growing colder, with less to eat. Then the man grew desperate and he went just to find something to eat and the woman was desperate, too. She got up, left the old woman to take care of her baby, and went into the city to sing for some money. The woman became so cold she put the baby in bed and went home. Then a boiler blew up in a big factory beside the little house and set it on fire. A piece of iron was pitched across and broke through the roof. It came down smash, and cut just one little hand off the poor baby. It screamed and screamed; and the fire kept coming closer and closer.

"The old woman ran out with the other people and saw what had happened. She knew there wasn't going to be time to wait for firemen or anything, so she ran into the building. She could hear the baby screaming, and she couldn't stand that; so she worked her way to it. There it was, all hurt and bleeding. Then she was almost scared to death over thinking what its mother would do to her for going away and leaving it, so she ran to a Home for little friendless babies, that was close, and banged on the door. Then she hid across the street until the baby was taken in, and then she ran back to see if her own house was burning. The big factory and the little house and a lot of others were all gone. The people there told her that the beautiful lady came back and ran into the house to find her baby. She had just gone in when her husband came, and he went in after her, and the house fell over both of them."

Freckles lay rigidly, with his eyes on the Angel's face, while she talked rapidly to the ceiling.

"Then the old woman was sick about that poor little baby. She was afraid to tell them at the Home, because she knew she never should have left it, but she wrote a letter and sent it to where the beautiful woman, when she was ill, had said her husband's people lived. She told all about the little baby that she could remember: when it was born, how it was named for the man's elder brother, that its hand had been cut off in the fire, and where she had put it to be doctored and taken care of. She told them that its mother and father were both burned, and she begged and implored them to come after it.

"You'd think that would have melted a heart of ice, but that old man hadn't any heart to melt, for he got that letter and read it. He hid it away among his papers and never told a soul. A few months ago he died. When his elder son went to settle his business, he found the letter almost the first thing. He dropped everything, and came, with his wife, to hunt that baby, because he always had loved his brother dearly, and wanted him back. He had hunted for him all he dared all these years, but when he got here you were gone—I mean the baby was gone, and I had to tell you, Freckles, for you see, it might have happened to you like that just as easy as to that other lost boy."

Freckles reached up and turned the Angel's face until he compelled her eyes to meet his.

"Angel," he asked quietly, "why don't you look at me when you are telling about that lost boy?"

"I—I didn't know I wasn't," faltered the Angel.

"It seems to me," said Freckles, his breath beginning to come in sharp wheezes, "that you got us rather mixed, and it ain't like you to be mixing things till one can't be knowing. If they were telling you so much, did they say which hand was for being off that lost boy?"

The Angel's eyes escaped again.

"It—it was the same as yours," she ventured, barely breathing in her fear.

Still Freckles lay rigid and whiter than the coverlet.

"Would that boy be as old as me?" he asked.

"Yes," said the Angel faintly.

"Angel," said Freckles at last, catching her wrist, "are you trying to tell me that there is somebody hunting a boy that you're thinking might be me? Are you belavin' you've found me relations?"

Then the Angel's eyes came home. The time had come. She pinioned Freckles' arms to his sides and bent above him.

"How strong are you, dear heart?" she breathed. "How brave are you? Can you bear it? Dare I tell you that?"

"No!" gasped Freckles. "Not if you're sure! I can't bear it! I'll die if you do!"

The day had been one unremitting strain with the Angel. Nerve tension was drawn to the finest thread. It snapped suddenly.

"Die!" she flamed. "Die, if I tell you that! You said this morning that you would die if you DIDN'T know your name, and if your people were honorable. Now I've gone and found you a name that stands for ages of honor, a mother who loved you enough to go into the fire and die for you, and the nicest kind of relatives, and you turn round and say you'll die over that! YOU JUST TRY DYING AND YOU'LL GET A GOOD SLAP!"

The Angel stood glaring at him. One second Freckles lay paralyzed and dumb with astonishment. The next the Irish in his soul arose above everything. A laugh burst from him. The terrified Angel caught him in her arms and tried to stifle the sound. She implored and commanded. When he was too worn to utter another sound, his eyes laughed silently.

After a long time, when he was quiet and rested, the Angel commenced talking to him gently, and this time her big eyes, humid with tenderness and mellow with happiness, seemed as if they could not leave his face.

"Dear Freckles," she was saying, "across your knees there is the face of the mother who went into the fire for you, and I know the name—old and full of honor—to which you were born. Dear heart, which will you have first?"

Freckles was very tired; the big drops of perspiration ran together on his temples; but the watching Angel caught the words his lips formed, "Me mother!"

She lifted the lovely pictured face and set it in the nook of his arm. Freckles caught her hand and drew her beside him, and together they gazed at the picture while the tears slid over their cheeks.

"Me mother! Oh, me mother! Can you ever be forgiving me? Oh, me beautiful little mother!" chanted Freckles over and over in exalted wonder, until he was so completely exhausted that his lips refused to form the question in his weary eyes.

"Wait!" cried the Angel with inborn refinement, for she could no more answer that question than he could ask. "Wait, I will write it!"

She hurried to the table, caught up the nurse's pencil, and on the back of a prescription tablet scrawled it: "Terence Maxwell O'More, Dunderry House, County Clare, Ireland."

Before she had finished came Freckles' voice: "Angel, are you hurrying?"

"Yes," said the Angel; "I am. But there is a good deal of it. I have to put in your house and country, so that you will feel located."

"Me house?" marveled Freckles.

"Of course," said the Angel. "Your uncle says your grandmother left your father her dower house and estate, because she knew his father would cut him off. You get that, and all your share of your grandfather's property besides. It is all set off for you and waiting. Lord O'More told me so. I suspect you are richer than McLean, Freckles."

She closed his fingers over the slip and straightened his hair.

"Now you are all right, dear Limberlost guard," she said. "You go to sleep and don't think of a thing but just pure joy, joy, joy! I'll keep your people until you wake up. You are too tired to see anyone else just now!"

Freckles caught her skirt as she turned from him.

"I'll go to sleep in five minutes," he said, "if you will be doing just one thing more for me. Send for your father! Oh, Angel, send for him quick! How will I ever be waiting until he comes?"

One instant the Angel stood looking at him. The next a crimson wave darkly stained her lovely face. Her chin began a spasmodic quivering and the tears sprang into her eyes. Her hands caught at her chest as if she were stifling. Freckles' grasp on her tightened until he drew her beside him. He slipped his arm around her and drew her face to his pillow.

"Don't, Angel; for the love of mercy don't be doing that," he implored. "I can't be bearing it. Tell me. You must tell me."

The Angel shook her head.

"That ain't fair, Angel," said Freckles. "You made me tell you when it was like tearing the heart raw from me breast. And you was for making everything heaven—just heaven and nothing else for me. If I'm so much more now than I was an hour ago, maybe I can be thinking of some way to fix things. You will be telling me?" he coaxed, moving his cheek against her hair.

The Angel's head moved in negation. Freckles did a moment of intent thinking.

"Maybe I can be guessing," he whispered. "Will you be giving me three chances?"

There was the faintest possible assent.

"You didn't want me to be knowing me name," guessed Freckles.

The Angel's head sprang from the pillow and her tear-stained face flamed with outraged indignation.

"Why, I did too!" she cried angrily.

"One gone," said Freckles calmly. "You didn't want me to have relatives, a home, and money."

"I did!" exclaimed the Angel. "Didn't I go myself, all alone, into the city, and find them when I was afraid as death? I did too!"

"Two gone," said Freckles. "You didn't want the beautifulest girl in the world to be telling me.———"

Down went the Angel's face and a heavy sob shook her. Freckles' clasp tightened around her shoulders, while his face, in its conflicting emotions, was a study. He was so stunned and bewildered by the miracle that had been performed in bringing to light his name and relatives that he had no strength left for elaborate mental processes. Despite all it meant to him to know his name at last, and that he was of honorable birth—knowledge without which life was an eternal disgrace and burden the one thing that

- 424 -

was hammering in Freckles' heart and beating in his brain, past any attempted expression, was the fact that, while nameless and possibly born in shame, the Angel had told him that she loved him. He could find no word with which to begin to voice the rapture of his heart over that. But if she regretted it—if it had been a thing done out of her pity for his condition, or her feeling of responsibility, if it killed him after all, there was only one thing left to do. Not for McLean, not for the Bird Woman, not for the Duncans would Freckles have done it—but for the Angel— if it would make her happy—he would do anything.

"Angel," whispered Freckles, with his lips against her hair, "you haven't learned your history book very well, or else you've forgotten."

"Forgotten what?" sobbed the Angel.

"Forgotten about the real knight, Ladybird," breathed Freckles. "Don't you know that, if anything happened that made his lady sorry, a real knight just simply couldn't be remembering it? Angel, darling little Swamp Angel, you be listening to me. There was one night on the trail, one solemn, grand, white night, that there wasn't ever any other like before or since, when the dear Boss put his arm around me and told me that he loved me; but if you care, Angel, if you don't want it that way, why, I ain't remembering that anyone else ever did—not in me whole life."

The Angel lifted her head and looked into the depths of Freckles' honest gray eyes, and they met hers unwaveringly; but the pain in them was pitiful.

"Do you mean," she demanded, "that you don't remember that a brazen, forward girl told you, when you hadn't asked her, that she"—the Angel choked on it a second, but she gave a gulp and brought it out bravely—"that she loved you?"

"No!" cried Freckles. "No! I don't remember anything of the kind!"

But all the songbirds of his soul burst into melody over that one little clause: "When you hadn't asked her."

"But you will," said the Angel. "You may live to be an old, old man, and then you will."

"I will not!" cried Freckles. "How can you think it, Angel?"

"You won't even LOOK as if you remember?"

"I will not!" persisted Freckles. "I'll be swearing to it if you want me to. If you wasn't too tired to think this thing out straight, you'd be seeing that I couldn't—that I just simply couldn't! I'd rather give it all up now and go into eternity alone, without ever seeing a soul of me same blood, or me home, or hearing another man call me by the name I was born to, than to remember anything that would be hurting you, Angel. I should think you'd be understanding that it ain't no ways possible for me to do it."

The Angel's tear-stained face flashed into dazzling beauty. A half-hysterical little laugh broke from her heart and bubbled over her lips.

"Oh, Freckles, forgive me!" she cried. "I've been through so much that I'm scarcely myself, or I wouldn't be here bothering you when you should be sleeping. Of course you couldn't! I knew it all the time! I was just scared! I was forgetting that you were you! You're too good a knight to remember a thing like that. Of course you are! And when you don't remember, why, then it's the same as if it never happened. I was almost killed because I'd gone and spoiled everything, but now it will be all right. Now you can go on and do things like other men, and I can have some flowers, and letters, and my sweetheart coming, and when you are SURE, why, then YOU can tell ME things, can't you? Oh, Freckles, I'm so glad! Oh, I'm so happy! It's dear of you not to remember, Freckles; perfectly dear! It's no wonder I love you so. The wonder would be if I did not. Oh, I should like to know how I'm ever going to make you understand how much I love you!"

Pillow and all, she caught him to her breast one long second; then she was gone.

Freckles lay dazed with astonishment. At last his amazed eyes searched the room for something approaching the human to which he could appeal, and falling on his mother's portrait, he set it before him.

"For the love of life! Me little mother," he panted, "did you hear that? Did you hear it! Tell me, am I living, or am I dead and all heaven come true this minute? Did you hear it?"

He shook the frame in his impatience at receiving no answer.

"You are only a pictured face," he said at last, "and of course you can't talk; but the soul of you must be somewhere, and surely in this hour you are close enough to be hearing. Tell me, did you hear that? I can't ever be telling a living soul; but darling little mother, who gave your life for mine, I can always be talking of it to you! Every day we'll talk it over and try to understand the miracle of it. Tell me, are all women like that? Were you like me Swamp Angel? If you were, then I'm understanding why me father followed across the ocean and went into the fire."

CHAPTER XX

Freckles' voice ceased, his eyes closed, and his head rolled back from exhaustion. Later in the day he insisted on seeing Lord and Lady O'More, but he fainted before the resemblance of another man to him, and gave all of his friends a terrible fright.

The next morning, the Man of Affairs, with a heart filled with misgivings, undertook the interview on which Freckles insisted. His fears were without cause. Freckles was the soul of honor and simplicity.

"Have they been telling you what's come to me?" he asked without even waiting for a greeting.

"Yes," said the Angel's father.

"Do you think you have the very worst of it clear to your understanding?"

Under Freckles' earnest eyes the Man of Affairs answered soberly: "I think I have, Mr. O'More."

That was the first time Freckles heard his name from the lips of another. One second he lay overcome; the next, tears filled his eyes, and he reached out his hand. Then the Angel's father understood, and he clasped that hand and held it in a strong, firm grasp.

"Terence, my boy," he said, "let me do the talking. I came here with the understanding that you wanted to ask me for my only child. I should like, at the proper time, to regard her marriage, if she has found the man she desires to marry, not as losing all I have, but as gaining a man on whom I can depend to love as a son and to take charge of my affairs for her when I retire from business. Bend all of your energies toward rapid recovery, and from this hour understand that my daughter and my home are yours."

"You're not forgetting this?"

Freckles lifted his right arm.

"Terence, I'm sorrier than I have words to express about that," said the Man of Affairs. "It's a damnable pity! But if it's for me to choose whether I give all I have left in this world to a man lacking a hand, or to one of these gambling, tippling, immoral spendthrifts of today, with both hands and feet off their souls, and a rotten spot in the core, I choose you;

and it seems that my daughter does the same. Put what is left you of that right arm to the best uses you can in this world, and never again mention or feel that it is defective so long as you live. Good day, sir!"

"One minute more," said Freckles. "Yesterday the Angel was telling me that there was money coming to me from two sources. She said that me grandmother had left me father all of her fortune and her house, because she knew that his father would be cutting him off, and also that me uncle had set aside for me what would be me father's interest in his father's estate.

"Whatever the sum is that me grandmother left me father, because she loved him and wanted him to be having it, that I'll be taking. 'Twas hers from her father, and she had the right to be giving it as she chose. Anything from the man that knowingly left me father and me mother to go cold and hungry, and into the fire in misery, when just a little would have made life so beautiful to them, and saved me this crippled body—money that he willed from me when he knew I was living, of his blood and on charity among strangers, I don't touch, not if I freeze, starve, and burn too! If there ain't enough besides that, and I can't be earning enough to fix things for the Angel——"

"We are not discussing money!" burst in the Man of Affairs. "We don't want any blood-money! We have all we need without it. If you don't feel right and easy over it, don't you touch a cent of any of it."

"It's right I should have what me grandmother intinded for me father, and I want it," said Freckles, "but I'd die before I'd touch a cent of me grandfather's money!"

"Now," said the Angel, "we are all going home. We have done all we can for Freckles. His people are here. He should know them. They are very anxious to become acquainted with him. We'll resign him to them. When he is well, why, then he will be perfectly free to go to Ireland or come to the Limberlost, just as he chooses. We will go at once."

McLean held out for a week, and then he could endure it no longer. He was heart hungry for Freckles. Communing with himself in the long, soundful nights of the swamp, he had learned to his astonishment that for the past year his heart had been circling the Limberlost with Freckles. He began to wish that he had not left him. Perhaps the boy—his boy by first right, after all—was being neglected. If the Boss had been a nervous old woman, he scarcely could have imagined more things that might be going wrong.

He started for Chicago, loaded with a big box of goldenrod, asters, fringed gentians, and crimson leaves, that the Angel carefully had gathered from Freckles' room, and a little, long slender package. He traveled with biting, stinging jealousy in his heart. He would not admit it even to himself, but he was unable to remain longer away from Freckles and leave him to the care of Lord O'More.

In a few minutes' talk, while McLean awaited admission to Freckles' room, his lordship had chatted genially of Freckles' rapid recovery, of his delight that he was unspotted by his early surroundings, and his desire to visit the Limberlost with Freckles before they sailed; he expressed the hope that he could prevail upon the Angel's father to place her in his wife's care and have her education finished in Paris. He said they were anxious to do all they could to help bind Freckles' arrangements with the Angel, as both he and Lady O'More regarded her as the most promising girl they knew, and one who could be fitted to fill the high position in which Freckles would place her.

Every word he uttered was pungent with bitterness to McLean. The swamp had lost its flavor without Freckles; and yet, as Lord O'More talked, McLean fervently wished himself in the heart of it. As he entered Freckles' room he almost lost his breath. Everything was changed.

Freckles lay beside a window where he could follow Lake Michigan's blue until the horizon dipped into it. He could see big soft clouds, white-capped waves, shimmering sails, and puffing steamers trailing billowing banners of lavender and gray across the sky. Gulls and curlews wheeled over the water and dipped their wings in the foam. The room was filled with every luxury that taste and money could introduce.

All the tan and sunburn had been washed from Freckles' face in sweats of agony. It was a smooth, even white, its brown rift scarcely showing. What the nurses and Lady O'More had done to Freckles' hair McLean could not guess, but it was the most beautiful that he ever had seen. Fine as floss, bright in color, waving and crisp, it fell around the white face.

They had gotten his arms into and his chest covered with a finely embroidered, pale-blue silk shirt, with soft, white tie at the throat. Among the many changes that had taken place during his absence, the fact that Freckles was most attractive and barely escaped being handsome remained almost unnoticed by the Boss, so great was his astonishment at seeing both cuffs turned back and the right arm in view. Freckles was using the maimed arm that previously he always had hidden.

"Oh Lord, sir, but I'm glad to see you!" cried Freckles, almost rolling from the bed as he reached toward McLean. "Tell me quick, is the Angel well and happy? Can me Little Chicken spread six feet of wing and sail to his mother? How's me new father, the Bird Woman, Duncans, and Nellie—darling little high-stepping Nelie? Me Aunt Alice is going to choose the hat just as soon as I'm mended enough to be going with her. How are all the gang? Have they found any more good trees? I've been thinking a lot, sir. I believe I can find others near that last one. Me Aunt Alice thinks maybe I can, and Uncle Terence says it's likely. Golly, but they're nice, ilegant people. I tell you I'm proud to be same blood with them! Come closer, quick! I was going to do this yesterday, and somehow I just felt that you'd surely be coming today and I waited. I'm selecting the Angel's ring stone. The ring she ordered for me is finished and they sent it to keep me company. See? It's an emerald—just me color, Lord O'More says."

Freckles flourished his hand.

"Ain't that fine? Never took so much comfort with anything in me life. Every color of the old swamp is in it. I asked the Angel to have a little shamrock leaf cut on it, so every time I saw it I'd be thinking of the 'love, truth, and valor' of that song she was teaching me. Ain't that a beautiful song? Some of these days I'm going to make it echo. I'm a little afraid to be doing it with me voice yet, but me heart's tuning away on it every blessed hour. Will you be looking at these now?"

Freckles tilted a tray of unset stones from Peacock's that would have ransomed several valuable kings. He held them toward McLean, stirring them with his right arm.

"I tell you I'm glad to see you, sir" he said. "I tried to tell me uncle what I wanted, but this ain't for him to be mixed up in, anyway, and I don't think I made it clear to him. I couldn't seem to say the words I wanted. I can be telling you, sir."

McLean's heart began to thump as a lover's.

"Go on, Freckles," he said assuringly.

"It's this," said Freckles. "I told him that I would pay only three hundred dollars for the Angel's stone. I'm thinking that with what he has laid up for me, and the bigness of things that the Angel did for me, it seems like a stingy little sum to him. I know he thinks I should be giving much more, but I feel as if I just had to be buying that stone with money I earned meself; and that is all I have saved of me wages. I don't mind paying for the muff, or the drexing table, or Mrs. Duncan's things, from that other money, and later the Angel can have every last cent of me grandmother's, if she'll take it; but just now—oh, sir, can't you see that I have to be buying this stone with what I have in the bank? I'm feeling that I couldn't do any other way, and don't you think the Angel would rather have the best stone I can buy with the money I earned meself than a finer one paid for with other money?"

"In other words, Freckles," said the Boss in a husky voice, "you don't want to buy the Angel's ring with money. You want to give for it your first awful fear of the swamp. You want to pay for it with the loneliness and heart hunger you have suffered there, with last winter's freezing on the line and this summer's burning in the sun. You want it to stand to her for every hour in which you risked your life to fulfill your contract honorably. You want the price of that stone to be the fears that have chilled your heart—the sweat and blood of your body."

Freckles' eyes were filled with tears and his face quivering with feeling.

"Dear Mr. McLean," he said, reaching with a caress over the Boss's black hair and his cheek. "Dear Boss, that's why I've wanted you so. I knew you would know. Now you will be looking at these? I don't want emeralds, because that's what she gave me."

He pushed the green stones into a little heap of rejected ones. Then he singled out all the pearls.

"Ain't they pretty things?" he said. "I'll be getting her some of those later. They are like lily faces, turtle-head flowers, dewdrops in the shade or moonlight; but they haven't the life in them that I want in the stone I give to the Angel right now."

Freckles heaped the pearls with the emeralds. He studied the diamonds a long time.

"These things are so fascinating like they almost tempt one, though they ain't quite the proper thing," he said. "I've always dearly loved to be watching yours, sir. I must get her some of these big ones, too, some day. They're like the Limberlost in January, when it's all ice-coated, and the sun is in the west and shines through and makes all you can see of the whole world look like fire and ice; but fire and ice ain't like the Angel."

The diamonds joined the emeralds and pearls. There was left a little red heap, and Freckles' fingers touched it with a new tenderness. His eyes were flashing.

"I'm thinking here's me Angel's stone," he exulted. "The Limberlost, and me with it, grew in mine; but it's going to bloom, and her with it, in this! There's the red of the wild poppies, the cardinal-flowers, and the little bunch of crushed foxfire that we found where she put it to save me. There's the light of the campfire, and the sun setting over Sleepy Snake Creek. There's the red of the blood we were willing to give for each other. It's like her lips, and like the drops that dried on her beautiful arm that first day, and I'm thinking it must be like the brave, tender, clean, red heart of her."

Freckles lifted the ruby to his lips and handed it to McLean.

"I'll be signing me cheque and you have it set," he said. "I want you to draw me money and pay for it with those very same dollars, sir."

Again the heart of McLean took hope.

"Freckles, may I ask you something?" he said.

"Why, sure," said Freckles. "There's nothing you would be asking that it wouldn't be giving me joy to be telling you."

McLean's eyes traveled to Freckles' right arm with which he was moving the jewels.

"Oh, that!" cried Freckles with a laugh. "You're wanting to know where all the bitterness is gone? Well sir, 'twas carried from me soul, heart, and body on the lips of an Angel. Seems that hurt was necessary in the beginning to make today come true. The wound had always been raw, but the Angel was healing it. If she doesn't care, I don't. Me dear new father doesn't, nor me aunt and uncle, and you never did. Why should I be fretting all me life about what can't be helped. The real truth is, that since what happened to it last week, I'm so everlastingly proud of it I catch meself sticking it out on display a bit."

Freckles looked the Boss in the eyes and began to laugh.

"Well thank heaven!" said McLean.

"Now it's me turn," said Freckles. "I don't know as I ought to be asking you, and yet I can't see a reason good enough to keep me from it. It's a thing I've had on me mind every hour since I've had time to straighten things out a little. May I be asking you a question?"

McLean reached over and took Freckles' hand. His voice was shaken with feeling as he replied: "Freckles, you almost hurt me. Will you never learn how much you are to me—how happy you make me in coming to me with anything, no matter what?"

"Then it's this," said Freckles, gripping the hand of McLean strongly. "If this accident, and all that's come to me since, had never happened, where was it you had planned to send me to school? What was it you meant for me to do?"

"Why, Freckles," answered McLean, "I'm scarcely prepared to state definitely. My ideas were rather hazy. I thought we would make a beginning and see which way things went. I figured on taking you to Grand Rapids first, and putting you in the care of my mother. I had an idea it would be best to secure a private tutor to coach you for a year or two, until you were ready to enter Ann Arbor or the Chicago University in good shape. Then I thought we'd finish in this country at Yale or Harvard, and end with Oxford, to get a good, all-round flavor."

"Is that all?" asked Freckles.

"No; that's leaving the music out," said McLean. "I intended to have your voice tested by some master, and if you really were endowed for a career as a great musician, and had inclinations that way, I wished to have you drop some of the college work and make music your chief study. Finally, I wanted us to take a trip through Europe and clear around the circle together."

"And then what?" queried Freckles breathlessly.

"Why, then," said McLean, "you know that my heart is hopelessly in the woods. I never will quit the timber business while there is timber to handle and breath in my body. I thought if you didn't make a profession of music, and had any inclination my way, we would stretch the partnership one more and take you into the firm, placing your work with me. Those plans may sound jumbled in the telling, but they have grown steadily on me, Freckles, as you have grown dear to me."

Freckles lifted anxious and eager eyes to McLean.

"You told me once on the trail, and again when we thought that I was dying, that you loved me. Do these things that have come to me make any difference in any way with your feeing toward me?"

"None," said McLean. "How could they, Freckles? Nothing could make me love you more, and you never will do anything that will make me love you less."

"Glory be to God!" cried Freckles. "Glory to the Almighty! Hurry and be telling your mother I'm coming! Just as soon as I can get on me feet I'll be taking that ring to me Angel, and then I'll go to Grand Rapids and be making me start just as you planned, only that I can be paying me own way. When I'm educated enough, we'll all—the Angel and her father, the Bird Woman, you, and me—all of us will go together and see me house and me relations and be taking that trip. When we get back, we'll add O'More to the Lumber Company, and golly, sir, but we'll make things hum! Good land, sir! Don't do that! Why, Mr. McLean, dear Boss, dear father, don't be doing that! What is it?"

"Nothing, nothing!" boomed McLean's deep bass; "nothing at all!"

He abruptly turned, and hurried to the window.

"This is a mighty fine view," he said. "Lake's beautiful this morning. No wonder Chicago people are so proud of their city's location on its shore. But, Freckles, what is Lord O'More going to say to this?"

"I don't know," said Freckles. "I am going to be cut deep if he cares, for he's been more than good to me, and Lady Alice is next to me Angel. He's made me feel me blood and race me own possession. She's talked to me by the hour of me father and mother and me grandmother. She's made them all that real I can lay claim to them and feel that they are mine. I'm very sorry to be hurting them, if it will, but it can't be changed. Nobody ever puts the width of the ocean between me and the Angel. From here to the Limberlost is all I can be bearing peaceable. I want the education, and then I want to work and live here in the country where I was born, and where the ashes of me father and mother rest.

"I'll be glad to see Ireland, and glad especial to see those little people who are my kin, but I ain't ever staying long. All me heart is the Angel's, and the Limberlost is calling every minute. You're thinking, sir, that when I look from that window I see the beautiful water, ain't you? I'm not.

"I see soft, slow clouds oozing across the blue, me big black chickens hanging up there, and a great feather softly sliding down. I see mighty trees, swinging vines, bright flowers, and always masses of the wild roses, with the wild rose face of me Ladybird looking through. I see the swale rocking, smell the sweetness of the blooming things, and the damp, mucky odor of the swamp; and I hear me birds sing, me squirrels bark, the rattlers hiss, and the step of Wessner or Black Jack coming; and whether it's the things that I loved or the things that I feared, it's all a part of the day.

"Me heart's all me Swamp Angel's, and me love is all hers, and I have her and the swamp so confused in me mind I never can be separating them. When I look at her, I see blue sky, the sun rifting through the leaves and pink and red flowers; and when I look at the Limberlost I see a pink face with blue eyes, gold hair, and red lips, and, it's the truth, sir, they're mixed till they're one to me!

"I'm afraid it will be hurting some, but I have the feeing that I can be making my dear people understand, so that they will be willing to let me come back home. Send Lady O'More to put these flowers God made in the place of these glass-house ilegancies, and please be cutting the string of this little package the Angel's sent me."

As Freckles held up the package, the lights of the Limberlost flashed from the emerald on his finger. On the cover was printed: "To the Limberlost Guard!" Under it was a big, crisp, iridescent black feather. Limberlost Guard!" Under it was a big, crisp, iridescent black feather.

THE END

HISTORICAL CONTEXT

INTRODUCTION

The 20th century was a period of enormous turbulence, both for society and literature. Forever marked by the two world wars, a worldwide economic Great Depression, the subsequent disintegration of the British empire and resultant transformation of global politics, and the continuing technological and scientific advances made for an almost unprecedented time of cataclysmic change in human history.

Leaving the Victorian era behind, the turn of the century saw the emergence of the Georgian and Aesthetic movement poets; realism was a prominent feature of the modern novel; a new unsettling and more challenging style of poetry emerged in the aftermath of World War I; Imagism and Modernism emerged in the inter-war period; while the post-World War II period introduced various responses to Modernism, such as the Postmodernism movement.

MOVEMENTS AND LITERATURE

THE EDWARDIANS

By the turn of the century, marked as it was by the death of Queen Victoria in 1901 and accession of Edward VII, there was a sense of disenchantment with and movement away from the former inflexible Victorian certainties and conservatism. Influential philosophical, scientific and political thinkers of the time included Albert Einstein, Charles Darwin, Sigmund Freud, Friedrich Nietzsche and Karl Marx, whose works had a profound and ground breaking impact on Western culture, beliefs as well as humanity's understanding of itself and its origins.

- *H.G. Wells, modernism and a new era*

The start of a new century brought with it both an optimism for the new, and an apprehensiveness about what change could bring, as a new millennium and an unknown future approached. This mood was expressed in early Utopian works by English writer H.G. Wells including his *Anticipations of the Reaction of Mechanical and Scientific Progress upon Human Life and Thought* (1901), *Mankind in the Making* (1903) and *Utopia* (1905), exploring and anticipating the impacts and transformations which science and technological development could deliver.

- Realism and a new role for the arts

The Edwardian era saw many writers make a deliberate move away from pure Aestheticism, with its slogan of "Art for Art's Sake", as championed by Decadent writers and artists towards the end of the 19th century. such as Oscar Wilde, Algernon Charles Swinburne, and Dante Gabriel Rossetti. Writers, particularly of dramatic works, now began using their writing and productions as a platform for debate and exploration of the key moral and social issues of the day, covering such diverse subjects as politics, the role of women, marriage as a social construct, and the morality of war.

Heavily influenced by the realist and naturalistic approaches of 19th century dramatists and writers including Ibsen, Balzac and Dickens, Irish playwright George Bernard Shaw's comic works *Man and Superman* (1903) and *Major Barbara* (1907), John Galsworthy's exploration of the morality and politics of industry in *Strife* (1909) and Harley Granville-Barker's critique of class hypocrisy in *The Voysey Inheritance* (1905) are good examples of this new more didactic approach visible in the arts.

- Transition and traditionalism

Thomas Hardy is an example of a writer who, like Rudyard Kipling and G.K. Chesterton, had achieved literary acclaim in the previous century, and can be seen as something of a transitional figure, bridging the gap between the Victorians and Edwardians via his efforts to maintain traditional literary forms and approaches. Similar efforts to revive traditional methods and themes can be seen in the pastoral poetic works of A.E. Housman. During the early years of the 20th century the Georgian poets as they were known, who included Rupert Brooke, Robert Graves, and Edmund Blunden, similarly preserved a more traditional, moderate poetic style via their continued use of romantic and sentimental styles.

- Henry James and Joseph Conrad

Another key transitional figure in literature, also bridging the gap between realism and modernism, Henry James was an American-born British author whose works famously concentrate on the clash between the Old World and the New, and Americans and Europeans. His late novels *The Wings of the Dove*, *The Ambassadors* and *The Golden Bowl*, published between 1902-1904, feature an air of dissatisfaction and despondency with a new world order in which both the old social structures and moral certainties were dissolving. Joseph Conrad's work express a similar dismay with the world, as he explores the cost of human arrogance and shortcomings in ground breaking works such as *Heart of Darkness* (1902), *Nostromo* (1907) and *Under Western Eyes* (1911).

MODERNISM

The early 20th century was a time of experimentation and innovation in literary style, as writers and poets largely sought to free themselves from the post-Romantic traditions of the previous century, and felt the influence of new philosophical, pollical and scientific approaches.

- *Imagist movement*

This new modernist attitude is expressed well in the work of the imagists, a group of American and English poets brought together under the banner of principles espoused by Ezra Pound in his poetry anthologies *Ripostes* (1912) and *Des Imagistes* (1914); key members included T. E. Hulme, Richard Adlington, Hilda Doolittle and Amy Lowell. Their poetry was experimental, making use of free or irregular verse.

- *The modernist novel*

The shattering impact of World War I can be felt in the style and themes of literary and poetic works produced after its outbreak in 1914. D.H. Lawrence's modernist approach can be seen in his innovative use of a stream of consciousness style, as displayed in *The Rainbow* (1915) and *Women in Love* (1920) and in his assessment of the disastrous effects of industrialisation. In 1922 James Joyce's trailblazing novel *Ulysses* also used the stream of consciousness technique, and successfully epitomizes the modernist literary movement as a whole.

- World War I Literature

World War I evoked an outpouring works by poets including: Rupert Brooke, who successfully evoked the idealism of the conflict's opening months in his patriotic poem *1914*; Wilfred Owen whose poems powerfully depict both the comradeship and the moral dilemmas of war; and Siegfried Sassoon who captured the mounting feelings of anger and wastefulness as the war raged on. It wasn't until the 1930s however that many of these works became known and achieved acclaim.

- T.S. Eliot and The Waste Land

American-English poet T.S. Eliot is seen as a leading member of the modernist poetry movement, with his use of experimental diction and style. In two of his most celebrated works published in the post WWI period, *Prufrock and Other Observations* (1917) and *The Waste Land* (1922), Eliot brilliantly expressed the disillusionment and antipathy felt from the post-war viewpoint, via his use of a disjointed style and dissonant allusion to a wide array of literary and cultural works. Identifying spiritual emptiness as the cause of the current psychological sickness affecting civilisation, he nevertheless held out hope through use of mythology and symbolism, offering opportunity for renewal and rebirth.

- Literature in the 1920s and 1930s

American drama reached its pinnacle during the inter-war period with the works of modernist playwrights such as Eugene O'Neill, whose experimental techniques and use of naturalist and expressionist practices in his stage productions were hugely influential at this time. Popular modernist poets of the period include E. E Cummings and Wallace Stevens, whilst non-modernist writers who achieved great acclaim include Theodore Dreiser, Ernest Hemingway, Scott Fitzgerald and John Steinbeck. Key British writers publishing in the 20's and 30a include Scottish poet Hugh MacDiarmid, novelists Virginia Woolf and E. M Forster, Evelyn Waugh and P.G. Wodehouse.

Aldous Huxley's dystopian classic *Brave New World* was released in 1932, with Henry Miller's controversial work *Tropic of Cancer*, about his life as a struggling writer in Paris, published two years later in 1934. Graham Greene's *Brighton Rock* (1938) and James Joyce's *Finnegans Wake* (1939) were also released.

- Post World War II Literature

The defining focus, in terms of a central and unifying literary theme emerging immediately after the second world war, was on a renewed desire for spiritual connection and religious belief, exemplified in works emerging from such diverse writers and poet as W.H. Auden, T.S. Eliot, Evelyn Waugh and Christopher Fry.

- The Novel: the 1940s onwards

The novel 1984, George Orwell's dystopian classic on totalitarianism, was published in 1940, while the first four volumes of Anthony Powell's 12-volume classic cycle of novels *A Dance to the Music of Time*, appeared in print during the 1950s. William Golding's *Lord of the Flies* (1954), Muriel Spark's *The Prime of Miss Jean Brodie* (1941), *A Clockwork Orange* (1962) by Anthony Burgess, *Watership Down* (1972) by Richard Adams, Ian McEwan's *The Cement Garden* and Alasdair Gray's *Lanark* are other key works spanning the years between the mid 1950s and late 1980s.

KEY HISTORICAL EVENTS

- Archduke Ferdinand Assassination

In 1914 the European super powers were divided between the Triple Entente on one side – including France, Russia and Britain – and the Triple Alliance – comprised of Germany, Austria-Hungary and Italy – on the other. On 28th Jube a Bosnian Serb student assassinated Archduke Franz Ferdinand, the heir to the Austro-Hungarian throne, and his wife, escalating tensions in the Balkan region. When Austria-Hungary declared war on Serbia in 28 July 1914, the other countries were drawn into the conflict via their alliances: the Ottaman Empire, Germany and Austria-Hungary forming the Central Powers on one side, and the Alies formed from Italy, Britain, France, Russia and Serbia.

- World War I

German plans for a quick victory over France failed, with their advance checked outside Paris, and their troops forced back. Both sides proceeded to dig trenches extending from the English Channel to Switzerland, creating the Western Front which would be the position for the long and bloody battle for the next three years, with the major German attack on Verdun in 1916 and the British offensive of the Somme the same year, achieving little progress and massive casualties for both sides.

On the Eastern Front the war raged across many regions, known as the Middle Eastern theatre, the Italian Front and the Balkans Theatre. Submarine warfare initiated by Germany following the Allied naval blockade brought the United States into the war in 1917, and Russia exited the conflict the same year following the October revolution, freeing up German troops to be transferred to the Western Front.

Despite this German Army was unable to stop the advance of the Allies, and following the abdication of Kaiser Wilhelm, the new Germany government signed an Armistice in 1918, with similar agreements being signed by the other Central Powers already, bringing the conflict to a close.

In 1919 the League of Nations was created in a bit to prevent future conflict, but heavy financial and territorial losses imposed on Germany by the Treaty of Versailles resulted in nationalist fervour and desire to reclaim these lost territories and, arguably, combined with political and economic instability, eventually to the rise of fascism and accelerated rearmament under Adolf Hitler.

- World War II

World War II started on 1st September 1939 when Germany invaded Poland, led by the German dictator Adolf Hitler; the United Kingdom and France joined the fight, declaring war on Germany two days later. Quickly gaining control of Poland, the German and British navies continued the battle at sea, with German U-boats attacking and sinking merchant ships heading for Britain.

In 1940 Germany successfully invaded Norway and advanced through Belgium and the Netherlands to France. Italy joined the war against France and Britain as Germany forces marched on Paris, who signed an armistice agreement days later.

Now in preparation for the advance on Britain, German Luftwaffe bombed the country extensively in what became known as the Blitz, and were eventually defeated by the Royal Air Force in the Battle of Britain, forcing Hitler to postpone invasion.

While Hitler successfully invaded the Balkans and prepared his invasion of the Soviet Union, he also drew up his "Final Solution" plans for extermination of the Jews throughout Europe, with over 4 million Jews dying in death camps in occupied Poland over the next 3 years. Hitler's soviet invasion was stalled by a Soviet counter-offensive combined with harsh weather in October of 1941.

Japanese aircraft attacked Pearl Harbour naval base in Hawaii in December 1941, bringing the US into the war. Japanese victories following but the US fleet's success at the Battle pf Midway in Jun 1942 provided a turning point in the war in the Pacific, with further US victories between 1942-1943.

In North Africa Allied troops had defeated the Italians and Germans by 1943, and after their invasion of Sicily and Italy, Mussolini's government fell in July 1943. On the Eastern Front the soviet counteroffensive successfully ended the Battle of Stalingrad in 1942 and the remaining German troops had surrendered by
early 1943.

On D-Day, 6 June 1944, the Allies launched their invasion of Europe, landing hundreds of thousands of troops on the beaches of Normandy in France. Following intensive aerial bombardment of Germany by the Allies in February 1945, they invaded Germany by land, and the country was forced to formally surrender on May 8th 1945.

US president Truman, fearing further heavy casualties from a land invasion of Japan, authorised the atomic bomb to be dropped on Hiroshima and Nagasaki on 15 August 1945, leading to Japanese surrender on September 2nd.

- *UK women win right to vote*

Following a lengthy movement fighting for women's right to vote in the UK, led by campaigners including suffragette Emmeline Pankhurst, it finally succeeded and an Act was passed in Parliament in 1918. The *Representation of the People Act 1918*, enfranchised all men over the age of 21 and all women over the age of 30. In 1928 the government passed the *Representation of the People (Equal Franchise) Act 1928* granting equal franchise to all men and women over the age of 21.

- *The fall of the Berlin Wall*

The fall of the Berlin Wall on 9 November 1989 was a critical event in world history, marking the thawing of the Cold War and fall of the Iron Curtain; the Cold War was declared at an end three weeks later at the Malta Summit. It also foreshadowed the end of communism in Eastern and Central Europe. German reunification was officially announced on 3 October 1990, just under a year after the fall of the Berlin Wall.

Made in United States
Orlando, FL
06 February 2024

43360981R00275